Readers love the Brandt and Donnelly Capers by XAVIER MAYNE

Frat House Troopers

"Yes, this is a highly erotic novel (which I loved) but it's about human sexuality, not sexual exploitation."
—The Book Vixen

Wrestling Demons

"This book is so much more than an MM romance novel…"
—Prism Book Alliance

A Wedding to Die For

"This full length novel is going in my permanent library and I will be reading it again."
—Love Bytes

Spring Break at the Villa Hermes

"This story was sweet, funny, and hot, while still bringing up and addressing serious issues such as being honest and true to yourself, and the struggle for equal rights."
—The Novel Approach

Bachelors Party

"Once again Xavier has given me a story that topped the charts. If there was a way to give it more than five hearts I definitely would."
—MM Good Book Reviews

By Xavier Mayne

The Accidental Cupid
Husband Material

BRANDT AND DONNELLY CAPERS
Frat House Troopers
Wrestling Demons
A Wedding to Die For
Spring Break at the Villa Hermes
Bachelors Party
Destination, Wedding!

Published by Dreamspinner Press
www.dreamspinnerpress.com

DESTINATION, WEDDING!

XAVIER MAYNE

Published by
DREAMSPINNER PRESS

5032 Capital Circle SW, Suite 2, PMB# 279, Tallahassee, FL 32305-7886 USA
www.dreamspinnerpress.com

Destination, Wedding!
© 2017 Xavier Mayne.

Cover Art
© 2017 L.C. Chase.
http://www.lcchase.com
Cover content is for illustrative purposes only and any person depicted on the cover is a model.

ISBN: 978-1-63533-197-4
Digital ISBN: 978-1-63533-198-1
Library of Congress Control Number: 2016915094
Published January 2017
v. 1.0

Printed in the United States of America
∞
This paper meets the requirements of
ANSI/NISO Z39.48-1992 (Permanence of Paper).

For J. Ours was the original destination wedding.

ACKNOWLEDGMENTS

THANKS ARE due as always to that extravagantly indulgent first reader, George Schober, who helped me shape my longest book ever with his honest and meticulous feedback. I've learned over the years that if it works for George, it just works.

CHAPTER ONE

Saturday, Three Weeks until the Wedding
Prelude

GABRIEL DONNELLY rearranged the piles of laundry on the bed for the third time. "So, who are you going to be presenting to this time? And remind me why you're going to San Diego while I'm stuck here where it won't stop raining?"

"It's a conference for trauma doctors," Ethan Brandt answered. "And when I asked you if you wanted to go, you showed me a list of things you had to get done that was actually as long as your arm."

Donnelly sighed. "It's gotten longer since then, with the wedding just three weeks away." But then he perked up. "You'll be back before we need to fly to New York to get on the ship, right?"

"Absolutely. Fly out Wednesday, present Thursday, fly back Friday. We'll pack up and head to New York Saturday so we can get on the ship Sunday morning. We'll cruise across the ocean and land in the loving arms of every single member of both of our families—even the ones we can't stand sitting next to at Thanksgiving—plus as many friends as we can stuff into a drafty castle in merry old England. We won't have a moment to ourselves, plus we'll have to smile endlessly because everyone has a camera, and we'll do it all wearing kilts. Sounds like a festival of awesomeness, doesn't it?"

"It all ends with us finally being husband and husband, and that's all I care about," Donnelly said with a smile. "The rest of it is just a bunch of details. Lots and lots of details." He sighed again. "Hundreds of little details."

"I know it seems like a lot of work, but what we're doing is an immense task. Moving an entire wedding across an ocean, in the space of two months, is herculean. Wendell did a lot, and James has been amazing paying for it all and helping out, and Bryce and Nestor have pitched in all over the place, but the hardest parts of it have fallen to you. And you have kept calm and carried on, and you've been amazing." Brandt kissed his fiancé on the nose. "And I love you for it. You're my hero."

"You're just sweet-talking me because you're guilty about running off to play with doctors in the Southern California sun."

"Maybe a little. Honestly, I'd rather be here with you. But Greg worked really hard to set this up. If the ER docs who took care of Peter had been made aware of how to support gay and lesbian spouses, Greg might have been able to be with him when he died. It's really important work."

"I know, I know. I'm just being selfish, trying to have you all to myself." Donnelly smiled as he dug deeply into the laundry basket. He pulled out a tiny bright red Speedo. "Taking this along to San Diego or saving it for the honeymoon?" He waggled the shiny bit of fabric at Brandt.

"Let's say I'm saving it," Brandt replied, rolling his eyes.

"All right, it goes in the honeymoon pile," Donnelly sang happily.

"No, I don't want to take it on our honeymoon," Brandt said.

Donnelly looked crestfallen. "But you promised."

Brandt leaned in close and whispered into Donnelly's ear. "The pool at the Villa Hermes is clothing optional." He stepped back to take in Donnelly's shocked expression. "I opt for none."

"Get over here," Donnelly growled, yanking Brandt to the bed. "Packing can wait."

CHAPTER TWO

Thursday
Convention hall, San Diego

PUBLIC SPEAKING hadn't come naturally to Brandt, but every time he walked to a podium in front of a large group of people, it got a little easier. As he stood half listening to his introduction to the hall full of trauma surgeons, he thought back to the first time Greg Sampson had asked him to speak on behalf of his organization.

It was a group less than a tenth the size of the one he now faced, and he was deeply terrified—as scared as he had been facing an audience of one, Nick, when he undressed for the first time during his undercover work in the frat-themed cam house. Standing before a couple of dozen public-school administrators to discuss how marriage equality was impacting child custody, he had felt just as naked, just as much an imposter. He had fumbled badly through his talk that day (Greg was too much of a gentleman to offer anything more critical than "you seemed a little nervous") but every speech, every event since then had been a little easier.

For a long time—until recently in fact—his anxiety stemmed not from doubting his knowledge or his authority to speak on these issues, but from his discomfort at being introduced as one of the first openly gay officers on the state police force. Brandt's inability to come to rational conclusions about his sexuality meant that any introduction that focused at all on his identity would always make him feel uncomfortable in his own skin. He looked forward to the day when he would simply be able to say that he was Gabriel Donnelly's husband and leave aside any consideration of what that said about his sexual identity. And that day would be here in a little more than two weeks, a thought that made him grin like a lovestruck goofball every time he thought of it.

"And now it is my great pleasure to introduce Officer Ethan Brandt, one of our state's leading authorities on marriage equality and the changes it will bring—is already bringing—to our country." Though he had retired from the nightly newscast, Sampson's voice was still deep and television-perfect. "And I am thrilled to be able to call him a dear friend. Please join me in welcoming Officer Brandt." Sampson stepped to Brandt and shook his hand warmly, then stood aside as Brandt took the podium.

"Thanks, Greg, and thanks to all of you for inviting me to speak today." Although his voice lacked the professional timbre of Sampson's, Brandt sounded sure and confident. He took a deep breath, smiled to the group, and began his speech.

That evening, Brandt met Sampson in the hotel bar.

"Great job today, buddy," he said as Brandt approached. He stood and hugged Brandt in welcome.

Hugging other men in public was another thing to which Brandt had not been accustomed when this adventure began, but he was now able to give Donnelly a run for his money in the public displays department. The men sat.

"Seemed like a good group," Brandt replied. "And some of those questions—man, I was glad I'd done my homework on medical powers of attorney."

"It showed they were listening and really taking you seriously," Sampson said with a smile. "You just get better and better at this stuff."

Brandt blushed, as he always did when anyone complimented him on anything. Somewhere underneath his tough exterior there would always be a puppy wagging its tail and begging for praise. "Thanks. I've learned from the best." He raised his glass to Sampson, then sipped. "Whoa, that's different." He held the glass up and looked at it, then at Sampson. "What did you order for me?"

Sampson smiled. "A little something special. I know you like a whiskey sour in the evening, and the whiskey in this one comes from a shelf so high it can't even be seen from the top shelf. It is the whiskey of the gods." He grinned and sipped his own drink. "I am, of course, a scoundrel, plying you with pricey hooch because I have a favor to ask."

Brandt set his drink on the table, shaking his head. "You don't need to buy me off—I'd do anything to help you."

"Well, this is a big one. I know you're dying to fly back to Gabriel's loving embrace, but I managed to get us some time at the ER directors' postconference meeting. I've been after them all year to get a slot on their social issues track, but it's only in the past few months that they seem to have realized that implementing marriage equality isn't going to simply take care of itself once the law changes. All of a sudden, they are desperate to hear how to change their policies to stay ahead of potential issues, and they want to hear from us. From you in particular."

"When is the gig?" Brandt asked.

"Saturday morning," Sampson said with a bit of a wince.

Brandt nodded, a frown working its way onto his face despite his effort to hide it. "Gabriel will kill me. We're supposed to be flying to New York on Saturday to get on the ship."

"Which doesn't leave until Sunday. I've already looked into the arrangements—your talk ends at ten in the morning, the limo takes you to the airport, and by noon you're on a direct flight to New York. First class, I might add. Meet Gabriel there and have an amazing dinner in your suite at the most expensive hotel in the city. My treat."

"I don't think you realize the stress he's been under, planning this wedding. My coming here for just a couple of days was already stretching things. Another one might just push him over the edge." Brandt's phone rang, and he pulled it from his pocket. As he glanced at the screen, he thought he caught a glimpse of Sampson looking guiltily away.

Brandt answered the call. "Hey," he said softly.

"Hey," Donnelly replied. "Did you send any of the trauma surgeons to the hospital with your heart-stopping charm?"

"Hardly. They were a good group, though. I think it made a real difference."

"That's my man, saving the world one speech at a time."

Brandt took a deep breath. "So, Greg was just saying—"

"That he needs you to stay for another day. I know. He called me a little while ago."

In the two-second silence that followed, Brandt's heart sank and refused to beat.

"I swear, Ethan, you must make me out to be some kind of storybook evil queen. Of course you should stay. Think about how an enlightened ER administrator might have made Peter's last hours better. Don't even think of saying no."

Brandt gave a sigh of relief. "Good God I love you," he murmured into the phone. "I'm the luckiest man in the world."

"Second luckiest. Now go be amazing, and I'll see you in New York on Saturday. Greg's booked us a suite with a whirlpool on a terrace overlooking Central Park. The use we will make of that is going to live in legend—on that you may rely."

"Boing," Brandt whispered.

"Then my work here is done. Keep that boner to yourself, mister. I shall require its service on Saturday. Love you."

"Love you too," Brandt said, then hung up and tried to both pocket his phone and adjust his growing erection to a more comfortable angle. It didn't really work. *Dammit, Gabriel.*

"So...?"

"So Gabriel's the sweetest guy in the world, and you know it. Of course he wants me to stay."

Sampson smiled broadly. "My troopers come through again," he said, raising his glass. "Now drink up. I ordered another round, and each of these costs as much the car I drove in college."

They had finished their third round of the large, pricey cocktails when Brandt decided he had better head up now if he was going to have any chance of negotiating the elevator buttons successfully.

"Oh, no, wait," Greg called as Brandt stood to go. "There's someone I want you to meet." Sampson waved in the direction of the bar, gesturing for someone to come over. "You're going to love Kerry. We were absolutely inseparable in college."

Brandt had met a number of Greg's extensive acquaintance—he found them a rather elite lot. He had only met those who knew Greg after he became famous, though, so perhaps his college buddy would be a more down-to-earth character.

Greg sprang to his feet. "Kerry! Get over here, you," he called into the crowd.

Through the now-crowded bar, Brandt at first couldn't tell to whom he referred.

"Kerry Stansfield, I'd like you to meet Ethan Brandt."

"Oh, it's Mercer now... again," a female voice replied, startling Brandt, who had been expecting to be introduced to a college buddy, not the tall woman with the brilliant smile who had stepped out of the crowd and now stood next to him. She was objectively beautiful.

"What?" Greg asked, clearly startled. "What the...?"

"A story for another time," Kerry replied. "A drunker time." She extended an elegant hand to Brandt. "Ethan, I'm very pleased to meet you."

"Likewise," Brandt managed as they shook hands.

"Please, sit," Greg said, pulling out the third chair at the table.

"Are you sure I'm not intruding?" she asked with an impish inflection, winking at Greg.

"Alas, no, you're not," Greg replied with a chuckle. "Ethan's wedding isn't for another week, but he's already the most married man I know."

Kerry smiled at Brandt as she sat. "You must be very married indeed. I've known plenty of men—and women—who got significantly less married the longer they spent in Greg's company."

"Now, if you're going to tell all my secrets I may have to disinvite you," Greg scolded with a grin. He turned to Brandt. "One of the risks of keeping in touch with friends from college is that they can tell stories about our awkward first gropings toward adulthood."

Kerry's musical laughter rose above the din of the bar. "Awkward gropings indeed! This guy," she said, pointing at Greg, "had a line out the door and down the dormitory hall, all desperately hoping they might be the next one to get an awkward groping."

Brandt raised an eyebrow at Greg. This was a side of him he hadn't heard of before.

"It wasn't like that at all," Greg protested. "The first couple of years, I was pretty much lost and confused, trying to make it work with women, most of whom—"

"Most of whom would have given their left boob to be the first to hang a tie on your dorm-room door."

"Yeah, it always seemed to fall apart after the third date," Greg said. "That was when certain difficulties arose for me."

"Or didn't arise, as the case may be," Kerry rejoined, casting a wry look at Brandt. "Poor Greg was simply desperate to put his square peg into a round hole. No wonder it wasn't working."

Greg fixed his friend with a judgmental squint. "I don't remember you being so sassy."

"You don't remember me after a couple of drinks. Speaking of which," she said, glancing around the table, "it looks like it's time for another round. What are we drinking?" Kerry waved to a passing server.

"Expensing this to big pharma?"

"You know it. A conference like this is pretty much a gold mine for us, so the bean counters don't blink at a bar tab until it hits the mid four digits."

Greg looked at Brandt. "Kerry here is in sales for one of the big drug companies."

"I used to be a bench chemist," she explained to Brandt. "But it turns out there's less money in coming up with the drugs than there is in smiling prettily to doctors about them, so now I'm the VP of North American sales." She turned back to Greg. "I've pretty much sold out, which is something my friend here knows all about, having turned his promising career as an award-winning investigative reporter into a cushy job reading the teleprompter. And now he's enjoying semiretirement as a philanthropist." She reached over and mussed his hair. "So proud of you, by the way."

"The feeling's mutual," he replied, beaming.

"So, Ethan, what brings you here? No, wait, let me guess." She looked him up and down. "Judging from the musculature, I'm going to say… ortho?"

He shook his head. "I'm afraid not. I'm just a state police officer. I help Greg out with talks on behalf of his organization."

Her eyes widened. "Wait, you're the one who spoke to the group this afternoon? About marriage equality in the emergency room?"

Puzzled, Brandt nodded.

"Oh wow. It's all anyone could talk about for the whole rest of the day. I was working in my company's booth in the trade area, and usually when one of the big speeches finishes up everyone rushes the floor to see who's giving away iPads and drinkable chardonnay. But you've never seen such long faces. I counted three who were still blotting tears—trauma surgeons, crying!—because of what happened to…." She took a sharp breath and laid her hand on Greg's, her bright eyes instantly welling with tears. "Sorry, love."

Greg smiled a bit mournfully and put his hand on hers. "Thanks."

"I wish I'd had a chance to meet him," she said softly.

"He was the love of my life, and I'm grateful we got to spend a few years together. I think I heal a little bit every time we do one of these events in his name. And I'm very lucky to have Ethan along to tell the story. I don't think I'd be able to keep it together if I had to do it alone."

She turned back to Brandt. "You must be some kind of speaker. I wish I'd had a chance to see your talk."

Brandt—blushing deeply, of course—chuckled self-consciously. "I can't do anything like what Greg can at the podium, but I do my best."

"Handsome, muscly, and modest. Someone very lucky is going down the aisle with you."

"I will tell him you said so," Brandt said with a smile. Their drinks arrived to save him from having to deal with any more compliments.

"So, at the risk of bringing the room down," Greg said once they'd all had a sip, "what's this about going back to your maiden name?"

Kerry sighed and set down her drink. "Remember that thing you warned me about before my wedding? When I accused you of being a jealous drama queen and told you he would never in a million years ever do such a thing, ever?"

Greg put his hand to his mouth. "He *didn't*!"

"Did he ever. Then slunk away in the dark of night. Only heard from him one time after that, when he called to offer me a good chunk of his trust fund to keep it quiet. Well, I'm not one to go advertising my poor taste in men, so I never would have breathed a word, but I may have neglected to point that out. So much on my mind at the time, you know." Kerry laughed. "Next day the papers arrived, I signed, and once the fantastically complicated financial operation had ground slowly to its conclusion, I started my new life as a single lady—as of a month ago. Now all I need," she concluded, looking about the room, "is to find a nice trauma surgeon to spend a little time with."

"As hunting grounds for rebound guys go, you could do worse than a bar full of doctors far from home," Greg advised. "Just be warned that most married trauma surgeons don't usually wear wedding bands, so watching for a tan line on their ring fingers won't help you much."

Kerry laughed. "After what I've been through, I think my sleaze detector is pretty finely honed. Turns out that every single buddy of my ex had something going on the side, from a weekly rubdown courtesy of a night nurse to an entire second family the next town over. I know all the signs." She scanned the room, a sniper acquiring targets. "There's a bachelor surgeon out there who's going to crawl to the breakfast buffet tomorrow with the last bit of strength I've left him." She snapped back from sniper to charming pharmaceutical executive in the blink of an eye. "But first, a drink with my college buddy and his strapping but very taken friend." She held her glass up, and the men joined her in toasting friendship.

CHAPTER THREE

TWO DAYS later, Kerry had apparently remembered her whiskey-induced threat to attend the session with the hospital administrators to see Brandt "work his magic." On Saturday morning she arrived as Brandt was pacing the room, trying to work off his nerves. The ballroom was empty except for a silent band of chair arrangers plying their craft, conjuring neat rows of hundreds of seats from the stacks that kept emerging from closets at the back of the room.

She watched him for a moment as he paced. "This really does make you nervous, doesn't it?"

He looked up, glad of the distraction. "Frantically. I hardly have to do cardio anymore, given that my pulse doubles every time I even think about what I have to do up there in an hour." He jerked his head toward the dais at the front of the room. "And this one's even worse—it's my first panel discussion."

She looked at the raised platform. "I would think it would be easier that way, since you're not up there all alone."

"Yes, but the people I'm up there with are all smart, and expert in their field, and they probably do this all the time. I'm going to look like I accidentally wandered in from the valet stand."

She stepped toward him and put an empathetic hand on his arm. "You will be charming and eloquent, and what you say up there will change the lives of the people in this room. I've seen the aftermath of one of your talks, remember."

He smiled, glad to be pulled away from his obsessive dread. "Thanks. I needed to hear that, and normally Gabriel's the one to tell me. I would have called him, but he's on his way to the airport by now and doesn't need to bother with my insecurities." He shook off his moping. "Greg and I missed you at brunch yesterday."

Kerry laughed. "Remember my plan to completely exhaust some strapping trauma surgeon? Well, let's just say he had more stamina than I was expecting. We were still a bit involved when that brunch date rolled around." She looked a little sheepish. "Truth be told, I was lucky to get dinner. Thank God for room service." A hint of blush appeared on her cheeks.

"So you were looking for a rebound guy but found something more?"

"Oh hell no," she retorted with a laugh. "Don't get me wrong, we rebounded for nearly twenty-four hours straight. But every time he opened his mouth, I remembered why I don't like surgeons. The only time he ever said anything that didn't start with 'I' was when he was telling me what to do. To him. Luckily we spent most of the day in an incoherent tangle, and I was spared a third telling of how he rebuilt the cheekbone of a major-league baseball player whose name I didn't recognize, much to his disappointment."

"So no second date?"

She shook her head vigorously. "But if I ever change my mind, he left me a glossy eight-by-ten headshot with his office number on it," she said with a roll of her eyes. "Plastics guys somehow view their own beauty as a testament to their skill. Not to say he wasn't beautiful. And strong. He had muscles in some amazingly convenient places…." She drifted off dreamily.

"Good for you," Brandt said, genuinely happy for her. "Now, would you like to accompany me to find some coffee? Somehow being blitzed on caffeine helps me be less nervous."

"It would be my pleasure, Officer Brandt," she replied with a broad smile.

Somewhere inside Brandt's autonomic nervous system, an ancient relic of hetero chivalry swung into motion, and his arm extended for her to take as if they were a prom couple. He looked down at his elbow in no small surprise, but if Kerry was fazed by it, she gave no sign; in fact, she smiled warmly as she slid her arm through his. They walked together to the coffee bar in the hotel lobby.

Along the way, Brandt caught sight of their reflection in several of the mirrors mounted on the walls. They made a striking couple, evidenced by the number of heads turning to watch them walk by. The part of Brandt that was gratified ran smack into the part of him that was mortified to know everyone who watched them pass surely considered them a couple. A man and a woman. Together. Brandt suddenly felt the heavy weight of guilt press into his chest as they approached the coffee counter.

"What's your drink, Officer?" Kerry asked, looking at the menu card. "My treat. Least I can do after standing you up for brunch."

"My taste in coffee is pretty simple," he managed to reply. "It's Gabriel who can go on and on about coffee in its many and varied forms. All of which, apparently, make a big difference to fancy coffee people, but I can't really tell the good stuff from whatever comes in a can at the grocery store. I sometimes think he can divine from the first sip the name of the plantation where the stuff was grown." Now he was just rambling.

"You really are nervous, aren't you? You didn't even take a breath there." She smiled and again put a hand on his arm. "You'll be okay. We'll get some coffee in you and it will all be fine." She looked up at the waiting barista. "Two Americanos, please, extra shot?"

Brandt tried to breathe normally.

"I think he was disappointed you didn't order," Kerry whispered conspiratorially. "He hasn't taken his eyes off you since we walked up, the poor boy."

Brandt glanced up at the young man making their coffees. He seemed to be about the same age as Jonah and Casey, the wrestlers from Woodley who were now finishing their first year at university. As Brandt caught his eye, the barista immediately broke into a flattered grin that stayed—just barely—on the side of professionalism.

"And now you've disappointed the cashier," Kerry continued, glancing at the woman about the same age as the barista who was busily running Kerry's card for the coffee purchase. "She seemed hopeful that you would smile at her instead of the coffee boy."

Brandt looked from the barista to the cashier, aghast at the drama he was causing.

"Oh, don't panic, dear," Kerry said warmly as the barista put lids on their drinks. "Surely you're used to this."

"I never...." He had no idea what to say.

"That's an Americano, extra shot, for the gentleman," the barista said, gazing into Brandt's eyes with a force that made him blink in surprise.

"Thank you"—Brandt glanced at the young man's nameplate—"Luke."

Luke blushed, fidgeted, and nearly dropped Kerry's coffee. "And one for the... lady," he added distractedly.

"Why, *thank you*," Kerry exclaimed, as if he had laid his coat across a puddle for her. She made a not-terribly-successful effort to stifle a giggle.

They walked halfway across the lobby to a pair of ornate armchairs hidden behind a planter full of orchids. Brandt offered the chair with the intricately decorated pillow to Kerry and sat down in the other.

She sipped her coffee and regarded him appraisingly. "Now, when I met you, I knew you were modest. But my goodness, man, have you no clue the wake of roiling hormones you leave behind you as you stride through this world?"

"Now you're just having fun," he replied. "And since I am a good sport and you bought my coffee, I will allow you to." He raised his cup to her and took a drink.

"Ethan, please," she replied with a hint of an eye roll. "I am having fun, but you can be assured that the little melodrama played out at this hotel lobby coffee bar is just the latest in a long, long line. Surely you've noticed it?"

Brandt considered this for a moment. "It's not that I've never noticed anything like that," he said slowly, "but only among a pretty distinct community of people. See, there's this friend of mine by the name of Bryce who just goes on and on about me and Gabriel, but that's just his way. Well, him and his... friend? Partner...? Well, I'm not sure what to call Nestor, but he and Bryce are kind of birds of a feather. A pretty fabulous feather, actually. But aside from them... and our wedding planner this one time... oh, and there's Nick, but he's straight. Sort of. I guess...." He wound down and slumped in confusion. "I really am kind of clueless."

"I'd still call you modest, not clueless," Kerry replied. "If you took notice of everyone who looked at you like our poor barista, you'd not have time to do anything else. And I can assume that Gabriel has a similar effect on people?"

"Oh yes," Brandt answered immediately. "Now, guys *throw* themselves at him."

Kerry nodded, clearly feeling vindicated. "And he would doubtless say the same about you," she summed up. "But does he also attract the attention of the fairer sex, as you did with our desolate cashier over there? I only ask because it's a rare gay man who can draw the ladies the way you do. Greg could pull it off in college, but that was because he was still in denial, and there were many, many women who wanted to help him nail that closet door shut. But once he decided which team he truly plays for, the ladies in waiting... well, they gave up waiting."

Brandt's head was swimming again. Every question this woman asked sent him into a tailspin. But a moment's reflection made clear that she was spot-on. As Donnelly had grown into his skin as a gay man, the hungry looks that came his way came entirely from men. "I guess you're right," he said. "It's men who follow him across the room. But it is—and I'm not kidding here—every single one of them."

She nodded sagely. "And yet you," she said, narrowing her gaze, "you pull in everyone. So what that says to me is—"

"That this is about to become a therapy session rather than a friendly chat over coffee?" he interrupted with a smile that showed he meant no offense.

"Your requisition for a change of subject has been declined," she replied. "What this says to me is that—despite your impending marriage to another man—you somehow manage to, shall we say, engage both men and women. That makes you… bisexual, perhaps?"

"Wow, when you analyze someone, you really go for it, don't you?" Brandt shook his head and tried to think through all of the things that were wrong with her statement, but kept tripping over the things that were right in it. It was a mess.

"It's probably too late to say that I don't want to pry, isn't it?" she said impishly. "But it's just that I'm a pretty good judge of people—my horrid ex to the side—and I also lack any sort of filter to keep every thought in my head from rolling right out my mouth like some demented gumball machine. So, I have to ask: honestly, Ethan, do you even live in that amazing body of yours?"

"I'm starting to think I don't," he said, seriously and with no small amount of distress plain in his voice.

She sat back in surprise. "It… it was just a joke—"

"No, I'm serious. I think you're exactly right." He looked at her, studying this person who had shown up out of nowhere to jostle his entire self-concept. "Not about the bisexuality, though—you're completely up a tree about that. But about not living in my body. That's something Gabriel said to me recently, and he's known me for years. You got that after being in my presence for a grand total of less than a half an hour."

"Well, this may sound trite," she replied, "but women know things."

"I guess they do," Brandt said, sitting back in his chair.

Kerry took a breath as if she were about to launch into another inquisition about his identity, and Brandt knew he had to keep that from happening.

"Well, I should get in there," he blurted, standing abruptly. "Thank you for the distraction. And the coffee. And the psychotherapy."

"It was my pleasure," she assured him, rising as well. "You don't mind if I stick around for the panel, do you? I desperately want to see the Ethan Brandt magic in action for myself. I mean, you have the strapping young barista demographic completely on board, but I would love to see you work a room of hospital administrators. One imagines that a smile—and a shirt full of pectoral muscle—won't put them over the moon quite so easily."

"I would be delighted to have another friendly face in the audience. May I escort you back to the room, then?" he asked, holding his arm out again. She took it with a graceful nod, and they made their elegant way through the lobby, once again drawing the eyes of most hotel guests. Brandt let it roll over him, as he had reached his self-reflection limit for the morning.

As the panel began, Brandt was distracted by the presence, in the front row, of Greg and Kerry, who sat together and fixed him with remarkably similar looks of appreciation. Either their early history together had shaped them in ways that were still visible a decade after college, or they thought the same things when they looked at Brandt. That, more than the pressure to say the right thing at the right moment, made him nervous as the panel discussion got underway.

But he soon found his bearings and was able to tell the story of Greg and Peter and the horrible drama that played out at the hospital after their wedding, when Greg was prevented from ever seeing his husband of only a few hours on his deathbed because their marriage wasn't recognized by the laws of that state. As was the case with the trauma surgeons two days before, there were more than a few tear-dampened faces among the hundreds in the conference hall. Brandt was more keenly aware of this effect than he had been previously, and it gave him a sense of accomplishment that surprised him—not because he could make people cry but because the crying would likely make them remember the import of his talk long after they left the room.

At the end of the panel discussion, Greg and Kerry hovered near the dais while Brandt shook hands and fielded quiet questions from the other panel members—including one who, early in the discussion, had tried to defend the refusal of religiously affiliated hospitals to recognize visitation rights for gay spouses. The panelists took a few pictures, trading their phones around so everyone would get a shot of the group. Brandt was handed business cards from several administrators who wanted to talk with him about making a presentation at their hospitals, and he cheerfully promised to make himself available if his schedule allowed it.

Finally he was able to detach from the group and join Greg and Kerry.

"Great job, as always," Greg said, crushing Brandt into a hug.

"You're damn lucky I packed waterproof mascara, you brute," Kerry teased, clutching a tissue in one hand while she embraced him with the other arm. "That was a master class, my good man. You won them all over within the first two minutes, and even that dick from Saint Whatever's knew he was in the presence of a higher power. Dude." She hugged him again.

"Now, I made a promise to a certain Officer Gabriel Donnelly that I would get you to the airport in plenty of time to get on the plane to New York, so I must now march you right out the front door. Got your luggage?"

Brandt reached behind the curtain that covered the wall behind the dais and pulled out his rolling duffel. "Good to go, chief," he said smartly.

"So, I'm also flying out today," Kerry said. "Can I hitch a ride to the airport with y'all?"

"You're welcome, of course, but it's just Ethan flying out this morning," Greg said. "I need to work the rest of the meeting to make sure I ruthlessly exploit every tear shed in this room for the good of mankind."

"You go," Kerry replied. "He set 'em up, now you knock 'em down, buddy." She socked Greg on the arm, then turned to Brandt. "Ready to go?"

"Don't you need your luggage?" Brandt asked.

"I have everything I need right here," she said, pulling a small rolling bag from behind her chair. "I can pack for a five-day trip in this bag, including cocktail wear and something casually elegant in which to rock a walk of shame like a boss. I tell you, what the modern woman must do to keep all of this up." She held her arms glamorously wide, as if she were a spokesmodel gesturing next to a very expensive car.

Brandt and Greg exchanged a look and a shrug.

"Oh, right," she said, dropping her arms. "Forgot that my siren song falls on deaf ears in this group. All right, then, let's fly," she said, then hugged Greg. "Love you, buddy. I'll see you soon?"

"You will," Greg replied, holding the hug a long moment. "You take care, Ms. Mercer."

"I will. And for at least a little while, I'll have this hunk of man to take care of me."

"You don't strike me as a woman who needs taking care of," Brandt said with a laugh. "In fact, I'm a little scared to be setting out without Greg to protect me."

"You two," Greg said, laughing. "Get going. Have a great trip, and I'll see you at the wedding."

"Which reminds me," Brandt said as he tucked his notes into his rolling bag, "Gabriel mentioned last week that you still hadn't told him whom you were bringing."

"That's because I hadn't decided until last night."

Brandt waited a moment. "And that decision is…?"

"You're looking at her," Kerry said, once again holding her arms dramatically aloft. She looked at their faces, then dropped her arms and slumped. "I have to stop doing that."

"That's awesome," Brandt said, genuinely pleased. "I can't wait to introduce you to Gabriel. And I trust you will save me a dance?"

"Of course," both Greg and Kerry answered, and all three cracked up laughing.

A first-class lounge

"YOU KNOW, the drinks are free," the man said as he sat down next to Donnelly.

"Oh, thanks," Donnelly replied distractedly. This was his first time in the first-class lounge. And likely his last time, given the travel budget of police officers.

"You look like you could use one."

Donnelly looked up, surprised. "Is it that obvious?" he said with a chuckle.

"Looks like you've got a lot on your mind, is all."

"I guess I do. And I guess I could use a drink."

"No, don't get up. No sense shuffling all of those papers around." The man stood again. "What can I get you?"

"You don't have to—"

"Please. I'm already up. What'll it be?"

Donnelly smiled gratefully. "A gin and tonic wouldn't go amiss right now, I guess. And thank you."

"No worries. I'll be right back. You just try to keep all your papers in order until I return." He smiled warmly, his voice light.

The man was back shortly with a tall, elegant glass in which a lime wedge bobbed and glistened, surrounded by tiny bubbles. "I hope Tanqueray's okay—I took a chance that you're not a Sapphire man."

Donnelly took the glass from him. "Thank you so much. And I'm afraid my gin preferences are determined solely by what's on sale." He looked around the room. "Though that's probably not something that gets said out loud much in a place like this."

The man laughed. "It can be a pretty stuffy place, all right," he said, sitting in the chair perpendicular to Donnelly's, setting his own drink on the low square table in the corner their chairs made. He tucked his messenger bag between himself and the arm of the chair, the strap remaining around his shoulder. "That's why I often try to find someone who looks like he's here for the first time. Much better conversation that way." He extended his hand. "Name's Sandler."

Donnelly grasped the other man's hand. "Gabriel. Pleased to meet you, Sandler."

"Likewise." Sandler took a sip of his drink. "Traveling for business?"

"Pleasure, actually," Donnelly replied. Then he looked at the piles of paper in his lap, and on the seat next to him. "Though it probably looks like I'm planning something on the order of the invasion of Normandy, it's actually just a wedding."

Sandler's eyebrow lifted. "Yours?"

Donnelly nodded. "It's in two weeks. It was supposed to be a small event at a local church with a few friends and family, but suddenly it's turned into this huge, out-of-control Frankenstein's monster of a thing." He took a big drink of the gin and tonic. "As an example of how insane it all is, I'm about to fly to New York to get on a ship. A ship. Who does that anymore? But apparently that's how one arrives at a wedding in a castle."

"Wow." Sandler looked around the room. "Is your fiancée already there, waiting for you?"

Donnelly rolled his eyes. "Not exactly. He's at a conference in San Diego, and got stuck there for an extra day. So instead of coming home yesterday and making the trip with me, he's going to fly there directly and meet me this evening, assuming everything goes perfectly to plan." He sighed. "I'm sure it will be a lovely voyage straight out of a 1940s movie, but getting there with my faculties intact is the challenge."

"Well, congratulations," Sandler said, holding his glass to Donnelly. "I wish you every happiness."

"Thank you, kind sir." They drank, and then Donnelly looked up from his stacks of paper. "What brings you here?"

Sandler's small smile seemed well practiced. "I kind of live here," he said. "I travel a lot for work."

"Ah, I see. I don't know how you do it. I hardly ever travel, and I think you can see already it stresses me out a little. Especially when I'm on my own. If Ethan were here, he'd be pacing and fidgeting and getting me another drink every five minutes." Donnelly shook his head. "It's funny, but his mania kind of relaxes me. If I know he's worrying over everything, then my job is to keep him calm, and that kind of keeps me calm too."

"You guys been together a long time?"

"It's been about four years. But for the first two of those, we were just partners on the job. Still, I count them because we were basically together 24-7."

"Let me guess," Sandler said, rubbing his chin and looking at Donnelly through narrowed eyes. "Police?"

Donnelly nodded. "Very good."

"Must be a pretty progressive police department if they hire enough gay officers to provide a decent dating pool," Sandler said with a laugh.

"The department's been great, but we were pretty much the first to be out. Then again, I'm not actually sure how progressive they were when we joined up. We were straight when they hired us."

"Ah," Sandler replied thoughtfully, then sipped his drink. He stopped before swallowing, looked at Donnelly with a tipped head, then swallowed awkwardly. "I'm sorry... what?"

"We were both straight at the time."

Sandler smiled, but his brow was furrowed. "So I did hear you correctly. I just have never heard anyone say that, I guess...." He stumbled to a stop and shrugged in confusion.

Donnelly grinned. "Yeah, I get that a lot. I should probably come up with some other way to say it, or maybe not say it at all."

Sandler laughed. "No, please don't try to be boring. Anyone can be boring. Especially in a place like this." He looked around at the relentlessly sedate furnishings, the soft lighting, the hushed conversation going on in scattered groupings of suited-and-tied businessfolk. "But you are obligated now to tell me how it happened."

"Nothing really earth-shattering," Donnelly replied. "We worked together for a couple of years and got to be best friends. Then we had a kind of stressful undercover assignment, and we were forced to face just how close we'd become. Ultimately the thought of losing him scared me more than the thought of not being straight anymore."

"That's actually really beautiful," Sandler said, his grin turning a little melancholy, just for a moment, before it reset into a more blandly positive configuration. "Good for you. So, tell me about the wedding."

Donnelly sighed. "Which one?" He chuckled and shook his head. "We'd been planning for more than a year, and then last month the whole thing got ripped out from under us, so now we're working on 'Wedding 2.0: The Destination.'"

"How does that happen? What could possibly rip your wedding out from under you?"

"That's kind of a complicated story. Short version is that by doing our jobs, we managed to piss off someone very powerful, who decided to take a bit of revenge by getting our reception venue to cancel our reservation. The one we'd made a year in advance."

"Good for you," Sandler replied.

"Hmm?" Donnelly inquired through his sip of gin and tonic.

"If you pissed off someone who's that much of an asshole, then you clearly did the right thing. So good for you."

"Thanks, I guess. Hadn't really thought of it that way before. But, it turns out to be no easier to plan a wedding from the moral high ground."

"But you're taking a cruise across the Atlantic and getting married in a castle. In terms of romantic nuptials, that pretty much takes the cake."

Donnelly smiled wryly. "I guess we lucked out there. James, the person who got us involved in the case in the first place, felt bad about how our wedding got ruined, so he set this all up for us—cruise, castle on the coast of Devon, the works. I didn't think it would have been possible to do on such short notice, but that's the thing about money. If you are willing to throw sacks of cash at a problem, the problem usually goes away. Or becomes someone else's problem."

"Well, I think it sounds lovely. I'm heading for London today, and I'm sure you're going to enjoy the trip much more than I will. Your troubles are no doubt behind you, and it's all going to go flawlessly from this moment on."

It was at that moment that the public-address system interrupted the luxurious quiet of the first-class lounge.

"May I have your attention, please" came the dulcet tones of the concierge's deep British/Indian voice. "We regret to inform you that due to volcanic activity in Iceland, all aircraft are being held on the ground at this time. We expect that flights will resume within a matter of hours, except for those bound for airports in the Northeastern United States, including the New York and Boston metropolitan areas. We apologize for the delay, and if there's anything we can do to accommodate you in the meantime, I hope you will let us know." The microphone clicked off, and about half of the people in the room rose and walked toward the desk.

"Oh, that's not good," Sandler said.

"If the problem is over Iceland, why can't we get to New York?"

"Because most flights over the Atlantic begin or end there. They'll have flights incoming, but no flights able to depart for Europe, which means there'll be a whole lot of planes on the ground, and then the overflow will be diverted to Boston and the other airports in the region. They'll be hard-pressed to handle all of that congestion even without domestic flights coming in and out. Same thing happened last time Iceland erupted. It took days before the first flight could go, and weeks before schedules returned to normal. Flying around ash clouds takes a lot of extra fuel, so the airlines tend to cancel rather than reroute."

Donnelly sat back, aghast. "So there's no chance I'm getting to New York today?"

Sandler took in a tactful breath, clearly aware he was delivering bad news. "I'm afraid not, Gabriel. If you skip the cruise, you could try to get a flight through Atlanta or Miami, fly across to Rome or Madrid, and then connect to London by rail. It would be a long couple of days." He glanced up at the concierge desk, now swamped with travelers. "Though you'd have a lot of company."

"But the ship is in New York. Ethan's going to New York."

"Not today he's not." Sandler stood. "Let me get you another drink. And then we'll get this figured out. Don't worry," he said with a bracing smile. "We'll get you to the church on time."

Not quite the airport

BRANDT LEANED forward, certain he had misheard the driver. "What was that about the flights?" he asked. The limo had been snaking its way slowly through traffic approaching the airport but hadn't moved at all in the last twenty minutes.

"They say that all flights to the East Coast are being held on the ground because of a volcano blowing up in Greenland or something," the driver said, turning back to make himself heard. "That's why there's all this backup. Apparently they're holding everyone here until they figure out which planes can go where. They expect to start moving planes within an hour or so. Unless you're going to New York. You're not going to New York, are you, sir?"

"As a matter of fact, I am," Brandt said miserably.

"Well, at least you don't have to worry about missing your flight because of this traffic," the driver said with mock cheer. "Because that plane's not going anywhere."

"Yeah, that's awesome." Brandt sat back in the luxurious leather seat, from which he took no comfort. He turned to Kerry, who was madly typing away on her phone. "What am I going to do?"

She looked up, her eyes kind but her expression not hopeful. "My travel agent says it's going to take all day to sort out the rest of the country, and not to even hope to get to New York until tomorrow evening. And you can forget about getting across to England; the volcano is apparently just clearing its throat. They expect a much larger eruption within the next twenty-four to forty-eight hours."

"Oh." Brandt's voice was small, and even to his own ear sounded defeated.

"Oh!" Kerry jumped and pointed at her phone excitedly. "My guy has a plan."

"Your travel agent has a way to get me to New York?"

"Ah, no. That one would take an act of God, apparently. But here's what he can do. He can get you on a flight from Tijuana to Mexico City, and then he thinks you could get a plane from there to Madrid. Then you'd have to find a way to get from Madrid to London, probably by train since the flights in and out of London are just as screwed as those in New York." She looked up from her phone. "You won't make it for the cruise, but you'll at least get to your wedding."

"But we're not in Tijuana. We're in San Diego."

Kerry leaned forward to confer with the driver. "What would it take to convince you to take us to Tijuana? I would of course cover your expenses."

The driver smiled. "It would be my pleasure, señorita," he replied with a grin. "Beats sitting in this traffic for another few hours." He immediately swerved onto the shoulder and began to make his way off the gridlocked boulevard.

"But you need to get to the airport," Brandt cried. "You can't just go gallivanting off to Mexico on the spur of the moment."

"Listen to you, grandpa. *Gallivanting.* You need to live a little, my good man, and take life as it comes. All I was going to do when I got back to New York was wash my hair, order Chinese, and binge watch *Orange is the New Black.* Again. Does that sound healthy to you? A little run south of the border is exactly what the doctor ordered. And once we get to Mexico City, maybe I'll just hop a plane to a beach somewhere."

Brandt laughed and shook his head at this free spirit Greg had unwittingly hooked him up with. "You are a piece of work," he said when he caught his breath.

"Nine out of ten people who've met me would agree," she said, joining in his laughter.

Soon they were rocketing south, heading for the border crossing. They busied themselves digging their passports out of their luggage and preparing for the crossing.

"I have to let Gabriel know about this," Brandt said, pulling his phone from his pocket. "He's going to—" He stared at his phone. "Oh, shit."

"What's wrong?"

"This isn't my phone."

"But you just pulled it out of your pocket."

"I know. It looks like my phone, but it isn't mine. Look." He held the phone up for her to see that the lock screen displayed a picture of a somewhat grand building, clearly a hospital, that dated from early in the last century. He dropped it to his lap and stared down at it miserably. "We must have gotten them mixed up when we were taking pictures."

"Well, I'm sure you'll be able to get yours back," she said bracingly. "Though that doesn't really help you now, does it? Here let me—"

"Border ahead," the driver called. "The guards are coming over."

They pulled their ID and passports together, and aside from the extra twenty minutes of conversation that Brandt's badge and gun occasioned (the guards had never seen a biometric case—it only opened in response to Brandt's thumbprint), the crossing was simply a matter of filling out the right paperwork for the charter of the limousine and paying a customs fee that Brandt suspected was somewhat inflated. But they were soon on their way.

It was only about a half hour later that Brandt remembered that Donnelly had no idea he was on this odyssey. "Kerry, can I borrow your phone?" he asked.

"Certainly," she said and dug it out of her bag. "Here you go—oh, crap." She looked at the screen.

"What is it?"

"I wasn't planning on leaving the country. This phone doesn't have an international card in it. My company revoked all of those after a sales meeting in Winnipeg a couple of years ago that got a bit wild. If I'm going to travel abroad, I need to swap out the sim card, or it just won't work." She held the phone up for him to see that it was not operational.

Brandt sighed. "It's a good thing he's the levelheaded one when it comes to travel. I'm sure he's fine, and he'll probably be getting to New York any minute now."

"Wasn't he flying in today too?"

Brandt closed his eyes. This just kept getting worse. "He was. I just hope he got underway early enough that his plane was able to get in before the shutdown. I have his flight info here." He picked up the phone in his lap and only then remembered it wasn't his. "Crap."

"I'm sure he's fine, Ethan. Plus there's really not much we can do to help him at this point, is there?"

"I guess you're right. I'll just look for a way to call him from the airport."

The airport at Tijuana was a smaller and humbler affair than its counterpart in San Diego, but it did have the advantage of actual flights taking off. The ground stop affected flights to and from the US, but domestic Mexican flights were still running on schedule. On their way to the ticket counter, Brandt searched for a pay phone that would allow him to call Donnelly, but the intricacies of the key sequences required to do so surpassed his ability to guess the Spanish words for things like "dial" and "credit card." The voice coached him patiently, but he kept reaching dead ends. He had to give up and hope he found a more amenable facility in Mexico City.

Thanks to Kerry's travel agent, by the time they reached the ticket counter they both had reservations for the next flight to Mexico City. They hoped that once they arrived in Mexico City they might be able to make arrangements for the next leg, putting Brandt on the way to Europe and his wedding date.

What they found at Mexico City, however, made them feel anything but confident.

The airport

DONNELLY SAT staring at the line of increasingly impatient denizens of the first-class lounge. No one had yet seemed to get a satisfactory answer to their queries, so he didn't see the point in getting up from his chair. His destination was the city most affected by the shutdown, so it hardly seemed worth asking if there was anything that could be done.

Sandler still held his phone to his ear, as he had for the last half hour. Donnelly was unaware whether Sandler had been speaking during that time; he hadn't been listening, too wrapped up in his own dismal thoughts.

Suddenly, Sandler spoke.

"Okay, thanks. I appreciate the help, sir." He pocketed his phone and looked at Donnelly. "Get your stuff together, Gabriel. I'm breaking us out of here." He stood and buttoned his jacket, then adjusted the strap of the leather messenger bag that had never left his shoulder.

"What?"

"I told you we'd find a way to get you to the church on time, and so we shall. Now gather up your papers and to-do lists and let's get moving. And grab a sandwich on the way out—we have a rather complicated day ahead of us." Sandler hefted his compact duffel bag over his other shoulder and walked to the table that still bore a tasteful array of small bites for those whiling away the hours before a flight. He picked up a paper plate and began loading it up.

Donnelly, trying mightily to come to grips with the demolition of his itinerary, carefully slotted the stack of papers into his portfolio—a sleek leather one Brandt had surprised him with when his manila folder had simply given way under the strain of so many well-thumbed plans—put it into his carry-on, and picked up his sweater. He checked his phone one more time and again saw no indication that Brandt had even received his texts. He hoped that meant Brandt was sequestered in a conference room deep in the structure of the hotel and out of range, rather than any of the several dozen doomsday scenarios he'd been running in his head. One disaster at a time, he thought to himself.

"Here, grab a couple of these," Sandler said by way of greeting when Donnelly joined him at the refreshment table, handing him several bottles of water. "It's always good to have water on the way."

"On the way where, exactly?" Donnelly asked as he began to stack little sandwiches on his own paper plate. "I didn't think any of the planes were moving yet, and certainly not to New York."

Sandler smiled at him conspiratorially. "You're right, planes aren't moving yet. That's why we're not taking a plane to New York. I've got a different plan to get us there."

"But if you're trying to get to London, aren't you going to do the Atlanta or Miami thing you talked about? You don't need to go to New York."

"I think it would be rather rude of me to leave you to your own devices, especially when you've got so much on your mind." Sandler nodded toward the stuffed portfolio Donnelly held under his plate. "So I changed my route."

"You can do that? I thought you were traveling for business. Won't your employer want you to get to London as soon as possible?"

"I'm not traveling for business; traveling *is* my business." Sandler seemed to note Donnelly's confusion. "I'll explain on the way—we really should get going." He pocketed a couple of water bottles himself. "Ready?"

Donnelly nodded and fell into step behind Sandler. They made their way past the concierge desk and through the doorway to the terminal, thick frosted-glass door panels silently sliding out of their way and then closing behind them again.

"This way," Sandler said, leaning in close to Donnelly's ear to be heard over the hue and cry of the terminal. He put a hand on Donnelly's elbow and guided him toward the baggage-claim area. They managed to thread their way through and out the doors to the pickup zone at the curb. Sandler swiveled his head rapidly, making several scans of the area, and then froze. He pointed into the distance. "There."

Donnelly had no idea what they were walking toward, but followed along closely as they veered between idling cars, which seemed, like the airplanes, frozen in place, awaiting clearance to move.

Finally, they reached the outermost lane of the wide boulevard that ran between the terminal and the towering parking structures opposite. As they approached, a man stepped out of the front seat of a sleek black town car and walked around to the back door to open it.

"You are a sight for sore eyes," Sandler called in greeting. "Can't thank you enough for rescuing us."

The driver smiled widely. "Always a pleasure to help out another member of the service," he said, in an accent that Donnelly recognized as African, but which part of Africa he couldn't place.

"Gabriel, this is Freeman Dewatti, a colleague of mine. Freeman, Gabriel's on his way to get married, and we need to get him to New York by tomorrow."

Freeman's face turned instantly serious. "That is not going to be easy," he said. "I can only get you to the District, and from there even the man himself could not get a flight out today."

"No worries," Sandler said cheerily. "I think I have a way to get us there."

Freeman's wide white smile returned. "Then get there you shall, of that there is no doubt." He turned to Donnelly. "Your bride shall not be disappointed, Gabriel. Not with Sandler as your guide. Please, get in, and I will take you as far as I can."

"Thank you," Donnelly said as he stepped into the backseat of the town car. Not wanting to appear ungrateful, he swallowed his reaction to being reassured as to the emotional state of his "bride."

Sandler sat next to him and shut the door as Freeman started the car. Donnelly could see no way that they could possibly merge into the solid mass of immobile traffic, but Freeman apparently had already worked that out. He placed a red and blue flashing light on the dashboard of the car and simply drove on the sidewalk—luckily empty of any pedestrians at the moment. Once he had bypassed the lines of stopped cars, he returned to the roadway, switched off the flashing lights, and sped out of the airport.

"Sandler, what is it exactly that you do?" Donnelly carefully tried to avoid giving away his concern about what line of work this man he'd known for all of two hours might be in.

Sandler laughed. "I guess it does look a little strange, what with the black car and flashing lights. But it's really nothing glamorous at all. Or sinister, if that's what you're thinking."

"I'm just wondering what 'service' you and Freeman are both part of."

"You listen like a police officer, even when you're off duty," Sandler replied approvingly. "He meant the diplomatic service. Freeman is an attaché at the Liberian embassy, and I knew if anyone could get us out of there and on our way, he could."

"No need for flattery," Freeman called back. "I happened to be passing through on the way back from a long drive—a mission for the ambassador—and I was happy to make a minor detour to pick up a friend."

"Thank you again," Donnelly replied.

"Delighted to be of service," Freeman said with a bright smile.

They traveled a few miles in silence.

"At the risk of being tiresome—" Gabriel began.

"You would still like to know what I do," Sandler finished the thought for him.

Gabriel smiled. "Unless it's classified or something."

"Nothing that important, alas. I'm simply a courier. I pick up something from one place and take it to another. That's about it, really."

"Not to sound thick, but isn't that what the postal service is for?"

"For most things, the mail works fine. For almost all of the other things, there are many specialized delivery services that will fit the bill. But once in a great while something needs to be carried in person because it simply cannot be left unattended. For that, they call a courier like me."

"And that's why your messenger bag never leaves your shoulder?"

"Exactly. Some of the time I carry things like jewels or rare coins or financial instruments that for some reason are irreplaceable. Then there are cases like this one, when I'm carrying a diplomatic pouch. That's why I was able to call upon my friend here to help."

"You're carrying a diplomatic pouch for Liberia?"

"No, not this time. But the diplomatic services watch out for each other—kind of an informal mutual-aid agreement—and Freeman here was generous enough to come to my aid."

Donnelly leaned over toward Sandler. "So, what's in the pouch?"

"Can't tell you," Sandler replied mysteriously. Then he laughed. "Because I don't know myself. Diplomatic pouches are sealed, and it's sort of an international incident to open one in transit—and my daddy didn't raise me to violate the 1961 Vienna Convention on Diplomatic Relations! Honestly I think it's better for me not to know. I might get too nervous if I knew I was transporting nuclear launch codes or something. Ignorance is bliss when it comes to diplomatic pouches. And because I'm not actually a member of the diplomatic corps myself, I never actually get to find out what's inside, though sometimes by catching the news afterward I can piece it together."

"Well, it sounds like pretty exciting work," Donnelly observed.

"On the whole it beats squiring a Stradivarius to Vienna, like I did last week. The violin had its own business class seat and everything. But it couldn't make conversation, and it's a long flight to Vienna if there's no one to talk to."

Donnelly glanced out the window at the landscape blurring past the window of the car. "Seems like a pretty glamorous life, especially to someone who grew up in a small town in the middle of nowhere. Even though I live here in the city, I'm still only a couple hours away from that small town. I've never even been to Europe, in the company of a violin or otherwise."

Sandler fell silent, and he spent a long moment looking out his own window. "I thought it was glamorous too, for a few years. As someone who grew up in your typical American suburb, I got caught up in the thrill of being whisked through the back door of Buckingham Palace so I could place a parcel in the hand of the prime minister between courses at a state dinner. I once slipped through the loading dock of a museum carrying a diamond as big as my fist while decoy armored trucks parked out front. But there were some really sad moments too. I've carried astronaut remains and threats of war and vials containing samples of diseases that could wipe out the population of entire cities. I've traveled the world bearing the highest achievements and lowest impulses of our species, and I'm worn out." He turned to look at Donnelly. "That's why helping you today is so important to me. If I can make one person's day a little better, then I've accomplished more than I could in a year of lugging priceless objects." He fell silent for a moment. "That probably sounds ridiculous."

"No, not at all. I think it sounds noble, and I don't know how to thank you."

Sandler smiled, every trace of sorrow erased in an instant. "Just be yourself. I'm so happy to have a conversation with someone that lasts longer than it takes for the next taxi to arrive."

They settled in for the drive north.

"So, how does one choose a career in carrying rare and sometimes dangerous items to the far corners of the globe?" Donnelly asked when he tired of watching the landscape slip by through the tinted windows.

Sandler turned to him and raised an eyebrow. "It's not a very interesting story."

"It's less interesting than several more hours of watching trees go by?"

"You have a point. I guess what I meant is that it's not a story I tell to many people, mainly because I don't come off looking very good in it."

Donnelly regarded him skeptically. "What part of not looking very good results in your being sent to Buckingham Palace? I kinda think anything that lands you at the Queen's back door is probably not something you need to be ashamed of."

"You really don't want to hear it."

"I think I really do. This may be my only chance to live a vicarious life of intrigue, so it would be the height of cruelty to keep it from me."

"Okay, you win," Sandler replied with a laugh. He smoothed the seam of his khaki trousers for a moment as if searching for how to begin. "It started when I was in college. I was pretty desperate for tuition money, not to mention rent on my little garret on the wrong side of campus. I'd always wanted to travel, and when I saw an ad in the student newspaper for a courier gig, I tore it out and stuck it on my fridge. Then when the fridge died—spoiling the last of my food budget for the month— and my slumlord refused to fix it, I called the number. My first job was carrying a briefcase to St. Bart's."

"When's the part where you don't come off looking good? Was St. Bart's unfashionable that season or something?"

"No, it's not that. It's just that the job wasn't really carrying the briefcase. I only found out once I got there I'd actually been hired to accompany the owner of the briefcase to St. Bart's."

"Wait—so your job was to carry a briefcase for someone who was going along on the trip too? Was it a really heavy briefcase or something?"

"Turned out what I was being paid for wasn't what I carried, but what I brought with me." He gestured vaguely at himself, up and down his body. "I was more like a personal assistant. To a pretty high-profile businessman who had stumbled on the courier thing as a way to employ college-age guys who could come along on his 'business trips' to provide services of a more… personal nature."

Donnelly sat back in surprise. "So, you were an escort?"

Sandler nodded.

"Did you know that going in, or did he spring it on you suddenly?"

Sandler looked out the window for a long moment.

"Come now, Sandy," he said to me. "You had to see this coming."
I hadn't.

"Looking back, I guess I should have seen it coming."

And another thing I hadn't seen coming: him walking out of the bathroom with a towel around his waist. A towel that quickly hit the floor, sort of like my stomach felt it did at that moment.

"Sir, I came here to help you with—"

"This," he interrupted, pointing at the slab of cock that jutted from his groin. "Are you going to tell me you aren't at all interested in touching this? Tasting it?"

I studied it for a moment, because where else was I going to look?

"I, uh...."

He stepped closer. "Now, son, let's be honest with each other. This is not my first rodeo. And unless I miss my guess, this is not the first time you've been presented with a hard dick."

Every faculty of speech failed me at that moment, and I could invent nothing to say other than the truth. "No, it's not."

"Did he rape you?" Donnelly asked, putting a hand on Sandler's arm.

"No, it wasn't like that."

"You like cock, don't you, son?" His erection throbbed at me, lunging higher as if hungry for my words, my consent. My submission.

"I guess I... yes, sir. I do."

"Good, good." He smiled, and put a hand on my shoulder. "Now, why don't you get acquainted with mine. I think you'll find it's larger than most you're likely to run across. And once you two have gotten to be close, close friends, we'll go get a nice dinner, and I'll buy all the drinks my very obedient young man could want. Okay?"

The pressure on my shoulder increased. My knees gave way, not because of his physical force, but because he had somehow awakened in me a need I hadn't felt before. He had an air of authority that somehow both demanded my compliance and made it thrilling for me to give it. It was like he was taking all the responsibility for what I was about to do, and all I had to do was go along. It helped that though he was twenty years older than me, his body was in amazing shape. And that cock—well, he was right about it too.

"So you were okay with it?"

"Yeah, I was. He wasn't my first—I'd known I was gay since I was about five."

"Wow, that young?"

"Oh yeah. The first time I caught a glimpse of my cousin watching MTV's *Spring Break*. She giggled and joked with her friends about the shaving-cream Speedo contest, but I was dead serious about watching every drippy move those guys made."

"Sounds like you were a pretty advanced five-year-old."

"Just a lucky one, I think. Never had to spend a moment wondering about whether I liked girls or not. Not that it made it a picnic to grow up gay, but at least I could strike confusion and denial off my to-do list."

"So when he propositioned you…?"

"Let's say I was surprised but not disgusted."

"That's it," he murmured, guiding my head toward his crotch. "Be a good boy and kiss it."

I looked at it, straight on, and realized it had every bit the same air of authority as the man to whom it was attached. It both beckoned me and challenged me, and it was a challenge I wanted to take on.

"Ahh, that's my boy," Mr. Big whispered with a groan of pleasure that thrilled me. I was, suddenly, intensely proud of being able to make him rock back on his heels and hold on to my head for balance. I was going to give him exactly what he brought me here for. And mister super businessman, the power player who was always in control, lasted all of a minute and a half. My tongue made that captain of industry my bitch. The orgasm startled him—I could tell by the way he gasped and whimpered.

Donnelly looked Sandler up and down, trying to fit this new information into the impression the suave courier had made on him.

"See, this is why I don't tell this story," Sandler said. "You probably think I'm a complete slut."

"No, not at all. Remind me to tell you sometime how my fiancé and I finally realized we were in love with each other. We all have stuff in our closets others could judge us for. I'm just surprised you were so… adaptable, I guess."

"Well, when you're as poor as I was, the idea that someone would pay a considerable chunk of money to spend a week with you is pretty ego-inflating."

"You're the best I've ever had," he said as he lifted his cocktail to me at the bar an hour later. "How did you learn to do that?"

"Just a born talent, I guess."

"I've been bringing boys down here for years. None of the others seemed to know what to do. They always hesitate at first, and then they don't know how to keep from scraping me with their teeth."

"I think the circumference is working against you there, actually," I said with a laugh. "Maybe you should try finding men to date, rather than hiring college students whose motivation is more monetary than sexual."

"So, he turned out to be an okay guy?" Donnelly asked.

"Yeah, he did. Priorities all out of whack, but decent enough in his own way."

He looked down at his hands for a moment. "I don't expect you to understand," he said slowly.

"Understand how the people who invest in your company would react if they found out you like to get frisky with frat boys in St. Bart's? Yeah, I can get a pretty clear picture of that. But here's what I don't understand: You are a handsome man. You are tan and fit and you smell good. You have a little gray at the temples that honestly

just makes you hotter. You could have any number of guys—grown-up, real men who could run circles around me when it comes to blow job technique—but you choose to sneak away with random college boys who grudgingly supply you with semicompetent fellatio."

He looked down at his hands again.

"Actually, I have a hard time imagining you being the escort type," Donnelly said. "It just doesn't seem to fit you."

"I kind of decided that myself," Sandler replied. "That was my first and last gig as an escort, and I don't think it turned out exactly as he thought it would."

"You want me to what?" he asked, even though I'd already said it a second time. His voice was deeper now, more assertive.

But he wasn't saying no.

"Get on the bed," I ordered. "Now." I was scared shitless, but I needed to do this. "I'm going to fuck you."

His eyebrows leapt up. "No one fucks me," he spat, real anger lighting his eyes.

I stepped up close to him, grabbed his tie with both hands, pulled him close. "Then I'll be your first," I growled right into his face, full of bravery I didn't feel.

"You can't do this." His voice was calmer now, as if he thought he was getting the upper hand. As if he sensed weakness.

"I can and I will." I set my jaw and stared him down. "And you will beg me to."

"Fuck you."

"No, I'm going to fuck you. And you will beg me to," I repeated.

"Why would I do that?" he said with a sneer. "Are you going to blackmail me? Let me tell you how that works out. Or, better yet, I can tell you where to find the last whore who tried that. He's in a halfway house somewhere in Oklahoma. Turns out he wasn't very good at extortion."

"After he made it clear to me what he wanted, I made it clear to him that I wasn't going to play the role of the call boy. So we renegotiated the terms of our agreement."

"How did he take it?" Donnelly asked.

"Turns out he took it pretty well."

"I'm not going to blackmail you into giving up that ass to me. You are going to give it up because no one's ever demanded it before now. There's a reason you only open your bedroom to clueless boys you're paying to be there. It's not that you want to be in control, it's that you're scared of what will happen if you're not." I could see his eyes widen, just for a split second, as I struck a nerve. "Well, you're not in control anymore. I am. And what you're going to do is exactly what I want."

"Bullshit," he said, but his voice wasn't nearly as strong as it had been.

"All those boys, over all of those years, and all you really wanted was a man. A man who would throw you on that bed and take what he wants. Whether you want

to give it to him or not. But—spoiler alert—you do want to give it to him. To me. Right the fuck now."

"I... don't," he offered, but I didn't believe it and neither did he.

I grabbed the front of his handmade shirt and tore it apart. The shredding of the fabric seemed to tear the last bit of resistance right out of him, and he slumped a little, staring at me agape. Then, obediently, he loosened the tie that held the remains of the shirt's collar around his neck. I stepped back to let him undress, watching him the way a fat tourist watches the lobster he's chosen get lowered into a pot of boiling water. The power was all on my side now.

He was quickly naked and laid out on the bed. I threw off my clothes and straddled his back. I leaned down to whisper into his ear.

"What do you want me to do?" I murmured.

He was silent.

"So he was okay with his escort pushing back?" Donnelly asked.

Sandler smiled. "Actually, in the end, he seemed to want me to."

I slid down his back, and once I'd reached his legs, I shoved them roughly apart. His ass was a work of art, a perky bubble with a promising split right down the middle. I leaned forward and pulled his muscular cheeks apart, revealing the tightest pucker I'd ever seen. He was not kidding about nobody fucking him. But that was going to change.

I spat dead center, and he jolted as if I'd bitten him. I spat again and rubbed it all around his clenched asshole. Then I stuck my finger in my mouth to get it all slick, and I just shoved it right through that knot of flesh.

He let out a yowl that he quickly clamped down on. It became a nonstop growling, grunting string of expletives as he cursed me and all my progenitors. But I put a stop to that when I found his prostate. He sucked in a surprised breath, and I started to work that button like it was Play-Doh. His legs went rigid, and he hardly seemed to be breathing.

"I'm going to ask you again," I said softly. "What do you want me to do?"

He was still silent.

I reached between his legs and wrapped my fist around his iron-hard cock. I yanked it back until it pointed straight at me. The more I pressed on his P-spot the more glistening fluid appeared at the tip of his dick, and I began to rub that around with the thumb of my other hand. I felt his hips twitch, and I knew I had him.

"This is your last chance. Say it, or I leave you right here, right now, and I'm never coming back."

He drew two pained, shuddering breaths. Then a low whisper.

"What? What was that?" I spat again on his ass and drove a second finger in.

He whimpered. Then I could just barely hear his voice: "Fuck me."

"I didn't quite catch that," I taunted, my fingers grinding into his prostate. With my other hand, I released his slick cockhead and flicked lightly at his balls. That got his attention.

"Fuck me," he said with a groan. "Please, fuck me."

I couldn't help but smile. "No."

"Didn't it seem kind of risky?" Donnelly asked. "Since he'd taken you so far from home and you were depending on him to get you back. He could have just abandoned you there."

Sandler laughed. "I think there are many opportunities on St. Bart's for a young man of certain talents, so I probably wasn't in danger of starving to death. But I'd already decided that accompanying rich older men for money wasn't really my thing. That's what I learned about myself from the experience: that a relationship needs to have a balance of power in order to work."

He was stunned. I could tell by the way his shoulders dropped and his head hung low. "Please, God, please fuck me. Sandler, please, you have to fuck me. Now!" His hips thrust as if I were already inside him, stretching him, pounding him into the bed.

I yanked my fingers out of his ass, and reached for the condoms by the side of the bed. I rolled one on, covered it with lube until it dripped a puddle onto the bed, and then covered my fingers with the stuff and jammed them back inside. He sucked in a sharp breath and then began moaning again.

"Fuck me, fuck me, fuck me," he muttered, like it was the mantra that guaranteed his ascension to Nirvana.

I placed my cock at his asshole, which had loosened not one bit despite my prying fingers. This was going to hurt.

"Make me feel it," he moaned, as if we were connected by our minds as well as our bodies.

"Oh, you're going to feel it," I promised him. I didn't really want to hurt him, but honestly there was no helping it. I was too big, and he was too small, for it to be any other way.

"Well, I guess it turned out the best way it could for you," Donnelly said.

"You're right. Once it became clear that he was okay with our new equal status, we actually had a pretty good time that week."

The next morning he woke me with a kiss on my forehead. "Sleepyhead, it's time to get up," he whispered.

I opened my eyes and saw him, standing in a robe, smiling down at me.

"You can walk," I said, a little surprised.

He chuckled. "The first few steps were a bit delicate, but I seem to be okay now. You were a force of nature last night."

"You were no slouch yourself," I said, sitting up in the bed. "There's no way I expected a repeat performance, but three times? Man, you are tough."

"Me? All the boys I've brought here, and you are the first who's ever stood up to me that way. It was amazing." He sat down on the bed next to me. "And I trust you will amaze me several times a day for the rest of the week." He kissed me softly. "Now, they've set up breakfast on the terrace, so let's fuel up. Being amazed really takes it out of a guy."

He stood, and I saw something in him I'd not seen before. He was happy. Like a weight had been lifted from him, and he was suddenly buoyant. What had weighed him down was what I had taken from him last night: control. Having given that up—even just for a night—he could finally be at peace.

"What?" he asked, looking at me with a puzzled expression.

"You're... beautiful."

He smiled, and his cheeks pinked up a bit. "No one's ever told me that," he said softly.

"You've been hanging out with the wrong people," I said as I pulled back the covers and stepped out of bed. I kissed him in passing as I walked toward the terrace, naked. He followed, letting the robe drop as he joined me for breakfast.

"So after that...?"

"After that I decided even though I wasn't going to be an escort, I'd always wanted to travel, so I looked for legit courier opportunities. My businessman—who's happily married now to a fitness model you've no doubt seen if you've ever shopped for underwear—gave me a glowing reference as to my courier abilities, and so the next jobs came pretty easily. Being on planes for so many hours gave me plenty of time to get my homework done, so I was able to graduate with honors even though I missed class quite a bit. Then I could start taking jobs full-time, and I've been on the road ever since."

"Where's home, then?" Donnelly asked.

"You're looking at it," Sandler replied. "Everything I own is packed into a bag that fits the overhead bin on any plane in the world. I do laundry on layovers."

"But you must go somewhere for holidays."

Sandler shook his head. "Nope. Family didn't really work out for me, so I spend holidays carrying stuff that really needs to get somewhere on Christmas or New Year's or whatever. For which the pay is astronomical, by the way." He looked out the window again for a long moment. "But lately I've been thinking...."

"That it might be nice to have a home somewhere and someone to come home to?" Donnelly ventured.

Sandler nodded, slowly and a little sadly. "I must be getting old, Gabriel."

"It's not that," Donnelly said with more certainty in his voice than he had intended. "You've done amazing things, and that's great. But I've come to realize that without someone to share my accomplishments with, they just aren't... real? I guess that's it. Until I share something with Ethan, it just doesn't fully exist to me. That's the best way I can describe it." He looked at Sandler, searching for comprehension in his eyes. "Does that make sense?"

Sandler met his gaze, held it for a long moment. "It does," he said finally. "That is exactly what I've been feeling." He shook his head slightly. "How lucky am I, to have you show up and tell me just what I needed to hear?"

Donnelly smiled. "Ethan would die laughing if he heard you say that. He's always after me for meddling. Thank you for not telling me to keep my busybody advice to myself."

"Never. But I do want to find out more about this amazing man you've landed." Sandler shifted in his seat, turning toward Donnelly. "Now, tell me how it all began."

"Are you sure you're up for it? It makes your story seem pretty PG-13."

"All the better," Sandler replied, eyebrows peaked expectantly.

"So, TWO straight guys, best friends, end up having video sex with each other?" Sandler laughed as Donnelly wrapped up his story of how he and Brandt had discovered their feelings for each other. "That's the most ridiculous thing I've ever heard. Hot as hell, but ridiculous."

"It didn't seem ridiculous at the time—I thought I'd gone completely crazy. You don't know how lucky you are, knowing that you were gay from the time you were five. It hit me all at once, and at twenty-six. And it took my best friend on the other end of a sex-cam line to make me see it."

"What else did he make you see?" Sandler asked with a wink.

Donnelly grinned. "Everything except what he kept under his bright red jockstrap." He paused for effect. "And then he took that off too."

Sandler fanned himself like a Southern belle struck with the vapors. "This fiancé of yours, is he... like you?"

Donnelly couldn't help but catch the innuendo. "Oh, he's much more than me," he replied with a laugh. "In general, and in the part that the red jockstrap covered. Well, barely covered." He reached for his phone and flicked to his photo albums. He found a picture of Brandt taken during their recent vacation at the Villa Hermes, reclining against a sheer black granite wall. He was shirtless (and pantsless as well, though Donnelly had cropped the photo to keep it relatively dignified), with his powerful arms up and hands clasped behind his head. Donnelly held the phone up for Sandler.

"Oh fuck," he breathed. Then he startled as if slapped. "I'm sorry, Gabriel, I didn't mean to—"

Donnelly held up a hand. "No worries—I still say that myself sometimes. You should have heard what I said after our video-sex thing, as I pounded my head on the bathroom floor and tried to keep from throwing up."

"Wait, I thought you said it was the video thing that got you two together."

"It was, ultimately. Eventually I was able to pick myself up from the bathroom floor, and I went to his place to wait for him to come home." Donnelly shook his head, lost for a moment in the memory. "That was the hardest thing I've ever had to do."

"But just like that you went from being buddies to being a couple?"

"It wasn't quite that easy. But our families were wonderful—well, all except my mother, who still isn't speaking to me—and we've got a lot of great friends."

"I don't mean to pry," Sandler said, his voice dropping an octave as he leaned closer. "But if you two had been straight all your lives, how did you figure out all the bedroom stuff? Did you have to get a book or something?"

Donnelly laughed. "We were pretty innocent, looking back on it. After that first night, we woke up and hardly knew what to say to each other. And, given the amount we'd had to drink, we didn't even remember what we had done once we'd gotten into bed together—if anything. We may have just passed out. But there we were, clearly on the other side of a pretty big boundary, and we had no idea what we'd gotten ourselves into, or what to do next."

"I imagine typical straight dudes would have tried to laugh it off—'I was so drunk, man, I don't even remember last night!'—and then never spoken of it again."

Donnelly nodded. "It was terrifying. But after the first few shocked seconds, I realized that what terrified me most was the possibility of losing whatever it was we'd started to build between us, and that possibility was worse than anything we'd face as partners. That much I knew, even the first morning. Ethan, though, seemed like he might be perfectly willing to pretend it had never happened. He's always had a harder time finding his way around the 'traditional masculinity' thing than I have. In fact, to this day he describes himself as a straight man who fell in love with a guy."

"Ouch," Sandler said, wincing.

Donnelly, startled by Sandler's reaction, shook his head in confusion. "Why do you say that?"

Sandler took a breath, as if he didn't really want to say what came next. "Well, doesn't that kind of mean he's not completely committed?"

"No, it's not like that," Donnelly replied, searching for the right words. "To me it means that he loves me more than labels, or whatever abstract concepts of sexual identity he grew up with. It means what we have is unique. Though I've learned in the years we've been together that there are a lot of best friends in the world who might enjoy adding physical intimacy to their relationship, but they're terrified to even admit the thought."

"Huh. Hadn't thought of it that way."

"And it also means that I get to sleep with a straight guy every night. Every time feels like the first time, if you know what I mean." He winked at Sandler.

"Okay, so that's completely hot," Sandler said, adjusting himself slightly in his seat. "You, Gabriel Donnelly, have the perfect life."

"Yep. That's exactly right. The perfect life is what stranded me on the way to my emergency destination wedding, relying on the kindness of strangers." He put his hand on Sandler's knee. "For which I am eternally grateful, of course."

Sandler beamed. "I am deeply honored to be of service to you, sir."

"As am I," chimed in Freeman from the front seat.

Donnelly had completely forgotten about Freeman and how he could hear everything they were talking about in the backseat. He blushed.

"Oh, don't worry about Freeman," Sandler said with a laugh. "We go way back, don't we?"

"We do, my friend, we do," Freeman replied, then met Donnelly's gaze in the rearview mirror. "And of all the men Sandler's had in my backseat, you are the most handsome."

Donnelly noticed they both were now blushing. They rode in silence for several miles. "So, what's the back door to Buckingham Palace look like?" Donnelly asked with a grin.

They spent the next several hours trading anecdotes from their respective professional lives. Their arrival in Washington, DC, surprised them both.

"Is this the Liberian embassy?" Donnelly asked, surveying the corrugated iron building behind which the town car had pulled up.

"No, they actually have a beautiful building north of the Mall. This is a freight depot out back of Union Station." Sandler opened the door of the town car and stepped out onto the dusty gravel.

Donnelly got out of the car as well and looked around at the graffiti-covered walls and rusted roll-up doors. "At the risk of sounding like I doubt your abilities, I cannot help but wonder what you have in mind." He jumped as one of the doors screeched into reluctant motion. "Not that I don't trust you, but I am intrigued."

Sandler smiled broadly as Freeman opened the trunk of the town car. He grabbed up his duffel and handed Donnelly's pack to him. "You're going to love this."

Freeman closed the trunk and turned to the voyagers. "Gentlemen, I wish you easy travels. And Gabriel, may you find every wedded happiness with your beloved." He paused and smiled. "He sounds like a good man," he said with a wink.

"Thank you, Freeman," Donnelly replied, shaking Freeman's hand warmly. "I cannot tell you how much I appreciate your help. I doubt the rest of the journey will be as pleasant as you have made the first part."

"Your service to the Crown is recognized and appreciated," Sandler said, taking Freeman's hand after Donnelly released it. "Give my regards to his excellency."

"Until we meet again." Freeman bowed deeply and then turned to get back into the driver's seat.

As the town car pulled smoothly away, Donnelly was struck by the quite bizarre situation he was in: he stood in a desolate, semi-industrial wasteland somewhere in the nation's capital, waiting for a man he'd met only hours ago to tell him exactly how he would miraculously get to New York before his ship sailed.

He took a deep, calming breath and let it out slowly.

"Ready?" Sandler asked.

"I was born ready," Donnelly replied, shouldering his bag and giving a confident nod. "Lead on, sir."

Sandler smiled. "I like your style. Follow me."

He led Donnelly through the doorway opened by the retraction of the roll-up door a moment before, and they stood before what looked like the shipping desk of a recently abandoned factory. It wasn't decrepit, exactly, but it certainly didn't look like it was in active use.

"Gunny?" Sandler called into the dark recesses of the building.

No answer.

"Gunny!" Sandler shouted. This was less a request than a military order.

"Sir!" came a voice from somewhere in the back of the building.

The sound of shuffling feet grew slowly but steadily louder in the succeeding minute and a half. Finally a stooped man in black-streaked overalls appeared, wiping his hands on a red kerchief. He appeared to be in his sixties, someone who would be more at home running a kiddie railroad at a third-rate amusement park than doing whatever he was doing in this warehouse.

"Behold what the cat dragged in," the old man exclaimed as he neared the doorway. "Sandler, boy, let me look at you. How long has it been?" He extended a freshly wiped hand to Sandler.

"It's been a week, Gunny. A week. But it's great to see you too. Now, I'd like you to meet my friend Gabriel Donnelly. Gabriel, this is Gunnery Sergeant Tommy Maxwell."

"Call me Gunny, son, everyone does," Gunny said as he shook Donnelly's hand. "Good to meet you." He turned back to Sandler. "So, you have two articles to transport today, eh? The pouch and this strapping young man?" He winked broadly at both men.

"Exactly. Can you get us to New York by tomorrow before noon? We need to see Gabriel off to his wedding in England."

"Hate to be the bearer of bad news, son, but there ain't gonna be any planes leaving New York for London tomorrow, or for the next three or four days for that matter. One of my buddies knows a guy who knows a guy at the FAA, and they're not letting anything even attempt to fly around that Icelandic ash cloud. One of the flights en route when the eruption happened didn't get out the way soon enough, and they just barely made it to Shannon. Engines were destroyed—just ground down. They're going to have to be replaced before that plane will fly again. So now they're locking the whole north Atlantic down." He turned to Gabriel. "Sorry, son."

"We still have a shot, Gunny," Sandler said. "Gabriel and his fiancé are crossing on a ship. They'll make it, as long as we can get him to the pier in time."

"Well, that's a horse of a different feather," Gunny said with a wheezy laugh. "Why didn't you tell me that?"

"You didn't give me a chance, as usual!" Sandler protested.

But Gunny was already on his way around the shipping desk. From under the piles of paper and scraps of cardboard he pulled out a laptop, flipped it open, and began typing with startling speed. He pulled out a pair of lopsided cheater glasses and squinted at the screen. "Got it," he grunted and unleashed another barrage of typing.

Suddenly an unseen printer rattled to life, and several sheets of paper slid out through a slot on the front of the desk. They glided across the floor, and Sandler stooped to pick them up.

Gunny snapped the laptop shut and then reburied it under the random scraps of paper and packing material that littered the desk. He stowed the glasses again and turned to Sandler and Donnelly. "They've already got the car ready—you've been pulling some diamond-encrusted strings, my boy," Gunny said with a wheezing laugh. "Now, it may be slow going today with the extra passenger service they've been trying to add. But you should hit New York in the early afternoon at the latest. The car is due to be shunted onto the main in an hour, and then Bob's your uncle."

"Thanks, Gunny. You're the best," Sandler said, folding the papers. "And enjoy your granddaughter's birthday this weekend, okay?"

Gunny laughed, clearly delighted that Sandler remembered this detail. "I'll give her your best." He turned to Donnelly. "She's turning four. Smart as a whip and cuter than shit." He laughed raucously. "Best of luck to you, sir. Congratulations on your upcoming nuptials."

"Thank you, Gunny," Donnelly replied, shaking his hand again.

"Let's roll," Sandler said and led the way out of the warehouse and across the graveled expanse that separated Gunny's domain from the endless complex of tracks and switches leading out of Union Station.

"I don't want to question your plan," Donnelly said as he fell into rapid step beside Sandler, "but if we're taking the train, wouldn't it have made sense to just buy tickets and get seats ourselves?"

"On any other day, yes. But when the planes can't fly, trains take up the slack. If you think the airport was chaos this morning, it's nothing compared to the Dantean scene you'd find at the passenger terminal in Union Station right now. It'll be standing room only on every train heading for New York until this time tomorrow, and only those who got in line hours ago will even have a shot at being able to stand."

"So what are we going to do? Hop a freight train like hoboes in a movie from the forties?"

Sandler laughed. "You're actually not far wrong. Because diplomatic pouches can't travel without an escort, the railroad keeps a couple of freight cars here that can carry couriers as well as cargo. We'll get on one they're holding here for us, and they'll hook us up to a freight train that's passing through on its way to New York." He consulted the paperwork Gunny had given him. "That'll put us in the city with plenty of time to get you to the pier."

"This is amazing," Donnelly said, astounded at what Sandler was able to accomplish.

"Well, I would reserve judgment until you see what the accommodations are like. We'll be the only passengers, but the freight car isn't exactly built for comfort. It'll get us where we're going, though."

"Thank you," Donnelly said. "I know I keep saying that, but you've just been so... thank you."

"It's my pleasure, Gabriel. This is the best way I can imagine to spend the day. If I hadn't met you, I'd be just sitting in that airport lounge drinking too much, waiting for the embassy to figure out a way to get me to London. This is much more fun."

Sandler launched himself onto a rusted, ancient stairway that led up to a pedestrian bridge; Donnelly could see that it ran over the dozens of crisscrossing tracks separating them from a grouping of sheds. The stairs groaned as Sandler climbed them, two at a time.

"Yeah, fun," Donnelly said under his breath as he too began to climb.

The pedestrian bridge was barely wide enough for one man to pass, and Donnelly was sure he could feel it shake and start to tip as they hurried across. They reached the far end quickly, much to his relief, and then climbed down to earth.

"Diplomatic desk is over here," Sandler said, pointing to a shed whose only distinguishing mark was a blob of what seemed to be splattered white paint.

As they approached, however, Donnelly could see that it was actually a collection of white stickers, each an oval that bore the abbreviation of a country's name.

"When a diplomatic pouch moves by freight, one of those stickers goes on the outside of the container. Someone got the idea to peel them off of incoming containers and stick them there—kind of like a scrapbook." Sandler rapped smartly at the big metal door.

Donnelly looked at the collected stickers, seeing countries he recognized, and some he didn't—and some that didn't seem to exist anymore. He was startled by the metal door squealing into motion and then was somewhat surprised that anything startled him anymore.

A small, birdlike man in impressively tidy dark-blue coveralls silently held out his hand, and into this Sandler placed the packet of paper that Gunny had given him. The birdman shuffled through it rapidly, eyes darting over the sheets as if he knew exactly where to look on each of the densely printed forms. He nodded—to himself as he hadn't looked either Sandler or Donnelly in the face—and scurried to his desk, which bore no resemblance to Gunny's piles of paper with a desk somewhere underneath. This desk had only three things on it: a self-inking stamper, a large plastic envelope, and a key ring with one huge key. The birdman picked up the stamper and, in a blur of motion that would have put an African secretary bird to shame, stamped no fewer than eleven times on various sheets in the bundle Sandler had given him. He then pulled two of the sheets off, slid them into a drawer, and placed the remaining paper into the clear plastic envelope. He sealed it by pulling off a long adhesive strip, carefully folding closed the plastic flap.

He stood, studied the envelope carefully, then picked up the large key and marched around the desk and to the doorway.

"Come." It was the first word he'd said to either of them, and he didn't wait to be sure they understood.

Sandler shrugged to Donnelly, who had watched these proceedings with fascination, and they followed. They had to jog to catch up with the birdman, who was already skittering down the yard between two lines of freight cars.

"We're not going in one of these, are we?" Donnelly asked, looking into the dark, rusty interiors of the box cars they passed.

Sandler laughed. "No. Not really." They jogged a bit farther. "Well, kind of, in a way."

"You're not making me feel any less claustrophobic," Donnelly grumbled.

Ahead of them the birdman suddenly stopped his scurrying. They had arrived at a boxcar about half the length of the others. There was nothing else to distinguish it from those around it; it even had graffiti splotched across its brown corrugated skin.

The birdman used the large key to unlock the door of the boxcar. He shoved it with the vigor of a far larger man, and it slid open. A set of stairs extended from the opening. The birdman stood to the side and gestured for Sandler and Donnelly to enter. As they did so, he peeled a sheet of backing paper off the plastic envelope and pressed it to a flat area next to the door.

If from the outside the boxcar was almost indistinguishable from its brethren, on the inside it could not have been more different. It was light, for one thing, with small square skylights in the roof as well as small, rather dim light fixtures on the walls. To the left of the doorway was clearly a cargo area, with a flat floor and tie-downs spaced evenly across the floor and walls. To the right, two pairs of passenger seats faced each other over a table as if they had been lifted directly from a 1940s Pullman coach.

While Donnelly was taking in these strange surroundings, Sandler stood by the doorway and nodded to the birdman, who handed him the big key. He then folded the stairway back up into the car and slammed the door shut. Sandler slid the key into the large, intricate lock and turned it several times until it stopped. Donnelly heard bolts slide into place with every turn.

"So, welcome to the red-eye to NYC. What do you think?"

"I think that the world is full of stuff I've never even imagined," Donnelly replied. "This is completely James Bond."

Sandler laughed. "I'd prefer to travel by rocket-powered Aston Martin myself, but this will do." He stepped over to a low console Donnelly hadn't noticed before and opened the door. "Let's see what Mr. Happy put in here for the trip." He pulled out a thermos, several cups, and a paper sack bearing the name of a deli Donnelly didn't recognize. These Sandler brought over to the table, and then he sat in one of the seats and gestured to Donnelly to sit across from him.

"I just realized I haven't eaten since those little sandwiches at the airport," Donnelly said. "This was really nice of him."

"Yeah, he's an odd bird, but he comes through on the details." He opened the deli bag and pulled out a startling number of containers with foods both everyday and exotic. "Nice," Sandler pronounced and then opened the thermos bottle and sniffed. "Ah, that's the stuff. Kenyan, unless I miss my guess."

Donnelly jumped at this. He pulled the bottle to himself and took in the powerful aroma of fresh coffee. "That's it," he said, smiling broadly, "I'm only going to travel by freight car from now on."

"If you'd like to wash up before dinner, there's a bathroom behind you," Sandler said, continuing to lay out the food. "Through that door."

Through that door Donnelly found a small but tidy bathroom, far nicer than he had expected to find on a train—particularly a freight train. He returned to the table, refreshed and even hungrier.

"I think he was trying to make up for the fact that he never eats," Sandler said, sweeping his hand out over a table laden with all manner of food.

"It looks like when my high school international relations club put on a dinner," Donnelly said. "Because our little town was about as far removed from anything international as it could possibly be, we tried to make up for it by cooking a dish from every land." He glanced up at Sandler as he sat. "I drew Kyrgyzstan. Do you want to know what they eat in Kyrgyzstan?" He stuck his tongue out. "No, you do not want to know what they eat in Kyrgyzstan."

"I'm sure if you made it, it was delicious," Sandler said as he swabbed up some hummus with a triangle of pita.

Donnelly smiled. "That's something Ethan would say." He reached into his pocket and pulled out his phone. "Nothing," he said sadly, setting his phone down. "Still nothing."

"He probably dropped his phone into a puddle or something," Sandler said in what was clearly a willfully upbeat tone. "Or, better yet, he's found a way to get to New

York and can't use his phone. Like he's on a chartered plane, or a long-distance bus in an area with no coverage."

Donnelly shook his head. "He'll find a way. I just have to stop worrying about it and trust that he'll get there."

A short while later, a groaning rumble in the distance made Donnelly stop chewing. "What's—"

He was cut off by a sudden jolt as the train car lurched several feet. He was thrust back in his seat, while Sandler was thrown toward the table. Donnelly caught the thermos of coffee (he saw now why Sandler had put the lid back on it after pouring them a cup), and Sandler grabbed at several containers of food that threatened to slide to the floor. As suddenly as they had crashed forward, they stopped with a great thud. Donnelly looked at Sandler for an explanation.

"Wait for it," he said, holding his hand up. Then another, smaller jolt, and the car sat still once more. "Shunting engine. They're getting ready to haul us out to the main for the train to New York to pick us up. We'll start moving in a minute."

Just as he had foretold, the freight car gave another shudder about a minute later, a gentle nudging motion rippled through, and this time there was no complementary halt. But a great noise emanated from the floor as the train car negotiated what sounded like a balletic sequence of switches and crossings. About five minutes later, they felt the car slow and come to a gentle halt.

"Now we wait for the train to come by. It'll take a while for it to pass—some of these trains are hundreds of cars long—and then it'll stop and they'll hook us up. Then there's nothing between us and New York City but a couple hundred miles of freight track. Simple!"

"Simple," Donnelly said with a wry smile. "This is all so overwhelmingly complicated I can't even believe you'd use that word. But thank you for getting it all figured out."

"It's my pleasure," Sandler said, pouring more coffee. "Now, how do hoboes pass the time between stations?"

Mexico City

THE MEXICO City terminal was packed with people, all apparently trying to make some kind of change to their reservations. The flight delays that plagued the US had spread while Brandt and Kerry made their way from Tijuana to Mexico City, and now only select flights were being allowed to leave. Most had been cancelled altogether.

Brandt stood before the departure board, looking morosely up at the listing of nearly comprehensively cancelled flights. "Everything that isn't cancelled is delayed. And everything that's only delayed isn't going anywhere near New York. I'm no closer to getting to that ship now than I was in San Diego. And we thought this was a good idea... why, exactly?" he asked Kerry.

She studied the board as well, silent, her jaw set. Suddenly, she jumped. "That," she said, pointing. "That's why we thought this was a good idea."

Brandt followed her finger, then squinted at the board. Finally, he saw it. It was a flight to Madrid, whose status had just gone from "cancelled" to "delayed." Next to this new status was a revised departure time less than thirty minutes away.

"Let's go," Kerry whispered. "Let's get you on that flight." She tore off in the direction of the gate listed for the Madrid flight, with Brandt following right behind.

"But I don't want to go to Madrid," he called after her.

"At least you'll be in Europe, and the rest of the trip you can make by train or bus or something," she replied as they jogged through the terminal. "Hell, you'll have nearly two weeks—you could buy a backpack and walk to the wedding."

"There's got to be a way to get to the ship. I don't want Gabriel to have to make the trip alone. I have to get there."

Kerry stopped, grabbing him by the elbow so he stopped as well. "Look, hon, there's no chance you're getting to New York tonight or tomorrow, or probably for the next few days. This is your best shot. If we can't get you on the Madrid flight, we'll work on plan B. Okay?"

He reluctantly nodded, and they resumed their quickstepping progress to the Madrid gate.

The agent at the ticket counter had a lilting accent that reminded Brandt very much of Nestor's, but whereas Nestor only ever spoke gently and flirtatiously, the ticket agent wielded his voice with devastating effect.

"No, sir," he said over and over again as Brandt asked for a seat—any seat—on the flight to Madrid. "Flight is full. No seat is not taken for this flight. Try mañana."

Brandt stepped away from the desk. "Well, it looks like it's not going to happen today. I guess I can camp out here and see what I can get tomorrow."

"I don't like your chances, buddy," Kerry replied. "My guy said that unless we got you out tonight, it could be days. Everybody and his *hermano* is going to be down here trying to work the southern crossing. He said Miami was already swamped, and it was only going to get worse every minute that New York and Boston are closed. This is your shot."

Without another word she scurried over to the crowd of milling passengers waiting to board the flight to Madrid. Brandt was too busy clutching his temples and running worst-case scenarios to hear what she was saying, but she returned to the ticket counter five minutes later with a middle-aged couple in tow.

"Ethan, darling, I'd like you to meet Juan and Esmerelda."

"Kerry, what are you—"

"They have graciously agreed to give us their seats so that we can start our honeymoon. Isn't that lovely?"

He gaped at her, too stunned to speak.

Kerry leaned over to Esmerelda. "Men, right? The only time they stop telling us what to do is when we actually need them to speak." The women shared a conspiratorial giggle, then quickly regained their composure.

"Now, we just need to arrange for the ticket change," Kerry said, guiding the couple to the ticket counter and beginning to explain to the ticket agent what they were proposing to do.

Fifteen minutes later, Brandt and Kerry had taken Juan and Esmerelda's place in the queue for the plane to Madrid.

"Are you going to tell me why you wanted a seat on the plane? I mean, I'm glad to have the company, but Mexico City was already a bit out of your way. Now you're going to Madrid?"

"Well, I was getting nowhere asking for a single ticket. Then it struck me— surely someone would be willing to give up a couple of seats to honeymooners, right? I only had to ask three couples before I found someone willing to take pity on us. So suddenly we had to be married, and both of us were going to Madrid."

"I can't believe you'd do that for me," Brandt said quietly.

"I am a somewhat eccentric person, but I am a romantic through and through. This is the best chance we have to get to your wedding, and I wasn't going to stand in the way of that. Besides, I've been working too much lately, so I'm just going to take some time off. In Europe, apparently!"

"This is amazing. Thank you."

She nodded graciously. Then she seemed to become aware that people were looking expectantly at them, and she leaned in, a little awkwardly, and kissed him on the nose.

Brandt was startled, but kept it from showing as best he could. What startled him perhaps more was the reaction among the assembled passengers to that little peck on the nose. Immediately there were smiles and warm glances and little nods of approval. It was as if the entire crowd shared the joy at seeing the newlyweds show their affection for each other.

Brandt knew full well, and felt it in his heart like the stab of a knife, that had he been there with his actual betrothed and they had shared this casual intimacy, the looks would have been different. Maybe here and there a younger face would have softened, but Brandt knew what kind of reaction a kiss between men was likely to provoke. Especially in a more traditional country than his own. He felt a little sick at the realization.

"I need to call Gabriel," he said. He stepped out of the line, but was immediately stopped by the gate agent.

"Please, sir, we will board shortly. You must stay in the boarding area."

"I just need to make a phone call," he protested.

"There is no time," she responded. At that moment the boarding door swung open, and the gate agent gestured to it. "You see, sir, we begin now."

Brandt looked helplessly at the agent, at the door, and at Kerry.

"He'll be fine," she said softly, putting her arm through his. "You'll be fine. It'll all be fine." They began to shuffle forward to board the plane.

"I just wish… I just want…." He fell silent. "I just need… him."

"I know, I know," she said, pulling his arm tighter. "You'll be with him soon."

"Soon I'll be in Madrid," he said miserably. "That's not even close to where he is." He paused. "At least to where I think he is. Who even knows at this point?"

"You're right," she said as they found their seats, together in a pod on the left side of the cabin in the first-class section. "The best we can do is get you there. And as soon as we land, we'll be able to find out exactly where he is."

"I hope you're right," he said, trying to smile even though he felt like punching something. Or crying.

"Me too," she said, mostly to herself. "Me too."

It was late in the day when the flight finally took wing on its way to Madrid; several hours had been added to the itinerary due to having to route around the ash cloud that was blocking the northern Atlantic.

En route, after dinner had been served and the lights dimmed to allow the passengers to sleep, Kerry turned to Brandt. The long, wild day they'd had showed in the tired corners of her eyes as she yawned and looked at him for a while.

"What?" he asked lightly.

"Just seeing how you're holding up," she said, a sleepy heaviness in her voice.

"I honestly cannot tell you how I'm doing," he said, shaking his head. "I thought the panel discussion would be the biggest challenge I would face today. It seems like a week ago, and everything that's happened since dwarfs it completely. I've been sitting here hoping that I would just wake up and find myself on the plane arriving in New York. But I keep opening my eyes, and here I am, winging my way across the ocean instead of sailing across it with Gabriel. And who knows what will happen once we land. At this rate I'm never going to get married."

"I've only known you for a couple of days, but here's something I know for sure: once you put your mind to something, you get it done. And I cannot imagine your darling Gabriel is any different. You will be married. All will be fine. And this will be a thrilling tale you will tell your kids every year when they make you two a special dinner for your anniversary. It will become a family tradition, and you will laugh and laugh at how you circled the globe looking for each other."

He smiled. She had a way of making everything okay. Not the way that Donnelly did, by bending reality to his will, but by picking up a situation and turning it over and around until she saw its good side. And then making him believe it would turn out that way.

"Thank you," he said. "That sounds perfect. I hope that's how it turns out."

She nodded sleepily. "It will. Now you should get some rest, and tomorrow we'll go get you a happy ending." She reclined her seat until it was flat, pulled up her blanket, and closed her eyes.

Brandt watched her fall asleep, her long, slow breaths evidence of a peace he didn't think he would be able to attain. It was the last conscious thought he had before being awakened by the flight attendant bringing breakfast just a few hours later.

"It feels like I just fell asleep," he said as Kerry's seat whirred into an upright position on the other side of the discreet polished-wood divider.

"That's the joy of flying eastbound," she said with a weary shake of her head and an ill-concealed yawn. "We're basically thrusting ourselves into the face of time at half the speed of sound. That's why I always fly to the West Coast on Monday and back East at the end of the week. Give myself the weekend to sleep it off."

A heavily accented message on the PA system interrupted their breakfast to announce that the flight had been routed farther south than normal "out of an abundance of caution," and the plane would therefore arrive in the late afternoon rather than midday as scheduled.

"Well, there goes another day," Brandt grumbled.

"I like the part where the captain assured us that they had taken on extra fuel in case this happened," Kerry said with a chuckle. "I thought it would go without saying that they would look at the fuel gauge, you know, before deciding to stay airborne for several more hours."

"I'm with you. That they felt they had to say it at all makes me a little more concerned than if they hadn't."

"Control freaks like us shouldn't fly," she said wryly and stabbed at a strawberry in her breakfast yogurt.

He nodded. "Gabriel is the one who reels me in when I get this way. I can just look at him, smiling back at me, and I feel the stress just melt away."

She smiled. "He sounds amazing."

"He is. You'd never imagine he's the same man who shot a guy straight through the heart after Greg and Peter's wedding."

The blood drained from Kerry's face. "That... sounds...." She stumbled and looked blankly at him. "That happened?"

Brandt nodded. "Actually, our bullets ended up in his heart together. But that was only after Gabriel shot him in the shoulder and charged at him. He was about to shoot a defenseless man—for the second time."

Kerry shook her head. "Wow. I can see why you want him by your side."

"He's really the sweetest guy you'd ever meet. As long as you aren't a bad guy, that is."

"Noted, Officer," she said with a serious note in her voice—and a salute for good measure.

They finished their breakfasts and waited for the plane to loop its long way to Madrid.

Evening, on the railroad to New York

THEY WERE on their third hand of gin rummy (the birdman had thoughtfully provided a deck of cards along with the food and coffee) when they heard the rumble of the approaching freight train. Its horn sounded just as the engines roared past, and for the next several minutes, the men were treated to a steadily lowering pitch of rumbling and wailing as the train slowed. Then, as the noise finally died away, they were once again in motion.

This time the jolting was side to side as they were switched across what felt like several tracks. Then Donnelly could sense them slowing, and they drifted along for some time, motion barely noticeable. Next, without warning, a clunk and shudder as they came to an abrupt halt. From the front of the car came a vigorous knocking and clanking, as if the freight car were being bolted permanently to the back of the train. Finally, silence.

"This is my favorite part," Sandler whispered, his head cocked as if scanning for distant sounds.

"What is it?" Donnelly whispered back.

"When the engines pull forward, the slack gets taken out of the train couplings. Each car moves forward a little, and then tugs the one behind it. You can hear it coming—listen."

Donnelly turned to the side, trying to imagine what the sound would be like. He shook his head, but then he heard it—in the distance, but getting closer. It sounded like when he was a kid, listening to a hailstorm as it approached through the summer heat. Louder and louder the booming crackling came, until finally it was so loud they just had to be next—but it got louder still. And then they jolted forward.

"Awesome, right?" Sandler asked, smiling broadly. "It's like motion itself, realized in iron, turned into sound. Gives me a chill."

"You really love traveling, don't you?" Donnelly asked as the freight car picked up speed.

"I do, but especially when I have someone to share it with. Which is almost never. I mean, I make small talk in lounges and things like that, but I never get to spend this much time with someone. It's just kind of a relief to be able to say the things I think out loud and have someone hear them." He looked at Donnelly a little sheepishly. "I must sound insane."

"Not at all. I'm experiencing the complete opposite right now, because Ethan and I normally spend every single minute of every single day together. Honestly, the silver lining in this whole travel mess is that when I see him tomorrow, I'll have things to tell him that he won't already know."

"You know, you guys seem pretty married for people who are about to get married."

"We get that a lot. But honestly, I wouldn't want it any other way."

"Even if it means he's the only guy you'll ever be with, your whole life?" Sandler shuffled the cards for a moment. "You can tell me if I'm being too personal, but I figure we've got hours locked in a train car, and what else are we going to do? If I had ended up married to the first guy I slept with, I wouldn't be very happy right now."

"Ethan and I were partners for two years, and best friends for a year and eleven months of that before we ever even touched each other. I probably would have been ready to marry him even if we hadn't started having sex—I just couldn't imagine my life without him in it."

"That's really sweet. I guess I figured that since you grew up trying to be straight, it would be understandable that you would hang on to the first guy you were intimate with. But you went about it the other way round. Good for you."

"So, you're glad you didn't end up with the first guy you slept with." He met Sandler's eye. "Do tell."

Sandler smiled. "Gabriel Donnelly, you know a gentleman would never tell such things." He consulted his cards insouciantly. "You're fortunate I'm not a gentleman."

Donnelly put his cards down and settled himself back in the creased leather of the old train seat, all rapt attention. "As my dear, somewhat excitable, friend Bryce would say, 'Give, girl!'"

Sandler burst out laughing. "You may have his line down, but until you can deliver it with a sassy snap, I imagine you haven't captured his essence."

Donnelly's mouth dropped open. "You've... met Bryce?"

"We've all met Bryce. It's like Article 3 of the Gay Agenda: Every gay community shall be issued a man so fabulously flamboyant that his mere presence causes the Kinsey scale to bend back upon itself into a perfect circle of glittering queerness, which he shall wear as his tiara. He shall ascend his throne and from a great height judge everyone who comes before him—and their shoes."

"So you *have* met Bryce." Donnelly chuckled as he shook his head in disbelief. "Anyway, you had a story to tell."

"Yes, I promised you that. Let's see." Sandler gathered the cards and shuffled them idly as he spoke. "It was my sophomore year in high school, almost at the end. The spring musical, *Hello, Dolly!*, had just finished its two-week run—you're sitting across from the greatest Cornelius Hackl ever to grace the stage of Eleanor Roosevelt Senior High, I'll have you know—and summer was just around the corner. It's trite to say that in spring a young man's fancy turns to thoughts of love, but this young man's fancy was turning all right. All the damn day and night."

"Let me guess," Donnelly interjected. "You and Barnaby missed the cast party on account of being otherwise entangled?" He raised an eyebrow in good-natured insinuation.

"No, though Barnaby did make it clear he was available. As did several of the waiters at the Harmonia Gardens. But I was at that perverse age when I didn't want anyone who wanted me. You know how teenagers can be—always pining for what they can't have and turning their noses up at everything within reach."

Donnelly nodded. "Just another thing to look forward to."

Sandler gasped dramatically. "Are you telling me that you *have* to get married, Officer Donnelly? That there's a little Gabriel on the way?"

"Shut up," Donnelly replied, smacking Sandler's elbow across the table. "Now, let's get back to you being all horny for what you can't have."

"Ah, yes. What I couldn't have went by the name of Trevor Hendricks. Oh, man, I rubbed myself raw nightly thinking of every move he made. He had gone to another junior high, so I didn't know the world contained such wonders until the first day of freshman year when I saw him across a crowded lunch room. He was beautiful, and so damn smart. I studied myself into exhaustion so I'd be placed in the advanced classes with him. Sophomore year I switched my whole schedule around so we'd have gym together. That was when I had to start stockpiling Vaseline under my bed, because he changed clothes next to me every day after PE, and I couldn't get to sleep until I had worked that out of my head and collapsed into a wet heap." Sandler looked up at Donnelly. "Sorry, too graphic?"

Donnelly shook his head. "You have a way with words. Please, don't be delicate on my account—you have already turned compulsive adolescent masturbation into something close to poetry. I can hardly wait to hear what happens when you and Trevor finally get to it."

"Alas, Trevor didn't seem to know I existed. Actually, I'm not sure he knew other people existed in general. He was polite to a fault; he would answer questions, or discuss an assignment, but then he would just fall silent. He had no idea he was so beautiful, no idea that his voice was my own personal Viagra. It wasn't just that he kept to himself; no one I talked to ever saw him outside of school at all. It's like he walked to school and then walked back home and that was it. So the last Friday of the school year, I decided to make my move. I stationed myself outside the school and pretended I just ran into him randomly. I had some questions prepared about the final exam for our honors chemistry class—I was barely passing—and he gave me answers that I mostly understood as we walked toward his house. I probably would have comprehended more if his sparkling blue eyes hadn't caused my brain to reboot every time he looked at me.

"So pretty soon we're at his house, and we walk up to his porch. He turns to me, and suddenly he's a completely different person. He smiles at me so sweetly, and invites me in to get a snack. He even holds the door open for me. Like, just when I thought he couldn't get any more amazing, he suddenly breaks out this suave gentleman act. I smile and walk in as smoothly as I could with a sudden erection snaking down the leg of my jeans."

Donnelly laughed, then clapped a hand over his mouth. "See? I was right—the dirtier it gets, the more fun it is. Please, continue."

Sandler nodded his thanks for the compliment. "So we go into his house, and he leads me into the kitchen, which is seriously like the set of a cooking show, and sets his backpack on a chair. Then he turns to me and holds out his hand. I have no idea what he wants me to do, but then he nods toward my backpack, so I hand it to him and he puts it on the chair next to his. Like, snuggled up next to his. All I can think was how I hope I will get as lucky as my damn backpack. But before my book bag has a chance to make a move on his, he starts asking me questions about what I'm allergic to. He's standing in front of the fridge throwing questions full of words like 'lactose intolerant' and 'gluten sensitivity' over his shoulder. I tell him I can eat anything, anything at all, anything he might want to feed me—I kind of blather a bit, tossing every bit of innuendo I can summon up on the spur of the moment. And then it happens. He swivels his head around and gives me the Look. You know, the one that tells you the person you've been flirting with understands what's going on, and he's not entirely opposed. And maybe a little into it. But then again, Gabriel, you're already so married you probably have no idea what I'm talking about."

"I'm not dead yet, mister. Please, go on."

"Glad to hear that. So he turns back to the fridge and starts pulling stuff out, and in like five minutes he's made this amazing sort of... salad? I don't know what to call it. I think there was quinoa. Anyway, it's delicious. So we sit there in his kitchen and eat and drink some Italian sparkling water, and we just talk. For like an hour, maybe two. He tells me everything I'd ever wanted to know about him, and because he's like a super sweet guy he keeps asking me questions and then actually listening to the answers. Then his dad gets home and comes into the kitchen, and he seems absolutely stunned that Trevor has a friend over—or has a friend at all, for that matter. Trevor introduces me, and he shakes my hand and keeps looking at me like he can't believe I'm really in his house. Then Trevor says, 'Sandler had some questions about the chemistry final, so we're going to my room now,' and he gets up and leads me down the hall to his bedroom. He shuts the door behind us, and I turn to see he's got this look on his face that I've never seen before. I mean, he'd already shown me a new Trevor in the kitchen, but this one's different again. His eyes kind of burn through me, and he takes a step toward me so aggressively that I actually take a step back. I'm completely flummoxed now, and I blurt, stupidly, 'We forgot our books in the kitchen.' And he just grins at me, this sexy hot smile that makes my knees turn to rubber, and shakes his head slowly. He takes another step toward me and this time I don't step back."

Sandler shuffled the cards. Donnelly sipped his coffee and waited, silently.

"Well?" Donnelly finally asked.

"Well, then we kiss. It's the first time I've ever kissed anybody, and I have no idea what I'm doing. But it's the most innocent, slow, loving kiss I've ever experienced, even to this very day. I stand there, my arms around this guy I'd never even shaken hands with, tasting his sweet lips, and can hardly believe this is my life. All my dreams, even the ones I was too inexperienced to wish for, come true in that moment. The kiss lasts forever, and still I don't want it to end. Finally, his hands slip down from where they've been, wrapped around my neck, stroking the little hairs on the back of my head, and he pulls back a little. He stands there, looking into my eyes, and he's crying. Tears well in his eyes and start running down his cheeks. 'What's wrong?' I ask him, terrified that now I've finally managed to kiss a boy I've clearly fucked it up so badly that the guy is reduced to tears. He just shakes his head, and whispers, 'Thank you.' I ask him what he's thanking me for, and he just says, 'For making me real.'"

Donnelly drew in a sudden breath. "That's… sad. And so beautiful."

"My thoughts exactly," Sandler replied. "Not at the time, of course. I didn't have much time to think anything because at that moment, Trevor leans in for another kiss, and I'm about to find out what sex is like, and then his bedroom door flies open and his mom and dad are both standing there, gaping at us. And then the shrieking starts. Holy hell that man could scream. His mom just stares at us with her arms crossed and her eyes shooting out flames. She tells me—in a voice that would make Satan soil himself—that I need to get out of their house that very instant, and I do, because she was a scary, scary woman. The last thing I hear as Mr. Hendricks hurls my backpack at me is Trevor calling out that he's sorry. I ran out their front door, and I didn't stop running until I was eight blocks away just in case she sent flying monkeys after me."

Sandler, a bit winded, took several deep breaths, then seemed to calm himself by shuffling the cards again.

"So that was your first time?" Donnelly asked, tipping his head sympathetically.

Sandler chuckled, shaking off the intensity of the story he'd told. "No, that wasn't it. Once I was sure Mrs. Hendricks wasn't going to swoop down on her broom and smite me, I started to think about how unfair life was turning out to be for sixteen-year-old me, so I decided right then and there that I wasn't going to take it lying down. I knew where I had to go and what I had to do."

Donnelly sat back in surprise. "You turned around and confronted the Hendrickses about their homophobic reaction?"

"Oh hell no. I went and fucked Barnaby until neither of us could walk."

Donnelly's mouth dropped open, and though he was able, eventually, to close it, it dropped open again. Finally, he was able to find words. "I did not see that coming."

Sandler shook his head and held his hands up. "Like I said, sixteen-year-old drama. I was so freaked-out by what had happened at Trevor's, and still so horned up because of what had happened at Trevor's, that I needed to get it out of my system. Barnaby had expressed interest in the past, and when I showed up at his house, he was still interested. And so he was my first. I was nowhere near even his dozenth—guy was a total slut. But he was up for it, and he showed me what to do. And I did it. And then did it again. And then one more time. I stumbled out of his house half an hour after I walked in, no longer a virgin and no longer having any self-respect when it came to sex. Never even saw Barnaby again—he was a senior, and he graduated and moved somewhere out West for a theater program of some kind. Last I heard he was an understudy for some B-list actor in a touring company of some show everyone's already seen."

"Ah, so that's what you meant about not having a future with the first guy you slept with," Donnelly said. "But what about Trevor?"

A sad smile appeared on Sandler's face. "Ah, Trevor. Yes. Well, the next week after the chemistry final, he asked me to come with him before heading to the cafeteria for lunch, and we ducked into a classroom down the hall that was empty. He said his parents had come unglued and made him tell them that what had happened between us was a mistake, and that it would never happen again. I asked him if that's what he wanted, and he said no. Then he kissed me again. And my world started turning again. And I knew in that moment that I would never love anyone the way I loved him."

"That's so sweet," Donnelly said with a smile. "Good for you."

"Yeah, it was good. For a while. All that summer and through junior year we snuck around, seeing each other whenever we could, staying one step ahead of his parents—my parents had pretty much already given up on me and didn't much care what I got up to. I hated sneaking around, but that year we had together... well, it was the happiest of my life. Every day I learned something new about him that made me love him more. Even though a bunch of our friends and some teachers knew about us, we managed to keep it from his parents because they were basically hermits, like Trevor used to be. I felt like the luckiest guy in the world. Then the night of the junior prom, our luck ran out. We'd arranged to double-date with a couple of girls who were also keeping their relationship secret from their parents, and it was the first time we'd ever been actually able to be together without having to hide from Trevor's parents. It was awesome. And then...."

Sandler looked to the side, as if he could see landscape passing by a window that wasn't there. He sighed.

Donnelly waited patiently, seeing the emotions storm across Sandler's face. He put his hands on Sandler's, which had fallen still, cards frozen in midshuffle. No words, but a gesture that spoke them all.

Sandler took a deep but shaking breath. "We were driving home from the dance, and Trevor was holding my hand and smiling at me the whole way. God, he was beautiful—all the more in the tux that fit him perfectly. There was a warm summer breeze blowing through the window, even that late at night, and a lock of his hair flopped down over his eye. I reached over to lift it, so I could see his eyes sparkling at me for as long as I could make this evening last, when suddenly he wasn't there anymore. The whole side of the car wasn't there anymore."

Donnelly's hands flew up to his mouth, and he gasped in shock.

"A couple of our classmates decided to celebrate prom by racing their trucks down a stretch of highway with their lights off. They had just stopped and were arguing about who had won when I slammed into the back of a truck that was blocking the road. Sliced my car in half, and the part with Trevor in it crumpled up so that the engine was where the passenger seat used to be. He was wearing his seat belt, and the airbag did its thing, but he was thrown around pretty badly. I woke up in the hospital the next afternoon, and he'd already been taken by helicopter to the university hospital several hours away."

"Was he okay?"

Sandler shook his head. "I don't know."

"What… what does that mean?" Donnelly asked.

"He was in a coma for several months after the accident—that much I know. But once his parents found out from the police report that we'd been riding in the front seats together, they could do the math. Then our dates for the evening, both of whom were banged up but not seriously injured, decided that their brush with death was a sign that they needed to live truthfully. They came out, and that was all the Hendrickses needed to know. They never let me see him. They wouldn't even tell me whether he survived or came out of the coma. They sold their house and moved to the city where they could hold vigil at Trevor's side. That night, when I brushed the hair out of his eyes, was the last time I ever saw him."

Tears were running down Donnelly's face. "I can't imagine how much you suffered," he whispered.

"It's not a story I tell," Sandler said softly. "That year is like a chapter from someone else's life. For years after I think I actually convinced myself that it never happened. It was the only way I could deal with the loss. I think it would have been easier to deal with, really, if he'd been killed in the accident. That way I could remember him as perfect and beautiful, and know that he didn't linger on in a vegetative state, his body punctured by tubes and bound with wires."

"And they never let you know what happened to him?"

Sandler shook his head. "Not sure I want to know at this point." He began shuffling the cards again, as if the motion distracted him from the pain of recollection.

"But there's a chance, isn't there, that he recovered?"

Sandler shrugged sadly. "Here's how I think about it. If he died, then he's gone, and there's nothing anyone can do. I mourned, and the only healthy thing for me to do is move on. If he is still in a coma, then there's no way for me to reach him, and even if I could, he wouldn't know I was there. And if he recovered, then he could have found some way to let me know in the ten years since the accident. Three options, all of which lead to the same reality: I'll never see him again."

Donnelly looked for a long moment into the sad face of his new friend. "What if I could find out? Would you want to know?"

Sandler took in a sharp breath, then blew it out slowly, a long sad sigh. He made no answer.

"I won't if you don't want me to. But I could ask for a records check, see if anything comes up."

"I spent years wishing I could find out, but with no money to hire an attorney or an investigator or whatever, I figured there was nothing I could do. By the time I could have, I'd pretty much come to the conclusion that it's better not to know." He looked at his hands, as if watching them shuffle. "But maybe it's time to find out. Clearly the universe has brought us together for good reasons, and perhaps this is one of them. I'll have to think about it. Thank you for the offer, though." Sandler toyed with the cards in his hand idly. "You just kind of show up in people's lives and help them, don't you?"

"My secret's out. I'm old-fashioned that way, I guess. It's why I chose to go into law enforcement in the first place. If I ever get to the point where it becomes more important to do paperwork than to help people, I'll go grow wheat or something."

"Great," Sandler said with a chuckle. "Now I'm imagining you in overalls."

"Think I could pull off the look?" Donnelly asked with a grin.

"Oh hell yes." Sandler suddenly dropped the cards. "Wait—your fiancé isn't going to pistol-whip me for flirting with you, is he? I'm trying not to, honestly I am."

Donnelly shook his head, still grinning. "Don't stop. No one ever does it when he's around, so it's kind of nice, actually. My buddy Malcolm is the only one who's risked it, and he just about peed himself when he found out Ethan was my partner. But Ethan's fine with it. He knows he's the only man for me."

"I think that's awesome. You two sound like you have a great relationship."

"We do. It's completely impossible to explain it to anyone, since we both started out straight, but it's the best thing I can imagine."

The boxcar shuddered as it leaned into a curve, and a riotous squealing issued from the wheels below them.

"Now, I believe it's your deal?" Sandler said, pushing the cards toward Donnelly.

"Yes. Prepare to meet your doom, sir."

"Care to make it interesting?" Sandler said, a light challenge in his voice.

Donnelly laughed. "This is already the most interesting thing I've ever done, but if you mean you want to put a price on your complete humiliation at gin rummy, count me in." He dealt out the cards.

"Oh, it is on," Sandler growled, sorting his cards for the first of several dozen hands they would play as the train rattled its way north.

CHAPTER FOUR

"PASSENGER BRANDT, passenger Ethan Brandt, please see the gate agent for an urgent message." The voice over the PA system as Brandt and Kerry deplaned in Madrid startled them out of their semiconscious postflight daze. So many hours of breathing recirculated air had made Brandt somewhat sluggish, but he shook that off immediately when the hope of good news—any news—presented itself.

"I'm Ethan Brandt," he blurted upon reaching the desk at the gate. "There's a message for me?"

"Yes, sir," the gate agent replied and shuffled through a stack of papers on the counter. "Right... here," he said, and handed over a sheet with a few lines printed on it. "It must be very important, sir. It was sent to every ticket desk in the system, as the sender did not know which flight you might be on."

"Thank you," Brandt said, taking the paper.

"What's it say?" Kerry asked as they walked away from the desk.

"It's from Greg's travel agency. Apparently Gabriel has been pinging them nonstop for news about where I am, and because you finagled the flight, they didn't know what to tell him. They wanted to let me know that he found a way to get to New York." He looked up from the paper, joy and sadness competing inside him. "He's going to make it to the ship. He's actually coming."

"That's awesome," Kerry sang out, smiling broadly.

Brandt nodded. "It is. I just wish... I just wish I could be there with him. Or at least be able to let him know I'm on my way to meet him."

Kerry looked at her watch. "I don't have scratch paper, so don't necessarily trust my math on this, but you said the ship sails in the afternoon, right?" Seeing Brandt nod she continued. "It's not that late in his time zone—I think. You should call him, see if you can get through."

"You're right! Let's see if we can find a pay phone."

Brandt raced through the terminal, looking for anything that resembled a telephone. Finally, just before baggage claim, he found a dingy and apparently largely overlooked example of the type. He picked up the receiver and inserted the coins Kerry had gathered by asking somewhat flirtatiously at various food and services counters. He patiently dialed, and dialed again, and finally reached Donnelly's phone. Or rather, his voice mail. The outgoing message cheerfully told that Donnelly would be out of reach for the next ten days as he and his fiancé sailed across the Atlantic. He remembered Donnelly making that recording, and remembered asking why that much detail was needed.

"Because on the ship our phones will be expensive toys," he'd explained, "suitable only for playing games or reading. There's no cell service in the middle of the ocean. Won't that be awesome?"

Brandt shook his head as the message played. "No, not awesome," he muttered. "Definitely not awesome." Then the beep. "Gabriel, it's Ethan. I don't have my phone, and it's nearly impossible to use these pay phones, and I'm in Madrid, and I'm going to Southampton so I can meet the ship. I'm so sorry I missed it. I tried really hard." He wiped the tears from his eyes and continued, "I love you so much, honey. I love you. I'm sorry. I hope you're okay, and I'll see you as soon as you get there. I love you." A harsh rattle from the phone announced he had reached the end of his allotted time. He set the receiver down and closed his eyes for a long moment.

He felt Kerry's hand on his shoulder. He stood still for a moment, taking comfort from the touch that somehow warmed him more than he'd thought possible. He took a deep breath, nodded to himself—*you can do this*—and turned around.

"So, that was the worst voice mail I've ever had to leave anyone," he said with an overwhelmed roll of his eyes. "It's gotta get better from here, right?"

Kerry smiled. "Right you are. Now, we've just got to find the best way to the train station." She looked around the terminal. "Take Spanish, my father said. You can use Spanish. When will you ever use French? But did I listen? *Mais, non!*" She sighed and shook her head, then jumped a bit and pointed. "There." She started off in the direction she'd pointed out.

"Are we sure we can't fly, at least part of the way? I really just want to get there."

Kerry stopped, turned, and stepped back toward Brandt. "Two things. First, I checked, and there are just no flights going north from here. We can't even get to Paris—apparently they shut that down just a few hours ago when the wind picked up and brought the ash cloud halfway across the country. The train is our best bet, but I'm thinking we need to hurry if we want to get a ticket. And second," she continued, then took a deep breath as if reluctant to make this second point, "Gabriel won't get to Southampton for a week. It won't do you any good to get there tonight." She stepped closer, her voice low and a little sad. "He won't be there."

Brandt sighed, then sighed again. He nodded. "I know. I know. It's just...." He rubbed his brow, feeling suddenly very tired. "I don't do helpless very well. It's not something I'm used to."

"Roger that," she replied, socking his arm gently. She seemed to sense that he needed bucking up more than a soft shoulder to cry on. "It sucks. Just fucking sucks. But when his ship comes in, you will be there, and it will be such a reunion that *Life* magazine will use my pic of it instead of that old Times Square sailor-and-his-girl photo they've been running for the last seventy years. It will be epic. Now let's go make it happen, okay?"

He managed a smile. "Thank you. I'm glad not to be going through this alone."

She nodded, no words needed.

Kerry's rough approximations of Spanish—built mostly on the rickety framework of her high school French, combined with a smile that seemed to make Spanish men want to move heaven and earth for her—soon had them on their way to the rail station, located in the terminal farthest from the one at which they had landed. But on their arrival, they found it closed, and even Brandt could tell what the sign saying 0530 meant. As it was now nearly midnight, they had more than five hours to kill before the gates rolled up and they could get on their way to the city center.

Kerry scouted out a comfortable location for them to crash for the evening while Brandt collected every brochure and timetable he could find outside the rail station.

"I found a great spot over there next to those columns," Kerry said, pointing to where she had pushed together several sets of chairs, making a surprisingly cozy-looking arrangement that would be their hotel for the evening. The rest of the grand and modern terminal was deserted, as if everyone else somehow knew that coming to the rail station at this hour would only end in disappointment.

"Looks great, thanks," Brandt replied distractedly. He studied the booklets in his hands, willing them to cohere into a plan to get him to Southampton.

She smiled as if she had expected this reaction. "Come on, chief. Let's get settled in, and we can spring at the gates as soon as they open." She pulled him by the arm, and he followed. They sat on the chairs nearest the window. "It's actually kind of beautiful here," she said, looking around at the undulating ceiling and tall swathes of windows. "I had no idea an airport could be this quiet."

"Mm-hmm," he said, not taking his eyes from the timetable in his hands.

She got up from her makeshift bunk, comprising four terminal chairs pushed together, and sat down lightly next to him. She peered over his shoulder. "What's that?" she said, a lemony look on her face.

"It's the Chinese version of the timetable," he replied. "It has the best map. But I can't quite get the times and stations to match up. The one in… Dutch? I think?" He shuffled the stack of booklets. "This one has a section showing the connections from the main rail station in Madrid, but it's dated almost a year ago, so I'm not sure it has the correct schedule. Then this one"—he shuffled again—"is dated just a month ago, but it's in Hebrew, so I have no idea how to read the tables because they all run the wrong direction." He looked up at her, feeling helpless all over again.

She put a hand on his jumbled stack of papers, looked him in the eye, and shook her head. "None of this is going to make his ship go faster," she said sympathetically. "None of it is going to launch you out over the ocean waves to him. You are doing the best you can, and you've come this far, and the rest is going to be easy. Just relax, and we'll figure it all out in the morning. I'm sure the ticket agent will have all the answers. We have nearly a week to get you to Southampton, and nothing will stop us." She raised her eyebrows and pursed her lips a little sternly. "Okay?"

He took a deep breath and let out a defeated sigh. "Okay," he said and tried to smile. Tried to mean it. He didn't, and he could see she knew he didn't, but she seemed willing to accept this little fiction. He pretended to as well.

"Good. Now, since we've had about three hours of sleep in the past thirty-six, I think we should try to get some shut-eye before we have to start elbowing our way to the front of the line for trains tomorrow morning at 0530. Sound good?"

He nodded. "I'm going to find a bathroom and brush my teeth," he said, picking up the toiletries kit from his carry-on.

"Over around that corner, on the left," Kerry said, pointing the way. "I'll go when you get back."

"Thanks," he said, then stopped after only a few steps. He turned back to her. "And, seriously, thank you. I wouldn't have made it here without you."

She shook her head. "Come on, now. We both know you would have found a way here. I just got us here smiling helplessly and telling little white lies rather than flashing a badge and waving a gun around."

"Well, your way is better. So thanks."

She nodded, and he went on his way.

NYC

THE LURCHING of the boxcar woke Donnelly—or at least he thought he had been awakened, as he didn't remember falling asleep. But he sat up with a jolt from the reclined train seat just as Sandler did from the one next to him. Then he recalled that they had decided, as their final, pointless game of gin wound down, to crank back the seats and see if they could get a little sleep before their arrival in the great freight yards of the city. And now, apparently, they had arrived.

"Morning," Sandler said sleepily and then flopped back onto the seat. "What time is it?" He must have noticed Donnelly reaching for his phone.

"Nearly noon," Donnelly replied. "I guess what they say about the motion of trains is true—I was out cold."

"Getting any signal yet?"

Donnelly shook his head. "Maybe once they let us out of our box."

"Should be any minute now. They don't usually leave pouches alone very long." Sandler sat up again and shook sleep off. "Now to make myself presentable," he said somewhat grandly as he stood and pressed the wrinkles out of his clothes with his hands. He ran his fingers through his hair, gave his head a shake, and stretched.

"Wow. You look like you got eight hours of sleep, had a shower, and ironed your clothes. You have got to teach me that."

"I give all credit to miracle fabrics and low expectations," Sandler replied with a gracious bow. "You, though, look amazing. If this is how you weather an all-night stakeout, I might take up a life of crime just to be able to see it."

Donnelly rolled his eyes. "As baseless compliments go, that was one of the weirdest I've ever heard. But thanks." He stood and stretched as well.

A grinding from the front of the boxcar announced their decoupling from the rest of the train. Two mighty metallic clangs rang out, and they shifted backward a few feet. At almost the same moment, a thud and a shudder emanated from the back end.

"Shunting engine," Sandler announced. "Won't be long now."

The boxcar was in constant rocking motion for several long minutes, crossing switches and other miscellaneous bumps in the railroad, the horn on the shunting engine bleating constantly. Then they ground to a halt.

"Grab your socks, mister, we're about to be sprung," Sandler announced as he picked up his messenger bag.

Donnelly scooped up his duffel. "Hey, I just noticed. You actually took off the bag last night. Is that allowed?"

Sandler smiled. "I was in a sealed boxcar with a police officer. That counts as one of the few times I would be forgiven for ducking out of the harness, I think."

"I'm flattered to be an exception to the rule," Donnelly replied with a laugh.

Four sharp raps on the door brought Sandler right back to business. "Showtime," he said as he stepped over to the lock. He inserted the key and turned it until all of the bolts retracted from the perimeter of the sliding door. He gave it a shove, and it slid back, letting in a wide swathe of early morning light. He and Donnelly blinked into the brightness.

"Afternoon," barked the man who had knocked on the door, his voice a foghorn of pure New Jersey. With a lightning stroke, he flipped a knife out of his pocket and slashed at the plastic document pouch stuck to the side of the boxcar. He glanced at the documents, then up at Sandler and Donnelly.

"Courier, escort, and pouch," he counted off, jabbing a fat finger at Sandler, Donnelly, and the messenger bag Sandler held out before him. "Present and accounted for." He folded the documents roughly into quarters and stuffed them into his breast pocket. "Welcome to New York, gents," he said jovially as he extended the stairs. "Your car is waiting just over there." He pointed over to a black car that idled just on the other side of an imposing metal gate festooned with concertina wire.

"Thank you, sir," Sandler said as he stepped briskly down from the boxcar.

Donnelly followed, and they picked their way nimbly over several sets of rails on their way to the gate. As they approached, it slid open enough for them to slip through and quickly clanged shut behind them.

An imposing man wearing a black suit and black sunglasses emerged from the driver's seat as they approached and silently opened the back door of the long Mercedes sedan. He held out a hand to take their duffels from them, but of course made no move to relieve Sandler of his messenger bag. They settled into the backseat as the driver placed their duffels in the trunk.

"Strong silent type, eh?" Donnelly whispered to Sandler.

"He's a very nice guy when he's not working. But on the job? He's fearsome. He's less a driver than a one-man security force."

The driver settled into the car and looked at Sandler in the mirror. "Where to, sir?" It was the voice of a devoted but angry servant to the tsar.

"We're heading for the cruise dock in Brooklyn, Yevgeny," Sandler replied. "We need to get this one on his way to England."

Yevgeny nodded curtly, as if providing cruise shuttle service were a matter of urgent national security he had been entrusted to perform. The car roared forward and snaked through the ramshackle sheds of the freight yard, prompting Donnelly to reach around for his seat belt.

As they rocketed out onto the streets of the city, Donnelly's phone chimed several times.

"That's him!" he said excitedly as he pulled his phone from his pocket. "Or… at least a voice mail from him, anyway." He jabbed at the phone and then held it to his ear. The message, recorded by a sleep-deprived Brandt in a phone booth in a crowded airport across the largest ocean, was not what he had hoped to hear. He listened to the message twice before putting his phone down.

"He's not coming." He turned to Sandler, unable to say anything more.

"What? What happened? What did he say?"

Donnelly sighed and closed his eyes. "He managed to get to Madrid, and he's going to meet the ship in Southampton."

"But that's a good thing, right? He found a way to get there despite the flights all being cancelled, so he won't miss the wedding." Sandler paused for a moment, as if waiting for a reaction of some kind, before continuing. "It's pretty amazing he was able to get that far. According to my network"—he held up his phone, its screen covered with new messages and more rolling in—"all the flights that haven't been cancelled are booked solid for most of the coming week. I didn't think it was possible that he'd get to Europe before you."

Donnelly managed a weak grin. "Well, that's Ethan. The impossible doesn't usually stand a chance against him." He wished that bit of good news actually made him feel better.

"I know it kind of sucks that he won't be making the trip with you, but at least he'll be there. You don't have to worry about postponing your wedding."

Donnelly looked out the window at the city blurring past. "I know I should be happy, but the last twenty-four hours have kind of left me with whiplash. I've been looking forward to this day for weeks. It's been the light at the end of the twisty tunnel this wedding has become, and all I wanted was to be on board with Ethan, sipping champagne as the Statue of Liberty wished us bon voyage." He put his head in his hands. "Sorry I'm such a sap. An emotionally exhausted sap."

Sandler put his arm around him. "You have nothing to apologize for. You've been through a lot, and most people would have been reduced to curling up into a fetal position and moaning by this point. But you're almost there. All we need to do is get you on that ship, and then it's smooth sailing until you are reunited with Ethan. The hard part is over."

Donnelly lifted his head and fixed Sandler with a skeptical gaze. "You haven't known me long enough to know this, but the hard part is never over, especially when it comes to Ethan and me ever finding our way down the aisle." He managed a weak smile. "But thanks for the pep talk. I appreciate it."

"That's the spirit. Now, just sit tight and we'll get you on that boat."

As they snaked through traffic near the cruise terminal, Sandler's phone rang. He pulled it from its clip on the strap of his messenger bag. "Sir?" he said without preamble. He listened, nodding slightly, as if being given a long and somewhat complex set of instructions. Finally, after several minutes of this, he said simply, "I understand." He lowered the phone and clipped it back onto the strap.

"That sounded official," Donnelly said.

Sandler chuckled and rolled his eyes. "You're never going to believe this."

"Try me. And please, make it improbable. That's the only kind of thing that happens to me or anyone around me anymore."

"That was my employer. They've been tracking my movements, and he wanted to let me know that they're very impressed with how I've managed to get to New York when most of the transport options are completely seized up. I decided not to mention that it was all in the service of getting you to your wedding."

"Probably a prudent omission. So it was just a congratulatory call?"

"Not exactly. He—"

"Cruise terminal," Yevgeny announced suddenly as the car lurched to a stop. He sprang out of the seat with startling speed for a man his size and pulled open the back door for the men to step out of the car. Then he was suddenly by their side, holding out their duffel bags to them.

"Thank you, sir," Sandler said.

Yevgeny nodded. "Will there be anything else?"

"No." Sandler drew himself up to full height. "The Crown thanks you for your service."

Yevgeny nodded with great ceremony and had already begun to walk around the car to the driver's side when Sandler called out to him.

"And, Yevgeny?"

He stopped and snapped to attention. "Yes?"

"Give Alexei my best. I'd love to see that great apartment you two were working on so hard last time we had dinner."

A smile—something Donnelly had not been able to imagine even being compatible with Yevgeny's face—opened, sparkling white. "Call when you come back in town. Stay with us couple of days."

"Finally get a guest bed set up?" Sandler asked teasingly.

"No, still just one. But is big enough," Yevgeny said with a wink. He got into the Mercedes and drove away.

"See? Nice guy." Sandler said to the stunned Donnelly. "Come on, we'd better get moving."

Donnelly shook his head to clear it of visions of what might happen in Yevgeny's big bed and followed. "You were about to tell me what your employer said on the phone," he said as he caught up with Sandler.

"Right. Well, it looks like there's a cruise in my future as well."

Donnelly shook his head, certain he had heard incorrectly. "What?"

"He's arranging for me to cross to England. Otherwise the pouch would have to wait for a week or more while the ash cloud clears."

"He can just do that?" Donnelly asked, amazed at the strings that kept getting pulled for Sandler. "How?"

"See that flag?" he said, pointing at the red flag at the stern of the massive ship that lay before them at the dock. "That's how. This ship is flagged in Bermuda, and you know who's the head of state of Bermuda."

"So this is what it's like to have the Queen of England in your corner. Wow."

"Well, that and the fact that with the disruption to the entire transport network, there are a lot of vacationers who aren't going to make this sailing. So the United Nations is working to slot in diplomats who need to get home. The standby area in the cruise terminal is going to look like the lobby of the General Assembly."

They reached the doors to the large terminal building and stepped into yet another chaotic scene of disruption, delay, and distemper. Sure enough, there was a cordoned-off area on one side where a large group of men and women in serious suits were standing, looking very much out of place in a room full of tourists. Everyone in the cavernous hall seemed to be standing in a line, though none of the lines appeared to be moving or even pointing toward a discernible goal.

"Wow. In all my years traveling, I've never gone by cruise ship. Now I can see why."

Donnelly scanned the cavernous space, then found what he was looking for. "Follow me," he said and started off for the far corner of the terminal.

"But I should probably go check in over at the standby pen with the ambassadors and all their sour-faced hangers-on, some of whom I'll be bunking with for the next week. They're, like, my people." He stuck his tongue out and gave a queasy roll of the eyes in their direction.

"No, you're my people now," Donnelly said. "I have a plan. Come on."

Sandler seemed genuinely startled, but he fell in step behind Donnelly as they slipped gracefully through the crowd.

"Here we are," Donnelly announced when they'd reached the front of the room. He pointed up at the sign that indicated they were in the reception area for passengers who had reserved (and paid dearly for) the largest suites on the ship. He walked to the counter and presented his passport to the smiling clerk.

"Good morning, Mister"—she glanced at his documents—"Donnelly." She began typing with elegant precision and consulted her computer monitor. "And Mr. Brandt, I presume?" she inquired, casting her beaming smile at Sandler.

"Alas, as much as I'd like to be Mr. Brandt, I am instead Mr. Birkin."

"My fiancé," Donnelly explained, "was trying to get here from the West Coast and was unable to. He's going to meet the ship in Southampton. However, Mr. Birkin also needs to get to England, on a rather important matter, and I would be delighted to have him take Mr. Brandt's place."

Sandler turned a surprised face to Donnelly, who simply motioned that he should hand over his identification. He did so, and the clerk seemed astonished to find herself holding a diplomatic passport.

"Well, this is quite irregular," she said slowly, looking at the extravagantly stamped passport. "We don't really have a way to—"

"I know it's an unusual circumstance, but if you will allow me to make a quick phone call," Sandler said, unclipping the phone from the strap of his messenger bag. He dialed and held the phone to his ear. "Sir? Yes, I'm at the desk in the ship terminal and…. Yes, sir, of course." He held the phone out to the clerk.

She looked at him in alarm but reached out hesitantly for the phone. Gingerly, as if expecting it to explode, she held it to her ear. "This is—"

She fell silent. That seemed to happen whenever anyone spoke to Sandler's boss, Donnelly noticed. She started nodding, just as Sandler had earlier. After a minute or two of this, she finally found her voice. "But sir, we would need some documentation of—"

"Excuse me, Miss Prentiss, this is a matter of some urgency." A tall man had appeared next to her, holding several sheets of paper in front of him.

She set the phone down on the counter as if she'd been hung up on. "Yes, sir," Miss Prentiss said absently, clearly overwhelmed.

"You are to keep alert for a Mr. Sandler Birkin, who will present a diplomatic passport. He is to be granted passage with the highest priority."

"Yes, sir. This"—she pointed vaguely at Sandler—"is he... him. Mr. Sandler Birkin, I mean."

"Ah!" the man cried. "Excellent work as usual, Miss Prentiss. Now please complete the check-in so that Mr. Birkin and his guest may get underway."

"Actually, this is Mr. Gabriel Donnelly, and I am his guest," Sandler said, smiling at Donnelly.

"Very good, sir," the man replied with an obsequious smile that quite nearly obscured an appreciative flicker of his eyelids as he appraised the two men and perhaps speculated on the nature of their relationship. "I leave you in Miss Prentiss's capable hands, and I trust you shall have a delightful crossing."

The two men filled out several forms, had their pictures taken, and were issued their boarding packets in soft leather portfolios. Then Miss Prentiss personally escorted them to a lounge area that was as far removed from the hue and cry of the general boarding terminal as could be imagined. There were only a dozen or so other passengers present, not one of whom seemed to be under the age of seventy. They found a pair of chairs next to a small table in the corner of the room beside a window overlooking the pier; the ship, from this vantage, was simply a vast black wall.

"May I offer you gentlemen a cup of tea?" asked a tuxedoed waiter bearing a gleaming silver pot.

"That would be lovely," Sandler said.

"I don't suppose you have... coffee?" Donnelly asked.

"But of course, sir," the waiter said. With a flickering glance across the room, he summoned two more waiters who walked briskly over, one bearing a coffeepot and the other bringing a tray laden with cups, little pitchers and bowls, and a plate of sandwiches cut into triangles with anal-retentive precision.

There was a discreet flurry of activity, and in under a minute Donnelly was sipping a very fine cup of coffee indeed. "Ah, that's the stuff," he groaned as the first caffeine of the day entered his deprived system.

Sandler lifted his steaming cup with its delicate saucer and sipped cautiously.

"Too hot?" Donnelly asked.

Sandler swallowed and set the cup back on its saucer with a smile. "No, it's perfect. It's just that the tea they make for the household staff at the palace has spoiled me. I never drank much tea before, but there's just something about the way they do it there." He sipped again. "I'm sorry, that sounded arrogant and awful."

"Not at all. I love hearing about your travels and experiences. My only brush with the glamorous elite was being thrown up on by the lieutenant governor at a wedding reception. That's not a story I tell much, for obvious reasons. Yours are so much better."

Sandler smiled and looked around the room. "So, it seems as though the experience of crossing the Atlantic on a ship hasn't changed much since the *Titanic*.

The great unwashed masses mill about like cattle, and the smart set sip tea and talk about the Queen."

"So it would seem. This is the first time I've done this, and almost certainly the last. I have some idea how much this trip must have cost, and it's easily more than I've spent on every vacation I've ever taken, combined."

"Then we must be sure to enjoy it," Sandler said with a chuckle. He picked up one of the precious sandwiches and popped it into his mouth. "Oh, dude, you have to." He held the plate over to Donnelly. "They killed it with the egg and cress. Just fucking crushed it."

Donnelly's laughter drew more than one stern look from the other passengers. He stifled it as soon as he saw their reaction but still smiled broadly. "Let's be sure to let the waiter know that they 'fucking crushed it,' okay? They probably don't hear that very often."

"You kidding me? That one, over there," Sandler said, tipping his head toward a stately woman who had to be ninety, and who regarded the room from the needly tip of her Edwardian nose. "She probably drops the f-bomb on the regular. 'Jeeves, bring me the fucking newspaper, and a fucking crumpet while you're at it, you old poofter!'" he said in the arch tones of congenital nobility.

Donnelly dissolved into helpless laughter while struggling desperately to stifle any sign that he was laughing. When the waiter returned with the coffeepot, he asked if he could be of any further assistance.

"No, I'm just fine," Donnelly replied, lifting the freshly filled coffee cup toward the waiter in gratitude for its replenishment.

Sandler watched him glide away. "Poor guy thought he'd have to run and fetch the defibrillator. I imagine that happens daily with this crowd."

"Now behave," Donnelly scolded with good cheer. "We'll probably be seated next to her at dinner."

"Don't worry, I won't ask her to pass the fucking salt," Sandler said solemnly, holding his fingers aloft as if swearing to try his very best.

"That's better," Donnelly replied with a grin. He slugged back his coffee in a gulp, and then it struck him. Out of all of the chaos of the last twenty-four hours, this was the first normal thing he'd done: drinking coffee and laughing.

"What's wrong?" Sandler asked suddenly, setting his cup onto its saucer with a clatter and leaning toward Donnelly.

"Nothing," Donnelly replied, not even convincing himself. "I just... forgot. Just for a minute, I let myself forget."

"Forget what?" Sandler's voice was full of concern.

"That he's not here. That I'm about to take this trip of a lifetime alone."

Sandler nodded. It was clear from his face that he knew a thing or two about going it alone. "I know it's hard. But he pulled off a miracle getting to Madrid, and you'll be together soon. The best thing you can do is to try and salvage what you can from this situation. You are about to embark on an amazing journey, and he would want you to enjoy it, wouldn't he?"

Donnelly smiled sadly for a long moment, then nodded.

"And you aren't alone." Sandler said this in a low voice, and put his hand on Donnelly's knee.

Donnelly put his hand on Sandler's and nodded. "Thank you. I wouldn't have gotten anywhere near here without your help."

"And I wouldn't be on my way in the lap of luxury without you, so that makes us even. Now, the least we can do is use the sacks of cash that your friend blew on this trip to some good purpose and enjoy it a little, right?"

"You're right, of course. I just miss Ethan so much. This will be the longest we'll have spent apart in… well, since we first met."

"I can hardly wait to meet the man you love so much."

"That's a very sweet thing to say. I'm sure he'll be happy to meet the person who made it possible for me to get there at all."

"Good. Now, let's snarf these sandwiches. I saw some cake being passed around over there."

Donnelly nodded grandly. "I say, I believe I'll have some of the fucking cake."

It was Sandler's turn to dissolve into laughter.

Meanwhile, back at home

"THEY SAY the air, it is full of ass?" Nestor asked, his expression puzzled. Intrigued, but puzzled.

"Not ass, *ash*," Bryce replied, stabbing at the news reports on his phone with increasing alarm. "An obstreperous volcano, of all things, is attempting to derail our dear troopers' impending nuptials."

Nestor stared blankly, then shrugged helplessly.

"This bitch of a mountain in Iceland," Bryce said, turning his phone for Nestor to see, "has decided out of pure spite to blow up, and the ash in the air means we cannot fly to the wedding tomorrow." Bryce had invited himself and Nestor to come nearly two weeks early, just to see to details. Of this particular manifestation of his dedication to service, the troopers were, as of this moment, unaware.

Nestor again shrugged, holding his palms outstretched in a gesture of accepting what one cannot change.

Bryce gave a mighty—yet piercing—harrumph. "This is what holds your people back," he snapped. "A dictator starves the entire island for decades, and…." He held his hands out just as Nestor had done and gave a surrendering shrug. "The entire world gives up on both communism and the Catholic church, but"—he shrugged again—"you manage somehow to hang on to them. And now in the face of the worst thing to happen to a wedding since heterosexuality?" He shrugged a third time, arms stretched to heaven. "It's almost as though you would prefer to yield quietly to whatever the world throws at you, like Buddhists contemplating a river, or the French army hearing gunfire."

"But, my love, it is a volcano. There is nothing we can do—"

"Nestor, I will not have that flaccid attitude in this house. In this—as in all adversity—I prefer to think there is never nothing we cannot keep from *not* doing."

Nestor's eyes crossed a bit.

"I will not stand idly by while some 'natural disaster,' as the alarmists on the news are calling it, keeps me from getting to that wedding. Our dear boys need us, darling. How else are they going to get down the aisle with the pleats of their kilts perfectly pressed? I will not have them mussed as they say their vows. Even if I have to reach under there and straighten things out myself."

Nestor nodded gravely. "Is a skirt, with something... extra."

"My point exactly! Now you know our boys will be testing the tensile strength of that plaid fabric even before they say their vows and all of that talk of commitment gives them a marriage boner. We must be vigilant. And we must get there, darling, we simply must."

"What do you plan, my love?"

"I'm glad you asked. It's simply too brilliant. In fact, I have no idea why no one else seems to have thought of it. The ash cloud is currently over the Atlantic Ocean. That means planes flying east cannot get through. So, what we're going to do is fly *west*." He stood back to give this idea—and Nestor's impending accolades—the room they deserved.

Nestor stared for a moment. "But is not England east of here?"

"Yes, but by going west, we avoid the whole mess!"

"We fly around... the whole world?" Nestor whispered, eyes wide.

"Now you've got it," Bryce cried, clapping his hands and bouncing excitedly.

Nestor's uncomprehending eyes followed him: up and down, up and down.

"Genius, right?" Bryce prompted. Nestor's delay in celebrating his brilliant solution was getting tiresome.

"Yes, *henius*. That is the word I was wanting," Nestor cooed.

"There we are. Thank you. Now, I have many arrangements to see to. Reservations to change, tickets to buy—"

"But, my love, how will we pay for?"

"Leave that to me, honey, leave that to me." Bryce paused for a moment's thought. "Actually, not entirely to me. Open up your suitcase and toss out anything that says 'I played a footman on *Downton Abbey*' and replace it with some 'I forgot to pack underwear' and a little 'I wouldn't mind a spanking.'"

Nestor nodded. These were directions he understood. He hurried off to the bedroom to modify his wardrobe for the week.

"Never fear, my beloved troopers," Bryce swore to the ceiling. "I am coming to you."

The dock, New York

"MESSIEURS DONNELLY and Birkin?"

In a room full of tuxedoes, this man moved with an even more extravagant formality. He was dressed in white tie and morning coat, with spotless white gloves.

"Yes...?" Donnelly replied, somewhat uncertainly.

"So pleased to make your acquaintance, sir. I am Rutherford, your butler. Are you ready to board, sir?"

Donnelly rose. "I guess so," he said, looking to Sandler with eyebrows raised.

"Good to go, chief," Sandler replied, hefting his duffel.

"Please, sir," Rutherford objected gently. "Allow me." He reached out and relieved the men of their duffels. He turned and handed them to a very young man dressed in a way that Donnelly would have considered cliché even for a bellboy in a 1940s hotel comedy. Then he reached out for Sandler's messenger bag, but a subtle shake of Sandler's head was enough to dissuade him from asking to take it as well. "This way, gentlemen." He held an elegant, gloved hand out to point the way toward a door that now stood open.

The butler spoke in the hushed, proper clarity of British Empire, which had doubtless ruled over the island of his birth. Donnelly couldn't quite place the undertones that lurked beneath the BBC-issue accent, but Rutherford's ebony skin spoke of a tropical origin. The man could have been forty or seventy; his bright eyes and brilliant white smile gave no sense of age whatsoever.

As they walked, Rutherford led the way through several more doors. "Your luggage, Mr. Donnelly, has already been brought aboard. I have taken the liberty of unpacking for you."

"Thank you," Donnelly replied, completely overwhelmed by the strange world of privilege he had suddenly stepped into.

"How'd you manage to get your luggage here?" Sandler asked.

"We had our suitcases sent in advance so we wouldn't have to lug them around. I completely forgot about it, actually. I had been trying to think of how I could meet the dress code in the dining room with just what I have in my carry-on."

"Have no worries about that, sir," Rutherford said suavely. "Your tuxedos are the finest I think I've ever seen."

Donnelly stumbled a bit. "Tuxedos? We don't own tuxedos."

Rutherford nodded, as if something that had been nagging at him had suddenly been cleared up. "They arrived separately from your luggage. There seemed to be a gift card attached to the box. I set it aside for you—unopened, of course."

Donnelly shook his head. He had been completely unprepared for things to suddenly start working out perfectly. Perhaps his luck really was changing.

They made their way through the almost completely empty ship—clearly the masses had yet to begin boarding—and arrived at a bank of elevators in the main lobby. The four of them—butler, bellboy, and Donnelly and Sandler—boarded one that stood open, and they rose several decks before the doors opened again. As they proceeded through restaurants and shops toward the front of the ship, Rutherford turned to explain. "Your elevator is far forward, on the starboard side." Donnelly nodded, overwhelmed by the size of the ship, and was simply trying to remember the path they were taking so he could find his way later.

Finally they reached a small alcove with just a single elevator in it. Rutherford drew a card from his waistcoat pocket and touched it to the brass plate where a button would normally be. Instantly, the doors glided open.

"Gentlemen," Rutherford said, sweeping his hand out and stepping to the side.

Donnelly and Sandler entered the elevator, and the two uniformed men followed them. Only as they began to rise did Donnelly realize that the back wall of the elevator car was glass. They suddenly had a view of the entire pier and the hundreds of passengers who were beginning to shuffle toward the ship.

"The elevator is keyed to your cards only," Rutherford said. "It will take you to decks 7 through 11. Your suite is on deck 10."

At that moment the doors slid open. They had arrived. Rutherford and the bellboy stepped out of the elevator and stood aside once again, and Donnelly, awestruck, stepped directly from the elevator into the suite that would be his and Sandler's home for the voyage. Rutherford showed them around the bedroom, the sitting room, the dining room, and the two bathrooms. Finally, they arrived at the large plate-glass doors that led out to the balcony.

"You'll notice," Rutherford said as they stepped out onto the teak expanse, "that because of the solid walls on both ends, no one can see onto your balcony once we're underway. Should the weather be conducive to sunbathing, you needn't worry about anyone intruding upon your... privacy." He set this word down gently, with the practiced inflection of discreet service.

"Thank you," Donnelly replied a little awkwardly. He was recalling the use that he and Brandt had made of the balcony at the Villa Hermes and willing himself desperately not to blush at the memory.

"If it suits, it would be my pleasure to pour the champagne." They nodded, and Rutherford glided back into the suite, leaving them on the balcony.

"This is amazing," Sandler said, leaning on the railing and taking in the commanding view of the ship and harbor. "It would have been so romantic." He looked at Donnelly and seemed to realize his mistake. "I'm sorry, that was really rude."

"Don't worry about it. This is so far beyond anything I'd ever imagined that it's not possible to be disappointed. I mean, it would be awesome to have Ethan here, but it's hard to look at all of this and feel anything but lucky."

"Gentlemen?" Rutherford stepped back out to the balcony with a silver tray bearing two flutes of champagne. The bellboy emerged from his wake with a silver ice bucket on a stand, which he set near the railing.

They each took a crystal vessel.

"Should you require anything—dining in your suite, reservations, or anything else—please touch 1 on any of the phones. That is my direct line."

"Thank you, Rutherford," Donnelly said, momentarily panicked that he should be tipping everybody.

But Rutherford simply smiled, set the silver tray on a table, and nodded to both men. He and the bellboy let themselves out.

"Well," Sandler said, holding his flute aloft. "Here's to smooth seas and the reunion that waits on the other side."

"I'll drink to that," Donnelly said, touching his glass to Sandler's.

About an hour later, after they had polished off the bottle of not inexpensive champagne, Donnelly got a little unsteadily to his feet. "Well, there are two showers in this palace, and I think I'm going to make use of one of them. You are welcome to the other, of course, should you feel the need to freshen up."

"It's been thirty-six hours and a thousand miles by car and boxcar since I showered. I think it's high time." Sandler rose as well, and they made their way back into the suite.

Suitably refreshed, they took in the spectacle of the lifeboat drill and then decided it was time for dinner. They had to change, of course, as the dress code for the restaurant dedicated to denizens of these rarified suites was stringent.

"I don't actually have anything posh enough for this," Sandler said when they returned to the suite. "I normally stay in the background, and my entire wardrobe is chosen for wrinkle-resistance rather than style."

"No worries," Donnelly replied as he opened the closet into which Rutherford had unpacked Brandt's baggage. "You're close to Ethan's size. I'm sure he wouldn't mind you wearing his dinner jacket and slacks. He wasn't exactly looking forward to wearing them himself, truth be told."

"Not much for fashion, is he?"

Donnelly rolled his eyes. "You could say that. Given the choice, it would be jeans and a sweatshirt and some awful baseball cap every single day for him."

"Sounds like you'd prefer he dress up a bit?"

"Hardly. I prefer him naked, actually." Donnelly winked roguishly, which made Sandler burst out laughing. "Now, he's about your height, but he has a bit more… bulk."

"You mean he actually works out?" Sandler asked as Donnelly held a shirt up to him.

"It shouldn't be too bad. He carries most of his weight in his chest, and arms. And those shoulders. Oh, and that butt of his…." Donnelly looked off into the distance.

"Need a moment alone with your memories?" Sandler asked with a wink.

"Later, when I have time to reflect," Donnelly replied with a Mae West growl. "Here—try these. And if nothing fits, we'll hit the gym in the morning and see if we can't get you filled out a bit."

Soon they were dressed and on their way down to dinner on deck 7, to which their private elevator whisked them instantly.

"Now, remember," Donnelly cautioned as they entered the restaurant, "if we're seated at the duchess's table, let her drop the first f-bomb. It's only polite."

Sandler laughed and crossed his heart to make his vow of decorousness.

"Ah, Messieurs Donnelly and Birkin," the maître d' intoned as they approached the podium. "This way to your table, please."

They followed the lanky, elegant man through the restaurant, all the way back to the far corner where a table for two was set some distance from the others next to a large window. The crystal vase of red roses declared to all present that this was the honeymoon table. The maître d' pulled out one of the chairs, and Donnelly motioned for Sandler to take it. He took off his messenger bag and set it next to him as he sat. Then Donnelly was seated and more champagne was poured.

"So, what exactly did you do for the guy who paid for all of this? Because it kind of seems like you must have given him a kidney or something," Sandler said as he sipped the champagne.

"It wasn't quite that extravagant," Donnelly replied. "We just helped him get himself out of an awkward situation."

"Awkward like a mafia hit squad?"

Donnelly laughed. "No, a marriage that had turned bad. But you're not far off with that mafia hit squad thing. James's soon-to-be ex-wife had pretty much set out to ruin him, and we did what we could to help. It's not like we saved his life or anything—we were just in the right place at the right time, through a run of coincidences that no one would actually believe. But her father felt like he should take a swipe at us just out of spite and ruin our wedding reception. So James set this whole destination wedding thing up at the last minute to make it up to us."

"And you say I live an exciting life," Sandler said with a grin. "You've got some complications of your own there."

"You know, now that you mention it, the last two years have been unbelievably complicated. Life wasn't like that before. I swear, sometimes it feels like we're characters in the most ridiculous book you can imagine. Who would read this stuff?"

Sandler laughed. "I would. I totally would." He reached his champagne flute across the table. "Here's to more adventures, even more unbelievable than the ones that came before."

"Careful what you wish for there, mister," warned Donnelly. But even as he worried about tempting the fates, he touched his glass to Sandler's and drank more expensive champagne.

When they returned to the suite after dinner, it had in their absence been prepared for a romantic evening; there were rose petals on the bed, heart-shaped chocolates on each pillow, and yet another bottle of champagne icing in a silver bucket. The two men stood at the foot of the bed, staring at the spectacle.

"Well, isn't this romantic?" Sandler said, the irony in his voice rendering the question rhetorical.

"Wow. Rutherford's on his game."

Sandler picked up the bedside phone. "Good evening, Rutherford. Would you be so kind as to make up the sofa bed for me? Yes, thank you." He set the phone down. "He sounded a little disappointed, but he'll be here momentarily."

"Poor guy," Donnelly replied. "This is probably the first time he's had people in this suite who wouldn't be risking a broken hip just getting into bed together."

Sandler laughed. "My hip would probably be only the first of many things Ethan would break if I even came close to this bed."

"Oh, now, he's not that sensitive about other guys. In fact, he hasn't shot anyone in the kneecap for weeks now." Donnelly hooted with laughter until he was interrupted by the gentle chime of the doorbell.

Sandler backed out of the bedroom, looking a little fearful for the safety of his kneecaps, and opened the door to admit Rutherford.

"It will take me just a moment to make up the sofa, sir," he said to Sandler as he got to work moving couch cushions. "Did you enjoy your dinner?"

"Yes, we did, thanks," Sandler replied.

"We actually may have enjoyed dessert a little too much," Donnelly added, coming in from the bedroom.

"Oh, Mr. Donnelly, you look like a man who doesn't enjoy dessert often enough," Rutherford said with a smile. "And you too, Mr. Birkin." He turned back to making the bed, with perhaps a slight sadness on his face.

"Rutherford," Donnelly said, a little awkwardly, "I feel I should tell you that Mr. Birkin and I are not… together. In fact, my fiancé was supposed to be with me on this voyage, but he was unable to get to New York in time, so he's meeting the ship in Southampton."

"Ah," Rutherford said. "I apologize. The reservation said that you were about to be married. I do hope I caused no offense."

"No, none at all," Sandler said, smiling warmly. "We thought it was very sweet. And if Mr. Donnelly were not marrying a handsome and dangerous man to whom he is forever devoted, I might have been inspired by your rose petals to… well, let's just leave it at that, shall we?" He winked at Rutherford, who with a hint of a grin returned the gesture.

"There you are, sir. I will return in the morning to take care of the sofa, so don't bother with the sheets and blankets. I hope you will find it comfortable."

The men thanked him and saw him out.

"He seemed disappointed that we wouldn't be rolling around in his rose petals, didn't he?" Donnelly said as they closed the door.

"I think Rutherford is a little sweet on you, actually," Sandler teased.

"Again, I think it's down to our being fifty years younger than his usual guests. But it's nice of you to say."

"Drink before bed?" Sandler asked, walking to the wet bar and opening the cabinet. "We've got some nice Scotch here, and—oh, some Tanqueray."

"Tell me there's tonic and a lime and you've got a deal."

"This is your lucky day." Sandler set to work making gin and tonics.

As Donnelly stood looking out at the dark, flat horizon the sea had become, lost in his thoughts, Sandler appeared at his elbow with a tall glass.

"Your Tanqueray and tonic, sir?" he asked in his best approximation of Rutherford's dry patrician accent.

"Fucking delightful, my good man," Donnelly replied, his jaw aristocratically tight. He took the glass and reveled in the first sip. "That, sir, is a finely crafted beverage. It is precisely what I needed." He turned back to the window, his smile fading as he watched a few more stars sparkle into view.

Sandler stood next to him, as if trying to see what it was Donnelly was looking for in the twilight. After a long moment, he spoke. "He's probably feeling exactly the same way right now," he ventured softly.

Donnelly nodded, not looking away from the window. "If I know Ethan, he's charging north from Madrid like a vandal horde, laying waste to everyone who crosses his path. I hope he has at least one moment like this along the way."

"I hope so too," Sandler replied.

"And I hope he's not alone," Donnelly continued. "I hope he has someone to stand by him the way you have stood by me."

"Something tells me you would have found a way here without my help," Sandler said. "You talk about how Ethan's the strong one, but I've seen you—seen your determination."

Donnelly finally turned away from the window. "You haven't just helped me with travel arrangements, though you've come up with some amazing stuff—and I do appreciate it more than you can possibly imagine. But it's not just that. It's… this," he said, lifting the drink. "You somehow know exactly when I need to have a drink and get mopey for a bit. And then you know exactly what to say to shake me out of it. I hope Ethan has someone to do that since I can't be there to do it for him."

Sandler blushed deeply. "It's not rocket science, Gabriel. You wear your love for him so transparently—I know exactly what you're feeling just by watching you. It's easy to know what to say to you because your emotions are so honest."

It was Donnelly's turn to blush. "I think you're being too modest. But it's a lovely thought, and I will treasure it." He tipped up his glass and finished his drink. "Now, I think I'd like to crawl between sheets that were no doubt woven by the angels themselves and get some sleep." He set the glass on the sideboard.

"I think I'll stare at the sea a little while," Sandler said, sitting down in one of the leather armchairs that faced the windows. "Good night, Gabriel."

"Good night, Sandler. Sleep well."

CHAPTER FIVE

Monday
Early morning, Madrid airport

AS THE clock on a nearby information panel counted out the minutes that slowly marched on after one in the morning, Kerry softly broke the silence.

"I can't sleep either," she said.

"My body has no idea what time it is," he replied, looking over at her, seeing how tired her eyes looked.

"That's a pretty fierce expression you have on your face," she said. "No wonder you can't fall asleep. You look like you're trying to think about him hard enough to make him feel it."

"That's definitely what I'm doing," he said with a dark chuckle. "I can't imagine why it's not working."

"Maybe it is. You never know—he may be sitting bolt upright at this very moment, wondering why he's seeing floating visions of a deserted airport terminal and transit maps in Chinese."

Brandt laughed. "Great. So now I'm making my fiancé think he's gone insane. I should stop before he ends up in an institution."

Kerry punched at the sweatshirt she was using for a pillow, then lay back down and wriggled in an obviously pointless attempt to make herself more comfortable. "Tell me a story," she said, once she'd given up wriggling.

"About what?"

"About him," she said simply.

He smiled. "You're probably tired of hearing about him by now."

She shook her head. "Not at all. I'm intrigued by the man who can make the strong, silent Officer Brandt lovesick. So tell me, sir, about the first time you knew you were in love with this amazing specimen of humanity."

"Hold up there," Brandt objected with a chuckle. "Part of the strong, silent deal is that no one expects you to talk about your feelings. Because no one expects you to have feelings."

She fixed him with a scolding glance, and shook her head slowly.

"Okay, so I'm clearly not going to get off the hook. Fine." Brandt shifted a bit, trying not to feel the armrest poking into his hip. "The first time I knew I was in love with Gabriel?"

"Yes. Now no more stalling. Tell." She looked at him expectantly.

Brandt took a moment to collect his thoughts. When had he known he was in love? He'd spent the last two years being in love, and it had happened so suddenly he'd never really reflected on whether there was a particular moment at which he knew it happened. Then it came to him, out of the depths he'd never spent much time plumbing.

"It was a little more than three years ago, right before Christmas," Brandt began. "Gabriel and I had been partners for a year and a half, ever since I graduated from the academy."

"Wait, so you two were together before you even joined the police force? Like, college sweethearts?"

"No, we weren't *partner* partners yet, not at that point. We had just been partners on the job for that long. We wouldn't actually get together for another six months or so. At this point, believe it or not, we were both straight. Never been with a guy, never intended to."

Kerry sat up and waggled her finger in her ear in a cartoon exaggeration of mishearing. "What, now?"

Brandt closed his eyes for a moment. This never got easier to explain. "We were straight when we met. We were straight right up until the time that we had this undercover job to do, and we suddenly... well, let's just say I showed him a side of myself I'd never let anyone see—even me."

"I would love to hear all about that—I mean, *all* about that—but right now you are going to tell me about the moment you knew you were in love with him, six months before you were actually in love with him. By the way, you're like the Robert Altman of late-night airport storytellers. I have a feeling none of this is going to make sense until I get to the end, and maybe not even then."

"Keep your expectations low. I've never told anyone this story, so I have no idea if it's going to make sense or not. I don't think I even understand it, to be honest."

"That's the best kind of story. Please, continue."

"So, we'd been together every day for a year and a half, except for when Donnelly's niece was born and he took a week off to help his sister out. We had our usual shifts during the week and every other weekend, and on our days off, we worked out and watched sports and generally hung out together. So, it's Christmas, and my family wants me to come home for the holiday, because I'd had to work it the year before. They all live on the other side of the state, so it's going to take me four hours to drive there and four hours to drive back, and I only have Christmas Day off, so it's a lot of hassle for a little bit of family time. So I'm not all that excited to go. At least that's why I thought I wasn't excited to go."

"The plot thickens. Nicely done."

"Thank you. I'm glad uncertainty about my own emotional state makes such satisfying narrative." Brandt propped himself up on one elbow, warming to his storytelling task despite his sarcasm. "Anyway, the end of our Christmas Eve shift finally comes, and Gabriel drops me off at my place so I can change and get on my way home. But then he shuts off the car and gets out with me, and I ask him what's up. He says he's going to make me some coffee for the road, because we've had a long day, and I need coffee to stay awake for the drive, and I'm shit at making coffee. All of which is true, by the way. So he comes up, and I change while he brews up some coffee. Five minutes later, after I've put presents for my family in my car, I come back into the apartment and he's got this thermos full of coffee, and he's made me a little snack in a paper sack—a sandwich and some carrots and a couple of cookies—and they're sitting on my kitchen counter like I'm a kid heading out for the first day of school. I look in the sack, and I can see that I had none of that stuff in my kitchen. He'd actually brought it all with him so he could send me on my way with a goody bag for the road. And the coffee."

"Oh, that's sweet," Kerry said, smiling a little sappily. "Is that when you knew you were in love?"

"No, that's when I knew my partner thought I couldn't take care of myself. Which, actually, I couldn't—I was going to stop at McDonalds along the way for terrible coffee and something that would make my arteries clog before I'd finished chewing. Anyway, he walks me out to my car, and I realize it's going to be, like, twenty-four hours before I see him again. A full day without Gabriel Donnelly. And the thought actually made me really sad."

"And that's when you knew."

"No, I just thought I was tired and not all that excited about having to drive across the state for less than a day with my family. But then he says Merry Christmas, and there was this note of sadness in his voice that so perfectly resonated with what I was feeling that I thought, just for a second, he knows what I was thinking. And that scares the crap out of me. Just flat-out panics me. So I say Merry Christmas back to him, and try to sound all jolly about it even though I'm completely freaked-out, and I jump in the car and drive away as fast as I can. Didn't even need the coffee after that, because I spent the entire drive trying to sort out why saying good-bye to him is the worst thing I've had to do in a long, long time. I kept telling myself—like out loud—that he's my best friend and of course I'd be sad to leave him, but mostly I'm not buying it because it's only for a day, and who gets choked up leaving their buddy for a day? Anyway, then I get home, and it's still dark because the sun won't be up for a few hours, and I just sit in the car in the driveway and drink the coffee he brewed for me and eat the snack he made for me and doing that makes me feel so close to him that I'm completely freaked-out all over again. As soon as the first light switches on in the house, when my mom comes down early to make cinnamon rolls and get the place ready for everyone to barrel down the stairs and open presents, I go inside and have what is probably the worst Christmas I've ever had because the entire time I'm thinking about Gabriel and about how his family doesn't seem to be all that close, and he wasn't going home for the holiday because they don't even talk to each other, though at that point I had no idea why. I get presents from my parents and brothers and sister that clearly show they have no idea who I am anymore, because they are the same things they would have given me when I was eighteen, but now I'm twenty-four and they're still giving me the same things as when I was in high school. I smile and pretend and give them the gifts that Gabriel had pretty much picked out for me to give them because he's amazing at gifts and I'm worse at it than I am at making coffee, and they are so happy with them and thank me, and the whole time I'm thinking that I'm not really a complete person without him around, and that not only scares me, it kind of makes me mad. Mad at myself for leaning on him so much that I couldn't even pick out presents for my own family anymore—not that I was ever any good at it, but still."

"Take a breath there, chief. You're kind of hyperventilating."

Brandt sighed. "Like I said, I've never told anyone this before. I didn't think how telling it would affect me. Sorry."

"No apologies needed. I asked you for a story, and you've got me completely wrapped up. Please, don't leave me hanging."

"Okay. So. We have Christmas dinner, and it's wonderful. At least the first two bites are before I start to think about how Gabriel doesn't have anyone to spend Christmas with except his sister, and he's never told me much about her, so I have no idea if they're even having dinner together. I can't even enjoy eating what has always been my favorite meal of the year. I should have brought him is all I can think at the moment. He should be here with me. And that starts another round of freaking out, so I give up, and halfway through dinner I say I've got to get back because I have an early shift in the morning, and they all wish me a Merry Christmas again, and my mom packs up this huge cooler full of leftovers, and everyone gets up from the table and waves as I back down the driveway. I drive like a maniac all the way back to the city and call Gabriel when I'm almost there to tell him I'm coming over. Didn't even ask him what he was doing, just said I was driving to his house. So I get there and drag that cooler up onto the front porch and bang on his door, and when he opens it, I yell Merry Christmas at the top of my lungs and basically tackle him with a hug. I think it was the first time I'd ever hugged him, and judging from the look on his face, he figured we'd die of old age before I ever did. Finally he staggers back into the house, and I let him go, and I stumble in with my cooler full of leftovers and tell him we're going to have Christmas dinner. So we load up plates with my mom's cooking, and all of a sudden, it's the taste of my childhood—everything's so good, even though I could barely swallow it when I was at home. Here, at his house, it's the best thing in the world. And he looks so happy, I just couldn't keep from smiling stupidly every time I look at him. And I still feel that freak-out feeling deep inside, but at this point I don't care anymore because seeing him happy is all I need."

"And so that's when…." Kerry ventured but then checked herself. "Never mind. You tell me when."

"Thank you. After dinner—it must have been ten o'clock by that point—he says that he has something for me. He gets up and goes over to this Charlie Brown Christmas tree he's put up in the corner of his living room, and picks up the only present under it. And it's for me. He hands it to me, and I feel like an idiot because it never even occurred to me to get him anything. But of course he tells me that he's enjoyed the dinner I'd brought more than any present I could have gotten him, because he's amazing and would never make anyone feel bad about anything ever. So I open the box, and inside is a coffee mug." Brandt fell silent, breathing deeply.

"He bought you a coffee mug for Christmas?" Kerry asked, seeming a little confused.

"It wasn't just a coffee mug. It was from this roadhouse that we'd raided a few months before. It was my first big bust in the department, and it got me noticed by the higher-ups. It was run by this biker gang with organized crime connections. It looked like a diner on the outside, but it was really a front for sex trafficking—ugly stuff. Anyway, when we did our initial surveillance of the place, we went and had breakfast at the counter, pretending to be tourists from up north. The cashier was a little twitchy and started asking us questions about where we were going and saying they didn't get many people in the place who looked like us. I was still new to the whole undercover deal and started to get panicky, and then Gabriel breaks in and asks if they sell the mug with the place's logo on it. Turns out he had overheard the cashier talking about how his son had drawn the logo, and all Gabriel had to do was say he liked it and wanted to buy one and the guy is suddenly all smiles. He even let his guard down enough for me to get a glimpse of the prison tattoo on his wrist that linked him to the gang we were tracking. That was the last piece of the puzzle, the piece I'd been missing, and now I had it."

"Ah," Kerry said. "So it wasn't just a mug...."

"No. Gabriel gave it to me to remind me of what I could accomplish, of the difference I'd made, of the new person I'd become. It was everything my family didn't understand about my career, my new life. But it was more than that to me. It reminded me of how much I owed him, of how we were truly partners."

"That's so sweet."

Brandt nodded, but was determined to finish his story. "So I take this mug out of the box, and all of this hits me: how he understands me better than my own family, how he saved me from being badgered by that twitchy cashier with the gang tattoos, how he helped me put the whole case together to close down that awful place. And I look at him, really look at him, and I realize that he's the person who means the most to me in the whole entire world. Of course I didn't want to be away from him for a whole day, because I'm only who I want to be when I'm with him."

"That's the moment!" she sang out.

Brandt shook his head. "You don't know how guys work. On the inside, I mean. We have an automatic defense mechanism that protects us if we start to get emotional about another guy. It's what makes us say 'I love you, man!' even if what we really mean is 'I love you.' But it's even deeper than that. It's like software that gets installed at the root level, and it subconsciously changes 'I think I'm falling in love with him' into 'I'm glad he's my buddy.' Even though what I was feeling in that moment was actually love—I see that now—at the time I was protected from the implications of that emotion by this deep wiring. And that's what we both had to overcome to reach each other, and that wouldn't happen for another few months, when we were caught up in a huge mess that left us no other way out. It takes a nuclear event to break out of the programming that our culture installs in the back of men's minds to keep us from feeling connected to each other."

"That's the saddest thing I think I've ever heard," Kerry said with a long sigh. "Sorry, go on."

"So I'm standing there, holding this mug, feeling all of the conflicting things that it brings up in my mind, and I look up at him, and he's just beaming at me. He tells me that now I'll have a proper mug for drinking that horrible coffee I make. And I just shake my head—don't know what to say, but know what I have to do. I walk into his kitchen, and I put the mug on the shelf next to his. He's looking at me like I'm insane, but I just tell him that only good coffee should go into it, and I only get that at his house, so I'm going to leave it there so I can use it when I'm over.

Which, again, is just about every day. He laughs it off, but just before he does I could see it on his face for just an instant. The look. The look that says he's happy that this little part of me will be in his house, just as happy as I am to have it there. It's like I've brought my toothbrush, like we're starting to move in together. Anyway, I see this flash across his face before the programming kicks in and he socks me in the arm and laughs. Then he says we've got a big day tomorrow and the shift starts early, and we should hit the hay. And honestly...." Brandt looked down, silent for a long moment.

"Ethan? You okay?"

Brandt nodded, feeling the tears already overflowing despite his best effort to blink them back. "He tells me that the guest bed is made up for me if I want to stay, and of course I want to stay—I don't know what else to do, or even what to think, but there's nowhere else in the world I want to be. I just nod, because I don't know what to say and probably couldn't say it without crying even if I did. He says good night and goes into his bedroom, and honest to God I want to go with him. I am too wiped out by the whole long day, the awful dinner with family and the amazing one with him, the terrible gift exchange at home and the amazing one with him, the awkward, distant, frustrating emotions of being with people I'm related to who don't understand me, and then him, the person who knows me best and accepts me and... loves me. And just for a second, maybe two, the programming falters and I see it. See it clearly. I love Gabriel Donnelly. Not as a buddy, not as a work partner, but as a person. As a man. I get this one moment of terrifying clarity, and then the darkness closes over it. But from that moment on, I knew. I wasn't ready to deal with it, couldn't even think about it or say it to myself, but... I knew."

He rubbed his eyes, wiped the wet tracks of tears off his cheeks. Having composed himself as best he could, he looked over at Kerry. She sat clutching the sleeve of her pillow/sweatshirt to her mouth, tears streaming down her cheeks. She shook her head slowly, with an infinite sadness.

"Hey, it's not that bad," Brandt said once he was sure his voice wouldn't break. "Our story has a happy ending, remember?" He gestured around the deserted airport terminal to prove his point.

"No, it's not you—it's a lovely story," Kerry said in a shaky voice between sniffles. "But I had no idea before... I... I've seen it. I didn't know what it was, but I've seen it." She squeezed her eyes shut tightly, forcing out more tears. "In the dorm. Greg wasn't the only one who struggled with it, sitting up all night on my futon searching for the words to describe the pain in his heart, the ache in his chest he would feel when a cute guy walked by. I thought they were scared about what their parents would say, about what would happen when they came out. But it's worse than that, isn't it? It's about what's already inside them, telling them what they feel is wrong, forcing them to believe they can't possibly be in love with another guy."

"It doesn't matter what your family will think if you can't even think it yourself," Brandt said quietly. "That voice in the back of your head is your worst critic, and it convinces you that you aren't really feeling what you know you're feeling. I talked myself out of loving Gabriel about a thousand times."

"I finally understand why it didn't really matter how liberal or compassionate or open my friends' parents were, or how many gay people there already were in the family. It was the voice in the back of their head that tortured them."

Brandt sighed. "I'm afraid inner turmoil comes standard with the Y-chromosome package."

Kerry nodded. "Never been happier to lack that optional equipment," she said with a small smile. "I could make out with girls in college and not torture myself about it."

"Not sure that makes up for all the ways that women get fewer opportunities and more discrimination on a daily basis, but at least you get 'I kissed a girl and I liked it' rather than 'I kissed a girl and now I'm in the throes of existential crisis.' That shit is what makes questioning guys throw themselves off bridges."

Kerry gave a halting sob. She nodded. "It was pills, not a bridge. But the end result was the same." She closed her eyes and let the tears flow. "I wish I had known what to say to him. I wish I had known what he was really struggling with."

Brandt reached across the small space they shared, and took her hand. "It's not your fault," he said. "I'm sure you were the best friend you could be. But even the best friend in the world doesn't stand much of a chance against that inner voice. It's not your fault." He held her hand while she cried, a long while.

As the night stretched into morning, they slept fitfully, exchanging half smiles when on occasion their eyes met.

Middle of the night, a truck stop

NESTOR LOOKED around the parking lot. "This is… not the airport."

"Oh heavens no!" Bryce replied. "It is just about impossible to get on a plane right now. It may be days before we could do that. No, what we're going to do is far better."

"But all I see are the trucks."

"Exactly right. We want to get to the West Coast ASAP, and what better way to see the highways and byways of this great land of ours than by tractor trailer?"

Nestor looked as though he would prefer to make the trip by pogo stick than truck, but he kept his peace.

"Now, I did my research, and what I discovered is that truck drivers can be friendly and accommodating to travelers such as ourselves. Assuming, of course, that one is willing to offer certain favors in return. You know, sort of like when that nice pizza delivery boy gives us extra sauce. And then doesn't charge us for the pizza."

Nestor nodded—this, he understood.

"We simply need to find a likely fellow who's heading the right direction and looking for some company. And who will be the least likely to throw us from a speeding truck once we've rendered our recompense. One would hate to end up in a shallow roadside grave—or worse, Kansas." Both men shuddered.

They stood near the truck stop's diesel pumps and shopped for a driver to approach.

"He look nice," Nestor said, pointing to one of the candidates.

"Mmm, I think not," Bryce said appraisingly. "No one's been wearing their jeans like *that* for months now."

"Or?" Nestor nodded toward a driver emerging from the convenience store.

Bryce shivered. "A man who tucks in that shirt is practically a serial killer already." He craned around, seeking more possible targets for his proposition. "Now, *there* is our man."

Nestor looked along Bryce's pointed finger to find a driver younger by at least a decade than all of the others. His milky-white biceps bulged powerfully from the cuffs of his skintight T-shirt.

Bryce nodded. "He's our trucker. Why, he's already given me a semi."

"Ah, *si*," Nestor agreed. He looked the man up and down, then up and down again. "Let us put our thumbs up."

"Well, look at you, getting into the hitchhiking spirit. But I think the proper term is putting our thumbs *out*. Although," he said, tipping his head as the man bent over to read the fuel gauge, "I'd put my thumb wherever he wanted." Bryce turned to Nestor. "Are we agreed?" Not that he waited for a response. He strode elegantly over to where the driver was putting the cap on his fuel tank.

"Excuse me, sir?" Bryce asked in his most importuning voice.

"Yeah?" The man stood upright and squinted at Bryce. His voice was deep and slow, drawing out one syllable into at least three.

"My friend and I are trying to get to the West Coast as quickly as possible. We were wondering if you might be willing—"

"You and your *friend*?" the driver interrupted, looking from Bryce to Nestor and back again.

"Yes, sir. I'm Bryce, and this is Nestor."

"And where, exactly, are you headed… on the West Coast?"

"Actually, that's a bit open-ended. You see, we have quite a long journey ahead of us, and simply want to get to an airport so we can fly our way across the Pacific to England."

The driver burst out laughing. Bryce was too distracted by the way his abdominals flexed into relief under the tight shirt with every guffaw to take offense.

"Do you know where England is?" he finally was able to say once he caught his breath.

"Of course I do," sniffed Bryce. "Though the British would never admit it, it's part of Europe."

"And you're going to get there by flying west?"

"Well, no one's flying across the Atlantic at the moment, so we made other plans."

The driver squinted at Bryce but offered no judgment of this rationale. "It just so happens that I am heading to Long Beach. But I'm not allowed to carry passengers."

"Oh, dear," Bryce replied, crestfallen.

"Officially, that is. But there's no way for them to know if I decide I might need some… company."

"Oh, oh! We can be *very* good company." Bryce nodded emphatically, and Nestor added a subtle wink.

The driver crossed his arms over his chest and nodded slowly. "Looks like I got me a couple of faggots here."

Bryce stiffened. "Now, there's no need—"

"Cut the crap. You two looking to provide certain services in exchange for my taking you to California?"

Bryce stroked his throat delicately. "Why… yes, in fact."

"Are you fucking crazy?" the driver erupted, face flushing with instant anger. "What the hell are you thinking, skulking around a truck stop in the middle of the night hitting on whoever comes by?"

"I assure you, sir, we didn't hit on just anyone. We chose very carefully."

"Just shut up and get in the truck, and don't let anyone see you." He looked quickly side to side, scanning the area before turning back to Bryce and Nestor. "Don't just stand there gaping at me—get in the fucking truck!" He stormed off to the cashier's booth.

"Well, isn't he just a take-charge fellow? I knew we'd picked well," Bryce said to Nestor as they climbed aboard. They stowed their suitcases behind the seat and settled in for the long haul. "Now remember our plan: I take care of anything that ends in 'job,' and you handle anything requiring lubricant." He sprawled over to the driver's seat to check the condition of his eyebrows in the huge side mirror and spied the driver returning from the convenience store with a small paper sack. "Oh, here he comes. This is so exciting!"

The driver's side door opened, and the trucker effortlessly bounded into the seat. He stuffed the paper bag under the seat and turned the key. The engine rumbled to life, and he put the truck in gear.

"Now, before we launch into the night," Bryce said, laying a delicate hand on the driver's knee, "will you do me a favor and promise that you aren't planning to dismember us? Because I'm more than a little attached to my member, and would like to continue to be so."

The driver picked up Bryce's hand and placed it roughly back in Bryce's lap as he merged onto the freeway.

Bryce looked down at his rejected hand and cast a confused look at Nestor, who shrugged in his accepting way.

"As I said," Bryce ventured as the truck gradually lumbered to cruising speed, "I'm Bryce, and my companion is Nestor." Met with stony silence, he continued. "And may I be so bold as to inquire whose strong biceps are so capably manhandling the wheel of this mighty vessel?"

The driver turned and squinted at Bryce, then leaned forward to see around him. "Does he ever shut up?"

Nestor shook his head with an adoring glance at Bryce. "Oh, no, no. If he stop talking, it mean he died."

Bryce returned the loving look. "You flatterer, you," he admonished, with a playful pat on Nestor's knee.

"I may have to give his mouth something else to do, then," growled the driver.

"I see we understand each other," Bryce cooed, sliding a little closer.

"You gonna do anything I ask you to?" There was a taunt in the driver's voice, as if challenging Bryce to specify the extent of his commitment to debauchery.

"I would consider it the height of rudeness to deny a gentleman's request," Bryce replied with great dignity—and a glance at the tightly packed crotch of the man's faded and worn jeans. "Whatever that request may be."

The driver nodded. He reached down to the exact focus of Bryce's fixed gaze and gave a little tug of adjustment. But then he reached lower, down under the seat, for the paper bag he had brought with him from the truck stop convenience store. This he retrieved from its stowage and handed to Bryce.

"A present?" Bryce cried. "You lovely man. I had no idea that gifts were customary in such circumstances. Nestor, we must remember this—we should carry something appropriate with us at all times."

"Open it," growled the driver.

"I can hardly wait to." Bryce opened the bag and reached inside. He glanced excitedly at Nestor as he felt around for its contents. With a great flourish, he pulled out a stack of... paperback books. "Oh, a man of culture! How lovely."

"Read 'em to me," the driver ordered.

Bryce and Nestor exchanged a bewildered look. "You want me to... read to you?" Bryce asked.

"That's right. But first, I've got two things to say. One, you are a couple of complete idiots, cruising a truck stop parking lot and throwing yourself at men. You could have gotten yourself into some very deep shit. Some of those guys play rough, and they would think nothing of fucking you unconscious and leaving you for dead. You are lucky you picked me."

"I assure you, we have already had occasion to celebrate our good luck," Bryce replied with another glance at the man's crotch. "And we take your advice to heart. No more truck stops for us."

"Promise?"

"Oh, I'd swear on my mother's grave if she had ever done me the courtesy of dying. On that happy day, however, you shall have my oath." Bryce crossed his heart solemnly. "Now, what was the second thing?"

"Virgil."

Bryce looked at him, confused. "What was that?"

"My name is Virgil."

"Oh, lovely! A name from antiquity, resonating with classical grandeur. We are so pleased to make your acquaintance, Virgil."

"Likewise. Now, get reading."

"Of course, it would be my pleasure." Bryce consulted the paperbacks he held. "Which would you like to start with?"

"I don't care," Virgil replied. "I just grabbed the three closest to the cash register."

"Well, let me see. We have shirtless cowboy, shirtless pirate, and shirtless... I'm going to guess... surgeon? The other details are a bit hard to make out. Is there a reading light of some kind?"

Virgil pushed a button on the dashboard and a reading lamp illuminated over Bryce's shoulder, casting a circle of light on the books.

"Oh, heavens no!" he shrieked, dropping the books as if they'd suddenly turned into spiders.

"What the—" Virgil asked, startled.

"These books. They have…." Bryce took a steadying breath, but could only continue in a desperate, hoarse whisper. "They have… *women* in them."

"Dios mío," gasped Nestor, fanning himself and looking heavenward.

"Look, they're right here on the covers," Bryce continued in scandalized tones as he fished the books up from the floor of the truck cab. "Observe the way this cowgirl is staring at him with longing in her cheekbones. She's clearly a slut. Then this piratical strumpet with the ridiculous push-up corset is undressing the swashbuckling captain with her eyes… or, finishing undressing him, I guess. And that nurse? Well, let's just say she looks the type to whip out a needle and have her tawdry way with his defenseless, unconscious body."

Virgil burst out laughing. "Of course they have women in them. They're romance novels. Don't tell me you've never seen one before?"

Bryce looked blankly at him. "People read books about heterosexuals?"

Virgil nodded, unable to speak through his laughter.

"Oh my stars. What this country is coming to? It's bad enough they do that sort of thing in the privacy of their own homes—and churches, from what I hear—but to force it on the rest of us this way? By putting a mostly naked man on the cover of the book to lure us in? Nestor, we have proof now of the heterosexual agenda. It's *real*."

Nestor crossed himself and sank back into an attitude of desperate prayerfulness.

"So pick one and start reading," Virgil said once Bryce's shock had ebbed and his breathing returned to normal.

"I don't know that I can do that," he replied solemnly. "I mean, when you said you wanted certain favors for granting us passage, I assumed you meant normal things, like a back rub, or a rusty trombone, perhaps a manicure. I had no idea there was such depravity packed into those tight, tight jeans."

"Bryce, you are homosexual."

"Well of course I am," Bryce replied. "Who isn't, these days?"

"And Nestor?"

"Honestly, now, it should be obvious to even the casual observer that one is as likely to find a straight man here as in a public restroom in Congress."

"Well, that makes three of us," Virgil concluded.

Bryce stared, amazed. He moved his lips from sheer force of will, but try as he might, he could make no sound. It was Nestor who finally broke the silence.

"I knew this," he said quietly.

Bryce turned, astonished. "You did?"

Nestor nodded placidly.

"Looks like your buddy has better gaydar than you do," Virgil said with a laugh.

"Pff. 'Gaydar,' I'll have you know, is of no use in our modern world. It's an artifact of an earlier time when we had to hide our sexuality and skulk about trying to determine who's gay without being able to say it out loud. I refuse to engage in such self-loathing spy games meant to silence us and keep us in the shadows."

Virgil sat back under the force of Bryce's pronouncement. "Wow. I hadn't figured you for a gay rights activist."

"Oh heavens no, dear. Nothing like that. Activism far too often leads to tragic results, such as mug shots under fluorescent lighting. I simply prefer to assume everyone's gay, and if someone I meet turns out not to know it yet, I am happy to show him the error of his ways. That way, I don't limit people's natural potential."

"Natural potential for what?" Virgil asked.

"For getting blow jobs, silly," Bryce replied with a roll of his eyes. "Honestly, Nestor, he says he's gay, but I'm beginning to wonder."

"I guess you can call me the old-fashioned kind of gay," Virgil said with a chuckle. "The kind that assumes everyone is straight until they get a little too drunk and a little too lonely and suddenly they're ready to go to town on the first accommodating body they find." He winked at Bryce. "That's usually me."

"Are you telling me you get your straight buddies drunk and then assail their virtue?" Bryce asked in shocked tones.

"Indeed I am."

"I knew I liked the cut of your jib," Bryce said approvingly. "But how do you do it when you're out on the road alone?"

"Luckily, the company I drive for doesn't pay for shit, so when we're on long dispatch and have to take a mandated rest between routes, we'll double up on a cheap motel room. We can't roll until twenty-four hours after our last drink, so we slam down as much as we can swallow as soon as we're out of the truck. Even the big burly ones get hammered when they bolt a fifth of something cheap."

"Ah, the thrill of illicit liaisons—I know it well. Sneaking around the back rooms of chic clubs with closeted celebrities. But of course I quite admire your blue-collar version, with drunk truckers in cheap motels."

Virgil's bemused look conveyed no gratitude for Bryce's admiration.

Bryce had no time for bemusement. "But, darling, if we are all playing with the same team, why in heaven's name did you burden us with these tawdry pulp novels full of heterosexing?"

"Have you ever read one?" Virgil asked.

"Oh my, no! The very idea."

"You don't know what you're missing."

"I know the outlines of it. They covered the basics in high school health class, and the parts I glimpsed through my fingers were more than enough to convince me I could go safely to the grave without firsthand knowledge of the female terrain betwixt neck and knee."

"These novels aren't about women—they're written *for* women, about men. If you want to know how straight guys think, you need to read novels written by women, for women, about men."

"But what could a woman possibly know about men?"

"That's not important. What's important is what men know about what women know about men."

Bryce turned to Nestor. "Is he making any sense to you?"

Nestor shook his head and shrugged.

Bryce turned back to Virgil with a sympathetic tilt of his head. "I suspect, dear, you've caught something from one of your straight trucker friends that has left you seriously deranged."

Virgil shook his head and patted Bryce on the knee. "Let me break this down for you. First, you must understand what motivates straight men. What makes them do everything, from the moment they wake up until they fall asleep at night—and pretty much dominates their dreams as well. That thing is… women."

Bryce and Nestor shuddered.

"It's true. It's like a nature documentary, a Darwinian struggle. If the species is to survive, then the straight ones must be driven by a primal need to pass on their genetic material. Now, because Mother Nature knows what's up, she gave straight men the overpowering desire to stick their dicks in any female willing to allow them to do it."

Bryce clapped his hands over his ears. "Stop! Stop this horror story!"

"I'm almost to the good part. Now, how does a man convince a woman to let him impale her?"

Bryce lowered his hands. "Convince her? Really? All I hear from those conservative ninnies in the media is that heterosexuality is natural and normal, and now you're telling me that women have to be argued into bed?" Bryce stopped for a moment to consider this. "I guess it is just punishment, if they insist on being straight."

"Yes, it's a straight man's sad lot in life: he can only have sex with women when he negotiates the terms of their relationship beforehand. And how do you think he's going to approach this negotiation? How will he behave in order to convince the woman to consent? He's not going to do it by being himself, or by being what he thinks a man should be. No, he's going to be the man he thinks the woman wants him to be."

"So in order to have sex with a woman, a man has to stop being a man and start being what he thinks a woman thinks a man should be?"

"Now you're getting it," cried Virgil. "Men work so hard to adapt their behavior to women's expectations that pretty soon they don't even realize they're doing it. It becomes part of who they are. And these romance novels show exactly what women think men should be. So I read them to be able to understand straight guys."

"And with that understanding, you can ruthlessly exploit their weaknesses in order to have sex with them!" Bryce called out, clapping his hands. "Well played, sir, well played."

"I knew a man of culture such as yourself would appreciate the genius of my plan."

"But, just a moment," Bryce said, pursing his lips. "If the men are trying to be what they think women think they should be, what are the women doing?"

"Ah, that is the real tragedy. For generations women were taught to define themselves by what men thought they should be. So now, whether they know it or not, most women make themselves into what they think the men in their lives want them to be."

Bryce's brow was furrowed. "So, if I understand correctly, heterosexuality requires that men try to be the way they think women think they should be, while women try to be the way they think men think they should be. So both sides are trying to be what the other wants, but what the other wants is already based on what the other thinks the *other* other wants. It simply beggars imagination," he said with an exasperated flailing of his arms, "that heterosexuals ever have any sex at all."

"My point precisely. The chances that a straight man is getting as much sex as he'd like are about nil. And that makes my chances pretty darn good. Picture the guy who has a few dates with women who won't put out, and then he gets sent out on the road alone for a week. Then put him in a dingy hotel with a fifth of something high-proof and nowhere to go. That's when I break out my tablet with a hundred gigs of porn, which, generous soul that I am, I'm happy to share. Ten minutes of that and I'll be eating him out of my hand."

Bryce gasped. "That is a stratagem of uplifting depravity. I am furious I didn't think of it first."

"Something tells me you'll be able to put the information to good use, Bryce."

"Oh, I am already planning how I can adapt it to the seduction of the various straightish men in my life. The construction workers, the parcel delivery couriers, the angry closeted pastors. But let's start with the pirates, shall we?" Bryce picked up the novel with the bare-chested swashbuckler on the cover and waved it about. "Yo ho ho, ladies! It's time to pick up some sailors!"

He opened the book and began to read.

Still early, Madrid airport

THE CLATTER of the rail station gate rolling up startled him awake. Brandt looked at his watch and saw that it was precisely half past something—was his watch set for San Diego, or Mexico City, or Madrid? He glanced up at the clock on the wall and found that it was indeed five thirty. Time to get on the train.

Across the two-foot gap, Kerry was sleeping peacefully. Brandt decided to let her sleep while he went to purchase tickets. This he was able to accomplish quickly as the ticket counter displayed instructions in every imaginable language. It was, he sheepishly admitted to himself, exactly as easy as Kerry had predicted it would be. He picked up a couple of cups of coffee from the little espresso bar in the station and headed back to camp.

When he arrived, Kerry was finishing putting the seats back into their original positions. Her carry-on sat next to Brandt's duffel, tidy and ready to move. She held out her hands for the coffee he brought.

"Oh, thank you, you lovely man," she enthused as she smelled the sharp aroma of train-station coffee emanating from the little cup.

"You really do need to meet Gabriel," Brandt said with a laugh. "His eyes roll back in his head exactly that way when he gets his first sip of coffee in the morning."

"I love him even more now," she said with a smile. "Now, when does our train leave?"

"It runs every half hour, and there are only a couple of stops between us and the main railway station. It takes about forty-five minutes. First train is in twenty. From there," he continued, consulting one of his many booklets, "the express to Barcelona leaves every half hour and takes about three hours. So, we'll be in Barcelona by noon, looks like."

"Excellent. Then we'll see how far we can get from there." She paused for a moment, as if unsure whether she should continue. "What would you think about...?"

He stopped after picking up his duffel. "Think about what?" he asked.

"Now, I know you want to get to Southampton as soon as you can, but honestly there's no point in doing that if he won't be there for almost a week. What would you think about taking a day or two in Paris? Judging from the big train map over there, we're going to have to change trains in Paris anyway before we get to London, so we might just as well...."

He looked at her for a long moment. "You're right," he finally said.

She seemed surprised to have won him over so easily. "I am?"

He nodded. "It's like Gabriel's always telling me: if you aren't where you want to be, then you might as well enjoy getting where you're going. Or something like that—everything sounds better when he says it."

"He's right, you know," she said as she picked up her carry-on bag. "How many times in your life are you going to find yourself in Paris by accident? We might as well spend a little time looking at paintings or whatever while we're there."

He squinted at her. "Paintings or whatever? Seriously?"

"What? Are you implying I'm not a cultured person? I'll have you know I support my local public television station."

"Wow," Brandt said with a laugh. "Lucky me, being escorted through the Louvre by a card-carrying member of PBS."

"I'm no Gabriel Donnelly, but I shall do my best," she said with a gracious curtsey, then socked him on the arm on her way past him. "Shake a leg, Officer. The train's going to be boarding in a few."

He turned and followed her, laughing in spite of himself at her predawn dramatics.

It was slightly after noon when they arrived in Barcelona after two train rides. Kerry proposed that they stay overnight and add the Spanish city to their itinerary, but Brandt—for reasons he couldn't really explain—wanted to get to Paris, where at least he would be closer to where Donnelly would be. Eventually.

So when the high-speed train finally deposited them at the Gare de Lyon, they had been on the rails for more than fourteen hours. They stood on the sidewalk and looked tiredly at each other. It was an hour to midnight.

"Well, I suppose we should find a place to stay," Brandt said. "Maybe we should ask a cab driver for a recommendation?"

Kerry squinted at him. "Suddenly you want to live dangerously? Where do you think a Paris cab driver is going to deposit two American tourists at this hour of the day? We'd be sleeping in a brothel." She laughed as if this were the funniest thing she'd imagined all day, then turned without another word to hail a cab.

"Wait, I thought you said a cab was the wrong way to go," he said, a little indignant.

"No, you were right about the cab. It's just that I'm going to tell him exactly where to take us."

"I thought you hadn't been to Paris before?"

"I haven't. But I travel all the time for work, and I have a ton of points with all of the hotel chains. We'll go to one of these." She held out a stack of a half-dozen or more plastic cards, each showing the logo of a hotel—most of them far posher than anyplace Brandt had ever stayed.

A cab pulled up, and Kerry launched herself into it. A moment of consultation with the driver in her sketchily remembered high school French—combined with the cards as visual aids—soon got them on their way.

"Thanks for taking care of that," Brandt said as the cab wound its way through the streets of Paris. "I wouldn't have known what to do."

"We're in this together, buddy," Kerry said, leaning on his shoulder. "I'll take care of the hotel room, and you take care of any mimes who try to rough me up for spare change."

"It's a deal." Brandt shuddered. "Ugh—mimes."

They were soon in the spectacular lobby of a grand hotel. Brandt held their bags while Kerry spoke to the clerk at the desk. She returned and pointed him to the elevators.

"They had one room left," she said. "It's a good thing I worked so hard to land that French-Canadian exchange student in high school—I still remember how to flirt *en français*." She held up the card key as if it were an engagement ring. "Floor *neuf, s'il vous plait*," she said grandly.

He looked at her blankly.

"Nine. I think," she said, then shrugged and giggled.

The ninth floor was the pinnacle of the hotel, and the suite into which Kerry had flirted them was spacious and filled with more marble than the average sculpture gallery. There was, however, only one bed. It was, like the rest of the suite, executed on a grand scale, but it was the only place to sleep unless one counted the fainting couch on the balcony that overlooked landmarks Brandt surely would have been able to recognize were he able to look anywhere other than that bed. That one big bed.

Kerry opened the doors to the bathroom, which was, of course, palatial. "Oh my, yes," she whispered approvingly. "Now, if you'd like to take a shower before turning in, go right ahead, because I'm going to lounge in that enormous tub for like an hour."

"Are you telling me I need a shower?"

"The last chance we had to take a shower was in San Diego, remember? Do you even know how many days ago that was? I don't. Now if you'd like to take one, please do, because I'm serious—you may not be able to get me out of that tub."

"All right, all right," Brandt said, laughing. "I'll take a quick one and you can have the place to yourself." He cast another glance at the bed. "So, about sleeping arrangements…."

"Look, I used to road trip with friends all the time in college—you should ask Greg to tell you about our trip to St. Louis sometime—and I have no problem sharing a bed. Is it okay with you?"

It wasn't. Not by a long shot. "Sure, yeah, it'll be fine." His only hope was to be asleep before she came to bed. That was the only way he'd be sure not to embarrass himself. He smiled to show her it was okay—it still wasn't—and took his duffel with him into the bathroom. The shower had a control panel that looked like it had been lifted from the space shuttle, but he managed to cajole hot water out of it. Kerry was right: he had no idea how long it had been since he'd taken a shower. It was heavenly, though he was true to his word and showered as quickly as possible.

As he stepped out of the shower, he realized he hadn't packed anything to sleep in. When he and Donnelly were together he never wore anything to bed since it would only get in the way. But now he would need something. He remembered that he had packed some running shorts and a T-shirt, which he grabbed out of his carry-on and slipped into. He strode back into the bedroom, clean and more than ready for bed.

"Better, right?" she asked.

"Much," he said, and he really did feel it. "Thanks for letting me play through. I imagine I'll be sound asleep in about three minutes, so soak as long as you like. I'll see you in the morning."

"Morning? Really? I'll *consider* noon... if you have room service deliver something unspeakably delicious."

"It's a deal."

She danced excitedly over to the bathroom and closed the door behind her.

He climbed into the large, soft, and luxuriously welcoming bed. As he settled his head onto the pillow, he felt certain he really would be sound asleep by the time she came to bed.

In this certainty he was very much mistaken.

A wedge of light from the bathroom awakened him and illuminated her form as she walked toward the bed. It was a shape Brandt had not contemplated for years—not since Donnelly and the masculine force he brought crashing into Brandt's life—and seeing it now, the past, his own history, rose up and stabbed him in the chest.

She was beautiful as she glided silently around the room, patting her hair dry, arranging her few clothes neatly in the armoire. Her movements were as sure as they were delicate, and even in the dim twilight of their Paris hotel room, he could see she was nude.

He closed his eyes, knowing he shouldn't intrude upon her privacy. She had been so good to him over the last few days as they made their way across the globe together, accidental traveling companions. This was the one thing she wanted to indulge herself in—a luxurious soak, a quiet moment—and here he lay violating that. Violating her. But he couldn't make himself close his eyes.

His mind, as minds will often do when we most need them to behave themselves, betrayed him. It brought up an image of Donnelly, his beloved Gabriel, walking through a darkened room naked. His tread would be heavier, he would block out the light with his broad shoulders. He would bring a waft of musky strength, not lavender. His silhouette would bulge with muscle where hers showed the graceful curve of her breast as she reached to hang a blouse.

Brandt clenched his eyes closed, bracing against the question that invaded his mind: would he be hard, right now, achingly hard, if it were Donnelly he were watching? Because he could no longer ignore the throb of his erection, its head jabbing the sheets.

He was hard. For her.

Fuck.

He managed to pretend to be asleep while she glided about the room, and even when she lifted the covers and slipped into bed wearing an oversize T-shirt. There was nothing sexy about what she wore, but the way she wore it agonized him. He could see, as she turned to rearrange the pillows, the gentle weight of her breasts, the delicate line of her clavicle.

That was his favorite part.

It hit him like a splash of ice water to the face.

His favorite part.

That place where the curve of the throat meets the collarbone, that soft concavity where the skin is so soft and so sensitive. He would kiss her there, every woman he had ever been with, and she would sigh with delight. It was a secret recess, a place he loved. Her scent would be strongest there, as if the perfume she wore lay in wait, released by the heat he inspired with his caress. That moment, a kiss at the base of the throat, was the moment when cuddling became something more. A kiss there portended more kisses, lower kisses, to come.

He had forgotten that.

Or, his betraying mind prompted, had he forced himself never to think of it? Had he chosen to deprive himself that heady thrill, that uniquely masculine experience? The feeling of power as he kissed that spot, the surge in his chest from hearing the surprised moan it brought from her delicate throat—these he had forsaken. Forever. Without a second thought.

Fuck. Is this what second thoughts feel like?

A pit, a heavy ache in his stomach, provided an answer. It wasn't the answer he wanted. It had to be the wrong answer. It had to be.

He glanced over at her, silhouetted by the dim light from the bathroom. She fell into a peaceful slumber almost instantly, and as she warmed the sheets with her body, the scent of an exotic bath oil rose to greet him. He listened to her breath, saw the soft rise and fall of her chest as she drifted away. She was as beautiful in slumber as she was awake.

Goddammit.

He lay there, tortured, agonized. He tried to be somewhere else in his mind but found himself inescapably here: in a bed in a picture-perfect Parisian hotel suite with a beautiful woman lying next to him. A beautiful woman who had spent the last who-knew-how-many days by his side as they rounded the globe on a ridiculous quest. She never complained, she never second-guessed. She simply smiled and laughed and cried at all the right moments.

As a fourteen-year-old he would have done anything to be here. Hell, three years ago he would have considered himself the luckiest man on earth. Now, he was in hell. Pure hell.

On the highway, America

"'BUT, BOLT,' she breathed breathlessly, 'I am promised to another!' Torchlight illuminated his strong cheekbones and danced on his face. 'Can another set fire to your loins the way that I, your pirate captain, can?' His eyes undressed her while his hands locked the door of the ship's basement." Bryce turned the page.

"Ooh, he gonna set fire to some loins," Nestor sang softly.

"I hope so," Bryce replied. "We keep hearing about how tight and manly his buttocks are, but we have yet to see them in action. Don't swordsmen have to thrust at some point?"

"I think you'll find that straight romance writers have little interest in the finer points of male buttocks," Virgil explained. "They're viewed as a sort of accessory, like strong shoulders or a classical profile."

"But the male posterior is the most versatile sex organ in the world," Bryce cried. "It can both give and receive—ideally at the very same time."

"Ah, lucky Pierre," sighed Nestor.

"Indeed," agreed Bryce.

"Can we please find out what Bolt sets fire to?" Virgil asked, drumming impatient fingers on the wheel of the truck.

"Yes, of course," Bryce said, flipping the book open again. "Bolt threw off his shirt, exposing his sweat-kissed chest, dripping with muscle. 'Come to me, Desirée,' he ordered, his voice heavy and moist with urgent command. 'No,' she ejaculated. 'Come to *me*, Bolt.' She reclined seductively on a sinuous coil of the jute rope Bolt's seamen used to hoist the ship's spanker and beckoned to him with her pert breasts. His powerful buttocks drove him toward her until their lips crashed together like a gallant man o'war fleeing before the wind, and a rock. She reached down and untied his tight leather pants; his ponderous manhood exploded into view, delighting her nether regions with its heft and beauty."

"Mmmm, heft," Nestor intoned dreamily.

"Though she doesn't deserve such a fine specimen, I guess I'm happy for her. So many times the big reveal just results in disappointment for everyone." He looked side to side at the other men. "Are we ready to continue?" Eager nods on both sides.

"'Bolt,' Desirée exhaled steamily, 'is that a great sea eel, or are you just glad to—' Bolt's engorged member wedged itself sexily between her molars, turning her words into groans and her tonsils into punching bags of pure passion. Her tongue swabbed the stalwart underside of his battering ram with a diligence that Mr. Sprat, the one-eyed deckhand, never brought to his work no matter how many times Bolt strapped him to the mast and had his way with the bullwhip. 'Desirée,' Bolt groaned muscularly, 'your mouth is a Charybdis.' Her eyes crossed with lust or confusion—or perhaps it was a giddy mix of both. The first of thirty-seven orgasms washed over her like the musical flames of an animal's passion." Bryce's brow furrowed as he reread that sentence to himself, lips moving slowly.

"Gonna have to hit the pause button," Virgil announced. "We need to pull in here for fuel."

"Ooh, how exciting," cried Bryce. "Now that I know what a hotbed of pent-up truckers these places can be, I'll have to try out what Bolt has taught me about straight men." He drew an eyebrow pencil from his clutch and began a quick touch-up.

"Hold the phone there," Virgil said, his voice serious. "You can't just flit in there and start mashing on every guy you see. It can be tricky—and dangerous. You two stay in the cab, okay?" He looked at them with a glare of warning that set them both back in their seats. "Good. Now, it'll take about ten for the tank to fill. Want something to eat?"

"Oh! Interstate cuisine!" Bryce hooted, bouncing up and down. "Yes, please. Just pick something that tastes like trucker so we can have the full experience."

Virgil laughed and shook his head as he jumped out of his seat to the ground. "You got it. I'll find something authentic and then slop chili over it."

"Sounds delightfully dire," Bryce replied. "Oh, and if they happen to be pouring mimosas?" He cast his best flirtatious look.

"Then I'll know I'm in the wrong place," Virgil replied and shut the door behind him.

"You know, I'm not at all sure that mimosas are in our future, Nestor," Bryce lamented. Nestor put a consoling hand on Bryce's knee and gave him a peck on the cheek. "Thank you, love. You are my rock."

About fifteen minutes later, when Virgil had not returned, Bryce began to grow impatient. "What can be keeping him? Does it really take that long to 'slop chili,' as he so colorfully put it?" He craned his neck over to the mirror and looked down the length of the rig. There, at the back bumper of the trailer, was Virgil. He was speaking with another man, and their conversation grew more animated as Bryce watched.

"I wouldn't mind eating that covered in chili," Bryce growled as the men talked. Nestor slid over to take a look over Bryce's shoulder.

It was at this moment that the man to whom Virgil was speaking reared back and slammed his fist into Virgil's jaw.

Bryce screamed. As he watched, Virgil steadied himself on the bumper of the trailer and managed to remain standing, but the other man lunged again and began pummeling him mercilessly. Virgil staggered under the hail of blows.

"Nestor, stay here," Bryce ordered as he flung open the door and leapt down from the cab of the truck.

"You. Fucking. Faggot!" the man beating Virgil yelled, and Bryce saw red (or, as he would recount it later, vermilion). He looked around desperately and spied a wrench under Virgil's driver's seat. He grabbed it up and dashed to the back of the trailer. By the time he got there, Virgil was on the ground being kicked savagely by the other man. Bryce hefted the wrench over his head, holding it precariously aloft until he brought it down with a mighty thud onto the back of the man's skull. The impact pitched the man over, stunned, and he staggered back.

"You goddam fucking faggot!" he bellowed, clutching the back of his head.

"That I may be," Bryce replied, straightening his back and glowering at the man with a haughty grandeur, "but I *dare* a bitch to kick my friend when he's down."

The ruckus caused by the fistfight had caused heads to turn all along the fueling islands. The assailant cast a wary glance to both sides, seeming aware of the attention the group was attracting. Virgil got to his feet and stood beside Bryce.

"How badly do you want to get beaten by two faggots, asshole?" Bryce growled, his voice an octave lower than his normal register, as he menacingly slapped the wrench into the palm of his other hand.

"Go to hell," the man spat, and he turned and stalked away, hand still clutching the back of his head.

"Are you under the impression that we aren't already there?" Bryce called, gesturing around the diesel-smelling truck stop with the wrench still in his hand. Upon realizing that he still held the grimy tool, he dropped it as if it were a snake. It clanged to the concrete. "And the name is Bryce, bitch."

If the man heard, he gave no indication. He opened the door of the truck stop's convenience store and disappeared inside. Once the door closed the spectacle was concluded, and the other truckers went back to minding their own business.

"Bryce... I can't believe...," Virgil said, blinking as if trying to focus. "You were amazing."

"Oh piff." Bryce said modestly. He nonchalantly smoothed the rumpled front of his blouse and then collapsed into Virgil's arms, unconscious.

At sea

"HOLY MOLY, do these people love bingo!" Sandler was reviewing the daily program of activities on the ship. "And art auctions. And wine tasting. Here I thought the point was to stare out at the ocean and reflect on one's life."

"I think bingo's just about as much excitement as most of these folks look like they could take," Donnelly said, toweling his hair before choosing a shirt to wear to breakfast. "At their age, reflecting may be too much, given reflections that stretch back to World War II."

"That does it," Sandler said, slapping the daily program onto the coffee table. "We are going to find someone else on this ship under the age of eighty."

"I don't like our chances," Donnelly replied, stepping out of the bedroom. "But I'm up for a scavenger hunt if you are."

Sandler poured coffee from the silver service Rutherford had brought at first light. "Excellent. Let the hunt begin." He handed Donnelly a steaming cup of black coffee. "After coffee, of course."

"Of course," Donnelly replied, sipping from the fine porcelain. "Oh, and after breakfast. I looked at the menu, and they're serving American-style pancakes with artisanal blueberry compote. I'll happily forgo all the bingo in the world for those."

"Well, let's get to it, then," Sandler said, tipping back his coffee cup and standing. "And after we have hunted down pancakes, we will scour this ship until we find someone who isn't old enough to have voted for Churchill." He walked over to the safe bolted to the wall of the walk-in closet and placed his messenger bag inside it. He shut the door with a clang and punched in a combination. "Ready for pancakes."

After breakfast—which exceeded even Donnelly's high expectations for pancakes—Sandler led the way to the beauty salon and spa complex at the front of the ship.

"Feeling like a hot stone massage and a cucumber facial?" Donnelly teased as they approached the frosted-glass doors.

"As intriguing as that sounds," Sandler replied, "this is merely the first stop on our scavenger hunt."

"We're starting at the spa?"

Sandler nodded and pulled the door open. He walked up to the reception desk and had a brief conversation with the young woman who smiled with professional zeal as he approached. He returned a moment later.

"So?" Donnelly inquired.

"So, we're going to get haircuts," Sandler replied.

"Are you telling me I look unkempt?" Donnelly demanded with fake outrage.

"Not at all. But I'm afraid good grooming is the price we have to pay for information."

They were soon seated in salon chairs that faced both mirrors and large windows looking out over the sea. A pair of sharply dressed, whippet-thin young men with impeccably groomed eyebrows came up behind them. They exchanged a glance after they had looked Donnelly and Sandler up and down.

"Good morning, gentlemen," the taller of the two softly sang in a voice that managed to be both elegant and lilting at once. "Since you're in our chairs, I have to assume that you somehow expect us to improve on what God has wrought. A daunting challenge indeed, but we shall do our best not to disappoint."

"We deliver ourselves into your capable hands," Sandler replied smoothly. Donnelly noticed a slight rise in his inflection that he hadn't recalled hearing before. The smile on the faces of both hairstylists indicated they'd heard it as well.

"My capable hands are delighted to welcome you," the young man replied, and he and his partner set to work. It was nearly an hour later, after Sandler and Donnelly had been shampooed, dried, cut, and even shaved, that they were released from the clutches of the two stylists.

"That took longer than all of the haircuts I've had in the past year combined," Donnelly said with a laugh as they made their way out of the salon.

"Totally worth it, though," Sandler replied.

"Do you think it made that much of a difference?" Donnelly asked, running his fingers through his brilliantly shiny hair.

"Of course it did. But not just in the way you look. While my guy was taking his time massaging my scalp, I asked about places on the ship where we might be able to find passengers who are not yet pensioners."

"That's some pretty good detective work there. What did you come up with?"

"Two things: first, some ideas of where to look on this vast vessel for signs of life, and second, the exact place our two stylists will be meeting us when their shift is over tonight."

Donnelly stopped in his tracks. "What?"

Sandler smiled. "Well, I'd asked about places to go, so it's kind of natural that he offered to show us some."

"I was thinking about a place to get a drink and talk with people somewhere nearer our age, not going clubbing with those barely legal fashionistas."

"Well, listen to you, ready to be consigned to the old folks' home." Sandler smiled slyly at Donnelly. "You said it yourself, mister: you're not dead yet."

"But I am engaged and on my way to my actual wedding." Donnelly's voice took on a harsher tone, revealing the frustration he was feeling.

Sandler took a deep breath before continuing, his voice soothing. "This is not a double date. I asked them where we could have some fun on this stately boat, and they offered to show us around. That's all." He studied Donnelly's face. "Gabriel, I'm not setting you up to cheat on that amazing man of yours."

Donnelly shrugged. "I know. I just... I don't know how to do this."

"Do what?"

"Go... out. Without him."

Sandler took in a breath as if a puzzle piece had finally fallen into place. "Oh, I get it. You skipped this part, didn't you?"

"What part?"

"The part where you go out and have fun and have a drink or two. Maybe even dance. You wouldn't know this, because you jumped right from straight to committed, but this is what guys do."

"Yeah, if they're looking for another guy."

"Yes, but this is also what guys do when they just want to spend some time with other guys. It doesn't mean you're looking for someone to take home with you."

"Are you sure?" Donnelly asked, squinting at Sandler. "Are you sure those guys aren't expecting us to be... available?"

"I'm sure they're hoping you might be, but it's not like they're going to run screaming away when they find out you're engaged. I think your guy mostly wants to sit and watch you smile—I tell ya, every time you smiled in the mirror he lit up like a Christmas tree. On fire."

Donnelly laughed in spite of himself. "Okay, if you promise me this won't get awkward, I'll give it a try. But if things get weird, I'm out. Deal?"

"Deal." Sandler extended his hand, and Donnelly shook it with ridiculous vigor, as if they were concluding the Louisiana Purchase. "Now, where can two well-groomed gentlemen get some hot bingo action?"

That evening, after another unspeakably elegant dinner at their secluded table for two, Donnelly and Sandler made their way to one of the ship's nightclubs.

"Good evening, Mr. Donnelly, Mr. Birkin," the bartender said as they sat. "What can I get for you?"

"A whiskey sour, my good man," Sandler replied jovially. The bartender smiled and turned to Donnelly.

"I'll have the same," Donnelly said, "and one thing more. How did you know our names?"

"I wish I could tell you it was magic," the bartender replied, his voice suddenly laced with a lilting Irish accent, as if he had thrown off the proper British his employer required. "But for the guests in our royal suites we make it a point to welcome you personally."

"So there are mug shots of us circulating among the staff?"

"Aye," the barkeep said and flipped his tablet toward the men. On it were the pictures they took at boarding, along with the name of their suite, their butler, and every drink they had ordered since getting on the ship. Including, now, whiskey sours.

"Well, that's personalized service taken to a frightening extreme," Donnelly said cheerfully. "Thank you…?"

"Emmet, sir. And you're welcome." Emmet winked. "To anything you like," he added slyly as he turned to make their drinks.

Sandler leaned close. "I think Emmet's taken a bit of a shine to yeh," he whispered in a leprechaun brogue.

Donnelly rolled his eyes. "He was just being friendly."

Sandler tucked the corner of his mouth up cynically and shook his head.

"If I may be so bold, gents," Emmet said as he laid the drinks before them, "Dax didn't do you justice."

Sandler laughed. "Mentioned our conversation, did he?" Emmet nodded. "Well, it's his doing. I was a frightful monster before he plied his trade on me this morning."

Emmet chuckled. "I have a hard time believing that, sir. But he was very excited that he might see you tonight."

"Tell me," Donnelly broke in. "Is it okay for staff and passengers to… fraternize?" That was a far more loaded term than he had intended, but he didn't know how else to ask the question.

"This hallowed line is one of the few that still provides gentlemen hosts so that our single ladies have someone to dance with," Emmet explained. "They could hardly begrudge our single gentlemen the same kind of attention, now could they?"

Donnelly stiffened and turned to Sandler, who seemed to know exactly the objection he was about to make.

"*If* we wanted someone to dance with," Sandler said emphatically, "just dancing, nothing else. That would be fine, wouldn't it, Gabriel?"

Donnelly wasn't at all sure it was fine, but he would feel a little silly bugging out of a social situation just because someone mentioned dancing. He nodded and took a drink.

"Though I think Dax and Stanley would be pleased to expand the definition of 'gentleman host' beyond the dance floor," Emmet said discreetly, then turned to take another patron's order.

Donnelly glared at Sandler. "I don't know about this."

Sandler took a deep breath. "I'm going to tell you something, and I need you to hear me out, okay? You've lived a very sheltered life. What we're doing here— flirting innocently with our refined and honestly strikingly attractive bartender, is perfectly normal. It's what our people do. Whether it leads to something more is

entirely dependent on whether one is fully committed, heart and soul, to another"—
he pointed to Donnelly—"or one is perhaps willing to entertain the possibility
of entertaining the advances of a refined and strikingly attractive bartender." He
pointed to himself. "Or a sharply dressed hairstylist. For example. I speak in a
purely hypothetical sense, of course." His grin indicated that purity was not entirely
his aim.

"I just don't want to lead anyone on," Donnelly said, his native modesty requiring
this to be whispered.

"Gabriel, look around you," Sandler whispered back. "Dax sent us to the
'friendliest' bar on the ship. The fucking duchess is conspicuously absent, and in her
place is every confirmed bachelor this ship has to offer. And all of them have been
looking at you the way Emmet does whenever he passes by. Most of them are discreet
about it, though those two"—he tipped his head toward the windows—"look ready to
drag you back to their cabin right now."

Donnelly turned and glanced in the direction Sandler had indicated. The couple,
dapper gentlemen in their early fifties, sat in deep leather club chairs near the window,
and though Donnelly expected them to look away when he caught their eyes, they
simply smiled and returned his gaze. He quickly turned back to Sandler.

"Well, that was awkward," Donnelly muttered.

"Awkward? That's what men do when they see a man who looks like you. You
should probably be used to it by now."

Donnelly shrugged nervously. "But Ethan's always right next to me. He's the
one who attracts all the attention."

Sandler shook his head. "I don't believe that for a second. I'm sure he's a
specimen of manhood, but you keep selling yourself short. You just need to take a
deep breath and accept the fact that you are a beautiful man, and other men are going
to appreciate that. And even though you are getting married in a week, that doesn't
mean you have to stop appreciating beauty where you find it either. I mean, honestly,
look at that."

Donnelly looked back over to the appreciative couple, who were at that moment
being served another round of drinks by a waiter in unreasonably form-fitting slacks.

"Now, I know you're the most engaged man in the world, but tell me that
perfect bubble butt doesn't do anything for you. No, really get a good look. Take in the
gentle curve that marks the lower border of his back. Follow the seam of his pants as
it separates those two perfectly round globes. Now, that is a sight to raise the pulse of
any red-blooded man."

The waiter stood and turned toward them.

"Fuck me, the front is as fine as the back," Sandler whispered. "Drink trays are
not all he's been lifting."

"This is really embarrassing," Donnelly muttered as he turned back to his drink.

"Why?" Sandler asked.

"Because you're trying to turn me into some kind of dirty old man, ogling
waiters in tight pants."

"You're not old. You're certainly not dirty. And waiters wear tight pants in bars
like this because oglers tip better. It doesn't hurt anyone for you to look, Gabriel."

Donnelly just shook his head, unable to explain his discomfort more fully.

"Can you honestly tell me you felt nothing when you looked at him bending over?"

Heat flashed across Donnelly's face.

"Yeah, I thought so. Why does that freak you out so badly?"

"It's just awkward, okay?"

Sandler sat back a bit, looked Donnelly up and down. Something seemed to fall into place. "Ah, I get it now. You never had a candy store phase."

"A what?"

"A candy store phase. It's what just about every guy goes through when he comes out to himself. All of a sudden you give yourself permission to look at other guys after years of feeling ashamed and wishing that seeing a waiter bend over didn't make your pants tight. It's the freedom that comes from finally admitting that guys make you feel the way that you could never convince yourself to feel about women. You, though, went right from straight to Ethan, and you never candy-stored."

"Well, what's the point?" Donnelly asked, getting a little tired of being psychoanalyzed over whiskey sours. "I have Ethan. Why do I need candy?"

"It's not about candy. It's about liberation. Just because you skipped over this phase doesn't mean it's not important."

"What I don't get is why."

Sandler sighed. "Here's why. When you see an attractive guy, what do you do?"

"I don't really notice attractive guys."

"That's my point. What you're doing is acting as though you are still in the closet. Yes, you have the most amazing handsome, muscular man in the whole world, though if there's any justice in the universe he's hung like a canary—"

"No justice on that one," Donnelly replied with a chuckle. "Sorry."

"Dammit!" Sandler spat theatrically. "Anyway, just because you have Ethan doesn't mean you have to never look at another man."

"But I never looked at other men before Ethan."

Sandler nodded. "That's my point exactly. Now, I'm not going to advance any theories about whether you were in denial, or not self-aware, or simply waiting for the amazing Ethan to show you his red jockstrap and suddenly change your entire hormonal system. But you are a gay man, Gabriel, and for a gay man to pretend that waiter over there doesn't have a fine ass, or that Emmet here doesn't have dimples that just make you want to kiss him, well, that just goes against nature."

"Amen to that, sir," Emmet said, beaming with a dimply grin.

"Thank you for allowing me to use your dimples to make a point, Emmet."

"Yeh can use them for more than that, sir," Emmet said with a wink. "I put them at your disposal."

"I shall remember you said that, barkeep," Sandler replied with a subtle growl in his voice. Emmet smiled even more broadly and set down another round of whiskey sours before turning back to his work.

Donnelly rolled his eyes at the flirtation being performed in front of him and returned to their previous discussion. "Why is this so important to you? What does it matter whether I look at guys the same way you do?"

"Because it's human nature, that's why. If we don't appreciate beauty, we aren't fully human. Beauty is truth."

"Thanks, Mr. Keats."

Sandler smiled. "For a man with a poetic spirit, you fight awfully hard against the beauty of the human form."

"Ethan's beautiful, and I throw myself at him every night. Sometimes twice."

"For which I congratulate you on both your good taste and your good fortune. But if you try to convince yourself that only Ethan is beautiful and no other man in the world will even draw your eye for a moment, then you are fighting a losing battle."

"Again, what does it matter to me if the world is filled with godlike men?"

Sandler put his drink down on the bar with a thump. "It matters because if you deny that you find men attractive, you are denying you're a gay man."

"Because finding men attractive is the only thing that defines us," Donnelly replied sarcastically. "That sounds like a pretty limited view of what it means to be gay."

"Okay, then, what does being gay mean to Gabriel Donnelly? Tell me." Sandler folded his hands in his lap and looked attentively at Donnelly.

Donnelly cleared his throat. "Well," he said, uncertainly, "I guess it means, first, that… well, that you're a guy who falls in love with another guy."

"Good start. What else?"

"That people have opinions on the fact that you fell in love with another guy. Sometimes they are happy for you, and sometimes they throw you out of the house and tell you never to come back. But everyone seems to have something to say about it."

Sandler nodded, eyebrows up, clearly expecting more.

"And… that's about it." Donnelly picked up his drink because he didn't know what else to do.

"That's it?"

"Yeah, I guess."

Sandler sighed. "You've left out the most important part."

"Falling in love with a guy, everyone else in the world getting to tell you what they think about it. That's pretty much it, from my experience."

"Okay, look at it this way. When people want to get a crowd whipped up into a homophobic frenzy, what do they say all gay people are up to?"

Donnelly rolled his eyes. "The gay agenda."

"Right. And when people are supportive of equal rights, how do they refer to us?"

"As the gay community?"

"Right again. Now, what do those two terms have in common?"

Donnelly squinted at Sandler. "They both have 'gay' in them?"

"Ooh, got it. Now for Double Jeopardy. What else do they have in common?"

Donnelly thought for a moment. "What?"

"They both refer to us as a group. Either the kind of group that gets together and forms a militant action plan—as if you could put five gay men in a room and get them to agree on the right shoes for an outfit, much less a plan for world domination—or a community of people who have things in common. But both the haters and the allies refer to us as a group. Now, do you feel like you've joined a group since you became aware that you're gay?"

"No, I don't. I mean, I've met some very nice people, but I don't know that I would call them a community."

"Then look around you. Would you call the men gathered here a community?"

Donnelly glanced around the room. The older couple by the windows smiled when his eyes met theirs again—he surprised himself by smiling back before continuing his sweep of the room—but he saw nothing other than a collection of people who seem to have ended up at the same bar at the same time.

"Not really. It's like you said this morning about the bingo players—I wouldn't presume to have much in common with these guys, as nice as they seem."

"All right, so not much in common. Now, pretend I'm Ethan for a moment. I know you'll have to squint pretty hard, but humor me."

"Okay, you're Ethan." Donnelly pulled his arm back and landed a solid punch on Sandler's shoulder.

"Ow! What was that for?" Sandler clutched his arm and rubbed it up and down.

"For missing the ship." Donnelly smiled. "Thanks for letting me get that out of my system."

"You're welcome," Sandler replied ruefully. "Now, assuming you don't have any more hidden aggression to take out on me, let me ask you this: would you feel comfortable kissing me right now?"

Donnelly scowled. "What?"

"Pretending I'm Ethan. Would you feel comfortable leaning over right now and kissing me? Not a peck on the cheek that could pass as European, but a real kiss?"

"Ethan and I don't normally do that kind of thing in public."

"Kissing? You don't kiss in public?"

Donnelly shook his head in frustration. "You make it sound like we're ashamed. We're not. We just don't want to make anyone uncomfortable."

Sandler nodded. "Point taken. So, let's assume that you're in a bar, later in the evening, aboard a romantic ocean liner. Would you kiss him then?"

"I don't know. Not if it would—"

"Make anyone uncomfortable. I know. So let's say another couple kisses—they're celebrating their seventy-fifth wedding anniversary, and feel a little frisky. So now someone else has done it. Do you?"

Donnelly was out of answers.

"Right. You've made my point. You'll only kiss your hubby-to-be when it's appropriate. How will you know it's appropriate? By what the other people in the room do. And what signs will they give you? Well, first and foremost, you can see whether that delicious waiter draws their eye. If he does, then you know you're safe. You're among friends. You're part of a community. And it may strike you as superficial or outrageous or simply ridiculous that that sense of community is built around the appreciation of a young man's buttocks, but you cannot deny that the effect is real. The community is real. And for previous generations who were rejected and jeered and beaten for who they were and whom they loved, that sense of community was a lifesaver in every sense of the word. It is their legacy to us. A lingering glance at a waiter's ass, a casual reference to a Broadway show, any opinion at all about Barbra Streisand: these were the signs of safety, the secret signal that it was okay to be who you are. And to ignore them, or pretend they don't matter, is to betray their legacy."

"Wow."

Sandler stared at him for a long moment. "Wow?"

"Yeah, just… wow. I had no idea there was this whole… culture? I guess?" He looked around, feeling as thought Sandler had given him x-ray specs that revealed what was really going on in the room. "I feel like you've just told me I joined a club two years ago, and I didn't even know it." He turned back after completing his survey. "I had no idea."

Sandler smiled. "And that's a sign of the progress we've made. You came out late, and aside from your mom being an asshole to you, you've had a pretty easy time of it, right?"

Donnelly nodded. "We definitely made some new friends—Bryce the Fabulous being one of them—but I never considered them to be a subculture or anything."

"That's because they don't really have to be anymore, in major cities at least. The initiation ritual for this club you've joined used to be giving up your family, your religion, and often your job and friends. Now, because of the progress we've made as a society, you don't have to give up most of that—again, asshole relatives excepted—and all you gain is a new group of friends and bars with better music."

"Who knew so much depends on the peach-like curve of a waiter's ass?"

Sandler smiled. "You effortlessly mashed up William Carlos Williams and T.S. Eliot in an offhand remark. Amazing."

"That is a peach I shall not eat," Donnelly said with a smirk, nodding at the waiter as he again leaned over a table to serve drinks.

Sandler looked appraisingly at the young man's callipygian beauty, the way one might when walking behind Michelangelo's David. "We must agree to disagree on that," he mused.

"Well, this evening has been exhaustingly introspective," Donnelly said as he stood. He tossed back the last of his drink and set the empty glass on the bar. "As heartbroken as I am to miss Dax and Stanley, I'm going to turn in. But please don't let my departure keep you from your peach harvest."

Sandler laughed. "You assume I'd be able to persuade him to share his peach with me."

Donnelly leaned close. "You could have any man on this ship, and you know it." He stood upright again. "Now, I'm going to brush my teeth and fall instantly into a sound slumber. You needn't worry about disturbing me when you get in." He winked to make his meaning clear.

"Now you're just flattering me."

"And you're just fishing for compliments. So I'll simply say once again that you are welcome to the boisterous use of the cabin tonight and every night. Someone should be getting lucky in the honeymoon suite." He clapped Sandler on the shoulder as he made his exit.

"Thank you, Gabriel," Sandler called after him, even as his gaze turned to hail a waiter.

On the highway, a little farther west

WHEN BRYCE opened his eyes, the rig was already well down the freeway from the truck stop that had been the site of the altercation. He awakened with his head in Nestor's lap.

"My hero, he wake," murmured Nestor as he stroked Bryce's forehead lovingly.

"You okay there, champ?" asked Virgil, taking his eyes off the dark road ahead for just a moment to check on his supine passenger.

"What happened?" Bryce asked. "All I remember is harsh lighting and some kind of tool." He gasped. "Oh dear lord, please don't tell me I did manual labor."

"No, you coldcocked a guy who was beatin' the shit outta me. For which I owe you big time."

"Coldcocked, you say?" Bryce asked, sitting up. "Brrr. Sounds refreshing."

"You never quit, do you? You just got into a fight at a fucking truck stop, and you completely owned that guy. And there you are, still making witty little sex jokes. Bryce, you are more man than any six truckers I know."

"Goodness, you could turn a lady's head with that kind of talk."

"I intend to," Virgil said with a smile. "I'm gonna give you boys a special treat."

Bryce gasped. "I feel like Desirée Demornay, about to unleash the beast in Bolt's tight leather pants."

"I promise you won't be disappointed," Virgil said with a wink.

"Nestor!" Bryce barked. "Condoms! Stat!"

"Now hold on," Virgil said. "You saved my ass back there, so I'm going to take my time showing you my gratitude. We're going to stop in at a little motel I like and spend a few hours before we get back on the road. Does that sound good to you?"

"A few hour?" Nestor asked. "I only bring twelve condoms."

Virgil laughed. "Well, it's a start. Let's see how many we can burn through."

"You are a true gentleman," Bryce said. "But first, I do have one question. Why was that awful man attacking you back at the truck stop?"

Virgil sighed and shook his head. "I'd never met him before, only knew him by reputation. Name's Archer. He's pretty well-known for being an ornery son of a bitch. Turns out he's also the brother-in-law of a guy I spent some recreational time with last month. Now, I don't seek out married men as a rule. Don't like being caught up in domestic drama. But he didn't let slip that he was married when he slipped it to me, so I didn't know until later. Well, apparently his wife found out what he'd gotten up to with me, so now he's telling people a story about how I raped him, which is completely untrue—all I did was 'accidentally' show him some porn with bi dudes in it and he was all over me. Anyway, his wife's brother got all lathered up about defending his virtue or reclaiming his good name or whatever. So when he recognized my rig, he thought he'd pay me a call and kick my spleen for a while. It ain't the first time something like this has happened, but it's definitely the worst beatdown I've ever had the pleasure of experiencing. If you hadn't come along with that wrench, I might'a ended up in the hospital—or worse."

"It was nothing," Bryce said with perhaps a bit too much modesty. "Please don't tell anyone about it. I don't want people thinking I go around knowing how wrenches work."

"People are not going to think anything bad about you, Bryce, because they'd be too scared that you're gonna whip out your wrench and crack some heads. By tonight you're going to be a truck stop legend all up and down the highway."

"I have always said that there are only two things in this life a man can truly call his own: his reputation and his moisturizer. And now," Bryce said, touching a delicate hand to his throat as if receiving the best-actress Oscar, "truck drivers will know my name. *Truck drivers.* This is the greatest day of my life."

Virgil cast a look toward Nestor, eyebrows raised. Nestor shook his head subtly. "He always say that. Every day."

Virgil grinned widely. "You the man, Bryce. You the man."

"Oh my," Bryce gasped. "No one's ever called me *that* before." He said it to himself several times, trying it on for size. He quite liked it.

About an hour later, Virgil pulled off the interstate toward a small knot of buildings clustered near the off-ramp. Bryce, who had fallen into a dreamy daze thinking about truckers mouthing his name, roused himself as he felt the truck slow. Virgil guided the rig into the parking lot of an old but well-kept motel that stretched, low and long, away from the frontage road. He parked at the far edge of the lot, and the rumbling diesel engine fell silent.

"Welcome to paradise," Virgil announced as he swung the door open and hopped down. He held up a gallant hand to help Bryce and Nestor out of the cab.

A buzzing neon sign showed Virgil's characterization to be literally true: Motel Paradise, it read, in lurid reds and blues. They walked to the office where Bryce noticed a tiny rainbow flag tucked in the corner of the front window. Virgil opened the door, and a melodic tinkle announced their arrival.

From an office behind the front desk appeared a short, muscular man with a tight T-shirt and a broad smile. "Virge!" he called, jogging around the desk and grasping Virgil's hand in his.

"Michael, it's always great to see you."

"Listen to you," Michael scolded. "You talk like we ain't buddies." He grabbed Virgil's jaw with both hands and pulled him into a kiss that was both athletic and passionate. The men stayed clinched together for a long minute.

"The great plains are full of wonders, Nestor," Bryce whispered.

Nestor made no reply other than to adjust his pants.

"Can you take a little time?" Virgil asked, once he had the use of his mouth back.

"And disappoint the desperate hordes of weary travelers clamoring for a room?" Michael pointed out to the parking lot, in which no car—or anything else—stirred at this hour. "Hell yeah, I can take some time if you've got some to give." He winked, making clear the kind of "giving" he was interested in receiving.

"In that case, I'd like you to meet Bryce and Nestor, my companions for this trip to the coast."

"So pleased to make your acquaintance," Bryce bubbled as he shook Michael's hand.

"And I yours," Michael replied. He took Nestor's hand next. "Oh, what soft hands."

Nestor beamed. "And yours, so strong," he murmured.

"Well, gentlemen, shall we?" Michael took a key from the pegboard behind the desk. "Your favorite room is available," he said to Virgil, shaking the key ring.

"As long as you're willing, I'll work myself in anywhere."

"Oh, fuck, the way you talk," Michael whispered, wiping his brow. "Follow me, gents!" He held open the door to the office and then locked it behind them.

Virgil's favorite room was all the way at the end of the motel, farthest from the street. Michael jiggled the key in the knob and shoved the door open. The men stepped into a gleamingly clean and spacious room containing a wide bed and a whirlpool tub in the far corner, surrounded by mirrored walls. It was the roadside motel version of a honeymoon suite.

"Ah, even better than I remember it," Virgil said, looking around the room. "Love the new color."

"I'll tell Trish you approve of her interior design skills," Michael said as he shut and locked the door.

"Where is the lovely ball and chain?" Virgil asked.

"She's at one of her artistic retreats. You know, where a bunch of women get together, tell feminist stories around the fire, and don't shower. I assume there's lots of weed 'cause she's always very relaxed when she gets back from one of those. I think it does her good to go be a hippie lesbian for a while. Plus, it frees me up for visits from old friends like yourself."

Virgil smiled. "You two really have married life figured out."

"Am I to understand," Bryce said after clearing his throat delicately, "that you are… married? To a woman?" He was unable to suppress a wince.

"In fact I am. To the best woman in the world. Been ten years now."

"But I had assumed, since you and Virgil…."

"Oh, don't misunderstand. Virgil's definitely going to pound my ass until I forget my own name. It's part of the arrangement Trish and I have. She goes to her retreats where they spell *womyn* with a *y*, and she can munch all the pussy she wants. And I occasionally entertain transportation specialists like Virgil here."

Bryce, whose eyes had rolled back in his head at the mention of the P-word, managed to remain upright through sheer force of will.

"He was my first," Michael continued. "And still the best." He pulled Virgil to him and they kissed again, clutching at each other with greater purpose.

This was just the tonic Bryce needed to recover his senses. "Nestor, be a dear and run a bath," he instructed. "I think the show's starting."

Nestor stepped lightly over to the whirlpool and turned on the taps. He availed himself of the bubble bath that sat on the edge of the tub, and soon a mountain of suds rose into view.

"Delightful," Bryce said, managing to tear his eyes for just a moment from the athletic grappling at the foot of the bed. "Thank you, dear." He turned back to watch

Virgil pick Michael up and throw him without ceremony onto the bed. He pounced like a jungle cat, full of raw but sinuous energy. He tore Michael's shirt open, then threw the scraps of fabric to the side. Well-worn jeans followed, and then Virgil threw off his dingy white T-shirt.

"Ooh," Bryce exclaimed at this sudden vigorous motion. "Nestor, love, is the bath ready?"

Nestor reached through the bubbles to feel the water, then nodded. "Is ready."

"Excellent," Bryce replied. "Shall we?" They began removing their clothes.

"You two aren't going to join us?" Virgil asked, removing his mouth from Michael's for the first time in a long while.

"Oh, of course we will, dear," Bryce replied. "But there is really nothing better than relaxing in a nice tub and watching two manly men handle each other. Nestor and I are specialists of a more delicate type, and our particular skills will come into play once you have worked out your more aggressive appetites."

"Your friend talks pretty," Michael offered from under Virgil. "Let's give him something to talk about."

Virgil made answer by pouncing again, pressing Michael flat against the mattress as he devoured him with an onslaught of kisses and nips all along his neck and chest. Michael groaned and swore when Virgil bit down on his nipple, and as he arched his back in ecstatic surprise Virgil lunged, taking most of the man's meaty pectoral muscle into his mouth and sucking the flesh against his teeth.

"Oh my," Bryce whispered to Nestor from across the mountains of bubbles in the tub. "I have a new appreciation for our country's transportation infrastructure."

Just then Virgil, scrambling for better purchase on the slick bedspread, splayed his legs wide and attacked Michael's other nipple. The view from the foot of the bed was expansive.

"And to think," Bryce remarked, staring at Virgil's mounded buttocks as they strained at the faded denim that covered them, "he spends all day just sitting on that lovely mass of muscle, rather than using it for the purpose God intended. Such a pity."

"But he gonna use it now," Nestor sang lightly.

"Of that I have no doubt." Bryce settled back into the tub to watch the show.

Virgil reared back, grabbed Michael under the knees, and lifted his legs nearly up over his head. He pushed the smaller man's legs wide, and looked down at him with a grin. "You been savin' yourself for me?" he asked with a growl. "That ass of yours is the tightest thing I've ever seen."

Michael looked up, his face contorted with lust. "Bust me wide open, you motherfucker."

"That's the only way I know how to do it." Virgil let go of Michael's ankles and drove his fingers into the slender gap between Michael's obscenely spread buttocks. He tugged the man's cheeks wide open. "But first, I need a taste of that ass."

Bryce and Nestor jumped in surprise at the sound of Virgil's mouth smacking into Michael's ass, but then craned forward to see the stubbled friction that was making Michael squeal in delight. Virgil slurped and smacked and chewed, his cheeks pulling in from the force of his suction, his jaw working open and closed feverishly as he ground his face into Michael's ass. Without warning he pulled back, and the sudden release of suction made a wet popping noise that filled the room. With a growl he lunged forward again, tongue already fully extended before making contact between Michael's twitching buttocks.

"Such raw power," Bryce murmured. "I haven't seen anyone suck like that since… well, when was the last Vin Diesel movie?"

"All muscle, no acting," sighed Nestor, shaking his head mournfully.

Back on the bed, Virgil had apparently concluded his asshole appetizer, for he pulled off and this time simply stared down at Michael's no doubt well-chewed ass. "Are you man enough?" he asked, jeering, as he held up his middle finger.

"Fuck yeah," Michael replied, as if he'd been asked whether he wanted another beer.

Virgil stuck his middle finger into Michael's mouth, then pulled it out slowly, dripping a string of spittle with it. He looked at it for a moment as it gleamed, and then without further ceremony, he jammed it into Michael's ass.

"Well," murmured Bryce. "That escalated quickly."

Virgil withdrew his finger, then slammed it roughly back into Michael's ass. He repeated this motion several times, each more quickly than the last, until his hand was a blur of motion. Michael's grunting began to quiet.

"Are you man enough for two?" Virgil asked.

Without warning Michael lurched up and slammed his fist into Virgil's solidly muscled chest. "Make me feel it this time, bitch."

Virgil's reply was to yank his finger out of Michael's ass and then shove it brutally into his mouth, forcing the smaller man back down onto the mattress. He jammed in his index finger as well, and forced both fingers in and out of Michael's mouth. Michael's voice could be heard, but with Virgil's fingers in his mouth he could not be understood. Finally, Virgil withdrew.

"Come at me, motherfucker," Michael yelled, his face red and furious.

"Fuck you," Virgil replied, and with corded muscle standing out the length of his entire arm, he drove his fingers into Michael's ass.

In the bath, Nestor leaned his head on Bryce's shoulder. "The way they talk," he whispered. "So romantic."

"It is a moving sight, isn't it, darling?" Bryce agreed.

Virgil twisted his arm wildly, corkscrewing his fingers into and out of Michael's ass. "You like that, fucker? You like that?"

"Is that all you got?" Michael jeered. "Pussy."

"You man enough for three?" Virgil snarled back.

"I could hardly feel two, so do your worst."

Virgil yanked his fingers out and with lightning speed jammed them into Michael's mouth. This time two more joined in, stretching Michael's jaw as they worked their way between his lips. After just a few seconds of this Virgil pulled his hand back. "You want all four, fucker?"

Michael's response was to spit a huge glob right into Virgil's face. It ran down his cheek, until his tongue darted out and he spat it right back into Michael's open mouth. He jammed his fingers together into one impossibly large battering ram, placed it against Michael's already bright red pucker, and pushed. Hard.

Michael let out a shriek that he quickly clamped down on, but his fierce eyes never lost contact with Virgil's. "Fuck you!" he bellowed as Virgil's fingers disappeared with agonizing slowness into him.

Virgil grunted with the effort of driving his spit-slicked fingers into Michael's writhing ass, but he was unrelenting. He brought his full weight to bear, and gradually his knuckles pressed against the buttocks that could spread no wider to accommodate him. He let out a vicious yell, glorying in his accomplishment as Michael struggled, red-faced and grimacing, to adjust to the intrusion.

Virgil, however, did not pause to allow the other man to catch his breath. His biceps gathered into melon-sized mounds as he wrenched his hand, twisting and jabbing, forcing Michael's ass open from every angle. "You dirty little fucker," Virgil growled. "You want this, don't you? You want me to tear you open."

"Fuck you," Michael retorted, his voice still gruff but growing ragged with the strain. "You ain't man enough."

Virgil's response was a guttural yell that filled the motel room with incoherent animal lust. He yanked his hand out of Michael's ass, but then used both hands to pry the man open even wider. Two, and then three fingers of each hand wriggled into the bright red ring of muscle, and with the muscles of his back arching with effort, he pulled his hands apart. Michael's voice leapt up an octave as his eyes rolled back in his head and his spine arched as if he were trying to get away from the prying hands.

"Gotcha, fucker," Virgil taunted. He spat mightily into the yawning gap opened by his fingers, and laughed out an unhinged, bestial roar of victory. "Your fuckin' ass is mine, bitch." He hocked another glob of spit into the chasm.

"Shut up and fuck me," Michael spat back, "if you even can, you fucking pussy."

A sinister snarl spread across Virgil's face, and he chuckled ominously as he spat once again into Michael's ass. He finally released his grip on Michael's legs, allowing them to drop to the bed on either side of him. He shuffled himself back, placing his feet on the pink carpet, and yanked Michael's legs toward him.

Michael raised his legs to give Virgil access to his ass, but Virgil shook his head. "I don't want to see your faggot face when I fuck you," he grunted as he grabbed Michael roughly and flipped him over onto his belly, then yanked his hips up until he was on his knees. "That's better." He quickly unbuttoned the fly of his jeans and slid them off his slim, naked hips. A truly enormous penis stabbed out from his body.

"Oh captain, my captain," whispered Bryce reverently.

Virgil grinned at Bryce as he placed the tip of his enormous uncut cock against Michael's inflamed and hungry ass.

"Nestor, quick!" Bryce called as he launched himself out of the tub. As he reached the bed he looked back and with the sure hand of a veteran fielder caught the foil square Nestor had whipped toward him. In one fluid motion, he tore the packet open and popped the condom into his mouth, then grabbed Virgil's cock authoritatively. Virgil took a step back, clearly startled. Bryce smiled politely as he quickly and professionally skinned back Virgil's foreskin. Then he leaned down and swallowed half the organ in one sure swoop. Just as quickly he pulled back, leaving the condom perfectly placed on the bobbing erection. He straightened up, smiled brightly again, and patted Virgil on the head. "There. You may now bust him open, motherfucker." Bryce giggled and stepped lightly back to the tub.

Virgil shook his head in smiling wonder as Bryce settled back into the suds to watch the main event. But Michael's crouching ass soon drew his attention back to the job before him. He spat into his hand and rubbed it once down the length of his hard cock, then placed it at the entrance to Michael's once-private place. He leaned forward and landed his hand on the back of Michael's head, pushing him down to the mattress and pinning him there as he lunged forward.

The invasion of Virgil's cock into his ass seemed to push all of the air out of Michael's lungs. Virgil reared back and threw himself forward again, violently driving his hips against Michael's buttocks with a mighty slap. For the first time since their grappling began, Bryce saw a flash of fear streak across Michael's face, as if he were genuinely uncertain whether he could accommodate Virgil's massive member. But he closed his eyes for a moment, and when he opened them, they had the familiar fire of lust resurgent in them. He reached back and grabbed Virgil's buttocks, his grasping fingers leaving trails of white skin that bloomed pink, driving Virgil even harder into him.

"Is that all you've got?" he taunted Virgil, his strong hands now leaving claw marks on Virgil's muscular ass as he pulled him into ever harder penetration. "I thought you were going to fuck me."

Virgil made answer by pushing Michael's face into the pillow and thrusting more savagely into him than he had previously. His powerful buttocks striated as the muscles beneath the pale, smooth skin drove his cock forward again and again, impaling Michael viciously. Michael released his grip on Virgil's straining ass, and he flailed wildly, seeking a handhold to keep from being pounded flat by the animal force on top of him.

"Unless I miss my guess," Bryce murmured to Nestor, "we'll see the first beads of sweat grace those lovely, lovely buttocks right about... now." As if he had summoned it by his incantation, Virgil's flesh began to glisten and shine in the glare of the motel room's lamplight. "Ah, right on time. Boy knows how to work it."

Spurred on by Bryce's appreciation, Virgil began jackhammering Michael with rapid, deep strokes. Michael's voice could be heard screaming into the pillow, though the particulars of his discourse were unintelligible. This machine-gun fucking continued for several astonishing minutes, during which time Bryce and Nestor simply gaped in wonder as they watched. Finally, whether through an exercise of mercy or mere exhaustion, Virgil pulled back and detached himself from the panting form below him.

"Roll over, motherfucker," he grunted, short of breath.

Michael complied without a word, flipping himself over with surprising agility. He raised his legs, surrendering himself silently, entirely. A crooked grin broke across Virgil's face as he looked down at the accommodation Michael offered him. This time he didn't spit angrily, but rather let a long strand of saliva drizzle down from his mouth onto his cock, still sheathed in the condom Bryce had applied earlier. It was hard enough to burrow slowly into Michael's ass without Virgil even having to put his hand on it. As his cock entered, he laid himself down onto Michael, and they lay eye-to-eye as their hips found each other. Michael wrapped his arms around Virgil and held him tight as he thrust gently, swiveling his hips in random, sensuous gyrations. Michael lifted his head and used his tongue to trace the outline of Virgil's lips. Virgil groaned and kissed Michael passionately as his hips and buttocks continued their slow dance of thrusts and twists.

Finally Virgil broke their long kiss. "I want to feel you come," he whispered huskily. He reached down and gripped Michael's hard cock. Precum, the product of Virgil's brutal battering of Michael's prostate, pooled on his lean lower belly. Virgil spread the slick liquid all over Michael's cock and began to stroke in earnest. "I want to feel you squeeze me when you come."

"Oh, fuck," Michael grunted. He tipped his head back, eyebrows raised in incipient ecstasy. "I'm so close."

"Come for me, come for me," Virgil chanted, stroking and thrusting in a coordinated assault on Michael's body, front and rear.

Michael's body went rigid and then began to twitch all over. "Oh fuck, oh fuck, oh fucking fuck!" he called in time with the increasing cadence of Virgil's thrusts and strokes.

"It's starting," Virgil said, wonder in his voice. "I can feel you twitch inside. You're so fucking tight!"

The two men writhed together, beyond words, for a long moment. Then a mutual gasping, squealing ecstasy overtook them. Their motions became spastic as orgasm locked them in its iron grip. Michael screamed as if he were ejaculating fire; Virgil grunted as if his cock were being severed by the tight ring of Michael's ass.

Then… silence.

Neither man moved for several seconds before they both took a deep, heaving breath. Their lips found each other, and they kissed slowly, gently, as if the crisis had passed and they had all the time in the world to luxuriate in its afterglow. Their sweat-glazed bodies relaxed, and they rolled onto their sides and embraced, nuzzling tenderly, beyond the need for words.

"I think they're warmed up nicely," Bryce whispered into Nestor's ear. "Shall we?"

Nestor nodded, and they stood, bubbles clinging to their lean bodies. They dried off using the rather rough motel towels—"Ooh, drying and exfoliating in one step!"—and stepped lightly over to the bed. The mirrored wall showed the contrast between the two pairs of men: Virgil and Michael solidly built with farmers' tans, while the elegant city boys were free of sinew and muscle. Bryce was a statue in white marble, ready to be worshiped by Greek philosophers; Nestor's smooth skin was the color of a sweet, hot mocha. They approached the weary men who sprawled, entangled, on the bed.

They each knelt on one side of the two men, and with light fingertips traced arabesques on their glistening skin. Bryce brought a finger to his mouth to sample the salty essence he found on Virgil's strong back. Nestor began to massage Michael's exhausted body, paying special attention to his lightly furred cheeks that had been rent so wide.

"Mmmm," groaned Virgil. "You have amazing hands."

Bryce, were he capable of blushing, would certainly have done so.

"He's nothing compared to my guy," Michael replied, his voice laboring under the weight of such pleasure. "Fuck...." He leaned back and looked up at Nestor, who beamed down at him. Michael reached up, wrapped a hand around Nestor's neck, and pulled him down. Michael kissed him with a gentle sweetness that was nothing like the athletic mauling he had exchanged with Virgil.

Bryce and Virgil watched the other two make out for a bit; then they looked at each other and exchanged a sly smile. But instead of kissing Virgil, Bryce leaned down and took his flaccid penis into his mouth. Virgil jumped and squirmed, laughing.

"Whoa there, boy—I need some time to recover. Busting this guy open put a bit of a strain on the old fella."

Bryce smiled up at Virgil and winked. He did not, however, let go. He gently slid up and down Virgil's soft but still sizable cock, easily swooping all the way down to the base when he felt like it.

Virgil's head lolled back. "Oh fuck," he groaned through gritted teeth. "I can't... I can't...."

Bryce let Virgil's cock slip out from between his lips. "Yes, you can, darling." He got right back to work.

Nestor seemed to take inspiration from Bryce's industrious dedication to duty, and he swooped down upon Michael's similarly soft-but-lengthy cock. And Michael, perhaps seeing how ineffectual Virgil's objection had been, made none on his own behalf. He simply stretched out luxuriantly and exchanged a smile of deep satisfaction with Virgil.

"I can't believe I'm startin' to get boned up already," Virgil said in a husky whisper. "After fucking you half to death, I figured I'd be done for the night."

"I believe in you, darling," Bryce said once he had pulled Virgil's growing cock from his lips. "Erections are self-fulfilling prophecies, and I forecast great things for you." He kissed the tip of Virgil's manhood delicately. "And for me, of course."

"Fuck," Virgil groaned, throwing his head back in surrender to Bryce's abiding belief.

"Now, Nestor," Bryce said, between long lollypop licks, "isn't this better than flying?"

"Is about the journey," Nestor agreed with a tickling nip at the tip of Michael's cock.

"I am so glad to hear you say that," Bryce replied, beaming while his strong-but-elegant fist made vigorous transits from the base of Virgil's erection to the tip and back again. "Though I think I'm going to reach the end of my journey before you reach yours,"

Nestor cocked a skeptical eyebrow. He made no answer but doubled the pace of his stroking. As Michael writhed under the onslaught, Nestor lifted his mouth off for just a moment. "Is on, bitch," he said sweetly. He spat a huge glob of slippery saliva on Michael's cock and clenched it in both hands, throttling it with a vigor that made its owner clench up in surprise.

"Aw, shit," Michael yelped, looking down his heaving torso in shock. "Take it easy there, okay?"

Nestor fixed him with a glare that would have set fire to an entire field of sugar cane, and neither his pace nor his grip slackened. Michael flopped back on the bed, giving himself up to be tugged toward ecstasy.

"Ooh, I applaud your effort, darling, but there's simply no chance you'll get there before I do." Bryce's voice was courtly, but his eyes glinted with purpose. Under the pretense of daubing at the corner of his mouth, he slipped his middle finger between his lips, wetting it thoroughly. He brought his hand down into the dark, hot recesses under Virgil's balls. With instincts honed over the years, his fingertip instantly found Virgil's tight pucker.

"Whoa there," Virgil shouted, legs stiffening. "Nothing goes up there, you hear me? Nothing—"

"Oh, but, darling, it's already in." Bryce smiled sweetly. "I'm honestly a little insulted you think I'd barge into your delicate orifice like some kind of sex-crazed trucker."

"I've never had anything up there," Virgil protested, the indignation in his voice softening.

"Then you've never felt this," Bryce said, and with a twist of his wrist he changed Virgil's life. He dipped his head back down, taking in the cock that surged even more stiffly before him.

"Oh... oh... oh, *fuck*!" Virgil tore at the sheets and kicked his legs ineffectually, as if he could battle the pleasure that Bryce's finger brought him with its sinuous invasion.

Bryce winked victoriously at Nestor. But the battle was not nearly over, as Nestor released his grip on Michael's cock and brought his hands down to the large balls that bounced there. He gripped them expertly, his fingertips dancing over them; then, without warning, he cinched his fist around Michael's scrotum and pulled down. The effect was electric. Michael seized up, a strangled wail gurgling in his throat.

Startled by Nestor's dedication, Bryce thrust his finger into Virgil with renewed vigor, sending him into even greater seizures of ecstasy.

It was a dead heat. The men lying supine writhed and shouted, while the lithe demons besetting them gave no ground. The room was filled with the sound of deep grunting and wild suction as Virgil and Michael fell into a rhythm of thrusting abandon.

"Almost there, motherfucker," Virgil taunted Michael as his legs stiffened with impending orgasm. "We're gonna kick your ass."

In response, Michael's eyes rolled up into his head and his pelvis snapped into manic motion, battering Nestor's welcoming throat. "Fuck...." he wailed, voice weak and reedy as if choked by pleasure.

As the rules of this game dictated, Bryce and Nestor each pulled the cock out of their mouths and pounded away at them, knuckles white with the hardest work the two of them had ever done in their lives. Their eyes locked, the fierce competitors crashed toward the finish line.

Bryce was so intent on winning, in fact, that the first surge escaped his notice completely until semen suddenly filled his nostril. He startled back but didn't lose a stroke, the sting softened by the knowledge that he had won. But not by much—a quick glance over at Nestor showed a near photo finish as Michael ejaculated wildly, scattering cum all over the bed as Nestor pulled and squeezed.

"Fuck, fuck, fuck," the recumbent men chanted, their unison seeming nearly as practiced as that of Bryce and Nestor. They looked into each other's eyes as they came, their expressions of surprised pleasure mirrored in each other.

Bryce and Nestor were nothing if not thorough, and they yanked and licked and kissed until the last drops emerged and the members in their hands began to soften. Nestor leaned over and kissed Bryce on the cheek, leaving a pearly lipstick print. Bryce accepted the gesture with a regal nod.

"You ran a good race, dear," he said generously. "I'm sure you'll come even closer to winning the second heat."

Nestor looked down at the sweat-drenched and panting men. "They tired," he said.

Bryce glanced from Virgil to Michael and back again. "You know, you may be right. Let's get them some water and let them rest for five minutes or so. They deserve that. And then round two!"

"Round two?" Virgil whimpered.

"Five minutes?" Michael moaned.

"That's the spirit," cheered Bryce. "Nestor love, I'll get the water, you get the condoms."

It was just four and a half minutes later when Bryce and Nestor climbed atop their respective mounts and began gently to ride, cowgirl style, toward bliss.

CHAPTER SIX

Tuesday
A day in Paris

"OH GOD, I was snoring, wasn't I? I am so sorry. It happens when I get overtired."

Kerry stood on the balcony of their suite in a bright white hotel robe, blinking into the Parisian noon.

Brandt looked up at her from the chaise lounge where he had dragged a pillow and a blanket in the wee hours of the morning when he could stand it no longer. He couldn't sleep in hell, so he came out here. Where he didn't sleep much either.

"No, not at all. I just... I guess I have trouble sleeping in strange rooms or something. I needed some fresh air. I guess." He stood and gathered up the bedding, wadding it into a huge ungainly ball that he didn't know what to do with.

She smiled and took it from him. "Here, let me," she said. "You look like you didn't sleep very well, which I simply cannot imagine given how comfortable this wrought-iron patio furniture looks." She shook her head and stepped back into the suite.

"Fuck," he groaned, then followed her in.

She stood next to a side table, pouring steaming coffee into a pristine white cup, which she handed him. "Here. You'll feel more human in seconds—these guys know coffee."

He sipped, and it was indeed good.

Gabriel would love this.

Fuck.

Gabriel.

He blinked hard and then noticed she was staring at him.

"I know what's going on," she said quietly, her voice serious.

If his heart intended to ever beat again, it gave absolutely no sign. He took an awkward step to the side, trying to regain his balance.

"I am so sorry." She set down her own coffee cup and stepped over to him, took his hand in hers. "But I promise you this. He will never know. Not from me."

"Wha-what?"

"I've never met him, but I cannot imagine Gabriel would be happy knowing about it. So if he asks me, I'm going to tell him you never had a moment of doubt. You can tell him whatever you want when you're ready. That's your call."

"Doubt?" It was the only word Brandt could force himself to say. His head was spinning; his knees were ready to buckle.

"That we'd get there for your wedding. I guarantee you he's spending all his time hoping you're okay and that you're just crushing this *Amazing Race* thing we're doing, striding mightily across continents to get to him. Just let him believe that until after the ceremony, okay? He'll feel awful if he glided across the Atlantic in first class and you… well, you slept on balconies because you were punishing yourself for things out of your control." She smiled, clearly intent on bucking up his spirits.

Out of his control. She had that right.

"Thanks," he said, whipping up his best effort at a smile to match hers. "I'm so glad you understand."

She smiled more broadly and patted him on the shoulder. "There ya go, chief. Now, in my effort to impress room service with my Frenchy skills, I may have accidentally ordered a dozen croissants—sorry, not sorry—so eat up and then let's hit the *musées*, mmm-kay?" She tossed him a pastry and took a huge bite of another as she walked to the bathroom, humming a song she probably remembered from high school French class.

Yep, this is hell.

He took a bite, washed it down with some coffee. Then he set his shoulders and got on with it.

After the first hour in a museum, he'd reached his limit. Kerry flitted from painting to painting for two more hours, taking it all in before moving on to sculpture, while he walked stolidly through the galleries. He hardly even saw the artwork. Instead he saw couples holding hands, young sweethearts babbling excitedly, elderly companions walking slowly without need for more words, having exchanged a lifetime of them already. Everywhere he looked he saw men and women in love. He was nearing the edge of his sanity when he finally saw a pair of young men standing closer than friends would stand, before a huge canvas. He stopped to watch them, to see them express some tenderness to each other, to remind him what men can mean to each other. But when the one on the right spoke to the one on the left, the one on the left turned and left. The one on the right, left alone, stared at the painting intently for another minute, then wiped his eyes and left in the opposite direction.

Brandt sat down hard on a bench as if he'd been punched in the gut.

"Had enough?" Kerry said, plopping down next to him.

"I think so," he replied, trying to scrub the pain from his voice.

"All right, then, let's go find one of those charming sidewalk cafés you always see in books about Paris. We'll get some crusty bread and some creamy Brie and a sassy pinot. I may buy a beret."

"Now you're talking," he said. They found the nearest exit.

An hour later they were finishing a bottle of wine and watching tourists stream past their small marble-topped café table. They laughed at the little dogs and smiled at the babies, and for a moment Brandt forgot that he was having the worst day of his life.

"I know what we'll do," Kerry said suddenly once the last of the wine was gone. She stood, a little unsteadily, but soon regained her balance. "Come on."

"Where are we going?" he asked, knowing before speaking that it didn't matter. He would go anywhere with her because anywhere was better than another night in the hotel was going to be.

"No self-respecting woman can come to Paris and not do a little shopping," she said. "I could tell you were getting bored with the art thing, so let's mix it up a bit." She pulled a small folded map out of her purse and unfurled it, taking her bearings from the street signs on the corner. "This way," she pointed, then turned 180 degrees and headed off the other direction.

"Do you have any idea where you're going?" he asked, following her lead.

"Of course I do. According to this map, the main shopping district is just a couple of blocks over this way."

"What are you shopping for?"

She stopped in midstride and looked at him. "Well, that's a guy question. People don't shop *for* things. 'To shop,' I'll have you know, is an intransitive verb. It requires no object. It is complete in itself."

"Oh, goody."

"If you aren't careful, you're going to have your gay card revoked with an attitude like that."

He shook his head. She had no idea the kind of card he was carrying.

She ducked into the first shop they came to, which offered a wide range of—to Brandt's eye at least—identical dresses. But Kerry seemed determined to look at all of them.

Every. Single. One.

"What do you think?" she asked, over and over again, holding one of the dresses up to herself and turning to him.

"Nice," he said, over and over again, varying the word until he'd run through his mental thesaurus and started over again, back at "Nice."

"Well you're being no help at all," she finally blurted. "I'm going to have to try these on. Here." She handed him several dresses on hangers. "Let's go." She strode purposefully over to the fitting room and swept the door wide open. She stood aside expectantly. "Well, come on."

"In there?" he asked, aghast.

"Yes, in here." She rolled her eyes. "You have to help me choose."

"But—"

"But nothing. Move it, mister!" She pointed authoritatively into the fitting room.

As he entered the small room, holding a pile of dresses, he wondered how he had managed to descend from hell into something worse. He dropped that line of thought when she dropped the dress she'd been wearing and stepped out of the puddle it made at her feet.

She stood before him in her bra and panties, holding out her hand for the first dress.

He couldn't move.

Brandt had never had what he would consider a long-term relationship before Donnelly came into his life. He'd been too busy finishing college in three years and blasting his way through the police academy to have much time for more than a date once in a while, mostly when his brothers bugged him about the monk-like life he was leading. He didn't consciously avoid dating, but between the intensity of his studies and his dedication to duty, he met a limited number of eligible women—and the ones he did date tended to be those who introduced themselves after a spin class when he tugged the cuffs of his T-shirt down over his biceps. Though most turned out to be far more interested in his body than his mind, the main advantage these women brought was that he didn't have to go looking for them. The main drawback was that there was nothing for them to say once their limited pool of conversation topics (kale, hot yoga) had been exhausted.

So he had little experience with smart, funny, thoroughly good women, especially the kind who stood before him in simple but sexy underthings—sexy not because of their design or fabric but because of the confidence with which she wore them—and asked him to hand her a dress.

He blinked hard and handed her the dress on the top of the stack draped over his arm. She smiled, took it from him, and stepped into it. After she pulled it up, loosely arranging it on her shoulders, and swept her golden hair to one side, she turned her back to him. He had no idea what to do.

She looked up and met his gaze in the mirror. "Zip me up?" she prompted, as if he should have known what he was there for.

"Oh yeah, sorry," he blurted, then spent the next agonizing thirty seconds trying to make his fingers work. He finally got the zipper pulled up, up to the base of her skull, where the fine hairs softly brushed his hand....

He stepped back, dropping his free hand to his side.

She flipped her hair, and it somehow flowed back into perfect, glamorous order. She turned to him, eyes bright. "Well?" she asked, putting a hand on one hip.

"You're... beautiful," he said softly.

She rolled her eyes. "Well, thanks for the compliment, buddy, but what about the dress?" She turned to look into the mirror. "Is it the right color? What about this neckline?" She turned side to side. "Now that I see it on, I'm starting to think that this pattern is a little last-year. I have a sinking feeling that all anyone's going to think is Anne Hathaway at the Tony awards. Remember that amazing thing she wore, the one with the flowers and all the stuff around...?" She wiggled her fingers around the neckline, eyebrows up, as if he surely must know what she was talking about.

He shook his head helplessly. "I think it looks amazing on you. Anne Hathaway never even occurred to me." This was the truth.

"Oh, you," she scolded. She turned and swept her hair out of the way again. "Here, undo me and I'll try the others. And if you tell me they all look amazing on me, I am totally firing you." She smiled into the mirror and laughed as he fumbled with the zipper.

The next four dresses all looked amazing to him, though they all reminded her of some celebrity he should have immediately thought of as well. It was exhausting.

The fifth dress seemed to catch her fancy, as she kept it on longer than the previous four and did some additional turn-and-looks in the mirror.

"No, seriously," she said, dismissing his initial evaluation of "looks nice," and tucking up the corner of her mouth as she studied her reflection, "what about the way this one fits up top?" She tugged at the sides of the bodice, frowning. "I love the fullness of the skirt, but I'm afraid it leaves the girls on their own." She ran her hands under her breasts, pulling the fabric taut. "Although, a dart at each side might take care of that...." She chewed her lip and studied the effect from several angles.

"Yeah, that could do it," he said, hoping what she said was something she would want him to agree with.

"I know what's wrong," she blurted, clapping her hands in a eureka dance. "It's the bra. It's never going to work with this bra." She stepped over to where he was trying to disappear into the corner of the fitting room and turned her back to him, hair pulled aside.

This he was ready for. He knew his role well enough at this point to unzip her.

She shucked the dress down off her shoulders, then unhooked her bra and tossed it onto the chair over which she had draped the rejected dresses.

This he was not ready for.

She pulled her hair to the side again, and Brandt was greatly relieved that the dress was back in place before he caught sight of her braless reflection.

She stood before the mirror, considering again. "Hmm. What do you think? Better?"

He tried hard not to think about her breasts, free and full, brushing against the fabric of the dress as she casually stepped side to side. He tried hard not to think about how he was getting hard.

"Much—" His voice failed him, and he had to clear his throat and start again. "Much better."

"Do you think I can pull it off at my advanced age? Not getting too saggy?"

"Your breasts are beautiful," he said, shocked at the husky note in his voice.

She glanced at him in the mirror, eyes bright. "You're such a sweetheart." She studied herself more, then nodded. "This is the one," she said definitively.

Brandt glimpsed his exit from hell.

"Now, unzip me, and then we can go find *you* something." She presented her pale, shapely neck one last time, and he unzipped the final dress. She carefully lowered it and stepped out of it, then turned to hand it to him.

She stood before him, wearing only panties and the bright smile of the successful shopper. Time stopped for Brandt.

He had seen her breasts from the side, he had seen them silhouetted in the dim midnight of their hotel room. He had not seen them in their full splendor, in the thorough lighting of an elegantly appointed fitting room.

He was fourteen again.

Breasts are, to the adolescent boy, the most powerful things in the world. They are everywhere visible, but nowhere exposed. The very possibility of seeing bare breasts—in person—would inspire most teenage boys to crawl across broken glass, to make any imaginable deal with the devil. They are his constant thought and his goal in life, his dream and his reason for being.

Brandt at fourteen had been outwardly more mature than his peers, but he was no less intoxicated by the idea, the outline, the potential heft and wiggle of breasts. And all of that adolescent yearning came crashing back into his chest, bringing with it the embarrassed flush he could see rising in his cheek, the tightness he could feel continuing to grow in his pants.

He had forgotten about breasts. He remembered now.

She reached for her bra, humming happily as she celebrated her shopping victory. He hoped she would turn away from him as she put it on, but she seemed to have forgotten he was in the room. He busied himself with gathering up the reject dresses, arranging them with a consuming diligence so he wouldn't have to look anywhere else. Mercifully, by the time he had exhausted every distraction at hand she had finished dressing and was picking up her purse, tucking a stray ringlet behind her ear.

"Good to go," she said, smiling.

He smiled back, but all he could see were her breasts. He bowed and motioned for her to precede him, mainly so they would stop pointing their perky nipples at him accusingly. They knew his secret.

Get a grip, Brandt.

She made her purchase, and he handed off his armful of dresses to a whippet-thin young man who reminded him of Nestor, particularly with his eyes fixed on the front of Brandt's jeans, still awkwardly tightened by the semiboner caused by those breasts. That he was being ogled by a man because of the erection caused by a woman made his head spin; he couldn't help but smile in surrender to the sheer insane irony of it all.

"Glad you're enjoying yourself," Kerry said as they stepped out onto the sidewalk. "I was starting to worry about you in there, looking overwhelmed by a half-dozen little dresses."

"I'm out of practice, I guess," he replied as they walked. "I like the simplicity of things like jeans. I only have to know two numbers, waist and inseam, and I can just grab the color I want. Don't even have to try them on."

"And they end up looking like that," she said, falling back a half step and glancing down at his ass. "Lucky bastard."

"Lucky? Because I don't have to shop? I thought you loved shopping 'as an end in itself.'"

"I do. I meant Gabriel's the lucky one." She winked at him and laughed that damn musical laugh of hers.

"I'll be sure to remind him of that."

She suddenly stopped walking. "Now, here's the place for you," she announced, looking into a shop window.

Brandt stood beside her and looked in as well. The display held three mannequins, arranged as if they had just stepped off the catwalk at a runway show for a designer whose main style note was "skintight."

"Yeah, I don't think so," Brandt demurred. "My style is more... well...."

"Butch?" she suggested, her voice laced with irony.

"Sure. Let's call it that." He looked desperately up and down the boulevard for another store, and luckily spied one two doors down that seemed to specialize in things like hats and shoes. "How about there?" he asked, pointing.

She smiled knowingly. "Shoes, right? I knew we had a lot in common. Let's go." She marched smartly off toward the men's furnishings shop, swinging her parcel gaily as she went.

Brandt followed, practicing his deep breathing as he walked slowly and calmly behind.

Once in the store, Kerry was in frantic motion, picking up shoes, exclaiming over them, and putting them down once the next one caught her eye. Brandt made a beeline to the scarf-and-leather-goods section, thinking to find Gabriel something cashmere, or perhaps a wallet or something. Anything that would keep him out of the fitting room.

"I found it!" Kerry called suddenly. She was holding aloft a colorful moccasin-style shoe, which also—for reasons Brandt could not fathom—boasted sections of black patent leather.

He grimaced. "It looks like something a clown would wear to a funeral."

She burst out laughing, surprising Brandt and utterly terrifying the shop employee who had been hovering near her. "I know! I just had to see what you'd think of it—you guys are always so quick with the snappy judgment." She was still laughing and shaking her head as she set the gaudy shoe back in place. "Clown funeral, oh my God."

You guys.

He knew exactly what she meant. She hadn't meant to offend him, he knew that as well. But he couldn't pretend to be her gay best friend and shopping companion much longer.

"I like this," he said, holding up a scarf made of three different layers of soft cashmere fabric in cool, slaty tones of blue and gray. What he really meant was that Donnelly would like this.

Wait. He really would like this, Brandt knew. He'd never known such a thing before, at least not with this certainty. When he told Kerry that he was terrible at picking out gifts, he wasn't kidding—he'd always dreaded having to guess what Donnelly would like and usually ended up getting something that he was sure would end up in the bottom of a drawer somewhere. Not that Donnelly would ever let on that it wasn't just exactly what he'd been hoping for, of course, but Brandt was never confident in what he chose.

Until now. This scarf, he knew—he just *knew*—was perfect.

"I'll take this," he said to the clerk, who had retreated behind the counter to be a safe distance from Kerry and her shoe-related outbursts.

"Oui, monsieur," he replied, taking it from Brandt. "Est-ce un cadeau?"

Brandt looked helplessly at him, and then at Kerry.

"Oui," she answered on his behalf, and the clerk pulled out a box and began wrapping the scarf in tissue. "I'm assuming this is penance to Gabriel for experiencing Paris without him?"

"Oui," Brandt replied. "How did you know?" Though the fact that it was mostly for experiencing a boob-induced boner in Paris, he didn't say.

She winked at him. "We know men, don't we?"

"Indeed we do." *It's women I can't figure out.*

The clerk took Brandt's card and soon handed it back, along with a small shopping bag containing the scarf, neatly wrapped in a box with a tidy bow.

"Thank you," Brandt said, grateful to have made a purchase that did not require a trip to the fitting room.

They walked a little farther down the boulevard, then caught sight, between two buildings, of the river. They exchanged a quick nod and soon were strolling along a tree-lined riverbank, laughing at squirrels and squinting in the bright sunlight. For a moment, Brandt forgot about the anxieties and general panic he'd been experiencing for the last twenty-four hours.

"How about we head back," Kerry suggested, "and get a little nap before we go looking for an amazing place to have dinner?"

A nap. In bed.

Shit.

"You know, I may grab something to read." Nodding toward a newsstand at the next corner. "I have a hard time sleeping during the day."

"I'm beginning to think you have a hard time sleeping in general," she said. "It's like you're always 'on.' I know you're stressed about this whole situation, but it might help if you relaxed a little." Her tone was helpful, not critical, and she looked genuinely concerned.

"I'm trying, I really am," he said. "This whole thing has been such a mess. But since Gabriel often has to give me the same pep talk, I should probably reflect more on my general stress level, shouldn't I?"

She nodded thoughtfully. "As a sort of medical professional, I prescribe rest. Let's go crash for a bit—I promise you'll feel better."

He smiled and agreed, though he knew full well it was only going to get worse.

Back at the hotel room, Kerry immediately put her new dress on—again, sans bra—and looked at it from every possible angle in every possible mirror. "Do you really like it?" she asked as she studied it in the mirror.

Brandt knew from watching his younger sister discover fashion that this was an integral part of the shopping experience—the postgame critical commentary and second-thoughts session. Even though he suspected that Kerry was still quite pleased with the dress, he knew he must indulge her in this moment of pretend doubt. He perched on the edge of the bed and tried to be supportive.

"It's lovely, and you look amazing in it. You'll have them falling at your feet when you wear it."

She looked deeply pleased. "I certainly hope so, given what I paid for it." She turned to view the back in the mirror. "Maybe I should wear it tonight to dinner, see how it performs?"

Brandt held up his hands. "You do not want to get that dress anywhere near me and a bottle of wine," he warned. "Nothing good will come of that, given my general clumsiness."

She turned to look at him, her face far more serious than he expected. "Why do you do that?"

"Do what?"

"Run yourself down that way. You're clumsy. You don't know anything about fashion. You didn't make it to New York in time." She leaned against the armoire and looked at him hard. "When I look at you, I see a genuinely good man with a charming personality and a body that was sculpted by the angels themselves." She studied him for a moment, then stepped aside so he had an unobstructed view into the mirror behind her. "What do you see?"

He looked at his reflection for a long moment, something he rarely—never, really—did. What did he see? He saw a man alone. Even in this city, even with Kerry right here next to him, watching him right now, he was utterly alone. No one knew the struggle inside him, no one except Donnelly, and even he could only listen to Brandt's anguished utterances and say loving, reassuring things—he didn't really understand what it was like. Donnelly had gone from thinking he was straight to knowing he was gay, and he'd never looked back. Brandt, however, had gone from knowing he was straight to thinking he was gay, and though he never for a moment doubted his love for Donnelly, he had come to realize that he was not, and would never be, gay. At least not in the way that Donnelly—and, heaven forbid—Bryce and Nestor were. He was something in between, or perhaps he was nothing. Like no one ever. Brandt didn't know anything but that he was alone.

"Oh my God, what's the matter?" Kerry asked, sitting on the bed next to him, seeming not to care that she was wrinkling her new dress.

Brandt shook himself out of his bleak musings to notice his reflection again. His eyes were red now, and a tear was making its way down his cheek. He'd had no idea he was crying. He closed his eyes for a long moment. He tried to think of something witty to say, something that would reassure her—and himself—that he wasn't slowly going insane, but he couldn't. All he could bring himself to say was the truth.

"Without him, I'm afraid I don't exist."

Well, that certainly sounded insane.

But she didn't seem fazed by it. She put her hand on his knee and looked into his eyes. "I know exactly what that feels like," she said quietly.

"You... do?" He was stunned.

She nodded. "I do."

He shrugged, completely confused.

"You know full well that Gabriel is feeling exactly the same way as you are right now. You two... you two made each other. He changed your life when he came into it, and you changed his. Like, forever and ever. Right?"

He nodded, stunned that she could sum them up so effortlessly, so completely.

"So of course you're feeling adrift without him. But I'm going to let you in on a secret—it's something women have to learn and most men never even dream of.

Ready?" She waited for him to nod. "All right. You can be changed by someone—transformed into something completely new—and still be yourself. When you're with him you feel like a new person, but you have to know that when you're not with him, you are still a person. The people who are important to us change us, Ethan. That's not a bad thing. It means we're human, and humans weren't meant to be unchanging and eternal."

She paused, but he was so overwhelmed by the idea of the impossibility of disentangling his identity from Donnelly's that he could hardly take anything more in. So she continued.

"I dated a physics major for a while in college. He was super nerdy and super hot, which was an amazing and rare thing in itself, but his best quality was his ability to take the most obscure science facts and make them almost philosophical. Late one night as we were lying on the grass in the quad outside our dorm, looking up at the stars, he said, 'Do you know what a beam of light looks like as it travels through space? Like, completely empty space?' And of course I had no idea, so I just said it probably looked like the lasers in *Star Wars*. He kind of smiled at me—that superior smile is the reason I dumped him, if you must know—and said 'Nothing.' I must have looked exactly as stupid as I felt at that moment, because he went on to tell me that light is invisible until it hits something. In the emptiness of space, there's not even a speck of dust to scatter the tiniest part of that beam of light, and so it just continues in a straight line, at the speed of light and completely invisible, until it hits something. So now I'm all set if the physics of light comes up in Double Jeopardy, right? Yay."

Brandt chuckled, and this seemed to encourage Kerry.

"But then he got this faraway look—which is the reason I waited so long to dump him, because that faraway look was sexy as hell—and he started down this really philosophical road, saying that people are the same way. You don't really know what anyone's like until they come into contact with other people, and then you see who they are. That's why when you said you were afraid you don't exist, I thought about that beam of light. Because in some ways it doesn't really exist when it's all by itself, like a tree falling in a forest when there's no one to hear it. But that doesn't mean it's not real, or that it's any less bright. It's just waiting to be revealed when it hits something."

"If you start singing 'This Little Light of Mine'...." he warned with a smile.

"Not a chance—I hire people to sing 'Happy Birthday' so I don't have to," she said with a laugh. "But I really want you to know that I see the amazing person you are, even if you feel you aren't who you really want to be when he's not with you."

"Thank you," he said, leaving aside the question of whether he was really who he wanted to be when he was with her either.

"Good," she said, rising and smoothing the winkles out of her dress. "Now, I'm going to get a little snooze in before unleashing this incredible dress on an unsuspecting populace. Help me out of it?" She turned and swept her hair to the side once more.

He got up from the bed, unzipped her dress, and didn't even look at the smooth skin of her neck, paid no mind to the sweet smell of her hair. He walked over to his side of the bed, took off his shoes, and lay back on the bed. Staring resolutely at the ceiling, he tried not to picture her as he heard her slip out of the dress, hang it up, then pull something out of the drawer below the armoire.

"I'm going to turn the temp down a bit, is that okay?"

Make it freeze, I beg you. "Sounds good."

He felt the bed dip as she lay down. He was as far toward the edge of the mattress as he could be without risking a fall to the floor, but he could still feel her next to him. She must have been a foot away, and yet the hairs on his arm rose up as if she had brushed against him.

"You know," she said after a silent few minutes, "aside from the whole escaping a volcano and nearly missing your wedding thing, this isn't a bad adventure. We're in Paris, we saw some amazing works of art, we shopped, we had *le déjeuner* in a sidewalk café, and now we're being incredibly lazy, resting up before the hard work of eating an amazing dinner. This beats the hell out of most of the vacations I've ever taken."

"I'm not the adventuring type," he replied, still fixing his gaze at the ceiling, "so if you'd told me a week ago that I could survive even half of what we've been through, I would have thought you were crazy."

"Turns out I'm not crazy?"

"Didn't say that," he said with a laugh. "But this has been a pretty amazing adventure, and though I would trade you in an instant for Gabriel—oof!" Her elbow jabbed his ribs with a lightning blow. "Sorry, but you know what I mean."

"I do," she said. "I just felt it necessary to defend my honor."

"Understood. Now, what I was saying is that though I would love to be having this adventure with Gabriel, you're excellent company, and I am really glad Greg introduced us."

"Me too," she said. "I hadn't realized how much I miss having friends like you and Greg. My gay buddies were such a huge part of college, but when I entered the professional world, I suddenly found myself surrounded by polo-shirt-wearing, golf-playing mouth-breathers. If I didn't need dick once in a while, I'd write off the entire straight male population. Being with you fulfills a need that I had kind of forgotten I have."

I know what you mean.

"So," she said, turning on her side and placing her hand on his arm, "thank you for coming into my life. I was getting frustrated and exhausted by everything—my job, the people in my life, all of it—and you've brought me back. Thank you, Ethan."

Brandt's congenital passion for being useful completely overwhelmed his angst at being in bed with a woman, and he turned and smiled at Kerry. She was beautiful, he knew that, but with her hair casually tousled and her eyes bright with the emotion of their conversation, she was breathtaking.

"And thank you for helping me get this far. I couldn't have done it without you."

She glowed, and her smile grew even wider. "All right, enough sappy stuff. Let's get a little rest, and tonight we take the town!"

"Watch out, Paris," he said, and they shared a laugh.

As silence fell over the room, it was just him and the ceiling. He stared for a long, long time.

At sea

"Do you like it when I do this?" Brandt asked, a fire in his eyes, a gloss of exertion on his forehead. His whole body bucked with the fervor of his thrusting as their bodies ground together.

"Fuck. Yeah." His breath came in short bursts now, the sweet agony of repeated blows on his prostate almost more than he could bear. They kissed, and even his shallow breath was taken.

"Then you're going to love this," Brandt growled, and in one fluid motion caught him up in his strong arms and flipped him over, spinning him on the spindle of his enormous cock, dropping him back to the tangle of sheets their bed had become— without withdrawing.

From this angle, he knew, Brandt could thrust more deeply and wildly. Those slim yet powerful hips gyrated crazily and then without warning began pounding away with an almost brutal power. He was losing control, shuddering under the onslaught, his own cock grinding into the bed, bringing him ever closer to the edge of his own orgasm. He bit his lip, trying to keep from shaking.

"Are you sure I should come inside?" Brandt asked, but in a voice that was odd, different, higher.

"Yes, I want you to," a voice replied that wasn't his own.

Donnelly writhed, the sheets gripped in his fists.

"But won't your... friend mind?" That wasn't Brandt's voice at all. He had heard that voice somewhere, but he wasn't sure where.

"He's fine with it. Promise. Now get in here."

When the door clicked shut, Donnelly sat up, suddenly wide-awake.

He was alone.

Brandt wasn't here.

He was on a ship. Oh.

He listened for a moment to the sound of Sandler and the peachy waiter in the other room, whispering to each other urgently enough that their voices carried as well as if they'd been speaking in normal voices.

Good for you, Donnelly thought. He settled back into bed and closed his eyes.

"What would you like, Mr. Birkin?" he asked, the cheeks on his face as pronounced and beautiful as the ones farther south I'd already been admiring.

I smiled at him, and he smiled back—the smile that says he knows full well why I'm smiling, but he's not going to let me know he knows. Which he knows I now know. Let the games begin.

"What do you think I'd like?"

He paused for a moment and knitted his brow as if we've known each other all our lives and he's searching back through the high school yearbooks for a clue

as to what I'd be drinking. "I think you'd like something that tastes of... peach?"
He delivered this line with such practiced nonchalance that I almost considered it a
coincidence, but then there it was again, that hint of a grin. He had been listening to me
and Gabriel, the little scamp.

"You know," I replied, "I think I am in the mood for peach. Is there something
you would recommend to satisfy my craving?" I flicked my eyes downward to let him
know what would really satisfy me.

"I have just the thing," he answered with a wink, and turned to walk slowly
away, allowing me ample time to watch the luxuriant cadence of his buoyant buttocks
rising and falling. I was hard in an instant.

"Are you allowed to take off your uniform?"

Donnelly smiled at the playful flirtatiousness of Sandler's question. He was
trying not to listen, but the instincts of a police officer are not easily switched off.

"I'm off duty, so I can wear what I want," the waiter replied.

"Can I make a suggestion?"

In the silence, Donnelly imagined the waiter's nod, playful and expectant.

"Take it off. Take it all off."

"Yes, sir."

He brought me the drink in a tall, slender glass. It was a deep orangey-pink at
the bottom, rising to a pearly white at the top. He set it before me, then stepped back,
eyes aglow with anticipation.

"What is it?" I asked.

"Something no one's ever had before," he replied, a quiver of excitement in his
voice.

"Like you?" Clumsy, yes, but he was young enough that a veiled reference to
sexual inexperience would flatter, not offend.

"You'll have to taste it before I tell you any of my secrets."

He may be young, but he knows how to flirt. I lifted his drink to my lips and
tasted it, slowly but fully, just like I would taste him. I held the glass like I would hold
him. Our eyes met.

"Well?" he asked, his slick manner giving way to eagerness to witness my
pleasure.

"Delightful," I replied, and that was no flattery. "It's perfect."

"Do you want to know what's in it?"

"Not yet. Let me taste it all and discover it for myself."

He looked a little crestfallen. "Okay. I'll leave you to it, then."

"No, please, stay for a bit." I looked around the room. "The place is clearing
out—surely you can spend a few minutes?"

That smile again. He glanced over to Emmett, who gave a quick nod and a
wry smile. He perched on the barstool next to me, the one Gabriel had occupied,
his eyes darting back and forth as if he were doing something scandalous. Perhaps
he was.

"I'm Ankur," he said.

"I know."

He looked surprised for a second, then glanced down at his name tag and smiled at me. "Sorry, I forget sometimes that we're labeled."

"Surprise me, then. What's describes you that's not on the label?"

He looked furtively around again before leaning over the table. "Interested," he whispered.

The thick sound of dropping uniform—unforgiving fabric cast from a standing height.

The gasp of contact, of hidden skin caressed, flesh and muscle grasped by strong hands.

The throaty mumble of urgent kisses, stubble scraping stubble.

"Turn around." Sandler's voice resonated with lust and command in equal measure.

Donnelly rolled over, restless.

"Turn around," I said.

He looked a little disappointed, as if I had decided he wasn't worth kissing. I kissed him again, to let him know. He smiled then and turned around. I sat on the edge of the bed, and watched him turn, saw that beautiful peach come into view. Covered by his stiff black pants it had seemed a wonder, but now… now it was perfection itself. Perfectly round, perfectly tight, perfectly covered with a fine, downy, perfect dusting of hair. I kissed one cheek—who could resist?—and then the other one. Goose bumps rose all over his body, and he gave a little shiver.

"Is this okay?" I murmured into his flesh, my lips pressed to his warm skin.

"Yes, please," he replied, a confirmation and an invitation all in one.

"Bend over."

Slowly, achingly slowly, he leaned forward, arching his back. His buttocks became spherical—not just round, but geometrically uniform—as he did. And then, as his back reached a perfect ninety-degree angle, they parted. Those perfect globes of muscle opened, just slightly, to let me see the paradise they guarded.

"Oh fuck," I whispered, without intending to. When presented with an ass that perfect one must simply say, "Oh fuck."

He stepped his feet apart, first the left and then the right, and opened wider. The invitation was clear.

I kissed him again on the right cheek, and then the left, and then the right again, back and forth, each time edging a little closer to my goal in the dark recesses of that perfect ass. With each kiss, I felt him take a little breath, urging me on, letting me know how close I was getting to what he and I both wanted. Finally I reached the middle and placed a delicate kiss right on that obdurate ring of muscle. It was both indescribably soft and drum tight, and it responded to my kiss with a little twitch, a convulsion of desire that I could taste as much as feel. I kissed him again, and then I entered him.

"Oh," he moaned as I pressed the tip of my tongue through the center of that magic ring. He bent farther and pressed back against my face. "Oh."

"Oh." The sound was so soft, so plaintive, so… tender. Donnelly couldn't help but hear it, and hear in it the innocent hunger, the thrill of having a dream come true. It repeated, soft as a sigh, its meaning clear as a bell. Then silence, as if the one who made the sound had forsaken breathing altogether.

Donnelly realized he was holding his breath.

I pulled my tongue back and the knot of flesh snapped shut, closed tight against any intrusion. If he hadn't flirted so effortlessly and accompanied me back to the suite so willingly, I would have sworn that I was looking now at a virgin enclave, an unexplored mystery. But perhaps he was less experienced than I had assumed. If he hadn't been so tight, I might at this moment have slipped a spit-slicked finger inside and begun to tease him open. But the way he closed in on himself, like a sea anemone in the tide, made me want to seduce him, to insinuate myself gently, so he would open naturally to me. Instead of sliding a finger in, I kissed him again, softly, just brushing my lips against the tidy but irregular pleats of muscle that surrounded an opening no longer visible. I tickled my tongue in a dizzy circle all around it, zigzagging in a crazy random circumnavigation. Then I kissed him, my lips pressed against his opening, my tongue probing for reentry.

His gentle sighs of pleasure were replaced with something sharper, more urgent.

I sucked hard right at the center of his ass, and as I drew in more of his flesh, I felt it open to me—it unfurled its mysteries as my cheeks pulled in with the effort of maintaining the suction. He opened, and the sweet heat of his innermost place was revealed to my tongue as I drew him into me, trying to turn him inside out.

His breath grew ragged, and his knees began to quiver as if I really were sucking the life out of him. But he pushed back harder on me, forcing himself on me, pulling me in deeper. Into the hot, yielding muscle I pushed my tongue, and he welcomed me inside. I pressed my cheeks against his, shoving my tongue into him as far—and as wide—as I could. I gripped his slender hips and held him against my face, feeling his legs tremble as I fucked him with my tongue.

"Fuck… me… now," he panted. "Fuck… me… please."

Like there was any other way.

"Please." He said "please." Donnelly heard without trying to hear but then realized he had been listening all along.

What Sandler was about to discover, a strange land he was about to explore for the first time, was something Donnelly had experienced only once in his life. With Brandt. Which was enough for him, he reminded himself.

He heard Sandler shuffling and imagined the creaking of the sofa-bed springs were the waiter mounting it, making himself ready on hands and knees while Sandler tore open a condom wrapper. He could picture it as clearly as if he were in the room watching.

And then he realized he was lying in bed, alone, naked, picturing two men having sex.

He'd never done that before.

He was on his hands and knees, that beautiful ass thrust back and upward, still shiny from my spit. I could still taste it on my tongue. I came up behind him, running my hands all along that perfect flesh.

He sighed and shifted his weight impatiently, a colt eager to be saddled, tamed— or to seduce an unsuspecting rider into mounting. For the ride of his life.

I slid my arm under his hips and lifted—he was so light—and flipped him on his back.

"I want to see you," I said. "I want to kiss you."

He smiled so widely I was charmed all over again by his sexy sweetness.

I rolled the condom on, slicked it up, and then—gently, slowly—introduced a lubed-up finger. He closed his eyes and sighed as my finger entered him, and I played for a little while with him, opening him, warming him up. I didn't want to hurt him.

His smile faltered only for a moment, as his lips formed a silent "Oh." But then it broadened out again, and his eyes opened.

"Okay?"

"Yessss," he whispered.

I slipped a second finger in. He lurched up but settled right back down, wiggling his hips as he adjusted to the fullness. A new expression formed on his face, this one eager, hungry. I pushed a little harder, in and toward me, and found the hint of a prostate right where I knew it would be. I felt around it, then pressed my fingertip into it, just a little, and watched his eyebrows peak in surprise. He arched his back, and his palms flattened against the bed as he leveraged himself up even higher, pushing himself toward me while also squirming away as if the stimulation were too much for him to bear. He danced like an adorable puppet on my fingers for a while until finally he opened his eyes and spoke the word I'd been waiting to hear.

"Now." Ankur's voice was deep and strong, all of his youthful reserve evaporated by the heat of his excitement.

I did as I was told.

"Now."

That word. Donnelly was suddenly back in his bedroom—the bedroom that he now shared with Brandt—but before it was "our" bedroom. Before they knew.

He could see Brandt on the screen, nervous, anxious, pretending to be excited— but Donnelly knew him better than that. He was ashamed, mortified. He was naked.

Naked because Donnelly had just commanded him to take off the bright red jockstrap he had been wearing. The one Donnelly had chosen for him to wear. He had slipped it off, and now he lay naked, facedown, clearly terrified.

Donnelly had seen him naked hundreds of times over the two years they'd been partners on the force, but never like this. Never could he have taken a long moment to trace the muscles of his legs all the way up to where they blossomed into full, powerful buttocks. Never had he let himself acknowledge the beauty of his best friend.

But now there was nowhere to hide those feelings. His emotions were no more hidden than their bodies—he had taken off his clothes so Brandt wouldn't be alone in his nudity. He could no longer deny what he felt for this man he knew so well but had never really seen before.

Having studied his back in all its masculine wonder, he wanted to see the front. He had to know if Brandt was as inexplicably excited as he was, had to see whether he was erect as well from this insane game they were playing. For the first time in his life, he wanted—needed—to see another man's penis. No, that's not right. He needed to see Ethan Brandt's penis. He needed to see it erect, hard, obscene. He had to know he wasn't alone. And so he commanded him to turn over.

"Now."

I lifted his legs and touched my painfully hard cock to his winking ass. I pushed, just a little, and felt him open to me. He sucked in a little breath, but his eyes widened with pleasure, not pain, and so I pushed a little more.

I bent down to him, and he wrapped his hands around my neck, pulling me close. Our lips touched, gently, and I slowly nibbled my way from one corner of his mouth to the other, like we had all the time in the world.

My penis thought otherwise.

As we kissed, our bodies aligned somehow, and I slipped farther into him. His intense heat enveloped another inch of my cock, then another.

"Come on," he whispered. "Come on."

I lifted my head, and with my nose almost touching his so I could watch his eyes, I tensed my hips and felt more of my cock enter him. The corners of his eyes crinkled a little—he was smiling. Then he reached down and grabbed hold of my ass.

"Oh my," I said, sounding stupidly prim in my surprise.

"Come on," he said, more certainly now, his voice lower. He wasn't encouraging me; he was commanding me. His strong hands pulled me into him.

I hesitated. I know it sounds arrogant, but I've been here before. I've had guys be enthusiastic about me fucking them until I get a few inches in, and then things fall apart. The bottom line is, I get pretty thick at the base—one guy said the first four inches were heaven, and the last four were hell.

We were about at the four-inch mark.

But his grip on my ass didn't slacken—I think it's going to leave a mark, actually—so I pushed forward. I saw it in his eyebrows first: they rose in the middle, the creases between them ragged and twitchy. Then a growl from his throat, deep and urgent. But his fingertips, strong from stacking glasses and bussing heavy plates, dug into my ass and spurred me on.

And then my hips met his lovely round ass, and I was fully inside him.

"Fuck," he said, drawing out the word to about seven syllables on an exhalation that seemed to evaporate every tension in his body. He released my ass from his iron grip and threw his arms around me, pulling me close again, overwhelming me with kisses.

I know better than to pull back right away—I wanted him to get used to me inside him—so I just rotated my hips a little, giving him a wiggle-wiggle rather than a thrust. He moaned and matched my motions, and we spent a long while just grinding on each other.

"Okay?" I asked.

He nodded—he knew exactly what I was asking—and smiled, as if anticipating what was to come.

I drew back a little, and pushed forward a little, and he smiled even more widely. He nodded, just to be sure I got the message.

"Come on," he said again, and this time it was a challenge.

Oh, it was so on.

I started slowly, pulling back a little more, and when the head of my cock brushed his prostate he gave a jolt, his face an explosion of joy. I pushed forward a bit to hit that spot again and was rewarded with another spasm of pleasure that seemed to electrify his entire body. I fell into an easy rhythm of slow transits, hitting that magic spot every time, rewarded every time with a tightening twitch of the muscles in his ass. With my elbows on the bed next to his shoulders, I could cradle his head in my hands. We were in contact along our entire bodies, and every thrust I made was answered by the tightening of muscles and sinews everywhere on him. This was his entire essence: perfect skin and pure muscle, a broad smile and lively eyes.

"Okay?" he asked.

"More than okay," I answered, kissing him again.

Then I felt it. He was clamping down on me, using his ass in some tantric voodoo super-Kegel thing that took my fucking breath away. His ass gripped my entire cock, from root to tip, in a way I'd never felt before.

"Now," he said once more. This time it was with the assurance of a thousand-year-old Buddha, a god who knows fulfillment inheres in the utterance of his command.

I had no choice. The orgasm was upon me before I knew what was happening, was forced on me by the milking of his mystical ass. To stave it off for a moment, to make it last a little longer, I gritted my teeth and grunted against it, but it was no use. This orgasm wanted me, and it would have me.

Donnelly had only ever heard Brandt orgasm, and from the first—which he hadn't even seen firsthand, captured as it was on video by a sex-cam website—to the last, he knew the sound of every breath he took, every kind of pleasure of which his body was capable. Brandt was his entire world when it came to sex. And yet he recognized instantly the sound of Sandler reaching an anguished climax.

Donnelly was hard in an instant.

As Sandler's voice rose in pitch and his gasps came more frequently, Donnelly's erection began to bob in time. He reached down to it and found to his surprise that the head of his cock was already wet.

Sandler's moaning grew more plaintive and was filled with such a yearning that Donnelly felt it in his own loins. He stroked harder now, banishing all rational thought about how perverted it was to jack off while listening to a friend have sex in the next room. He'd been away from Brandt for only a few days and hadn't touched himself during that time. Now his cock was demanding attention, and he had no choice but to give it.

He threw back the covers. In the soft glow afforded by the night-light in the bathroom, he could see his cock silhouetted, standing ruler straight as he gripped it tightly at its base. He spat into his hand, and his saliva mixed with precum to slick up the entire length. He stroked in time with Sandler's grunting, growling moaning, and they both sped up as the end drew near.

Donnelly felt Sandler's voice deep in his muscles, as if the other man were conjuring his orgasm. The thrill of this forbidden connection shocked him.

But it wouldn't keep him from coming.

I came.

That doesn't begin to describe what it felt like, but it's the best I can do, since there just aren't words to describe the orgasm he created for me. It was enough to make me ponder taking up a life on the sea so Ankur and I could travel the world and I could fuck him every day just like this, and he could do that thing with his ass and all would be perfect in the world.

I kept coming.

It seemed to last forever, until I was sure the condom would burst from the sheer Niagaric volume of my semen. I pictured the tip blown up like a balloon animal at the circus.

Finally I had come.

"That was... amazing," I said with a sigh, collapsing onto him in elated exhaustion.

"You are the best I've ever had," he whispered, then kissed my ear softly.

"I'll bet you say that to all the passengers," I replied.

He looked stricken. "No," he said, shaking his head slowly. "No."

He was so sweet and earnest that I couldn't help but be charmed by him all over again. "Wait until you see what else I can do," I whispered into his ear, then kissed my way down the side of his neck, and over those perfect mounds of pectoral muscle, and then down across his hard and still panting abs, then down.

His cock was hard—diamond-cutting hard—and perfectly shaped along its six or so inches. He was uncut, and his foreskin slid easily up and down, gliding effortlessly on the shiny slickness my jabbing of his prostate had produced. I stroked him, entranced by the motion of his skin—like most Americans of my generation, I was robbed of mine soon after birth—and he moaned as if my rough caress was the best thing he'd ever felt.

Determined to repay him for the pleasure he'd given me, I swooped down on his cock and took it all in, all the way to the base, holding the slender stiffness in my mouth for a long moment before coming back up. He writhed, clutching at the sheets, and bucked up and down, ab muscles tensing in and out of view with every motion.

I plunged down again, pressing my nose against the soft hair of his groin, desperate to get every bit of him into me. I growled out my pleasure, knowing the vibration would transmit into him, rumble his very core. The high, needy whine he was making told me all I needed to know.

I lifted up and let him go, just for a moment, so I could suck his lovely smooth balls into my mouth. He gasped in a desperate breath, but I held them, swirled my tongue around them, tugged a bit at them before letting them plop out of my mouth.

I gobbled down his cock, tasting its renewed slickness as I felt it pass between my eager lips.

A precious few moments of slurping at his erection brought him to a frantic ecstasy, kicking and scrabbling at the sheets. As he thrust into me, hips rising off the mattress in his frenzy, I slipped a finger into his still-loose and still-lubed ass and his prostate came right to my fingertip, firm and more pronounced than before. He was close. I ran my finger over it, and his gasping let me know he felt it. I pushed. Hard.

The spasms started instantly. I felt them at my fingertip, in my hand, in my mouth. His taste changed in that moment, from light and sweet to salty and tangy. He was coming.

His body had been in frantic motion the entire time I'd been sucking him, but at this moment he took a deep breath and the frenzy left him. It was like he hadn't come but rather arrived—in Nirvana. I felt the tension leave his body, his spine relax. He sighed softly.

"Oh."

It was a sound of surrender, of relief. As if his body had found peace.

His cock, however, was still all business. Hard and hot, it commandeered my mouth, filling it, thrashing and sloshing about. I swallowed, and it replenished me, then twice, and again. He'd been saving himself for me.

I sucked and licked and swallowed, and as the storm subsided, I pulled up and kissed the pearly droplets that remained on the head of his cock. I didn't want to miss a bit of his sweet essence. I looked up at him, and he was watching me, a look of puzzlement on his face.

"You don't have to...," he said, haltingly.

"Don't have to do what?" I asked. I smiled up at him, because making someone come is about the best thing in the world, and I always get kind of giddy about it.

"I can clean up," he offered quietly.

"Don't you dare," I replied, and kept lapping at his only slightly softening cock.

"I can't believe you would do that," he finally said, his voice mystified.

"I'm doing it because I want to. Because you're amazing, and you taste so good, and you are about the sweetest person I've ever met."

"No one's ever—" His voice caught, and there were suddenly tears in his eyes.

I kissed the lovely tip of his cock one last time and then kissed my way up his body, his beautiful body. I nuzzled the delicate stubble of his strong jaw and kissed his trembling mouth.

"What is it?" I asked, looking into his eyes.

He shook his head and blinked out the tears.

"Tell me, Ankur."

"I've been with a few passengers," he said softly.

I nodded encouragingly.

"Not many. Five or six over the year."

I had assumed the number would be higher—he certainly would have no shortage of offers—but simply nodded again.

"They didn't care, like you do. Mostly they just wanted me to leave once they had... finished. They didn't kiss me, or touch me the way you did. And not one of them ever called me by name."

I didn't know what to say. Tears filled his eyes again, and he closed them tight and nuzzled my neck. The purity of his emotion, the innocence of its expression, filled me with a humble warmth.

"You deserve better than that," I whispered, then kissed his neck, and his jaw, and his lips.

We kissed. We kissed for a long time. We kissed until his tears dried and his expression lightened. We lay there and smiled a little stupidly at each other for a long, long time.

"And that's why I found you spooning like prom dates this morning?" Donnelly asked, then sat back and sipped his coffee.

Sandler smiled. "As one-night stands go, it was kind of sappy. But he's such a great guy. And the sex was un-fucking-believable."

Donnelly blushed and looked out the window.

"Oh my God, did you hear us?"

"It was fine. I told you not to worry about it." Donnelly felt a cold sweat creep up his neck.

"What's the matter?" Sandler asked, concern in his voice.

Donnelly hesitated, unsure what he should say, or whether he should say anything at all. "It's just that... when I heard you and Ankur... I kind of...." He shrugged helplessly.

Sandler raised an eyebrow. "You kind of... *hmm hmm*?" He made a subtle wanking motion with his hand.

Donnelly felt the fire in his cheeks flare to three-alarm level. He closed his eyes. "I can't believe I'm saying this, but... yes." He opened his eyes to see Sandler beaming at him.

"Awesome."

"What?" Donnelly asked, bewildered.

"Awesome. After all that talk last night about what it means to be a gay man, I'm really glad that you took advantage of the... opportunity... my adventure with Ankur afforded you."

"I felt like I was cheating on Ethan," Donnelly blurted.

"Cheating? How do you figure that?"

"Because I heard you. And your voice made me... hard." He took a deep breath. "And when you came, I came."

"Wow." Sandler's voice was soft with surprise. "That's even awesomer."

"But I've never done that before."

"Well, I assume you don't go skulking around listening to people have sex. But really, it's not any different than looking at porn for a quick wank when you need one."

"It was different."

"Why?"

"Because it wasn't watching anonymous people on the Internet have unrealistically well-lit sex. It was listening to you—hearing you. At first all I could hear was Ethan, and then I started to hear how you were different from Ethan, and then it was like I could feel your voice inside me. When you grunted, I could feel it. It wasn't like I even chose to touch myself—I couldn't help it."

"That's incredibly sexy," Sandler said, a hint of a grin playing at the corners of his mouth.

"I feel like I cheated on him."

Sandler reached out and put his hand on Donnelly's. "You didn't cheat. You are human, and you had a human reaction. An incredibly sexy one that, quite honestly, is making me a little light in the head right now, but leaving that aside, you did nothing wrong. You're a gay man, Gabriel, and gay men sometimes get turned on by other gay men having gay sex in the next room. It doesn't mean you cheated."

"It's just never happened before. I think our talk in the bar beforehand jarred something loose. Ethan's the only man I've ever had a sexual thought about." He looked hard at Sandler. "Until last night."

"I'm honored to have complicated your sex life," Sandler replied. "But Freud was right about one thing: having sexual thoughts is what makes us human. It's the bond we share, the communal weight we carry. That you had one makes me happy, because not having them... well, it's not good. I was worried that you were still resisting coming to grips with being gay, but now I know you're fine. So congratulations. You now are like every other married gay man in the world, surrounded by beauty he can look at but cannot touch. Unless," Sandler raised an eyebrow, "he agrees to touch with you."

Donnelly laughed. "If you think my development as a gay man has been delayed, you have no idea what you have in store for you when you meet Ethan."

"I look forward to that more with each passing day."

"Speaking of which, how shall we pass this day?" Donnelly, eager for a change of subject, tossed the daily program over to Sandler, who looked at it but didn't pick it up.

"First I need to stop by the salon and apologize for not waiting in the bar long enough to meet up with Dax and Stanley. Bad form there."

"But you would have missed your chance at Ankur."

"Right you are. And you would have missed my epic performance last night."

Donnelly tossed a tasteful accent pillow at his head. "I shouldn't have said anything."

"Don't say that. I like being able to talk with you about this stuff. And I kind of love the idea of seeing Ankur again. So let's lay out in the sun, or work crossword puzzles in the library, but for God's sake we have to be back in that bar again tonight. There are things I need to do to that strapping lad."

Donnelly rolled his eyes. "I'll stop by the shop for earplugs."

"Like hell you will."

Donnelly shrugged sheepishly. "Yeah, I probably won't. But if you breathe a word of this to Ethan...."

"The muscular guy with a gun? I don't think you have to worry about that. But if I know you, you're going to tell him everything, and then you two will have impossibly gorgeous sex that will drive any thought of my little escapades with Mr. Peaches right out of your head."

"Damn right," Donnelly replied. "Now, get a move on. There are pancakes to be had."

Motel Paradise

"VIRGIL. HEY, Virgil."

Michael's whisper brought no response from the dark form of the man lying next to him. He kicked at him gently under the covers. "Virge! Virge, wake up."

"Might I be of service to you, sir?" Bryce's voice, cheerfully emanating from the heart-shaped loveseat by the window, startled Michael so desperately that he jumped and shivered.

"Wha—Oh, it's you." He rubbed his eyes as if Bryce were a bad dream he was trying to wipe away. "You stay over there, you succubus."

"Oh my, you country folk do have a way with flattery. Thank you, darling."

"He say you a devil," Nestor offered from the loveseat, where he had moments ago been sleepily entangled with Bryce.

"Not just a devil, love, but one who preys on sleeping men to extract their seed." Bryce turned back to Michael. "You charmer, you."

"Just stay where you are," Michael said, his voice tense. "I don't have a drop of seed left to give you, and it feels like my dick's been sandpapered."

"Oh pish," Bryce tutted. "I used plenty of lube, and you were still producing several drops during rounds six and seven."

"Six and seven?" Michael's voice cracked. "Oh my God. How many times did you do that last night?"

"Oh, seven was the end last night. You seemed to need a little rest. Which was fortuitous because you won it for me in a sudden death overtime bonus round this morning, darling. Thank you for that, by the way."

"There was more this morning?"

"Yes, rounds eight through ten were after midnight, so technically—"

"Ten?" Michael shouted, managing to bring himself upright with great effort. "You did that to us ten times? How could you?"

"Oh, I can't take all the credit, darling. You played a large role yourself, of course. Though right at the end I will admit that while the spirit seemed willing, the flesh was a bit weak. But I persevered, and we arrived at our happy ending."

"Ten times?" Michael's shouting was growing steadily more unhinged.

"Ten fuckin' times," Virgil said with a chuckle. "How fuckin' awesome was that?" He sat up, punched his pillow into shape, and reclined easily against the headboard, which was carved with hundreds of little Cupids.

"You're okay with this?" Michael asked.

"Me? Fuck, you were all revved up about it. You were all like 'if you stop now, you forfeit,' and 'don't be a fucking wimp, Virgil.' I gave in because you were like some lust-crazed beast." He leaned over and kissed Michael on the nose. "Which I love about you, by the way. That was all kinds of fun." Virgil lay back again with a groan. "Oh fuck. My balls feel like a punching bag." He looked down at his red, somewhat swollen scrotum, then up at Bryce. "Totally worth it. By the end I couldn't even tell when one orgasm stopped and the next one began."

"Luckily you were in the hands of experienced professionals," Bryce replied modestly. "Your amateur practitioners will often stop when there's no more spunk to be had. What a waste—that's when the fun begins! There's nothing more gratifying than seeing a burly man such as yourself straining every muscle trying to achieve an orgasm his body is simply too drained to accomplish. It clears the mind and allows the body to achieve what it thought impossible. I like to think of it as the purest form of meditation."

Virgil laughed. "Zen and the art of the dry orgasm. You are brilliant, Bryce. Just brilliant."

"Oh, stop," Bryce said, halfheartedly holding up a hand. "Eventually."

Virgil laughed even harder and was joined by Michael, who seemed to be slowly coming to forgive the succubi who had drained and exhausted him overnight.

Finally Virgil sat up and swung his legs over the edge of the bed. "Well, I gotta get on the road." He stood, a little unsteadily. "But first, I need a shower. Who's with me?"

Three hands were raised, and soon the large shower was full of men discovering they weren't as exhausted as they had thought. The road could wait for another couple of hours.

Evening, Paris

THE RESTAURANT didn't look like much from the street—just a heavy oaken door with medieval hardware and a discreet brass plaque that announced its presence through a deep patina.

Brandt pulled open the door and motioned for Kerry to enter. She glided past him in her stunning new dress, and he followed closely behind. Inside, the restaurant was stark in black and white, punctuated by aggressively colorful artwork on the walls, brilliantly lit from above and below. The canvases appeared to have been painted by an artist who tripped on acid and remembered being Kandinsky in a previous life. Or a really angry Pollock.

They were shown to a table for two—the rarity of which the concierge at the hotel had stressed several times when describing the reservation he'd been able to secure for them. The menus they were handed presented an overwhelming range of indecipherable wonders. Brandt looked helplessly at Kerry over the top.

"Any ideas?" he asked with a shrug. "I'm not sure I'd be able to understand it even if it were in English, honestly. I'm more of a diner guy."

She nodded in sympathy, but then her expression brightened. "We're saved," she said. "There's a *prix fixe dégustation.* And it comes with wine pairings, so even if we have no idea what we're eating, we won't care."

He sighed in relief. "Thank God. I would have needed to go back to school just to be able to order dinner."

Three hours later they were wending their way toward the dessert course. The wines that had accompanied the seven preceding courses had done their job, and the two of them were laughing as they shared stories from their lives.

Brandt had told Kerry things that only Donnelly knew, and he suspected that she was telling him secrets as well. It felt good to unburden himself this way, even if he had not felt himself to be laboring under any discernible burden previously.

The dessert arrived, and like all of the previous courses, it looked gorgeous and tasted even better. As they traded bites of the two different dishes, Kerry suddenly grew quiet.

"Ethan, I need to tell you something," she said, setting her fork down.

"Whoa, sounds serious."

"It is," she said. "I've been thinking about our conversation earlier today when I said I'd forgotten how nice it is to have gay friends."

"Yeah, about that," he broke in, emboldened by her sudden honesty. "I have something to tell you as well, once you're done."

She nodded. "So here's the thing: I think I realized today why I always had gay friends."

"Uh-huh?"

"Because there was some part of me that needed validation."

He thought about this for a second and wondered whether the wine was clogging his brain. "I don't get it."

"It's like this," she continued. "And I'm not proud of this, but I feel like I can tell you. It's because there's some part of me that wanted to see if I could, um, attract some… interest?"

Brandt stared at her for a long moment. "Interest?"

"Stupid, right? And pointless. But sometimes being young and insecure makes you do stupid, pointless things."

"Okay, so let me get this," Brandt said slowly, hearing his words slur a bit. They had had too much to drink, he thought, as if he hadn't known that already. "You liked hanging out with gay guys because you thought maybe they weren't… gay?"

"No, not that they weren't gay, but that maybe they would find me so breathtakingly attractive that they might… have second thoughts about being gay. Like they might be straight, just for me."

He stared at her. "You *are* breathtakingly attractive. And completely insane."

"I know. That's why I said I wasn't proud of it. But being with you today, in the dressing room, it reminded me of those times, and the ridiculous things I used to fantasize about. I mean, honestly, in college the hottest guys were gay—sharp dressers, and they worked out all the time—and I guess I thought that if I were hot enough to make one of them find some… flexibility? That would mean I was like the sexiest girl in the world. So, yeah, I know it's insane. And you helped me realize that, because today I could tell from your face that seeing me change clothes did absolutely nothing for you. So on behalf of the former me, I would like to say I apologize for what I did before I knew you."

He was still trying to figure out what she was saying when she polished off the rest of the muscat in her glass, set it down, and blurted, "So, you were going to tell me something, which I hope is equally embarrassing."

Brandt's regret at having mentioned that he had something to say was strong enough that he tried to swallow it along with the rest of the wine in his glass. But once he had swallowed, she was still there looking expectantly at him, and he had to go on.

"Okay," he said, mainly to steady himself. He took a deep breath. "Okay. You know how you said you could tell that seeing you change clothes did nothing for me?"

"That was thirty seconds ago. I remember it like it was yesterday." She giggled at her lame joke but quickly composed herself when he didn't join in.

"Well, it wasn't exactly true." He paused for a long moment, trying to figure out how to explain. "The fact is, seeing you change clothes was actually really hard to do. For me to do, I mean."

"Am I that horrible to look at?" she asked, her expression stricken.

"No, that's the problem." He took another deep breath, mostly to give himself something to do other than talking. He was about to hyperventilate. "It's not you, it's me. I'm not... I'm not as gay as you think I am. I'm actually... not gay at all."

Her mouth dropped open. She closed it, but then it dropped open again. Finally, she was able to make a sound and shortly able to form words. "But, Gabriel" was all she managed to say.

"Yes, Gabriel." Brandt's damnation of his own conduct was heavy in his voice.

"Gabriel's a man."

"Yes," he said.

"And you are about to get married to him."

"Yes."

"And you are a man."

"Last I checked," he said.

"And the two of you are... intimate?"

"Spectacularly so."

She stared at him, searching his face in sheer confusion. "So when you say you're not gay," she said, carefully enunciating each word, "I think you must be working with a definition of which I am unaware. One I don't think I understand. I...." Her shoulders slumped, and she braced herself with an elbow on the table. "I have no idea what you're talking about."

This was not a surprise to Brandt, of course. He had told few people about his struggle with sexual identity, and those he had told were uniformly baffled. The only people who seemed to understand it at all were Donnelly, of course, because he seemed able to understand everything about Brandt without his having to say anything, and their friend Will, who had experienced something very similar when his wife left him and Lucas came into his life. Everyone else gave him the look of utter befuddlement worn by Kerry at the moment, even when sober.

"I don't know if I can explain it," he said quietly. "And it may not make sense to you even if I could. I guess the simplest way to say it is that I'm a straight man who fell in love with another man. I love Gabriel, and I love being with him in ways that I cannot imagine being with anyone else, man or woman. Back in San Diego, before my talk, when I said you were wrong about me being bisexual? This is why I said you were wrong. I'm not bisexual. I'm Gabrielsexual."

Her jaw, which had been dropping steadily as he spoke, snapped back into place and a smile burst across her face. "That's the most romantic thing I've ever heard." She grinned goofily and clapped her hands like a kid on Christmas morning. "That you would be so dedicated to one person that he defines your sexuality is pretty amazing." Then her brow furrowed a bit, and she settled into a more serious attitude. "But does that mean you're not attracted to anyone else, ever?"

He sighed. "That's what I needed to tell you. Since I've been with Gabriel, our social lives have been centered on the group of friends we've made as a couple. Just about every single one of them is a gay man. I mostly feel like an imposter in that group because I don't see myself as gay. When they go on and on about some cute new produce guy at the supermarket, I just hang back—I'm just not attracted to guys that way. But this trip with you…." He shook his head and looked down at his hands.

"This trip with me… what?"

He sat, fiddling with his fingers, trying to find the words. Finally, he began. "This trip with you is the first time I've spent any time at all with a woman—at least a straight woman—in what seems like years. And when you asked if I wasn't attracted to anyone else, ever? Yeah. Before this trip, I would have said that."

She sat back in her chair, eyes wide. "And now?" Her voiced was flat with shock.

"And now I have to realize that my lack of sexual attraction to anyone other than Gabriel was less the result of my superhuman virtue and more a product of the complete lack of women in my social circle." He lifted his gaze from his hands. "I am so sorry. Sorry to not be the person you thought I was—the person I thought I was."

She goggled at him for a long moment, as if he had sprouted another head. Then finally, she rolled her eyes dramatically. "Oh, shut up."

He stared at her, stunned. "What?"

"If you torture yourself for a single second because your sexuality doesn't behave the way you want it to, I will reach across this table and slap you." She raised her hand suddenly, waving at the waiter. "Garçon?" The waiter came to the table, eyebrows up. "En plus?" she asked, pointing at their empty glasses. He nodded and hurried away. "Now, where were we…? Oh, that's right. Shut up."

"Heard you the first time."

"Yes, but I want to make sure you really get it. Don't apologize for your sexuality. No one gets to choose who they love, or what gives them a boner. Desire is a divine bit of crazy the gods give each of us, to delight us and derange us in equal measure. You can't explain it to anyone who isn't you, and a lot of times you can't even understand it yourself. But never think it's your burden alone. We all have it, mister, and we all think we're the only ones."

"Wow," he said, surprised by her sudden vehement eloquence. "I guess 'divine bit of crazy' pretty much nails it."

"And my bit of crazy is what I told you before—that I used to hang around with gay guys because they weren't supposed to be interested in me, so if I could make them interested that meant I was some kind of superwoman. It was ridiculous."

"Ironic, isn't it, that you relived that experience by spending the day with a guy who discovered he actually could be kind of... interested."

She fixed him with a withering glare. "Oh, shut up again. We both know that there is nothing on this earth that can compete with Gabriel for your affection." She sat back for a moment while the waiter poured more wine. "But thank you for saying you were at least aware that I was there, which was more than I was ever able to accomplish before." She took a drink, then set her glass down and stared at it for a moment. "I need a new hobby."

Brandt smiled at her resignation. "Or you need to meet some straight guys who aren't already in love, with themselves or anyone else."

"If you know of such a unicorn, please send him my way."

"Don't come across many straight men lately, I'm afraid. Myself excluded, of course. But then I guess there aren't many like me in the world either." He sighed, weighed down by the barren loneliness of that statement. "I think 'straight guy who fell in love with a guy' has got to be the rarest sexual orientation ever."

"You know, I'm proud to call myself a feminist—always have been. And despite our inability as a gender to close the wage gap, this is one of the rare cases where women have it better than men. I could fall in love with any number of women, especially during college, and never have to think of myself as anything other than a straight gal with curiosities. Just like every other straight gal. Making out with my roommate on a lonely Saturday night in the dorm didn't mean I was suddenly a lesbian. But guys get that pressure, and it never lets up. Kiss one guy and you're gay forever, right?"

"That seems to be the way it works. For most people."

"For most *men*. But somehow women don't seem to work that way. And either this is one of those fundamental biological differences between the sexes, or it's a result of a social stricture that requires something from men that it doesn't from women. In case you're wondering, the answer is 'B.' So you're not strange or somehow defective— you're just not limited by social strictures on sex and gender. Congratulations." She held up her glass and toasted his lack of limitations.

He drank to that, as little comfort as it offered him. It certainly wouldn't make tonight any easier to face. "So, there's something we need to talk about."

"Well, when you change the subject, you just go for it. Good for you. Fire away."

"Where should I sleep tonight?"

"Oh, okay, you really are going for it. All right." She drained her wine glass and set it on the table with a clunk. "Let's think this one through. If we keep the same arrangements we had last night, is my virtue at risk?" She failed to keep a straight face, bursting into giggles almost immediately.

"Virtue. Funny." He rolled his eyes; then he too drank the last of his wine.

"Yeah, so we're agreed that I haven't exactly saved myself for marriage. But I don't see a reason to send one of us to the couch. I mean, we're grown-ups—and just because you're straight doesn't mean you're going to throw yourself at me, right?"

"You may rest assured I'm not going to do that," Brandt replied. "But sleeping next to you causes a certain… reaction. And that may be uncomfortable."

"Only if you roll over on it!" She hooted with laughter at her dirty joke but regained her composure quickly. "Seriously, though, lying next to you gives me a boner too. You seem to have no idea what a beautiful specimen you are, my friend. But I managed to keep my hands to myself, and you did as well. I think we're good, as long as I can have a nice long bath before climbing in the sack with your gorgeous self."

"You don't need to wash up before you get into bed," he said but then stopped as the realization dawned on him. "Oh, it's not about washing up, is it?"

She shook her head slowly. "In the spirit of perfect candor, I only thought about you twice. The other three times I thought about Gabriel."

"But you've never met him!"

"I know, I know. But I figure if he can land a man like you and keep you that bewitched, he must be un-fucking-believable. So I may have spent some time picturing him. And maybe you with him. A little."

He blushed and scowled at her, then smiled at the ridiculousness of the whole thing.

"Oh, come on. Tell me you haven't found a quiet moment during this great adventure to think impure thoughts about Gabriel Donnelly."

The blush rose in his cheeks again.

"Yep, thought so. Good for you, chief."

"I can't believe we're talking about this," he said quietly.

"We're both grown-ups, Ethan. The circumstances are a little convoluted, but as long as we are honest with each other we're going to be fine." She picked up her purse. "So, shall we?"

He got to his feet and lent her a steadying arm as she stood. "We shall. And I shall aspire to be as grown-up as you are about the sleeping arrangements."

"You know what they say," she remarked as they walked through the restaurant. "A boner is the sincerest form of flattery."

"Remind me to introduce you to Bryce at the wedding," Brandt replied. "You two will find you have a lot in common."

"He sounds delightful."

Late night, at sea

DONNELLY AND Sandler had decided to call it a night when Ankur got off duty, and he accompanied the men back to their suite—much to the dismay of Dax and Stanley, who were still obviously hoping to have their chance at them.

"This isn't a problem for you, coming back to our suite like this, is it?" Donnelly asked. He enjoyed seeing Sandler so happy but didn't want to be the source of complications for Ankur.

"No, not at all," Ankur said. "I covered for Emmett several times recently when there was a large group of conservative politicians on board for a seminar. He always says, 'the deeper the closet, the harder they fuck.' He was barely able to walk after an evening with that angry man from Fox News."

"I don't think I can close my eyes hard enough to stand being in the same room with someone like that, much less the same bed," Sandler said.

"Emmett's a very committed service professional," Ankur said wryly. "I couldn't do it either. My standards are too high." He reached out and traced along Sandler's jawline with his finger.

"Fuck," Sandler sighed. "You know you don't have to sweet-talk me."

"But I mean every word," Ankur said seriously.

"You two are adorable," Donnelly said, laughing at their earnest flirtation.

"And we'll try to be quieter tonight," Sandler said sheepishly.

"I told you before, you should have fun, and don't mind me. I'm a big boy."

"That's what *I* said," Ankur said. He smiled, seeming pleased to have contributed a joke that made the other men laugh.

They arrived at the suite, and Donnelly opened the door and stood aside to let the others in. Rutherford had made up the bed already, and the lights were low. "Well, I'm going to turn in," he said. "You two have fun, okay? Will you be able to stay for breakfast on the balcony, Ankur?"

Ankur turned to Sandler, eyes wide.

"I would love for you to stay," he said, seeming to understand perfectly what Ankur was too shy to ask.

"That would be lovely," he said, deeply pleased.

"All right, then," Donnelly said. "See you in the morning." He retreated to the bedroom and closed the door behind himself, smiling inwardly at the charming joy of Sandler and Ankur at having an evening to enjoy each other's company. He stripped off his clothes and took a short but relaxing shower—mainly to give the two lovers in the other room some privacy to start their evening off. He toweled himself dry and put on the plush robe that hung in the bathroom (Rutherford left a fresh one daily, whether he used it or not), then walked back into the bedroom. He could hear no sound coming from the other room—they were still on their best behavior—as he turned the lights down and tossed the robe over the chair that sat next to the bed. Naked, he slipped between the silky sheets and tucked a couple of the large pillows under the covers next to him. They weren't as firm as Brandt, but he needed to have something pressed up against him as he slept.

"Good night, Ethan, wherever you are," he whispered. "I love you."

He closed his eyes and was asleep within minutes.

CHAPTER SEVEN

Wednesday
Before dawn, at sea

"GABRIEL! GABRIEL!" *That voice could wake the dead.*

"I'm up, I'm up," *he called back, shouting so she could hear him downstairs in the kitchen. He threw back the covers only to discover, to his horror, that the sheets bore a dark spot where his still-erect penis had thrown a little party for itself in the wee hours of the morning. "Fuck, not again," he sighed. Luckily she didn't make his bed anymore. He got up and bundled up the sheets, wondering what she would think about him washing a third load of bed linens this week.*

He showered, dressed, and slammed down his breakfast in the space of the next fifteen minutes, and was at the bus stop with more than a dozen seconds to spare before the ancient school bus came wheezing up the street. His stop was the last before the bus turned and headed back into town, bearing its precious cargo of rural kids to the only high school for thirty miles.

They reached the city limits—if you could call this township of two-and-a-half-thousand souls a city—and stopped at the housing project that sat at its farthest reaches. There they picked up the usual cargo of truants in the making before continuing on to their final destination. They stopped; the door opened.

Unlike Gabriel, who dashed for the bus every morning still wiping sleep from his eyes, Cam boarded the bus looking like the world was his. He made a show of looking for open seats, but Gabriel knew which one he would pick for the five-minute ride to the high school parking lot.

"This seat taken?" *he asked—he always did—before sitting down.*

"It is now," *Gabriel answered, as he always did.*

"Good morning, Gabriel," *he said pleasantly.*

"Good morning, Cam," *Gabriel replied. Then he dropped his voice so the bus drive couldn't hear.* "Fuck this morning."

Cam's eyebrows shot up.

"Happened again," *Gabriel muttered.*

"You gotta get a grip, man." *Cam laughed but suppressed it quickly before anyone else could hear.*

"It's not like I can keep it from happening," *Gabriel objected.*

"Sure you can. If you don't want the pool to overflow, you drain some of the water. That's what I meant by getting a grip, dude." *He winked.* "Just think of me doing this." *He maintained an expression of utter boredom, looking blankly out the window, while his hand slipped over and onto Gabriel's crotch. He massaged what he found* there with a surreptitious vigor that got Gabriel's attention, then yanked his hand back before anyone could see what he was up to.

"That's exactly what I was thinking of when it happened, actually," Gabriel replied as he adjusted his jeans to accommodate his rising boner.

"Bullshit," Cam replied. "You were thinking about him, not me."

Gabriel blushed at the truth of Cam's accusation. "Well, it doesn't matter, does it? Not like he's gonna suddenly drop Cheryl Jenkins to be with me."

"You never know," Cam replied. "Maybe he'll get tired of boning the head cheerleader and decide to take a run at the star of the wrestling team. It'd certainly be more fun than rolling around on those huge boobs of hers."

"I think huge boobs are mostly what guys like him are interested in."

"Because they don't know better," Cam replied, shaking his head. "Now, take Ross over there." He nodded toward a massive guy in a varsity jacket two seats away. "In the locker room, all he ever talks about is the girls he's fucking. But after Friday night's fuckup that lost us the Woodley game, Coach made him spend Saturday cleaning the bathroom with a toothbrush. Well, I managed to get myself punished too, so Ross and I spent the day together. Turns out the only thing he likes more than fucking girls is getting blow jobs from this guy." Cam gestured to himself with his thumbs. "He's hung like a donkey. Course, he's as smart as one too." He looked over at Ross, who pointedly looked the other direction. Cam turned back, smirking. "I guess we're not on speaking terms anymore. Oh well, it wasn't the worst Saturday I've spent."

"Slut," Gabriel muttered as the bus lurched into the parking lot behind the high school.

"Really?" Cam replied, his tone showing no evidence of offense. "Please, sir, impress me with the dignity of your drooling now that he's here." Cam pointed out the window.

He was getting out of his car, a European sedan that surely exceeded in price the net annual income of the Donnelly household. The morning light struck his hair and Gabriel felt the pang in his chest of longing—fruitless longing—that seeing him always inspired. Then, from the passenger side of the car, Cheryl Jenkins emerged. Gabriel didn't hate her, of course—that wasn't in him to do—but he sure wished she would find a reason to transfer to some other school. Woodley, perhaps.

I'd make him happier, Gabriel thought. Bryan deserved to be loved.

As he passed the math exam back, their hands touched for just an instant. Gabriel blushed, but Bryan didn't seem to notice. Gabriel turned back to face the front and looked down at his hand, trying to figure out the divine magic that made it tingle after such a brief moment of contact. No one else made him feel this way. He looked down at his test and found mashed potatoes.

"Lunch lady seems particularly pissed off at humanity today," Cam remarked. "What the hell is this?"

"I think... chicken? Not sure," Gabriel replied, though his eyes weren't on his plate. It was a hot autumn day, and he was watching a group of guys testing the dress code with T-shirts that had been cut down the side to reveal their entire torsos.

Cam turned to follow his gaze. "Oh fuck. Someone's been working out." He tipped his head back, pretending to scrutinize the view through spectacles. "He's definitely filled out since last I laid eyes on him." He turned back to Gabriel with a wicked grin. "Or hands, for that matter."

"Basketball shorts are the best thing ever," Gabriel muttered, watching the globes of ass after ass bobbing by as the group passed the table.

"I like how you can slip your hand all the way up, and there's still plenty of room to move once you're there." He made a not-very-subtle wanking motion with his hand. "I bet I could get my whole head up there." He nodded at the last guy in the line, whose basketball shorts were both voluminous and well-packed.

"We could each take a leg and meet in the middle," Gabriel said with a flick of his eyebrow.

"I didn't think team sports were your thing," Cam replied, sipping his soda.

"You've forgotten that time after Homecoming?"

Cam's wicked grin grew wider and wickeder. "I'll never forget that. I spent the entire weekend scrubbing out the back of my dad's SUV, and it still smelled like cum."

"Not my fault. He swallowed most of mine, and you took care of the rest."

"See? Teamwork. Next time, though, we hold out for someone with their own car."

"Agreed."

"You're late for practice," a voice called, and when Gabriel turned around, he was in the gym. Everyone else was already scrimmaging, and he didn't have a partner. He looked to Coach to ask what to do.

"I'll be your partner," Bryan said.

He was in a singlet. Which means he must have joined the wrestling team. Which didn't make sense since he was the best running back on the football team. But Gabriel nodded, and they took up position on the mat.

"Ready?" Bryan asked.

"Ready."

It was supposed to be a warm-up, but Bryan hit him hard and knocked him to the mat. Then he reached around between Gabriel's legs and gripped his already hard cock. He stroked it through the thin fabric while staring into Gabriel's eyes.

"Like that?" he asked, his voice husky.

"Uh...." Gabriel couldn't form words, his throat was so dry.

"Would you like it if I did this?" Bryan leaned in for a kiss.

Gabriel felt joy surge through his chest. He was so elated he didn't even see the balled-up fist flying toward his face. It made contact, wrenching his head sideways with a sickening crunch.

"Faggot," spat Bryan. He stomped away, leaving Gabriel, bleeding and broken, on the mat.

Donnelly bolted upright, gasping. He brought his hands to his face, terrified to feel the broken bones and pulsing blood. He felt nothing out of place and only then began to realize he'd been dreaming. He sat, breathing hard, trying to will the adrenaline out of his system.

So that's what it would have been like, he thought to himself. I guess I'm better off not knowing I was gay back then.

Once he'd caught his breath, he could hear Sandler and Ankur in the next room, softly talking. Their peacefulness together made him smile, and he lay back down. Sleep came eventually, when he had finally convinced himself the dream wasn't real.

It was only five thirty in the morning when Donnelly awoke, but he knew once he'd opened his eyes that there was no going back to sleep. He hadn't had any more nightmares, but his body ached to tell him it needed a good stretch and a harder workout than he'd been giving it. He rose and slipped on a pair of running shorts and a light T-shirt, then picked up his running shoes—with socks tucked inside—and tiptoed silently into the outer room.

His worry about not waking the other men was misplaced, however. They were awake and were in fact fully engaged, at the moment, on the balcony. Sandler must have remembered what Rutherford had said about the privacy of the balcony, of which he and Ankur were currently taking full advantage.

Sandler fully reclined on one of the chaise lounges, Ankur astride him, sitting straight upright, back arched. He rose up a few inches and eased himself back down, a look of frank delight on his face. Sandler tipped his head back and huffed out several breaths as Ankur repeated his transit, up and down, then reached out, laid his hands on Ankur's hips, and held him down firmly. He bucked his hips upward, thrusting fiercely.

Donnelly took a step back. He meant to take more but didn't.

Sandler's cock, he noticed, was striking. It wasn't Brandt-sized, or even as long as his own, but it was substantial. Glossy and wide, it was illuminated by the rose-orange of dawn as it slammed into, and rapidly withdrew from, Ankur.

Impaled vigorously, Ankur bobbed atop Sandler, and his head lolled to one side. He was looking right into Donnelly's eyes.

Donnelly took another step back, mortified at being seen until he remembered that the glass was heavily tinted and from the outside presented a mirror rather than a window. Ankur could only see himself, the object of that cock's rough and repeated attention. The two men locked eyes, Donnelly watching as waves of passionate concentration washed over Ankur's face, Ankur transfixed by his own reflection—or, rather, the image of Sandler's thrusting cock burying itself in his ass over and over again.

Ankur's eyes rolled back, and he turned away from the window to focus his attention on Sandler, who was clearly reaching the point of no return. The expression on his face transformed from eager excitement to gathering tension; the sculpted concavity of his buttocks as he thrust up into Ankur grew deeper as he pistoned ever more rapidly.

Donnelly stepped forward.

Sandler's eyes squeezed shut. His thrusting ceased as the orgasm locked his body into a plank-like rigidity. Ankur, however, began a gyrating dance of rising-falling-twisting motion that astonished Donnelly with its sinuous, demanding intensity. Sandler jolted and brought a hand to his mouth in an apparent effort to stifle a cry. Donnelly watched as he bit down on his hand and writhed under Ankur's ministrations.

Donnelly took another step forward.

Ankur watched, a look of joy on his face, while Sandler shook and spasmed. He didn't let up until Sandler returned to himself and was able to draw several deep breaths. Ankur bent forward and kissed him, his hands stroking Sandler's face, his lips murmuring words that Donnelly wanted desperately to hear. Then Sandler pushed Ankur back upright and grasped his jutting cock with both hands. Ankur leaned back, putting his hands on Sandler's knees to brace himself, and closed his eyes as Sandler stroked him. His orgasm, Donnelly was fascinated to see, was of a completely different kind than Sandler's; he sighed, smiled, and finally seemed to float away on the current of it as he laced Sandler's glistening chest with white. Finally he folded himself over onto Sandler and they embraced, nuzzling each other tenderly in the golden glow of morning.

Donnelly withdrew from the room, feeling he had witnessed something almost sacred. Then the enormity of what he had done broke over him, and the breath in his lungs turned stony with shame. He had watched two people share the most private experience humans are capable of, and he had done so willingly, excitedly. Why had he not run from the room as soon as he saw them? Why had he stepped closer? Why was his penis hard, a wet spot spreading across the front of his shorts from its jutting head?

He had no answers, so he bolted for the elevator and jabbed the down button. The door slid open instantly, and just as he stepped inside, he heard the balcony door open, bringing with it happy, refractory voices. The doors closed, and Donnelly went down.

Airport, Los Angeles

"I CAN'T believe this is good-bye." Bryce dabbed theatrically at the corners of his eyes. "Now we'll never know whether Desirée finds enduring happiness with Bolt."

Virgil smiled. "Here," he said, handing Bryce the cheap paperback. "My gift to you."

Bryce clutched the book to his chest as if it were a trophy. "Thank you, my dear. You and Desirée have taught us so much already."

"You've taught me some things too," Virgil replied with a laugh. "Promise you'll text me if you ever decide to hit the road again, okay?"

"When I need my load hauled, you shall be the first to know," Bryce solemnly promised.

Virgil opened the door of the truck and stepped down. He turned back and held up his hand, inviting Bryce to follow. Bryce did, and Virgil caught him in a bear hug.

"Oh my," Bryce exclaimed, deeply thrilled to be embraced by the trucker. "I shall remember the strength of these arms around me for many nights to come."

Nestor followed, launching himself into Virgil's arms like a lovestruck puppy. Virgil bore his negligible weight easily and playfully mussed his jet-black hair.

"Nestor, my nuts are going to be shooting dust for a week. You have magic in your hands, and your mouth—"

"And up the butt," Nestor purred, nuzzling Virgil's neck.

"And up the butt," Virgil repeated, laughing hard as he set Nestor down. "Now, you travel safe, okay?"

"With Desirée as our guide, what could possibly go wrong?" Bryce waved the book merrily before stuffing it into his bag.

"Well, if you find your Captain Bolt, you send me pictures, okay?"

"On that you may rely," Bryce said. "What is panorama mode for if not long, long photos of long, long subjects?" He ran his fingers through his hair and smoothed the front of his shirt. "You've been our capable guide and a true gentleman, Virgil. Your rig provided me the best ride I've had in a long time. And your truck is nice as well."

Virgil laughed, and the men shook hands and took their leave. Bruce and Nestor walked across the street to the metro station where they would catch the train to the airport. From there, Bryce hoped, they would soon be winging their way across the Pacific.

Their arrival at the terminal, however, did not bode well. There were long lines at every ticket counter, and each was filled with passengers angry about the travel delays that had still not been corrected. As long as the volcano continued to belch ash into the skies, the lines would be full of desperate passengers stalking open seats. Bryce and Nestor walked the length of the building looking for their opportunity.

Bryce wasn't seeking a shorter line, however; his searching gaze was otherwise employed. Finally he saw what he was looking for.

"Excuse me, sir, might you have a moment?"

The young man in the pilot's uniform smiled warmly at Bryce, eyebrows up as if waiting only for the smallest request to be uttered so that he could gladly comply. "Yes?" he said, leaning down slightly as he towered a full foot over Bryce and Nestor.

"Well, aren't you just the sweetest?" Bryce replied, batting his eyes and looking up at the pilot.

The pilot blushed and looked to the side a little sheepishly.

"How can I help you?"

"We—myself and my limber yet quite durable friend here—need to book passage to the Far East."

The pilot's brow furrowed slightly. "Okay. Well, what you can do is get into one of these lines, and once you get to the front, you just ask for the destination you need. They take credit cards at the counter, and they'll give you your boarding passes."

"I see." Bryce turned to glance down the long lines of people. "It's just that, you see, we're missing something rather important."

"What would that be?" the pilot asked, his voice full of concern.

"A destination."

"Oh," the pilot said, then fell silent for a moment. "I don't... I guess I...." He stumbled to a stop again. "What?"

"To be perfectly honest, we're heading for England."

"Ah," the pilot replied but then seemed to grasp what Bryce had said. He shook his head quickly, then looked blank. "What?"

"Sometimes to get where one is going, one must go the opposite direction, don't you agree?" The pilot looked mystified, but Bryce forged ahead. "You see, we are going to a wedding in England, but that horrid mountain keeps blowing up. We were quite at loose ends until I was struck with the inspiration: instead of flying east with the benighted masses who cannot think outside the box, we'll simply go the other way and avoid the whole mess. We have traversed this great country of ours already by availing ourselves of the services of a friendly and quite muscular trucker, and now we appeal to you for assistance in making the next step in our journey. I can tell by your uniform that you are accustomed to command, and I assure you that we take commands quite well. I am Bryce," he concluded after this long monologue uninterrupted by breath, "and this is my dear friend and traveling companion Nestor." He presented his hand.

The pilot looked at the elegant hand Bryce extended toward him and shrugged as if shaking off the mist of illogic with which Bryce had filled the air. "Pleased to meet you, Bryce," he said, his voice deep and confident, as he firmly shook Bryce's hand. "And you as well, Nestor."

"Man in uniform," Nestor murmured wistfully. "So pleased."

The pilot chuckled, then looked from Bryce to Nestor and back again as if making up his mind. "Tell you what. Come with me, and I may be able to help."

"Oh, I *knew* you could help us, you lovely man."

"Please, call me Gary."

"I'll call you anything you like," Bryce growled with a comic leer. "Lead on, Gary. We are yours to command."

Gary laughed and shook his head but turned and led the way around the side of the ticket counters to an unmarked door. He opened it by swiping the badge that hung on a lanyard around his neck and held it open for Bryce and Nestor to walk through. The hallway they entered was glaringly lit by naked fluorescent tubes on the ceiling and extended into the distance without interruption of door or decoration. They walked a long way before the corridor made an abrupt right turn, revealing another locked door. This one said General Aviation in large red letters. Gary swiped his badge again, and the door clicked open.

They stepped into a large room that seemed to be a combination office, waiting room, and cafeteria. Its occupants were a half-dozen men and women attired like Gary in vaguely military uniforms with gold bars on their epaulets. Some chugged coffee, some consulted charts on their tablets; a knot of several stood near the microwave oven listening as one of their number finished telling what was, judging from the denouement, a vigorously scatological joke. Their laughter was met with glares from some of the more studious-looking crew.

Gary led them over to the man who had delivered the raucous punch line a moment before. "Rooster, I want you to meet Bryce and Nestor. Boys, this is Rooster, the best pilot I know."

"So pleased to make your acquaintance, Mr. Rooster," Bryce said, smiling brightly.

"Well, now," Rooster said in a drawl that still had the dust of west Texas on it, "what brings y'all to our little clubhouse?"

"They're trying to get to England by going the long way round," Gary explained. "I thought you might be able to help them on the next leg of their journey."

Rooster nodded. "It just so happens I'm on my way to Tokyo this morning. Gotta deadhead over to pick up some fuckin' Twitter-famous 'celebrity' who can't leave the house without her fuckin' Chihuahuas or whatever. Ferrying a herd of yappy little dogs and a blondie with more money than sense is not why the Air Force taught me to fly, I tell ya what."

Gary turned to Bryce and Nestor. "Rooster flies the big boys—the private jets that are actually airliners with all the coach seats ripped out and replaced with leather and gold plate. It's how the very rich and/or very famous get around while everyone else flies with their knees jammed under their chins."

"Such glamour," Bryce whispered, as if Gary had described a cathedral.

"But I can't take passengers on a deadhead flight," Rooster said.

"My company allows me to take service providers on deadhead trips," Gary said. "Now, I know I'm just a puddle-jumping prop jockey, but I thought maybe your big fancy company would let you do the same."

Rooster looked from Gary to Bryce. "What kind of services we talkin' about here?"

It was the question Bryce's entire life had prepared him to answer, and after years of practice he was able to answer it definitively with just a glance, a cocked eyebrow, and a hint of a smile.

"Ah, I see," Rooster said, nodding. Then a wide grin broke across his face. "Well, boys, it just so happens that I have not had the pleasure of a lady's company for more than a week, and this hop to Haneda starts a week on duty. I was planning to tug one out in the head before gettin' on board—and probably twice on the way—but I like your idea better." He grabbed at the substantial bulge in his crotch.

"I see we understand each other," Bryce said, with a quick glance down.

"Who's your right seat?" Gary asked.

"I got Ballard this trip." His tone conveyed a distinct lack of enthusiasm for his traveling companion.

"Think Ballard would go for it?"

"Like I give a fuck. That fuckin' goody-goody wouldn't accept a blow job from supermodel nymphomaniac if she were the last woman on Earth. I swear to God that boy is the most married asshole I know." He lowered his voice and grunted, "Loser." Then he straightened up, and his shit-eating grin was back in place. "Let's get you boys set up as interior maintenance crew, urgently needed on my plane to clean up the mess left when that Make-a-Wish kid puked all over it yesterday on the way back from Disney World."

Bryce recoiled.

"I'm just shittin' ya, come on," Rooster said with a guffaw. "The plane's spotless. But the guy who flew the dying kid and his family is a buddy a mine, and he'll say the thing got barfed up if I ask him to. Lemme go get the paperwork done, and we'll get on our way." He lowered his voice to a growl. "You two better be thirsty, though, because once I get going I can go like hell."

"You'll find us more than capable," Bryce assured him.

"Well, hot damn," Rooster said, clapping Bryce on the shoulder. "Looks like my lucky day." He ambled off toward the vending machines, dialing his phone. "Yeah, it's Rooster. I need a favor...."

"We cannot thank you enough for your help, Gary," Bryce said, putting his hand on Gary's arm.

Gary gave a wry smile. "One thing you should know before you thank me. The reason everyone calls him Rooster isn't because he's a morning person, or because he struts around looking arrogant. Both of those things are true, but the nickname comes from his most prominent feature, the thing that made him famous during academy."

"I shall be heartbroken if you are referring to his nose," Bryce said.

"I am not. It also explains why he's so eager to get you on his plane. According to him—and he spends a lot of time talking about it—only one woman has ever been able to take the whole thing. And she was a center for a WNBA team who only tried it because she didn't want to marry her girlfriend without giving it a shot with a guy. She picked him because he was the pilot of the team plane, and she figured if she was going to screw only one man in her life, she would choose the biggest of his kind. Rooster loved it. She, however, just got confirmation that she'd been right all along and left him a note in the morning saying so. Along with a hundred-dollar bill."

"Oh dear," Bryce tutted.

"No, that actually made it better for him. For a while there, all he could talk about was being 'Rooster for Hire,' like some action-hero gigolo. We were all happy when that blew over. Anyway, since the WNBA is not exactly a dating pool swimming with eager heterosexuals, Rooster sometimes goes back to what got him through the academy—dudes. He insists he's straight and only resorts to guys because women can't handle him." Gary rolled his eyes. "Whatever. It worked out for you guys, right?"

"He's exactly what we've been looking for," Bryce replied.

"Well, good for you. Look, I gotta get ready. I'm taking oil executives on a sightseeing trip over their rigs out in the middle of nowhere—cactus country—so I need to preflight soon. You two wait here, and Rooster should be back in a couple to get you set up as contractors."

"Thank you so much, Gary," Bryce said again. "And if there's anything we can do to show our appreciation...."

Gary smiled. "'Fraid not, boys. Rooster joked about Ballard being the most married asshole he knows, but I'm just as married. And the one I'm married to expects this asshole to be dedicated to his private enjoyment only."

"As you wish," Bryce said with a gracious nod. "But if you and your husband ever desire company...."

"You'll be the first to know," Gary replied with a smile. "I appreciate the subtlety with which you slipped your phone number into my pocket. Smooth."

Bryce touched his hand to his throat as if embarrassed to have been complimented. "Slipping into your front pocket was its own reward, dear."

Gary shook their hands and took his leave just as Rooster returned from his negotiations on the phone.

"All right, men," Rooster called out in a deep, resonant voice. "Let's move out. You have an awful mess to clean up on that plane, and it's going to keep you busy all the way to Tokyo."

"But you say was no barfing—" Nestor objected, but Bryce nudged him in the ribs. "Oh, *si*." Nestor cleared his throat before speaking up loudly. "We ready to be cleaning the plane now."

"Good enough. Let's get moving." He led them to a small office where they were each given a lanyard with a badge that said Temporary across the front, and then out to the hangar where the jet waited. At the far end, huge doors were sliding slowly open, admitting the morning sunshine into the dark, still hangar.

Rooster strode purposefully over to the airstairs that had been rolled up to the jet's forward door. Gesturing for Bryce and Nestor to follow, he charged up the steps two at a time and through the open door. Bryce and Nestor, struck by the enormity of the building and of the plane they were climbing into, took a bit longer to mount the stairway. The world they stepped into could not have been more different from the one they had just inhabited. Instead of the industrial gray steel of the hangar and its vast concrete floor, they were surrounded by a hushed luxury replete with leather and soft carpet and artfully glowing lights hidden under the sweeping arch of the ceiling.

"Nestor, darling, isn't this amazing?" Bryce whispered. "To experience this kind of luxury, one normally must be royalty, or at the very least the secret lover of a deeply closeted third son of an emir. Nice work, if you can get it."

"Now boys," drawled Rooster, "My copilot will be along any minute. All you have to do is pretend to get ready to clean the plane and smile nicely at him, but pretend you don't speak English. He'll pretty much ignore you, and after he gets settled in the cockpit, he never gets up. Once we're airborne and the autopilot is running things, I'll come back here to check on your work, and we can retire to the stateroom at the rear. Got that?"

Bryce nodded. "Smile, no English—which is nearly the case with my darling Nestor anyway—and then you'll take us in the rear. Got it."

Rooster guffawed. "Perfect." He bent down and looked through the windows toward the hangar office. "Here comes that Ballard asshole now. But before he gets here, I want to give you something to look forward to." Rooster quickly unzipped his fly and pulled out a cock so stupendously thick and long that even battle-hardened Bryce took in a sharp breath. Nestor had stopped breathing altogether. "And I'm a grower," Rooster said as he worked with both hands to tuck the massive member back into his pants. He zipped up just as Ballard's footsteps could be heard on the airstairs.

Rooster turned to the door as Bryce and Nestor walked aft and tried to look busy doing whatever airplane cleaners did when they prepared to get to work. The cold white light of the hangar was momentarily blocked by the hulking form of the first officer as he stepped through the door.

"Ballard," Rooster said in curt greeting.

Ballard simply grunted in reply, then turned his head to make a brief, professional sweep of the aircraft. "Who's that?" he asked, jerking his thumb at Bryce and Nestor.

"Cleaners," Rooster said. "Some kid puked all over the stateroom late last night. These two are going to be cleaning it on the way. Gotta be sure it's spick-and-span so a bunch of Chihuahuas can crap all over it on the way back, right?"

"Huh." Ballard didn't look as though he really cared about anything that happened behind his own seat in the plane. "Tell them not to open the cockpit door." He turned and walked through that door, then slammed it shut behind him.

Rooster gave Bryce and Nestor a thumbs-up and a big grin, then grabbed his heavily laden crotch and winked. "Take any seat you like, boys, and buckle up. They'll be towing us outta here in a minute, and we'll be on our way." He closed and latched the boarding door, then turned, let himself into the cockpit, and shut the door behind him.

"Now, as the emir's third son used to say, it's always better when you're strapped down." Bryce smiled cheerfully, took one of a pair of seats just in front of the wing, and motioned Nestor to take the one next to it. They settled into the soft leather and, with the push of a button, reclined comfortably. The plane jostled and thumped, then began to glide smoothly out of the hangar, propelled by a force silent and invisible. The left engine surged to life, followed by the one on the right, and after a moment's pause, the plane began to roll again. A quick turn, a brief pause, and the engines roared suddenly to full power.

Nestor's hand slipped over the armrest as the plane gained speed, and Bryce laced his fingers into those of his love. They shared a smile as the plane lifted into the sky.

Evening, at sea

"WELL, THIS is beautiful," Sandler exclaimed, taking his seat opposite Donnelly.

They were in the lounge at the absolute top of the ship, surrounded by huge windows and gleaming chandeliers and officious waitstaff who, at the moment, seemed to outnumber the guests. They sat at a table next to the largest of the windows, a silver champagne bucket on the table next to the flowers that overflowed a crystal vase. A tuxedoed waiter popped the cork on the champagne and filled their flutes.

As the waiter receded, Donnelly picked up his flute.

Sandler followed suit. "Now, if we were dating," he said, scrutinizing the fine bubbles scrambling to the surface of his glass. "I would suspect there was a ring in the offing."

Donnelly laughed. "My proposal to Ethan was nowhere near this fancy. I just sort of blurted it out on the sidewalk."

"I think that's much more romantic," Sandler said, taking a sip of the bubbly. "But if it's not a proposal—about the absence of which I am utterly devastated, but not at all surprised—I have to ask: what might be the occasion?"

Donnelly took a gulp of champagne and set his flute down on the table. "I'm not sure how to say this, so I'll just lay it out there." He took a deep breath. "I saw you this morning on the balcony."

"Oh." Sandler blushed and turned to look out the window. "You must think I'm some kind of exhibitionistic slut," he said dismally. "I'm sorry."

"No, I'm the one who should apologize," Donnelly said. "I got up early to go to the gym, but when I opened the door of the bedroom, I saw the two of you out there."

"And we were…?"

"Yes, yes you were," Donnelly said with a half smile. "Vigorously."

"Oh, I'm so sorry," Sandler whispered.

"No, you did nothing wrong. It was me. I saw you, and I just… stood there."

Sandler sat back, a look of utter bafflement on his face. "You just stood there?"

Donnelly nodded miserably.

A smile spread across Sandler's face. "Gabriel Donnelly, you scoundrel." He laughed and shook his head.

"I don't know why I did it," Donnelly said, looking down.

"I do."

"You do?"

"Of course I do. It's the same reason you listened to us the night before last. You've led a very sheltered life, and when you suddenly have access to the escapades of a willy-nilly slut like me, you naturally take advantage."

Donnelly, too ashamed to speak, looked out the window and shifted anxiously in his seat.

Sandler reached across the table and took Donnelly's hand. "You did nothing wrong, Gabriel. You just missed this part in your growing up as a gay man. You didn't get a candy-store phase, and this morning? Well, let's just call that the college-dorm phase. Everyone goes through some version of it—though not everyone gets to see the amazing thing that you did, if I may blow my own horn for a moment."

"It was pretty amazing. I couldn't look away, though I knew I should have."

"Ankur's like this… this spiritual being. He's not a party boy, obviously, but it's like sex is his church. I would never get tired of watching him come."

Donnelly felt the heat in his cheeks intensify.

"Ah, you saw it too," Sandler said with a smile. "Just so you know, while there are guys humping all over this ship, no one does it like he does. What you witnessed was transcendent."

"You sound like you might be falling for him," Donnelly hinted, glad for a topic of conversation that did not involve his sudden proclivity for voyeurism.

Sandler shrugged. "I'd be lying if I said it hadn't crossed my mind. In my line of work, getting to sleep with someone a second time is a luxury in which I've rarely indulged. I'm usually off to the next job before the sun rises. Of course, I don't think I've met anyone in a long time who I'd even want to see a second time. Not since…." He hesitated, as if afraid to say what he was thinking.

"Trevor?" Donnelly asked quietly.

Sandler took in a sharp breath, a visible sadness flashing across his face. He nodded.

Donnelly studied his face for a long moment. "He reminds you of Trevor, doesn't he?"

Sandler eyes widened, and his jaw went slack. "How did you know that?"

"Well, I am a police officer," Donnelly said with a shrug. "Observing people is kind of my thing."

"Am I being ridiculous? I fear I may be trying to recapture that feeling of being in high school and that first rush of falling for him." Sandler smiled, and then the sadness returned. "There's a place in my heart for Trevor, as hard as I've tried to let him go. Ankur's the first person who made me even consider that someone might take that place."

"That's good, right? You can't live your entire life holding back such an important part of yourself."

Sandler nodded, but not with much conviction. "I know I need to get over him… but, with the way it ended, I don't know if I ever will."

Donnelly took a deep breath. "Okay, I have one more thing to tell you."

Sandler raised an eyebrow. "You are an international man of mystery and intrigue, aren't you?"

Donnelly rolled his eyes. "If you knew me at home you'd call me a 'domestic man of duty and routine.' But after our conversation about Trevor on the train, I sent an e-mail to one of the detectives I work with. Gave her all of the info you mentioned about Trevor to see if she could figure out what happened to him. I know you said that you wanted to think about it, but since we were going to be out of phone range for a week, I just went ahead."

Sandler froze. "You did that? For me?"

Donnelly nodded. "I hope that's okay."

"Of course it is. It's just that… I had kind of given up on ever knowing what happened." He turned and studied the horizon, where sea met sky. "What did you find out?"

"Nothing yet. The e-mail finally sent from my phone once we got off the train, and all I got before the ship left was a message back from her saying she'd look into it. Once we get to Southampton, we'll be able to find out if she's come up with anything."

Sandler was quiet for a moment. "Do you think she'll find him?"

"She's our best detective," Donnelly replied. "If anyone can find out what became of him, she can."

"Wow," Sandler said with a long exhalation, as if he'd just run a race. "I don't know what to say." His eyes snapped up to look into Donnelly's. "Thank you."

"I hope we find out something good. Ethan calls me a hopeless romantic, but I tell him romance is actually all about hope. That's when he smacks me with a pillow."

Sandler grinned. "And you let him get away with that?"

"Oh hell no. He smacks me with a pillow, he knows it only ends one way."

"Do tell," Sandler replied, taking a sip of champagne and sitting back in his chair.

An hour later, after some spirited storytelling (the sexy details of which Donnelly found himself censoring less and less), they made their way down to the bar, where Sandler met up with Ankur, and Donnelly teamed up with Dax and Stanley to utterly dominate the trivia competition—he supplied answers for all of the sports questions while the others handled the Broadway musicals and celebrity gossip.

After being crowned captain of the winning team, Donnelly was ready to turn in for the night. "You and your buddy coming back to the suite?" he asked Sandler, who was for the first time that evening not in Ankur's company.

"I haven't even had the chance to sleep with anyone more than twice since… well, since Trevor." Sandler looked over to where Ankur was helping Emmett reset the bar for the next day.

"So you're not going to?"

Sandler turned back to Donnelly. "Are you fucking kidding me? You saw what he can do."

Donnelly, embarrassed, nodded guiltily.

"By the way, I told him you saw us this morning," Sandler added casually.

"You told him?" Donnelly was aghast. But he reconsidered that reaction immediately. Why shouldn't he know? "I should apologize to him as well, I guess."

"Not necessary. He thought it was outrageously hot. That's the phrase he used, 'outrageously hot.' He also asked if you would like to join us."

Donnelly gasped.

Sandler held up his hand. "I know, I know. But he wanted me to ask you anyway. He seemed to feel it was important—like it would let you know he really was okay with you seeing us. But honestly, I think he was serious. So I wanted to put that out there. Just, you know, so you… know." He looked up at Donnelly, clearly anxious about his reaction.

"Please tell Ankur I am very flattered, and still very taken. But he is welcome to spend the night in the suite, of course. I promise I won't spy on you again."

"Is it okay if I don't tell him that? It really seems to excite him to think you might be watching."

"You do whatever you want to, buddy. Though I kind of worry about either of you getting more excited than you seemed to be this morning on the balcony. He seemed pretty zen about it, but you—I'm not sure you could take it."

"I think you'd be surprised what I can take," Sandler said.

Donnelly stood. "I'm just going to leave that little double entendre on the table and head up to bed. I'll see you in the morning, sir."

"You shall. And I promise to be in a less compromising position when you do."

"Well, that doesn't sound like nearly as much fun," Donnelly replied with a wink. He turned and headed out of the bar.

CHAPTER EIGHT

Thursday
Morning, Paris

THE GOLDEN light of another Paris dawn broke into the room, awakening Brandt irreversibly. He scanned the sky for a moment, trying to judge the time, then turned his head toward the clock mounted on the wall opposite. To his surprise, he found Kerry looking back at him, wide-awake.

"Morning, chief," she said brightly.

"Good morning." He blinked a couple of times, adjusting to having a conversation in bed with someone other than Donnelly. "Been up long?"

"Not long," she replied. "There's such promise in a sky like that, don't you think? It's all golden and full of possibilities."

He turned to look at the sky again. The pinks of dawn were fading into gold, and would soon give way to the bright light of a blue sky over the city. He turned back. "It looks like it's going to be a beautiful day. What are we going to do with it?"

"First I will slip daintily out of bed, so you don't have to get up first and risk showing off the boner that waking up next to me no doubt has inspired. Though I would naturally consider it a compliment, I imagine you'd rather avoid the entire spectacle."

"Now you really are being ridiculous."

She raised an eyebrow. "Are you trying to tell me you do not, in fact, have an erection?"

He laughed. "Hell yeah, I have an erection. But it wasn't waking up next to you that did it. It's just habit, since I normally wake up with it wedged between the loving buttcheeks of my darling Gabriel."

She grinned. "Good for you. But I will still take the high road and get up first. I'll be in the bathroom for a half hour, so you may deal with that buttcheek boner however you see fit." She launched herself energetically out of bed and walked to the bathroom, her oversized T-shirt flowing behind her. "Wasn't me that did it... *as if,*" she muttered sarcastically and cast him a theatrically offended look as she disappeared into the bathroom, cackling, and shut the door behind her.

He rolled onto his back and stared at the ceiling, unsure whether to ask the heavens whether he had been cursed or blessed by her appearance in his life. What he was sure of, however, was the ponderous heaviness in his groin as his erection rubbed against the silky sheets.

A half hour, she said? Hmmm.

Brandt had always viewed jerking off in much the same way a race-car driver might view changing his own oil—a necessary job when there's no one else to take care of it, but not the primary reason to own a race car. But this morning, lying in a bed in Paris, alone for the first time in a long while, he decided to take his race car out for a spin. Reaching under the covers, he wrapped his hand around his achingly stiff cock and then squeezed the flared head, just the way Donnelly loved to do first thing in the morning. He closed his eyes and pictured him there in bed, heat rising from his naked body, a wicked smile on his handsome face as he tweaked and squeezed the head of Brandt's erection.

Fuck. Gabriel, why aren't you here with me?

There was something Brandt shared with very few people in the world: he had been paid thousands of dollars to do exactly what he was doing now, but on camera. In the aftermath of that undercover assignment, he was unable to touch himself in that way and feel anything other than a rush of shame and regret. Thankfully, it was also during that time that Donnelly became his lover, not just his best friend and partner. Donnelly's perpetual randiness meant that Brandt had little occasion for this kind of self-indulgence, and so over the last three years, he had taken matters into his own hands only a very few times, and most of those times were with Donnelly right next to him, watching with a greedy intensity as Brandt brought himself to climax.

Brandt's cock surged at the memory of Donnelly's wide, delighted eyes roaming up and down his body, taking in the exertions and tensions that accompanied the growing pleasure caused by his stroking. He spat into his hand, and the slickness with which it slid up and down caused him to moan softly and writhe on the soft sheets. He was hard, his stroke was sure, but he felt no orgasm building.

There was something missing.

Donnelly, of course. But something else. Something he wanted to feel but didn't.

Brandt opened his eyes and looked over to the nightstand on Kerry's side of the bed. On it she had placed a little bottle of the exquisite lotion provided by the hotel. Brandt stared at it for a moment, listened to the shower still running, and made his move. He reached out and grabbed up the bottle, opened it, and tapped out a blob of lotion onto the fingers of his left hand. He reached down under the covers.

He had never done this before.

He jumped a little when the cool lotion touched that spot between his legs—the spot that Donnelly knew so well, but that Brandt had, until this moment, not explored on his own. This most private part of him was like an embassy in a foreign land; it was part of him, but it really belonged to Donnelly. To touch it without him was new, scandalous, thrilling.

He nudged his fingertip inside.

A flash of heat caused by the intrusion surged through his chest. His finger was dainty compared to Donnelly's extensive member, but Brandt still shifted a little awkwardly as he slid it in. His ass had been unexplored territory when Donnelly came into his life, and he was sure it would have remained so forever had they not found each other. And yet, when his finger grazed that secret spot inside, he felt certain he would have been missing one of the greatest pleasures in life. He pushed a little, right on the bump of his prostate, and his heart surged, skipping a beat or two and making his breath catch. He pushed again.

It was the highest sort of pleasure, the sort that demands nothing and gives so much. It was like scratching a mosquito bite without ever being irritated by an itch, like reveling in a cool breeze without having suffered from the heat. He rubbed in time with the stroking of his cock and soon fell into a rhythm that had him gasping.

The orgasm seemed to gather at his fingertip and radiate out through his unrelentingly hard cock. Lights flashed at the edges of his vision, even when he squeezed his eyes shut. His abdominals seized, bending him at the middle, wracking him with overwhelming pleasure. His prostate doubled in size, and he flicked and pressed and rubbed, every motion tingling through his cock in perfect synchrony.

Suddenly, he was growling, grunting like a rutting animal under the force of the orgasm he had wrought upon himself. He tried to stay silent but could not, as if overcome by the bestial force he had summoned. A dozen urgent, almost painful, spasms arced through him, but to his surprise only a few drops of white emerged from the deep red head of his cock. It was only when he let up the pressure on his prostate that the surge came, a river of cum flowing from him all over his still-tensed belly, gathering in the deep wells that separated the hard ingots of his abdominal muscles. He groaned again, feeling a second surge of spasms tear through him. He struggled to breathe, wondering if this orgasm would ever end. Not that he wanted it to.

Finally, after an eternity of delight, he collapsed back onto the bed and took several heaving breaths.

"Oh my God, oh my God," he murmured repeatedly, astonished that at the advanced age of twenty-seven, he could surprise himself this way. But even as he thought this, he knew it was Donnelly who had done it, who had shown him the wonders his body could achieve, who was here with him in spirit if not in the flesh.

"I love you, Gabriel," he whispered. He lay staring at the ceiling for a long moment.

He was stirred by the sound of the shower shutting off. He bolted upright and grabbed for the box of tissues next to the bed. He mopped up quickly, then darted over to the armoire to throw on a robe and stuff the tissues in the pocket. He ran back to the bed and had just put the lotion bottle back on Kerry's side when the bathroom door opened. He tried to strike a casual pose by the window, looking out over the city.

"Well, you look like the cat that just ate the canary," she said, laughing lightly.

"Just enjoying the morning," he said in a voice that impressed even him with its composure. He gestured grandly toward the bathroom. "May I?"

"You may," she replied, and stepped out of the bathroom doorway to allow him past. "Enjoy getting clean." She winked at him.

"I have no idea what you're talking about," he said with as much dignity as he could muster. As he passed by, he could feel his buttocks sliding sloppily against each other, lubed up by the excess lotion. It was an uncomfortable sensation, but he kept his head high, walked calmly into the bathroom, and shut the door behind him.

He could hear Kerry giggling through the door. Even with the social awkwardness, it was still the best time he'd ever had by himself. He began picturing how he would express his gratitude to Donnelly on their wedding night for the inspiration he'd provided.

Brandt took a longer shower than usual and scrubbed some things twice.

Emerging from the bathroom, he found Kerry on the terrace, reclining on a chaise lounge in the bright morning light, a tray of coffee and some pastries on the small table next to her. He poured himself a cup of coffee and sat on the next chaise over.

She opened her eyes slowly. "Whatcha feel like this morning?" Her voice was pleasant though not particularly energetic.

"I would love to go for a nice long walk. Let's find some miles-long tree-lined boulevard or take the metro out to a park."

"Already reached your limit of shopping and museums?" she teased.

"We spent more than *three hours* in that museum, and I think we've established that shopping is off-limits. Let's get some fresh air and move a bit."

"Sounds perfect," she replied, sitting up and stretching. "Give me five minutes, and I'll be good to go."

"Take ten. I need to have at least two more cups of this amazing coffee. French press, I tell ya what."

"Talk like that on your wedding night, and Gabriel will never let you out of bed," she said with a smile as she slipped back into the hotel room.

He laughed and poured himself another cup, then leaned against the wrought-iron railing and looked over the city. It would be a good day.

A couple of hours later, they were walking through a park on the outskirts of Paris that offered woods and ponds as well as lush picnic grounds. They walked for a long while, then perched on a low stone wall that surrounded a fountain. Across the gently sloping lawn, a group of young men had laid out several blankets and were reclining barefoot in the early afternoon sun. Though they talked and laughed, their attention seemed to be directed across the park. Brandt followed their sight lines and saw what had drawn their eyes—a group of men playing shirt-versus-skins football.

"I agree with them," Kerry said, lowering her sunglasses like a country-club cougar giving the once-over to a hot new lifeguard. She studied the football players as they ran and shouted, glistening under the sun.

Brandt looked from field to picnic blanket and back again, then cast a confused look at Kerry, who burst into laughter.

"You really are straight, aren't you?" she said, shaking her head and chuckling.

For the first time in his life, Brandt felt that saying so would be to admit a shortcoming of some kind. He scowled—playfully—at Kerry, and turned his attention back to the young men.

There were six of them, which immediately reminded Brandt of the six college guys he and Donnelly had met at the Villa Hermes back in March. But where they could hardly agree on anything, these Parisian picnickers gazed with a unity of purpose at the football field. They spoke among themselves as the ball was passed among the players, cheering when one made a particularly acrobatic move or flexed an attractive muscle. They reserved their most appreciative cheers for players who, after a goal was scored, spanked each other smartly on the ass. Brandt watched them for a long while, how they talked and laughed animatedly even when not looking at the playing field. They seemed, in that idyllic park in the midday sun, to be happy together in ways that Brandt did not think he had ever been with his own group of friends. Not, at least, since his life had changed.

Having grown up a natural athlete, he was accustomed to thinking of himself as one of the football players, with no clue that anyone would want to look at him, much less study his every motion. At least, that was, until the undercover work he had done three years ago put the lie to that way of thinking. He had been chosen for that particular assignment, and was successful in it, purely because of his physical attractiveness. It was the first time he'd had to confront how uncomfortable it was for him to be an object of desire and to know that his desirers numbered far more than six people on a picnic blanket.

In the aftermath of that assignment, he had made his peace as best he could with what he had done, and the violation he'd felt had faded. But did he now belong with those who watched the football game, following the surging gluteals of every player? He was certainly not at home there, though many people he now called his friends would be, with Bryce in the middle of it, awarding points to each player based on how much skin he had exposed. When he watched sports—as he often did—he watched for things that would bore Bryce silly, such as proficiency and teamwork. He was far more interested in box scores than a dick-slip in the postgame locker-room footage.

Uncomfortable being desired, and not driven to paroxysms of desire by athlete's bodies, where did he fit?

With a piercing whistle, the football game came to an end, and the picnickers began to pack up their blankets. One of the players, a great bear of a man, glossed with exertion and smiling at his shirtless victory, broke from his team after a congratulatory huddle and walked toward the group. As he approached, one of the picnickers set down his folded blanket and walked toward him. When they reached each other, they embraced, and there followed a kiss that was every bit as athletic as the football match had been.

Brandt looked quickly to each side to catch the reaction to this clinch. The spectators didn't appear to notice, and the soccer players, several of them with arms around their own—female—admirers, gave out a whoop of good-natured teasing and went on their way. The player and his boyfriend rejoined the group of picnickers, arms around each other as the player received the congratulations of the others in the group.

"Aww," Kerry said, looking at the embracing couple surrounded by their friends. "That's so sweet."

Brandt was too lost in thought to respond. The football player was embraced by the other picnickers, several of whom grappled his muscular frame long enough to stray from congratulation to groping. But he laughed with them and picked up the smallest and most voluble and spun him around wildly; once set back down, the smaller man laughed and staggered dramatically until bolstered by a pair of friends who kept him from falling over completely. There was much cheering and jostling, and Brandt half expected the soccer player to suddenly drop his butch manner and begin flitting about like the spectators were. He remained, however, the stolid, solid man who had been fiercely competitive on the field. But he smiled broadly and joked with the others. He didn't change who he was to be part of the group.

This was what Brandt had been trying to master the past three years. He had felt himself lost between two worlds, not realizing that he didn't have to leave one in order to be at home in the other.

"You okay?" Kerry asked, bumping his shoulder with hers. "You kinda zoned out there."

"Yeah, I'm fine," Brandt replied, meaning it for the first time in a long while. "Really good."

Kerry studied his face earnestly, then nodded. "I think you are. I guess some fresh air was all it took."

"And a football game," Brandt added.

She smirked. "I *knew* you were watching those guys. Guess you're not 100 percent superstraight after all, huh?"

"I couldn't explain it to you if I tried," he said, chuckling. "But I feel better than I have in a long time, and I owe that to you."

She sat back in surprise, though she was clearly pleased as well. "I'm thrilled that our spur-of-the-moment Parisian adventure has paid off for you, Ethan, I really am. I think we've helped each other a lot. Now we should do what I always do at the end of a productive therapy session."

"What's that?"

"Have a drink." She hooted with laughter as she got to her feet. "I saw a lovely boîte on the way into the park. Shall we give it a try?"

"Hell yeah," he said, rising. "No one told me about the drinking. I might actually be willing to give therapy a try."

They shared a long laugh on the way to the bar, thinking about Brandt on the therapist's couch.

Somewhere over the Pacific

THOUGH PILOTS at the helm of an empty aircraft tend to maneuver more aggressively than when they are responsible for a hundred souls on board, Bryce and Nestor enjoyed the giddy climb to cruising altitude. Once the plane was on a stable heading over the ocean, Rooster made good on his promise to rejoin them and show them to the rear of the plane.

"Shall we, gentlemen?" he asked, his voice courtly but laced with a ragged lust he ill suppressed.

"We shall," Bryce replied, rising to the full upright position.

Rooster led them through the galley, past the lavatories, and on through to the bedroom that occupied the rear of the plane. It was as luxuriously appointed as the rest, with piles of overstuffed pillows and soft fabrics. They entered the room, and Rooster closed the door behind them.

"Okay, here's the rules. No kissin', no cuddlin'. I ain't gay, and you ain't gonna 'turn' me by nursin' on my big ol' dick. Your job is to get me off, and my job is to choke you with the most fuckin' cum you've ever had in your life. You try anything with my ass, and I will fucking kill you. Got it?" While Rooster spoke, he loosened his tie, unbuttoned his shirt, and started unbuckling his belt.

"Yes, sir!" Bryce saluted smartly. "Permission to assist you with your disrobing, sir?"

Rooster's crooked grin gave his answer. He dropped his hands to his side, pelvis thrust forward in a posture of macho confidence.

In wordless unison, Bryce and Nestor dropped to their knees and set to work. In short order they had disposed of his belt, thrown off his shoes, and dropped his pants to his ankles. Rooster stepped out of them and stood before them in his socks and a pair of boxer briefs that was clearly overmatched by the manhood it attempted to restrain.

"Please," Nestor said, taking Rooster's hand and leading him to the bed.

Rooster sat down on the foot of the bed and raised his arms, placing his hands on the back of his head. Bryce and Nestor knew exactly what this posture demanded. They ran their fingers down his powerful arms until they reached his armpits, into which they nuzzled submissively, taking in the masculine scent rooted there. Rooster sighed contentedly.

"Good boys. You faggots love the stink of a man, don't you?"

By way of answer, Bryce pushed on Rooster's chest, and the man lay back on the bed. Nestor lifted his feet and pulled off the socks while Bryce tugged at the waistband of his black boxer briefs.

"Well, you boys get right down to it, don't you?" Rooster said with a husky chuckle.

"We are dedicated service providers," Bryce assured him. "Now lift." Bryce grasped Rooster's underwear, and as his pelvis rose from the bed, Bryce slid them gracefully off. Rooster's monumental cock slapped heavily against his flat belly.

Rooster now lay completely naked on the bed, his crooked grin never wavering. He looked at Bryce and Nestor, clearly eager to see the expressions of hunger and lust that his cock would inspire.

"Dios mío," Nestor breathed.

"Indeed, darling. The gods themselves had a hand in crafting it, and now we get to lay our hands on it." Bryce paused to lick his lips. "Among other things."

They exchanged a nod and went to work. Bryce wrapped his fist firmly around the base of Rooster's cock, his fingers not even close to touching on the other side. Nestor placed his hand right above Bryce's, and then Bryce did the same with his other hand. Nestor followed suit with his, and yet the very tip of Rooster's enormous cock rose above his grip.

"I win!" Bryce called, and bolted forward to take the head of Rooster's dick in his mouth. Nestor shrugged and contented himself with tickling his fingers down the length of the now fully stiff member until he reached the large balls in their loose sac.

"Mmm," he murmured. "Rooster eggs." He cupped them delicately, weighing them with his fingers.

Bryce, meanwhile, took more and more of the cock into his mouth; he had managed about six inches when he felt Rooster's big hand grip his neck and attempt to force him down farther. Bryce, however, jerked his head up. "I do not object in principle to such encouragement, darling," he said in a sultry voice, "but I ask you to reflect on whether any of the women you've been with were capable of as much as I was already doing."

Rooster grinned. "Naw, you got more in you than I've ever had before. Guess I got a little excited."

"I appreciate the compliment, sir. Now just relax," Bryce said as he lifted Rooster's hand off his neck and laid it next to him, "and let me do what I'm best at."

Rooster shook his head and smiled. "Fuckin' queers."

Bryce was as good as his word and in short order had Rooster's long prick once again tapping at—and then past—his tonsils. Rooster, for his part, began to grip the bedspread as his balls pulled up toward the base of his monstrous cock. Nestor, no longer able to grip them as the sac tightened, simply lapped at them like a puppy.

"Oh, fuck," Rooster called as his legs tensed up. Then, without further warning, he jolted and his cock blasted like a fire hose down Bryce's throat—who didn't lose a stroke, but simply closed his eyes and reveled in the flood he gladly received. In about twenty seconds Rooster gasped to a finish, and the tension left his body. It did not, however, leave his cock, which remained as hard and long as before it had erupted.

"That was fuckin' amazing," Rooster said with a sigh. "No one's ever got me to nut that quick."

"We're just getting started," Bryce replied with a smile. "Nestor?"

Nestor reached into the pocket of his impossibly skinny black jeans and pulled out a small flat silver case. He touched it on its edge, and it popped open, revealing a quartet of lube packs on one side and a half-dozen condoms in shiny foil on the other. Like a nurse in surgery, Nestor slapped a lube pack smartly into Bryce's open palm. Bryce tore off the neck of the pack with his teeth and squirted a dollop onto the angry red head of Rooster's cock. He swirled the slick gel around the helmet of flesh with his fingertips, bringing a content sigh from its owner.

"Ready for something more intense?" Bryce cooed, unbuttoning his pants with his other hand.

Rooster chuckled. "No way that little ass is gonna be able to take me. Bigger men than you have tried and given up, crying like little punks when I was less than halfway in."

Bryce slipped off his silky underwear, stood naked from the waist down, and smiled sweetly at Rooster. "There's no crying in sodomy, darling."

Bryce threw one slender leg over Rooster's thighs, facing the thick instrument that had apparently brought lesser men to tears. He extended his hand, and Nestor quickly slapped a condom packet into it. Bryce tore the packet open, and placed the rubbery ring atop Rooster's member.

"No condoms," Rooster grunted.

"Excuse me?" Bryce replied as he prepared to roll the condom on.

"No fuckin' condoms," Rooster growled. "If I'm gonna fuck you, I want to feel it. And I want you to feel it when I fill you up. Fags line up around the block to get at this man's cock, and if one of them won't take me bareback, I just go on to the next. I musta fucked a dozen fags in the last year, and not one bitched me out about condoms. Now, fuckin' sit on my dick, or I'll fuckin' hold you down and make it hurt."

Bryce regarded the man he straddled. An eyebrow slowly raised, reaching a fearsome peak. "I see," he said, his voice carefully calm. "Nestor, we shall require extra equipment." Nestor leapt up and hurried to the compartment where they had stowed their bags.

"What the fuck's going on?" Rooster growled, sitting up and thrusting Bryce off his legs.

"Here's what's going on," Bryce replied, kneeling on the bed. "I simply need a couple of things from my bag if we're going to do what you want me to do. And you do want it, don't you, sir?" Bryce rubbed a meandering hand over his smooth, perfect buttocks. Rooster's eye was immediately drawn, and his eyes widened without his seeming to notice.

"Huh," he said, taking a long look at Bryce's ass. "What kinda things you need? I could fuck you right now with just spit."

"How charming. I'm sure you could. But I'm kind of particular about barebacking, to be honest. Comes from having been raised in a very strict home. Every single day my parents would scold me. 'Bryce, you should try out for baseball! Bryce, those shoes don't go with that belt! Bryce, don't you dare take it up the ass without a condom!' Ugh, parents, right?"

Rooster stared blankly at him.

"Anyway," Bryce continued, undaunted, "I do so love barebacking, just like all of those fags who line up around the block, but it really helps if I'm... well...."

"What?" Rooster demanded. His hand found his cock and gave it a quick couple of strokes, as if he were worried it would soften during all of this talking.

"Tied down," Bryce whispered and batted his eyes coquettishly. "I just need to be tied down, spread-eagle, unable to close my legs to keep you from forcing your way in. In fact, I may need to be gagged as well, because I'll probably beg you not to be so rough." He leaned in and muttered, "I trust you will be rough."

Rooster's huge grin returned. "Aw, hell yeah I will be."

Nestor bustled in with a bundle of soft red ropes. "Who want to play Boy Scout?" he called.

Rooster leapt up and grabbed the ropes from Nestor. "Gimme those." He shook out the bundle into four separate lengths and reached under the bed to find tie-off points. He lashed ropes to the two corners at the head of the bed, then brushed past Nestor on his way to the foot. "You're next."

Nestor's face was that of a lottery winner, and he jumped up and down and clapped his hands softly.

"There," Rooster said, looking at the four lengths of rope anchored to the bed. "Now, get your ass up there."

Bryce took his time mounting the bed, knowing that Rooster would be fascinated by the sight of his bubble butt, waiting for the moment when he would spread his legs to the corners of the bed and his final secret would be revealed. So transfixed was he that he didn't notice Nestor quickly making slipknots.

Once Bryce was in position, and Rooster had gotten a good look, he leaned forward to secure Bryce's wrist to the rope at the left corner of the bed. Bryce pulled his wrist playfully away, but Rooster captured it and wrapped the rope tightly around it. Before he could make the knot secure, however, Bryce twisted away again.

"Fuckin' stop that," Rooster shouted, flashing to lust-fueled anger.

"Here, I help," Nestor said as he came around to the head of the bed. With lithe fingers he quickly completed the knot and pulled it tight. On Rooster's wrist.

"What the fuck?" roared Rooster, red-faced with fury. It was only as he tried to lunge at Nestor that he realized his ankles were already lashed to the foot of the bed. He had only one hand free, and as Bryce rolled out from under him he swung wildly, trying to strike either or both of them in his ferocious anger.

Both men leapt at his free hand and caught it in all four of their own. Nestor slipped the rope over it and cinched it tight. Now Rooster was the one tied naked and spread-eagled on the bed.

"Untie me! Fuckin' untie me!" he bellowed, struggling mightily against the ropes. They held securely—this was not Nestor's first rodeo.

"Shall we leave him for a while to see if he calms down?" Bryce asked as they stood at the foot of the bed looking at the struggling nude man.

"No! Don't fuckin' leave me here!"

"Then you need to calm down." Bryce folded his arms over his chest and tapped his foot.

Rooster stopped yelling, and his thrashing was reduced to the occasional yanking on the ropes, as if they might somehow have come loose since he last tugged on them.

"That's better." Bryce sat on the edge of the bed and patted Rooster on the shoulder. "Now, Mr. Rooster, here's something you need to know. Nestor and I do not, *ever*, have unprotected sex with anyone except each other. No self-respecting gay man would consent to what you asked. Now, I have no doubt that you have been able to find men who would do so, out of their own self-loathing or in some drug-addled state or simply because they didn't know better. But every time you had anal sex without a condom, you were committing assault. You were endangering your life and the lives of the men you fucked. Do you understand?"

"Fuck you," Rooster growled. "Like I care what some faggot wants."

"No, you will not fuck me. And it's a shame, because you really are stupendous. As am I."

Rooster kept his own counsel for a long moment. "Okay, you've made your point. Now, in case you've forgotten, I have to fly this fucking plane, so you'd better untie me right the fuck now."

"No, I don't think I will," Bryce said, standing. He picked up his clothes and started to get dressed again. "You need a little more time to reflect on your poor choices."

"I am the fucking pilot of this fucking plane!" he bellowed, but Bryce was unmoved.

"If you'll excuse us," Bryce said as he smoothed the wrinkles out of his shirt, "we need to have a little conversation with your copilot."

"What?" Rooster shrieked, clearly unhinged by this prospect. "No fucking way!"

"I'm sure we'll be right back, dear. You just stay where you are." Bryce and Nestor swept from the room as Rooster continued to thrash and holler.

Bryce marched through the airplane directly to the cockpit door.

"My love, are you sure of this?" Nestor asked along the way.

"Of course, Nestor, dear."

"But Rooster say the copilot, he stupid."

"I heard. But did you see the way they looked at each other before they went into the cockpit? There's more going on there than Rooster says. And unless I miss my guess, telling our Mr. Ballard about Rooster's bad behavior is exactly what we need to do." He rapped smartly at the cockpit door. "Mr. Ballard? Mr. Ballard!"

The cockpit door swung open abruptly, and Ballard's scowling face peered out at them. "What?" He clearly was not happy about being disturbed.

"Mr. Ballard, I am Bryce, and this is my associate, Nestor. So pleased to meet you, sir."

Ballard grunted and drew himself up to full height as if he expected a confrontation. "Look, I'm busy."

"Of course you are, sir. I would just like to let you know that the pilot, Mr. Rooster? He…. Well, I'm not sure how to say this," Bryce lied (he had ways to say things much more salacious than this). "But he made a rather unsavory suggestion to Nestor and myself, and we really had no choice but to… well, he's in the bedroom."

Ballard stared blankly for a moment. "What's he doing in there?"

"He's… indisposed."

Realization broke over Ballard's face. He slowly closed his eyes and shook his head. "Fuck. Not again."

"Excuse me, sir?"

"Let me guess. He brought you on board for this trip because he wanted you to suck his dick all the way across the Pacific, right? And then things started to get rough?"

"Well, aren't you the smart one," Bryce flattered.

"No, I'm apparently stupid, because I haven't been able to keep him from doing this. Last month two guys from the 'air-conditioning service' ended up getting pretty banged up. He said a duct cover fell on them, which was complete bullshit, but they wouldn't say anything about what really happened." His mouth curled into a disgusted frown as he looked past Bryce and Nestor toward the back of the plane. Then his gaze snapped back to them. "He didn't hurt you, did he?"

"No, not at all," Bryce replied, casually touching an already perfectly placed strand of hair. "His is a block we have been around before, alas."

"And you're sure you're okay?" Concern softened Ballard's expression as he looked Bryce and Nestor up and down.

"We're fabulous, thank you for asking. But we did leave Mr. Rooster tied up in the bedroom." Bryce shrugged and gave his best "que sera" look.

"You tied him up?" Ballard looked from Bryce to Nestor and back again. "You two together must weigh as much as that asshole's left leg, and you tied him up?"

"As I said, sir, we've had some experience with his kind."

"This I gotta see," Ballard blurted and charged toward the back of the plane. He turned back after a few jogging steps. "Jake, your plane," he called toward the cockpit.

"My plane" came a voice in reply.

"There are more of you?" Bryce looked in surprise at Nestor, then peered into the cockpit. "Is this an airplane or a clown car?"

"I'm just your humble relief pilot," the owner of the voice answered back. "Flights this long require us to rotate the grave responsibility of watching the autopilot do all the work." He laughed at his own joke. "Name's Jake. Pleased to meet you, Bryce and…. Nestor, was it?" Jake turned to look through the cockpit door.

Bryce registered blue eyes, a wide white smile, and cheekbones that spoke of hearty Midwestern heritage. A humpy farm boy in the sky. They stepped closer.

"*Si*," Nestor answered, eyes wide with the thrill of being noticed by the strapping young pilot who now flew the plane.

"So, Jake," Bryce said, his voice full of the sultry thrill of saying that manly name, "once Rooster is back in the cockpit, perhaps you can come see us, just to get better acquainted?"

"I'd like that a lot. As thrilling as being a relief pilot sounds, it's actually kind of a bore."

"We may be able to add some excitement to your duty," Bryce offered.

Jake answered with a deep, resonant laugh. "Sounds good. But once Ballard gets through with Rooster, he may not be up to flying. I think the dam broke this time."

"Oh dear," Bryce whispered. He turned to Nestor. "You don't think he might be angry enough to take advantage of Rooster's prone and vulnerable position?"

Nestor pulled his phone out of his pocket and turned on the camera.

"A prudent measure. We should go check to be sure they're getting along."

Bryce and Nestor slowed as they approached the closed bedroom door and tiptoed up to it. Silently, they pressed their ears against the highly polished wood.

"Give me one good reason why I shouldn't," Ballard spat angrily.

"Because if you do, I'll tell them about that layover in Singapore when you sucked my dick all night long. I'll tell your wife too, you motherfucker."

Bryce's eyes widened as he listened.

"Nothing happened in Singapore, or anywhere else, and no one will believe otherwise," Ballard replied. "You need some help, man. You need to learn that you can't just wave your dick at your problems and have them disappear."

"Fuck you."

"You know, that's not a bad idea. Maybe I should invite Bryce and Nestor back here to take a run at you. If they can truss you up like one of your Thai whores, they could probably wreck that ass of yours."

"Those faggots and their pencil dicks couldn't—"

"Well, now, that's just offensive," Bryce called as he pushed through the door into the bedroom. "And honestly, darling"—Bryce looked frankly into the gap where Rooster's widespread legs met—"it looks to me like you could take an entire box of pencils and hardly feel it."

"Oh snap," Ballard said, holding his palm high. Bryce slapped it with a giggle.

"So here's how this is going to go down, as it were," Ballard continued. "I'm going to take a few pictures of your… predicament, and then I'll take statements from Bryce and Nestor here about their experience. Now, if you don't contest their side of the story, the pictures will be our little secret. But if you ever—I mean *ever*—do anything like this again, I will make sure that everyone who's anyone will get a copy of this." He aimed his camera directly at Rooster's ass and clicked the shutter.

Rooster grunted, but spoke no more.

Ballard took pictures from several other angles, then pocketed his phone. "Now, gentlemen, let's retire to the lounge and have a little talk about what happened here." He turned back to Rooster, who still thrashed on the bed. "You stay right where you are, okay, buddy?" Ballard closed the bedroom door with a smile. He led Bryce and Nestor to the couches in the center compartment of the plane and motioned for them to sit.

"If you're going to take our statements on video," Bryce said, posing on a settee, "I'm afraid I must insist on being lit from the left. I think my left side is much more authoritative, don't you, dear?" He turned to Nestor, eyebrows up.

"I love the left and the right," Nestor replied, taking Bryce's hand and kissing it.

Ballard laughed, seeming delighted at the exchange. "No, I don't need a video statement. In fact, don't worry about making anything official. I only said that to scare him. He's such a coward he's probably in there trying not to shit the bed thinking about how much this could damage his career."

Bryce, a little crestfallen at not getting to play the wounded yet stylish victim on camera, was cheered by Ballard's description of Rooster's desperation. "I'm so glad we came to you, Mr. Ballard. You have saved us from the clutches of that horrible man."

"I rather think I saved him from you." Ballard chuckled. "I took a gander at those knots—that's some serious craftsmanship. No way he's getting loose from that."

"Well, we try to strike a blow for justice where we can," Bryce said modestly, as if he kept a superhero cape in his tasteful black clutch.

"Rooster's been needing to meet someone like you. He's been out of control lately." Ballard sighed and cast a look toward the back of the plane. "He's not a bad guy, but he lets his dick do his thinking for him. And as large as it is, it's still not all that smart."

"You've seen it?" Bryce asked, intrigued.

"Who hasn't? That guy finds more excuses to show off his junk than you could possibly imagine. We used to room together on layovers until I got tired of having him wave it in my face. He seemed to think that even though I'm married—to a woman, yet—I would make an exception for him because his dick is like a foot long. I don't know how he managed to convince himself that everyone in the world wants it, but that's how he lives his life. Or used to, now that you two came along. I've been hoping someone would stand up to him, but I'd kind of given up on it once the air-conditioning guys refused to make a complaint."

"We are so happy to be of service. And we are relieved that he won't be allowed to continue putting people at risk."

Ballard looked at Bryce, his face serious. "That was it, wasn't it? He wouldn't wear a condom?"

Bryce nodded.

"That bastard. I figured that's what was going on, but I had no proof—I'm not really the hide-in-the-closet-and-get-video kind of guy. But you took care of that for me, and now we can put an end to it." Ballard stood. "Well, I think I've let him stew for long enough. I'll go untie him and get him back in the cockpit. And don't worry—I won't let him out again. You'll be safe."

"Thank you, you gallant man."

Ballard smiled. "Save it for Jake—that line might actually work on him." He winked slyly and walked back toward the bedroom.

Ballard was gone for a few minutes, during which time Bryce and Nestor could hear voices, low and serious, through the wall. Eventually they emerged, Rooster wearing his uniform and a very grim face, Ballard following close behind. When they reached the lounge, Rooster stopped and glared at Ballard before turning to Bryce and Nestor.

"I owe you two an apology. I should not have pressured you to let me penetrate you without a condom. It was wrong of me, and I won't do it again." He glanced sourly back at Ballard to confirm that his stilted apology met his standards, and when Ballard nodded, he turned wordlessly and continued his march back to the cockpit.

Ballard followed but turned back as he left the lounge. "You two make yourself comfortable. I'll send Jake back, and you can, uh… feel free to make him comfortable as well." He smiled innocently, as if unaware of the innuendo, and left the room.

"You know," said Bryce, "I can see why airlines have such poor reputations when it comes to customer service. Really, when was the last time we were able to have sex with one pilot, much less two?"

"Even in first class, they don't sleep with you," Nestor agreed with a mournful shake of his head.

"We must make the most of this opportunity."

"Well, hey there, gentlemen," Jake said as he entered the lounge.

Bryce hadn't been able to fully appreciate the relief pilot when he was sitting in the cockpit, facing the other direction. He stood just under six feet tall and was built like a wrestler: lots of muscle, absolutely no fat. His smile was even broader now that he had been released from his duties in the cockpit.

"Can I offer you a drink?" he asked, opening a cabinet hidden in the bulkhead between the lounge and the dining room next door.

"If you would join us," Bryce replied. "But I don't imagine a pilot is allowed to get tipsy while he's on duty."

"Luckily, I've been relieved for the duration of the trip. Ballard said something about Rooster being a bigger than usual asshole and that I'd already put in more hours than a relief pilot should have to. Said I was free to relax back here with our guests, which I assume is you." Jake poured three glasses of a fine bourbon, neat. "Sorry there's no ice—the cabin crew usually gets that all set up."

Bryce took the heavy crystal tumbler. "No apologies, my dear. Anything served by a strapping buck like yourself will be a delight to bring to my lips."

"And to swallow," added Nestor, taking a long sip of his drink.

Jake laughed. "So Ballard was right. He said you guys would flirt the pants off anyone who came within ten feet of you."

Bryce tried to blush. "He said that?"

"Yes, he did. Ballard's a funny one." Jake took a sip of his drink as he sat on a couch opposite the one where Bryce and Nestor perched. "He comes off as totally conservative and kind of angry all the time, and I know Rooster pissed him off constantly. I figured he was just down on the gay thing—he seethed anytime Rooster would brag about how many guys he'd nailed on every trip. But turns out what bugged him wasn't that Rooster was fucking guys, it's that he treated the guys he fucked really badly. Ballard filled me in on what happened to you—that really sucks. I'm sorry."

"We are none the worse for wear," Bryce assured him. "When one hunts big dicks, one must assume that some will turn out to be big dicks. He's not the first we've run across."

"He not even the first we tie up," Nestor added, as if commenting on the weather.

"You two are amazing," Jake said, grinning. "I guess that's why Ballard sent me back here. I've been working with him for the better part of a year and he's never said anything about me being gay. I certainly wasn't going to bring it up, given how much Rooster pisses him off. So when he said I could come back here and kick back with you guys, I was kind of shocked. Even more so when he said he and Rooster wouldn't be leaving the cockpit until we land. And then he winked at me and gave me this little smile. Turns out Ballard knows what's up after all."

"He is a true gentleman," Bryce agreed. "It's a shame he thinks he's straight."

"Oh man. If you saw his wife, you'd be straight too. She's a knockout."

"I'll take your word for it," Bryce replied, his tone conveying how little he'd like to be straightened by Mrs. Ballard.

"Fair enough." Jake slugged back the last of his bourbon. "So, how shall we pass the time?" He sat back and spread his arms along the top of the couch, the muscles of his chest bulging through the thin white shirt of his uniform.

"On that topic, we may have some ideas," Bryce replied before downing his drink—Nestor did the same. "Shall we see if the bedroom offers us some diversions?"

Jake smiled brilliantly.

Ballard had apparently made Rooster return the bedroom to its previous pristine condition, for there was no evidence of its prior use other than the neatly coiled ropes Nestor had furnished. There wasn't so much as a wrinkle on the bedspread.

"Now, I don't want you guys to think that you have to do anything with me because of the whole deal with Rooster. I'll understand if you just want to—"

Bryce cut him off by kissing his adorable mouth. "Now hush," he said when he'd finished making his point. He ran his hands down Jake's impossibly muscled chest. "Rooster was nothing but an unfortunate detour from our progress toward the real prize. You are a beauty unrivaled."

"I'll bet you say that to all the guys," Jake said with a devastatingly modest grin.

"You're not wrong about that," Bryce said with a shrug, "but with you we really *mean* it. Don't we, Nestor?" Bryce turned to find Nestor already naked. Bryce made a stern *tsk-tsk*, and turned back to Jake. "I must apologize for Nestor. He's a bit eager when it comes to well-built, blond-haired, blue-eyed gods."

"I like the way he thinks," Jake replied, tugging at his tie and collar. He soon had his shirt off (and neatly laid over the back of a convenient chair) and his shoes, socks, and pants followed. He stood before Bryce and Nestor in tighty-whities and an even tighter white undershirt. The brickwork of his abdominals was clearly visible through the shirt, and the intensity of Bryce's gaze boring through the fabric seemed to catch his eye. "Something wrong?" he asked, looking down at his torso.

"Oh no, dear. Everything is completely right."

Jake rolled onto the balls of his feet and back down several times. "I guess I'm just a little nervous," he said. "I've never been with two guys before."

Bryce gasped in shock. "Well, that seems terribly inefficient. Given that there are millions of men who would love to have the chance, you could work through the backlog in half the time."

"I never looked at it that way," Jake said with a laugh.

"Well, in the future, see that you do," Bryce scolded, as if recommending annual prostate exams or tire rotation. He began slipping out of his clothes.

"So, um," Jake stumbled, "how do we... do this?"

"In sex, as in all things, it's important not to think," Bryce counseled. "Cast your mind back to, let's see—" His gaze wandered up and down Jake's body. "—wrestling practice, I want to say?"

"Yep. Wrestled high school and college. State champ twice."

"Of course you were, dear. Now, think about all of those times that you engaged in high-spirited horseplay with your teammates—perhaps after a big competition when everyone gathered to let off steam, all sweaty and elated and no-homo. Do I capture the experience?"

Jake grinned again. "That pretty much sums it up. Being a gay wrestler is like the hardest thing in the world."

"I'm sure it was," Bryce clucked, nodding sympathetically. "I'm sure it was. So now I want you to think of myself and Nestor as your wrestling buddies. Break out your best moves, and this time it's all-homo!" Bryce threw himself on the bed.

"Fuck yeah," Jake said and mounted the bed. He effortlessly picked Bryce up and flipped him over, then stretched his body out atop him.

"That's the spirit, dear," Bryce called from under the delicious weight of so much man. "Nestor, a little help?"

Nestor leapt into the fray, clearly eager to lend a hand to his fellow man.

Nearly three hours later, as the wrestling match ground to its climax—actually, its third—the sound of the plane's engines ebbed and the nose dipped slightly.

"I guess we've begun our descent," Jake murmured into Bryce's ear, then nuzzled his cheek gently. Their bodies were entangled such that he could nuzzle both Bryce's cheek and Nestor's buttcheek by simply turning his head. "I should make myself presentable." He tried to rise, but found himself still pinned beneath the other men.

"Oh, of course, dear, let me just...." Bryce extracted his limbs from the massive knot they had collectively become and then stepped lightly off the bed. He reached a hand back to help Jake up, but found him kissing his way across Nestor's round ass. "Now, darling, Nestor's posterior has no bigger fan in the world than yours truly, but don't you need to slip back into your uniform?"

Jake sighed sadly and planted one more kiss on each of Nestor's globes, then sat up. "You're right, duty calls." He got to his feet and stretched as far as the ceiling would allow.

Bryce looked him appreciatively head to toe and back again. "It's a wonder you were ever able to contain yourself within the confines of a singlet," he mused.

"It wasn't easy," Jake replied with a laugh. "I always had to use compression shorts that were two sizes too small. But even they didn't help when I had to wrestle the captain of the team. He had twenty pounds on me, easy, and half of that was cock. I would get boned up just seeing him walk out onto the mat, and by the time we actually started, my dick would be sticking out sideways trying to get at him. Fuck."

Bryce looked expectantly at him, waiting for more. "Well, did you?"

"Did I what?"

"Did you fuck? It's rude to leave an audience hanging like this," Bryce scolded good-naturedly.

Jake laughed. "Just once. I was finally getting used to the idea of being gay, and one night after a late practice, he kinda let it slip that he was struggling with it too. So I managed to convince him that if he did it once, he would know for sure. Man, he railed me that night—once he got started, he was unstoppable." Jake rubbed his ass as if recalling the experience. "After that night, he just disappeared—never came back to school. They said he ran away from home out to San Francisco, but I never found out for sure."

"Well, it must have been something drastic for him to never come back after one night with you. We've just had the afternoon, and I do believe there will always be a place for you inside of me."

Jake grinned. "You say the sweetest stuff. You're a complete beast in bed, but you're adorable." He walked over and kissed Bryce tenderly. "And now, I really have to go." He gathered up his clothes, put his pilot's cap on, and walked naked out of the bedroom.

"He does know how to leave a room," Bryce said with a sigh as he watched those powerful buttocks disappear around the corner.

"Is this England?" Nestor mumbled as he turned over in bed.

"We are almost there, my darling," Bryce cooed, sitting on the edge of the bed and petting Nestor's thigh. "We'll be in Tokyo soon, and then it's just a quick jaunt to merry old England, I promise."

"Mmm." Nestor wrapped himself around Bryce and sighed contentedly.

"Now, darling, I would love to start what we finished with Jake, but we must arise and prepare ourselves for the next phase of our journey."

"We buy tickets this time?" Nestor asked, sitting up and stretching.

"Why change now? We've come this far—and this many times—relying on the kindness of strangers. Who knows what adventures we would forsake were we to actually buy passage?"

Nestor kissed Bryce on the cheek. "Te amo."

"Oh! You're playing dirty. You know how your native tongue inflames me." Bryce threw his arms around Nestor. "I'm sure we have a little time before we must be in the full upright position." He looked down. "And you're there already. How lovely!" They found pleasant enough diversions to pass the remaining flight time and were able to make themselves presentable just as the plane taxied to a stop.

Ballard met them in the lounge. "Thank you for flying with us," he said as he shook Bryce's hand. "Now, you know where to find the next flight, right?" He shook Nestor's hand, still smiling warmly.

"Your instructions have been admirably detailed," Bryce replied. "I can't thank you enough for all that you've done."

"Well, I'm sorry about the mess with Rooster. I'll make sure he doesn't treat anyone that way again."

"Let's not keep him on too short a leash, shall we? It would be a shame to deprive the world of the proper use of his talents."

"You are a generous soul, Bryce. Best of luck to you."

"And to you, sir." Bryce regarded the only man on board he had not managed to have sex with over the last eight hours. "I hope to see you again."

"It would be my pleasure," Ballard replied.

"Indeed it would," Bryce murmured as he and Nestor walked down the airstairs to the limousine that awaited them on the tarmac. As they approached, the driver of the car stepped out and opened the rear door for them. He took their bags, and they took their seats on the soft leather while he placed the luggage in the trunk.

"One would think the company that hired Rooster, Mr. Ballard, and Jake would take greater care in their selection of chauffeurs."

"He got a belly," Nestor agreed.

"Well, every voyage must have its setbacks," mused Bryce, settling into the seat. "We can only hope the next pilots will make up for it."

"Mr. Ballard is nice to making arrangement for us."

"Yes, he was. The poor dear seemed distraught at Rooster's behavior, and I really think he felt this was the least he could do. We won't, however, have the place to ourselves this time. He said the plane was carrying the national men's gymnastics team of Australia to a competition in London and had a couple of empty seats. We're fortunate they were delayed leaving Tokyo because of engine trouble."

They drove in silence across the airport. Bryce noticed Nestor was staring vacantly at his hands.

"What is it, darling? You're all pale, which is not a good look for someone of your natural bronze hue."

"The engine, they fix it?"

"Oh, of course they will, dear. Why else would those sturdy men in coveralls be gathered around it?" Bryce pointed out the window at the plane they had pulled up next to; there were indeed six men in coveralls swarming around the open cowling of the engine in question. "I'm sure they'll have it working perfectly by the time we take off."

The flight from Tokyo was long—more than twelve hours, but enjoyably passed as they became acquainted with several of the gymnasts. Bryce had accompanied three of them to the plane's bathroom, where he offered a variety of physical therapy that was as unconventional as it was enjoyable for the gymnasts, and Nestor had helped several more release muscular tension they were not previously aware they suffered from.

They were only an hour away from London when the captain announced they would have to divert to Amsterdam as the repairs to the engine had failed to secure its proper operation. The sound of the engine on the right side of the plane died away, leaving an eerie quiet in the cabin as they descended.

Bryce looked over at Nestor and saw his eyes closed and lips moving silently. As if he could sense Bryce's stare, he opened his eyes and shrugged placidly. "I ask God for help with the plane."

"Honey, ask yourself: why would God allow a plane full of such beautiful specimens to crash? Why go through the trouble of artisanally crafting *those*"—he pointed out the blond twins who sat across the aisle from them, nervously looking out the window—"just to scatter their bits across the Netherlands? And trust me, I had the opportunity to become well acquainted—just an hour ago in the rear lavatory—with their nether lands, and they are some of the Big Guy's finest work." He smiled dreamily at the memory.

"Sometime God don't need a reason. Sometime he just do things."

"Well, if God wanted to smite us, he would have done so months ago when those upstanding Mormon boys came to our apartment to spread their gospel."

Nestor giggled, then slapped a hand over his mouth as if he'd committed blasphemy.

"You see my point. If chewing on Mormon boys is wrong, I don't want to be right. Anyway, I think we actually helped strengthen their faith. Just recall the number of times they called out to God during the weekend they spent with us."

"Oh God, oh God," Nestor said gleefully in the manner of a young Mormon missionary experiencing something overwhelming and new.

"That's right. Now, just relax, and if you're going to ask God for anything, you should pray that we're delayed in Amsterdam and have to share a hotel room with some of the gymnasts we haven't already… helped."

Nestor smiled peacefully and sat back in his chair, eyes closed and lips moving silently.

Their arrival in Amsterdam quickly extinguished hopes of a night full of pillow fights and fellatio. The plane, having fallen victim to engine trouble twice on one trip, was to be removed from service for an indefinite period for repairs.

"We'll have to make do overnight in the terminal," the gymnastics coach announced, standing at the front of the cabin as the plane limped across the tarmac, his exhausted voice gravelly and grim. "We'll see if they can get it sorted tomorrow."

The team filed out of the plane and looked around the mostly deserted terminal for comfortable benches on which to recline.

"Well, darling, we are once again on our own, making our way across the globe with just our wits and the few condoms we have left."

"Why we no stay with the team? They tired, and maybe saying yes where before they saying no."

"As delightful as it would be to seduce another dozen strong, flexible young men, we simply must get on our way. The wedding of the century is going to happen soon, and it shall not happen without us. Now, that darling ticket agent over there," Bryce said as he gestured toward a handsome gentleman in a uniform, "said the best way to England is to grab a ferry at the port."

Nestor beamed. "Sound like fun."

"Not that kind of fairy. A boat ferry."

"Oh." Nestor slumped a little but shrugged stoically.

"Patience, my darling. All we need to do is take the ferry and we're nearly there. Simple!"

Nestor nodded as if he believed anything Bryce set his hand to could possibly be simple.

But true to his word, Bryce shortly had them off the train and at the ferry terminal, buying passage to Newcastle.

"It sounds lovely, doesn't it?" Bryce said as he handed Nestor his ticket.

"The wedding, it is in the new castle?"

Bryce, desperate to keep Nestor's spirits up, skipped lightly over the truth. "Not exactly, strictly speaking. But we'll be able to get to the wedding lickety-split. After the ferry, we just need to take a train to another train and then a taxi or a horse or something. It's a little vague once we get out into the countryside. But we will get there, my darling, we will!"

Late night, at sea

DONNELLY TURNED over again, thrashing restlessly in his sleep. The creeping dread of a nightmare returning iced its way down his spine.

"Because you fucking punched me, that's why," Gabriel shouted, slamming the car door shut again.

"I can explain. But I can't do it here. Please, get in." Bryan again opened the passenger door of his sleek Euro sedan.

"So you can... what? Drive me to a meeting of your football buddies so they can all take their turns at me? You were the one who grabbed me, asshole. I should be the one who punched you in the fucking face."

Bryan stepped close. "We both know that's not what you wanted to do when I grabbed you."

"Fuck. You." Donnelly shook his head, snarling. "Just fuck the fuck off."

Bryan grabbed his wrist, held it tightly in his fist. "Gabriel, give me a chance."

"A chance to do what? Tell me why you grabbed my dick?"

He looked side to side as if checking to be sure no one was looking. "Yes," he whispered.

"Yes what?"

"Yes, I'll tell you. But you have to come with me. Look, I'm not going to beat you up or anything."

"And why should I believe you?"

"I... I just can't tell you here. Come with me, please. It's important." Bryan was pleading now, his eyes wild with desperation.

Gabriel looked up. "Where are we going?" The speedometer was about to hit ninety, so wherever they were going they would get there quickly.

"We have some hunting land about ten miles out," Bryan replied. His seemed to be more relaxed now that they were putting the town well behind them. He barely slowed down when the dirt road appeared on the right, sweeping a billowing cloud of dust behind the car as the back end fishtailed around before coming true out of the turn. The road dipped down into a little valley covered with trees, and he made another quick turn and slid to a stop where the road ended overlooking a wide green meadow. He switched off the car, then sat silently with his hands in his lap.

The sun, suddenly setting, glared orange in Gabriel's eye. He could wait no longer. "What were you going to tell me?"

Bryan huffed out an anguished breath. "It's not something I can just blurt out," he said quietly.

"Then why did we come all the way out here?"

"Because you have to stop."

Gabriel looked at him, looked for some sign that would tell him what he was supposed to stop doing. Bryan's face was utterly inscrutable.

"I have to stop... what?"

Bryan swallowed hard. "You have to... I need you to stop... doing what you're doing."

Still nothing. "What am I doing? What are you...?" Gabriel hammered his fists on his knees in frustration. "What the fuck are we doing out here?"

"I need you to stop looking at me, okay?" It was clear that blurting this cost Bryan greatly. He looked away, out the side window of the car, panting.

"Looking at you?" Gabriel felt the heat rising up into his face as the heavy weight of guilt settled onto his chest. He felt the truth of Bryan's accusation thickening in his arteries, and his heart struggled to keep beating.

"I see you." Bryan's statement was terse but devoid of emotion. "You think I don't notice, but I do."

"I don't understand." Gabriel understood perfectly.

"Look, I don't hate you. Until today I didn't know if I was imagining it, so I had to test you. I asked the coach if I could cross-train with the wrestling team, and I grabbed you to see what you would do. And when I did, I saw it in your eyes."

Gabriel was silent for a long moment. "Saw what?" He knew exactly what Bryan had seen, but there was some masochistic streak in him that wanted to hear it, needed his mortification to be completed by the uttering aloud of his perverse longing.

"I saw you wanted it too."

Gabriel had to play that statement back in his head several times before he fully understood the import of what Bryan had said. By the time he had, Bryan had opened the car door and stepped out. He strode out into the meadow and stood there, arms crossed adamantly over his chest as if he could withstand anything, fortresslike.

Gabriel must have gotten out of the car too, for he found himself standing next to Bryan.

"I wanted it... too?" he asked, laying emphasis on that final word. He stared straight ahead, afraid to even glance at the man standing silent next to him.

Bryan was silent for long enough that Gabriel had to break the tension. He turned and saw tears running down Bryan's cheeks. His stony expression hadn't changed—he looked like a statue of a classical virtue, like Fortitude or Valor, that had been rained on. The tears were the expression of an emotion deep enough not to show any other way.

"What does that mean, that... I wanted it too?" Gabriel asked.

Bryan exploded. "It means that every time I see you looking at me it is like a fucking knife in my heart. I know you can't walk past me without looking at me. And you know how I know that? Think about that for a minute. How do I know you're always looking at me? Because I'm always looking at you, asshole. That's why. Did you ever think of that?" He jabbed Gabriel in the chest, knocking him back a couple of stumbling steps. "Did you?" he screamed.

Gabriel was confused. And furious. He lunged forward, closing the gap between them in an instant, red lights flashing at the edges of his vision. "What the fuck are you talking about?" he screamed back, matching Bryan's anguished tone.

"I don't want to be like you!" Bryan bellowed, sobbing. Then, without warning, he bent double and threw up, monstrously, horribly. He staggered a few steps away, then fell to his knees, gasping.

Gabriel stepped back in shock. He had no idea what he was witnessing, other than that it was the most terrifying spectacle he could imagine. Bryan retched and cried until he could make no more sound, then collapsed onto his side, panting. Gabriel reached out and put his hand on Bryan's shoulder, not knowing what else to do.

"Are you okay?" he asked lamely.

Bryan groaned and twisted his shoulder out from under Gabriel's hand. "No, I'm not fucking okay," he muttered.

Gabriel sat silently for a moment. "I don't understand any of this."

Bryan slowly brought himself upright, sitting on the grass at the top of the meadow. He gave a long sigh and spat off to the side several times. "I don't either, to be honest."

Gabriel sat down next to him. "Then tell me the parts you do understand. I'm a pretty good listener. Tell me what you can, and we'll figure out the rest."

Bryan turned and stared into Gabriel's eyes as if searching for something. "Figures," he said.

"What figures?"

"That you'd turn out to be nice."

"Thanks, I guess?" Gabriel shook his head, frustrated by his inability to understand anything Bryan said.

"I kind of hoped you'd be an asshole. That I could tell you to stop, and then you'd get pissed at me, and then I'd beat the shit out of you, and then it'd all be over."

Gabriel's mouth dropped open. "That's what you hoped for?"

For the first time, a hint of a grin showed at the corner of Bryan's mouth. "Not really." He looked down at his feet. "I guess part of me really wanted you to be amazing, but that's the part of me I have to shut down."

"Why?"

"Because I can't be like you."

Gabriel shook his head. "What does that mean?"

"I'm not gay."

"Oh." Gabriel thought this over for a moment. "So when you said you look at me as much as I look at you, what you meant was... what, exactly?"

"It means that when I see you, I imagine what it would be like to... to be like you. To be able to look at someone the way you look at me."

Gabriel was starting to see. Maybe. He wanted to help Bryan, but doing so meant exposing himself completely. Could he do that? He looked at Bryan's helpless, tear-streaked face and knew what he had to do.

"Don't you look at Cheryl that way?" There. Now he knew. It was like an analogy on a standardized test: you are to me as Cheryl is to you. Simple. And deadly.

Bryan flinched as if Gabriel had punched him in the throat. "Why would you bring her into this?"

"Because of what you said about the way I look at you. Look, I'm being completely honest with you right now, and it's scaring the shit out of me. But now I've said it, so there it is. I look at you all the time because I cannot drag my eyes away from you."

A strangled moan wrenched its way out of Bryan's throat. He blinked hard, as if forcing back tears.

"I hear your voice in the corridor and I have to stop and look for you, because I need to see what you look like today, what you're wearing and how it fits you, who you're talking to. I have to see if you're smiling or serious because both of those are beautiful." Gabriel was shivering now in the cold light of truth-telling but could not stop. "Sometimes I turn and follow you even though it makes me late for class. I walk behind you and listen to you talk to your friends, or to Cheryl, hanging on every word you say because it's you saying it. And if it's too noisy in

the hallway to hear your voice, I just watch your amazing ass and dream about getting into those jeans. So if that's what you mean about not wanting to be like me, I totally get it because it sounds like I'm the most pathetic thing in the world, and creepy too."

Bryan was shaking his head. *"No, it's not pathetic and it's not creepy. You think I haven't done that before? I spent six months following Cheryl around before she finally said she'd go out with me. I used to watch her cheerleader skirt swish back and forth and dream of getting up in there."* He looked out at the horizon, just starting to pink up.

"Okay, I'm confused again," Gabriel said.

Bryan's head whipped around, the faraway look transformed in an instant to one of hawklike intensity. *"I've been chasing girls like Cheryl my whole life. Long as I can remember. My mom has a picture on the fridge of me in preschool with my arm around a girl, and she wrote on the bottom of it 'Bryan's first girlfriend.' I don't even remember her, but I see that picture every day. But then you...."* He turned and looked back out at the horizon.

Gabriel waited a long moment. *"I... what?"*

"You came along. When I started here freshman year, I didn't know anybody— just the guys on the football team, because my dad made sure I got on the team as soon as we moved to town. You were in my math class that first year. And every time Mr. Chandler made me get up at the whiteboard and work a proof, I could feel you staring at me. Everyone else was watching to see what bonehead error the dumb football jock would make, scanning my chicken scratch for any little mistake, but you—you were watching me. I could feel your eyes boring into my biceps."

Gabriel had been about to protest when that detail about the biceps came out. Then he knew Bryan really had noticed. His secret had never been a secret.

"In my defense, have you ever seen your biceps? They are like melons that fell from the garden of the gods and landed, still round and full of divine strength, on your arms."

"All of that poetry inside you, and that's what you waste it on? My biceps?"

"I won't apologize for appreciating your biceps," Gabriel replied with something that sounded like dignity.

"That's exactly what I'm talking about, right there. That's what I could never do."

"What, write a poem about biceps?"

Bryan grunted, maybe a laugh. *"No, doofus. I could never tell a guy that I thought his biceps were sexy."*

"I don't think I used the word 'sexy,'" Gabriel replied, mirroring Bryan's sly half grin. *"But of course you wouldn't do that. You're straight. Surely you're attracted to Cheryl's biceps?"*

Bryan laughed and shook his head. *"I'm straight except when you're around,"* he whispered.

Gabriel felt the smile evaporate from his face, just as he felt the breath leave his lungs. *"What?"* he managed to huff out.

"I guess that's what I needed to tell you," Bryan said, then turned away to look at the sunset.

"I don't know what that means."

"It means," he answered without turning his face to Gabriel, "you do this to me."

"I do what to you?" Gabriel felt the frustration that had finally been relieved by their light moment of laughter returning.

"This," Bryan answered, gesturing to Gabriel, and himself, and the entire meadow in which they stood. "Do you think I would drive out to the most remote place I know to have a heart-to-heart with any other guy? You do this to me, Gabriel. I have a girlfriend. I'm on the football team. I'm a normal guy. But not when you're around. When I see you, and I see you're looking at me, it's like a door opening on another world... another life. A life I am only part of when you're around. And then once you're gone, I can't get it back, couldn't even if I wanted to."

"Are you saying you... feel the same way about me?"

Bryan shook his head. Then, like a metronome with a failing battery, his head slowed its side-to-side motion. He began to nod. "It's that, and it's more than that. When you're there, I feel more myself than any other time. Like you're leading this life of truth and opportunity, and as much as I want to follow you, I can't because I'm not you. And there are times when I wish I was." He stared at Gabriel, hard, as if blinking would break the spell of truth-telling. "I'm only gay when you're around. I'm not... that way. But you made me."

"I haven't done anything to you," Gabriel protested. "We've been at the same school for almost four years, and this is the first time we've actually talked to each other. I don't know anything about you, and you know even less about me."

"That's not true and you know it. Who was my girlfriend before Cheryl?"

"Sarah," Gabriel answered without hesitation.

"And why did we break up?"

Gabriel paused, not sure he should reveal what he knew—what he'd heard through the grapevine. "Because she cheated on you with Troy."

"That's right. And I know that you and Cameron were together for most of junior year, but you cut him loose because he got with a guy in a car after the Homecoming dance."

Gabriel blushed at the recollection, but he decided not to point out that he'd been there with Cam in the car and that their decision not to be exclusive was a direct result of Gabriel's obsession with Bryan.

"How did you know I was with Cam? We never did anything at school to make a big deal of it or anything."

"Haven't you been listening to me? I was watching you. I saw the way you two would meet up after school and walk together. The way he lit up when he saw you coming." Bryan sighed softly. "I wanted to be him. I wanted to be able to smile like that and not care who saw me. I wanted... you."

"Bryan, I don't want you to get mad, but I have to ask this." Gabriel paused, looking for agreement. Bryan finally nodded, so he continued. "If I've been dreaming about you, and you've been wishing you were with me, then why are we standing here? Why don't we grab a blanket or something out of your car and just throw down right here, give it a try?"

"Because I'm not gay."

"Look, I don't care what we call it. We can do this and not have it change who we are."

"You don't get it. When I say I'm not gay, I don't mean that I'm not attracted to you. I don't mean that I don't like musicals or interior decorating or whatever. What I mean is that out of everyone I've ever met, in my whole life, you're the only guy I've ever been attracted to. At all. And I've tried. During spring break freshman year, I was home alone for a whole day while my family went to my dad's company picnic, and I decided to test whether what you did to me in the hallway was just you being you, or if it meant I was actually gay and just didn't know it. For months I told myself it wasn't me, and that you were just this kind of demon that God sent to test my faith or something. I pulled up some gay porn—a lot of gay porn, actually—and tried it out. I must have watched a hundred guys boning each other."

"And?"

"And nothing. It did exactly nothing for me. Couldn't imagine myself doing it, wasn't turned on by it, never looked at it again."

"Well, not everyone—"

"Gets off on porn? Yeah, I thought of that. So that summer I visited my gay cousin and got him to take me with him to a party so I could meet some actual gay people."

Gabriel looked him up and down. "They must have enjoyed meeting you."

Bryan gave a mirthless chuckle. "Not that it mattered. I didn't enjoy meeting them."

"What does that mean?"

"It means that none of them were you. That's what I went there looking for. You." His eyes, accusing, bore into Gabriel. "I wanted to meet someone just like you, someone who would make me feel the way you do. But all I saw were gay guys, and I was no more interested in spending time with gay guys at that party than I was any other time. They weren't you."

"I think you met the wrong guys."

Bryan shook his head slowly. "You don't get it, do you? I'm trying to tell you that you're the only guy I've ever felt this way about. And it's not some romantic notion I've created in my head like a lovestruck girl locked in her pink bedroom drawing pictures of the latest Disney-issue heartthrob. I've thought a lot about this. I've tried to find a way around it. I've had five girlfriends in the years I've known you, and you know why I broke up with the first four? Why I'll be breaking up with Cheryl soon?"

"Oh my God," Gabriel whispered. "Why?"

"Because. Of. You."

"You can't blame me for... whatever you're talking about. I haven't done anything."

"No, it's not your fault the only time I feel sane is during the summer when I'm working landscape and don't see you. It's not your fault when you're out sick and I drive myself crazy looking around the corridor for you. It's not your fault I dream about you every fucking night whether I want to or not. And in no way could it ever possibly in a million years be your fault that when a girl is giving me a blow job and I close my eyes, I can only see you doing it." Bryan's voice had risen to a brittle pitch, a pained shout.

"It is your fault. It's you. It's you I fucking see when I'm fucking her and realize that in my head I'm fucking you!"

Bryan fell silent, panting, wild-eyed, his hands flexing into fists and releasing with a frenetic rapidity.

Gabriel's heart was pounding as hard as he imagined Bryan's was. His entire world had been upended in this peaceful meadow, the landscape seeming to fold in on him as his secret, laid bare, was trumped by the secrets that came spilling out of Bryan.

He had nothing left to lose.

"Here I am." He stood, arms extended, offering himself to the man who had been his obsession, his dream, for years. *"I'm right here. You don't have to close your eyes. You don't have to have nightmares. Whatever you want to do, just do it."*

Bryan stared, looking like Gabriel had just dared him to step off a cliff. His lips began to move.

Gabriel leaned close. *"What?"* All he could hear was Bryan's anguished breath, the sound of dry tongue sticking to teeth. He leaned closer, his ear almost touching Bryan's lips.

"I can't."

"Why not?" Gabriel asked, stepping back six inches, no more. *"I get that it's hard to take that leap, to admit for the first time that you're attracted to a guy."*

"I'm not attracted to a guy. I'm attracted to you. Only you."

Gabriel took a deep steadying breath, and put his hand on Bryan's shoulder. This time, Bryan didn't twist away. He closed his eyes and tipped his head toward Gabriel's hand, then shrugged his shoulder to brush his cheek along it. It was an electric moment.

And then it was over.

Bryan snapped back upright, eyes wide open. He stepped back, letting Gabriel's hand fall off his shoulder. *"I just need you to stop, okay? I can't do this."*

"You want this," Gabriel replied, a statement of fact. This much he knew.

"That doesn't matter." Bryan heaved a deep breath. *"I can't live a life like this."*

"A life where you get what you want?"

"No. A life where you define me. Where I don't fit anywhere except with you. I can't keep a girlfriend, and guys don't do it for me. With you in my life, I'm not complete because you define me. So I am asking you, unless you want me to end up at the end of a rope, please, please for the love of God, leave me alone. Don't look at me, don't be anywhere near me. Just leave me alone. Please?"

Gabriel hadn't known what to expect when Bryan brought him out here, but he sure wasn't expecting this whiplash—he'd been rejected, then told his crush was reciprocated, then rejected again. What did Bryan want from him?

"Just kiss him," said a voice he recognized. It was his own. He turned to see a cliché miniature version of himself dressed as a Halloween Satan. He gestured at himself with a tiny pitchfork. *"He doesn't know what he wants, and you have to show him. Just kiss him. Do it."*

"Don't throw yourself at him," another version of himself said, just as he'd expected. He turned to see a tiny Gabriel with a tinseled halo glittering above his head. *"He says he doesn't want you to touch him, and no means no."*

"*Fuck that,*" the demon Gabriel grunted. "*He knows you're going to do it anyway. He expects you to. He'll think you're a pussy if you don't do it.*"

"*Don't you dare,*" admonished Saint Gabriel. "*Be a good friend to him. Be patient. And then when he blows you, it'll be because he* wants *to.*"

The demon and angel versions of himself high-fived over his head and disappeared in a puff of purple smoke.

Gabriel shook his head to clear it. He closed his eyes for a moment, trying to formulate exactly what it was he wanted to say. Finally, he opened his eyes. Bryan stood before him, bereft, his lower lip trembling. Gabriel saw him for what he really was in that moment: a scared boy, terrified in the face of a force that, though it was within him, was alien to him and threatened to upend his life. Gabriel knew what he wanted, but he also knew that he couldn't be the thing that destroyed what Bryan wanted—needed—his life to be.

"*Look me in the eyes and tell me,*" he said quietly. "*Tell me you don't want to be with me. Tell me you don't want to be near me. Tell me....*" His voice failed, and he had to clear his throat and try to forge on. "*Tell me you never want to see me again. Tell me, and I'll go.*"

"*I can't go on like this,*" Bryan said, his voice low and soft, like a prayer. "*I can't live another day like this.*" He wiped his eyes. "*I'm sorry, Gabriel. I'm sorry I'm not strong enough. You're like a cancer I have to cut out.*"

Gabriel willed his heart to start beating again. He let the pain sear through him, the utterly brutal blow resound through his body, and then he brought himself up to full height, back straight as a ruler. He nodded to Bryan, knowing words would be too much right now, fearing he would say all of the hateful, loving, desperate, wounded things that were bouncing around inside his aching skull, his empty heart.

He turned and walked away from the meadow, toward home. He heard Bryan calling after him, but he kept walking, and when Bryan's car pulled up next to him, he began to run. He ran across the fields where the roads don't reach, away from the yawning pit that Bryan had opened under his feet. He ran until he was completely exhausted, and he kept on running anyway.

CHAPTER NINE

Overnight
Dreamwork

DONNELLY JOLTED awake. In an instant he was upright, breathing hard, every muscle straining. The pillowcase was damp, as was his cheek, and it started to come back to him. A field, a fight, a gap that could not be bridged. It had something to do with a dream. He sat for a long moment, the only sound that of his harried breath.

The room was in gentle motion, as if the sea itself were encouraging sleep. It wouldn't be coming back for Donnelly, this much he knew.

The dream had shattered with his awakening into shards of emotion—mostly dread—that he would never fully be able to reconstruct.

Not that he wanted to.

He got up and put on a robe. In the dim night-light, he found his way to the door and opened it slowly, listening for the sound of breathing—or something more strenuous—but heard nothing. Sandler must not be back yet. Donnelly padded across the floor to the balcony doors, then slipped out into the night.

At the balcony rail, he looked up into a moonless sky that twinkled with more stars than he had ever seen. Somehow, seeing himself to be an infinitesimal part of such a vast universe calmed him a little. He took a deep breath of the sea air and let it out slowly.

BRANDT FELT Kerry pull back the covers and slip into bed, wafting along with her the rich perfume of the bubble bath provided by the hotel. He knew exactly what would come next: she would take three slow breaths, then sigh deeply, clutch her pillow to her chest, and fall right into a peaceful slumber.

He listened to her long, regular breaths, envying her for the effortless way she fit into the world. Her relationships with men might be complicated, at times, and she certainly had made some bad choices in the past, but she knew what she was looking for, and what would make her happy. All she needed was one good straight guy and a host of gay ones and her life would be complete.

That was what Donnelly had, he realized as he stared at the ceiling. Would that be enough for him?

As gently as he could, he pulled back the covers and slipped out of bed. He picked up his robe from a chair, tied the sash around his waist, and tiptoed to the balcony doors.

The streets of Paris at this hour were mostly empty, though the odd flower-delivery truck plied its trade far below. The Arc de Triomphe glowed in golden floodlight to one side while the top of the Eiffel Tower stabbed into the sky on the other. He stood for a long while, leaning against the ornately carved balcony railing, wondering how everyone else in the world seemed to be able to go about their daily lives free of the agonizing self-reflection with which he was saddled lately.

If only Donnelly were here, he thought. If only.

DONNELLY TURNED away from the rail and sat down on one of the plush loungers. He lay back and cast a lonesome look at the empty lounger next to him, the one that Brandt should have been lying on right now. He reached out his hand and stroked the cushion, imagining what it would be like to share this balcony, this star-filled sky, with him. It was what he wanted more than anything in the world.

A chill ran down him.

Was this what Brandt would want? Something in the back of his mind—a fragment of the nightmare that awakened him?—tugged at him with the heaviness of doubt, of dread. A straight man in the honeymoon suite with another man—the very idea was ridiculous.

Donnelly knew he was the only man Brandt had ever loved, or even felt attracted to. He was, in this sense, unique. Donnelly had somehow convinced himself that his unicorn status made their love special, unprecedented, impervious.

But here, tonight, staring at the empty chaise next to him, it felt empty, deluded, impossible.

When he looked back up at the sky, the stars had blurred.

BRANDT STEPPED back from the railing and lowered himself onto one of the ornate wrought-iron chaise lounges—the very one on which he had spent his first sleepless night in Paris. From here, with the monument floodlights blocked by the stone balcony wall, he could see the few stars that were visible through the glare of the city.

Across the balcony, the mate to the chaise he sat on lay unoccupied, as it had since they arrived from across an ocean.

Donnelly should be here.

Brandt flashed back to the football pitch at the park this morning, and how he would always be the one who sticks out, the one who isn't like the others. He would always be the straight man, and he was only now starting to feel that he had reached his peace with that reality.

But what about Donnelly? Didn't he deserve to have a partner with whom he shared something as basic as sexuality? Was it fair to saddle him with the only straight guy?

He wanted Donnelly here. But is that what was best for him?

Entre'Acte

ACROSS THE sky, a shooting star left a golden, sparkling tail in its wake.

He watched it cross the night, blazing, spectral, miraculous.

"I wish…," he said, closing his eyes and yearning with his whole heart, "to be the one who makes him happy."

CHAPTER TEN

Morning Light
Waking

"GABRIEL?" SANDLER stepped out onto the balcony. "You out here?"

Donnelly stirred, shaking off the restless drowse he had fallen into. "Yeah—yeah, I'm here. What time is it?"

"Almost two. Were you planning on sleeping out here?"

Donnelly rubbed his face, trying to clear his head of sleep and the shards of that nightmare. "No, I must have just dozed off. Came out here to look at the stars and be miserable for a bit."

Sandler sat down on the other lounger. Brandt's lounger, Donnelly thought. "Gabriel Donnelly, miserable?" He looked back at the door to the suite. "I must have stepped into an alternate universe."

"Sorry. I had this awful nightmare and couldn't shake it off."

"What was it about?"

"Well, as Freud was fond of saying, dreams aren't about what they are actually about. I was back in high school, I think, but I was completely different. I... I was gay, I think. In high school, I mean."

"Ah. From what you've told me about the town you grew up in, I imagine it didn't go smoothly."

Donnelly considered this for a moment, wondering whether the rattled state in which he'd woken up had been due to a dream of being bullied or worse. But that didn't seem to be it. "No, it didn't, but not because I was gay. I think it was because I'd fallen in love with a straight guy."

Sandler looked at him skeptically. "I would say that's the oldest sob story in the book, but then again you are in love with a straight guy in real life, and the two of you seem nauseatingly happy, so what do I know?"

"I don't think it was working out quite as well in the dream." Donnelly closed his eyes, trying to will the dream back into his consciousness. "I'm trying to piece it together, but there's only one thing I can really remember. At one point he said to me, 'you're a cancer I have to cut out.'"

"Ouch," Sandler replied. "So, not a very romantic ending."

"No." Donnelly studied the hem of his robe for a moment. "I guess I must be working through some stuff, huh?"

"Or you're missing him so much that you're spending all night worst-casing your relationship."

Donnelly rolled his eyes. Plotting out the worst-case scenario was usually Brandt's job. "I just hope I can be the person he needs—the person he wants to spend his life with."

"I think he told you that when he accepted your proposal."

"But I can't give him what he could get if he were with a woman."

Sandler shook his head. "You can't give him love? Commitment? A best friend? Amazing sex? I just don't see what he'd be missing by choosing you over any woman in the world. He's lucky to have you."

"I'm the lucky one. But he's straight—how long will my luck hold? How can he really want to be with me?"

Sandler took a deep breath, and his voice was calm and even. "Gabriel, you need to listen to me. Ethan chose you. He *chose* you over everyone else in the world, regardless of gender. He didn't just end up with you because you fit the general model of what he was looking for in life—he chose you because you make him happy. Honestly, I'd rather be with someone because they chose me, not because we look good on paper, or because our sexual orientations aligned perfectly. Everyone I've ever been with after Trevor has been out of convenience. We happened to be in town at the same time, or shared a cab and hit it off. We fit each other's opportunity, and it lasted as long as a layover. Trevor, though—he chose me, and we discovered who we are together. Ethan's with you because you awakened something in each other, something that only the two of you understand. You did that. You're not a cancer—you're a four-leaf clover, you're a unicorn, you're what he didn't know he was looking for. But he found you, and he chose you. Take a deep breath and let that soak in. He's with you only because he wants to be, not because you are what he was programmed to find."

Donnelly consulted the stars for a long moment, looking up into the depths of the universe. "There's a part of me that knows you're right—"

"Yes, yes I am," Sandler added with a grin.

"But I'm coming to realize there will always be a part of me that's going to worry about whether I'm the right person for him."

Sandler sighed. "That's life, buddy. We don't get any iron-clad guarantees, and even marriage licenses aren't carved in stone. But I'm convinced that knowing that is more than half the battle. He's been honest with you that his sexuality doesn't fit into a tidy little box. Don't view that as a problem, view it as a blessing. No one's sexuality is tidy, but almost no one is honest about it. Love him for all that he brings, and he will do the same. Because you are beautiful and amazing, and he knows he's the lucky one."

Donnelly smiled, embarrassed at the flattery but warmed by it as well. "Thanks," he said softly. "Thanks for being here to coach me through my midnight doubts." He stood and stretched. "I should get back to bed. Is Ankur coming over?"

"He should be here any minute."

"You two have fun."

"We almost always do," Sandler replied with a wink.

"I THOUGHT we were over the whole 'sleeping on the balcony' thing," Kerry said, crouching near Brandt and holding out a cup of coffee.

"If it makes any difference, I didn't sleep much," he replied.

She sat back on her heels and regarded him quizzically. "You, Ethan Brandt, are a puzzle. Your face to the world is the epitome of stoic masculinity, but dark complexities roil under the surface."

"That's far too Proustian a sentence for this hour of the morning."

"Sorry. I dated a poet once who told me that I roiled. I've been waiting to use it on someone."

Brandt chuckled. "Well, I would never have called anyone 'Proustian' before Gabriel told me what it meant."

"What does it mean?" she asked, hiking herself up onto the lounger next to his.

"I don't remember. The way he said it was so sexy that I kind of got distracted. Then by the time we were in the shower, I was too embarrassed to ask."

She laughed, but there was a sharper gleam in her eye. "It means a lot to you, doesn't it, what he thinks of you?"

It was not the sort of question one expects first thing in the morning, on a balcony in Paris.

He sipped and considered. "Of course it does," he replied, a little lamely. "Everything he thinks means a lot to me."

"But you're most concerned about what he thinks of *you*," she said, driving the point home with a poke of her finger.

He looked down at her finger pressed against his chest with no idea what to say.

"It's because you're straight, isn't it?"

He closed his eyes and sighed. It never got easier, explaining how he occupied the empty space at the middle of the Venn diagram of sexual identities.

"Don't give me that dramatic closed-eye sigh, mister. I get it."

"Please, then," he replied ironically, "enlighten me as to the nature of my struggle."

"I thought you'd never ask," she said brightly. "Okay, here's how I see it. First, you are in love with Gabriel, who happens to be gay. Second, you yourself are straight. Now, if I were to put myself in Gabriel's place—just as a thought experiment, not because I've been sleeping with you every night tortured by the presence of that perfect body next to me—about to be married to a man who, though he assures me he loves me, nonetheless describes himself as straight, what would I be feeling?"

He looked expectantly at her. Even if this wasn't a rhetorical question, there was no way he was going to go anywhere near it.

Luckily, she picked up without waiting for a response. "Would I be wondering whether he really loved me? Would I be concerned that he was in denial about his true sexuality, and I would someday soon find myself alone?"

This time she waited for a response.

"I think that's exactly what you'd be feeling," he answered, unable to keep a note of despair out of his voice.

She leaned over toward him. "You'd be wrong," she whispered.

"How do you figure that?"

"I figure that because Gabriel's a grown-up." She sat back and regarded him over her cup of coffee. "Look, I just got out of a marriage that will always rank as one of the worst mistakes I've ever made. The recently departed Mr. Stansfield—may Satan take him—entered into our nuptial commitment with every assurance that he would be, always and forever, the man he claimed to be—the man I took him to be. And do you know the worst part?"

He shook his head, suspecting there was no good way to answer this question.

"I should have seen it coming."

"That's easy to say now, but—"

"No, don't," she interrupted, her expression momentarily dulled by what looked like regret. "I don't mean that I should have believed what Greg warned me about. I mean that I should have listened to what my fiancé said to me. When he talked about what we were to each other, about what it meant to him to be married, it was never really about him and me. He waxed poetic about the institution of marriage, about the life we would be building together, about the importance of buying real estate in good school districts. But he never—not once, ever—talked about the personal commitment he was making. To me. To our marriage."

She sighed and looked into the distance for a moment.

"I know no one's perfect. I'm a big girl, and I can accept that everyone's got their faults. But what I didn't do was insist that he acknowledge his failings so we could build a marriage on a mutual understanding. What I got from him was platitudes—Hallmark-card sentiments about marriage. He never once told me how he was going to love me—for me—even though he had his own demons to face down. I will never again—" Her voice broke, and she closed her eyes for a moment before continuing. "I will never again enter into a commitment with someone who won't talk openly, honestly, about the foundation of that commitment, its challenges as well as its rewards."

"I'm so sorry, Kerry," Brandt said.

She shook her head. "I'm not telling you all of this to give you a big sob story. I'm telling you this so you know the emotional calculus Gabriel is running in his head. He knows you're straight, but he also knows you're committed to him. He knows he's the only man for you. He knows how much he means to you. And he's a big boy, going into marriage with his eyes open. Now," she said, taking his hand in hers, "this is the important bit. You are *both* going into this with eyes open. You've been honest with him, and he knows you're not hiding anything. And if at some point in the future you struggle with your sexuality, you can talk to him about it. You can work through it together. That's the commitment you'll be making next week when you stand at the altar with him. You're not committing to a perfect marriage; you're committing to working together to make your marriage work. That's the best foundation on which anyone can build a relationship, Ethan. Honesty, and commitment, and love. You are putting the best of yourself into your marriage. Never doubt that."

Brandt tried to take in all that Kerry had told him. It ran—as advice that derives from lived experience often does—contrary to what one was accustomed to hearing on the topic of marriage. But it did make him feel better.

"Thank you," he said, squeezing her hand. "I can't tell you how much you've helped me."

"All part of the deluxe Paris package," she replied with a laugh. "Baguettes and psychotherapy provided daily."

"So, this ex of yours…."

"What did he do to make me drop him like a hot rock?" she asked.

"I'd understand if you don't want to—"

"Would it surprise you to hear it had to do with sex?"

"Not really."

"Well, hold on to your croissant, because you're not going to believe this," Kerry began.

CHAPTER ELEVEN

Friday
Morning, at sea

"GABRIEL? GABRIEL, wake up."

Donnelly rolled onto his back and tried to open his eyes. Not much luck.

"Gabriel, the pouch is gone."

Donnelly was bolt upright in a split second. "What? Was there someone in the room? Was the safe pried open? Are you okay?"

Sandler dashed back out of the bedroom. "The safe was locked," he called, "but when I opened it this morning, it was empty."

"When did you last check it?" Donnelly was tying his robe as he ran into the room.

"Last night before I went to sleep. The pouch was still there."

Donnelly scanned the room, instinctively looking for signs of forced entry, but saw nothing out of place. He knew he should be delicate about asking this next question, but there was no time. "Was Ankur still here?"

Sandler's face was instantly clouded with anger. "Yes, he was still here. He just left, in fact."

"When was that?"

"About ten minutes ago."

"Was he carrying anything?"

"Are you serious?" Sandler's voice was getting louder. "The pouch has been stolen and the only thing you can do is accuse Ankur of taking it?"

"I'm not accusing anyone of anything," Donnelly replied, his voice conspicuously calm. "I'm just trying to get a sense of what happened. That's all."

"Fine," Sandler spat. He was clearly rattled by the theft, and Donnelly took no offense at his tone. "Ankur and I got sleepy around four. He got up to go to the bathroom, and that's when I checked the safe."

"Did he see you open it?"

"Ankur didn't steal the pouch, Gabriel."

"I'm not saying he did. I'm just trying to get a complete picture."

"Sorry, right," Sandler said with a despairing sigh. He rubbed his brow for a moment. "No, he wasn't with me any of the times I opened it."

"Okay. So he came back to bed, and then what?"

"I went to the bathroom, and then we fell asleep."

"And this morning?"

"He must have woken up before I did. He sat down on the edge of the bed and stroked the side of my face. He kissed me and said he'd see me tonight. Then he left."

"Did you watch him go?"

"Of course I watched him go. You know how he leaves a room."

"I'm going to ask this again. Please don't get upset, because it's important. Was he carrying anything when he left?"

Sandler bit his lip and squinted. Then a slow realization seemed to break across his face.

"What?" Donnelly asked. "What is it?"

"Oh, fuck."

Donnelly waited, his instincts telling him that questions wouldn't help at the moment.

"No. No, it—" Sandler stammered, his face growing red. "No. No, no, no. No!" He shook his head violently, then staggered back and fell onto the sofa. "Fuck."

Donnelly sat down next to him and waited.

Sandler took a deep breath. It didn't seem to be helping to calm him. "Ankur said…," he began, but then lost the thread and fell silent, shaking his head and mouthing "no," over and over again.

"What did Ankur say?"

Sandler grunted out a frustrated breath, then finally found his voice. "He said he noticed yesterday on the balcony that the cover on one of the seat cushions was splitting. So this morning he went out and got it so he could take it to the upholstery shop. He left with it."

Donnelly nodded. "Was the cushion large enough to hide the pouch in?"

Sandler nodded. "It was from one of the big chaise lounges." He cast a woeful look out through the balcony windows. "I can't believe he would do this."

"We don't know he did anything," Donnelly said, getting to his feet. "All we know is that he left here with a lounge cushion. We can't assume that he's guilty just because of that."

Sandler looked at him in surprise. "I figured you of all people would assume exactly that."

"Me of all people?" Donnelly repeated, bristling a little at the insinuation.

"You know, being a police officer and all."

"It may surprise you to know that police officers are the people who make 'innocent until proven guilty' happen. We take this stuff pretty seriously."

Sandler seemed to realize he was being kind of an asshole. "Sorry, Gabriel. I know you're not going to jump to conclusions. I've just never lost a pouch before. Sorry."

"Well, you may console yourself with the fact that whoever stole the pouch is not going to get far. We have three more days before we dock in Southampton, and until then, our thief isn't going anywhere."

"I hadn't thought of that," Sandler said, finally seeming able to get his breathing under control. "So, what do we do first?"

"Call Rutherford, and tell him the safe's been broken into, and ask him to send security to the suite. You can leave Ankur out of it for now—no sense involving him unless we need to. I'm going to grab a quick shower."

"Okay." Sandler picked up the phone receiver, his finger poised over Rutherford's call button. "Thank you for being here to help me."

"Happy to return the favor." Donnelly stepped into the bedroom, then leaned his head back out the doorway. "Oh, and one more crucial aspect of police work—can you ask Rutherford for some coffee?"

Sandler smiled for the first time this morning as he waited for Rutherford to pick up. "You got it, Officer."

Donnelly was thankful that Brandt's constant hectoring about the length of his showers had accustomed him to racing from lather to towel in under three minutes. He was shaved and dressed before Rutherford had even shown up with the coffee. The doorbell rang as he walked into the living room to find Sandler standing exactly where he'd left him: directly in front of the safe, looking ruefully at its empty interior.

"Ready?" Donnelly asked as he went to the door. When he saw Sandler nod, he pulled the door open.

It was Rutherford with a tray of coffee and a look of shocked concern on his face. "Sir, I most humbly apologize on behalf of the entire ship's crew. Such an occurrence is quite simply unheard of."

"We of course do not hold you or any member of the crew responsible," Donnelly replied, standing aside to allow the butler entrance to the room. "And a cup of coffee will do wonders to overcome the unpleasant surprise we've had this morning." To his delight, Rutherford set the tray down and in seconds had placed a steaming cup of strong black coffee in his hand. "Sandler, you should have some. Nothing like it to clear the mind."

"I just cannot believe it," Sandler replied, still staring into the safe. He turned to take the cup of coffee Rutherford offered. "Thank you," he said distractedly, then took a sip and resumed his vigil.

Rutherford looked positively pained to not have delighted Sandler with his coffee. Donnelly shrugged consolingly and took one of the small pastries Rutherford had brought along. It was, as usual, delicious.

The door chime rang just as Donnelly finished chewing his second pastry, and Rutherford opened it immediately.

"Sir," he said deferentially, and stood aside to admit a tall man with short-cropped salt-and-pepper hair and three gold bars on his epaulets.

"Rutherford, good to see you," the man said as he strode into the room.

"And you, sir."

"Misters Donnelly and Birkin, I presume?" He extended a hand to Donnelly and smiled warmly.

"I'm Gabriel Donnelly." They shook hands.

"Chief Security Officer Robert Lyndon. Pleased to meet you, and I'm sorry it's not under better circumstances."

Sandler stepped forward and extended his hand. "Sandler Birkin." His voice was stronger than it had been all morning, perhaps resonating with Lyndon's military bearing.

"I understand the article that is missing belonged to you?" Lyndon asked, stepping over to the safe. He squatted down to look inside.

"Not exactly," Sandler replied. "I am serving in the capacity of a diplomatic courier, and what is missing is a diplomatic pouch."

Lyndon rose quickly, his brow furrowed. "I see." He pursed his lips and looked down at the carpet for a long moment. When he looked up, his face had regained its composure. "Rutherford, two things. First, may I have a cup of your wonderful coffee?"

Rutherford poured, the seriousness of the situation competing with the compliment on his coffee for dominance in his facial expression. He handed Lyndon a cup on a saucer.

"Thank you. Second, could you ask Ankur Ramavastava to join us, please? He's waitstaff, forward."

Rutherford blinked twice, but then nodded, turned on his heel, and left the room.

The thump of Sandler's coffee cup hitting the side table startled Donnelly, who turned to see Sandler sink to the sofa, his face pale. He tried to speak, but though his mouth moved, no sound emerged.

"I would not presume to impose upon your privacy," Lyndon began gently. "But when Rutherford called me about a possible theft, I reviewed the security camera footage from the hallways outside your suite. It's standard procedure when a theft occurs. I noted Mr. Ramavastava's departure from the suite this morning and then pulled the recordings from last night. He appears to have accompanied you, Mr. Birkin, to this suite last night, as he had the two preceding nights. Is that true?"

Sandler, still ashen, nodded.

"I see. Is Mr. Ramavastava aware of your job as a diplomatic courier?"

Sandler shook his head.

"Had you at any point mentioned the contents of the safe?"

Sandler shook his head again.

"Did you leave Mr. Ramavastava alone in the suite at any point, even for a brief time?"

"Only for a minute or two at a time, when I was in the bathroom. But he was up before I was this morning—I don't know how long."

Lyndon nodded. "When Mr. Ramavastava left the suite this morning, he was carrying something rather bulky. Do you know what that was?"

"A cushion from one of the lounges on the balcony. It was splitting open, and he took it to the upholstery shop to be resewn."

"I see." Lyndon's expression was utterly unchanged. "Has anyone else been in the suite that you are aware of?"

"Just Rutherford, Ankur, and us," Donnelly replied.

Lyndon nodded. He took a deep breath, and when he turned back to Sandler his tone was light and conversational. "As you may be aware, Mr. Birkin, the diplomatic service makes up a far larger portion of our passengers on this voyage than is customary. We have diplomats from twenty-three countries on board, including some from countries who, one might say, are not on the best of terms. There have been some tense moments, particularly when a football match is underway, but this theft is unprecedented."

"Do you suspect this is a diplomatic incident rather than a simple theft?" Donnelly asked.

"I don't think we have enough information to make a judgment on that at this time," Lyndon said, using what was clearly a stock phrase for meetings such as this. "But I will say, given the incidents we've already seen, that it is a theory I'll be investigating."

"And will you also be investigating Ankur?" Sandler asked. "I can't believe he had anything to do with this."

"Mr. Birkin, one thing you must understand about discipline aboard a ship—"

Lyndon was interrupted by the doorbell announcing the arrival of Rutherford, followed closely by Ankur, who was clearly terrified.

"Mr. Ramavastava, please, come in." Lyndon's manner was warm, and he smiled politely.

Ankur stepped forward timidly, looking furtively around the room until he caught Sandler's eye. Tears welled immediately, and he shook his head as if to plead his innocence.

"Mr. Ramavastava—Ankur—do you know why you are here?"

Ankur swallowed visibly. "Mr. Rutherford said something has been stolen."

"Now, Ankur, I know you've spent the night in this suite for the last three nights."

A stifled cry made Ankur's distress apparent to everyone in the room. He nodded, tears running freely down his cheeks.

"Have you, during that time, noticed anyone or anything unusual, either in the room or in the hallways?"

Ankur's surprise was evident, as if he'd been expecting an accusation rather than a question. He gaped at Lyndon, an expression mimicked precisely by Sandler.

Lyndon chuckled warmly. "You look as though I were going to have you brought up on sodomy charges and given forty lashes at sunrise. Come now. We're all adults here."

"So Ankur's not in trouble for spending the night here?" Sandler asked.

"No," Lyndon replied. "We don't encourage such behavior, of course, but neither do we punish it. That Ankur was discreet speaks well to his character. We have had some young seamen who seem to relish gossiping about their relations with passengers more than they do the relations themselves. We quickly suggested other employment for them, off the ship."

"But is Ankur still under suspicion?" Donnelly asked.

"Not any longer. While we've been talking, my staff has been reviewing the security footage in detail, and they have updated me on their findings," he said, tapping his ear, from which a coiled wire could be seen running from a device in his ear down the back of his dress uniform. "They have observed that upon leaving this suite, Ankur made his way directly to the upholstery shop, where he deposited the cushion. The cushion has been examined, and there was nothing secreted inside it. We have also confirmed that upon leaving the shop, he went immediately to breakfast, where Mr. Rutherford found him. I have no evidence whatsoever that links Ankur to the theft."

Ankur very nearly collapsed upon hearing this news, and Sandler joined him on the couch, putting his arm around the trembling man.

"However, we may yet have questions for you, young man, relating to this case. In the meantime, I ask that you not mention the theft to anyone, crew or passenger. I'd like to have some time to gather information before this becomes widely known."

"Of course, sir," Ankur assured him.

"If I may ask the same of you, Mr. Birkin? Mr. Donnelly?"

"Yes, of course," Donnelly said, while Sandler winced a bit.

"I will have to let the protocol officer know," Sandler said. "Losing a pouch is a pretty big deal."

Lyndon nodded. "Of course." He pulled a card out of his shirt pocket and wrote a number on it. "He's in this cabin," he said as he handed Sandler the card. "The ship's operator will connect you."

"Thank you," Sandler said with a sigh. "This is going to be a tough call to make."

"Please assure him that while I acknowledge that this is an unfortunate situation, I have every confidence that we will resolve the matter before we arrive in England."

"I'm sure you'll do your best," Sandler said, shaking Lyndon's hand.

"We shall, sir. We shall." Lyndon shook Donnelly's hand as well. He strode purposefully from the room, followed by Rutherford, who bowed to the men before walking backward out the door.

"I am so sorry," Ankur blurted, his voice a tremulous wail.

Sandler wrapped both arms around him and held him close. "Shh. You have nothing to be sorry for. I know you weren't involved in this."

Sandler's assurance seemed only to unleash greater desolation in Ankur, who dissolved into sobs on his shoulder. They sat, entwined, for several long moments.

Finally, as Donnelly poured his third cup of coffee—trying to focus on the view out the window rather than on the canoodling couple—Ankur disentangled himself from Sandler's embrace and wiped his cheeks. "I must be getting to work," he said sadly.

"And I must as well," Sandler replied. "I need to start asking some subtle questions of my colleagues in the diplomatic service. It's all very well for Lyndon to wish for silence, but no one gossips with such ruthless efficiency as diplomats do. Word of the theft will be all over the ship by noon."

"Then we should get out there and make some inquiries before it becomes common knowledge," Donnelly said.

"Will I see you again?" Ankur asked, his voice small and a bit hopeless.

"Of course you will," Sandler replied. "We'll meet at the usual. I'm not going to let anything as trivial as a treaty violation come between us."

Ankur smiled, sweet and innocent, and Sandler kissed him delicately on the nose.

"Until tonight," Ankur said as he stepped to the door. He let himself out and shut the door behind him.

"Well, this has been quite a morning," Sandler said once Ankur had gone.

"And we have more ahead," Donnelly replied. "Gonna grab a shower before we head out?"

"Is that a hint?" Sandler asked, deadpan, as he sniffed his armpit.

"Of course not. I just thought you might want to freshen up before we go talk to all of the ambassadors. Is what I'm wearing okay?"

Sandler laughed. "You're fine—we're not being presented at court. Diplomats love the frippery and pomp of protocol, but once they're off the clock, they're pretty much regular people. From what I've seen, they've been treating this trip like a vacation, drinking too much and lounging around speculating on partisan voting patterns in sub-Saharan parliamentary by-elections."

Donnelly wrinkled his nose. "Sounds delightful. Now hurry up—I simply cannot face an ambassador without blueberry pancakes."

AS THEY exited the restaurant—after blueberry pancakes, of course—Sandler stopped for brief conversations at four different tables. Donnelly dutifully waited in the foyer for these hushed confabs to conclude, which they did in just a few minutes.

Sandler emerged from the restaurant and pointed down the colonnaded corridor to the aft of the ship. "Apparently there's a card room that's pretty much been taken over by the staff of several embassies. One of them may have been interested in that pouch."

"You didn't tell me how it went with the protocol officer," Donnelly said as they strode purposefully along the corridor. "I did my best not to listen in."

"He was, naturally, upset," Sandler replied, "as much about the theft as about my being the one who let it get swiped. I guess my record helped me out there—this is the first one I've ever lost."

"You were robbed," Donnelly said seriously. "You didn't lose it. Someone stole it from you."

"Still, it's not something anyone likes to have happen."

They walked along awhile. "Did he say anything about what you should do about it?"

"I told him Lyndon was on it, and that I'd be working whatever contacts I could find on the ship. He seemed okay with letting it go for a couple of days. But if we don't find it before we arrive, I think he's going to pat down every passenger personally."

"Sounds like fun. Let's hope it doesn't come to that."

"I have a few tricks up my sleeve," Sandler said, smiling for the first time this morning.

They arrived at the ornately carved doors of the card room, and Sandler grasped the massive brass handle and pulled. The room within was hushed and rather dimly lit for card playing. Heavy tapestries hung on the walls, and rich velvet curtains marked the placement of what were probably windows. The occupants of the room sat in knots of threes and fours, and many cast suspicious eyes at the doorway. No one was holding cards.

"Fun group," Donnelly whispered.

Sandler nodded but made no reply. He stepped into the room and looked purposefully about, seeming unaware of all of the eyes turned toward him. A quick nod let Donnelly know he had found the person he came to speak to, and he stepped briskly across the room, smiling widely. Donnelly kept right with him, a half step behind.

Sandler approached a group of three men sitting in closely drawn club chairs. Two of them held cups of tea in both hands as if partaking in a ritual of some kind while the one in the middle held a small leather-bound notebook, which he quickly but casually closed as he looked up with a practiced smile.

"Sandler," the man said softly, in a voice that seemed to Donnelly's ear that of a serpent rather than a diplomat, "what a delightful surprise to find you here."

"Oswald," Sandler replied with a perfunctory nod. "It's a pity I didn't know you were on board until this morning. We should be better friends than that."

"Yes," Oswald said with a soft sibilance. "We should be. There was, of course, talk of your being on board, if only because of the rarefied circles in which you have placed yourself. And this must be your… escort?" Oswald's milky blue eyes rolled in a graceful arc toward Donnelly but wasted no time looking at him before sweeping back to Sandler. It was the kind of glance one might give a precocious child—meant to acknowledge but not encourage.

"This is Gabriel," Sandler said. "He generously offered me passage when his partner was unable to make the trip."

"How lucky for you," Oswald replied, and this time cast a more serious glance at Donnelly from his head down. Donnelly suddenly felt naked under the man's scrutiny. "One imagines such a passage to be quite… pleasant."

Sandler yielded no acknowledgment of Oswald's insinuation. "Gabriel, this is Oswald. He's something of an attaché at-large, offering his services to governments unable to fully staff their own embassies."

Oswald gave a wan smile, devoid of both joy and modesty. "I do what I can to foster diplomatic relations."

"Pleased to meet you," Donnelly replied. It was as pure a lie as he had ever told.

"Now, what's this I hear," Oswald said, turning back to Sandler, "about a"—he leaned forward and whispered—"pouch going missing?"

Sandler smiled stoically, as one might when a cancer patient makes a joke. "Funny you should mention that," he said. "It's why I've sought you out. I figured that on a ship full of scheming, self-serving diplomats, you would naturally be the one with the best information."

The corners of Oswald's artificial smile hardened as if he were biting them, but he didn't so much as bat an eye. "I am flattered, dear friend. Flattered indeed."

"I'm sure you are, dear friend," Sandler replied through a smile just as tight.

"As it happens," Oswald mused, fingers idly tracing the razor crease of his trousers, "I heard something just this morning in the sauna." He looked up at Sandler. "I do love to start the day with a brisk massage and a sauna. So invigorating. If you are interested, I would be happy to share with you the name of the best masseur on the ship. And in exchange you might provide me the name of a service professional who meets your needs—a bar waiter, perhaps?" He smiled, and Donnelly half expected a forked tongue to flick out from between his tight, thin lips.

Sandler didn't acknowledge the jab. "You were saying you'd heard something this morning?"

"Ah yes, let me see." Oswald adopted the posture of a man trying to remember something of little importance to himself but of great value to his listener. "Someone—I simply don't recall who—mentioned that several of the ship's crew were quite violently attached to a rather repressive military figure in their native country and had been seen slipping out of the stateroom of its embassy staff quite late at night. They were apparently able to elude the notice of the ship's security cameras due to their knowledge of monitoring schedules and motion sensor placement." He shrugged. "It all sounded very complicated and frankly uninteresting. I've simply never had much experience with spiriting crew members out of my room in the wee hours of the morning." He blinked innocently up at Sandler.

"Yes, your life has been rather monastic that way, hasn't it?" Sandler said, pity thickly layered on his voice. He suddenly drew himself up to full height. "Well, thank you for that snippet of information, Oswald. It's not much, but it's better than we had before."

Donnelly considered this to be an unfair, and frankly rather rude, summation of their conversation, but he immediately saw he had misjudged Sandler's intent in offering it. Oswald, clearly stung by having his sauna-gathered gossip dismissed so coldly, recoiled like a dowager empress smelling a fart.

"There *is* one more thing," he said peevishly.

Sandler had already turned to take his leave, but now he swiveled gracefully back, a smile springing to his lips in a flash of insincerity. His expression was one of polite impatience laced with low expectations.

"If I were ever to misplace a pouch," he began, then paused to roll his eyes theatrically at the *very idea*. "My first order of business would be to speak with the ones who committed it to my care. No one simply *steals* a pouch, Sandler, and it hasn't walked off by itself. It's highly likely the person holding its leash works for the same government that gave it to you. Their motives, however, may well diverge significantly from the official ones."

Sandler blinked slowly, twice, as if letting this information wash gently over him. Then his expression was all diplomacy once again. "Thank you, Oswald. You've been more help than you know, and certainly more than you intended. Enjoy the rest of your cruise." Sandler turned briskly to Donnelly. "Shall we?"

Donnelly nodded, uncertain that he had understood any of what had just transpired. The men walked from the card room, Sandler leading the way back amidships. At one point Donnelly began to ask a question, but Sandler motioned that they should wait a moment until they reached the door to the promenade that circled the entire ship. They stepped out onto the sheltered deck, across which blew a cutting North Atlantic wind. Sandler began to walk the deck, and Donnelly fell into step beside him.

"I'm not going to be so paranoid as to think that our suite is bugged," Sandler said. "But on the off chance, I thought this might be more... secure."

"Difficult to eavesdrop on an entire deck," Donnelly replied. A quick look fore and aft confirmed that they were completely alone. "So did you get what you needed from that Oswald guy?" He shivered at the memory. "He kind of gave me the creeps, to be honest."

Sandler laughed. "He has that effect on pretty much everyone. Oswald makes his living by being indispensable at precisely the right moment. No one would choose to spend any time with him, except when he's the only one who can get something done. He's kind of a fixer for the diplomatic community. He knows everyone, and more importantly than that, he knows the dirt on everyone. Luckily he's the soul of discretion—at least until his secrets are worth more than his silence."

"Sounds like a great guy."

Sandler shrugged grimly. "He's a necessary guy. Sometimes things just need to get done, and he's usually the one who can do them. I met him years ago when relations between Britain and Ecuador were strained, resulting in my being held in a windowless office at the airport in Quito for a day and a half. Oswald showed up and had a word with the customs agents, and within twenty minutes I was on my way. I'd never seen anything like it. I asked him to have a drink with me at the hotel bar after I'd delivered my pouch, and he nursed one glass of absinthe for two full hours. He has the rare gift of telling stories of great intrigue that reveal nothing but his own prowess. He told me things that were quite frankly impossible, and I let him rattle on because he had freed me from that horrible little room."

They rounded the bow and began to walk back down the other side of the ship. After a quick glance around to confirm they were still alone, Sandler continued his tale.

"I asked around about some of the stories he told me and found he'd not embroidered anything but his own panache—he styled himself rather a James Bond, suave and dangerous. But the substance of his stories checked out, and it was honestly terrifying to have spent two hours in the presence of anyone who had seen, and done, the things he had. That kind of thing would have to hollow a man out after a while." Sandler gave a shiver, as if recalling specific instances of Oswald's hollow nature. "Well, he must have gotten up to even worse after that conversation, because the higher echelon of diplomatic missions won't have anything to do with him anymore; these days he puts his unique skill set at the disposal of smaller, more desperate governments who need a problem fixed and aren't terribly particular about his methods."

"Are we talking about crimes-against-humanity kind of stuff here?" Donnelly asked, wincing.

"No, nothing as blatant as that. But he has definitely made it easier for people who commit such crimes to remain in power."

Donnelly shivered as he came to realize they'd had an audience with the devil himself, or at least one of his devoted demons. He shook it off as quickly as he could. "So, what's the plan?"

"As vile as that little fiend is, he generally has good information. Not that bit about political unrest in a distant land causing ninja-like antics among the crew—that part was simply Oswald having a bit of fun with us."

"Why would he make up something like that?"

"Oswald is like a snake. He's only going to do the hard work of slithering up onto a warm rock if he's going to get something out of it. He wants us to poke around and make some trouble for those crew members, and I don't much care why he wants it. Lyndon didn't strike me as the kind of person who would countenance such shenanigans, so I think the whole story is highly unlikely. But the second part, that's what's got me worried."

"You think someone from the British government took the pouch so it couldn't be delivered to the British government?"

"That's exactly what I'm thinking. The diplomats on this ship may all have divergent views on how the world should be arranged, but all of them absolutely depend on the sanctity of the diplomatic pouch. That's why Oswald made up that story about the crew being under the sway of a rebel movement. He knew I wouldn't buy the notion that any of the recognized governments would do such a thing. It was only when I insulted his ability to deliver gossip that he told me what he really thinks."

"So, what do we do now?"

Sandler slowed and put a hand on Donnelly's shoulder. "What you should be doing is enjoying the voyage, getting a massage, or relaxing in the whirlpool. This is your pre-wedding celebration, remember?"

Donnelly shook his head. "I'd much rather keep busy than lay about thinking how I'm not with Ethan and wondering how he's doing. This whole spy-versus-spy thing you've got going is a great distraction. So what's next?"

"You're the best," Sandler replied. "All right, then, the first step is to find out who else in Her Majesty's government besides the attaché is on board. Someone knows what happened to that pouch."

"It's going to be a challenge to pick out the embassy staff from the rest of the people on board—seems like everyone's got a proper British accent."

"That's why we're going to pay a visit to the protocol officer. He'll have a complete list, both of the Brits and everyone else."

"So, I was going to ask you earlier. Aren't protocol officers responsible for which fork goes where?"

"Actually, they're responsible for who sits where, which is a much bigger deal. In any diplomatic situation, you have to know the rank of everyone in the room so that the introductions are made in the right order and to be sure you don't seat an ambassador next to a second assistant undersecretary."

"That matters?"

Sandler grimaced. "In the world these folks inhabit, it sometimes seems like nothing matters more. Now, in crisis mode like this, where all of the missions are kind of in a jumble, the protocol officers are going to keep pretty close tabs on everyone just in case they need to defuse a conflict or, you know, arrange a tea."

"Protocol it is," Donnelly said. "Let's roll."

"MR. MAGUIRE, I'd like you to meet Gabriel Donnelly," Sandler said, bowing slightly as if presenting Donnelly at court. "Gabriel, this is Bates Maguire, protocol officer for the British mission in the United States."

"Pleased to meet you, sir." Donnelly extended his hand to the severe gentleman who, out of all of the suited and serious men aboard the ship, struck him as the most serious.

"Delighted," answered Maguire, his tone indicating him to be anything but. He released Donnelly's hand after a brisk, firm shake. "And how may I be of assistance today?" It was less a question than an obvious formality; he looked back down at his portfolio without waiting for a response.

"It's about the pouch." Sandler said simply, as if he knew those few words would carry an outsize impact.

Maguire closed his eyes and opened them just as slowly, though now his eyes were trained on Sandler with a feline intensity. Feline in the sense of a jaguar spying a slow-moving baboon. "Have you found it?" he asked, an eyebrow raised critically.

"Not yet," Sandler replied coolly. "I was wondering if you might be willing to provide me with a list of embassy staff on board. Someone may have information that could prove useful."

"And this supposed person with their supposedly useful information," Maguire said slowly, scornfully, "they have not as yet come forward because...?"

"Because they may not realize the information they have is useful."

"But in your... capable hands"—Maguire's glance flicked disdainfully down to Sandler's tightly balled fists—"it will suddenly become so?"

Sandler took a deep breath, as if struggling not to strangle the sarcasm right out of Maguire. "Have I mentioned that Gabriel here is a police officer?"

"You hadn't." Maguire looked Donnelly up and down and, from his expression, found little to impress.

"If I can simply be allowed to review the list and ask some questions, with Gabriel's help I may be able to piece together what happened. And I think we can agree that it would be to our mutual advantage not to have this unfortunate situation go on any longer."

Maguire shifted in his seat and stared impassively at the wall above Sandler's head for a long moment. "I think we can agree that our mutual interest would have been better served had the ambassador's staff not trusted you with the pouch in the first place. Then I would be getting my work done, and you would be delivering ice creams to schoolchildren, as befits our respective abilities."

Donnelly glanced at Sandler and could all but see him counting to ten silently while he breathed with deliberate calm.

"As much as I would enjoy standing here trading witty barbs with you, I'm clearly overmatched. Perhaps if we could get started on that list, you'll sooner be at peace with your paperwork and I with my ice cream cart."

This sideward compliment seemed to placate Maguire, and he harrumphed resignedly. "Very well." He reached into a red box that sat on the desk next to him, retrieved a single sheet of paper, and held it out to Sandler. "This is the British delegation present on the ship." He snatched the paper back out of Sandler's reach. "As you pursue this folly of an 'investigation,' you shall not so much as ruffle a feather among the top three people on this list. Am I understood?"

"The top three shall remain unruffled. Got it."

"If any one of them mentions to me that they were annoyed—"

"You'll have me keelhauled." Sandler's calm was nearing the breaking point. "And the rest of the people on the list?"

"Oh, they don't matter," Maguire said casually as he handed the list to Sandler. "Numbers four through nine are functionaries, and the rest are civil service. Do what you will."

Sandler took a quick glance at the list, then looked brightly up at Maguire as if they'd just been having a pleasant chat over tea. "Thank you, sir. I appreciate your help. We will get this cleared up."

Maguire gave a courtly nod, but his voice laid bare the emptiness of the gesture. "That would bring a fitting end to your service to the Crown."

Sandler winced but swallowed any response he might have wanted to make to this brusque dismissal. He nodded submissively and backed out of the room, Donnelly by his side.

"That was horrible," Donnelly remarked once they were well out of hearing.

Sandler grinned. "Actually, that went really well. Maguire's a right bastard, that's for certain, but he gave us what we came for, and in terms of tongue-lashings, I've seen him give much worse over far less."

"So where do we start?" Donnelly asked as he followed Sandler back out to the promenade deck. Whipped by the wind, the paper struggled mightily to free itself from Sandler's grip, but he held tight.

"Maguire's warning about the top three people on the list doesn't really make a difference," Sandler said as they walked. "They wouldn't be any help to us anyway—they're too close to the ambassador."

"Aren't those the kind of people who might know something about the pouch?" Donnelly asked.

"Maybe I've spent too much time at the back door of embassies, but I always find the people with the best information are the ones who are high enough to know things, but low enough to be willing to get their hands dirty—or at least remember what it's like to be the guy at the bottom, trying to make things work. Now, here," he said, holding the paper up to Donnelly. He had folded the paper into a tidy rectangle, showing the names beginning with number four. "This one won't tell me anything, even if I wrote the questions on gold bullion and threw in a lap dance. He's super old-school—like Eton old—and to him my very employment besmirches the Crown."

"Besmirches? Really?"

"His word," Sandler replied with a roll of his eyes. "Like I said, I don't think he's going to be very helpful. But this one"—he pointed to number six—"has proven quite amenable in the past."

Donnelly raised an eyebrow. "Amenable's an interesting word. Someone you know well?"

Sandler grinned. "Someone to whom I may have neglected to mention my sexual orientation."

Donnelly raised his eyebrow even higher.

Sandler burst out laughing. "I may, in fact, have intimated that I was not only straight but ardently attracted to her."

"For *shame*," Donnelly scolded with all the mock seriousness he could muster.

"The courier business demands certain compromises," Sandler said in the strenuously dignified manner of a Boy Scout caught with his hand in the cookie jar.

"Well, I for one am quite eager to witness your star turn as a lovestruck Lothario. Where do we find the object of your lust for the fairer sex?"

"Unless I miss my guess, we will find her where there is easy access to both alcohol and men in various stages of undress."

"Pool deck?"

"Either that or lurking near the men's locker room, flask in hand. Let's hope it's the pool."

ONCE THEY'D reached the bow of the ship, they walked up several flights of stairs to the pool. Enclosed by a glass roof, it was the only pool in use during the transatlantic crossing, even in summer. Every elderly, leathery sun-worshiper on board seemed to be here, reclining under the sun's rather feeble rays or swimming languorous laps. Here and there a younger woman clutched a book with expensively manicured fingers, though whether anyone was actually reading was a mystery obscured by huge, stylish sunglasses. Clustered in one of the whirlpools was a group of fit young men who seemed determined to create a party atmosphere all their own despite the astronomically high average age of the population on the pool deck.

"Well, they liven the place up a bit," Sandler murmured. He cast a long look at their tanned, muscled forms.

"If your tongue rolls out of your mouth like a cartoon wolf seeing a flock of sheep, I'm going to tell Ankur."

"Tell him, tell him," Sandler replied. "Wolves hunt in packs, you know." He winked roguishly.

Donnelly laughed. "I don't think those pool boys would make elusive prey. Not one of them has as much as glanced at the woman on the lounger not ten feet away who just about fell out of her bikini top when she turned over to brown her back side. They're sitting awfully close together in that whirlpool. And when was the last time you saw a straight man in a Speedo?"

"Last summer, St. Tropez." Sandler shivered. "Looked like a Russian mafia family reunion. Bleached whales with hairy bellies that almost obscured their budgie-smugglers." He shivered again, as if shaking off a bad memory. "Almost."

"Eww. Thanks for that image."

"Feel free to cleanse it from your mind by looking at that," Sandler replied, tipping his head in the direction of the muscle-packed whirlpool. One of the men was leaning over the edge to take a drink from a waiter, hot water cascading down the round globes of his barely covered ass.

Donnelly wondered if the hot flash of embarrassment he felt when looking at an attractive man would ever fade. But he wasn't going to let that keep him from appreciating the beauty before him. It was liberating.

"Now, where we find muscle, we will find our quarry." Sandler scanned the pool deck. "Ah, there she is," he said.

"I can go wait over there if you'd rather work your charms solo."

"Hell no. I'm bringing you as extra bait. Just remember, we're straight."

Donnelly cast one more look at the whirlpool crew, then closed his eyes for a long blink. "Straight. Right."

Sandler led the way over to a table at the side of the pool deck, where a sixty-something woman sat with a cocktail glass in her hand. She was thin in the intentional, old-money way; her skin was tan and deeply lined, but with a glow of health and an aristocratic aura. Her blue eyes were sharp and bright, and—as Sandler had predicted—they were trained with predatory interest upon the whirlpool full of Speedos. She absentmindedly swirled the remains of her martini as she followed the splash and tussle. She didn't lose a drop.

"Madame Maillard?" Sandler managed to freight his voice with both masculine resonance and smitten submission, which Donnelly considered quite a neat trick.

With a blink she dropped the antics in the whirlpool and brought her imperious gaze to bear on Sandler. She smiled brilliantly, the lines on her face instantly doubling. "Dear boy," she said, her voice nearly as deep as Sandler's. She sounded like Vanessa Redgrave if she'd spent more time smoking unfiltered cigarettes and tossing back martinis before lunch. "Don't make me scold you, Sandy. Call me Fabienne." She extended a hand and turned her cheek toward him.

He took her hand and bent down to kiss the hollow below her prominent cheekbone.

"And you've brought me a present," Fabienne said, looking at Donnelly as if he were her next martini.

"Fabienne Maillard, I present Gabriel Donnelly."

She extended her hand and smiled. "Delighted," she purred, lifting her cheek slightly to Donnelly as she had to Sandler.

Donnelly bent forward and did his duty. She smelled like expensive gin and even more expensive perfume. "Pleased to meet you, Madame," he said, in what he hoped was his straightest voice. He gave her a peck on the cheek.

"You must call me Fabienne as well, of course." Her voice was dry and aristocratic, her accent difficult to place. It sounded like money and Europe, but beyond that Donnelly had no clue. "Now please, join me. But don't block my view of the local wildlife." She glanced at the whirlpool as if pointing out an exotic bird's nest she'd been diligently watching for signs of hatching.

Sandler took the seat closest to the grand dame, and Donnelly settled with relief into a chair on the opposite side. He studied Fabienne's reaction to Sandler's appearance. She regarded him like a farmer's daughter watching a lamb gamboling in the meadow: her enchantment with the adorable thing before her would not keep her from eating it up with relish later. Her eyes sparkled with delight as he pulled his chair close to hers.

"Now, Fabienne, why are you wasting your time on those mere boys?" Sandler chided suavely. "They may be entertaining for an evening, but can they hold up their end of the conversation?"

Fabienne's laughter was worldly and practiced, but her expression was one of sheer joy. "As long as they hold up *my* end for an evening, I don't care about conversation." She turned back to Sandler. "But given the strapping new options before me—" Her eyes flicked over to Donnelly and back again, quick as a whip. "—I have little need for them, have I?"

Sandler smiled broadly. "What need have you of any one man when you have your choice of all on board? And any of us would be fortunate to have the favor of your company."

Fabienne held a perfectly manicured hand to her throat as if Sandler's flattery had touched her to the core. "Sandy, darling, you've never been more full of shit than you are at this very moment." She cackled gleefully, and as she did so waved to the waiter who had been hovering nearby. "Three more of these, you lovely thing." The waiter nodded and dashed away while Fabienne laughed and daubed at her quite dry eyes.

"Fabienne, the things you say," Sandler admonished, though Donnelly detected a hesitation in his voice that hadn't been there before. This clearly wasn't going as planned.

"Oh stop, Sandy," Fabienne scolded back playfully. "Over the years I've been delighted with our flirtation, and I am touched by your persistence in keeping it up. But a woman of a certain age must face facts, and the facts are these: first, I am too old to attract the notice of a man of your age and beauty unless there is money involved. I am as glad that you are not the type to accept my money as I am happy to give it to those who will, like those scamps in the pool over there. Second, I am just as likely to sleep with a woman as you are. We may have tried it in our youth, but it turned out not to really be our thing, didn't it?" Fabienne was smiling, but her eyes were gimlets.

"I don't know what to say," Sandler finally managed.

"Start by introducing me to your friend. Who I suspect is more than a friend, unless I really have become a pointless old woman." She winked at Donnelly, who turned a panicked glance toward Sandler. Was he supposed to stick to the script?

Sandler laughed, shaking his head. "Fabienne, you are a wonder. You are right about me, and about Gabriel, though he's about to be married to the love of his life, who also happens to be frightfully handsome. We are, alas," he said, looking at Donnelly with a shrug, "just friends."

"You have always had impeccable taste in friends," Fabienne said approvingly before turning back to Sandler. "Now we have that all out of the way, we can get to—"

She was interrupted by the arrival of three large martinis.

"—our drinks." She picked up hers and motioned for them to do the same. "To old friends and new truths," she said.

"Not that old," Sandler said as he lifted his glass to her.

She smiled graciously and accepted his adulation as both genuine and entirely her due. She knocked back fully half her martini with no apparent effort and set her cocktail glass down. "Now, tell me, darling, what brings you to me today?"

"An ardent desire to bask in the radiance of your beauty?"

"You've already charmed me, dear boy. Let's move along to the reason you're here."

"It's about the pouch I was carrying," Sandler said, his voice conspiratorially low.

"Ah, so the tale of the purloined pouch is true," she replied, eyebrows raised dramatically. She seemed to notice his reaction. "Please, dear, don't pretend to be shocked. Gossip and gin are the only occupations left the older woman in our youth-obsessed culture."

"I hoped that you might—"

"Be able to help you find it, or at least find out who purloined it?"

Sandler nodded, his cheeks reddening. It was clear to Donnelly that having to ask for help was taking its toll on him.

"What do you know about the pouch?" she asked. Her demeanor had changed in an instant with the mention of the pouch. She was serious, almost businesslike, despite the quantity of gin that no doubt swirled through her every vein.

"You know they don't tell me what's in it," Sandler replied, a bit defensively.

"Of course not. But you know *something* about it. From whom you received it, for example, or to whom you were to deliver it?"

"It was a man I'd never seen before. My instructions from the Ministry just said where to meet him and gave me a code to exchange. He gave me the right code, so I took the pouch and got on my way."

Fabienne thought about this for a moment, frowning. "Where did this happen?"

"In a parking lot, of all places."

"How dignified," Fabienne sniffed. "But where, dear, was this parking lot?"

"In some little backwater I'd never been to. It was several hundred miles from Washington."

Fabienne's eye glinted, and she pursed her lips as if Sandler's information were a bitter sip of tea. "This little backwater didn't happen to be named Jefferson, I suppose?" she asked. It was clear to Donnelly she feared it was.

Sandler drew in a sharp breath. "Yes, it was." He scanned her face desperately, as if searching for a clue as to how she could possibly have known this. "Fabienne, what does that mean to you?"

"Oh, it means nothing to me," she said with the casual deflection of the practiced coquette. "But I would guess it means a great deal to someone on this ship. And now to you as well, it would seem." She picked up her martini and sipped significantly. Madame Maillard communicated primarily in gestures and gin, Donnelly reflected.

Sandler leaned in close—to Madame's evident pleasure—and in a whisper Donnelly could just make out above the noise of the pool deck asked, "Who is it?"

"How very forward, my boy. Now, please, sit back, and let me tell you a little story." She polished off her martini and waved for another round. "Once upon a time, entire branches of the foreign service were staffed almost exclusively with men of a certain… predilection. Knowing that they would be hounded out of public life were they to serve Queen and country at home, they chose instead posting in far distant outposts of the empire, where their interests would be, if not approved, at least tolerated."

"You mean they were gay?" Donnelly asked.

"Oh no, darling." She looked at him for a long moment. "You are as quick as you are handsome." She sighed distractedly, apparently unable to tear her eyes away from him.

"Madame?" Sandler prompted.

"Ah, yes. My fairy tale. Well, yes, of course they were gay. But that alone would not have meant permanent exile. After the law changed in the late sixties, they could at least have come home. They might not have been able to be open about it, but it wouldn't have meant a prison sentence any longer. No, if they had preferred the company of men, they would have been recuperable. But these men preferred the company of boys."

Donnelly sat back, disgusted. He felt like spitting, as he always did when such crimes were mentioned. He'd seen far too much in his career to feel anything else.

"Yes, my dear. It was horrid. And because they were abroad, in countries where such things are not viewed as criminally as they are in England, or where the pound sterling was still the coin of the realm when it comes to graft and corruption, they were able to get away with it. Recently, though, evidence of their crimes has finally started to emerge, sometimes from the diaries of those who died suddenly, before they were able to burn their personal effects. Few of their monstrous kind survive, or at least that's the hope. My guess is that you seem to have collected a pouch of great interest to one of the last surviving members of this ring of monsters."

"But the United States isn't exactly an imperial backwater," Sandler objected. "Why would one of them take refuge there?"

"Because his service had been in Bermuda, and though he needed to hightail it out of there, he feared coming home. He hoped they would simply forget about him as long as he stayed put. And it worked for a long time. I've heard whispers that he's not long for the world, and he'd hoped the unfortunate fact of his advanced illness would put a damper on any investigation. Fortunately, the Foreign Office has thus far not been prone to leniency in such cases."

"I'm a bit lost," Donnelly said. "What do you think was in the pouch?"

"Americans," said Fabienne with a sigh. "So direct. It is your greatest charm and your fatal weakness." She gazed absently at Donnelly for a long moment, as if he were a painting. "Yes, the pouch. There are two possibilities. First, that the pouch contains exculpatory evidence of some kind, and the old lecher wanted to be sure it got to the right person unmolested—which is more consideration than he ever gave his victims. Second, the pouch holds damning proof of his guilt and was sent in a pouch to keep the Americans from discovering it. With no disrespect to our friend here"— she nodded to Donnelly—"your countrymen tend to lurch into action whether or not action is called for."

Sandler, Donnelly noticed, did not rise to his defense. "So the person who stole it was either someone who didn't want the old lecher's name cleared, or someone who is trying to suppress evidence of his guilt."

"Precisely. Find the person on this ship willing to risk an international incident and you'll know which."

Sandler reached into his pocket. "It just so happens I have a list of embassy staff on the ship," he said, placing the list flat on the table and sliding it over to her. "Anyone seem likely?"

She gazed down her nose at it as if paperwork itself were somewhat beneath her dignity. She read down the list, then looked up at him. "I'm afraid you're out of luck, dear boy. No one on this list seems connected to the case we've been discussing."

Sandler was crestfallen. "Are you certain?"

She fixed him with a wry scowl but looked at the list again. "Perhaps if you had a list that began with number one instead of number four?"

"Oh, of course." He reached out and unfolded the paper.

Instantly, her precisely manicured fingertip stabbed at the second name on the list. "Him."

Sandler snatched the list out from under her sharp fingernail and stared at the name. "Are you sure? I thought you said he was terminally ill."

"Oh, it's not the man himself. It's his grandson, and from what I've heard his only living descendent. It's been a rather tragic family story. I only know the outlines of it, as it is never openly spoken of, even among the security staff. One of my dear friends in the service spent several years investigating his case and a few others. The things she discovered…." Fabienne shivered at the memory. "She kept it to herself most of the time, but once in Johannesburg, when we were at the World Cup, she unburdened herself to me."

"The World Cup?" Sandler asked. "I hadn't figured you for a football fan."

"Oh, dear no. I've never even seen a match all the way through. No, we went because we are fans of football fans. An entire city half-crazed with sporting hormones, nearly all of them male and youngish. Ah…." She drifted off for a moment, eyes misty with memory. Sandler gave an exasperated sigh.

"He has a family?" Donnelly prompted, never one to let a line of questioning get bogged down.

"Not in the traditional sense, no. There were rumors that at an early posting he attempted to prove his heterosexuality by sleeping with a call girl. As if being paid a pittance for having that sack of putrescence poke at her weren't insult enough, she was saddled with his child."

"That's terrible," Donnelly said.

"Oh, it worked out very well for him—the minor scandal was just the thing to throw everyone off the scent of his perversion for several decades. He packed her off to some remote village with a few coins, and thereafter made sure that at every posting the story somehow preceded him."

The waiter arrived with another round of martinis. Fabienne picked hers up, but the men didn't move. After a desultory sip, she set hers down and returned to her tale.

"So the girl had a baby daughter, who unfortunately followed in her mother's footsteps, such as they were. She was a little better businesswoman, however, because she managed to extract a proposal from the father of her own brat. The boy was about ten when his parents decided to make the laughably stupid maneuver of blackmailing the old man. They might have been successful, were it not for the notoriously slippery winter roads in their part of Eastern Europe. On their way to present their demands, their Soviet-made car set a new speed record, straight down the side of a mountain. For once the old man seems to have been moved, because he retrieved the boy from his postcommunist backwater and installed him in a boarding school. Luckily for him, several generations of brainpower that had been lacking in his progenitors concentrated in his skull, and he graduated from university with high acclaim."

"So it was a happy family reunion?" Sandler asked.

"Hardly. The bitter old troll refused to have anything to do with him. And for once the boy's intellect failed him, for instead of washing his hands of the whole affair, he decided to go into the foreign service himself, as if he could redeem his legacy or some such nonsense. You know men, always tilting at windmills."

Donnelly sat back in his chair. The wheels turning in his head were spitting out contradictory answers to overlapping questions. "So the pouch contains either damning proof or evidence that will clear his name. And if the grandson stole it, did he do so to suppress it or publicize it, to either clear his family name or destroy the man who disowned him?"

"Precisely," Fabienne said. "Now you see why I prefer to sit by the pool with my gin and my bathing beauties. Diplomatic intrigue is a young man's game, and I welcome you to it."

"It's a lot more to go on than we had before," Sandler said. "I feel hopeful for the first time since the pouch went missing."

"Least I could do darling," Fabienne replied, but at that moment her eye was caught by the group of barely clad men emerging from the whirlpool, steam rising from their wet and muscled bodies.

The group toweled off quickly and then walked toward the stairs, talking and laughing. One of the young men peeled off from the group and approached the table. He leaned down and whispered something into Fabienne's ear. Donnelly couldn't hear what he said, but it seemed to delight Fabienne, and she laughed and said, "*Oui, mon pétit, oui.*" It was only when the young man stood upright, smiling sweetly, that Donnelly noticed just how tightly packed his Speedos were. Fabienne certainly knew how to pick 'em.

She watched the young man rejoin his group, his tight buttocks undulating rhythmically, then raised her glass as if toasting his dedication to gluteal workouts. She tossed back the remaining half of her martini and with a flick of her wrist ordered another round from the attentive waiter. Only then did she seem to realize that the men at her table were staring at her with rather shocked looks on their faces.

"What on earth—are you that surprised to see me the object of cabana-boy attention?"

"No, not at all... um...." Sandler stumbled.

Fabienne gave another great peal of laughter. "Of course you are, darling. But you've seen me order drinks—did you think ordering a rent boy would look much different?"

"He's...?" Sandler turned to get another glimpse of the gaggle of pool boys just before they rounded the end of the deck out of sight. "But I thought they—"

"Were gay? Of course they are, Sandy. That is, when the right man opens his wallet. What you've been watching is their marketing campaign. They giggle like empty-headed sluts in the whirlpool to advertise their availability to every man on the ship whose wallet is the biggest bulge in his pants. It's rather like the lobster tank at one of those horrid American 'seafood' restaurants. One simply chooses from what's on offer. Frankly, I think they're quite relieved when a woman of means invites one of them to her cabin for an evening."

"He seemed quite full of relief," Donnelly remarked, then took a sip of his martini.

"At least his bathing suit was," Fabienne replied with a laugh. She'd clearly caught Donnelly's sly insinuation. "I do like your friend, Sandy. He's bright *and* handsome."

"Fabienne, I'm falling in love with you all over again," Sandler said with a laugh. "You've been a terrific help. Now, there's a conversation we need to have." He tipped back his cocktail glass and stood. "Thank you for the information, and for the pleasure of your company," he said.

"Very nice to have met you," Donnelly said, rising as well. Without being prompted, he leaned over and kissed her on both cheeks. She laughed joyously.

"The pleasure's been all mine," she replied. "I really must be going as well. I'll need a nice massage if I'm going to be limber enough for another evening with Aiden, or Jayden, or whatever that lovely boy is called."

At that moment, however, a new batch of scantily clad young men boisterously tumbled out onto the pool deck, making for the whirlpool.

"Or, perhaps another drink is in order," she said, settling back into her chair and gesturing to the waiter. "I hope I'll see you boys later," she said, but her eyes were already locked on the pool, scanning for the tastiest morsel.

DONNELLY FOLLOWED Sandler back to the stairs, making some effort to walk a straight line. Either the ship was rolling a bit in the waves, or keeping up with Madame Maillard's martini pace had taken its toll on him. "How about some lunch?" he asked, hoping that food would dilute the effect.

"Actually, that's just what I was thinking. But I won't be able to join you and your guest."

Donnelly stopped in his tracks. "What?"

Sandler smiled with equal amounts of charm and desperation. "The name she pointed to is the ambassador's cultural attaché. He knows me—I've carried pouches for him a number of times, as well as artwork, musical instruments, that kind of thing. If he's the one who stole the pouch, I can't just strike up a casual conversation with him."

"So you want me to do that?"

Sandler fell silent, a fragile expression of hope on his face. "I know it's a lot to ask. You've already done so much, and this was supposed to be a nice trip for you. Never mind—forget I asked."

"Oh hell no," Donnelly replied. "What you're giving me the chance to do is either help put a child molester behind bars or ensure that an innocent man's name is cleared. Just try to keep me away from that action."

"Gabriel Donnelly, I swear to God," Sandler said, clearly elated, "if you weren't engaged to be married…." He threw his arms around Donnelly and squeezed him hard. "Thank you." His words were a hot rush into Donnelly's ear, sending a chill down his spine.

"We're in this together," Donnelly whispered back.

The men stepped back from their embrace. "Now, tell me about this person I'm going to interrogate over cucumber sandwiches," Donnelly said.

"I don't know a great deal about him, and I'd certainly never heard what Fabienne told us just now. All I know about him is that he's a favorite of the ambassador and pretty well liked among the staff. On this trip, I've heard he meets the other senior staff every day for lunch, after which he goes to the same table in the lounge to work until it's time for tea. Which, by the way, he takes alone." Sandler glanced at Donnelly. "Until today."

"You seem pretty confident that he'd be willing to share his tea table with me."

"I think he'll be very glad to share his table with you."

"Why? Does he like Americans? Cops? Men who get married in kilts?"

"I think he likes all of the above. And though I lack Madame Maillard's decades of gossip, I do happen to know that you, in particular, will be his cup of tea."

Donnelly stopped again. "Let me get this straight, as it were. I'm supposed to seduce the information out of him?"

"You make it sound like I'm asking you to do something you wouldn't accomplish just by walking into a room."

"Flattery will get you nowhere," Donnelly replied, lifting a warning finger. "It will, however, get you a counterintelligence operative."

"Good man!" Sandler cried. "Now, let's get you the two things every agent going into the field needs: a compelling backstory and tighter pants." He led the way back to their suite.

A half hour later, Donnelly entered the lounge where his target was rumored to spend every afternoon. Sure enough, he found him at the window, reading one of a stack of many papers, a sleek laptop on the table next to him.

"Excuse me?" Donnelly said as he approached. "Would you mind sharing your table?"

The annoyed look on the man's face evaporated when he took in the sight of Donnelly towering over him. He smiled and gestured to the empty chair across from him. "Please," he said in a soft but resonant voice.

There were several other tables in the room that were completely unoccupied, a fact Donnelly was delighted to see the other man ignore. He pulled out the chair and sat. "I'm Gabriel," he said, extending his hand.

"Imre." The diplomat reached across the table and shook Donnelly's hand. "Would you like some tea?" He gestured to the waiter, then gathered his papers and closed his laptop.

Donnelly was pleased to see he had so completely distracted Imre from his work—it meant he might be able to get the man to open up. "That would be very nice, thank you."

"Yes, Mr. Romanov?" the waiter asked.

"Tea, please, for my friend?"

"Yes, of course." The waiter turned to Donnelly. "Is there a variety you prefer, Mr. Donnelly?"

Donnelly winced at the mention of his name, but their notoriety among the ship's staff had been taken into account in their planning of this operation. It's why they'd decided not to use a fake name. "Something green, please?" he asked. Normally, if it wasn't coffee he wasn't interested, but investigations sometimes required sacrifice. The waiter nodded and glided away.

If Imre were surprised that Donnelly was known to the waiter, he gave no sign, as if being recognized by the help were a normal part of life. "So tell me," Imre said once they were alone again. "What brings you on this long, uneventful voyage?"

"I'm going to Normandy," Donnelly answered. "My grandfather landed on the beach on D-Day, and I've never been. I figured this was a fitting way to make the trip."

Imre nodded. "It's a beautiful site, especially this time of year."

"I've read some of the books and seen the movies, but I don't think I'll ever really understand it until I've seen it for myself."

"It was a tremendous sacrifice. I wonder if we're capable of such undertakings anymore. Humans, I mean." Imre looked out the window for a moment, frowning slightly, but then seemed to shake it off and return to the conversation. "Was your grandfather able to return?"

"He went for the fiftieth anniversary ceremonies. I think it helped him, in a way. Afterward he was finally able to talk about what he'd done in the war. It's like I got to know a whole new person." Donnelly sighed, which Sandler had recommended he do when talking about his invented grandfather. Now it was time to bring it on home. "We lost him a few years later," he said, putting a little thickness in his voice. "He was a good man." It was Donnelly's turn to gaze morosely out the window, and he felt Imre's unblinking eyes on him as he did so. Perfect.

"May I, sir?" The waiter had returned with tea and a plate of sandwiches. Donnelly nodded, and the server poured a steaming cup of green tea and set the pot on the table. "Will there be anything else?"

Donnelly shook his head, and the waiter bowed and retreated.

"How's the tea?" Imre asked after Donnelly had tasted his first sip.

"Very nice," Donnelly replied. He set the cup down. "Are you traveling for business or…?" He looked down at Imre's stack of paperwork. "Business it is, I guess."

Imre smiled, clearly charmed. "Yes, I'm afraid so."

"Well, I won't distract you, then," Donnelly said, sitting back in his chair and looking again out the window.

"No, please," Imre said immediately. "A distraction is just what I need at the moment. And I cannot imagine a more pleasant one than a nice cup of tea and some stimulating conversation."

Donnelly smiled warmly and leaned in, elbows on the table. His napkin dropped to the floor as he did so. "I shall try to be stimulating," he said with a raised eyebrow. This is what Brandt referred to as his "secret weapon," and sometimes Donnelly thought he could get anything he wanted if he asked with a raised eyebrow. In this case, as at home, he seemed to be correct. A delicate color came into Imre's cheek as he returned Donnelly's smile.

Across the corridor, Sandler would have seen the napkin drop. The plan was underway.

"Are you traveling with family or friends or…?" Imre asked as he set his cup back down onto its saucer. He didn't meet Donnelly's eye as he waited for an answer.

"No, quite alone, I'm afraid," Donnelly replied with a note of sadness in his voice of which he was quite proud. "None of my friends were very interested in spending a week floating across the ocean to visit a beach where something happened more than seventy years ago."

"I pity those with no interest in history. Without it, there are lessons that have to be learned by every generation. Often at great price."

"I've often thought the same thing, just not as eloquently."

Imre's expression of flattered humility looked, to Donnelly's eye, a bit practiced—like an art history professor being told he had opened yet another student's eyes to the true genius of an Old Master. But then again, there was something genuinely charming about him that Donnelly began to glimpse under the diplomatic reserve.

"So, what do you do?" Donnelly asked.

"This, mostly," Imre answered, casting a downward glance at his tidy stack of papers. "Endless paperwork, punctuated with stilted conversation at unspeakably tedious formal events while being strangled by a black bowtie."

"You must be one of the diplomats everyone's been talking about around the ship. It sounds awful, by the way. Why do you keep doing it?"

"It wasn't what I set out to do," Imre said, tracing with impeccably manicured hands the intricate patterns of lace that ringed the doily in the middle of the table. "I became a cultural attaché to help bring culture to people who don't have access to it, and who could benefit from it. I had no idea that it would involve so much paper."

"Sounds like you're living the dream," Donnelly replied with a chuckle.

"Well, given that my father toiled in a mine from the age of twelve and then died in a car crash before the age of forty, I guess it's not so bad."

"Wow. That's really sad," Donnelly replied. He knew the outline of Imre's story, of course, but was struck by the blunt retelling. There was sorrow in Imre's voice, but it sounded like an objective sadness, as if he were describing bad things that happened, in general, to other people. "I lost my dad when I was twelve, and it's still hard."

"I didn't really know mine," Imre replied. "I don't mean that in a new-agey 'I didn't know the real person' way. It's more in a 'he spent every waking moment underground' way. I think he provided for us the best he could, but it was a hard life."

"What about your mom?"

"She was with him in the car. They'd only had it a week. It was a beat-up old Lada that my father inherited out of the blue from a relative he'd never even heard of, much less met. But he wasn't one to look a gift jalopy in the mouth, so he took my mom out for a spin on that very Sunday afternoon. They never came back."

"I'm so sorry," Donnelly said. "I can't imagine what that must have been like."

Imre shrugged, not carelessly but as if adjusting the weight that had been laid on his shoulders at the age of ten. "I don't know what would have happened if my grandfather hadn't appeared as mysteriously as that death trap Soviet sedan."

"Did he take you in?"

Imre gave a wry, dismissive flick of his head. "It was more like he took me on—as a kind of obligation he was only theoretically interested in. As a matter of fact,

I saw him only once, when he came to the village after the accident and packed me off to Switzerland for school."

"It's too bad you never had a chance to develop a relationship with him," Donnelly said.

"He's not much for relationships. He is, in fact, still very much alive and very much alone, and he appears to like it that way." Imre, who had been gazing at his tea leaves, suddenly seemed to remember he was sharing tea with the attractive man opposite him. "Listen to me, rabbiting on about my sad family. Not the kind of light chatter one expects over tea."

"It's been very nice," Donnelly said. "But I've imposed too much. Thank you for sharing your table with me, Imre." He stood, and extended a hand.

Imre rose as well and smiled with what seemed like unabashed delight at again seeing the full extent of Donnelly. They were precisely the same height, and their builds were remarkably similar as well—strong and lithe without excessive bulk. Imre was perhaps ten years older than Donnelly but kept himself remarkably fit.

"Gabriel, I hope you don't think me too forward," Imre said once they'd shaken hands. "Do you have plans for dinner? I'd like a chance to prove I can talk about things other than my bizarrely self-destructive family."

Donnelly felt the shy smile emerge, the one he'd practiced in the mirror with Sandler before coming to tea. That he now had a chance to use it meant that their preparation had been to good purpose. "I'd like that," he said. "Queen's Grill at eight?"

This was a risky move, taking charge of their dinner arrangements. Sandler had coached him that Imre had a reputation for managing his personal relationships with as much authority as his diplomatic responsibilities. But something gave him the inkling that he should turn the tables—as someone who didn't know he was dealing with the cultural attaché of the British Embassy might.

Imre's smile let him know he had made the right choice. "Queen's Grill," he said. "Well."

Donnelly saw the change in his expression, the one that signaled Imre's estimation of him was shifting. He had shown up as a passenger who had wandered into the tea room from steerage, a man who might be relied upon to offer bland and not terribly challenging conversation. But having casually mentioned the first-class dining room, Donnelly had provoked a new focus in Imre's eyes, as if he were now viewed as something approaching an equal.

"I'll see you at eight, then," Donnelly said. He turned and walked from the room with a callipygian stride that would have made Ankur proud—and perhaps a little jealous.

Ferry, North Sea

THEIR ACCOMMODATIONS on the ferry were to be in the only space available—a rather expensive stateroom that boasted, the port agent said with manic delight as if the very idea thrilled him to his core, its own bathroom.

Bryce was less impressed, as he made clear when he stalked away from the desk with a scowl. "What do the other passengers do? Squat over a bucket and then throw it overboard? It is simply scandalous that they charge so much for the privilege of lurching across the North Sea in that thing they call a ship."

"But you always say you love the cruising," Nestor said.

"Well, yes, when we're in the park looking for hot dads who want to go behind a tree and take a little break from heterosexuality. But cruising on the actual sea is going a bit far, in my mind."

It was at that moment that a couple of dashing men in sailor's garb walked purposefully through the ferry terminal, through the staff doors, and out to board the ship. Bryce watched them go, tracing the crease in their sharply pressed white pants up to the point where it broke over their buttocks.

"I may have been hasty in my judgments," he said thoughtfully. "I'm sure we will have a delightful passage, and the cost isn't all that much when you consider that we have flown so far for free."

A little while later, they were settled into their cabin, and the ship embarked on its overnight passage to Newcastle.

"One shudders to think of the cuisine that might be on offer, but I cannot remember the last thing I ate that wasn't dangling from a man," Bryce said after confirming in the mirror that his hair was still perfect. "Shall we go looking for our own Captain Bolt over dinner?"

"I too am hungry for the pirates," Nestor replied.

"That's the spirit, dear."

They walked the length of the ship and down a couple of decks to what was billed as the best restaurant on the ship. "Though in terms of achievement," Bryce confided, "'the best restaurant on the ferry' seems on par with 'the smartest Kardashian.'"

Their dining experience began inauspiciously when they found there were no tables for two available; the best that could be done was to place them at a table for four where an elderly woman sat stoically staring into the middle distance, her hand around a tumbler of deep amber liquid. The dining room host delivered the boys up to her with a simper, as if he'd brought around the dessert tray for her delectation. He handed them menus and evaporated.

"Well, it's marginally better than eating out of a vending machine and drinking 'beer,'" Bryce muttered to Nestor with a shudder as he perused the menu, searching for something edible.

"Not much," croaked their elderly tablemate.

"Oh, how lovely, you're conscious," Bryce said, peering over his menu. The old bird regarded him with ancient but sharp eyes and lifted her glass to her lips. "Is there something you'd recommend as being the least poisonous? Seeing as you have many, *many* more dinners under your belt than we do."

She swallowed her drink and narrowed her eyes. Then, without warning, she slammed the glass down and tipped her head back, letting out a guffaw that seemed to rise from somewhere deep in her diaphragm, down where tobacco and spite conspired to render her voice a reedy rasp. Her laugh was a rusty axe blade, wielded with reckless disregard.

"Well aren't you a saucy little miss," she spat when she had ceased her mirth-tinged hacking.

"Why thank you," Bryce replied with a tight smile. "That's high praise indeed from someone who must have met so very many people over the last century."

"But one thing never changes, you frivolous little butt monkey," she seethed. "Young dandies like yourself convinced you know everything because you think you invented cocksucking."

A waiter who had been approaching the table stopped dead in his tracks, then took a faltering step backward.

"We didn't invent it, you ancient darling," Bryce replied tartly. "But I daresay we've perfected it."

She looked Bryce dead in the eye. "Horseshit." She turned and waggled her empty glass at the clearly terrified waiter, who took it and scurried away. With a stately leisure, she turned back to Bryce. "Now, listen to me, you dim-witted sack of glitter. I knew men who were sucking cock when your grandfather was a mere boy out fucking sheep. Men who bent over and took it like a vicar and risked prison for the privilege. Men who weren't afraid to put on a dress and entertain a dozen sailors on shore leave and still show up for their twelve hours at the iron works the next day. Pfft," she concluded with a dismissive wave of her hand. "Pansy needs to learn respect."

The two of them, Bryce and the ancient lady, stared at each other for a long moment—long enough that Nestor, biting his lip and fidgeting, seemed ready to faint from the stress—until finally they broke into raucous laughter. Across the table they grasped hands as if they were long-lost relatives at a reunion dinner.

"You are a delight, you withered old bat," Bryce said, wiping a tear of hilarity from his eye.

"And you are an empty-headed sass-basket, God bless your soul," she replied. "Please, love, call me Mags. Everyone does."

"I'll remember because it rhymes with bags," Bryce replied.

"And fags," she chimed in, "with whom I've surrounded myself since Churchill's day."

"I'm Bryce, and this lovely gentleman is my companion, in travel and in life, Nestor."

Nestor, confusion at this turn of events evident on his face, nevertheless extended a hand across the table to shake Mags's.

"Lovely to meet you, dear," she said grandly. "Now, let's see what a lady has to do to get a bourbon around here." She gestured to the waiter, conveying her abject thirst through an arid pantomime.

"Yes, let's," Bryce said. "It's been *minutes* since you've had a drink."

"A lady doesn't drink alone," Mags replied, waving three fingers at the bartender, who immediately nodded and leapt into action. "We're in this together, possums."

The bartender, clearly terrified to risk making the lady wait, rushed back to the table bearing three tumblers brimming with bourbon. He set one in front of each person at the table, then scurried away before Mags could glare at him so fearsomely again.

She raised her tumbler and nodded imperiously at Bryce and Nestor to do the same. "To the journey, and the men who make it worthwhile," she said, then took a significant swallow of bourbon.

Bryce and Nestor attempted the same but were overwhelmed by the high proof and utter lack of subtlety in the alcohol and sputtered a bit as they set their glasses down. Mags didn't seem to notice.

"Now, how did the two dandies before me come to be on this tub bound for Newcastle? I insist on being entertained with a story both thrilling and improbable before my salad arrives, which," she said as she turned toward the waiter, "*had better be any second now*!"

The waiter let out a whimper and crashed into a busboy as he tore off toward the kitchen.

"Well, it just so happens that our story is both thrilling and improbable," Bryce said excitedly. "It's full of rough and ready truck drivers, men in uniform, and an Olympics' worth of gymnasts showing shocking flexibility."

"And blow jobs. Many blow jobs," Nestor added.

Mags cackled like a henhouse afire, then threw back her bourbon. "Well, get to it!" she demanded as she slammed her again empty glass on the table.

Behind her Bryce could see the bartender leap into action, slamming into the waiter who was bringing the salad, sending lettuce flying as if shot from a confetti cannon. Mags had no clue that cherry tomatoes were rolling in all directions behind her, and Bryce was not one to distract a captive audience by taking notice. "Our story begins in a churchyard, where one strapping state trooper proposes marriage to another...."

By the time Bryce's story wound its way to the present moment, their third dessert had arrived. All of the other diners had long since turned in for the night, but the waitstaff was too cowed by Mags to even suggest they be allowed to close the dining room for the evening.

"So you've traveled east by traveling west," she summed up, waving a fork bearing the last bite of chocolate cake, "and managed, until now, to pay for the entire journey with sexual favors? Out*standing*!" she thundered, slapping the table for emphasis, and then put the chocolate cake down the hatch to mingle with the quart of bourbon that had gone on before.

"We've simply made do with the humble talents we possess," Bryce replied with what he hoped sounded like false modesty.

"Humble my ass," Mags retorted. "You boys must be blessed with the sphincters of angels."

"They have inspired many to call upon the deities of their choosing, I will grant," Bryce said, dabbing daintily at the corner of his mouth with a napkin. "So now you know our story. You must tell us yours. Feel free to jump ahead to recent times—the last fifty years or so." He winked broadly at Mags.

She laughed volcanically. "My, aren't we the impudent whore? Let's retire to the bar, where we won't inconvenience these jackasses any further," she said, jerking her head at the cowering waitstaff.

She rose uncertainly to her feet, and for the first time Bryce noticed how frail she was. What came out of her mouth was pure piss and vinegar, but standing she looked to be ninety pounds of ancient brittleness. Bryce rounded the table and put out his elbow. Mags regarded it poisonously.

"Do you think, you insolent puke," she growled, "that I am incapable of making my own way?"

He took her arm and wrapped his around it. "Far from it, you bitter old coot," he replied in the sycophantic tone one would use with a hated elderly relative who, though terminal, still possessed the strength to change her will. "I think you could tumble your way to a broken hip all by yourself. But let's spare Nestor the spectacle, shall we? He's a bit delicate."

She winked at him and fell into step, and they made their way to the elevator, up one deck, and to the bar at the aft of the ship. There, under a steady rain of bourbon, she told them her tale.

"I grew up in the time between the Great Wars," she began. "England had been blasted out of its innocence—trench warfare will do that to you—and what was scandalous a generation ago suddenly seemed rather quaint. Oscar Wilde had done two years at hard labor for poking some urchins at the turn of the century, and now our boys in uniform were coming back from France, where they'd passed the time between German artillery salvos by having at the other boys in uniform. It's one thing to jail a dandy for his dalliances, but to tell men who've seen death and destruction that they shouldn't be allowed to fuck each other if it pleases them… well." She tossed back a shot of bourbon, looked for the next. It came immediately.

"By the time it was clear Hitler wasn't going to be content with just Austria and Poland and Czechoslovakia and the rest but wanted to yank the sword from the stone and make England kneel, I was old enough to go to war. And I did. My two brothers and I enlisted as soon as the call came, and off we went. They were killed in the opening weeks of the war, before I ever got to see them again." Mags's voice graveled away to a hoarse whisper, as if the edges of sadness had been blunted but not worn smooth. "Those two were the only people in my life who had accepted me for what I was, and Hitler took them from me." Her eyes glittered with tears that she refused to let fall. "Well," she said, once the veil of sadness had lifted, "we know how that worked out for him. I flew hundreds of sorties over France, over Belgium, over the *Vaterland* itself. And every bomb I dropped I prayed would find one of the soldiers who had killed my brothers.

"We sons of Britain returned victorious, again. But what we found at home was a society that had turned American. Puritans ruled the day, and even the meager freedom we had enjoyed between the wars was stamped out in favor of a new, manlier England. I had looked death in the eye every day to defend this country and was welcomed home with renewed sodomy laws and moral outrage over whom I chose to love. Well, as the kids say today, fuck that."

Bryce and Nestor tittered with delight.

"The last straw came on the first anniversary of the peace. There was a parade, of course, to allow those who didn't fight to wave their flags and sing along to 'God Save the King' and imagine they had had a hand in turning Hitler back. I marched, because I had not yet learned what my country had become. After the parade we retired to the local to have a drink with those of my mates who had returned home with their faculties intact, and in the back of the pub I was reunited, quite by chance, with the love of my life. He wasn't the love of my life yet, of course. We'd known each other only briefly during the war, actually just a few weekends in Paris during which we exchanged a great many things but not names. That's how it was then, between soldiers. We didn't indulge in the muck of sappy romance, calling out each other's names as we pounded away. But in those weekends, I saw enough of him, in his unguarded moments, to know he was special. As we said good-bye on our last weekend, I resolved that the next time we saw each other, I would tell him how I truly felt, and we'd find a way to be together, even if it meant we had to run away. The next week his plane went down over Dresden. Until that moment in the pub, I didn't know if he was alive or dead."

"Oh, how romantic!" Bryce gushed. "The drama of wartime assignations. When all's quiet on the front, the action is in the rear."

Mags chuckled. "You have a way with words, pigeon. Now, where was I? Right. The pub, after the parade. Well, we wasted no time getting reacquainted."

"Right there among all of the other soldiers?" Bryce was aghast, but intrigued.

"One thing you should know about men who have faced death together. They care only about living to see another day with the ones they love. In that room, among those men, with 'Rule, Britannia' echoing in our ears, it mattered not a whit when I kissed the man I thought I'd lost forever. Some of them may have looked away, but not one of them raised a voice to keep us from being happily reunited. No, it was what happened after, on our way home, that changed everything."

Mags picked up her next bourbon and held it to the light, swirling it a bit as if catching the right angle might show her the past. Then she slugged it down and waved for the next.

"We left the pub, he and me, and as it was just past closing time, we were arm in arm, mostly to keep each other upright but also because we couldn't keep our hands off each other. All we wanted was to get to my bachelor room off Piccadilly and pick up where we'd left off. We didn't hear them approach from behind."

Both Bryce and Nestor gasped at this sudden ominous turn.

"It was a lead pipe, I found out later," Mags said, staring into her newly arrived bourbon. "It didn't even make a noise when it hit my skull. I remember falling forward as if off a cliff, and then all was blackness. When I awoke, I was lying on the pavement, most of my teeth scattered around me, a pool of blood congealing on my face. He lay next to me, and for what seemed like eternity, I waited to see his chest rise. There was no sense getting up and facing life if he wasn't going to be a part of it. Finally he took in a halting, wheezing breath, and I knew he was going to be okay. If he survived Nazi captivity, he could certainly overcome a cowardly assault on the street. And so could I. I hauled myself to my hands and knees and found it can be devilish hard to draw breath when one's ribs have punctured both lungs. I called for help, but none came, not until a newsboy delivering the first edition of the day's papers happened by and screamed bloody murder—we must have looked quite a sight. Finally an ambulance came, and only then the police, but no one was at all interested in trying to find out who did this to us. They felt we deserved it, I could see it in their eyes."

She fell silent, staring at her bourbon.

"Oh, Mags," Bryce whimpered, eyes full of tears. "What did you do?"

She sighed, shaking her head. "We did what we had to." She swirled her bourbon, took a sip. "He and I committed ourselves that night, in the hospital, to each other. And we committed ourselves to doing whatever we must to carve out a place for our life together. We could either flee our homes and find a foreign shore that would allow us to be together—as if such a place existed in the forties—or find a way to be accepted. And so, as soon as we were released from hospital, we moved away to a village in the far north, and from the day we arrived there we were Harold and Mags, longtime sweethearts who had been married in Paris as soon as the war ended. And everyone accepted us, just like that. Which was astonishing, as I was rubbish at wearing a dress, at least at first. But people see what they expect to see, and they saw us as man and wife. We became part of village life, opened a little shop, had the occasional tea on Sunday in the vicarage. Every few weeks we'd take the train down to London, where no one knew us anymore, and find a few boys to knock about with. As the years went on, our trips to the city became fewer and fewer, and we found—to our great surprise—that we quite enjoyed being settled into village life. By the time it was safe to 'come out of the closet,' mine was full of dresses, and I couldn't work myself up for making a fuss. I came to enjoy the biweekly meetings of the garden club almost as much as picking up a sailor for a sweaty, dangerous weekend."

Bryce gasped.

"*Almost* as much, you ninny," Mags scolded. "I'll have you know I could still take on any seaman that might cross my path, well into my eighth decade."

"Good for you, dear," Bryce replied, relieved to hear that the desire to wrestle sailors never truly fades.

"We had a great many wonderful years, Harold and I. He passed on three years ago this weekend. Now, don't start up the waterworks again, you lily-livered fops," Mags warned. "We had over sixty years of wedded bliss, and it was his time. I've gone to Paris every year, to the places we first met, to remember him. And to have some time alone, which I guarantee myself by being as prickly as possible so no one dares to approach me unless he's bearing bourbon. Unfortunately, on this trip fate spoiled my plans and deposited these two empty-headed natterers at my table."

"Thank you, dear," Bryce replied warmly. "We've enjoyed it as much as you have."

"Now, it's nearly midnight, and I'm a frail old lady. But you are still in the blush of youth, and I daresay those two waiters haven't taken their eyes off of you all night."

Bryce turned to see a couple of black-aproned busboys looking their way. They immediately blushed at being noticed but did not look away. Bryce swung back to Mags. "You know, you may be right."

"I can see a hungry sailor at a hundred paces."

"But as fetching as those morsels are, we would be remiss if we didn't see you safely to your cabin first. Your poor old heart's pumping more bourbon than blood at this point."

"My dear Bryce...." Mags replied, her voice soft and low.

He leaned close to hear.

"Fuck. Off." She snarled theatrically and once again the battle-ax of her laugh chopped the air. "I've gotten by for nearly a century without your help, and I promise you I will somehow be able to find my way to bed. You must, however, swear on your honor that you will meet me for breakfast and give me every detail."

"My *honor*!" Bryce hooted. "You are a minx."

"It will be our pleasure to break the fast with you," Nestor murmured suavely, taking Mags's hand and kissing it.

"My goodness," Mags cried with a laugh. "Who knew this old broad could still get a boner so quickly."

Nestor beamed.

"Now off with you before I change my mind and drag this one down to my cabin." Mags lifted Nestor's hand to her lips and kissed it softly.

"Come, darling," Bryce said, rising. "Let us do to those boys all the things that Mags will enjoy hearing about over crumpets come morning." He looked at her with a smile. "Any special requests?"

Mags smiled mysteriously, then beckoned Nestor to lean down. She whispered something into his ear. Nestor's eyes bulged wide, but he swallowed hard and nodded to the old woman.

As they walked toward the still-smiling busboys, Bryce whispered, "What did she say?"

Nestor shrugged. "The words, they are too... much. I show you," he replied with a sly smile.

Bryce giggled. "See that you do."

Evening, at sea

DONNELLY SAT at his table, the one by the window, counting the seconds as the hands of his watch ticked toward 8:00 p.m. The long hand and the second hand had just rendezvoused at the twelve when the maître d' appeared with Imre beside him.

"Your guest, Mister Donnelly," the tuxedoed man said with a bow.

"Thank you," Donnelly replied, which sounded ridiculous, as if he'd been brought an appetizer.

Imre sat in the chair the maître d' pulled out for him.

"They are awfully formal here," Donnelly said apologetically.

"What else would one expect?" Imre replied, glancing around the strenuously tasteful room. "This is where the very wealthy come to spend their great-grandchildren's inheritance. And then there's Gabriel." He looked across the table with an amused expression.

In the golden light of the restaurant, Imre's smile glowed, his eyes sparkled. Donnelly, working a case, hadn't expected to see him this way. He wasn't sure he liked how it made him feel and sought refuge in looking down at the tablecloth, warmth in his cheeks. Diplomats, he reminded himself, trade on charm as much as linguistic or political acumen. And Imre was nothing if not charming.

"I don't exactly fit in here?" he asked with an ironic roll of his eyes.

"Quite the opposite, actually. You're very much at home in a room full of beautiful things."

Even an undercover operative as accomplished as Donnelly could not have willed his cheeks to pink up as brilliantly as they did under the onslaught of Imre's flattery. He hoped Imre would interpret his downward glance as graceful humility rather than the shame it was. Luckily, the waiter arrived at that moment to save him.

"Good evening, Mister Donnelly, Mr. Romanov," he said in a low, velvet voice. "Shall I bring you your customary?" He glanced at Donnelly expectantly.

"Yes, please," Donnelly replied, already feeling the cold gin and tonic in his hand. He would appreciate something to hold on to.

"And for you, sir?"

"I'll have the same, thank you."

The waiter nodded and glided away.

"You don't even want to know what it is before you order it?" Donnelly asked.

Imre shook his head. "If you like it, that's good enough for me."

"But what if you're allergic to gin?"

"One simply cannot be in the employ of the British government and not drink gin."

Donnelly seized this opening, leaning forward and resting his elbows on the table—which he predicted would convey reckless interest to someone accustomed to dining with ambassadors. "What's it like, working for the embassy? Have you met the Queen?"

Imre smiled. "It's mostly a lot of paperwork, and yes."

"Wow. That must have been amazing."

"The paperwork?"

"No," Donnelly said, playfully slapping across the table at Imre's arm. It was something he would have done to Brandt to stop him teasing. That it was not Ethan across the table should have made Donnelly sad, but instead it made him even more determined to be successful in this investigation. "The Queen. What's she like?"

"She's like the nation's stern grandmother. You know she loves you, but you get the sense she's always thinking you might have done just a bit better."

"I never knew my grandmothers," Donnelly said, a genuine sadness creeping into his voice. "The women in my father's family all seem to have died young, generation after generation, and my mother's mother never wanted much to do with us after my brother…." He stopped, having said more than he intended. Luckily their drinks arrived before he had to try to talk his way out of that very personal cul de sac.

"God save the Queen," Donnelly said, holding his gin and tonic aloft.

"I'll be sure to mention you were thinking of her," Imre said as he touched the rim of his glass to Donnelly's. He sipped, then set his drink down and folded his hands on the table. "That's perfect. Thank you."

"My pleasure," Donnelly replied as he plotted his next move to elicit information about the missing pouch. But he didn't get a chance.

"Your brother, then," Imre said lightly. "Bit of a black sheep, is he?"

Shit. Donnelly tried to conjure up a fictional brother who, for the purposes of this conversation, had a bad habit of stealing the occasional car or getting into fistfights. But then he realized he was profiling a video game character, and saw immediately that he wouldn't be able to keep it up. So instead, unexpectedly, he told the truth.

"He wasn't a black sheep to people who knew him. The people who matter." He took a deep breath and a healthy swallow of his drink and forged ahead. "He was a soldier and a scholar and the best man I knew growing up. He was killed in Afghanistan by an IED, after a couple of tours in which he saved many more people than he hurt. He was my hero. But he was gay, and that's all my mother and her batshit conservative family cared about. From the time he came out to them, all he got was hellfire and damnation."

He looked up at Imre, whose image had started to blur. Donnelly wiped his eyes. "So I think I will adopt your Elizabeth II as my new grandmother and be much better off for it."

He blinked hard and only then realized that Imre's eyebrows were peaked in sympathy.

"I'm so sorry," he murmured, barely above the sophisticated din of the dining room. "What an awful thing to have happen." He reached out his hand and put it on Donnelly's. "I am so sorry."

This was the part of investigative subterfuge Donnelly hated most. In order to be convincing, he tended to hew as closely as possible to the truth; it kept him from having to make everything up out of whole cloth and reduced the chance that he would be caught out in an inconsistency. But having told Imre something real—and emotionally raw—he allowed him the opportunity to offer real sympathy. The goal had been for Donnelly to prompt him to talk about his grandfather, but now that they had shared this moment of real connection, he wasn't sure he could get that opportunity back. He had to try.

"I think I'd have preferred the benign neglect you enjoyed from your grandfather over passive-aggressive birthday cards with a cake on the front and a message of eternal damnation on the inside."

"I'd have loved to get something from his own hand, even if it just told me to fuck off," Imre said, then slugged back his drink. The waiter arrived immediately, and Imre gratefully nodded at the unspoken offer of another. "He's never once sent me a personal note of any kind."

"Then why—if you don't mind me asking—did he get in touch with you at all?"

"That's a question I asked myself frequently during those first few years at school. I was completely alone there. My classmates had families that, at the very least, felt socially obligated to acknowledge their offspring with the odd letter and to collect them on the half terms and school holidays. I spent the first few such occasions hoping he would appear to take me home with him, but even a child can recognize when he's not wanted. Eventually an older couple, caretakers of the school gardens, began taking me in when everyone else jetted off for vacations in exotic locales."

"That sounds awful. I am so sorry."

"We do seem to be apologizing for the machinations of a cruel world, don't we?" Imre asked wistfully. "But the truth is, in time I began to appreciate what he had given me—the chance to rise. I was the only son of a poor miner and his long-suffering wife, orphaned by a cruel twist of fate, and in just a few years I found myself graduating from one of the most exclusive schools in the world, with universities seeking me out. What he gave me was opportunity, not love."

Donnelly shook his head sadly. "Not sure what the former is worth without the latter."

Imre looked a little startled, then chuckled softly. "It took me many years to see that, and you say it casually as if it's been clear to you all along." He shook his head. "Where have you been all my life, Gabriel Donnelly?"

"Well, I haven't been lurking in elite Swiss boarding schools, that's for sure." He looked up to smile his gratitude to the waiter for bringing another round of drinks.

"That's a shame," Imre said, lifting the glass to his lips. "I wouldn't have had to waste my time on all of those rich, arrogant boys."

"*All* of those boys?" Donnelly asked, eyebrow lifted.

Imre smiled, a devilish twinkle in his eye. "A dormitory full of boys, half of them already as power-hungry as their fathers and grandfathers, and the other half of a decidedly artistic bent? You can do the math on that one. It's a wonder we found time to study, what with all the buggery going on."

"What a charming British term for it," Donnelly said, struck again by how different his upbringing had been—rural, uncultured, straight. "Though one imagines many of them grew out of it?"

"Most, but not all, and not all of them are open about it even to this day. I'm always amused at reunions by the many ways some of them find to explain away what happened between all of us. Last winter, at Gstaad, one of the more... experienced... of my schoolmates actually claimed that he'd graduated a virgin. A virgin! I reminded him of that star-filled night in the depths of winter when I'd bent him over the footboard of his four-poster bed and pounded away until the wee hours."

"How'd he react to that little trip down memory lane?"

"Not well. But then again, neither did his fiancée, who was standing just behind him and to whom he had neglected to introduce me."

"Oh, that must have been awkward."

"You have no idea. Though it turned out all right—she's nobility, something like twelfth in line for some long-forgotten Prussian baronetcy, so she doesn't expect anyone to reach adulthood without having been railed whilst in boarding school. Plus, his family's money was needed to plug the holes in the roof of her family's castle. Win-win."

"I do love a happy ending," Donnelly said, laughing.

"I have a massage therapist to introduce you to."

Their laughter was perhaps more boisterous than the Queen's Grill was accustomed to.

Right, Donnelly thought, back to work.

"You said your grandfather went to the same school?" he asked.

Imre nodded. "And his before him and on into the mists of time."

"My grandfather was a widower the whole time I knew him," Donnelly said. "And he never so much as dated anyone after my grandmother died. Growing up I figured that people of his generation only had sex to make a family. It must be strange to think of your grandfather getting up to shenanigans at school."

Imre looked down at the tablecloth as if suddenly cast into somber thought. He was silent for a long moment. "My grandfather," he said, "was—"

He was interrupted by the appearance of the waiter, and the two men put aside their conversation and ordered dinner. When the waiter had retreated, Donnelly pondered the sad and musing face of the man across from him. He was trying to figure out how to get the conversation back on track when Imre took a deep breath.

"My grandfather never really left school," he began, his eyes fixed on the ice cubes in his glass. "At least in terms of his sexuality. I think his entire life has been a demented struggle to recapture those days of adolescent discovery."

"But he must have put it aside at some point to marry your grandmother, didn't he?"

Imre shook his head. "My grandmother was never his wife, and as far as I know, she was the only woman with whom he's ever had sex."

Donnelly layered his voice with a veneer of scandalized surprise. "I don't... I don't understand." This was going better than he'd dared hope.

"My grandfather, having spent his youth buggering schoolboys, seems to have decided to continue the practice into adulthood and finally senescence." Imre, for the first time since the conversation took a serious turn, looked up and met Donnelly's eyes with his own—bloodshot and desolate. "My grandfather, the man who gave me every chance in life," Imre said softly, barely above a whisper, "is a pedophile."

"What?" Donnelly didn't need to fake surprise this time, nor did he have to bother with arranging his face in an attitude of shock. The shock was real. How could someone state such a horrifying, monstrous thing as a simple fact? Imre's voice had been as devoid of emotion as if he'd said his grandfather was a plumber, not a rapist.

Imre's eyes filled with tears, and his hands began to rattle the ice in his glass. "I've never said that out loud," he whispered miserably. "It sounds just as awful as it has in my head since I found out."

"That's... horrifying," Donnelly managed, his voice rough and tinged with more anger than he'd tried to show.

"I don't think I've had a decent night's sleep since I discovered it." He reached, gratefully, for the third gin and tonic handed to him by the waiter. He seemed to Donnelly to be quite used to drinking heavily when he thought of his grandfather.

"When did you find out?" Donnelly asked, setting his third drink next to his second, which was still mostly full.

"There'd been talk for many years among the diplomatic gossip grapevine," Imre replied. Donnelly felt sure he had met one of the primary cultivators of that particular vine. "I was slow to believe it, given how much he had helped me."

"But you said he hadn't even seen you since your parents were killed."

Imre nodded. "I don't mean he helped me directly. He certainly never did that. But his reputation among the diplomatic service, the prominence of his name, those things did help me a great deal. He opened doors for me, even if it was ultimately up to me to walk through them. I owed him a tremendous debt, and it kept me from seeing the truth about him while I could still do something about it."

Imre sighed and rubbed his eyes, suddenly seeming exhausted and ten years older. "I found out too late to save any of them. By the time I knew what was going on, he'd stopped."

"How do you know he's stopped? Imre, kids could be in danger." Donnelly could no longer hold back the fury he felt rising in his chest. "You have to do something."

The upbraiding hit home: Imre sagged even further. "I wish I could have done something to help them, Gabriel, I really do. But by the time I finally came to see the truth, cancer had taken both his willingness and his ability to cause any more pain. He's in hospice now and not expected to last another month."

"When you reported this, what happened? Did they bring charges?"

Imre frowned. He studied the remains of his third drink as he swirled it in the heavy crystal glass, then downed it in one go. "I had no evidence they could use. I had pieced together enough to be certain—beyond certain—but I had nothing that would stand up in court. It seemed better to let it go."

"Better? Does it *feel* better to you? Really?" Donnelly's voice had an edge in it that he struggled to soften, but he wasn't entirely successful. "Are you certain he wasn't part of a ring of some kind? Your grandfather may not be able to hurt anyone now, but there may be others who still can. If you have any evidence at all, you need to get it to the police or constable or whoever it is that watches over you diplomatic types."

Imre stared silently at the table. Their soup arrived, and still he stared blankly, apparently unaware that he was expected to actually dine in the dining room.

"What if I told you I was trying to do exactly that?" he finally murmured.

"Trying to do what?" Donnelly leaned closer.

This last question, delivered in Donnelly's "hostile witness" voice, set Imre back in his chair. He shook his head slightly as if clearing it of the will to confess, and picked up his soup spoon. "Forgive me," he said, his voice back to its prior smoothness. "I've become a little morose. I must be hungry."

Stupid! Donnelly berated himself through most of the soup course for pushing too hard, all the while keeping up his side of the small-talky conversation. Imre seemed to be bucking himself up as he regaled Donnelly with some anecdotes from the glamorous life of a cultural attaché.

As the table was cleared in preparation for the arrival of the main course, Donnelly eased back into his questioning.

"So, you were going to tell me about something you'd done. About your grandfather…," he said with a carefully crafted nonchalance.

"Ah, yes. I suppose I did mention something about that." Imre looked around the room. "I probably shouldn't say anything. I wouldn't want to involve you in… an incident of any kind."

"Sounds intriguing." Donnelly took a deep breath. "But we've only known each other since teatime, so if you don't feel like you can trust me, I understand." He gave Imre a look that he hoped conveyed equal parts disappointed humility and Boy Scout trustworthiness.

"It's not that, not at all," Imre replied. "It's just that what I've done might not be considered ethical by all observers."

Donnelly spoke seriously, and he spoke the truth. "If you did anything that might help prevent more children from being victimized, the ethics are definitely on your side." He could see Imre starting to soften, so he pushed a little further. "Plus, if you're worried I might tell someone about it, you can rest easy. I don't know anyone on this ship—pretty much kept to myself since New York. You're the only person I've exchanged more than elevator small talk with." A flattered grin began to appear. Time to lighten the mood and get the disclosures going. Donnelly craned around the room like a summer-stock Poirot, then whispered loudly, "Your secret is safe with me." He winked to seal the deal.

Imre chuckled, and Donnelly knew he was home free.

"It would be nice to tell someone, and since I can't tell anyone I work with, it'll be nice to tell a friend." He laid particular emphasis on this last word. "But not here. Maybe we can have a drink after dinner? We could go to my cabin."

"I'd like that," Donnelly said, as an alien feeling of shame crept up the back of his neck. He had never been invited by a man back to "his place" before and had never intended to be.

"It's a date," Imre said, in a voice suddenly laced with a smoky warmth that hadn't been there before. It gave Donnelly a chill, but as he willed a pleased expression onto his face, he realized there was a part of him that was thrilled to have seduced a man. The purpose was to get his information, not his dick, but still. His head spun a bit with the power he felt.

Their main courses arrived, and again the conversation veered into less intense topics, which seemed like a relief to both of them.

THEY HAD lingered over dinner for hours, Imre talking as if he could finally unburden himself to a friend who knew most of his secrets—and would know the rest soon. Donnelly realized over dessert that he had been dragging things out a bit, not wanting to rush toward the moment that he would find himself alone with Imre in his cabin.

Now they were there.

"I was surprised at how small the cabins are," Imre said as he shut the door behind them. "I figured it would be like a hotel room, but this is like a hotel room in Tokyo."

Donnelly looked about. Imre's entire cabin would fit into the bathroom of his suite. "But the view is much nicer, I'd imagine," he said, looking out at the pitch-black night. "When the sun's up, I mean."

Imre smiled. "This room has never looked as nice as it does at this moment," he said suavely, pouring deep amber bourbon into two heavy crystal tumblers. He handed one to Donnelly. "You really dress up the place."

Fuck, fuck, fuck. Donnelly took a deep breath and reminded himself that he had a job to do. *Pretend he's Ethan.* He tucked a half smile into the corner of his mouth and raised an eyebrow. "That's a pretty smooth tongue you've got there," he said slyly. "It must get you into trouble."

"It has on occasion," Imre said with the same smoky heat in his voice that had panicked Donnelly so badly at dinner. "I hope it will tonight."

"We'll see," Donnelly replied, then took a steadying sip of the bourbon. He needed a way to slow this down. "How about some fresh air?" He stepped across the length of the cabin—about three strides—and opened the balcony door. A whoosh of chilly night air swept into the cabin, and he walked gratefully into it. He leaned his elbows on the railing and looked down to where the hull slashed the ocean into glowing white ridges. He took a deep breath of sea air, but before he'd had a chance to let it out, Imre was next to him, leaning on the railing, their shoulders touching. They stared out at the sea for a long moment.

"This ship is so grand, and yet one steps out here and sees how small it is against the entire ocean," Imre said. "It gives one a certain perspective. Out here we are simply a tiny artifice of man, surrounded by miles and miles and hundreds of miles of dark ocean under stars infinitely more vast."

"We are small, aren't we?" Donnelly replied, looking up at the twinkling stars. He took a drink and then played his hand. "It would be easy to realize how very small we are in the grand scheme of things and figure what we do with our lives doesn't really matter." He looked at Imre. "I think what we do matters. We may not understand the effect it has on other people, on the world, on all of this"—he gestured out into the endless dark—"but I think what we do matters, and we should always try to do the best we can for the people in our lives."

"I have tried," Imre said. He stared down at the surging splash where hull met ocean. "Do you want to know what I've done?"

"If it would help to tell someone, I'd be honored to hear it." He hoped Imre would respond to this light touch.

"I don't know how to...." Imre lifted his gaze from the churning water and looked deeply into Donnelly's eyes. "A kiss for good luck?"

Donnelly tried not to let the shock show on his face, to suppress the panic he felt in that moment. He took a deep breath and repeated his mantra—*you're a cop, you're doing a job*—and he leaned in. He closed his eyes, and on the deck of a mighty ship surging through the night sea, he touched his lips to those of the second man he'd ever kissed.

He closed his eyes and thought of Ethan.

When the kiss ended, Imre stepped back slightly, smiling in the glow cast by the lights in the cabin, his hair whipped back and forth in a brisk wind. "Oh my," he said softly.

"That bad?" Donnelly asked teasingly.

"Breathtaking, that was."

"Can't take credit. The waves, the stars, the bourbon...." Donnelly smiled modestly. *Now spill it, buddy.*

"So. Let's see." Imre took a drink, swallowing awkwardly as if the liquid burned him on the way down. "When a diplomat wants to send something secret to another diplomat, he uses what's called a diplomatic pouch. Once it's sealed, it can only be opened by the recipient—no country would allow another country's pouch to be opened in transit across their territory because they wouldn't want theirs to be opened."

Donnelly nodded as if he were learning about the Vienna Convention for the first time.

"So the fact that I stole one yesterday is likely to cause an incident."

"You… what?" Donnelly didn't have to fake disbelief at hearing Imre's confession—he had certainly not anticipated it coming out so quickly.

"Well, strictly speaking I didn't steal it, but rather arranged for someone who knows the ship well—and who could evade the security cameras—to steal it for me. I convinced him he was helping me sort out a domestic dispute straight out of a *telenovela*, so the poor boy had no idea he was actually stealing. But I think the finer points would be lost on a panel of inquest. They tend to be rather grim about their duty."

"Does this have something to do with your grandfather?"

"The pouch was from him. It's been nearly a decade since he was in active service, but he used his last measure of strength to arrange for one final pouch. And the courier who was dispatched to carry it is on this very ship."

"Well, that was quite a coincidence."

Imre chuckled and rolled his eyes. "Not exactly. The plan had to be made quickly, as I only found out that the pouch existed when the courier was sent. That volcano threw a bit of a spanner into the works, but in the end it was easier to steal it from a safe in a cruise-ship cabin than in an airport or while actually on a plane. I know the courier—he's far too good to let a pouch out of his possession under normal circumstances. When I found out he'd managed to get on board, I got here as soon as I could. There were so many diplomats who wanted to get on this sailing that I had to pull a few well-placed strings to get passage myself. He is a tremendously resourceful courier."

"That may be," Donnelly said, "but one imagines he's out of a job now, since his pouch has been stolen." Imre winced, clearly regretting that his theft might indeed have negative ramifications for Sandler. "Was it worth it? What was inside?"

"It's one of two things," Imre said somewhat mysteriously.

"You don't know?" Donnelly stared at him, mouth dropping open before he could stop it. "I can't decide which is crazier: that you stole it without even knowing what's in it, or that you've been holding it since yesterday and haven't opened it yet."

"I don't say this to in any way excuse my behavior, but I've been wracked with guilt ever since that pouch arrived in my cabin. I intended to open it immediately, but once I had it in my hands, the enormity of what I'd done overcame me, and I had to hide it and get as far away from it as possible."

"I don't think I understand," Donnelly said. "You went through all the trouble of getting on this ship with that pouch, then you managed to convince a member of the staff to steal it for you, and finally you have it… what's keeping you from opening it?"

"I'm afraid of what I'll find inside" was Imre's lame reply.

"You said it was one of two things," Donnelly prompted.

"Yes. My grandfather has been ill for some time. For him to arrange for a diplomatic pouch after all those years, well, it had to be a matter of extreme importance. He was well aware of the recent investigations into pedophile rings in the British government, and I think he feared he was about to be unmasked."

"What do you think he put in the pouch?" Donnelly asked, unable to choose from the possibilities swirling in his head.

"Evidence. One way or the other. Either my grandfather sent a confession—a literal deathbed confession—or he sent something that he ginned up to clear his name."

"You're sure there's no possibility that he is innocent?"

Imre shook his head gravely. "Not a chance. I recently found a story in the newspaper about a cricket team in Africa he'd helped start in the sixties that had grown over the years and last year won a championship. I showed it to my classmates at our reunion several months ago, proud to have a relation who had done some good in the world. Three of them, each independently of the others, pulled me aside and told me that they knew him. In the years before I got there, he'd been a benefactor of the school, returning to check on the progress of the students who benefited from his largesse— noble families fallen on hard times. The price he exacted for his generosity was paid late at night in the boathouse. Each was terribly ashamed and would never breathe a word of it to the school staff or their families. But in that bizarre fraternity, we had no secrets among ourselves, and so they let me know—without stinting any detail—how my grandfather had raped them. It was harrowing for them, and devastating for me." Imre took a deep breath, shaking as if the shock were still fresh. "So no, there's no chance he's innocent."

"What are you going to do once you open the pouch?"

"If it's a confession, I'll make sure it gets to the right people. The person to whom it's addressed may be inclined to keep it quiet, especially if a confession might cast a negative light on anyone else who's still alive. If it's fraudulent 'proof' of his innocence, I'll need some time to be sure I've got evidence against him and get that into the public record alongside whatever he's faked up. I don't think he'll face prosecution—he wouldn't last through opening statements—but the record must reflect what he's done."

Donnelly thought about this for a moment. "Here's what I don't understand. You're pretty sure you know what's in the pouch, one way or the other. You know what you're going to do with whatever it is you find." He paused, and Imre nodded to each of his points. "Then why the hesitation to open it?"

Imre sighed at the stars, then turned and walked back into the cabin. He sat on the small sofa, then set his empty glass on the coffee table. He was silent.

Donnelly, having followed him into the cabin, waited for a bit to see if the explanation was forthcoming, then walked over to the tray where the bourbon bottle sat. He picked it up and poured Imre—and himself—another drink. Imre nodded his thanks but remained silent.

Figuring he might be in for a wait, Donnelly sat down next to him and joined in, staring at the glass of bourbon as proxy for staring at Imre. It didn't work. Finally, he could wait no longer.

"Did your grandfather... did he—"

"Rape me?" Imre said under his breath.

Donnelly nodded with apprehensive encouragement.

Imre picked up the bourbon and took a long drink. He set the glass down and stared at it for a while longer. "No," he said.

Donnelly, hugely relieved but careful not to show it, took a healthy swig of the bourbon he'd poured himself. "Then what is it? What are you afraid you're going to find in that pouch?"

"Myself."

"But you just said he never—"

"Not myself as a victim. But myself as… him." Imre suddenly turned to face Donnelly, his eyes ringed with red, his expression desperate. "I don't want to be him."

Donnelly had always been a perceptive judge of character, and his time with Imre had led him to a confident conclusion. "You are not your grandfather," he said, slowly and soothingly.

"But you know what it's like," Imre said, growing more animated. "Growing up you hear all of these horror stories about how gay men are child molesters and can't be trusted. When I left school and had to face the fact that it wasn't just a phase for me, I had to convince myself I was still a good person." He looked at Donnelly pleadingly. "You said you grew up in a small town—you must have had it even worse than I did."

Donnelly couldn't answer. He knew what he should do—agree and keep the conversation going so he could finally understand what had made Imre steal the pouch—but in that moment he couldn't lie. Not about something as personal as this.

"I didn't, actually," he said softly. "I grew up… straight."

"What?" Imre was clearly startled.

"I grew up believing I was straight. Dated girls, went to prom, even had some girlfriends in college. It wasn't until I met… someone… that I even considered I might be gay."

"Wow. You're like the polar opposite of everyone I went to school with—most of them had sex every night, but never with a woman, at least until they graduated. I didn't know anyone did it the other way around." He smiled wanly. "He must have been an amazing guy."

"Indeed he was." *And still is.* "But I know very well the internal prejudice that gets built up over time that makes you think if you kiss a guy and like it you're suddenly a pervert. My mother was crystal clear on that."

"Well, two sons who turn out gay—I guess she was entitled to her tantrum. Any other siblings for her to pin her hopes on?"

"Just my sister, and she has a track record of making far worse choices in men than either my brother or myself did."

Imre chuckled, his angst about the pouch lifting. Donnelly saw his opportunity and decided to press on.

"So how about it? Let's bust that thing open."

Imre burst out laughing. "That's exactly what I was hoping to hear from you tonight, just not about the pouch."

"And there goes your dignified-diplomat façade," scolded Donnelly.

"I figured I had to take a shot," Imre replied, a sly grin on his face.

"We've got bigger fish to fry. Where's the pouch?"

Imre nodded. "You're right, I need to just do it. Thank you for being here with me." He patted Donnelly on the shoulder as he passed by on his way to the closet. From underneath his clothes, he pulled out Sandler's messenger bag.

Donnelly remembered it so clearly from the first forty-eight hours he and Sandler had been on this crazy journey. Its worn leather smell carried the essence of Sandler with it.

Imre set the pouch on the bed and sat next to it. Donnelly joined him, sitting on the other side of the bed, and they stared at it together. "Well, best be getting on with it," Imre said, unbuckling the messenger bag's metal clasps. He folded open the bag and withdrew an envelope with a discreet red seal on the front.

Imre set the envelope on the bed, and looked up at Donnelly. "I'm about to break a very serious law," he said.

"You don't have to," Donnelly replied. "You can take it to the ship's security officer right now, and he'll get it back to Sandler. I'm sure if you explain it to the ambassador, she'd understand. You had the right intentions."

Imre looked at Donnelly, the color draining from his cheeks.

"What's wrong?" Donnelly asked. "You look like you've just seen a ghost."

"Who did you say should get the pouch?"

"The ship's security officer. I saw him… during the lifeboat drill. Seemed like a nice guy."

"No, after that." Imre's eyes, unblinking, gave Donnelly a chill.

"Uh, the ambassador? That's who should get the pouch, right?"

"You said 'Sandler.' How did you know the courier's name, Gabriel?"

Fuck, fuck, fuck, fuck.

"You mentioned it yourself, a while ago, when we were talking about how he managed to find a way to get to England despite the volcano." Donnelly looked for any sign he was believed. He saw none.

"Something of which you may not be aware, being an American, is that when someone is in service, he is referred to by last name only. If I did mention his name, I would have called him 'Birkin.' I only recall his first name because it's unusual, and I certainly would never use it to refer to him."

One of the first rules of telling lies, Donnelly reflected in that moment, is to know when to stop telling them. He took a deep breath and gave up.

"You're right. I know Sandler. He's a friend of mine. And he is simply desperate to find out what happened to his pouch. We did some asking around and discovered the connection between your grandfather and the pouch. It was the only lead we had, and we decided to take our best shot at figuring out what happened. That's why I showed up at your tea table—to see if I could gather some information."

"And then once we'd spent almost the entire day together under false pretenses, you were going to… what? Grab the pouch and smash your way out of my cabin with it? Is that why you're doing this?"

"No, that's not what I was going to do—not at all. Imre, listen to me. What you've done you did for the right reasons. You had the protection of children at heart, and though you've made some questionable decisions in terms of the law, you have acted ethically in trying to ensure your grandfather's crimes are brought to light. If I'm ever forced to choose between the Vienna Convention and the welfare of children, I wouldn't hesitate to make the same choice you did." He put his hand on Imre's, trying to drive the point home. "I'm on your side, Imre."

Imre studied his eyes for a long moment, squinting as if trying to reach into the depths of Donnelly's soul and weigh the morality he found there. Then, abruptly, he blinked twice and took a deep breath.

Donnelly waited, hoping he was found worthy.

Imre looked down at the pouch, then back up to Donnelly, and back down again. "In my ethics classes, it never felt this way. They give you alternatives, and you have to reason your way to a course of action. But both choices just feel *wrong* here. If I open the pouch, I'm going against what I've devoted my career to preserving—the sanctity of Crown and country. But if I don't open it, my grandfather's crimes might never be known—or worse, he might be exonerated by false evidence. I don't know what to do."

"I can't answer that for you. I wish I could. All I can say is you should do what you think will cause the greatest benefit—or the least suffering—for the most people. Or the people who can't help themselves."

Imre seemed to ponder this for a moment, then closed his eyes and nodded, as if he'd answered the question for himself. When he opened his eyes, the confused desperation had been replaced with a new calm, a sense of purpose Donnelly could feel just by looking at him. He picked up the envelope and slid his finger under the seal. Having accomplished this diplomatic violation, he let out the breath he'd been holding and reached into the envelope. He pulled out a small packet about the size of a paperback book. It was covered in heavy green paper and bore a label inscribed in the flowing but tremulous hand of an elderly civil servant.

"I know this name." Imre said, reading the label. "It's an old friend of his in the Foreign Office. I think he's the only person still in service with whom my grandfather served—everyone else is either pensioned or dead." He stared at the packet, running his fingertips over his grandfather's cursive. He was lost in his reverie for some time before shaking it off. "Sorry, you must think me a sap just sitting here staring at my grandfather's handwriting."

"Not at all. Take all the time you need."

"What do you do, Gabriel?" Imre asked lightly, not taking his eyes off his grandfather's script.

"When I'm not sleuthing on cruise ships, you mean?"

Imre managed a chuckle. "Yes, though you are quite good at that, it seems."

"I'm a police officer—a state trooper, as we're called where I live."

Imre's laugh was loud, but largely mirthless. "Perfect. I've now committed a treaty violation in the presence of an officer of the law. This just keeps getting better."

Donnelly held his hands out in a shrug. "I'm afraid I have no jurisdiction here," he said. "The Vienna Convention will have to find other defenders."

Imre put his hand on Donnelly's knee. "Thank you," he said, with a not-very-convincing tone of irony. He was clearly relieved. He sighed and looked again at the packet in his hands. "I guess it's time to find out."

He tugged gingerly at the seal on the packet, teasing it open without ripping the paper. He unfolded it carefully and spread it open on the bed between them.

On top of the paper lay a box with a small envelope on top of it. This slid off to the side as Imre picked up the box and turned it over in his hands. It was made of paperboard, and had probably at some time in the distant past contained stationery for writing letters—likely with a fountain pen. Imre set it back down and gripped the lid of the box with trembling fingers. Slowly, he lifted it off. It made a barely audible groan, as if reluctant to give up its secrets. Imre set the lid aside and looked into the box.

It contained a leather-bound notebook, its corners frayed slightly. There was a monogram on the cover, over which Imre ran his fingers.

"It was his," he whispered, as if holding a relic of the man not yet dead.

He opened it.

Donnelly watched his eyes flicker over the first page, then the next, and the four or five after that. The corners of his mouth turned down—the disgust he felt was writ large on his face. He flipped through the pages with increasing speed, his look of horror deepening. He reached the end and dropped the little book as if it had bitten him.

"What is it?" Donnelly asked.

"He… he kept—" Imre bolted up from the bed and ran to the bathroom. Donnelly heard him retching, a violent noise of strain and disgust, only stopping when the sound of his throwing up was replaced by his sobs.

Donnelly walked gingerly over to the bathroom door and peeked in. Imre was sitting on the floor next to the toilet, panting, crying, looking like the world had been knocked out from under him all at once.

"You okay?" Donnelly asked as he uncapped the little bottle of mouthwash that stood sentry by the sink. He poured the contents into a glass and handed it to Imre, along with a hand towel.

"No," Imre replied. He tossed back the mouthwash, swished it for a moment, then spat it into the bathtub next to him. He handed Donnelly the glass and wiped his mouth. "Thank you."

Donnelly took the glass, rinsed it out, then filled it with water and handed it back to him. "Stress barfing can really dehydrate a person," he said.

Imre took a long blink, as if trying to fend off the silly remark, but a smile made its way onto his face. He drank the water, then got to his feet and put the glass on the bathroom counter himself. "Thank you, Gabriel. I'm glad not to have been alone when I opened it."

"Do you want to talk about what you found?" Donnelly asked.

"You don't want to know," Imre said, leading the way back to the bed.

"If it would help you to share it, I want you to. I can handle it."

"That's right, you're a police officer. You've probably seen some horrible things."

Donnelly nodded grimly.

"My grandfather apparently kept a running account of every young life he destroyed, every boy he robbed of his innocence. The first entries are from his own boyhood, but he seems to have kept at it all his life. Well, until the last few years, anyway, when his ill health finally ended his predations." Imre took a deep breath, looking very much like he was going to be sick again. "He kept very detailed notes—names and dates, but also how he seduced or threatened them, and what exactly he did to them. It's all preserved in his Edwardian script, as if he were recording bird sightings during pleasant walks in the Lake District." He swallowed hard. "He is a monster, Gabriel. An absolute monster."

"That's horrifying," Donnelly replied, shaken by what Imre had described. "How does someone do such things and then write them up in a tidy little notebook? Why would he keep such detailed records?"

"And more to the point, why was he sending it by courier? There's only one reason I can think of—he wanted to be sure it was out of the grasp of anyone who might want to investigate him."

"Why wouldn't he just burn it?"

"He's been confined to a sickbed for the last several years. He wouldn't have had a chance. This was his only way to hide the record of his crimes."

"Or maybe he wasn't trying to hide them," Donnelly suggested. "He sent them to someone in the Foreign Office—perhaps this was his confession?"

Imre shook his head gravely. "I've never seen any sign that he regretted his behavior at all. If he wanted to confess, wouldn't he have asked his only living relative to come hear it? If it was a confession, he had to know that I would be among the first to find out about it. And I'd be the one who would have his guilt on my shoulders for the rest of my career." Imre reached out for the well-thumbed black book, but then recoiled from it in renewed disgust.

"Imre?" Donnelly said softly. "There's something else you should look at." He picked up the envelope that had been cast aside when the box was opened. "It's addressed to you."

"What?" Imre looked at Donnelly with eyebrows raised in an expression of overwhelmed exhaustion. But he reached out and took the envelope from him. On its surface, his name was inscribed in a much surer hand than the one on the outside of the pouch, though it was still recognizable as his grandfather's bureaucratic script.

"I don't know if I can take another surprise," Imre said softly, turning the envelope over and over in his hand. "And how did he possibly imagine I'd be the one to open the pouch?"

"Only one way to find out," Donnelly said. "You need to know it all before you decide what to do about what your grandfather's left behind."

Imre pondered this for a moment, then set his jaw. He slid his finger under the flap of the envelope and withdrew a square of ivory writing paper. He unfolded it carefully, gently pressing the creases out of it until it lay flat on the bed before him. His grandfather's regimented cursive marched across the page in ruler-straight lines, evenly spaced and perfectly formed, as if the letter were a sample in a penmanship manual. Imre cleared his throat and began to read.

To my grandson, my dearest boy, my Imre—

His voice faltered at the end of the salutation and tears again filled his eyes. "I used to lie awake at night, dreaming of hearing those words," he whispered. "Only now, with his humanity obliterated, when he's proven that I am descended from a monster, does he assert our relationship." He shook his head, bereft. "Now that it's a curse."

"Take your time," Donnelly said. "Would you like another drink before going on?"

Imre shook his head. "Better to get through it, I think." He took a deep breath and began again.

This morning I watched as you were received as the new cultural attaché to this uncultured country we now both inhabit.

Imre paused, a somewhat frantic look on his face.

"I thought you said you hadn't seen him since he brought you to school?"

"I haven't. The day he's describing was more than three years ago, but I remember it clearly—he wasn't there."

The men shrugged to each other.

I couldn't be there in person, of course, but they were kind enough to film it and send it to your very proud grandfather. From what I hear, such a post was long in your hopes, and I congratulate you on attaining it. I wish I could have offered my congratulations in person.

Seeing the fine young man you have become has affected me far more than I could have predicted. It has changed me, in fact—changed me utterly. I hope you will understand I do not exaggerate in saying this.

Seeing your pure and masculine form today as your credentials were received, I realized what a monstrous thing I have done to so many young men not much different from yourself.

The person who delivered to you this letter has, if my wishes have been observed, also given to you a small notebook, one I carried with me from my earliest school days. It is a memoir of sorts—a devil's diary, I see now. It wasn't always. For years it has been my trophy, my secret gallery of triumphs. It is now my greatest shame.

What you hold in your hand is the best explanation I could ever offer for my absence from your life, Imre. Its pages contain the name of every boy I ever led astray, and how many times they suffered from my corrupted nature. I was determined that your name should never be among them. And so I was forced to stay away.

I barely knew your grandmother; she was a mistake I made early in life. I never laid eyes upon your mother—in fact, I never even knew her name until that horrid excuse for a man she married starting making demands. I hoped the car I sent would silence him.

Seeing you as an orphan—my flesh and blood—should have been enough to keep me from ever imagining you in the way I saw all boys your age. But I was weak in the face of my craven appetites, and once I had delivered you to school, I knew I could never see you again.

I wanted to forsake my monstrous ways, but I was not strong enough. Not until today.

You may ask yourself why, if I see my crimes clearly for what they were, I was unable to keep myself from committing them. I justified my actions to myself in myriad ways—that the boys I forced myself on enjoyed our contact as much as I did, that I was opening them to a world of physical pleasure they might otherwise never have known, that I was following in the classical footsteps of great Greek philosophers. In truth— and truth is all that is left to me now as I look back on a life filled with horrors—I knew, ab initio *and always, that what I did was wrong.*

I do not deserve the accolades that were heaped upon me when I withdrew from diplomatic service. I do not deserve the respect or even empathy of someone of your character. And I certainly do not deserve to enjoy an unsullied reputation after I have shuffled off this mortal coil. What you hold in your hand is my legacy. I will not destroy it, because I intend it to destroy my name after I am gone. I entrust it to you, Imre. Please see that it reaches those who will investigate my crimes and see justice done. It is my funeral pyre.

I came of age in a time when relations between men were outlawed. Because even a bare simulacrum of courtship and marriage was forbidden men like myself, my carnal as well as my romantic urges moldered inside me until they were forced out in furtive and criminal ways. I offer this, by way of explanation if not expiation: when all relations between men are forbidden, when there is no socially sanctioned structure in which men can build healthy relationships, the result will be dark, vile, criminal. Please understand me—I don't justify my crimes by blaming "society." I ask only that you reflect on this: yes, I should have been imprisoned for having sexual relations with boys. But I also would have been imprisoned for having sexual relations with men my age. And even once the criminal sanctions were lifted—and this did not occur until 1967!—I still would have lost my job, my pension, and all that I have worked to accomplish in my career.

But enough of an old man's confession. I did so much wrong to so many people during my life that I can never make restitution. I only ask that you now commit yourself to doing three things that may serve to reduce, however slightly, the suffering that I have caused.

The most distasteful task I will commend to you first. You must deliver the enclosed diary to the Crown Prosecution Service immediately. I trust no one else to accomplish this. I do not wish to burden you with descriptions of crimes you had no knowledge of and were powerless to prevent, but I will simply say that there is ample evidence contained in the pages of that book to indict several prominent members of the current government.

This will be difficult, Imre, and I am deeply sorry to have inflicted this heavy responsibility upon you. Some damage will, alas, accrue to your own good name from its association with mine. For that I apologize.

The second task will be more arduous but, I hope, less onerous. I have granted you power of attorney over the fortune I have amassed over my years (honestly, I must stipulate—my crimes have been carnal, not fiscal). I wish you to take one-half of those funds and disburse it among the young men I have listed in the diary. You may apologize on my behalf if you wish (I am truly repentant, though I don't expect you to accept my word), or you may join them in cursing my name—that is for you to decide.

If they have died, please deliver their allotment to their survivors. Each is to receive an equal portion, except for those marked with a double asterisk in the book; to them deliver a double share, for their suffering was accordingly greater. I shall not burden you with details.

The third task will, I hope, be for you a source of not only contentment but eventually pride. With the remaining half of my estate, I ask you to establish a foundation dedicated to protecting the youth of whom I have taken such shameful advantage. I preyed on both the indigent and the aristocratic, and children from all backgrounds deserve protection. I leave every detail up to you. I make only one condition: that you name it after someone you respect. Let my name accompany me into the grave.

I thank you for being willing to read the scribbles of an old and dissolute man. You have done me a great service, one that I did nothing to deserve. I wish you well, my dear grandson, in all that you do. Great things lie ahead for you, this much I know. May you have every happiness I was denied, and denied myself.

Imre fell silent, and stared for a time at the baroque signature of his grandfather. "I feel like he's dead already," he said finally. "It's hard to think of the man who wrote this lying alone in a hospital, breathing numbered breaths. I'd given up on the very idea of ever seeing him again, but now...."

"Do you think you'll go visit him?" Donnelly asked. He rose to pour more bourbon, sensing it wouldn't go amiss.

"I don't know." He took the glass from Donnelly with a faint smile, then took a long drink. "Imagine if your grandfather was on his deathbed, and before you went to him you found out he had been a Nazi. Not just a soldier following orders, but one of the really bad ones. Like he struck out on his own and set up an extra concentration camp, just for his own amusement. Sure, he says he's sorry, but does that really matter at this point?"

"I can't imagine having to figure that one out," Donnelly replied, shrugging empathetically. "But even if you never see him again, he has at least given you the ability to do some good. No one has to know he was the one who made it possible."

Imre gave a miserable grunt. "Yeah, that's going to be great. I get to spend the next who knows how many years tracking down the kids my grandfather fucked and giving them a few bucks for their trouble. Sounds like a great time." He covered his face with his hands, silent in his shock and grief.

"Someone I love very much tells me my optimism is both the best and the worst thing about me," Donnelly said, thinking of all the times Brandt had cast him that special look in response to some sunny-side-up comment. "But here's what I think. Your grandfather's wishes don't have to be followed in order. Set up the foundation first and start doing some good in the world. Then, once the criminal case is underway, you can start getting in touch with his victims. That way you can have support mechanisms in place for them, and they'll be able to see that life will be better for the next generation. They may also be more willing to cooperate with the prosecution of anyone else who still might be committing these horrible crimes." He smiled hopefully at Imre, who had lowered his hands and was listening attentively.

"You are amazing," he said, shaking his head and smiling—genuinely smiling—for the first time since the pouch had been opened. "This person you love is really lucky to have you in their life."

Donnelly grimaced sheepishly. "He's actually my fiancé."

Imre chuckled. "Figures. All the good ones are taken." Then his eyes grew wide. "Sorry about the kiss earlier. I clearly thought things were going a different way. Between us, I mean."

"I'm the one who should be apologizing. Sandler was desperate to find out what happened to the pouch, and he figured I might be able to, as he put it, 'turn your head.' I'm flattered that it worked."

"It did, it did," Imre assured him. "You are certainly in the right line of work. I think you could make anyone confess to anything if you kiss them like that."

"The department is surprisingly rather opposed to officers seducing suspects," Donnelly replied.

"Oh, so enhanced interrogation techniques are off the table all of a sudden?"

They shared a laugh, the tension in the room evaporating.

"Well, I guess I need to deal with this," Imre said, looking down at the horrid black book.

"I think if you tell the ambassador it was intended for you all along, she may be willing to overlook the entire thing," Donnelly offered. "I mean, in the end all you did was accelerate the delivery of something that was going to come to you anyway. With the added bonus that you can hand over the book to the proper authorities even more quickly. Aside from the treaty violation, no harm no foul, right?"

"For an officer of the law, you're a little fast and loose, aren't you?" Imre paused for a moment, frowning with concentration. "Though you may have a point. The Vienna Convention is an agreement among nation-states, so its provisions don't apply to individuals within the embassy staff of a single nation."

"Do you know the ambassador well?"

Imre nodded. "We're not friends, exactly, but we've worked together on several cultural projects over the last couple of years. Why?"

"Just wondering what's she's like. One hopes she's the kind of person who would look at the big picture and see that good purpose will be served by your having the pouch sooner rather than later."

"It wouldn't hurt to have you along to offer that justification on my behalf." His eyes twinkled mischievously. "Throw in a little kiss and I think you'll have her won over."

"She's not another Fabienne Maillard, is she?"

Imre burst out laughing. "I am happy to report that there is only one Fabienne Maillard. You've had the pleasure, then?"

"It seems like the pleasure was all hers," Donnelly replied with a roll of his eyes. "Everyone else in the world seemed to be merely decorative accents, viewed over the rim of her martini glass."

"That's her exactly!" Imre hooted with laughter. "The ambassador is a dear friend of hers, but she's of a much more serious bent. Plus, she's married to a man her own age, so that sets them apart pretty starkly." Imre looked at his watch. "Well, this evening got away from us, didn't it? Sorry for all the drama—every single day of my life before this one was absolutely normal, I swear."

Donnelly got to his feet. "Never settle for normal," he said as he pulled Imre into an embrace. "You have some heavy marching orders. It's a lot of responsibility, but you will do a lot of good for a lot of people. And remember this…." He released Imre to arm's length and looked him seriously in the eyes. "You are not your grandfather. His sins are not yours to carry, or to excuse, or to beg forgiveness for. You are your own man, and a damn good one."

"Thank you, Gabriel. You've appeared in my life exactly when I needed the help you have to offer. I hope you have a lovely time at Normandy."

Donnelly looked away sheepishly. "About that," he began.

"Let me guess, your grandfather was as much fiction as mine is unfortunately real?"

"No, I did have a wonderful grandfather. But the reason for my trip is… I'm getting married next week. In a castle in Devon. To Officer Ethan Brandt, the love of my life."

Imre smiled and practically vibrated with happiness. "I am so glad to hear that. I wish the two of you the very best."

"Thank you. Now, if you don't mind, there's someone who's waiting in agony to find out what happened to his pouch. May I let Sandler know that his responsibility for this pouch is complete?"

"Yes, please do. And give him back his messenger bag, along with my best regards. If he's interested, I'll be sure there are many more commissions in the future."

"I will." Donnelly beamed at Imre, then pulled him into another enthusiastic hug. "Good luck, Imre. And please, let me know if there's anything I can do to help you in the future."

"And you may likewise rely on me," Imre whispered. He kissed Donnelly on both cheeks. "Good night, Gabriel."

"YOU DON'T seem that relieved," Donnelly said, having just spent the better part of an hour describing what had transpired at dinner and in Imre's cabin.

"I'm still trying to take it all in," Sandler replied. "You have to remember I've never lost a pouch before, and now to have one stolen by none other than the very person it was ultimately destined for? That just doesn't happen."

"As someone who has had many things happen to him lately that just don't happen, I am uniquely prepared to give you advice. And my advice is: let it go. The universe has seen fit to yank you back from that particular precipice, so just let it go. You're still employable, and in fact I think Imre will seek you out for future courier duties. Your buddy Ankur turned out to be good people, and you can keep working up a sweat together all the way to Southampton. Life is good, my friend, very good."

Sandler smiled. "You're just whacked out on endorphins because you're going to be in the bulging arms of your fiancé in just over twenty-four hours. I think you'd tell a smoldering Joan of Arc to just let it go."

"Right you are," Donnelly replied, giving a joyful little bounce on his way to the bedroom. "And now I'm going to turn in. Give me about four and a half minutes, and I'll be so fast asleep, you and Ankur could bang away at each other until noon and I wouldn't have a clue." He stepped into the bedroom, then poked his head back out. "I will, though, insist on details."

"It's a deal," Sandler said. "And Gabriel, I can't thank you enough for all you've done for me. You've saved my career, such as it is."

"You are good at what you do, and you are good in general. You didn't need saving. I just helped things along a bit."

"Well, I owe you. Thanks."

"It was my pleasure. A bizarre, exhausting pleasure. And now, I bid you good night." He closed the door behind him, stripped off his clothes, and collapsed on the bed. He was, true to his word, completely unconscious four minutes later.

CHAPTER TWELVE

Saturday, One Week until the Wedding
Ferry, North Sea

THE NEXT morning Mags was back at her table in the restaurant, alone, drinking tea as if it were bourbon. If she was pleased to see Bryce and Nestor resume their seats before her, she gave no outward sign. With just an eyebrow—raised imperiously—she ordered tea for them as well, and once they each had a cup in front of them she finally spoke.

"Did we enjoy ourselves last night?" she asked in the tone of voice one would use to inquire about a knitting club meeting.

"We did," Bryce replied pleasantly. "Several times, actually."

"Ah, youth," she said wistfully. "One always hears that it is wasted on the young, but I rather enjoy watching the young waste it."

Bryce set his cup down, stricken. "Oh, darling, if you wanted to watch you need only to have asked." He turned to Nestor. "I feel just terrible we deprived her, don't you? Particularly given the somewhat acrobatic performances our guest stars were capable of."

Nestor nodded sorrowfully.

"Oh, piff," Mags replied. "I'm at that age where hearing about it later is just as good as seeing it in person."

"May God strike me dead before I reach that age," Bryce said solemnly, gazing heavenward.

"She shall, I daresay," Mags replied blandly, then sipped her tea and waited patiently for story time to begin.

They passed a leisurely breakfast while Bryce explained in great detail how he and Nestor had whiled away their evening.

"And so," Bryce concluded breathlessly, for describing the various bodily arrangements was nearly as exhausting as performing them had been, "that's when Nestor whispers in my ear, 'This is what the old señora wanted.' Well, you could have knocked me over with a feather. Not literally, of course, because those strapping waiters had me—both of us, actually—rather pinned in place. But as we thumped and crashed our way to the inevitable conclusion, all I could think was what a delightfully dirty old man that ancient broad turned out to be."

"No higher compliment has ever been paid," Mags sang out joyously. "Thank you for fulfilling an old gal's wish."

"The pleasure, it was ours," Nestor murmured.

"I should hope so," Mags replied and laughed until her voice was reduced to a raspy rattle.

The ferry's horn lowed plaintively.

"We must, I'm afraid, take our leave," Bryce said sadly. "We've got to take a train to get to the other train to jump on a camel or something."

"You two have been a delight to this old woman's heart," Mags said seriously, as she took their hands in turn. "Would you please give those constables of yours my best wishes for their long happiness together?"

"Of course, darling," Bryce promised. Then a light blinked on in his head. "You may join us, if you feel up to the trip. You could be the 'something old' for the ceremony."

"As charming as your offer is, I must refuse. I've got roses that are no doubt running riot all over my garden, and there's a church auction benefiting the local shelter for gay youth that I must help prepare for." She took a breath as if winded by the very mention of what she had waiting at home. "If you will allow an old woman her sentiment, I predict that the two of you will have as many happy years ahead of you as I enjoyed with Harold. Just remember to be kind to each other, and to share the special things in life—especially sailors."

"We shall, we shall," Bryce twittered, bestowing a scented cloud of air kisses upon the old dame. "We've been honored to meet you, Mags."

"Yes, yes you have," she replied. She picked up her teacup and gazed out the window, settling into a peaceful silence.

Bryce and Nestor made their way from the ferry terminal to the train station, where they secured a pair of seats in a first-class compartment and were soon rattling south toward the capital. The view out the windows offered a range of scenery, from charming hamlets to green dales, but Bryce had eyes only for the quartet of young men in the compartment opposite.

Morning, at sea

IN THE morning—or at least the last twenty-two minutes of it before the hands on the grand clock in the suite met at the top of the dial—Donnelly stepped out of the bedroom to find Sandler and Ankur snuggled together on the sofa bed. The sheets were seriously tangled, evidence of the lustful tarantella the two had danced through the wee hours of the morning. Donnelly smiled at them as he stepped to the phone and ordered brunch from Rutherford. He went out onto the balcony to await its arrival.

He looked out over the ocean, smooth as a mirror and extending miles and miles to a flat line where darker blue met lighter blue.

He's out there.

Donnelly had worked hard on putting Brandt's distressing absence out of his mind. At times like this, with nothing for him to focus on besides the distance between them, a heaviness crept into his chest. But, he reminded himself, they would be together soon. He imagined what Brandt must be feeling at this moment, and he smiled. Donnelly had beguiled this long week into passing quickly, pushing himself to think of other things, undertaking distracting cloak-and-dagger intrigue. Brandt, however, would kick and fight and struggle, determined to not just psychically but physically subdue the week. This morning he would be preparing his victory lap around the ring, glorying in having thrashed and beaten each hour into the past.

It was ridiculous. And Donnelly loved him for it.

Behind him, the balcony door opened. "Sir?" Rutherford said gently.

"Good morning, Rutherford."

"Would you like breakfast on the balcony, sir?"

"Yes, please."

The butler stepped back into the suite and reemerged with a huge silver tray. He laid out a white tablecloth and arranged an elegant table with such speed and precision that Donnelly couldn't help but be impressed.

"Join me for a cup of coffee before you go?" Donnelly asked once the preparations were complete.

Rutherford smiled and nodded. He poured two cups of steaming black coffee from the elegant silver pot (there was another on the cart in the suite, because Rutherford knew his stuff), and he handed one to Donnelly. They stood at the railing and sipped.

"I'd like to thank you for everything this week," Donnelly said.

"It's my pleasure to serve, sir," Rutherford replied modestly.

"I think we may have presented… challenges… beyond those you are normally called upon to handle."

Rutherford smiled. "Discretion prevents me from providing details, sir, but let me assure you that a significant number of previous guests have also presented interesting… challenges." He raised an eyebrow and sipped his coffee.

"I wish Ethan could have been here for this trip. He *hates* being waited on, but you're so good at it that I think you might have broken him of it."

"Perhaps he can make the trip next time," Rutherford replied. "I plan to be here for many years to come, and I have no doubt the two of you shall celebrate many years together."

"You say the sweetest things," Donnelly said. "I wish I could take you home with me."

"I doubt there will be room in your luggage, with Ankur already packed away for Mister Birkin." He winked over the top of his cup. "Thank you, sir, for the invitation. Now I must see to my duties, unless there's anything else?"

"Nothing else, Rutherford. Thank you." Donnelly finished his coffee as well. "Oh, if you could let Sandler and Ankur know that breakfast is here?"

"I will do my best to get them out of bed, sir." He smiled. "But I am only one man." With a warm chuckle, he headed back into the suite.

He may have been only one man, but Rutherford was somehow able to roust Sandler and Ankur from their slumber. They appeared, stumbling and blinking, just a few minutes later. The bright sun threatened to overwhelm them at first, and they stayed tucked close to the hull, looking mostly at each other and occasionally at the sea as they sipped tea. A fresh breeze ruffled the hems of their robes, and Donnelly was treated to an eyeful by the odd gust.

"You two seem to be having a pleasant day," he observed, tearing a morsel off the top of a blueberry muffin and popping it into his mouth.

"We are having the most pleasant of days," Sandler replied, and both he and Ankur beamed at Donnelly, radiating happiness.

"And the saddest of days," added Ankur, his smile instantly evaporating. Sandler nodded his head in melancholy agreement.

Donnelly stared at them for a moment, but they simply went back to sipping their tea and looking at each other. "Um, what?" he asked when it became clear they intended to offer no further thoughts on the matter.

"Today is your last day on the ship," Ankur explained gently, as if Donnelly might not have been aware.

"And Ankur and I won't see each other again," Sandler added.

Donnelly shook his head to clear it of the nonsense he had just heard. "Why in the world would you say that? There's no reason why you can't—"

Sandler held up a hand. "There is an insurmountable obstacle in our path, and so we must go our separate ways."

"And what could this insurmountable obstacle be?" Donnelly had seen people overcome long odds to find love together, and he was baffled as to why Sandler and Ankur thought they could not do the same.

"I am leaving the ship after this voyage," Ankur explained. "I must return home."

"Okay," Donnelly said, prompting him to continue toward the insurmountable obstacle.

"And then I am to be married."

Donnelly couldn't believe what he was hearing. But Sandler simply smiled at Ankur and ruffled his hair. "You're going to be adorable in your wedding outfit. I wish I could see it." Ankur blushed and kissed him.

"What the hell, you two?" Donnelly cried. "You're not making sense."

"My parents have arranged my marriage," Ankur explained. "I've worked on this ship long enough to be able to buy a place near my parents' home. After I am wed, my wife and I will live there."

"You're getting married to a woman?" Donnelly tried to will the shocked look off his face, but a quick glance in the mirrored window showed that he was not terribly successful. "I haven't known you long, Ankur, but I don't think many men spend the time before their wedding… well, the way you have with Sandler."

Both men burst out laughing. "I told you he would say that," Sandler said, and Ankur laughed even harder, nodding his head. "Look, Gabriel, I know it must seem strange, but Ankur and I went into this with our eyes open. The first day we met he told me about his upcoming marriage, and I backed off immediately, sure I'd gotten my signals horribly crossed."

"But I convinced him that I took this job so I could…." He turned to Sandler. "What is it you say? About the crops?"

Sandler laughed. "Sow your wild oats."

"That's right," Ankur cried. "My wild oats. It is expected that a man before marriage will harvest some oats. I chose to sow mine on Sandler's farm, that's all. I am sure I will love the woman that my parents have chosen for me—in the pictures they've sent me, she is quite beautiful."

"But she's a *woman*." Donnelly didn't mean to argue with Ankur about his own sexuality—he just wanted to understand.

"Yes, she is," Ankur calmly replied.

"But doesn't marrying her mean you won't ever be with a man again? Is that what you really want?"

Ankur disentangled himself from Sandler and stepped closer to Donnelly. "But, Gabriel, isn't that what marriage always means? That you choose to be only with the one you wed? Is that not what you plan with Ethan?"

"Yes, but—"

Sandler appeared next to Ankur, as if being five feet away from him were too much separation for him to bear. "And isn't the choice Ankur is making just like the one Ethan's making for you?"

Donnelly, caught off guard, could only close his mouth, it having dropped open at Sandler's remark.

"Sorry," Sandler said immediately. "That was rude of me."

"No, I...." Donnelly stumbled, then regained his train of thought. "But Ankur isn't choosing—his parents are choosing for him."

"In my culture," Ankur said, his voice gentle, "many marriages are chosen by the parents. And most marriages are happy because our parents know us well. You are right that I have not chosen the woman to whom I am betrothed, but I have the choice to accept my parents' choice. I choose to follow their will, and I know I shall be happy. Marriage and a family are what I've always wanted."

"When I saw you on the balcony a couple of days ago, it seemed like you wanted something else," Donnelly blurted. He immediately began to apologize, but Ankur's face showed no offense.

"I do very much enjoy my time with Sandler," he said, smiling. "But you must have a very limited view of what women and men can do together to think I will never... enjoy such pleasure in the future. Don't forget, we're the ones who brought you the *Kama Sutra*."

Donnelly spent a good couple of minutes coming up with objections to this entire view of things and then watching them crumble under Ankur's placid confidence in his plan to marry a woman he'd never met. During this time, Ankur and Sandler took turns feeding each other scones. They were adorable. They were happy. He wondered whether that was all that really mattered.

"Well, it sounds like you two have it all figured out," Donnelly said, watching them play idle lover's games. "Good for you. Who am I to judge?" He poured another coffee and toasted their happiness—for the next twenty-four hours, anyway.

"Now I must get to work—the last day is always very busy," Ankur said, brushing the scone crumbs from his robe.

"Will you come back?" Sandler asked. "For one more...?"

Ankur smiled sweetly. "It would be very late."

"I would wait until dawn." They kissed, and Ankur nodded before turning and going into the suite.

Sandler settled into a chaise lounge and sipped his tea. "Oh, what that boy does to me." He sighed.

Donnelly sat down next to him. "It's what you do to that boy that has me worried."

Sandler smiled placidly. "I know your instinct is to rescue people from the tyranny of social norms, but we're going to have to let this one go. He's happy to be going home to get married."

"I hope he will be happy. But when I saw the two of you on the balcony, he looked positively transported. I can't imagine anything making him as happy as you did."

"That's a very sweet thing to say. And I have greatly enjoyed our time together—in my line of work there's no time for second dates, much less any kind of relationship. It's been good for me to remember what it's like."

"You mean what it was like with Trevor?" Donnelly asked gently.

Sandler nodded. He closed his eyes for a long moment, and when he opened them, they were a little red. "First love. It never quite leaves us, does it?"

"I'm lucky that way. I consider Ethan my first, and he's never going to leave me again after the debacle that this wedding trip has become."

"I envy you. You don't know what I'd give to have a moment with Trevor, just to know he's okay."

They sat looking out over the water for a long while, each thinking of their first loves. The reappearance of Rutherford jarred them back to the moment.

"Sirs?" he said as he stepped out onto the balcony. "Would you like me to pack your bags for you?"

"That's the kind of sweet talk that can turn a man's head, Rutherford," Donnelly cried. "How will I go on without you?"

Rutherford chuckled. "You will find a way, sir. You will find a way."

That evening, Donnelly and Sandler sat down for their final dinner on board at their tucked-away table for two. There were fresh flowers and a chilled bottle of champagne waiting for them.

"I didn't expect all this on the last night," Donnelly remarked as the maître d' seated them.

"The flowers are compliments of a Madame Maillard, who sends her regards," he replied, "and the champagne is a gift from Mr. Romanov. Shall I pour?"

"Yes, thank you," Donnelly said.

"A toast, then," Sandler began, holding his flute aloft, "to our benefactors. Fabienne the Fabulous and Imre the Impulsive, and their shared delight in tearing open pouches."

Donnelly burst out laughing but touched his glass to Sandler's with a crystalline ring.

Once they had ordered, their conversation turned a little more serious.

"Where will you be off to, once we make landfall?" Donnelly asked.

"Well, assuming the volcano has settled down, I will probably have another job waiting for me when we get there. Either a pouch outbound or some commercial assignment. It'll be back on the road for me."

"I don't suppose I could convince you to stick around for a few days? Perhaps to come to a little ceremony I have planned?"

Sandler looked surprised and thrilled. "I would love to, but you can't just invite people to your wedding willy-nilly. I'm sure there's a seating chart and everything."

"There probably is. If there's some pompous and circumstantial detail to be attended to, I'm certain it's been handled. Either with cool efficiency by our wedding planner, or with hysterics and jazz hands by Bryce. Oh, and glitter. But nothing about this whole wedding has gone to plan, so I'm not going to worry about who sits where. Will you come?"

Sandler beamed. "I would be delighted to. But you simply must point your fiancé out to me the moment we step off the ship so I know who to hide from. Once he finds out we've been sharing a suite, who knows what he'll do."

"Ethan wouldn't harm a fly," Donnelly said with a laugh. "Though if he did, the fly would never see it coming."

Southampton, finally

"HOW'S IT feel?" Kerry asked as the train glided out of the station, bound for London. "You're finally on your way to Gabriel."

"I maintain an attitude of cautious optimism," Brandt replied. "You may think that this madcap adventure is a once-in-a-lifetime deal, but ever since Gabriel and I got together, it's been one ridiculous complication after another. It happens with such regularity I now just expect it to go sideways—at least then I'm not surprised by it."

"So you live in a constant state of 'hell's about to break loose'? That's gotta be rough."

Brandt nodded stoically. "The price of eternal watchfulness. I'm never caught completely by surprise, but it's probably bad for my blood pressure."

"On behalf of my company, which offers a complete line of pharmaceuticals for blood pressure management, I say thank you. On my own behalf, as your friend, I say you have to loosen up, bro."

"Gabriel's been telling me that for years. One thing I've learned this week is that sometimes all the worrying in the world isn't going to change things, and all I can do is make the best of the hand I've been dealt." He turned and looked out the window at the suburbs of Paris whizzing past. "I just don't think I can make the best of anything when he's not with me."

Kerry nudged his shoulder. "I wish I had somebody who made me feel that way. All I have ahead of me is a long spinsterhood."

Brandt looked at her skeptically. "You've been single for what, a month? Give yourself a little time. When you're ready, there will be no shortage of men eager for your company. And until that day, you can console yourself with an endless supply of athletic surgeons."

She giggled and slapped his knee. "You know all my secrets now. It's like I have a big brother watching out for me."

"Something tells me you aren't going to make it easy," he said with a laugh.

"Oh, have no doubt of that. But right now our job is to get you married to the most amazing man in the world. In less than a week, you're going to be Mrs. Gabriel Donnelly!"

Brandt's scowl made her jump back in her seat. "Kidding, kidding," she said, hands out, eyes wide in mock panic.

The train ride was smooth, and as long as Brandt didn't think about the technical impossibilities of riding a train underwater, he could actually enjoy it—every kilometer they traveled brought him closer to Donnelly, and for the first time since leaving San Diego, he felt hopeful. They were actually going to be together again. Tomorrow.

They changed trains in London and made the short trip to Southampton by midday. The ship wasn't due to dock until the following morning, so they settled into a hotel that was a decided step down from the penthouse suite in Paris but was comfortable nonetheless. In the restaurant off the lobby, they shared a fish-and-chips dinner with a couple of pints of proper British porter.

In the middle of a bite of fish, Kerry set her elbows on the table and stared across at Brandt, smiling and shaking her head.

"What?" he asked, startled by her sudden change of expression.

"I've seen Ethan in charge, Ethan in despair, even Ethan in a turmoil of sexual identity crisis. But this is the first time I've gotten to see Ethan in love. You're practically beaming, and I suspect you will glow even more the closer he gets." She grinned giddily. "I like this Ethan. I think he's my favorite one of all."

"Not that I don't appreciate the constant psychoanalysis, but I'm starting to see the advantage of not having any straight women in my life."

"Does that mean I'm disinvited from the wedding?" she asked with theatrical despair.

Brandt smiled—he could take any amount of teasing in his current state. In less than twelve hours he would be reunited with Donnelly after the longest absence they'd endured since their relationship began—hell, since they'd met each other. Nothing could shake his good mood. "I fully expect you to be there, in the front row so you can entertain the other guests at the reception with pithy observations on my mental state at every single second of the ceremony."

"Consider it done, my good man." She dissolved into giddy giggling.

CHAPTER THIRTEEN

Sunday
At sea, nearing Southampton

"MR. DONNELLY? Sir?" Rutherford's deep voice broke through Donnelly's slumber.

"Mmmmm?"

"Mr. Donnelly, I apologize for waking you so early, but it is disembarkation morning."

"Mmmmm-hmmmm."

"I've brought coffee, sir."

"Why thank you, Rutherford. You are a credit to your profession."

"It is my pleasure, sir."

A few minutes later, after coffee and then showering and dressing, Donnelly and Sandler sat down to breakfast in their suite for the last time.

"I expected to see Ankur," Donnelly said as he poured maple syrup on his blueberry pancakes. "Did he not make it here for his final go at homosexing?"

Sandler smiled. "He got here at about two and could only stay a little while. We made good use of the time."

Donnelly shook his head. "I hope he'll be happy. I'm not sure I could get out of bed with someone like you and know I would never get back in."

"Gabriel Donnelly, are you flirting with me?" Sandler replied in mock-scandalized tones.

Donnelly, by way of answer, stuck out his tongue. "You know what I mean. Being with you wasn't just a light dalliance with being gay—anyone who's going to take what you're giving has to be *committed*."

"I am flattered by your oblique reference to my endowment," Sandler said with a courtly bow of his head. "But don't worry about Ankur. He's actually remarkably mature about all of this, and he knows what he's doing."

"I wish him well," Donnelly said.

"So, how's it feel to be just a couple of hours away from seeing Ethan?"

"I can hardly believe it. And seeing him won't be enough for me to believe that we're actually in the same place at the same time. Until I can lay hands on him—all over him—it won't be real to me."

"When's the wedding ceremony? I wouldn't want to show up late."

"It's Saturday afternoon, but of course you'll be coming with us to the castle. We have the whole place for the week, and our families and friends will be arriving daily. You said you didn't have plans, right? There's plenty of room, and it'll be a nice break for you."

"That's a very generous offer. Thank you."

"Plus, it'll give you time to get to know Ethan," Donnelly added playfully. "I'm sure he'll be very interested to hear all about our voyage from your perspective."

"Um, yeah," Sandler said, looking deathly afraid of the very idea. "That'll be… great."

Southampton docks

IT WAS still well before dawn when Brandt gave up on sleeping, having stared at the ceiling for most of the night. He got up and showered, not waking Kerry who was sound asleep in the other bed. He dressed by the faint glow of the bathroom night-light and made his way out of the hotel and toward the water. Standing just above the docks, he looked out over the Southampton Water toward the sea. It was nearly five thirty when the riding lights of the great ship emerged from the misty distance, forming up into a brilliant city of the sea as it approached. Brandt could hardly stand still, his heart pounding as the ship grew larger, nearer. *Donnelly is on that ship*, he thought, *and soon he'll be right here next to me*. Brandt could smell him, just as clearly as if they were already shoulder to shoulder, and his knees grew weak as his pants grew tight. Soon they would be together again.

The ship slowed as it approached the dock, then turned elegantly and came to a graceful halt alongside. Knowing that disembarkation would take some time, Brandt turned and walked back to the hotel to get breakfast and try to keep himself from smiling like an idiot. It would be a challenge.

"So he's here?" Kerry asked when Brandt returned to the room. In his absence, she had gotten up and showered, and was finishing getting dressed when he arrived.

"He's here. Still on the ship, though. I kind of expected to see him dive off the side and swim to shore."

"That's insane."

"It's what I would have done," Brandt said with a sniff.

Kerry burst out laughing. "Let's get some breakfast. Something tells me that with this reunion ahead, you're going to need your strength."

After staring at breakfast and not being able to eat a bite, Brandt urged Kerry down the street at a pace that nearly had her flying headlong toward the pier.

"I think the people in the suites can get off first," he said, practically vibrating with excitement. "We should see him soon."

"Does he know he makes you this crazy?" she asked, watching him bob up and down.

"What do you mean?" Brandt asked, not tearing his eyes away from the ship to even glance her way.

She laughed and shook her head. "Never mind. I'll tell him myself."

The first to emerge from the ship were crew members, followed by officers with increasing numbers of gold bars on their shoulders. Finally, the first people who were clearly passengers started down the passageway from the ship. There was an elderly couple—she with a cane, he with a walker—who descended at a regal pace. Behind them strode several couples and small groups, who kept a polite distance while moving slightly faster than the first couple. Then a gap, followed by a single figure: a tall man in white tie, bearing baggage in both hands. Behind him was a man dressed far more casually than any of the preceding passengers, and next to him—

There he is.

"That must be him," Kerry observed. "You stopped breathing altogether."

"That's… him," Brandt whispered, more to himself than to her. "He's really here." He took two deep breaths. "Gabriel." He hardly made a sound.

Donnelly, more than a hundred yards away, instantly snapped his head toward Brandt, as if he had heard his name called. When he caught sight of Brandt, a wide smile burst across his face, and he waved energetically. Then he touched the elbow of the casually dressed man and pointed in Brandt's direction.

"Looks like Gabriel made a friend," Kerry observed. Then Donnelly tapped the formally dressed gentleman on the shoulder and repeated his gesture. "A couple of friends."

"He makes friends everywhere he goes," Brandt replied, his voice a little thick. "He's just amazing."

"Well, let's hope he gets down here soon, before you hyperventilate."

"I'm fine. It's all fine. Now he's here, it's all fine."

She put her arm around him. "I'm so happy for you."

He laughed. "Me too."

Dockside

THEY FINISHED their breakfast while watching the dock come nearer and nearer, until finally, with a groan and a shudder, the great ship came to rest.

"Never thought we'd get here," Donnelly said with a sigh of relief.

"In my line of work, arriving usually happens after I've already gotten ready for the next departure. It'll be nice not to have anywhere to go for a while," Sandler replied.

A few minutes later, Rutherford appeared at the door. "Gentlemen, that sad hour is upon us. It is time to disembark." He picked up their hand luggage and summoned the elevator. "As suite guests, you will be among the first to depart, and I will accompany you to the customs desk to ensure your efficient processing."

"That's very nice of you," Sandler replied, "especially since I no longer have the diplomatic pouch. I'm suddenly a tourist. Never been that before."

"Might I suggest cargo pants, a baseball cap, and a large camera to complete the look, sir?"

"Rutherford, you are having fun at my expense, and I love you for it." Sandler gave the butler a kiss on the cheek.

"My goodness, sir, they did *not* prepare me for this in butler school," Rutherford said with a roguish wink as he held the elevator door open for the men to precede him. "I do hope my virtue will be safe as we descend."

"I cannot guarantee that I won't be overwhelmed by your charm and do something foolish," Sandler replied. The three of them shared a laugh on the way down.

Rutherford led them through the ship, just as he had conducted them to their suite on the first day, and soon they were nearing the large door that led out through the hull.

They stepped into distinctly un-British bright sunlight, and Donnelly scanned the entire port area for a sign of Brandt. Then, without his even being aware of it, his head turned to the precise point where Brandt stood, and their eyes locked. Electrified by the sight of what he had been so long denied, he burst into a wild grin and waved energetically.

"There he is," Donnelly said to Sandler, touching him on the elbow and pointing.

He then tapped Rutherford on the shoulder and pointed again. The butler looked up, then nodded approvingly to Donnelly.

"Looks like he brought a friend," Sandler observed.

"She's probably a secret agent he recruited to help him cross borders without a passport or something."

"If your fiancé turns out to be just a nice, regular guy rather than some kind of superhero ninja, I'm going to be kind of disappointed, really."

"Don't worry," Donnelly assured him. "Ethan's both sweet and deadly."

"Awesome."

Southampton

AS DONNELLY and Sandler emerged from the customs area, Brandt sprinted toward them, nearly leaping over three rows of chairs. Donnelly surged forward as well, and they collided, crashing into each other with a mighty thump of muscle and yearning.

"Oh my God, I can't believe we're finally—" Donnelly began, but soon found his mouth commandeered by a frenetic, desperate kiss.

Their traveling companions stood off to the side for an awkward moment. If they were expecting introductions, it would be a long wait.

"Hi, I'm Kerry."

"Sandler. Pleased to meet you."

They watched the two men for a moment, then turned back to look at each other.

"So, have you known Gabriel long?" Kerry asked.

"No, we met in the airport when he was on his way to New York to get on the ship." Sandler took a sidelong glance at the two grappling men. "How about you? Longtime friend of Officer Brandt?"

She laughed. "Can't say that. I think I've known him about twenty-four hours longer than you've known Gabriel. We were introduced at a conference in San Diego by a mutual friend."

"And that's when you decided to travel around the globe with a man you'd just met?" Sandler asked with a grin. "Like I did?"

She nodded. "What is it about these two? Ethan and I somehow became like brother and sister almost instantly. And having spent a week with him, I can tell you that he's about the nicest guy you're ever likely to meet."

"I cannot describe how relieved I am to hear that," Sandler said with a deep sigh. "Gabriel is exactly the same. And how is it fair that the sweetest, hottest guy I've ever met happens to be getting married to an equally hot, sweet guy?"

"Right? This is the universe telling us to lower our expectations."

Their eyes darted over to where Brandt and Donnelly embraced, staring into each other's eyes, silent. Behind them a small group of elderly women, having come through customs behind the troopers, stood and watched, beaming at the two men so very much in love.

"This may take awhile," Kerry observed, plopping down into an open seat.

"Gabriel's been half-crazy with missing him," Sandler added, sitting next to her.

Kerry laughed and rolled her eyes. "Ethan's been full-crazy. I kind of expected Gabriel to be some kind of wizard or something with the way Ethan was pining for him. There's some strong magic at work here."

"I was worried Ethan might be upset that Gabriel and I ended up sharing a room on the way over."

"I wouldn't worry. He and I did the same."

Sandler turned and looked at Kerry, eyes wide. "But Ethan's…," he murmured, then leaned closer to whisper in her ear. "Straight," he hissed.

"Yeah, that came up once or twice," she replied, matching his conspiratorial whisper. "There was this one time when he—"

"Well, isn't this nice, our traveling companions are already gossiping like sorority sisters," Donnelly said. He and Brandt had materialized without warning not three feet away.

"Let's hope they're not telling each other all of our secrets," Brandt added.

"Sandler Birkin, I'd like you to meet Ethan Brandt," Donnelly said.

Sandler shot to his feet and stuck out his hand with a hesitant bravado. "I've heard so much about you, Ethan," he said and nearly managed to keep his voice from cracking.

"I may have some questions for you later," Brandt replied, shaking his hand and looking a little suspiciously into Sandler's eyes.

"Great," Sandler whispered, then dropped like a stone back to his seat.

"Stand down, Officer," Donnelly scolded, but his beaming expression hadn't changed a bit.

Brandt flashed a grin, then held out his hand to Kerry. "And I'd like to present Kerry Mercer," he said. "She's a friend of Greg's who somehow managed to put up with me all week."

Donnelly leaned forward and took her hand. "I shall be honored to support your application for sainthood."

Kerry burst out laughing. "No need. Your man handled every setback with grace and aplomb."

Donnelly shot a puzzled glance at Brandt. "Unless by 'grace and aplomb' you mean 'barely contained fury,' I'm not sure we're talking about the same guy."

"I see we understand each other," Kerry replied. "It is a real pleasure to meet you, Gabriel. I've heard so much about you. And, even more than that, I've seen the effect your absence has had on Ethan. You two are really something special."

Donnelly's response was to grab up Brandt in an energetic tackle hug, which was returned in kind.

"And we're off to the races again," Sandler said as the two troopers made up for lost time. He turned to Kerry. "Perhaps there's a café or something where we could wait out the hormone tsunami?"

"Good idea," she said, rising and sidestepping the intertwined Brandt and Donnelly. "It may be a while before they come up for air again."

Kerry and Sandler were halfway through their bitter dockside coffees when Brandt and Donnelly strolled into the café.

"They look so relaxed," Kerry observed as they walked up to the counter. "Ethan's not looked that calm the entire time I've known him."

"I've seen Gabriel relaxed—we were in a penthouse suite on a week-long cruise, after all—but I've never seen him glow like that. They are just perfect together."

"And, of course, completely hot."

Sandler rolled his eyes. "I'm glad I'm not the only one. I swear, that those two found each other—there's no justice in the world for homely guys like me."

"Homely? Pardon my German, but give me a fucking break." Kerry burst out laughing. "If you had a straight bone in your body, I would drag you back to the hotel and put it to use right now."

Sandler beamed. "That's about the sweetest thing any woman has ever said to me. And, if I may say, you're the first woman I've ever met that I would even consider breaking my perfect record for."

"Never given a gal a tumble, then?" she asked, her eyes sparkling with mischief.

"Not once. But keep being so charming and beautiful and my resolve may weaken."

"After a week of sleeping next to that"—she tipped her head toward Ethan—"I fear I may put your resolve to the test. Or at the very least you need to be my wingman—this girl's been pretty pent-up."

"I can't imagine what you've been through. Gabriel and I slept in separate rooms, and even then I was lucky to have the companionship of a crew member who proved quite... service-oriented."

"Good for you. You are now obligated to the wingman deal. It's only fair."

"It shall be my pleasure." He bowed graciously.

Brandt and Donnelly approached the table, coffee in hand.

"You two look thick as thieves already," Brandt observed as he sat.

"I have no idea what you're talking about," Kerry replied, a look of practiced innocence on her face. "Do you, Sandler?"

"Haven't a clue," he agreed, shaking his head as if he'd been asked a game-show question involving trigonometry.

"We'll schedule formal interrogations for this afternoon, then," Brandt replied with a growl that transformed into a grin before he'd even finished. It seemed simply impossible for him to be anything other than overjoyed that he was once again next to Donnelly.

"Now, since you're coming with us to Whitford," Donnelly said, "we'll need to arrange for—" He was cut short by his phone ringing. Clearly puzzled, he pulled it from his pocket. One look at the caller ID and he was on his feet. He flashed the phone toward Brandt, who nodded, and then he walked swiftly out of the café, phone to his ear.

"It's one of the detectives," Brandt explained. "It must be pretty important if she called him as soon as he turned his phone on. Probably just some detail that didn't get into a report." He smiled at Kerry and Sandler, then took a sip of coffee.

"Does he often leave details out of his reports?" Sandler asked.

Brandt blinked at him, twice. "Never."

"So what you're telling us is that you have no idea why a detective would be calling Gabriel during his wedding trip," Kerry said, "but you didn't want to worry us."

He cast her a critical look. "We've spent too much time together."

Sandler was looking through the windows out to the sidewalk. "He's pacing," he reported. "Well, at least now we know it's not good news."

Brandt shot him a look through narrowed eyes that could have brought the temperature in the room down fifteen degrees. "You seem to have gotten to know Gabriel quite well over the last week. I would love to hear how you two met." He leaned forward, his expression one of rapt attention—the kind an eagle might lavish on its small, furry prey.

"We—" Sandler began, his voice a high-pitched whisper. He cleared his throat. "We met at the airport...."

IT WAS a full twenty minutes later when Donnelly returned to the café table. He found Sandler glossed with what appeared to be nervous perspiration, Brandt in his trademark interrogation pose that brought his full muscular body to bear on the suspect, and Kerry looking helplessly between the two as if they were nitro and glycerin, headed for a collision.

Donnelly resumed his seat at the table just as Sandler was describing how they had managed to get to the ship when so many of the other passengers hadn't. "Well, this looks like a delightful exercise in third-degree storytelling, but I'm afraid I'll have to interrupt for a moment."

"What'd she say?" Brandt asked. He looked away from Sandler, who slumped forward and took the deep breath he'd clearly been missing.

"I had asked her to look into something for me as we left New York," Donnelly said, and he turned to Sandler.

The color drained from Sandler's face. He took a halting breath, then another. "Trevor?" he asked, his voice barely audible.

Donnelly nodded. "She found him."

Sandler blinked hard. "He's... he's alive?"

"He's alive."

Sandler doubled over as if punched in the gut. He panted with the exertion of taking in what Donnelly had said. He gave a small groan, as if hearing this was physically painful to him.

It may have been, Donnelly thought. But there was more he needed to know.

"Trevor is not well," Donnelly said, being as gentle as he could.

"Still?" Sandler asked. This was the first word he'd managed to speak out loud, as if the outrage of it had driven his voice back into action.

"He's apparently been in and out of various clinics and treatment centers ever since the accident," Donnelly explained.

"But... what's wrong with him? It's been so many years—how can he still be...?" Tears filled his eyes.

"She wasn't able to get his medical records, of course. But his parents have had to file custodial paperwork for him every few years to be able to keep him under their care. The last time this was done, there was a bit of controversy, and it ended up in court because one of the doctors who examined Trevor filed a dissenting opinion."

"Dissenting about what?"

"About...." Donnelly consulted his notes, wanting to be sure he got the wording right. "I asked her to text me the passages." He looked at his phone and read, "He was concerned about Mr. and Mrs. Hendricks's continued use of psychotropic therapies."

"What does that mean?" Sandler was crying now, but he steadfastly ignored the tears streaking down his cheeks.

"She said there was one sentence in his report she wanted to be sure you knew about. He wrote that 'every time Trevor so much as speaks the name Sandler, his parents seek out new doctors willing to try ever more radical interventions to expunge the memories that trouble him.'"

Sandler jolted and let out a gasp. The other three people around the table could only watch, horrified, as this terrible news sank in. "I think I'm going to be sick." He stood and, holding on to the backs of chairs as he went, rushed off toward the bathroom.

"I'd better go and make sure he's okay," Kerry said, getting to her feet.

"Shouldn't Gabriel go?" Brandt asked, turning to Donnelly. "You're his friend—you should be the one to help him through this."

Donnelly was touched that Brandt was so easily able to set aside his only half-pretend jealousy. "You're the best," he said, and kissed his fiancé on the forehead as he rose. "I'm sure he'll be fine—it's just a lot to take in."

He found Sandler at the bathroom sink, splashing cold water on his face.

"I'm sorry to drop all of that on you," he said.

Sandler gripped the sink as if it were a life preserver. He was still panting from shock.

"All these years," he said, shaking his head. "All these years."

"I know it must be hard to hear," Donnelly ventured. "But there's more you should know."

"Oh fuck, Gabriel, I don't think I can take any more," Sandler said with a defeated sigh. "Can you just give me a minute to try to fight my breakfast back down?"

"You should hear the rest of it." He handed Sandler a paper towel. "Take all the time you need to get yourself together, then come back to the table, okay?"

Sandler closed his eyes for a long moment, then nodded silently.

Donnelly withdrew, leaving him to decide when to face the rest of information Donnelly had gathered from the detective.

"He'll be out in a few," Donnelly said with an attempt at jauntiness when he returned to the table. "Just getting himself together."

"So, we're assuming Trevor was an early boyfriend?" Brandt asked, as both he and Kerry leaned in, expressions of deep concern on their faces. "And there was an accident of some kind?"

Donnelly briefly outlined the story of Sandler and Trevor, including the horrific prom-night accident.

"What kind of parent does that to their own child?" Kerry demanded, clearly furious at the Hendrickses, about whom she'd known nothing ten minutes prior. "They need to be stopped."

"There's probably a lot we don't know." Brandt's voice was soothing—something he could likely only accomplish with Donnelly's fingers laced in his own. "Situations like this can be very complicated."

"Situations like this," Kerry replied, biting off her words, "are a lot more common than you realize. I hear from doctors all the time about parents who demand meds for their kids—almost always it's the sons—because they don't pay attention in school, or they mouth off at home, or they get caught kissing a boy. Attention deficit, depression, antisocial behavior—they want a diagnosis, and they want a solution in a pill bottle."

"Kerry, take a breath," Brandt soothed, putting a hand on her arm.

She yanked it away. "And you know whose drugs end up being prescribed as some kind of cure for adolescence and family dysfunction? Mine. Medications that our chemists work and test and perfect for a decade or more to treat a real medical problem. The people who come up with these drugs never intended for them to be used to break the spirit of angsty teenagers, and the doctors know the only reason parents demand them is to make their kids docile, but they prescribe them anyway to keep everyone happy and keep the co-payments coming in. God, it's such a fucked-up system."

"That's horrible," Donnelly said. He thought about teenagers like Jonah Fischer, whose parents would have jumped at a drug that promised to keep their star wrestler son on the straight and narrow. And he never would have found that Casey Melville, his best friend, could also be the love of his life.

"Again, we don't know what's going on with this Trevor situation," Brandt said, maintaining his calming intonation. Kerry looked ready to seek out and strangle the Hendrickses, and Donnelly felt the same—or worse, because of what else he knew that had yet to be revealed.

"There's more to the story," Donnelly said quietly.

"Is it something you can tell Sandler? Because he's coming back now." Brandt tipped his head toward Sandler as he approached from the other side of the cafe.

Donnelly nodded but said nothing more.

"Sorry for the freak-out, folks," Sandler said with a smile and a willfully upbeat tone. "I promise I won't turn into a blubbering mess again."

Kerry put her arm around him. "You've had a shock—don't apologize for needing some time to take it in."

He smiled at her. "Thanks." Then he closed his eyes for a moment, and when they opened, he was looking straight at Donnelly. "You said there was more. So let's have it." He took a deep breath.

"As I said, Trevor's not well," Donnelly began, softly and slowly. "He's in a kind of clinic, seeing a psychiatric specialist. Seems the Hendrickses are doing exactly what the dissenting doctor said they would—seeking out anyone who will promise to make their son... well, straight, apparently."

"Oh God," Kerry and Sandler said at the same time. They turned and looked at each other in surprise.

Donnelly continued. "Right now he's in Geneva, at the clinic of Dr.—"

"Rauthmann," Kerry said. Her eyes were closed tightly, as if she were hoping not to hear even the slightest hint of confirmation.

Donnelly, stunned, sat back in his chair. "Yes, it's a Dr. Rauthmann," he said slowly. "How on earth did you know that?"

All eyes were on Kerry.

"He's been a... well, a problem for us—for my company—for years. We make a fairly comprehensive line of psychotropics, antidepressants, and other therapeutics for mental illness. And by and large the doctors who prescribe our products do so on-label."

She must have noted the blank faces looking back at her, because she took a deep breath and began again. "When a doctor prescribes a medication, he or she will normally prescribe it in accordance with the recommendations we make, based on the results of clinical trials and other research. A drug can also be prescribed off-label, such as when an antidepressant turns out to have a positive effect on chronic pain. It can't be marketed for that purpose unless we do another round of clinical trials, but doctors are pretty much free to prescribe a drug off-label if they think it will help their patients."

"That's actually kind of scary," Sandler observed.

"Again, the vast majority of doctors are responsible, and they are still subject to malpractice action if they aren't. But there are a very few clinicians who use drugs in a completely irresponsible way."

"And our Dr. Rauthmann is one of those?"

Kerry nodded.

Brandt shook his head. "I'm still stumped as to how you happen to know this damning information about a random Swiss doctor."

"It's not random. He's actually very well known to my company—in fact, we've been trying to get him to stop using our products for years. But every time we manage to pin him down and prove he's harming patients, he disappears and resurfaces somewhere else. Look, I shouldn't be telling you this because we're a publicly traded company and this is kind of insider info." She took a deep breath and plowed ahead anyway. "Every time we take action against a rogue doctor, the value of the drug we yank out of his hands drops a little because people read about it being abused, and then our stock takes a hit. But I'm glad to say that we're in the final stages with this guy." She shrugged grimly. "In a couple of months, he's going to be looking for a new way to screw people up."

"But you said Trevor's there. Now," Sandler said weakly, turning to Donnelly. "What's going to happen to him?"

Kerry took a deep breath, her distaste for what she was about to say evident. "Rauthmann offers parents like the Hendrickses hope. Hope that their kids can be made 'normal.' He uses high doses of one of our psychotropics—a dosage far in excess of what we recommend, an amount that's never been clinically tested—to achieve a permanent behavioral modification."

"What kind of modification?" Brandt asked as he picked Donnelly's phone up from the table.

"All I know is what I read in the attorneys' summaries. We get dragged in as a codefendant every time someone like Rauthmann gets sued for malpractice. It takes us a while to get removed from the suit, and during the hearings, we get to hear about the horrible things these maniacs use our drugs for. I don't know of any victims of Rauthmann who have sued him, but I've seen testimony about young men who have been treated by other doctors who follow a similar protocol. It's… horrifying."

"Oh my God," Sandler moaned.

"What, exactly, does that mean for Trevor?" Donnelly asked, leaning forward.

"It means his parents will get what they want. Rauthmann will ensure Trevor never again expresses any kind of feelings for Sandler. He may not even remember him. And he certainly will never have anything like a healthy emotional connection to anyone. Rauthmann essentially hollows them out, which is—and it fills me with disgust to even say this—apparently what some parents would prefer to having a gay kid."

"That's medieval," whispered Donnelly. This was so far beyond the realm of possibility that he could hardly believe what he was hearing.

"But it's actually happening," Brandt said, handing Donnelly's phone back to him. The web page of Dr. Rauthmann appeared, promising hope to families whose sons were experiencing "dysfunctions of the sexual identity."

Donnelly held up his phone for the others to see while he looked at Brandt. Wordlessly, they conferred and nodded in unison.

"We'll go with you," Donnelly said to Sandler.

"What? Where?" Sandler was clearly overwhelmed.

"To Geneva. We'll leave right now. We have to get to him before—"

"But your wedding," Sandler said, his confusion evident.

"Is in nearly a week. Plenty of time." Donnelly's voice conveyed exactly the tone he'd hoped for: brave, certain. He could be these things with Brandt next to him once again.

"You c-can't possibly—" Sandler stuttered.

Brandt stood, towering over the table, resolute. "We can, and we are. I'll go make the arrangements." He turned and strode out of the cafe.

Donnelly smiled and held his phone aloft. As if on cue, Brandt marched back into the cafe, plucked the phone from Donnelly's hand, kissed him on the head, and strode out again.

Kerry smiled at Donnelly. "He's not the same without you, you know."

A warmth spread across Donnelly's chest as Kerry beamed at him. He shook his head. "You should see what I'm like without him."

"You both are amazing, and I can't let you do this," Sandler said. "You should be in a castle, getting ready for your wedding, not skulking across Switzerland trying to help me rescue my high school sweetheart from some mad scientist."

"Sandler, I can't really explain it any other way than this: this is what we do. I don't know why, but the universe has seen fit to keep giving us these chances to help people—people who for whatever reason need just the help that Ethan and I can give. If we can help, we should. And so we do. It's as simple as that."

"But it's not like we're going to break into the clinic at night and steal him away," Sandler replied. "We just have to let the police or whoever know what his parents are trying to do and they'll stop them, right?"

Donnelly sucked in his cheeks and looked at Kerry. She simply sighed and returned his mournful look. The news wasn't good, and she seemed to be as reluctant as he was to deliver it.

"It gets complicated when it comes to medical issues," Donnelly said as kindly as he could. "His parents are likely to have a power of attorney to make medical decisions for him, and there's nothing illegal about what this doctor is doing. The drugs are legal—he's just using them in a way that the people who made them don't think is responsible."

Kerry nodded. "Hippocrates notwithstanding, it can be really hard to prove that medical treatment is doing harm. Think about chemotherapy. It's basically a treatment designed to kill the cancer a little more quickly than it kills the patient. To the casual observer, it looks like torture, and plenty of people who have cancer decide they'd rather not go through it. But the majority are going to fight it aggressively, no matter how painful it is. Now, if you're convinced, like the Hendrickses seem to be, that being gay is as bad as cancer, then an aggressive treatment seems like their only option."

Sandler looked bleakly from Donnelly to Kerry and back again. "Then what good does it do for us to even go to Geneva? If we're not going to be able to do anything...."

Donnelly smiled bracingly. "I'm sure there are things we can do. We just need to get there and see what our options are." He sensed Sandler needed something more concrete to occupy himself with. "Have you ever carried legal documents?"

"I've done some. Not as much as the diplo work, but a few times a year."

"Are there any attorneys you could call, see if they can give you some sense of what might be done?"

Sandler visibly seized the chance to have something to do that might be helpful. "That's an excellent idea." He pulled out his phone and started flicking through contacts.

Brandt walked briskly back into the cafe. "All set. The van that was sent to take us to Whitford is going to take us to London instead. From there I managed to get us the last four seats on the last train back to Paris. After a middle-of-the-night layover, we'll be on our way to Geneva. We should be there around noon." He held Donnelly's phone out to him, but Kerry snatched it from him.

"One of the lawyers who's been working on the Rauthmann thing is a friend. I'll check with her to see if there's any info she can give us that might help."

Donnelly nodded and let Kerry take the phone. She dialed, then got up to pace as she talked. She and Sandler crossed paths several times, as he too walked back and forth, tracking down someone—anyone—who might be able to help.

Brandt sat back down next to Donnelly, and they watched their new friends' progress across the floor, heads swiveling like they were observing two tennis matches at the same time.

"James's travel agent booked us into a suite at the best hotel in Geneva," Brandt said as the pacing continued. "He felt so bad about the mess we've been through that he's treating us to our little adventure. Nice of him."

"Indeed," Donnelly agreed.

"That means we'll finally get to share a bed again," Brandt continued casually.

"That'll be nice."

Brandt leaned over to whisper into Donnelly's ear. "I'm going to fuck you like there's no tomorrow."

Donnelly was powerless to prevent a devilish grin from spreading across his face. "You'd better," he whispered back. "Because at midnight we switch. I plan to give you as good as I get."

"I think you'll be completely exhausted by midnight."

"I think you're in for a big surprise."

Brandt playfully bit Donnelly's ear. "I've missed you so much."

Donnelly turned and looked into Brandt's eyes, suddenly serious. "I never want to be away from you again."

"Sounds like a deal."

They kissed.

"I'm just worried about one thing," Donnelly said. "How am I going to make it all the way to Geneva without tearing your clothes off?"

"I was just asking myself the same question. Be strong, Officer Donnelly. And in the meantime, I invite you to cop an inappropriate feel anytime you like." He slipped his hand under the table, along Donnelly's thigh, and up to his very full crotch. "That's what I'll be doing."

"Oh, fuck," Donnelly moaned. It was going to be a long journey.

Chapter Fourteen

Monday
Hôtel Genève

FOR ONCE, all the mechanisms of travel meshed perfectly for the newly constituted foursome. The train left London on time, and while spending the wee hours of the morning in a train station was a bit tedious, the ride into Geneva was both scenic and smooth. Their hotel was a short walk from the train station, allowing them a welcome opportunity to stretch their legs.

The hotel elevator conveyed them to the very top of the historic hotel, and through double doors at the end of the grand hallway was their suite. The two bedrooms that opened off the luxuriously appointed parlor boasted commanding views of the lake.

"Dibs on the room with the twin beds," called Kerry, after bustling from room to room. "Then Sandler won't be able to make a move while I'm sleeping and defenseless."

"I think we established when you fell asleep on me on the train that you're not my type," Sandler replied. "And we further established that you snore."

"You are such a charmer," she said with a laugh as she chucked his cheeks like a doting grandmother. He laughed with her, his anxious mood seeming to lift under the influence of Kerry's joviality.

"So I guess we get the big bed," Brandt said with a wink at Donnelly.

"Make sure you check for structural integrity before y'all let loose on it," Kerry warned, then broke into giggles.

"Thanks for your concern," Donnelly said drily. "But I assure you my fiancé will be a perfect gentleman this evening." He smiled at Brandt, mischief in his eyes.

"We're well out of your jurisdiction here, Officer," Brandt replied, a husky growl underlying his voice. "Your assurances, among other things you hold dear, are subject to violation."

"Welp, good night, everyone!" called Donnelly as he seized Brandt by the arm and began dragging him to the bedroom.

"See you in the morning," Brandt added over his shoulder, not even making a show of resisting Donnelly's firm grip.

"You two have fun," Kerry said as the door to their bedroom slammed shut. She shrugged at Sandler as the two of them stood in the parlor, suddenly alone.

"Here's a suggestion," he began, "how about we head down to the café in the lobby and plot some strategy for tomorrow?"

"Excellent idea," she replied as she picked up her bag. "That way we'll be out of the impact zone." She rolled her eyes toward the bedroom door.

Sandler laughed and held the door open for her. "After you, m'lady," he said with a bow.

"Such a gentleman," she said as she stepped with regal grandeur through the doorway. Behind her, not-very-gentlemanly noises began to emanate from the bedroom. They were getting out just in time.

The hotel lobby was suffused with the golden light of the late afternoon sun, laced with the quiet conversation of the wealthy. They found a high table at the café that occupied a windowed corner of the lobby, overlooking the street, and soon had steaming mugs of strong coffee laced with even stronger liqueur. The sky darkened as a storm approached from across the lake, and gentle rain began to fall on the city as streetlights blinked on and pedestrians began to hurry on their way.

A delicious warmth spread across Kerry's chest, both from the coffee and the high-proof enhancement it was spiked with. They watched the street in silence for several long minutes. Then she turned to study the man across the table from her. Sandler's expression was distracted, not by the street scene Kerry had been watching but by a deeper mix of emotions that etched his face with worry. She thought about asking him something, though she had no idea what she could possibly say that would be appropriate, given what he'd been through in the last twenty-four hours. So she waited.

Finally, after nearly a quarter hour of staring blankly ahead, he spoke. "Do you think he's really out there?" he said quietly, looking out the window.

She saw the desolate expression on his face, heard the utter lack of hope in his voice, and knew that blithe words of optimism wouldn't be enough. She reached across the small table and put her hand on his arm. "I do," she said solemnly.

He turned at her touch, looking first down at her hand and then up to meet her gaze. He seemed no less lost than he had before.

"He is here," she said slowly, seriously. "And you will get to him before anything bad happens."

He closed his eyes for a long, dismal blink. When he opened them, he seemed to be, if anything, even more hopeless. "It's been ten years since the accident, and his life is still entirely in his parents' hands. I think bad things are the only things that have happened to him."

"I know it seems grim, but you have to be hopeful," she replied, as gently as she could. "Maybe his parents have been keeping him prisoner against his will."

He looked at her, startled. "How is that in any way hopeful?"

"Because it means he may be fine, physically and mentally, but his parents have managed to convince everyone—well, not everyone, but Dr. Rauthmann at least—that he's sick."

"And that's supposed to be better than actually being sick?" His furrowed brow clearly showed he wasn't buying this pep talk at all.

"It is," she answered decisively, "because you are here now to save him from them. Once he's rescued from their clutches, he'll probably be fine."

"Sure, because people who've been institutionalized against their will for nearly a decade just bounce right back. I'm sure he'll be making witty jokes about it over drinks at this very table tomorrow night." He screwed his eyes shut, squeezing outraged tears from them before turning his head back toward the window.

She hadn't moved her hand from his arm, and she didn't intend to. "Sandler, we've known each other a little more than twenty-four hours. If you're asking me whether everything's going to turn out just peachy for Trevor, I will honestly tell you I have no way of knowing that. But hear me out," she said, talking over the objection he was opening his mouth to make. "Hear me out. Trevor has been absolutely controlled by his parents since the accident. You didn't even know whether he was alive or dead. But look who he has on his side now. Two police officers who have experience with rescuing gay people from horrible parents. Me, who knows more about the therapy that Rauthmann uses than just about anyone else on the continent. And most of all, you."

"Most of all me?" Sandler replied dismally. "Because what someone held captive by his parents really needs is a messenger. Right."

"No," she said emphatically. "What Trevor needs is someone who loves him. And he has that and better, because the person who loved him more than anyone else in the world is here for him. His parents have confused love with control, but you—you knew him and loved him as he really was—as he really *is*. When he sees you, and sees you have come here to save him, his life will be transformed. Miraculously transformed. You have the chance to work a miracle in his life, Sandler. A miracle. That's why you're here. That's why I'm here. That's why Ethan and Gabriel are here. Saving Trevor is the reason we have all ended up here, through a series of unlikely events and even unlikelier coincidences. You have to see that. And that should give you hope."

"I thought you were a chemist—a scientist," he said. "You can't possibly believe that stuff about our being brought here for some kind of greater cosmic purpose. You sound like the lady who reads tarot cards outside the British embassy in Budapest."

Kerry laughed at the image, but then leaned closer over the table. "Do I believe that some divine hand guided us here? No. I believe we make our own destiny, and that's what we've done." She was warming to her subject now, speaking more forcefully with every sentence. "I hopped on this crazy train because I saw such goodness in Ethan that I had to help him if I could. I think you did the same with Gabriel. And they chose to come with you on this adventure because they believe they can—and should—help you. It's not cosmic forces—it's *people*. A group of people who made a series of well-intentioned choices, each one building on the last. Small choices that add up to a big insane plan, with the end result that we're in fucking Geneva about to bust your first love out of that clinic of the damned." She realized her voice had been climbing in volume, and she took a breath and sat back in her chair once again. "Luck didn't bring us here, hon. We did. And we're going to do what we came here to do."

Eyes wide, Sandler seemed unable to form words.

She grinned bracingly. "That's where hope comes from, doll. Not from wishing for something good to happen, but knowing that you are going to do everything you can to make it happen. And having friends who would rather pitch in with you, thick or thin, hell or high water, than be off in a castle getting ready for their own wedding. You should have hope because the three of us are in this with you, and we will be with you no matter what happens. So stop moping and start thinking about what you're going to order to toast Trevor's first night of freedom."

His mouth opened and closed, then opened again, but no words emerged. He swallowed hard, then looked back out the window for a long moment. "A week ago I was carrying a pouch for the millionth time and wondering what I should do with my life. I knew people all over the world but had no friends. Every man I've been with since Trevor has been a shadow of him, and I've made damn sure that not one of them has gotten anywhere near the heart I wrapped in barbed wire after I lost him. And now...." He sighed deeply and shook his head. "I just can't believe I'm here."

"*We're* here," Kerry said, squeezing his arm again. "This is your adventure, big guy, but we will be with you every step of the way." She cast her eyes upward. "Well, I will be, and once those two exhaust themselves, they will be too."

Sandler smiled. "Still not fair those two found each other and the rest of the world gets to struggle along with the leftovers."

Kerry raised her cup. "To the leftovers!" she cried merrily.

Sandler raised his as well. "Some things are better the second time around." A note of hope sounded in his voice for the first time.

"Now we need to get a plan together," she said once they had toasted. She pulled out her phone. "My friend in legal gave me some good background on Rauthmann and his fucked-up 'therapy,' but I don't have much on this clinic he's working out of. Did you find anything?"

He nodded tentatively. "One of the lawyers I've worked for was able to find a case from several years ago when someone sued for malpractice, and I got some info from the lawyer who handled it." He tapped and swiped at his phone for a few seconds. "He said it's a kind of co-op place, where the individual doctors rent facilities and the use of some support staff, but they manage their own patients. There's apparently a law that shields the owners of the clinic from liability if one of the doctors who uses it does something wrong, as long as they can show they didn't know about it."

"So all we need to do is let them know what Rauthmann is up to, and they'll throw him out?" Kerry asked.

"I don't think it's that easy. We'd have to sue him and win before they'd be likely to do anything. In the case he told me about, the firm won their case, and the doctor who lost was basically thrown out. But until the verdict was reached, he was allowed to keep practicing there. So filing a lawsuit would help Trevor in a couple of years, not tomorrow."

"So what we need is to find some reason for the clinic to throw Rauthmann out immediately."

"How are we going to do that? He basically says on his website that he's willing to completely fuck people up in order to make them straight, and they're apparently okay with that. What could we tell them that would change their mind about him?"

Kerry pursed her lips and mulled this over. "Maybe we don't have to change their mind about Rauthmann. Maybe we need to make them think about the effect he could have on the reputation of their little clinic. But first we'd need to visit the man himself and get him to admit that he's still using the protocol we think he is." Her brow furrowed. "Though we couldn't just walk into his office and demand that he give us the details. We may need to be a little... devious."

Sandler narrowed his eyes. "What are you thinking?"

"What I'm thinking is that if we stage a little drama, we can get him to give us what we need." She looked at him with a conspiratorial gleam in her eye. "Too bad we don't know anyone who dabbled in the dramatic arts… say, in high school?"

"You're scaring me with that wicked smile," Sandler said suspiciously.

"Thought so. I can spot the high school theater type a mile away."

"Not all gay men have trod the boards, you know. It's kind of a stereotype."

Kerry sat back in her chair. "Wait, you did… *musicals*, didn't you?" She slapped her hand on the table. "You did. You did musicals. Tell me I'm wrong."

Sandler gave her a look that was frankly terrified. "How did you do that?"

"It's been said that I have weapons-grade gaydar," she said modestly.

"Said by whom?"

"Oh, that's a long story. Bottom line is I told a friend in college he was gay before he'd realized it himself, and though he denied it up and down and spent weeks telling me I was wrong, he finally forced himself to try it. Ended up pounding on my dorm-room door at two in the morning, breath smelling like the soccer player he'd been chewing on, and he pretty much accused me of being a witch." She shrugged. "You'll be happy to know that he and his soccer player are happily married to this day."

"That's heartwarming, but I tend to agree about the witch thing."

Kerry laughed. "I've been called worse by people I like less, so thanks."

"So what's this drama you've got planned?" He gave a movie-star flip of his hair. "What's my motivation?"

"I need to work on the script a bit, so I'm a little light on the details. How's your self-loathing? Got anything along that line?"

"There was a haircut in college that I regret. I looked like I escaped from a prison work farm in Alabama."

"Excellent. Have that anguish in your back pocket when we go see the horrid Dr. Rauthmann. We may need it to seal the deal."

"Like they say in bad movies, it might just be crazy enough to work. Or, you know, get us arrested."

"I'm stickin' with crazy," Kerry said with a laugh. "You know I'm up for adventure, but spending time in a Swiss jail is going a bit far. Let's just get your boy rescued, shall we?"

Sandler smiled, looking genuinely hopeful. "You know, I think we just might."

The bedroom, Geneva

BRANDT PUSHED the door shut with his foot—his hands were otherwise engaged. They were, in fact, grappling with all of the parts of Donnelly's body that he had been sorely missing for the last week. Now that they were finally alone together, Brandt felt Donnelly's presence everywhere, coursing through his entire body and being. He had been missing the better part of himself, and his soul delighted in being reunited with its complement.

He pushed Donnelly back toward the bed, gripping him tightly around the neck as they kissed. Donnelly's hands roamed his back, lifting his shirt, slipping into his jeans.

Donnelly pulled back and looked at Brandt, a twinkle in his eye. "A week in Paris with a girl sure got you riled up."

"It was pure hell," Brandt breathed. "It killed me not to be able to get to you." He kissed Donnelly's cheeks, his eyes, all along his strong jaw. "You are the only man for me."

Something in the way he said that made Donnelly flash back to a horrible dream he'd had. Something in a meadow, someone named… Bryan?

"Can I ask you something?" Donnelly asked softly.

"Anything. Anything for you."

"If you and I hadn't…. If we hadn't gotten together the way we did… would you be with someone like Kerry?"

Brandt froze, just for an instant. He willed himself to breathe, hoping Donnelly wouldn't notice how the question startled him.

Donnelly noticed.

Brandt closed his eyes for a moment, wanting to get the words right. "Gabriel, when you came into my life, you changed me. I became something I never imagined I could be, because I never imagined I would meet someone like you. I'm not the same without you. That's what this week showed me. I'm only the person I want to be when you're with me."

The words that were meant to reassure Donnelly only served to deepen his doubt. He released Brandt from his hold and sat on the bed. "Is that a good thing, really? That you're a different person when I'm around?"

Brandt sat on the bed next to him. "Not a different person. A better one. The one I want to be."

Donnelly looked into Brandt's eyes. "You didn't answer my question. If we weren't together, would you be with someone like Kerry?"

"You mean, would I be with a woman?"

Donnelly looked down to the bed and nodded. He didn't want to see the struggle on Brandt's face as he tried to answer this question.

Brandt saw the pained mix of fear and uncertainty on Donnelly's face. But he knew he had to speak the truth.

"Yes."

Donnelly exhaled, feeling the life flow from him. "Then why do you want to be here with me?"

"Because I love you. I love you more than I thought it was possible to love someone. I'm here with you because I've spent the last week being without you, and if I needed any confirmation that with you is where I want to be, I got it. I was a mess without you, Gabriel, a complete mess."

"But you weren't a mess before we got together," Donnelly replied, shifting on the bed. Saying this was awkward and uncomfortable, but not saying it was worse. "Did you ever think maybe you feel like a mess when we're not together because we're not supposed to be together? That by being with me you're defying your own nature?"

"Gabriel, my love," Brandt whispered, running his fingers along Donnelly's jaw. "What the fuck are you talking about?"

As anxious as he was about this conversation, Donnelly had to smile a bit at Brandt's ability to deliver that line with such sweetness. He really was a different person than he had been when Donnelly met him.

"Donnelly," the sergeant barked. "Your new partner is here. Try not to break this one, okay?"

Donnelly grunted his disapproval of the joke the sergeant was trying to make. His previous partner had been placed on long-term disability after finding his way under a Rolls-Royce that had been stolen and taken for quite an elegant joyride around the greater metro area. His new nickname was Speed Bump, which he might appreciate if he ever returned to the force to hear it.

"If you're worried, why are you giving me a virgin?" Donnelly asked. No one liked getting a partner fresh out of the academy, even one whose reputation preceded him like this Brandt guy's did.

"He's downstairs," growled the sergeant. "Just go get him and try not to fuck him up too badly, okay?"

Donnelly got up from his desk, to which he'd been exiled for two months after the accident—the department wanted to be sure the horror of watching his partner slide under a three-ton car was compounded with the boredom of filling out three tons of paperwork. This Brandt would be his third new partner in two years, and he hoped he would be the last. Getting to know someone that well—during long days of utter boredom punctuated by random eruptions of sheer adrenaline—was exhausting. It would be nice to find someone... nice.

He walked out to the desk and saw the new guy immediately. He stood stick straight, uniform creased to a razor's edge, hat tucked under his arm as if he were standing at parade rest. He didn't move.

"Officer Brandt?" Donnelly said as he approached, though the blinding glint of light reflected off Brandt's nameplate provided answer without the need for speech.

"Yes, sir," Brandt said, extending his hand.

"I'm—"

"Officer Donnelly. Pleased and honored to meet you, sir." His grip was steely, his smile bright.

"Yep, that's me. And please, call me Gabriel." Donnelly shook his head. He'd heard through the grapevine that Brandt was an overgrown Boy Scout, but this display of sheer eagerness nearly overwhelmed him. "Come on back, let me show you around."

"Thank you, sir."

"Stop that," Donnelly snapped.

"Sorry, s—" Brandt bit down and kept himself from saying it. He remained silent but still vibrated with enthusiasm.

"Here's my desk," Donnelly said, pointing to the battered metal surface by the window. He'd "inherited" it from Speed Bump, since a guy in traction doesn't really need a desk. "And there's yours." He pointed to the one right next to his own, which used to be his before his sudden seniority bumped him up to a seat with a view.

"Thanks," Brandt said, unable to disguise his excitement at the sight of the cracked oak surface of the ancient desk. He didn't even seem to care that it wobbled precariously when he set his briefcase on it.

A briefcase! Donnelly shook his head. "I'll give you a tour of the place first, and then we'll head down to the range for weapons check."

"I've passed all my checks," Brandt replied, reaching for his briefcase.

"I know—I've read your file. But if we're going to work together, I need to see you shoot first."

Donnelly had indeed reviewed his file, and knew that his performance on the shooting range at the academy had been record-setting. But sometimes the best marksmen started to think they were simply gifted when it came to firearms and got cavalier when it came to handling weapons. He wanted to see for himself that Brandt was as good as his reputation.

Brandt nodded, and for the first time, Donnelly saw something under his eagerness to please—a little wrinkle of resentment at the corner of his mouth. This was a guy who, young as he was, wasn't used to being challenged. The reaction, little more than a tic, a poker tell, vanished almost as soon as it appeared. But Donnelly was heartened to see it at all. It meant Brandt was more than a Boy Scout—there was assertiveness just under the surface. If Donnelly had seen no reaction, he would have worried that Brandt wasn't ready for the street; a stronger reaction would have hinted at cockiness rather than confidence.

This guy's got potential, Donnelly thought.

His performance on the range was, as promised, blisteringly accurate. Donnelly had never seen anyone shoot the way Brandt could. But he was no cowboy—his stance was steady, his breathing controlled; he blinked in preparation for a shot rather than in reaction to it. He was a consummate marksman, one day out of the academy.

A little later, as Donnelly settled into the driver's seat of their cruiser, he took another look at the young officer to his right. Brandt was clearly pumped to finally get out into the real world, to wear the uniform among the people he was sworn to protect rather than amid a sea of blue caps at the academy.

Donnelly knew that Brandt was two years his junior, but already he projected an aura of calm capability. Donnelly realized as he watched the new officer that some part of him had been expecting to find Brandt too green, too eager, or too arrogant to do his job well, especially on the first day. But Brandt was none of those things.

Maybe Donnelly hadn't drawn the short straw to replace Speed Bump after all. There was one way to know for certain.

"See the game last night?" Donnelly asked as he pulled the cruiser out of the lot behind headquarters.

"Hell yeah," Brandt replied, grinning broadly. "Whoever said Warner is the new Sanchez didn't figure on Johnston."

"Right?" Donnelly replied. "That last inning was like a fire drill at the asylum." He burst out laughing, and Brandt joined him enthusiastically.

The new guy was going to work out just fine.

At the end of their first shift together, Brandt buttoned up his uniform and picked up his briefcase. "Thanks for everything today," he said to Donnelly, who was finishing up a report.

"Hey, I'm heading down to the gym in a couple if you're interested," he said, looking up from his computer. "I try to get a workout in every day. Helps put a nice close on the shift."

"That'd be great," Brandt said, but then seemed to have second thoughts. "I didn't bring anything to work out in, though."

"I've got stuff you can use. Just did laundry this weekend and brought in a pile of stuff. You'd actually be helping me—my locker barely closed this morning."

Brandt beamed. "Thanks. That's really.... Thanks."

"No problem. It'll be nice to have someone to work out with for a change," Donnelly said as he closed his laptop and stowed it in his pack. Then he raised his voice so his nearby coworkers could hear clearly. "The rest of these dullards seem to think that lifting donuts is the same as lifting weights, which is why they're all tremendous fat fucks."

"Screw you, Donnelly" came the reply from more than one of the tremendous fat fucks.

"I work out with your mother plenty," one shouted from across the room.

"Neanderthals," muttered Brandt, low enough that only Donnelly could hear.

An officer expects his partner to have his back, but this Brandt guy was already protective. Donnelly, to his surprise, wasn't bothered by this at all—in fact, he was touched by it. What's more, Brandt had pronounced the term correctly—with a hard "t" rather than a "th." Well, the guy had not slept through college; that was certain.

"Gym's this way," Donnelly said, leading Brandt out of the office area and down the stairs. "I'm the only one who uses it, even though the state outfitted it with brand-new stuff just last year as part of their initiative to keep us all from being tremendous fat fucks." He switched on the light, and the small but very well-equipped workout room came into view. "Clearly, it's not working. I don't think anyone's been in here since I turned out the lights last night."

"You work out on weekends too?" Brandt asked.

"I'm currently between girlfriends—like, a long way between—so working out is kind of my only hobby these days," Donnelly explained as he led Brandt into the locker room off the gym. "There's a changing room without a shower on the other side of the hall for guys who don't like to lift heavy things. This is kind of my own personal locker room."

"I'm not intruding, am I?"

This Brandt guy was courteous to a fault.

"Not at all. I'm happy to share it with anyone who is willing to spot me on the bench." Donnelly set his pack down, opened his locker, and whipped off his shirt. He reached into his locker and pulled out an extra pair of shorts and a shirt for Brandt and handed them over. It was only then that he realized Brandt was staring.

"What?" Donnelly asked. "Something wrong?"

"You must really be between girlfriends," Brandt said, eyebrows raised.

Donnelly looked down at his admittedly ripped torso. He chuckled self-consciously. "Yeah, I've been working some stuff out."

"Well, whatever you're doing, it's working." Brandt started to unbutton his starched uniform shirt.

Donnelly, used to having the locker room to himself, threw his clothes off and pulled on his workout gear in a blur of motion, not caring where things landed. Brandt, meanwhile, carefully folded every article, and even found an abandoned hanger in one of the lockers on which to hang his uniform.

"I'm gonna go warm up on the treadmill," Donnelly said as he walked past Brandt on his way to the door. "There are socks and an extra pair of shoes at the bottom of my locker."

"Thanks," Brandt called after him.

Donnelly was already running his second mile when Brandt emerged from the locker room. He mounted the other treadmill and swiftly fell into pace alongside Donnelly, matching his stride exactly. They ran wordlessly for fifteen minutes, and then Donnelly hit the stop button and coasted back to the floor. "Let's get to it," he said as Brandt stepped off the treadmill as well.

It was only then that Donnelly noticed he had handed Brandt his most shredded workout shirt. It was sleeveless, and he had ripped the collar out last year after snagging it on the latch of his locker door. This Brandt guy was hiding some serious muscle under that uniform. Donnelly looked away before Brandt could notice his stare, but he couldn't keep himself from checking out a few different angles in the mirrors that lined the free-weight area.

They lifted for the better part of an hour, then stretched on the mats that occupied the far corner of the gym. Throughout, they said perhaps a dozen words to each other—they both approached physical training seriously. But as they stretched, Donnelly realized that simply having someone to work out with had made him push himself even harder than he normally did, and his muscles were already letting him know about it.

"Be honest—how much time did you spend in the gym at the academy?" Donnelly asked.

"Not much. Just the time that my squad spent out drinking, or watching porn, or shooting the shit about political stuff they didn't really understand." He smiled. "So, yeah, I guess you could say it was a lot of time."

Donnelly couldn't help it—he glanced down at Brandt's brickwork abs, visible where the torn shirt gapped open as he stretched. "You can't possibly be between girlfriends, though."

Brandt rolled his eyes. "Not so much 'between' as 'not ever.' I don't think a girl you date twice or three times counts, and that's all I've ever had. Too busy cranking through school and the academy to have time for a girlfriend."

"Plus all that time in the gym," teased Donnelly.

"Exactly. Why spend time with a woman when a dank, smelly gym is waiting for you?" Brandt laughed.

"I've got some bad news. The dank, smelly shower was remodeled when they put in all the equipment, so instead of the festival of exotic mold that it used to be, it's actually quite nice." He got to his feet and stretched his arms one last time.

"Sounds great. I'll catch one after you."

"You're in luck—there's two stalls. No waiting." Donnelly turned and headed back to the locker room.

Standing in front of his locker, he threw off his workout clothes and grabbed a towel. He tossed one to Brandt and walked past him to the tiled shower area. *"Oh, huh,"* he said. *"That's weird."*

"What's weird?"

"They took down the shower curtains. They must finally have noticed that they hadn't been cleaned since they were put up last year." He cranked on the water. *"Oh well. The shower still works, and that's what's important."*

There were two showerheads in the small bathroom, facing each other from opposite sides of the far end of the room. The shower alcoves were separated by a small tiled space, and delineating each was a shower curtain rod; these boasted a dozen wire rings, bereft of their curtains. Donnelly entered the stall on the left and cranked on the hot water. Behind him he heard Brandt turn on the taps in the other shower.

A steamy minute or two passed.

"Any soap?" Brandt asked.

Donnelly reached down and grabbed the gallon jug of all-purpose wash that the department had thoughtfully supplied. As he was the only person who used this shower, it had lasted him the entire year and was still half-full. *"Here,"* he said, turning around for the first time to hand it to—

Brandt.

All of Brandt. Fully naked Brandt.

It wasn't his impressive musculature that struck Donnelly, for he had gotten glimpses of that during their workout. It was rather the combination of two outstanding features: Brandt's bright, genuine smile, and his absolutely enormous penis.

"Thanks," Brandt said, taking the jug from Donnelly. He set it in the tiled no-man's-land between the shower stalls, then took a big pump and began scrubbing his short, spiky hair.

"Yeah," Donnelly grunted.

Donnelly was not unacquainted with male genitalia. He had been a powerful high school wrestler, in a part of the state where wrestling was more a religion than a sport. In the course of his athletic career, he had showered hundreds of times with the other guys on the team; any shyness he might have had about being naked in a room full of naked men had been boiled out of him two weeks into his freshman year. He had seen plenty of penises, of all sizes. Or so he thought. He had, until today, never seen one like Brandt's.

He turned around and lathered up, closing his eyes and trying to shake the image of Brandt's thoroughbred member out of his mind's eye. His mind's eye, however, had other ideas. He saw it in great detail, every inch after inch of it, and then his perverse subconscious piled on. How big do you think it gets? He shoved this thought, and several others that he didn't even have words for, out of his mind.

"Thanks for everything today," Brandt said from his side of the room, not three feet away.

"No problem," Donnelly managed to answer, though he wasn't sure what he was being thanked for. *"Glad to have a partner again."*

"I just hope I don't end up under a Kia or something."

"Very funny," Donnelly retorted, inwardly relieved to be thinking about something other than... Brandt's huge penis. Dammit.

"I mean it, though. I'd heard at the academy that a lot of guys are really hard on virgins, and you've been decent about it. You treated me like a colleague, and I wanted you to know how much I appreciate it."

"Well, you'd have to admit any plans I had about hazing would be pretty awkward right now," Donnelly said, looking across the narrow space that divided them.

Brandt laughed, a deep, joyful laugh that seemed to come over his whole body. Including his penis.

Get a grip, Donnelly. He's your partner, and he's a guy, and so are you. Stop being perverted about this.

"What would you think about a run tomorrow before shift?" Brandt asked, turning away to rinse under the shower.

"Sounds great. Do you run a lot?"

Look at that ass—of course he runs.

"Try to. Maybe do 5K before the day gets going?"

"Sounds like a plan." A daily run would give him an ass like Brandt's in no time. And that's what this was all about, after all. Brandt simply had the physique that Donnelly would like to have, and that's why he kept feeling his eyes drawn to him. Workout goals—that's what this was about.

Donnelly felt his chest lighten, now that he'd figured out what was bothering him. Got it all sorted out now. (Except for the part about how he couldn't stop looking at Brandt's tremendous endowment, but his subconscious let him off that particular hook.)

They dried, dressed, and walked out through the now-quiet office area. The day shift had gone home, and only vital areas like dispatch and the break room were occupied through the night.

"See you tomorrow at five?" Brandt asked as they walked out the main doors.

"Dream come true," Donnelly replied with a grin. Then, without knowing he was going to do it or why, he added, *"Hey, want to grab dinner and watch the game? There's a bar just over that way that takes a dollar off the price of a pitcher for every run."*

"Beats going home and watching it on the small screen," Brandt replied with a broad smile. *"Thanks."*

They fell into step together as they walked down the street toward the bar.

"Hey, um," Brandt said, a little awkwardly, *"back in the shower?"*

A cold dagger stabbed into Donnelly's chest.

"I meant what I said. I really appreciate how you... welcomed me. Thanks."

"I think you're going to be an amazing cop, Ethan." Donnelly was relieved to feel his heart still beating. This could be, he reflected as they continued their stroll, the start of a beautiful friendship.

"I'm talking about how you were a normal guy before we met. And so was I."

"We changed. People change," Brandt replied.

"I didn't change. I just admitted to myself what I'd buried for a long, long time. You changed. I changed you."

Brandt nodded. "People change each other." Like beams of light. "It's a big part of what makes us human."

"But maybe it wasn't fair of me to… change you that way. Maybe you'd be happier if you had just gone on being what you were."

Brandt leaned close, so his lips touched Donnelly's ear. "What I was," he whispered, sending shivers down Donnelly's entire body, "was waiting for you." He kissed Donnelly's ear softly. "You didn't just change me. You awakened me." He kissed down Donnelly's neck, bringing a moan from his throat. "I needed you without knowing what I lacked. I felt complete and independent. And absolutely alone." He ran his open lips along Donnelly's clavicle, summoning waves of goose bumps and sending them radiating across his muscular chest. "The day I met you"—he kissed Donnelly's already-stiff nipple—"and every day since then"—he kissed the other—"you've shown me life is so much bigger and better than I ever thought it could be."

He kissed Donnelly's lips, the lips he'd been dreaming of for a week. "Being away from you—not able to get to you no matter what I tried—made me see what I am without you. That's not how I want to live."

"But that's exactly what I'm talking about," Donnelly maintained, reluctant to keep objecting but not comfortable yielding the point. "If you're different when I'm not around, then who are you, really?"

"Of course I'm different when you're not with me." Brandt kissed him again. "I was terrified the first few days, not knowing who I was without you." He put his finger on Donnelly's mouth to stem his protest before he could voice it. "But," he said firmly, looking into Donnelly's eyes, "*but*, I realized I'm a fully functioning human being, even when you're thousands of miles away. I'm not as confident or as smart or as calm as when you're with me—Kerry has some stories to tell you, I'm afraid—but I can exist on my own if I have to. I don't want to, and I never want to be separated from you by a fucking volcano ever again, but I'm still a complete person. Just not the best person I can be."

Donnelly looked at him, trying to see whether Brandt really had survived the week with his faculties intact. "Are you sure? You aren't going to wake up one morning and realize you'd rather be straight?"

Brandt tucked the corner of his mouth up in a sly smile. "I am straight, remember? But out of all of the people in the whole world—male, female, all the genders for that matter—I choose you. Because you are the one person I've ever met who knows my entire heart and loves me anyway. Because I look at you and I see everything I ever want in life. Because we changed each other, and for the better in every way. I am going to marry you, Gabriel Donnelly, and we will be together all the days of our lives."

"I love you so much, Ethan." Donnelly's voice was low, almost a moan.

"I've loved you since before I had a word for it, since before I could admit it to myself. And I will always love you."

They kissed for a long while, wordless in blissful reunion.

"I just have one more question for you," Donnelly said when they finally had to stop and catch a breath.

"What is it, my love?"

"When do we get to the fucking?" Donnelly gave his best coquettish smile.

"Right the fuck now, is what I'm thinking," Brandt replied.

Donnelly threw off his shirt, then flopped back on the bed and began shucking off his pants. He kicked them off, and his boxer briefs and socks joined them, arcing gracefully through the air. He was suddenly fully naked, and he pushed himself farther up on the bed, coming to an elegant recline against the mountain of pillows at the head of the bed.

Brandt stood for a moment, looking down upon this wonder of a man, the one who had somehow come into his life and decided he would stay forever. He gracefully inhabited the body Brandt preferred above all others in the world, despite being the only male body he'd ever been attracted to in any way at all. How that happened, he didn't pretend to understand; why it happened, he knew with a certainty that occurred to him as if from another world. He was born to love this man, the only man he had ever loved, the only person he would ever love.

He took his time unbuttoning his shirt, the one he had so carefully chosen the morning before because it was Donnelly's favorite and he'd wanted to be wearing it when they saw each other for the first time. He pulled it open and let it slide down his muscular arms.

Donnelly gazed, rapt, at his torso and nowhere else. "Poor Kerry," he said, looking up at Brandt and shaking his head.

"Why do you say that?" Brandt asked as he carefully draped the shirt over a chair.

"She had to spend a week with you knowing that all of that"—he gestured at Brandt's heavily muscled torso—"was off-limits."

Brandt chuckled. "Want to hear something funny?" He unbuttoned his pants slowly.

"Make it quick because as soon as those pants are off, I won't be paying attention to anything that happens above the waist."

"That's my boy," Brandt said with a laugh. "Anyway, Kerry apparently figured since I was marrying a man, I must be gay."

"What a strange assumption," Donnelly replied, eyes wide with ironic puzzlement.

"Right? So we ended up in a dressing room in some supercouture dress shop, and she starts throwing off her clothes. Which was bad enough, but then she wanted fashion advice. Fashion advice! From me!" He draped his jeans over the same chair and stood before the bed in just underwear.

"I would be mad at her, but I'm sure the poor girl suffered enough. I hope she didn't buy something horrifying on your recommendation."

"Nah," Brandt said as he cast his underwear over his shoulder. They landed atop Donnelly's. "She just wanted someone to agree with her. But I thought you should know that I was alone in an enclosed space with those amazing boobs of hers, and I lived to tell the tale."

"You are a hero, sir. Now get over here and collect your reward."

Brandt wrinkled up his nose. "I hope it's not boobs. I'm pretty much over those, actually."

"I think you'll find a distinct absence of boobs here. But I have my own charms to offer." He rolled most of the way over, arching his back to proffer his exquisitely muscled ass to Brandt. "See anything you like?"

"Fuck," huffed Brandt. The sight of Donnelly's perfectly round ass always gave him a savage twist in the gut, which today erupted into a desperate hunger. He leapt onto the bed, pinning Donnelly down flat, his shoulder pressed firmly into a decidedly solid left buttock.

"Oof," Donnelly groaned. This—this was what he'd been craving all week. The heaviness of Brandt's unabashed desire, the weight of his strong body. He ground his rock-hard cock into the bed and then pushed back, thrusting his ass up into Brandt.

"God, Gabriel," moaned Brandt. He nuzzled Donnelly's right buttock, tracing a line of gentle kisses along its flawless porcelain surface. "Your ass is the most perfect thing in the world."

"And to think I've just been sitting on it all this time."

"That's a damn shame. An ass like this demands special treatment."

"That's fine talk, mister, but what are you going to do about it?"

"First I'm going to get comfortable," Brandt said, lifting himself up and insinuating himself between Donnelly's outstretched legs. "Then I'm going to get reacquainted." He kissed the left cheek, paralleling the line of kisses he'd made on the right. "Hello, you perfect globe of manly vigor."

Donnelly tried to keep a straight face, and failed—good thing his face was pressed into a pillow.

"And greetings to you, sweet hemisphere of masculine beauty." Brandt returned to kissing the right side.

Donnelly lost his battle to keep from laughing delightedly.

"And now for the part I think I may have missed the most," Brandt said grandly.

"Oh, I hope it's the butthole," called Donnelly giddily. "Please, oh please, be the butthole!"

"That's right, it's your friend and mine, Gabriel's butthole!" Brandt placed his hands firmly on Donnelly's cheeks and pulled. In the lightly furred cleft in between, Donnelly's tight hole winked into view. "There you are, my love." Brandt leaned close and bestowed a delicate kiss directly on its wrinkled surface.

"Oh, fuck," exhaled Donnelly into the pillow. The featherlight touch of Brandt's lips on his most private place sent an arc of pure electricity sizzling through his body. Underneath him, pressed into the lace coverlet, his cock surged anew. He twisted and writhed, desperate for more vigorous contact.

In this he was not to be disappointed.

Brandt lavished a dozen kisses on Donnelly's ring of muscle, kissing his way around it in a tightening spiral before finally reaching the center again. He pulled back, looked up at Donnelly's body, marveling at how he had come to desire this masculine form with an urgency that was as physical as it was emotional. After all the time Brandt had spent agonizing over how he had come to choose a man over all of the women in the world, it was really this simple: here, before him, naked and welcoming, was the only person in the world he loved. And it wasn't that this perfect, loving soul happened to be wrapped in the body of a man, forcing Brandt to look past the masculine exterior; in fact, Brandt knew in this moment, he loved that body as much as he loved the mind and the spirit and the heart it sustained.

While Brandt had been pondering the nature of attraction, he had been tracing spirals on Donnelly's buttocks with his fingertips, and now he looked down at the powerful mounds that shivered with delight and desire.

Yes, this is where I belong, Brandt thought.

He kissed his way up Donnelly's spine, feeling a twitch of pleasure ripple through the muscles of Donnelly's back with every feather touch of Brandt's lips. Finally, he reached Donnelly's neck and nuzzled it as he laid himself down and pressed their bodies together, his now rock-hard cock warming itself in the cleft between Donnelly's legs.

"You are the entire world to me," Brandt whispered into Donnelly's ear.

Once again blanketed by the overwhelming strength and extent of Brandt, Donnelly had never felt so secure and loved. The anxieties of the past week flowed out of him. All of the worry about the nature of their relationship, about how their individual pasts had brought them to this amazing present—it all faded away. And in its place there was just… love. They didn't need to explain themselves to each other or to anyone; they simply were, together, something greater than they could ever be apart.

Donnelly, his wrestling moves still ready at hand, rolled suddenly to one side and flipped Brandt over. He pounced atop him, covering him as completely as he had been covered a second ago. He placed his hands on both sides of Brandt's handsome face and held him tight. "I love you so much, Ethan," he whispered. "We will have our entire lives to whisper sweet devotions to each other. But right now, there's just one thing I want to hear from you." He sat up astride his recumbent fiancé.

"And what would that be?" Brandt asked, certain he already knew the answer.

"A surprised groan as you suddenly remember how tight my ass is," Donnelly answered with a wicked grin.

"Nothing would delight me more," Brandt said in the manner of James Bond being offered an extra-large martini.

"Remember when we were at the Villa Hermes, and you carried a bottle of—"

"Right here," Brandt replied as he reached for his jeans. He pulled his hand out of the pocket and brandished a small bottle of lube. "I thought we might have need of this today."

"Right you are, as always," Donnelly said. "Hand it over." He fixed Brandt with a serious glare, one that conveyed an intensity of desire that made Brandt's cock twitch.

"Yes, sir," he said dutifully. He dropped the bottle into Donnelly's impatient hand. Anything that involved the two of them and lubrication he was definitely up for.

Donnelly flipped the cap on the bottle, then lifted himself up and moved down until he was straddling Brandt's strong thighs. Their fullness was immediately apparent. "Someone managed to find time for leg day even while flitting about Paris."

"Flitting demands considerable hamstring and quadriceps involvement," Brandt said with a haughty dignity that Donnelly found quite amusing.

"Officer Ethan Brandt, flitting," Donnelly said, shaking his head. "I never thought I'd see the day."

"Officer Gabriel Donnelly, flirting instead of using that bottle of lube I so kindly provided him. I may take it back and show him how it's done."

"Like hell you will," Donnelly said with a determination as steely as the cock he now gripped in his hand. He drizzled a generous amount of clear gel onto the head of Brandt's cock, a little surprised not to hear it sizzle. He flicked a slick thumb over the tip, knowing exactly how Brandt would react.

"God, I've missed your touch," Brandt groaned, arching his back in sudden pleasure.

"And I have missed this guy," Donnelly said, beaming down at the extensive hard-on he held in his hand. He worked the slick gel up and down, covering the entire shaft. It dripped down onto Brandt's balls.

"A hand job isn't exactly what I had in mind," Brandt wheedled impatiently. "Though given my level of deprivation, I'll gladly accept one."

"I'm not going to let you off that easy," Donnelly said with a smirk, quite pleased with his wit. Satisfied with the slipperiness of Brandt's cock, he rose up onto his knees, arched his back, and reached around to grip Brandt's cock behind him. He held it straight and true as he lowered himself down toward it.

"Ahhhh, fuck!" groaned Brandt as his cock touched Donnelly's ass. "You're so tight."

"It's been a lonely week," Donnelly replied, backing up against Brandt's hardness.

"And you didn't have even a moment alone to see to your own needs?"

A crooked smile emerged on Donnelly's face. "I may have indulged once or twice," he said slyly. "The shower in the suite was amazing—great water pressure and so many ways to direct the deluge." He sighed at the memory. "But even then I saved my ass for you."

It was Brandt's turn to give a sly smile. "I'm afraid I'm not as pure as you are when it comes to that."

Donnelly's eyes lit up with the scandal of what he'd just heard. "But you *never* do butt stuff when you jerk off."

"I do now, I guess," he said with a sexy shrug. "Call it just another step in my progress as a sexual being."

"Fucking hot is what I call it. Good for you. Now here's something special to reward your flexibility." He took a breath and pushed down, hard. Brandt's wide battering ram of a cock breached the stubborn ring of muscle and surged inside. "Oof," Donnelly grunted. "I guess I did tighten up a little during the week. It feels like the first time."

"Every time feels like the first time," Brandt said as he raised his hips to continue his burrowing progress. He had a fleeting thought of asking if Donnelly was okay with him thrusting in, but deep down he knew—he knew exactly what Donnelly wanted, and it was precisely the same thing he did: for the two of them to be joined as completely as two people can be.

Brandt reached up and grabbed Donnelly's hips. As he thrust upward with his powerful buttocks he pulled down with his muscular arms, and between the two forces, Donnelly was impaled, possessed, fulfilled.

"Fuck," Donnelly said, stretching the single syllable until it trailed off in a moan. His eyes rolled back in his head, and he gave himself to the monstrous invasion, feeling Brandt assail all of the sensitive places in his ass at once.

Finally their bodies met, Brandt's groin pressed into Donnelly's obscenely spread buttocks.

"I'm home," Brandt sighed, looking up at Donnelly with an awestruck wonder. "This is my place in the world—mine alone."

"Always," Donnelly whispered, eyes closed for a moment as he got reacquainted with the feeling of being taken so completely. Then the time for gentle reacquaintance was over. He opened his eyes and stared into Brandt's—he wanted to watch the change come over him. Slowly at first, then with increasing purpose, he lifted his hips, feeling the thick pillar of flesh pull at him as it retreated.

Brandt's eyes widened, then lost focus for a moment as Donnelly ascended to near the apex of his eight-inch transit. Just as Donnelly felt the flare of the tip reach the tight grip of his ass, he stopped. Brandt's eyebrows peaked, and he took in a soft breath, as if he were about to lose what he wanted most in the world. Donnelly hovered there, teasing, hesitating, until finally he worried that Brandt had stopped breathing altogether. He lowered himself smoothly, feeling the fullness overtake him again.

Brandt looked up at him with a mischievous smile. "The way you stopped had me worried. Thought you were out of practice and I was a little too much for you."

"You are too much," Donnelly groaned as he reached bottom. "I swear I can feel it pushing the air out of my lungs." Then he smiled. "And I wouldn't want it any other way."

"I'll try to be gentle," Brandt said with a warm chuckle.

"Now, let's not get crazy. Gentle isn't exactly what I need right now."

"That's all I needed to hear," Brandt growled as he reached out and took hold of Donnelly's hips again, pulling him down onto the root of his cock. He twisted his hips side to side in a vigorous gyration that would make any pole dancer proud.

Donnelly experienced this motion as a forceful grinding right on his prostate, and it took his breath away. He brought his hands down and planted them on Brandt's meaty pectorals, his fingertips digging into the taut flesh, indenting the muscle.

This was exactly what Brandt had hoped to see, had craved for all the time they'd been apart. This moment, when their union became almost too much even for his strapping fiancé to handle, was intoxicating. He glanced down at Donnelly's cock, bobbing and jutting before him, and saw a strand of crystal fluid drip in slow motion from its tip. What he felt on the inside, his cockhead ramming Donnelly's prostate, he now had visual confirmation of. He looked up and watched Donnelly's head tip back, his eyes closed.

Unable to resist the urge any longer, Brandt bucked his hips forward, clenching his ass tightly to throw every ounce of his strength into Donnelly. Powerful fingers raked his chest, letting him know without question that he was hitting all the right places deep inside the man who sat astride him.

The rumble began deep in Donnelly's chest, a rumble summoned by the friction of Brandt's probing cock as it stretched his ass. As much as he wanted this to last, he wanted even more to push Brandt headlong into the orgasm he'd been dreaming of the entire time they'd been apart. He took a deep breath and pulled hard, clenching all of the muscles he had control over—the involuntary ones were already spasming to life under the onslaught.

"Oh," Brandt cried out softly, eyes wide. "You *have* to teach me how to do that."

"And give away all my secrets? Not a chance, mister." Donnelly repeated the motion, knowing that Brandt would not last long.

Brandt groaned and thrashed, but he continued to thrust determinedly. "It won't be that easy," he growled. "I can go all night."

"I'm sure you can," replied Donnelly lightly. "It's one of the qualities I like most about you. But though you may go all night, you're going to come"—clench—"right"—clench—"now."

"Oh *fuck*," Brandt roared, and his pelvis hammered into Donnelly in a blur of ecstatic thrusting. He may have been at Donnelly's mercy, but he was going to lean into it. Donnelly would know how much he had missed him by his unhinged frenzy. But he also knew that his fiancé was intensely visual, so he decided to give him a special treat.

Brandt released his hold on Donnelly's thighs, raised his hands up, and then joined them behind his head. He continued thrusting, but did so as if he were in the gym doing ab crunches of a particularly enjoyable kind. Every contraction brought his head and his pelvis up off the mattress.

Donnelly looked down and saw the deep cuts between Brandt's abs throbbing into and out of relief, the veins standing out from his bulging biceps, utter determination glowering on his brow. This man—the most man Donnelly had ever known—was all his, and would never share this most intimate experience with anyone else, male or female. He took it all in, this sculptural specimen laid out beneath him, from his sweat-spiked hair to the deep V of his pelvic muscles. And whether it was from the unparalleled vista before him or the unrivaled cock within him, he knew that he would last no longer than Brandt would.

He pitched himself forward so that Brandt's manic crunches caused his cock to rub against that divinely muscled torso. It was just the friction he needed.

"I love you, I love you," he chanted, overwhelmed with the sensations of their reunion.

"Fuck, Gabriel," Brandt huffed, "I love you so—" What followed was an incoherent growling, a soundtrack from a wilderness documentary showing what happens when two grizzlies claim the same stretch of salmon-rich river. He jackhammered into Donnelly, feeling the inevitability build deep inside his loins. The crescendo of their lovemaking echoed around the room and probably across the entire floor of the hotel. They held each other tight as they were both consumed and reborn through their passion.

After a week apart, they came together.

Brandt filled Donnelly, and Donnelly soaked Brandt, and they were very, very happy together.

Together.

A little later, Geneva

"WHERE DO you suppose Kerry and Sandler got to?" Brandt asked as he delicately plucked grapes off the stem. The remains of their room-service tray of delicacies lay between them, demolished by their passion-fueled hunger.

"I think they're afraid we're going to fuck each other right through the wall or something."

Brandt's eyebrow shot up. "Hmmm...."

"We are *not* going to try fucking against the wall—not here. I had to replace the drywall the last time you got that gleam in your eye—think of the damage you could do to a historic building like this."

"These walls must be a foot thick," Brandt replied. "You don't really think I could do them any harm just with my little ol' penis, do you?"

"To badly paraphrase Voltaire," Donnelly said as he stood and picked up the tray from the bed, "it ain't little, it ain't old, and it's only a penis in the same way that the *Titanic* was a dinghy."

"If my history prof had delivered a lecture on the Holy Roman Empire looking like you do now, I might have gotten that allusion," Brandt replied, popping the last grape into his mouth with a satisfied grin.

"Hmmm. A naked history professor," Donnelly said, placing the tray on the dresser and returning to the bed. "I don't think I'd have wanted to see any of my professors naked." He sat next to Brandt. "You, though, should remain naked at all times."

"I think the holster would chafe," Brandt retorted. He ran his fingertips along Donnelly's arm. "Now that you've had a light snack, can we get back to what we were doing?"

Donnelly grinned. "What we were doing was racing the room-service waiter to see if you could come before he did. Congratulations on that, by the way. You almost made it."

"Luckily, room service always rings twice."

"Yes, but *you* didn't have to answer the door while recovering from your vigorous efforts. I'm glad those robes are so thick. I hope he couldn't see my legs shaking."

Brandt frowned sympathetically. "I wasn't that hard on you, was I?"

"You're just lucky I like you hard. In fact," he said, snaking a hand down Brandt's recumbent body, "I can't help but notice that you are once again ready to rumble."

"I could be persuaded to—"

"That's horseshit and you know it," Donnelly scolded with a laugh. "Persuasion has nothing to do with it." He kissed Brandt on the nose. "Now, I want you standing right here." He tugged on Brandt and directed him to the side of the bed.

"Oh, this is getting interesting." Brandt did as he was told. When Donnelly and sex were involved, it was always rewarding to do as he was told.

Donnelly placed him standing next to the bed, while he sat on it facing him. "Yes," he said, then leaned forward and sucked Brandt's entire erection into his mouth.

"Oof," Brandt groaned, trying to keep his knees from buckling. "I don't know how you do that."

Donnelly pulled back, feeling Brandt slide along his tonsils. "It's a simple matter of deciding that one wants cock more than one wants oxygen," he lectured, a crooked grin on his face. "It's a trade-off I'm happy to make."

"You are demented, and I am the luckiest man in the world." Brandt leaned down and kissed Donnelly. He tasted of brie and cock.

Donnelly winked at him and returned to his devil's bargain of trading air for dick, and soon had Brandt moaning.

"Perfect," Donnelly proclaimed as he withdrew Brandt's cock from his throat. It jutted, slick and throbbing. Donnelly stood, turned, and bent himself over the bed. Reaching behind him, he guided Brandt's cock back into his ecstatically tender ass. He moaned as he felt the massive thing slide into him once again.

Brandt, looking down at where their bodies joined, smiled to himself. Donnelly was a man capable of taking down gang members at a dead run, strong enough to lift people out of the burning wreckage of their cars. And yet here he was, offering himself up to the battering ram Brandt was proud to wield. Crouched on all fours, he backed onto Brandt until they touched, and then he surged forward to begin the cycle again. Between Donnelly's obscenely splayed buttocks, Brandt could see the tight ring of muscle clinging jealously to his cock, as if reluctant to let it slip out even an inch.

He knew what Donnelly wanted, and he was pleased to give it to him. Rather than thrusting, he simply stood strong and let Donnelly fuck himself on Brandt's hard cock. Giving up this measure of control was a thrill for Brandt, who so rarely let go of any bit of command in his daily life. Plus, the end result would be just as devastatingly pleasurable; this would end with Brandt blasting yet another load—his third tonight—into his partner. He was happy to get there any way that Donnelly wanted to go.

Donnelly rocked back and forth on the bed, controlling the pace and angle with the sole purpose of pushing his prostate unto madness. And it was working. He was breathing so hard he almost didn't hear the cuckoo clock strike midnight. He had thought it inexcusably kitschy when they first entered the room—that a cuckoo clock would be standard-issue furnishing for a Swiss hotel seemed ridiculous—but now he was grateful for the twittering, bonging cacophony from the other room. Once the clock ceased its clamor, it was the next day.

His day.

He lunged forward, startling Brandt. With an audible pop, they were separated.

"What the—" Brandt howled.

"It's midnight," Donnelly interrupted, getting up off the bed. "Remember our deal."

"Oh shit. Really? Now?" Brandt moaned.

"Really. Now. We just need to make one small adjustment, and all is well," Donnelly said brightly as he drew up next to Brandt and kissed him softly.

"Well, if you put it that way," Brandt conceded.

"I am about to put it that way," Donnelly replied, running his hand down to Brandt's ass. Without further warning, he placed a firm hand on Brandt's neck and gave a shove, sending him sprawling across the bed.

"Dude, fuck!" cried Brandt as he landed heavily on the bed, but some part of him was thrilled by Donnelly's brutish hunger.

"I intend to. Up on all fours," he ordered.

Brandt hesitated. Not because he didn't want Donnelly to fuck him—he did, he did without doubt—but to see how far he was willing to push to get what he wanted. Brandt hoped he would push hard.

"Now," Donnelly said, low and quiet.

That was what he said, Brandt thought, that night on the live cam session. The same word, the same commanding tone. Brandt felt a chill flash through him, and suddenly he was back in that first moment when their friendship had turned into something more—something terrifying and thrilling and uncertain and promising. He felt himself back on that bed in the sex-cam house, under Donnelly's hungry glare on the video screen. Then he had been mortified; now, he was as turned on as he had ever been in his life. He arched his back, pushing his ass up slightly, just enough to give Donnelly a teasing glimpse. His buttocks parted, opening him to Donnelly but just out of reach.

Donnelly tossed the lube bottle onto the bed, between Brandt's wide-spread legs. "You have thirty seconds to get ready. Then your ass is mine."

This—this was new.

Brandt reached between his legs and found the lube bottle. He flipped the cap, and tried to figure out how to squirt some onto his fingers from this fucked-up angle.

"Twenty seconds," Donnelly said quietly, but there was iron under his words.

Brandt gave up trying to be tidy with the lube. He grabbed the bottle, reached around his back, and positioned the nozzle at the top of his ass, just where the globes of muscle split. He squeezed hard, and a small river of lube oozed down the crack toward his anus. He brought his other hand up between his legs, and with it he rubbed the lube around his tightly clenched hole.

"Ten seconds. You'd better get some up in there or this may be... strenuous for you." A growling, guttural chuckle signaled Donnelly's ineluctable intention.

With a grunt, Brandt dug his middle finger into his ass. He tossed the now-empty bottle of lube to the side and used both hands to poke into his ass, jamming as much of the lube in as he could. He was making progress, but he needed more time. He knew how to get it.

Reaching both hands behind him, he dug both index fingers into his ass at the same time, and pulled them apart. He felt the cool air of the hotel room hit his now obscenely exposed inner passage.

"Fuck," Donnelly groaned, his eyes trained on what Brandt had never shown him before. He lost count entirely.

Brandt worked his fingers in and out, stretching his muscle and spreading more lube. He began to rock back and forth, and as he worked his fingers in and out, he felt himself begin to loosen—maybe enough to accommodate Donnelly, maybe not.

The uncertainty sent a thrill through his pounding chest. He would soon find out. He was suddenly grateful for his explorations that lazy morning in a Paris hotel room; he had been like a bride preparing for the practicalities of her wedding day. The very idea nearly brought a laugh to his throat before he swallowed it back—he wouldn't break Donnelly's horned-up concentration for anything. With a grunt, he worked a third finger in.

"They say travel broadens the mind," Donnelly said as the bed sagged slightly under his weight. "Let's see if it works on other things."

Brandt felt the heat radiate from Donnelly's body as it drew near. Then the invader was at the gate—the massive bluntness of his cock pressed against Brandt's recklessly slicked-up hole. It was unbelievably hot and impossibly big. There was no way it was going to fit.

"Fuck!" Brandt's guttural cry startled Donnelly, who would have reacted by pulling back had not Brandt at that moment thrust himself backward.

If men climb Everest because it's there, Brandt was going to fuck that enormous cock for an even better reason—not just because it was there, but because it was attached to the man he loved most in the world. He crashed backward, feeling himself split open, the momentary hot flash of pain overwhelmed by the certainty of having Donnelly so far, so unbearably far, inside him.

When their bodies collided, he was complete, and the pain and anxiety of their weeklong separation left him, never to return.

"Unf," Donnelly groaned, pushing back now against Brandt. What choice did he have? Brandt's unhinged thrust would have thrown him from the bed entirely.

Brandt panted, motionless, trying to put out the fire Donnelly had ignited inside him. His body cried out against the abuse he had just perpetrated upon it, but there was nothing in the world he wanted more than to experience it again. And again. He lurched forward a little, and the dragging friction of Donnelly's concomitant withdrawal was like sandpaper. He sucked in a sharp breath of shock at the rough sensation and froze again.

"You okay?" Donnelly murmured, his voice once again soft and full of warmth. It was the Donnelly he knew and loved, the gentle, caring man.

This was not the Donnelly he was looking for.

"Come at me," he grunted—a jeer, a challenge—in his voice. He wanted the riled-up Donnelly, the one who would take what he wanted. Brandt wanted to be taken. He craned around and looked behind him to see Donnelly's face drop and harden; his solicitous eyebrows furrow into gritty determination. A shiver shot through Brandt, emanating from the place where they were still joined. He wasn't sure he could bear the strong thrust he hoped Donnelly would make. He knew he couldn't bear it not coming at all.

Donnelly knew exactly what Brandt needed—needed, not wanted—and he was more than ready to fill that need. He surged forward, and in one pistoning motion, he brought his flat, smooth lower belly back into contact with Brandt's strong, gaping buttocks.

Brandt grunted into a pillow, smothering his outburst lest Donnelly stop what he was doing. Brandt certainly didn't want that. What he did want to do was breathe, and that was increasingly difficult since every available space in his body was now completely full of Donnelly's cock. Brandt was swept away, and never wanted rescue.

"God, you're so fucking tight," Donnelly said with a groan. The sweet heat of Brandt's deep-inside consumed him. He wished his cock were as long as Brandt's so he could push even deeper into the inferno—that there was even one more inch he might possess sent a twinge of loss up his spine. He jabbed his pelvis forward despite being already pressed up against Brandt's ass. The muscle gave, a little, just enough for him to claim a few more millimeters of territory that would now and forever be his. He twitched hungrily, aching to reach more deeply, but he could go no farther. He unclenched and slid back.

Brandt inhaled, feeling like a snorkeler who has gone too deep and barely reaches the surface before his lungs burst. Donnelly's retreat let him relax enough to take a breath—the rush of oxygen brought heightened sensation, and he keenly felt every inch that Donnelly had stormed through. It was twitchy-achy-amazing, and Brandt wanted more. He nudged back, letting Donnelly know he was ready.

He wasn't in any sense of the word ready, but he needed more. Now.

Donnelly watched, rapt, as Brandt pushed back. The strained ring of muscle folded in on itself and then slurped up one, two, four inches of Donnelly's achingly hard cock. Donnelly pulled back a little to halt Brandt's progress—he was in charge now, not Brandt—and then jolted forward to the hilt once more.

"Yes," Brandt hissed. He wanted to spur Donnelly on but could form no more complex sound than this through his tightly gritted teeth.

Donnelly, satisfied that Brandt was with him, embarked on a slow but inexorable transit, pulling back until he felt the flange of his cockhead nearly emerge through the iron grip of Brandt's inner sphincter. He reversed course without stopping, as if he were easing a heavy set of weights almost back onto the stack before pushing into the next rep. He knew orgasms, like endorphins, lay at the end of constant motion, of unstinting exertion. He would get there sooner than he would normally like, but no force on Earth could make him halt his progress toward completion.

He picked up the pace, sliding smoothly now in and out of Brandt, closing his eyes to try to feel every bit of sensation. He heard Brandt's ragged breath, felt hot friction along every millimeter of his length as he drove it in and out.

Just as Brandt would adjust to Donnelly's pace, it would quicken, then quicken even more, until he finally had to stop even thinking about how it felt, how he could accommodate that insistent invader—had to stop thinking altogether. He relaxed every clenched thing in his body and just let Donnelly come at him. He kind of hoped he would come in him—soon.

An inspiration struck: he contracted his hips, clenched his abs. His back rounded up like a bear getting ready to charge. The next thrust brought Donnelly crashing against his prostate, and a shock of pleasure arced through his groin and ricocheted along the length of his cock. He wasn't sure he could take many more impacts like that one.

Donnelly, meanwhile, felt the reconfiguration of their bodies as a threshold he tripped over and found himself falling toward heaven. The passage he'd been drilling with his cock suddenly shifted, and the landscape was new; he was gripped in ways he hadn't experienced before, and every bit of it added up to one thing: the end. Before he was even aware that he was coming, the first stream blasted out, covering his cock with a new, hot slickness. Then there was more—much more. He opened his eyes, which he had screwed shut when the orgasm sideswiped him, and saw the root of his cock flecked with his own cum, drilled out of Brandt by his rapid, eccentric thrusting.

Without warning, Donnelly pitched forward, exhausted from laboring under so much pleasure. His cock gave one last, exhausted jab at Brandt's prostate, and, as Donnelly's weight was added to his own, Brandt's cock was pressed against the bed. It twitched twice and erupted. Brandt spasmed, his pulsing grip on the unsubsiding cock in his ass sending waves of overstimulation through Donnelly's body. They shuddered and grunted together, hands clasped tight, bodies locked together in shattered elation.

Eventually, finally, their breathing slowed, their muscles ceased twitching. Donnelly, with great effort, lifted his head and then lowered it again to kiss his way along Brandt's neck, up to where he could nuzzle his ear.

"That almost made it worth it," he whispered between nibbles. "Nearly two weeks apart, followed by an orgasm that reduces me to a twitching wreck. I might be persuaded to take that bargain again sometime."

Brandt turned his head so he could press his cheek against Donnelly's. "I'm happy to tell you that the waiting period is permanently waived. You can do this every night of our lives if you want."

Donnelly sighed as his cock slid out of Brandt. It came to rest atop Brandt's balls, which were now very wet.

"We'll just need to come up with some kind of code phrase," Brandt said as he neatly flipped himself over while remaining nestled under Donnelly. "Like 'how about a nice cup of tea,' which sounds very innocent, but only you and I will know it really means 'get on all fours because I'm going to fuck you until your teeth rattle.'" He kissed Donnelly on the nose, quite pleased with his solution.

"I never want to be doing anything other than fucking you," Donnelly said, kissing all over Brandt's face. "Unless it's getting fucked by you. Or snuggling on the couch watching movies with you. Or doing pretty much anything in the world, as long as it's with you."

"Works for me," Brandt replied, beaming. "You've ruined me for other men." He glanced downward, at the soppy mess they'd made of the bed. "I mean that literally. My ass is literally ruined. I don't think I'd even feel any other man after you."

Donnelly smirked. "I'm happy to report that you are still as tight as a drum, sir. There were a couple of times you clamped down so hard on the poor fella, I thought he'd come out shaped like an hourglass." He kissed Brandt tenderly on the lips. "But just so we're clear, you won't be trying anything like that with any other man."

Brandt shrank back a little from Donnelly's suddenly fierce glare, then laughed. "You're lucky I'm straight."

Donnelly smiled. "Indeed I am."

CHAPTER FIFTEEN

Tuesday
Plotting rescue

KERRY STUMBLED into the parlor of their suite, hair crazily askew in the early morning light. "Gentlemen," she mumbled, and then her nose pointed toward what she sought: a silver tray with a brilliantly polished pot. "Please tell me that's coffee."

"It is indeed," Donnelly replied, jumping up to pour a cup for her. "You look like you could use some."

"And you look like you just ran a marathon," she cracked, taking in his rosy and glistening presence. "You two *are* going to stop exhausting each other with sexy times at some point, aren't you?"

"It wasn't sexy times," Brandt groused from where he stood near the window. "We hit the gym before the sun was up."

She narrowed her eyes at him. "Hit it pretty hard, looks like. Is there anything left of it?"

"Let's just say that Gabriel was a bit aggressive this morning."

"I'll just bet he was," Kerry replied, a catty tone in her rough morning voice. She turned and took another view of Donnelly. "Lucky you."

Donnelly smiled. "Don't I know it." He handed her a steaming cup. "Have some coffee. We have a big day ahead of us."

She gratefully took the cup and saucer from him, then sank down onto the antique sofa and slurped luxuriantly. She couldn't keep a freshly caffeinated smile from spreading across her face. "You are a gentleman, Gabriel. Though I suspect you aren't always. Am I right, Ethan?" She smiled brightly, though with a hint of teasing in her voice.

"Let's add Gabriel's sexual prowess to the list of things we won't be talking about, ever," Brandt replied and went back to looking out the window.

Kerry laughed. "Well, now that list has precisely one thing on it. It's not really a list at all, is it? No sense even keeping it around." She set her coffee down on the table and pantomimed crumpling up a piece of paper and tossing it over her shoulder. "There. Clean slate."

Brandt rubbed his eyes. "In answer to your inevitable question, Gabriel—yes, she's always like this. Always."

"I think she's delightful," Donnelly replied, then turned to Kerry. "You keep right on giving him a hard time." Then he lowered his voice to a whisper. "And I'll do the same." He gave a silent-movie wink, which reduced both of them to laughter.

"Great. Now there are two of you," Brandt grumbled, then shoved off from his windowsill perch and strode over to pour more coffee. He threw it back in one go, then straightened up and was all business. "We need to get a plan together—tomorrow has to run like clockwork. Everyone get dressed and ready, and we'll meet here in an hour?"

"It takes an hour for you to get dressed and ready?" Kerry teased.

"It does when Gabriel's in the shower with me," Brandt replied archly. "He's very thorough." He laughed and set down his empty coffee cup. "Are you coming, love?" His voice was suddenly warm and deep.

"I will be shortly," Donnelly replied as he followed Brandt out of the room eagerly.

An hour later the foursome was gathered in the parlor, the remains of breakfast scattered across the long coffee table around which they sat.

"So what you're proposing is a three-pronged attack?" Brandt asked once Sandler, Kerry, and Donnelly had all chimed in on their brainstorming.

"I think it gives us the best chance," Donnelly replied. "We cover the doctor, the clinic, and the Hendrickses themselves. We only need one of those to be successful."

"But it spreads us pretty thin, doesn't it?" Brandt asked. "If something goes wrong for one of us, the others won't be there to help."

"Kerry and Sandler will be working together," Donnelly said, "and I think you'd agree they're pretty resourceful." Kerry nodded her thanks at the compliment, while Sandler continued staring anxiously into the middle distance. "And you and I will be working alone, but it's not like we've never done that, right?" Brandt conceded the point with a curt nod. "So I think this is probably the best use of the tools we have available, given the time pressure we're under."

Brandt sighed testily. "This is a shotgun plan, blasting everything we've got at once, hoping something hits. I'd much prefer a sniper attack—a surgical strike." He stood and paced the length of the room a couple of times. "But we don't have the luxury of time to pull something like that together." He sat again, and looked from face to face around the table. "All right, let's do this."

A cheer went up, but as Kerry looked from face to face she saw all present seemed to be fully aware that what they were about to do would be difficult indeed.

CHAPTER SIXTEEN

Wednesday
Dr. Rauthmann's office, Geneva

"I'M SO glad you could see us on such short notice, Doctor," Kerry said. She was particularly proud of the way she managed to imbue her voice with a tone of moneyed groveling. "We are only in Geneva for the day."

"It was fortunate indeed," Dr. Rauthmann replied, smiling broadly. "Tomorrow I shall begin a course of treatment for another unfortunate young man, and I expect he will require all of my attention for the next several days—a terrible case, a tragic case." The doctor arranged his fleshy face into a posture of suitably clinical empathy, and then the smile returned. "Please, tell me what brings you to see me today."

"Well, I've—I mean, we, we both, have heard such wonderful things about your treatments." She shot Sandler a sharp glance. "Haven't we, dear?"

"Uh, yes," Sandler replied tepidly.

"May I ask from whom?" Rauthmann asked, the smile fading instantly from his face. He was clearly suspicious.

"Well, I don't know if it's proper to speak about the medical treatment of others, but through an online support group I got in touch with a former patient of yours. He told me all about how you helped him overcome his"—she shot another look at Sandler, judgment in her eyes—"difficulties. He didn't know where you had moved your practice to after leaving Akron, but I tracked you down!" She beamed at her good fortune in finding him.

Rauthmann's expression didn't change a bit. "And what might be the name of this 'patient' of mine?"

"Oh, well," Kerry said, hand pressed delicately to her throat. "I only knew him by his username in the online forum where we talked, but he said you would recognize him from that. Ricky G. says hello."

Rauthmann's face brightened considerably at this.

Kerry breathed a sigh of relief that the name, given to her by her friend in the legal department, seemed to work like a charm. It had been discovered in court documents relating to one of the malpractice suits, and belonged to a patient of Rauthmann's who offered his support of the doctor's methods in written testimony.

"Ah, yes. His was a particularly gratifying result. I trust he is well?"

"Oh, he is, he is," Kerry assured him. She hoped that poor Ricky G. hadn't resorted to suicide, as so many seemed to after the full effect of a "successful" treatment was felt. "Now, Doctor, can we discuss what you can do for my darling?" She cast a sickly smile in Sandler's direction.

"We shall see, we shall see," Rauthmann said. "Would you leave us alone for a few minutes, Mrs. Newman? I'd like to speak frankly with Mr. Newman, and I find it's best to have such conversations in private."

"Yes, of course," Kerry gushed, getting to her feet. "I'll be right outside, love." She kissed him lightly on the forehead, then took her leave.

Out in the hall, she closed her eyes for a moment and hoped Sandler would be able to finish what she had started. It was a long shot to hope Dr. Rauthmann would admit to a clinical recklessness that they could use to lodge a complaint that would allow them to get his license revoked immediately, but they had to try. She hoped Sandler would be able to deliver.

AS THE door closed, Rauthmann turned his attention to Sandler. "Now tell me, young man, why are you here?"

Sandler cleared his throat. He didn't have to fake being nervous—he was truly terrified. But he closed his eyes for a moment and thought of Trevor, and that seemed to focus him. "Well, as my wife said—"

"No." Rauthmann's voice was suddenly imperious. "Why are *you* here? There is nothing I can do to help you if you cannot tell me why you have come to me for help."

"I...." Sandler swallowed. "I have these... thoughts." He fell into a miserable silence.

"Go on."

"Thoughts about... men."

"I see. What are these thoughts you have about men?"

Sandler paused, hoping he was doing this right. "They're... intimate thoughts."

"Sexual thoughts?" Rauthmann probed.

"Yes," Sandler whispered. Though he had never had a sexual thought that wasn't about a man—and he'd never been ashamed of them—he felt a kind of phantom shame creep over him as he made this pained utterance. This conversation was turning into a vicarious closeting.

Rauthmann leaned back in his chair, a slight smile slithering onto his face. "When did these thoughts begin?"

He was not, Sandler noted, asking him when did he first think these thoughts, but rather when did the thoughts themselves arise—like poltergeists—to trouble him.

"I... I don't remember."

"Think back. When were you first aware of these sexual thoughts about another male?"

This, Sandler could answer.

"Move! Move! Move! Get your suits on and get out onto the pool deck now! Now!"

No one bellows quite like a gym teacher. And this asshole had a set of lungs to make Pavarotti spit with envy. I yanked on my swim trunks, nearly crashing headlong into my own locker when my big toe caught on the elastic. I righted myself, then tied the waist string tight—wouldn't want to have it slip off when I dove in like happened to that poor kid last year who changed schools after everyone saw his wiener.

I slammed the locker shut, and that's when He *was revealed to me.*

He stood six lockers down, and he was beautiful. I'd seen him once or twice around campus, but never like this. He was just pulling his suit up over his ass, and it was like the light had gone out of the world when those brilliant globes were stifled by mundane navy-blue nylon.

I read once where they used to require you to swim naked at the Y back in the fifties. I was born too late.

He snapped his locker shut and walked away down the aisle of lockers. I watched him go.

I had sexual thoughts.

"It was in high school," Sandler said.

"Did it trouble you?"

"Not really. I didn't think it was anything weird because when you're in high school you're kind of horny all the time, so sometimes it happens in the locker room."

Rauthmann nodded. "And were any of these thoughts manifested in reality?"

"What do you mean?" Sandler asked.

"I mean," Rauthmann replied, leaning forward on his desk, "Did you partake in any sexual activity with other males?"

Part of Sandler's mind was focused on trying to guess what would be the most effective answer—the one that would get Rauthmann to detail what he would do to cure him—and part was flying back a decade to that night he and Trevor did indeed partake.

"Are you sure your aunt and uncle won't be home all weekend?" Trevor asked. Again.

"I'm sure," I said, unlocking the door and welcoming him to my home-slash-bachelor pad. "Are you sure your parents bought the story about you hiking with the guys from your young man's prayer circle or whatever?"

He smiled that crooked smile that made my knees get a boner. "Yes, they did, because we've done it the first week of summer vacation for the last three years."

"And they'll back you up? What if your parents ask them about whether you were there?"

"They'll do what we always do when parents ask questions. 'Was Jacob with you all weekend, boys?' 'Yes, he was, Mrs. Williams.' 'Did Aiden behave himself?' 'Yes, Mr. Johannsen, he led our big hike on Saturday.'"

I smiled. "And what were Jacob and Aiden actually up to?"

Trevor laughed. "Jacob spent the weekend boning that girl Brittany from our chemistry class, and Aiden never left the tent because he was stuck under his boyfriend the entire time. Man, that guy could just go and go—I don't know how Aiden could even walk come Monday."

"I like this prayer circle more and more," I said, closing the door behind Trevor. I grabbed him around the waist and pulled him close. "Now tell me, Mr. Hendricks, and you have to be perfectly honest with me...."

"Always," he said, kissing me on the nose. He was fucking adorable.

"How many prayer circle weekends have you spent getting boned in the pup tent?"

This stopped him cold. He looked at me as if I'd accused him of walking the streets in fishnet stockings and unfortunate eye shadow.

"None," he said, his voice just above a whisper. "Why would you even think that?"

"I'm sorry," I blurted, embarrassed to have embarrassed him. "I just figured since you were so casual about the other guys, you probably had done some of that yourself."

He shook his head slowly. "No," he said solemnly. "I've never even...." He blinked, swallowed, and took a deep breath. "You're the first guy... the first person... I've ever even kissed."

I felt like crap for even asking, and I was about to tell him so, but he continued.

"I've never felt like this for anyone," he said, looking searchingly into my eyes. "I've never even noticed other people. I kind of see now why I haven't had crushes on any girls, but you're the first guy I've ever even thought about." There was a sort of hopeless smile on his face now. "You're the first... the only one."

All I could think to do was crash my mouth into his as exuberantly as I could because he was just so sweet and so humble and so fucking sexy. We kissed for, like, ever, and then we had to stop just to be able to breathe, and he looked at me with a kind of suspicious grin on his face and said, "How about you?"

My mind was pretty scrambled with hormones by that point, so I sort of stared dumbly at him.

"How many times have you... you know... done it?"

As euphemisms for fucking go, that one's a retro classic. He was so adorable. "Just once. And it was your fault."

"My fault?" he cried, "How could it possibly have been my fault?" He didn't wait for me to answer. "Oh, and by the way, you're a slut."

I would have been offended, but he said that with this growly voice he used when he was fired up, and then he kissed me, so we were good.

"It was after that time at your house. I was a little frazzled after fleeing from that harpy you use for a mother—"

"Understandable."

"Thank you. So when you kissed me, you sent me into blue-balled permaboner hell, and running six blocks from your house didn't help things a bit. So I brainstormed all of the things I could do to alleviate my... condition—"

He snickered at that—he clearly understood the compliment I and my unflaggingly erect penis had paid him.

"And I basically came up with two things: duck into a public bathroom and wank until only dust came out, or hit up the only person who had ever expressed an interest in me sexually."

"I'd like the record to reflect that I had also expressed interest in you sexually."

"So stipulated. But this other expression of interest didn't come with the added bonus of a mother who can summon the demons of hell with a single shriek of her infernal voice, so you have to kind of give me the benefit of the doubt on that."

"Granted. Proceed."

"So I called him—"

"Who him?" Trevor demanded.

"*No one you know. The guy who played Barnaby in* Hello, Dolly!*"*

"*That skank?" Trevor shrieked, sounding uncomfortably like his mother.*

"*You know him?"*

"*No, of course not. But he got his hands on you when I couldn't, so I hate him."*

"*Aww, that's so sweet." I kissed him, which led to another kiss, and suddenly it was a half hour later.*

"*So," he said, wiping his amazing lips, "you were telling me about your first time. And I was being gracious and listening, no matter how much it pains me to hear about you in the arms of that horrible skank."*

"*Do you want me to gloss over the details?"*

"*Of course not! I want to hear every sweaty, disgusting, amazing moment. Go!" He plopped down on the sofa in my living room and leaned forward attentively.*

"*Okay, so I called him and asked him if he wanted to hang out, and he said yeah."*

"*'Hang out'? Did he know you were asking him for buttsex?"*

"*Well, he had practically come right out and asked me for exactly that a couple of weeks ago at the cast party, so he caught on pretty quick, especially once I got there and we went to his room and I asked if anyone could hear us. He asked if I came to make some noise, and I said hell yeah, so he locked the door of his room and we got to it."*

Trevor stared at me, waiting for more.

"*I was so boned up after kissing you that even a half hour later I was still rock hard, and he jumped right on it. He grabbed a condom out of his dresser, rolled it on, and mounted up."*

"*How did you know what to do?"*

"*I didn't have to. He basically took care of everything. Given the hair trigger I was on, I came in like twenty seconds but didn't even let him know. He kept riding, and I just held on the best I could. The second time I came, I kind of shook and thrusted, so he knew what was happening. And oh man did his ass clamp down on me. He jerked himself for like three strokes and then just busted all over the place. He hopped up and smiled at me as he cleaned us both up, then he gave my cock a squeeze and said 'Good to go again?' and I just nodded, and we were off to the races one more time. After that time, I had to get out of there before he came at me again. I mean, I guess you could say he came at me a second time—dude shot far enough for it to land in my hair—but it was three times for me, and I needed to stop. So I pulled my pants up and said thanks. He said it was his pleasure, and that was the last time I saw him. The end."*

Trevor sat silent.

"*What's wrong?" I asked him after about a few seconds went by.*

"*Promise not to be mad?" he asked softly.*

"*Of course," I said, but I didn't mean it. I mean, I wouldn't have been mad at him no matter what, but I figured he was building up to telling me that he didn't want to be with me since I clearly made poor choices under the influence of an erection lasting longer than an hour. He was going to tell me he was leaving.*

"*I don't want you to put it in my butt."*

And just like that, the angels were smiling on me again. "I don't want to put it in your butt," I said, sitting next to him on the sofa. He looked at me with an awkward combination of relief and indignation on his face. "I mean, I totally want to put it in your butt someday," I stumbled, "and I totally want you in my butt. Honest." His expression now morphed into one of alarm. "I mean, I want us to do everything together. But we don't have to do anything right now. We can just do what we're comfortable with, and what we want, and we'll see about the other stuff."

He smiled shyly. "What do you want to do? With me, I mean?"

"This," I said and leaned forward to kiss him softly. "If this is all we do, I'm good with that."

He kissed me back. "I don't think I'll be good with that," he said, that little growl back in his voice.

"Then you tell me. What do you want to do?"

"I want to see your bedroom."

I stood up and reached back to take his hand. He looked at me, and then at my hand, and then back at me. Looking back on it, it was a kind of silly romantic gesture—I mean, he didn't really need my help to get up off the sofa—but he took my hand with a little grin that let me know he was okay with it. I led him down the hall to my room. I was a little nervous about opening the door, honestly. We'd been planning this day for a week, so I'd cleaned up and vacuumed and put new sheets on the bed (my heart was pounding as I did so, contemplating the use we would make of those!). But my room just wasn't nearly as nice as his. Then again, mine didn't come with a banshee ready to break the door down because her son might actually be kissing somebody, so I think I got the better deal.

I opened the door, and though I'd painstakingly dusted every surface, Trevor only had eyes for the bed. He sat down on the edge of it and held out his arms for me. I sat next to him and pulled him to me. We sat there in silence for a while.

"I didn't think I'd ever get to do this," he said softly.

"Hug someone? Scandalous."

He pulled back to look me in the eye. "No, this," he said. "I never thought I'd have someone to just hold."

"Why would you say that?" I can't imagine someone as sweet as Trevor going through life alone.

"My parents have drummed it into my head that you're supposed to save yourself for marriage and not have any physical contact at all with anyone until then. It makes even hugging someone seem so far away, like something you can't even consider until you're married."

"It sounds so lonely."

"I was. Until you." That shy smile came back.

"But the guys in your oversexed prayer circle weren't waiting for marriage. Why did you think you had to?"

He thought about this for a moment. "I guess being an only child I feel kind of responsible for my parents' hopes and dreams, you know? Like if I can't do what they expect, no one else is going to."

"That's a lot of weight to be carrying around."

He nodded and gave a helpless shrug. "We all have our baggage, I guess."

I wrapped my hand around the back of his neck, feeling the strong sinews that held up that lovely head. "You don't have to carry it alone anymore."

He blinked hard and brought those beautiful eyes up to mine. "You're the dream I'd given up on coming true," he said softly.

"I could say the same of you," I replied. "I can't believe you're here."

"I can't believe I'm here either. I'm in the bedroom of a notorious slut, and he hasn't even ripped my clothes off yet."

"Be careful what you wish for," I warned him.

He closed his eyes. "I wish for a dick. Full-size, low mileage, handles well. Reliable starter, likes to be driven hard."

"Fuck me, the way you talk."

"It's more than talk," he said, then started to unbutton his shirt.

This. This was the moment I'd dreamed of all through sophomore year while I watched him undress and then—alas—get dressed again in the locker room; my daily dose of yearning and boners. Which meant I was always late for class because I had to wait for my dick to deflate before I could finish getting changed.

"Why are you looking at me that way?" he asked, folding his shirt neatly and setting it on top of my dresser.

"Because I can't believe this is happening."

"Oh, this is happening," he replied with a laugh, then unzipped his pants.

All I could do was sit and watch as he reenacted my daily torture. He slid his jeans down and whipped his socks off, then stood there in just his blindingly white briefs.

"I hate these things," he said, looking down. "My mom actually bleaches, starches, and irons my underwear. She says that morality starts with not giving in to our body."

I gave in to his body long ago. "I love those things," I replied. "Seeing those luminescent tighty-whities in the locker room was the highlight of every fucking day for me."

"Why?" he asked, brow crinkled in adorable confusion.

"Because when I saw them, it meant I was about to see what's under them."

"People teased me for changing into a jockstrap for gym. They obviously don't have a mom who complains about sweat stains in their drawers."

"Teasing you? I seriously considered sending you flowers. I thought that once swim season ended, I'd never get another chance to see that amazing ass."

"Amazing?" he asked, turning to the side and looking in my full-length mirror. "Really?"

"Really," I said, getting to my feet—I didn't want to be even two steps away from him for another second. I pulled him to me, wrapped my arms around him. He smiled, but his eyes widened when I slipped my hands under the waistband of those virginal briefs.

Had I harbored any lingering doubt about my sexual identity, it would have evaporated under the heat of that first touch of what had been, until that moment, forbidden. I had spent an entire school year terrified that someone would catch me gawping at the fulsome muscularity of Trevor's buttocks. Now I had them in my hands.

From a distance of six locker-widths, they had looked smooth, round, and firm. From a distance of zero millimeters, they were all of that, and hot. They were like sculpture come to life, burning in my hands.

"Sandler," he whispered, the shock of violation tinging his voice.

"If you're going to ask me to let go, I'm just going to tell you now that's not going to happen. They will pry your asscheeks from my cold, dead hands."

He laughed, still apparently unable to believe that these muscular wonders—clearly stolen from a sculpture of Apollo somewhere—were anything special.

Right now, they were everything special in the world to me.

I grabbed meaty handfuls of his ass, causing him to pitch forward into me and emit a squeaking noise that made me laugh for weeks after. He shook and shivered as I ran my hands in giddy circles, raising goose bumps and causing him to grind into me in a way I found most pleasant.

Soon enough, though, he let go of my shoulders and fell to the task of ripping my clothes off. And I mean ripping. I'll admit my T-shirt was a little tight—I'd wanted to give him a preview of coming attractions today—so I wasn't that surprised when the seams gave way. I was surprised by the way the sound of shredding fabric made my knees weak. He yanked the remains of it off my shoulders, then started on my pants. These, luckily, held together, but were soon pooled at my ankles. I kicked them off.

I caught sight of us in the mirror, and we made quite a pair. Him in his starched and ironed tighty-whities and me in my brand-new boxer briefs. Was it creepy of me to have chosen the color to match his eyes? Maybe. But now that his eyes were glued to them, mission accomplished.

"Look at us," I whispered, tipping my head toward the mirror.

He turned and looked us over top to bottom. "We're like some archbishop's wet dream," he muttered, with a grin that would certainly have made his mother clutch her pearls.

"I kind of hate you for how amazing your shoulders look," I said. "I've been working on mine all year, and nothing."

He ran his fingertips across my shoulders, sending a delicate shiver down to my... well, all the way down. "My shoulders are nothing compared to this," he said, bringing his other hand in front of me and tracing the V-line of my lower abs down to the waistband of my boxers. "I'd love to have your V."

"Good news," I said. "You do have my V. It's all yours. And here's a pro tip: at the end of the V, there's a D."

Oh, that crooked grin. I hope he never does that in public, because then I'd do something that would get us both kicked out of any reputable establishment.

"Thank you," he replied graciously. "I will take you up on your most generous offer." He kissed me, and then, with that devilish grin still firmly in place, he began to slide down.

I watched him descend in the mirror. He ran his fingers down my torso, taking my breath away and turning my nipples into hardened munitions that would pierce armor. Kneeling before me, he ran his fingers along the waistband of my boxers and looked up at me with wide, imploring eyes.

"Like you even have to ask," I chided him. "The boxers are brand-new, but you are free to fucking chew your way through them if that's what gets the job done."

"And what job is that?" he asked, his fingers beginning to edge under the elastic.

"The job of getting your hands on my penis. Or, you know, your mouth or something. Your call."

"Let's see what we're working with here," he said, smiling slyly. I felt him begin to pull down, the fabric of my boxers sliding along my hardness. A moment later, my cock popped free.

Though its length was no secret—he could see it clearly outlined through the material—its reach still seemed to surprise him. It bounced out and whacked him on the nose.

"Someone's eager," he said with a laugh as he shucked my drawers down to my ankles.

"Someone's been waiting an entire year for this moment, so yeah, I think you could call me eager."

"Well, I won't make you wait a second longer." He reached out and laid hold of my member, then looked up at me. "This is the first one I've ever touched," he whispered.

"You've never touched your own?" I teased.

"Oh, I've touched it plenty. Especially in the last week, thinking about you."

Fuck. The things he says. I think my dick grew an extra inch.

"It's so hot," he said, sliding his hand up and down my length. "And it's... huge."

"Thanks, but it's not nearly the largest I've seen."

He squinted at me. "How many have you seen? I thought Barnaby was the first and only."

"Dude, we were in the same locker room all during swim season. You can't tell me you didn't notice Colin, or Neal, or even Allen for that matter. They were all enormous. And you—you're bigger than me."

"Maybe when I'm soft, but you—you're a grower. Those other guys probably don't get any bigger when they get boned up. Plus," he continued with a grin, "I used to see Colin tugging at it before taking his underwear off—like he wanted to be a little plumped before showing off the goods."

We both laugh at Colin, whose attitude in the locker room seemed to stem entirely from the size of his dangle.

"But I don't care about other dicks because I have the best one right here," he said. Then, leaning forward just slightly, he opened his mouth and without warning slurped the head of my cock into his mouth.

In movies, when someone's dream comes true, they look heavenward and smile, and the music swells and all is right with the world. When my dream came true—there was no other way to think about what getting my dick sucked by Trevor Hendricks meant to me—I basically collapsed. Like, knees buckling, hands flailing collapsed. It was mortifying.

Well, except for the part about landing naked on Trevor. That part was nice.

"You okay?" he asked. As concerned as he looked, I noticed he hadn't taken his hand off my dick. The dream lived on.

"You're just so...." I struggled for the words. "I can't believe you're here. Still can't."

He pulled me into a sitting position, and put his hands along my jaw, cradling my face. "I'm here. And I don't want to be anywhere but here. Okay?"

I nodded. "Okay."

"Good talk. Now I gotta get back to what I was doing." He placed a hand on my chest and pushed, and I fell back to the floor. "Perfect," he said, and took his place between my legs.

As my cock entered his mouth for the second time, I closed my eyes and just let myself feel this moment—the man I had crushed on for a year was now here, with me, doing something to me that a week ago I couldn't have imagined in my wildest fantasy.

Well, I had imagined it. I just never thought it would actually happen.

This was happening.

"Oh my God, how... do you know how to do what you're... amazing, oh my God that feels... so good best blow job ever." At least that's what I think I said. I may not have been quite that articulate in the heat of the moment.

He pulled back, kissing the slick head of my cock as it left his lips. "Better than Barnaby?"

With my cock free of his mouth, my power of speech returned. "First, I believe it was Miss Manners who said that it is rude to inquire about former lovers while giving a blow job. Second, Barnaby didn't put his mouth anywhere on me, which was actually fine with me because he kind of reeked of cheap cigarettes. Third, you are a fucking natural at this cock-sucking thing, because damn."

"You say the sweetest things," he murmured, then got right back to it.

It was then that I discovered another untoward side effect of having one's most fervent dream come true. It makes one ready to come in about twelve seconds. Which, at the moment, I was not necessarily opposed to. But I wanted my first time with Trevor to last a little longer than it takes to work a long-division problem, so I tried to work a long-division problem in my head (I know you're supposed to think of baseball, but the only reason I watch baseball is for the hot players, so that wouldn't really have helped me right then). By the time I came up with a remainder, I was on my way back up Orgasm Mountain, so I needed to have a new plan.

I pulled him off of me as gently as I could. He looked deprived and disappointed until I kissed him. He rose up, laid me back down on the carpet, and kissed me with such soft urgency that I thought I might come anyway. Then I tasted my own precum in his mouth, and I just about lost it.

"I want you on the bed," I managed to say around his tongue, which was thrashing about in my mouth, making concentration impossible.

He pulled back and smiled.

"Now," I said. My struggle to keep from shooting all over his leg gave my voice a gravelly drill-sergeant bark (a scenario we would explore later, when my aunt and uncle went back East for a wedding). He got to his feet, which left me briefly at eye level with his briefs, and I took a moment to silently thank the universe for bringing me that particular gift. I was looking forward to unwrapping it.

He sat on the bed and then, with an adorably shy look on his adorable face, laid himself back. He was giving himself to me, trusting me with his first sexual experience. I was touched, I was honored, I was so hard I could barely stand it.

"You're beautiful," I whispered, crawling up the bed until I was over him, face-to-face.

"I'll bet you say that to all the boys," he replied with a quiet snicker.

"Just one." I kissed him, kissed him again. "Just you." I lowered my hips to his, felt my naked cock brush against his fabric-covered one.

"I think I'm going to have to wash these myself," he said.

I looked down and saw what he meant—a dark spot where precum was oozing from his erection had appeared on the front of his briefs, and seemed to be spreading fast. I was probably making it worse by contributing my own drops, since I'd been leaking ever since he first walked into my bedroom. "We can do it together," I said, "in the bathtub."

He smiled and appeared quite content to let his briefs continue to dampen. I, however, wanted them off before another second went by.

"I'll just set them carefully aside," I offered, as I slid down his body and hooked my eager fingers under his waistband. I yanked them off and threw them over my shoulder—I wouldn't find them until the following Thursday when I put my hand in the pocket of my hoodie and pulled them out. On the plus side, it was an obscene reminder of my first real sex; on the minus, I was at the end of the year picnic for the swim team at the time. Luckily Trevor had come with me, so we had a good laugh about it. Then we made out behind the snack bar.

There he was, my idol, my dream come suddenly true. Trevor Hendricks was laid out before me, fully naked, fully hard, and fully into letting me do anything I wanted with everything I could lay my hands on. He was outfitted top to bottom with lush but not showy muscle; he looked athletic rather than bulky. But, I discovered as I laid my hands on his rounded pectorals, there was plenty of strength there.

"You feel as good as you look," I murmured. He blushed, but there was still a sexy smile on his face.

"How do I taste?" he asked teasingly.

I was startled by the boldness of his question and warmed by the hunger in his eyes. For all his reserve in public—he was practically a cipher to those around him in school—now, here, he was intense and frankly lustful. It was a good look for him.

"I'll have to find out," I said, licking my lips. "This may take a while—I want to be thorough."

His eyes rolled back and fluttered closed. Permission, clearly, for me to take him with my tongue. He would not be disappointed.

I started with the soft hollow at the base of his throat. There I kissed the softest skin I'd ever felt—I swear I could feel his heart beating on the other side. I moved across his clavicles, ran my lips along each as they swept delicately out to his strong shoulders. Now his nipples were stiffening, and I closed my mouth around the first one I came to—on the right, as it happened. He moaned and arched his back, and I took the opportunity to wrap my arms around him, crossing them where they met in the hollow above his ass. Holding him tightly, I kissed my way down his flat, muscled belly, stopping in my downward progress only when I came to his belly button. I knew myself to be ticklish there, and it was a good thing I had my arms around him to hold him tight, or he might have bucked right off the bed when I stuck my tongue into his innie.

I released my grip and arrived at the main event. The soft slope from his belly button to the region beneath I covered with my kisses, and I soon found myself nuzzling at the base of his cock. His pubic hair was soft and light brown, and it smelled of vanilla and lust—a heady combination of lotion and precum. His cock, still as hard as when I had unveiled it, I grabbed firmly with both hands. A sharp intake of breath let me know he was keenly aware that he was about to get manhandled for the first time in his life. And I intended to do the job right.

As long as I live, Trevor's cock will always be my first cock, just as mine will always be his. And I have never had another in my hand, or in my mouth, or in my ass, that I loved more. Trevor was more than a cock to me, of course, but there was something essential about him that his cock expressed. I felt I knew him better in that moment, holding him in my hands, than I ever had before.

I leaned forward and kissed the tip, then lapped up the little droplet of sparkling precum that emerged in response to my kiss. It was sweet and slick and just about the best thing I'd ever tasted.

"I'm happy to report," I said, licking my lips, "that you taste just as amazing as you look."

"Are you sure?" he replied, looking down at me, his face flushed. "I think you should try again, just for… science."

That's my boy. *"You're right—it was reckless of me to jump to conclusions. I'm going in." I again kissed the firm head of his cock, then opened my mouth and proceeded to cram as much of him in as I could. It wasn't much—probably only half of his six inches would fit—but it was the first time I'd ever had a mouthful of dick, and it was all I could have hoped for. His writhing on the bed was a nice bonus.*

"Oh fuck," he huffed, his back arching.

I had a feeling he was, like me, on a hair trigger. Not that I had any objection to coming early and often—we had all weekend, after all—but my experience with Barnaby left me wanting a little more. And now that he was here, I wanted our first time to be everything we'd ever imagined.

So I slurped up another delicious drop from the tip of his cock and then kissed my way down the smooth shaft. He continued to moan and wriggle, though he sucked in a sharp breath when I reached the place where the hardness of his cock met the softness of his balls. Unlike my balls, which tend to be pretty tightly gripped to my body, his were draped elegantly below his dick, and were gently sliding up and down as if excited to meet me. I was definitely excited to make their acquaintance.

"I watched these balls from across the room all year," I said. "They were the highlight of my day." I put my hand over them, then continued in a whisper. "Don't tell them, but your balls were a close second—after your dick, of course."

Trevor laughed, sending his balls churning under my hand. "I promise not to say anything."

"Thank you, sir. I do want to maintain good relations with the boys, since I'm about to introduce myself." And with that, I opened my mouth and slurped in the one on the left, which hung a little lower and danced a little more energetically than the other.

"Oh my God," Trevor blurted, sitting upright in an instant. I think he was afraid I was going to bite it off or something.

To reassure him, I slowly ran my tongue around the smooth ball, gently exploring it while being careful not to apply any pressure. I looked up at him as his face softened from terror to woozy delight. "Oh my God," he said again, but with a rather different inflection this time. He sank back down to the bed, but I could feel his thighs twitch every time I made a circuit around his ball with my tongue. Reluctantly, I opened my lips and let his ball slip out.

"You okay?" I asked.

He propped himself up on his elbows and looked down at me. "When I first started to wonder if I might be gay, I figured my balls had kind of lost their purpose—since I figured kids weren't in my future. But now I know they do have a purpose. They belong in your mouth."

"Damn right."

"So can you do that for me, please, like right now?"

"I'm on it." This wasn't as easy as it sounded—each of his balls was a healthy mouthful by itself, and they had plenty of room to move around. But with determination all things are possible, and I was determined to get both of his testicles into my mouth at the same time. I slurped up Mr. Right, forcing another moan from Trevor, then went after Mr. Left. He proved to be a slippery character, but when I trapped him with my fingers, he knew the game was over. He joined his brother in my mouth, and it was a happy family reunion for all involved.

Trevor panted a bit and moaned rather maniacally, but I think he was generally supportive of my efforts. I grabbed his ass with both hands, gripping the hollows formed by his frantic thrusting. Though my mouth was full, I still managed to suck my cheeks in around his balls, feeling their smooth resilience against my tongue.

After a couple of minutes of this, I was worried Trevor might hyperventilate, so I pulled back, stretching his ball sac a little—just some gentle traction that I thought he might like.

"Oh fuck fuck fuck fuck fuck...," he chanted, his head thrashing side to side.

I let go of Mr. Right, and pulled back a little more to feel Mr. Left slip out between my lips.

"Oof. Fuck." The tension flowed out of Trevor's glistening body, though his panting was still making his abs flash in and out of view. He opened his eyes. "Please?" His cock twitched at me, telling me what he wanted.

"It would be my pleasure," I replied. I cradled his cock in my hand and kissed it delicately. Then, summoning all my powers of concentration, I relaxed my throat as much as I could and took him into me. When he hit my tonsils, he exploded. There was no other word for it. I could feel every pulse surge through his cock, and then hot wetness blasted into my mouth. I pulled back—not wanting to suffocate on the product of his first non-solo orgasm—and let him fill my mouth while I continued to suck and pull on him.

He growled and thrashed and shuddered until it seemed like this was less an orgasm than a new lifestyle he'd suddenly adopted, like coming would be his new way of interacting with the world. Which I would have been totally fine with, by the way.

Finally he stopped erupting, stopped writhing, and stopped sounding like a bear in a trap. His cock didn't soften a bit—a sign of good things to come—but I let it slide out of my mouth. I kissed the last bit of cum from it (I'd been worried about the taste, but damn, everything about him tasted good), and then set it gently back against his belly. It throbbed there, and I silently promised it I'd be back for more. Lots more.

I slid my way up his body until we were face-to-face again. I was expecting a little postorgasm cuddling, but he gripped my head with both hands and kissed me with a strength that startled me. He wrapped his legs around me, cinching us into a full-body hug.

"That was amazing," he said, once he'd finally let go of my lips. "I've never felt like that before."

"Me either."

"Now I want to make you feel that way." An excited grin broke across his face. But instead of getting up to let me take his place, he started to shimmy down the mattress, leaving me on all fours above him. He ran his hands down my back, sending shivers all over me, and then continued down my buttocks and thighs. I was starting to wonder where he was going when he moved his hand around to grip my cock and pull it down toward the bed. Then his mouth closed over it and I was on my way.

Now, I had just given my first blow job ever, and I was self-aware enough to credit its efficiency to Trevor's desperation for release. There was just no way I was that good the first time out—it seemed like I suddenly had too many teeth, and I was constantly worried I was going to bite him. Trevor, though—he rose to the occasion and went at his task with the mouth of a practiced whore and the work ethic of a lumberjack. It was like his mouth—and, to be honest, his throat—had been shaped and formed for the express purpose of bringing my cock to ecstasy. There were stars dancing around my head as I simply tried to keep my knees from buckling. I fought with all my might to keep from collapsing into him.

I didn't fight long.

The orgasm he pulled me into was like nothing I'd ever experienced. It started deep inside, with a cold seizure that gripped parts of me I hadn't even been aware of before. Then my balls pulled up, threatening to return to their ancestral home, and the icy sword that had penetrated me turned into fire, spreading heat from the base of my erection to somewhere deep inside Trevor's throat. It was then that my cock turned into an obscene fire hose. I wasn't aware of individual spasms, but rather a constant, overwhelming pressure that opened the tip of my cock and held it open as everything I had created flowed into him. I shook all over, and though I seem to recall a somewhat less-than-masculine whimpering, I held strong.

Until I collapsed on top of him.

He took it well, bless him. I don't know if I could have handled a cock being driven down my throat by the full weight of the body it was connected to, but Trevor did it. He lifted my hips slightly to ease me out past his tonsils, and then I was able to roll onto my side. He kissed the head of my cock, lapping up the last dribbles of the load that had blasted directly down his throat.

It took me a minute or two to catch my breath.

"How do you know how to do that?" I croaked. "That was the most amazing thing ever. I think I died a little at one point."

He smiled and gave my cock one last kiss before sliding up the bed to look me in my no doubt bloodshot eyes. "Don't think because you flatter me on my first try I'm not gonna keep practicing on you," he replied with a grin. "But I guess when your parents have drummed it into your head that the only sex you're ever going to have is with a woman, and only after you have married her because otherwise you'll make Jesus cry, you tend to fantasize a bit about other ways the whole sex thing might work out."

"I've fantasized too. What you did was well beyond fantasy."

"I may have studied some porn too," he said with a laugh. "I figured I might never get a chance to do it for real, so I spent a lot of time working out what my technique would be like if it ever happened."

"You nailed it," I told him, then kissed him. "I will never experience anything better than that."

"I wouldn't be too sure," he said, wrapping his arms around me. "We have the whole weekend."

"Yes, I did partake. I mean, I was sexually intimate with other males during high school."

"Ah," Rauthmann replied, nodding sagely. "Many men experiment at that time in their lives."

"I did more than experiment," Sandler said in a voice that he managed to tinge with equal measures of pride and regret.

"I see." Rauthmann stood, walked around the desk, and leaned against it meditatively, looking Sandler up and down. "Are you currently troubled by thoughts of intimacy with men?"

Not currently, Sandler thought, because looking at your ugly bigoted face has pretty much taken care of that. "Yes... yes, I am."

"Even when you are intimate with your wife?"

How unhappy Rauthmann's patients must be if they come to him because they hate themselves for picturing men when they are having sex with their wives. He felt bad for everyone involved. Except Rauthmann. "Yes, especially then."

"And you wish to be free of these... thoughts?" Rauthmann asked gravely.

"I would do anything, try *anything*, to be free of them."

"What have you tried in the past?"

"I went to counseling in my church, and then to a psychologist. Those didn't help, and I was pretty depressed by my failures there, so then I went to a psychiatrist who prescribed medication. When that didn't help, I felt I was out of options. Then my wife heard about you. I think...." Sandler paused to daub at his eyes, thankful that his high school drama career had left him with the ability to cry on demand. "I think you are my only hope. I just want to be normal, Doctor. Is that too much to ask? To be normal?"

"No, of course it isn't," Rauthmann replied, something like compassion creeping into his voice for the first time. "There is a protocol I have developed that may be of some help in cases like yours."

"Has it helped other people?" Sandler looked up at the doctor, his eyelashes heavy with tears.

"While the mainstream psychiatric profession will tell you it's impossible, I have achieved positive results even in the most extreme cases."

"And these men you treated, they went on to be straight and happy?"

"I can tell you that not one of them ever expressed an interest in being intimate with a man again. Even in cases where the habit of homosexual intimacy was well established."

Sure, if you count the dead ones as straight, Sandler thought, but he managed to keep his disgust from showing on his face. "That sounds like the answer to my prayers."

Rauthmann beamed.

"Can you tell me what this protocol involves? Just so I know what to expect."

"Certainly. Under clinical observation, I administer a drug that is known to be effective in altering the sexual identity. I will observe you throughout the day to ensure that the correct dosage has been administered, and you'll stay the night for additional observation. By the end of the second day, you should be able to return home—not necessarily a new man, but a better one."

"And this treatment is entirely safe?"

"Absolutely. The drug is one that has been approved in the United States, and by the relevant authorities here as well. It's taken—in smaller doses—by hundreds of thousands of people every day."

Sandler wasn't at all sure he'd gotten anything from Rauthmann that would justify revocation of his license. But he felt to probe more would arouse suspicion, so he simply looked up at Rauthmann. "I had almost given up hope of ever being truly happy."

"What you must understand is that homosexuality does not offer happiness. Homosexuals are interested only in gratifying their sexual urges. There is nothing in the way of emotional attachment in their coupling, only the satisfaction of base, animal desires. For happiness you must look to your wife, for there is no love between men."

"You're beautiful, you know," Trevor said as I brought a bowl of popcorn into the living room.

We were spending a blissful Sunday morning watching old movies, entwined on the couch. We were, of course, naked.

"You're just saying that so I'll sleep with you."

Trevor laughed. "We hardly slept at all last night. I'm a little sore, and I think I fell asleep during the last part of Heathers. *Now I'll never know how it ends."*

"I hardly watched it myself. You started snoring, which was distracting enough, but then you started to get hard, so I just sat here staring at your dick for like a half hour. It was mesmerizing. Then you woke up, and I got hungry." I kissed him on the nose. "Now you're all caught up."

Trevor cuddled up, tucking himself under my arm with his head resting on my chest. "I could stay here forever," he purred contentedly.

"I wish you could."

He looked up at me. "Why can't I?"

"Because my aunt and uncle are going to get home eventually, and they may have something to say about us lounging about naked."

"For you I might even put clothes on. Eventually."

"Very dignified." I sprinkled some popcorn on his head. "There. Even better."

He laughed and flicked the kernels at me. "Seriously, though, I love being here. With you." He paused for a moment. "I love... you."

Warmth surged through my chest, fluttering up into my throat. He'd said what I'd been thinking all weekend, afraid to say it. "I love you too." It was a huge relief to finally give voice to what had been on the tip of my tongue for what seemed like forever.

"Did we just... say that?" Trevor asked, his voice awestruck.

"We did. And the world didn't come crashing down upon us. We're guys, and we love each other. And it's okay."

"More than okay," Trevor said. "It's perfect."

We never did see the end of Heathers. We debauched my aunt's sofa for a good solid hour, then collapsed again in a tangle of blankets and some stray kernels of popcorn.

Flushed and glistening with hard-earned sweat, Trevor kissed me and then looked me seriously in the eye. "Are we really doing this? We're really in love?"

"Yes. You keep asking that as if you expect my answer to change."

He shrugged. "I've sort of been conditioned to fear the worst when it comes to sex. Especially this kind of sex."

"Trevor, you have to accept the fact that we are normal. We fall in love, we mess around; then maybe someday we get married and have six kids. The usual stuff. Relax."

"Six kids? Oh my God."

"I'm just teasing you. It's not like I'm going to run out tomorrow and tattoo your name on my chest or something."

"You're not?" he said with a pout. "That's heartbreaking."

"Shut up, you," I scolded, whacking him with a sofa pillow. "I'm not really the tattoo type, anyway."

Trevor looked at me thoughtfully. "Let's say you were going to get a tattoo. What would you get and where?"

"I just told you—your name across my chest."

"No, seriously. Come on, this is the stuff people talk about when they're... in love."

He was adorable. Clearly he'd been convinced by his parents or their church or whatever that he wasn't worthy of love, and he was having a hard time reconciling that with the fact that he was sitting next to a naked man who both loved him and wanted to rub his dick all over him.

"Okay, a tattoo. Let's see. Something dignified and classic." I pondered this for a long moment while the opening credits for the next movie we wouldn't actually watch started up. "I'd probably get a tattoo of the winged sandal of Hermes."

"Why?"

"Because I want to travel someday. Hermes was the messenger of the gods, and so he was always on the move. I think it would be a good reminder that in order to really live, you need to see new places and do new things."

"Where would you put it?" he asked.

I had to think about that for a minute. "It would need to be someplace where people wouldn't see it until I wanted them to," I replied.

Trevor ran his hand down my chest to my hip. He drew a little circle with his finger along the V-line, just above where my pubic hair began. "Here," he said. "Put it here, and only I will see it."

I looked down and saw my cock beginning to stir, even though it was still damp from the last adventure. Just the proximity of his finger was all it took to get me going again. "Well, if I ever get over my pathological fear of needles, I'll keep your suggestion in mind." I shuddered. "You should see me at the blood drive—giving blood's a good thing, but I have to do it with my eyes closed. If I ever caught sight of them sticking that needle into me, I think I'd scream, barf, and faint, and not necessarily in that order. I'm kind of a mess that way."

"You're not a mess, and I'd still love you even if you were," Trevor said, edging his hand inward from my hip. He quickly encountered a substantial—and growing—obstacle, and that was fine with me.

"I love you Trevor Hendricks."

"I love you, Sandler Birkin."

"Right. Sex, not love. Just so. Doctor Rauthmann, you are exactly what we've been looking for."

"Excellent," Rauthmann replied, standing and gesturing toward the door. "Let's join your wife in the outer room, and give her the good news."

Clinic director's office, Geneva

"THANK YOU for taking the time to see me, sir," Brandt said as the man behind the sleek imposing mahogany desk stood and extended his hand. The chamber they stood in was the epitome of a stultifyingly dignified office, heavy with dark paneling and armored against natural light by heavy brocade curtains that blocked any hint of the sun. Even sound was muffled—by the thick Persian carpet and voluminously stuffed chairs—as if to discourage any possible objection.

Brandt took the doctor's hand. Though his hands were small, they were as strong as steel traps, and the firm grip surprised Brandt.

"Mr. Brandt, is it? I am Dr. Galen Schwegler, director of the clinic. How may I help you today?" the doctor asked, sitting back down behind the desk and smoothing the white lab coat that overlaid his sharply tailored suit.

"I've come to talk to you about one of the doctors who works here," Brandt began.

"First, I must clarify," Schwegler broke in. "The doctors who practice here are not employees. They are independent practitioners who contract with the clinic. We provide space and support staff, but we do not in any way monitor or control their work."

"I understand that, sir," Brandt replied, "but surely if one of the doctors who practices here is the subject of a lawsuit, the clinic would wish to avoid any implication that you in any way sanctioned his work."

Schwegler nodded and opened his mouth to respond, but Brandt forged ahead.

"Or that you were warned of potential malpractice and did nothing to address it."

Schwegler's eyebrows lifted. "There is always the chance that anything a doctor does, no matter how proper, may be viewed by someone with imperfect understanding as malpractice. This is particularly true of Americans, I have found." Schwegler's words were polite but his tone made clear the implication—that Brandt was a troublemaker from overseas. "We cannot let the lamentable state of jurisprudence keep doctors from doing what they know is best for their patients."

"But surely you have an obligation to act if you are informed that one of the doctors working here is acting irresponsibly."

Schwegler's eyes narrowed. "Let us leave behind this vague talk, Mr. Brandt, and deal with particulars. Are you here to make an accusation?"

"I am simply here to inform you that one of your doctors continues to use a therapy that has been discredited in every study that has examined it, and that the pharmaceutical company that makes the drug he uses in his protocol is taking action to stop him."

Schwegler sat back in his chair—if he was startled by Brandt's statement, he made no sign. He took a deep, measured breath and let it out slowly. "Do you know why this clinic exists, Mr. Brandt?"

Brandt shook his head, wondering what Schwegler was getting at.

"It exists to offer treatments that people may not have access to in their own country—pioneering therapies that face a long and bureaucratic approval process. National health care systems are by nature conservative, slow to adopt promising new procedures. Switzerland is different because we rely on private practitioners and hospitals. We can innovate in ways many other countries cannot."

"But that's also true in—"

"The United States?" Schwegler interrupted with a condescending smile. "I can tell from your accent. The United States presents a challenge of a different kind. With no national health system, one would think that innovation would abound. And it does. But it brings two untoward side effects: lawyers and charlatans. There's a charming phrase in English… let me see… ah, yes. 'Snake oil salesman.' Americans are beset by medical fraud, which then encourages an infestation of lawyers. Real physicians, the ones who want to advance medical science to benefit their patients, suffer from the presence of both. If real doctors offer real hope, they are accused of being grifters. And if their results are not perfect—and they never are, not on the frontiers of medicine— they get sued out of existence. And so we open our doors to the pioneers, Mr. Brandt, to give them a place to innovate for the benefit of their patients. Patients with nowhere else to turn."

"But a doctor who pushes the bounds shouldn't endanger patients by doing so."

"That is an objection often made by those without an understanding of how medicine works. Breakthroughs are not made by incremental clinical trials. Small, halting progress is, but not real, paradigm-shattering breakthroughs. The advancement of medicine requires risk. And doctors must be free to undertake such risk on behalf of patients with no other options. Tell a man whose son is dying of rapidly metastasizing cancer that a new therapy will be available—once clinical trials conclude, sometime in the next decade. That's not medical progress, that's a death sentence. If a doctor can offer another option—even one that carries with it some risk to the patient—is that really an option you wish to see suppressed, whether by government regulation or by fear of lawsuits?"

"Are you actually claiming that no amount of documented negative outcome is enough to compel a doctor to stop offering his 'option' to desperate patients? How many have to die, Dr. Schwegler?"

Schwegler's face hardened. "Again, I must insist that if you have a specific accusation to make, you make it. Otherwise I have more pressing matters to see to this morning."

"Dr. Rauthmann. I'm here to talk to you about Dr. Rauthmann."

Schwegler pursed his lips and lowered his gaze to the desktop. It was a momentary gesture, but it told Brandt all he needed to know. He was not the first to talk to Schwegler about Rauthmann.

The doctor recovered quickly. "And what is it that concerns you about Dr. Rauthmann?" His tone conveyed his utter lack of curiosity in any answer Brandt might make.

"Are you familiar with the work that he does?"

"My familiarity with the work of any particular doctor who happens to contract with this clinic is immaterial, Mr. Brandt. I do not review his work, nor am I in any way responsible for the results of it."

"So you're saying you are not aware of the nature of the work that Rauthmann does here?" Exasperation was creeping into Brandt's voice.

"We have quite stringent patient privacy rules here. I'm afraid I am not at liberty to discuss anything related to Dr. Rauthmann's work."

"Then let me provide some of the details for you," Brandt replied. "About a year ago, when Dr. Rauthmann was practicing in a clinic outside Mexico City, a young man was brought to him by his family. They claimed to have a diagnosis of psychiatric illness, and Dr. Rauthmann treated him with a regimen of psychotropic drugs that involved dosages far in excess of those considered safe by the drug's manufacturer. The result was that the young man was, in the eyes of his parents, cured of the persistent delusions that had been haunting him, and he returned home."

Schwegler sighed. "And this is the part of the story where you tell me that all was not well and it was entirely Dr. Rauthmann's fault."

"Dr. Schwegler, the persistent delusion that the young man was treated for happened to be that he believed himself to be homosexual. His 'cure' entailed the complete eradication of any sexual identity, whether physical or emotional. His parents considered him cured and were certain Rauthmann had worked a miracle. The patient, however, had a different interpretation. Six weeks after his return from Mexico City, he walked in front of a train and was killed."

"And for this unfortunate accident you blame Dr. Rauthmann?" Schwegler's tone was again dismissive.

"No. The young man did that himself. In the note he left before his suicide, he made it very clear that Rauthmann's treatment had destroyed any hope he had of happiness."

Schwegler's expression turned to one he had likely learned in medical school: professional compassion that admits no responsibility for the loss experienced by another. "That is indeed a tragic outcome. But as I have already made clear, when one works at the frontiers of medicine, one must expect that on occasion—"

"It wasn't one occasion, Doctor." Brandt pulled himself upright—he was taller by a head than the other man, and even sitting was the more imposing figure. "We know of seven more 'tragic outcomes' from Dr. Rauthmann's treatment. And those are just the cases that have been made public. There are very likely more." He took a breath, let this information sink in. "And so I ask you again, Dr. Schwegler, how many patients have to die before you are willing to step in?"

Schwegler took a long moment, staring at his hands as he brought his fingertips together slowly, in a rhythm only he heard.

"What you must remember is this," the doctor began, his voice once again clear and definite. It was the tone of a professor. "People are only likely to seek out radical therapies when they have exhausted all other avenues of treatment. These unfortunate eight patients you speak of were very likely distraught and perhaps presuicidal at the time they sought out Dr. Rauthmann. We cannot necessarily blame him for their outcomes."

Brandt sat back. "Do you believe that homosexuality is something that should be treated as a delusion or a psychiatric disorder?"

"Of course not. You may not be aware that Switzerland was the first country in Europe to remove legal strictures on homosexuality. The vast majority of our citizens believe in equal rights for homosexuals, as do I."

"So it is not illegal. I'm happy to hear that. But would you consider it a disorder?"

"No, I would not."

"And yet you provide Dr. Rauthmann the facilities to perform a clearly dangerous therapy in an effort to cure a disorder that does not exist?"

Schwegler was silent.

"Let's suppose that Dr. Rauthmann was in the habit of providing dangerous doses of psychotropic drugs in an effort to cure illnesses that resulted from patients being born under the wrong astrological sign."

"That's ridiculous."

"Why?"

"Because astrology has no basis in reality."

"Granted. But would you allow Dr. Rauthmann to perform his therapies on those afflicted by astrological disorders?"

"I don't see how this is relevant—"

"It is perfectly relevant, Doctor, because it makes no more sense to treat astrological disorders than it does to treat homosexuality."

Schwegler fell silent. Brandt pushed ahead.

"The pharmaceutical company that makes the drug Dr. Rauthmann uses is suing him. They want to keep him from having access to it. They will have their day in court next month, and they will very likely succeed, as they have with a dozen or more physicians in the past who have misused the drug."

Schwegler held up his hands in an exasperated gesture. "Then that will solve your problem with Dr. Rauthmann. I don't see why you would need to involve me or the clinic at all."

"Because next month will be too late for the patients already under Rauthmann's 'care.' He's seeing patients right now—patients who are suffering from no disorder. Patients who will be irreparably harmed by his treatment."

"And would you happen to be personally acquainted with one of these patients?" Schwegler's eye was sharply trained on Brandt, clearly evaluating his reaction.

"Let's say one of them is a friend of a friend."

"So this is personal for you."

"That doesn't mean it's not the right thing to do. He needs to be stopped before he drives anyone else to suicide."

The doctor looked down and began to carefully align the pads of paper on his desk and then tidy a cup full of identical black pens. He surveyed the order he had brought to his desk, lips pursed in thought. Then, after sitting motionless for longer than Brandt thought sane, he picked up the sleek telephone that sat to his left. Without any hint of salutation, he uttered two or three sentences. Brandt thought he heard Rauthmann's name once or twice, but he couldn't be sure. He wasn't even sure what language Schwegler spoke.

Schwegler set the phone down silently and turned back to Brandt. "I will meet with Dr. Rauthmann. I will look into the allegations you have made." He picked up a pen from the cup. "How may I reach you should I have questions?"

He told Schwegler the name of their hotel. "But I'm not staying in Geneva long," he said. "I'll be here for two days. After that I can leave my contact information, but I have a commitment in England this weekend."

"Harassing clinic directors there as well?" Schwegler replied, the barest hint of irony in his voice.

"No. I'm getting married."

Schwegler gave a little shake of the head, as if he were sure he had heard incorrectly. Then some reserve of courtesy welled up. "Congratulations," he said, haltingly. "I wish you and your bride every happiness."

Brandt stood. "It's a two-groom wedding, but I appreciate your good wishes."

"Ah," Schwegler said, nodding. The pieces seemed to have fallen into place for him. "Thank you for coming to see me, Mr. Brandt."

"And thank you for helping prevent Dr. Rauthmann from harming anyone else." Brandt extended his hand.

Schwegler nodded as he shook Brandt's hand, but his face clearly conveyed that he was not looking forward to having to deal with the Rauthmann issue.

Brandt walked from the clinic director's office with a smile on his face. Things were looking up.

Another hotel

DONNELLY TOOK a deep breath and got into character. Sandler had given him all he needed to know about the role, but stage fright always reared its ugly head before he did anything remotely undercover. He just needed to stay calm.

From the concierge at their hotel, he'd been able to find out the location of the hotel where patients coming to the clinic most often stayed. Conveniently located across the street from the facility, the hotel was far more modern than the one Donnelly and the rest of the foursome were staying in. Donnelly had made an inquiry at the desk about the Hendricks family and found out that they were in fact staying there.

Through the magic of social media, he had reasonably recent photographs of both parents (though he came across no visual evidence that Trevor even existed). He was pretty confident he would be able to recognize them, so he settled himself in the lobby—in a chair facing the elevators—to wait.

He was just finishing his second cappuccino when one of the elevators opened to reveal Mrs. Hendricks, who made her way across the lobby with deliberate steps, eyes straight ahead as if she had blinders on. She didn't seem to notice Donnelly as he approached.

"Mrs.… Hendricks?" Donnelly exclaimed, planting himself directly in front of the scowling woman. "Is that really you?" He smiled as if finding a long-lost relative.

Her facial expression didn't shift, but she did come to a halt. She looked him up and down. "Who are you?" she demanded.

"Randy Filkins. Wow, it's been years. It's so good to see you."

"I'm sorry…," she said, though her brusque tone belied her apology. "I don't think I—"

"We only met once, when you picked up Trevor after one of our forensics competitions. That was the year we went to State, remember?"

Whether she actually remembered or not, she nodded vaguely. Donnelly felt relief waft through him—Sandler's backstory had felt solid, but until it was believed there was always the risk that it wouldn't work.

"I never got to tell you how sorry I was about what happened to Trevor," Donnelly continued somberly. "That must have been terrible for you."

"It's not something one ever gets over," she replied, her dour look starting finally to fade. She did not, however, offer any hint of what happened to Trevor after the accident. Then, as if she had flipped a switch, her expression changed to one open to grudging small talk. "What an interesting coincidence that we should meet here of all places. What brings you to Geneva, Randy?"

"I'm looking at graduate programs," Donnelly replied smoothly. "Some of the best schools are here, so I wanted to come take a look. And what about you? On vacation?"

Her lips pursed a bit, as if she were debating internally. She was silent long enough for Donnelly to worry that she was on the verge of dismissing him completely.

"Can I buy you a cup of coffee, Mrs. Hendricks?" he asked, putting on his best innocent, high-school-debate-student smile. "Unless you have somewhere to be...?"

His kind offer seemed to surprise her into courtesy. "I would like that. Thank you," she said with a smile that looked like it didn't get much use. "I don't think I've talked to anyone who knew Trevor since... well, in a very long time."

Donnelly led the way to the café, where he purchased two coffees and found them a table near the far wall, away from the traffic of midmorning in the lobby. She sat opposite him, and sipped the coffee that she had filled with milk and artificial sweetener. He struggled not to wince at the grave injustice done to the drink.

"You asked what brings me to Geneva," she said after setting her coffee cup down on its saucer.

He nodded encouragingly.

"We're here to see a specialist about Trevor," she said quietly.

Donnelly leaned forward. "Trev's alive?" His voice was shocked unto hoarseness; this, combined with the nickname that Sandler had told him the forensics team always used, seemed to have the desired effect.

Mrs. Hendricks nodded. "We always felt badly about how we had to leave town so suddenly, but the medical services available in the city were just so much better. And Trevor needed so many specialists." She closed her eyes stoically.

"We all thought he never woke up from the coma," Donnelly said, reminding himself to speak on behalf of his high school class. "How is he now?"

She sighed. "He's never really recovered from the accident. Once he was freed from the coma, we were able to bring him home and care for him, but I'm afraid the effects—physical and mental—have persisted."

Donnelly the police officer would have made a gentler approach in his questioning, but as Randy Filkins, who had just discovered that a friend from high school long presumed dead was actually alive, he forged ahead. "So, is he in a wheelchair, or a vegetable, or what?" He suspected that Trevor was frozen in time for her as he was at the time of the accident, so he tried to communicate as a high school junior might— clumsy and a little overwhelmed.

Mrs. Hendricks flinched as if he had slapped her.

"I'm sorry, I don't know the right words for any of this—it's all so bizarre. Please don't think me rude."

She managed a weak smile. "No, not at all. As I said, I haven't talked to anyone about Trevor outside of our little circle of doctors and support groups in so long, I forget what a shock it can be." She took a sip of coffee and composed herself. "Trevor is conscious, and often aware of his surroundings, but he is... limited, in some ways. We're hoping that a specialist we're here to see will be able to take care of the psychological issues that have been holding him back from making a fuller recovery."

"So, he's physically okay? Is it posttraumatic stress or something?"

"Something like that."

"And you're saying he's here, in Geneva?"

"He's here in the hotel. I was just going out to sign some papers at the clinic, and then I'll be going up to relieve Mr. Hendricks so he can take a little rest. Caring for Trevor is a twenty-four hour a day job, I'm afraid." She sighed again, this time a little more dramatically.

"Trevor's really that bad off?" Donnelly shook his head sadly. "He was always so… so strong, I guess is the word I'd use. Can't believe he's been like this for so long."

"It's not as bad as all that, most days," she said with something that was probably supposed to sound like comfort in her voice.

"Do you think… do you think I could… see him?" Donnelly asked this with downcast eyes, exactly how he'd imagine a seventeen-year-old buddy of her son's might ask if he could come see a movie on a school night. He saw on her face that it had worked—at least a little.

"Well, I don't know about that," she said, creasing the corner of her napkin thoughtfully. "We're trying to keep him calm before he goes to the clinic tomorrow."

Tomorrow! He needed to pull out all the stops. He sat back in his chair as if the tragedy of Trevor's situation had finally hit him. "I can't believe he's here. Seems like just yesterday we were in the bus on the way back from a forensics meet and I was telling him that my sister had a wicked crush on him. He laughed it off, but he blushed like a fire hydrant. My sister was heartbroken by the accident. I don't think she ever really got over him."

He looked up to see if it was working. He had dangled heterosexuality in front of her and now could only wait to see if she would take the bait.

She looked a little misty at the mention of Trevor's high school days, her face softening. "I suppose it wouldn't hurt if you came up for a couple of minutes. Just to say hello."

It's lucky bigots are usually stupid. "That would be so nice. But weren't you on your way somewhere?"

"Oh, that can wait a bit. Would you like to come up now?"

He nodded, beaming at her, though he felt a shiver of trepidation down his spine as they stood. Getting this far had been easy compared to what lay ahead. He had no idea what to expect, nor what would happen if Trevor saw through the paper-thin ruse that he and Sandler had concocted. Though Sandler assured him that Randy Filkins was practically his doppelgänger, there was still a chance that Trevor wouldn't buy it. Worse still would be finding him in such bad shape that he couldn't be reached at all. There were many ways for this to go wrong.

Donnelly swallowed his anxiety and followed Mrs. Hendricks to the elevator. They rode in polite silence.

"Would you mind waiting out here for a moment? I want to be sure he's not in one of his moods this morning. Seeing someone from high school may be a bit shocking, and he won't handle it well unless he's perfectly calm." He nodded, and she opened the door to the hotel room, nearly the last in the long hallway. She slipped inside.

Putting his ear close to the door, Donnelly could hear quiet conversation between Mrs. Hendricks and a deeper voice that he assumed belonged to Mr. Hendricks. He listened hard but couldn't make out a third voice. He stepped back from the door when the voices began to rise in volume.

"He was a friend from high school," Mrs. Hendricks spat, her voice angry. "I think it would do him some good to see someone from a happier time."

Mr. Hendricks's response was muffled, composed only of furious mumbling.

Their conversation concluded without Donnelly being able to make out any more words, and he retreated to a more casual stance in the hallway as he heard her footsteps approach. She opened the door, wearing a smile that nearly scared him with its breadth and intensity, as if she were positively willing the entire situation to a successful conclusion.

"Please, come in, Randy."

"Thank you, Mrs. Hendricks." He stepped into the hotel room. "Mr. Hendricks," he said with a respectful nod.

Mr. Hendricks took two purposeful strides toward him, eyes narrowed, brow creased. "Randy... Fisker, is it?"

The bastard was testing him. "Filkins, sir," Donnelly replied, extending his hand. Certainly the real Randy Filkins wouldn't even consider the possibility that the mistaking of his name would be a gambit to rattle an imposter.

Mr. Hendricks grudgingly took Donnelly's hand and shook it. "Quite a coincidence, isn't it, all of us being in Geneva at the same time."

Donnelly's heart pounded as the possibility of the charade unraveling yawned wide in front of him. What would Brandt do, he wondered? He knew immediately. He would double down.

"I don't think it is a coincidence, sir," Donnelly replied, his smile never wavering.

Mr. Hendricks was clearly taken aback. "You don't?"

"No, sir, I don't. I think things happen for a reason. I think God wanted Trevor to see a friend right now, and so he put it in my heart to be here. Simple as that." He worked his features into what he hoped would be a convincing arrangement of placid resignation in the face of fate.

Bingo.

Mr. Hendricks's face lit up, and he smiled for the first time since Donnelly entered the room. "That's a wonderful way of looking at it," he said warmly. "I think you must be right."

The Hendrickses exchanged a long look and then nodded to each other.

"Trevor's doing well this morning," Mr. Hendricks continued. "He's right through here."

Mrs. Hendricks went ahead of them to the door that connected their hotel room to the next. She opened it, stepped through, then closed the door behind her.

"She'll let him know you're here, and then you can go in," Mr. Hendricks said. "We try not to surprise him. Surprises trouble him."

Donnelly nodded. The risk of an untoward surprise weighed heavily on him, but at least he had the consolation that if Trevor freaked out because a stranger had appeared claiming to be a long-lost high school friend, his parents would not immediately jump to the conclusion that Donnelly was a fraud.

At least, that's what he hoped.

Mrs. Hendricks reappeared in the connecting doorway. "Randy, Trevor perked right up at the mention of your name. I think it'll be fine for you to come in."

Showtime.

Donnelly followed Mrs. Hendricks back through the doorway into a room that, while a mirror image of the one next door, was dimly lit and appeared not to have been disturbed since it was made up by housekeeping. In a chair near the window (Donnelly assumed it was a window, though the heavy curtains obliterated any hint of daylight), a frail-looking young man sat staring blankly ahead. He was wrapped in a blanket and was wearing a stocking cap.

"Trevor," Mrs. Hendricks called, her voice just above a whisper. "Trevor, dear, Randy's here now."

Donnelly approached, searching Trevor's face for any sign of recognition—or alarm. Slowly Trevor turned his head, and finally their eyes met. But though he stared right at Donnelly, his facial expression didn't alter.

On the plus side, he wasn't screaming bloody murder at the appearance of an imposter claiming to be one of his friends from high school, so Donnelly took a steadying breath and pushed ahead. He moved slowly to the chair opposite Trevor and sat slowly down. Trevor's eyes followed him as he moved, but did not so much as blink.

"Trev?" Donnelly said softly, leaning toward him. "Trev, it's me, Randy. Randy Filkins."

Trevor stared, still perfectly devoid of expression.

"Trevor, are you all right, honey?" Mrs. Hendricks asked, leaning toward him as well.

Trevor jerked and started, and his hands flew up to flail at his mother. He made a strangled, wailing sound that Donnelly found simply heartbreaking. Without thinking, he put his hand on Trevor's knee.

Immediately Trevor fell silent. His gaze snapped down to Donnelly's hand, and then he looked up and met Donnelly's eyes once again. This time there was something… different. Donnelly wasn't sure what it was, but something had changed.

"Oh, now, Trevor," his mother scolded, "Let's not—"

Trevor again flailed at his mother, and this time his voice was stronger—less a wail than a full-throated protest. She recoiled, her face clouded with confusion.

"Trev?" Donnelly said soothingly. He rubbed Trevor's knee with his hand, pressing the connection between the two of them. Again, Trevor calmed immediately and returned to looking at Donnelly.

Mrs. Hendricks stepped back, arms falling limply by her side. "I don't understand."

As if driven to madness by even this bewildered utterance, Trevor barked again in her direction.

Donnelly turned to her. "Mrs. Hendricks, do you think Trevor and I could have a moment or two alone? It seems like one person at a time may be as much as he can take."

Mrs. Hendricks drew herself up. "I think I know what my son—"

She was cut off by more frantic flailing and guttural noises from Trevor. She stepped back again, eyes wide with confusion. As she retreated, Trevor calmed.

"I promise I'll call you if anything happens," Donnelly said, not taking his eyes off of Trevor. "I'm sure he'll be fine if I just sit with him for a few minutes."

Mrs. Hendricks seemed to debate within herself for several long moments. She watched as Trevor slowly reached out and took Donnelly's hand in his own. Donnelly held his breath, hoping that the gesture wouldn't alarm Mrs. Hendricks with its intimacy. But Trevor simply shook Donnelly's hand, as if they'd just been introduced. That seemed to placate the paranoid Mrs. Hendricks.

"Well, I guess it wouldn't hurt to leave you two alone for a bit," she said, her voice uncertain. "I'll just be in the other room. Call me if you... well...." She backed herself into the door that stood ajar and then awkwardly stepped around it and disappeared from view.

Donnelly turned back to Trevor and looked into his eyes. He didn't know how much time they might have, and he needed to make a connection—needed to see what they were up against.

"Hey, Trevor," he began, a little stiffly. "Great to see you."

Trevor blinked at Donnelly then, twice. Slowly he brought his finger up to Donnelly lips, and pressed it there. He shook his head slowly. Then his own lips began to move.

"What?" Donnelly whispered, leaning close. "I didn't hear you." He leaned forward until his ear was nearly pressed against Trevor's lips. Then he could hear, and the words sent a shiver down his back.

"Help... me."

Donnelly swallowed hard. "I came here to help you, Trevor."

He looked for any sign of recognition on Trevor's face but saw none—at least at first. Then he saw it: a tear formed at the corner of his eye and ran down his cheek.

"Help me," he said again.

"Yes. I'm here to help you."

"Everything okay in there?" called Mrs. Hendricks from the other room.

"Yes, Mrs. Hendricks," Donnelly called back dutifully. He wouldn't have much time.

"Trevor," he said, leaning in close again and whispering quietly, "do you know why you're here? In Geneva?"

Trevor blinked hard, forcing more tears from his eyes.

"Do you want them to take you to the doctor tomorrow? Do you want to be treated?"

Mrs. Hendricks popped her head back into the room. "We should probably let Trevor rest," she said. "He's got a big day tomorrow."

"All right, Mrs. Hendricks," Donnelly replied. "Can we have just one more minute? I think Trevor's really enjoying our conversation."

Trevor, eyes focused on his mother, strained to make something that looked like a smile.

"Oh my, look at that," she said, holding her hand to her chest. "I haven't seen a smile like that in I don't know how long." She gave an embarrassed little laugh. "I guess it wouldn't hurt for you boys to take another couple of minutes." She ducked back out.

Donnelly was out of time. He knew he needed to make his move if this whole charade was going to work.

"Trevor, I came here with someone. Someone you know."

Trevor looked at Donnelly, frozen, listening.

"Sandler is here."

Trevor gasped, then quickly stifled the sound. He struggled visibly to get himself back under control.

"Sandler came here because he found out you needed help. He's here to help you, Trevor. We all are."

His eyes wide in wonder, Trevor's lips began moving again. Donnelly leaned in close once more.

"Sandler," Trevor said softly, then repeated the name several times, like a mantra.

"Now we should let Trevor get some rest," sang Mrs. Hendricks as she sailed back into the room. "I'm sure this has all been very exciting, but we need to be rested for tomorrow."

Donnelly stood. He took Trevor's hand again and shook it, then placed it back in his lap. "Bye, Trev. I hope we can see each other again soon."

Mrs. Hendricks led him through the doorway to the other hotel room. "That was simply amazing," she said as they passed through. "I've honestly not seen him smile like that since the accident."

"We're very lucky that you not-so-coincidentally showed up in Geneva," Mr. Hendricks said. "Your visit was just what he needed."

"Do you think I could see him again?" Donnelly asked. "Could we maybe have dinner together tonight?"

The Hendrickses exchanged a look.

"I don't think that would be a…," Mrs. Hendricks began.

"You see, Trevor can't really eat in restaurants," Mr. Hendricks said. "Being around that many people really seems to bother him."

"Maybe I could come up, and we could have dinner here?" Donnelly wheedled. He had to find a way to get back here.

"Well…," Mrs. Hendricks said, tipping her head to one side, appraising this Randy Filkins and his radical ideas.

"You said he was going in for a treatment tomorrow. They say people respond better to medical treatment when they are in a good mood"—he was making up whatever he could to press his case—"and my being here really did seem to do him some good."

"You're right about that," Mr. Hendricks said, turning to his wife.

"I really think this is what I was brought here to do," Donnelly offered solemnly. "I would be honored to come back and have dinner with him, and you two could go get dinner downstairs. You probably don't get a chance to do that very often, do you?"

"Not at all, young man," Mr. Hendricks replied. "Not at all."

They both turned to Mrs. Hendricks.

"All right, all right," she said, holding up her hands in surrender. "Randy, if you could come back at about six, we'll order up some room service for the two of you."

She took his hand in hers. "And please make sure you tell him about your sister. You'll do that for me, won't you?"

"Of course I will, Mrs. Hendricks," Donnelly replied with a laugh he hoped sounded less forced than it felt. "I wouldn't pass up the chance to give him a hard time about that!"

They all shared a laugh, and then Donnelly was on his way. Now he just had to figure out how to turn a dinner date into a rescue operation.

Hôtel Genève

"SANDLER," DONNELLY called from across the lobby. They were on their way for a progress check over lunch in the hotel restaurant. Brandt and Kerry had already gone in, but Donnelly wanted to catch Sandler to give him the news about Trevor alone.

"Gabriel!" Sandler clapped a hand on Donnelly's shoulder. "How'd it go?"

Donnelly said as he put his arm around Sandler, "Let's sit for a sec so I can tell you before we go in."

Sandler stopped cold. "Is it that bad?"

"No, it's good," Donnelly assured him as they sat down. "I saw him today."

Sandler's mouth dropped open. "You saw... Trevor?"

Donnelly nodded.

"Like, in the distance? Through a window?"

"No, I sat next to him. I talked to him."

Tears sprang to Sandler's eyes.

"I talked to him about you."

Sandler's hand flew up to his mouth, covering a gasp. "What did he say?"

"He said your name—he said it like a prayer."

"Oh my God," Sandler said softly, tears flowing freely down his cheeks now. "Oh my God, oh my God." He clutched his head in his hands and rocked back and forth, completely overwhelmed.

Donnelly sat silently for a few minutes, letting Sandler absorb what he had said. "He repeated your name over and over again. It brought him such joy."

Sandler took another few moments before he was able to speak again. "How... how is he?"

Donnelly took a deep breath. "I don't know. He seemed... delicate? He didn't seem well, but he was clearly aware of his surroundings. He asked me to... help him."

"We have to rescue him," Sandler said. "We have to find a way to get him out of there."

"We will. I promise you that."

Sandler nodded, but though he tried to speak several times, he was unable to form words.

"I'm going to go join Ethan and Kerry. Take as long as you need, okay? Then we'll get to work figuring out how to get Trevor free."

Sandler nodded and sat back in the chair, eyes to the ceiling.

Donnelly went into the restaurant and found Brandt and Kerry sitting at a table in a far corner, away from other diners.

"Did Sandler get lost?" Kerry asked as he approached the table.

"I wanted to tell him about my morning before he came in—give him some time to process it."

"Bad news?" Brandt asked, his brow furrowed empathetically.

"No, I think it's pretty good news, actually. But we need to figure out what comes next." He brought them up to speed on his morning with the Hendricks family.

Sandler joined them just as Donnelly was wrapping up, and they listened to Brandt describe his conversation with Schwegler. Then Sandler summarized their conversation with the doctor himself.

"He's still taking new patients," Sandler said.

"And he's still making promises about how his protocol will cure them," Kerry added.

"I'm surprised he would admit that," Brandt said, "given that your company is pursuing legal action. I would have thought he would be a little more circumspect in talking to you about it."

"Well, we were very subtle about that aspect of things," Kerry replied, looking at the tablecloth. "It didn't make sense to go in with those guns blazing if we wanted answers, right?"

"Kerry was terrific," Sandler blurted. "Now, what's next?"

"Well, here's what we know. Dr. Rauthmann is indeed implementing his protocol despite evidence provided by Kerry's company that it causes irreparable harm. The director of the clinic is concerned, but his concern won't stop Rauthmann in the short term from continuing his horrible work. Finally, Trevor is here, at the hotel near the clinic, and has an appointment at the clinic tomorrow for a treatment that we have every reason to believe will leave him mentally and emotionally damaged, and likely suicidal. Gabriel will be having dinner with him tonight, which may be our only chance at him before he's taken to the clinic tomorrow." He looked around the table. "Does that about sum it up?"

There were nods all around, though Sandler's was slower than the rest—the part about Trevor being suicidal had clearly shaken him.

"The question before us, then, is how can we keep Trevor from being taken to the clinic tomorrow?"

"We could phone in a bomb threat," Kerry said casually.

Donnelly jumped and stared across the table, stunned.

"Let me rephrase that," Brandt said sternly. "How can we keep Trevor from being taken to the clinic tomorrow without committing a felony?"

"Oh, so now there are all kinds of conditions," Kerry replied. "I thought we were brainstorming." She smiled, and even Sandler got a chuckle out of her attempt to lighten the mood.

"Is there a way we can bring more attention to his work, to embarrass the clinic into shutting him down immediately?" Sandler asked.

"I don't get the sense that Dr. Schwegler is likely to be swayed by the media spotlight," Brandt replied. "The guy is pretty unflappable. I was only able to get him to look into Rauthmann's practice when I calmly pointed out the number of suicides that have followed his treatment. He didn't respond to emotion, only logical argument."

"Plus, time is pretty short," Donnelly added. He looked around the table. "I think we really have only one option."

They all looked at him expectantly.

"I'll warn you up front that those of you who are sticklers for proper legal procedure are probably not going to like it...."

And then all eyes were on Brandt, who rolled his eyes and heaved a sigh. "Can we just do this without all the drama, please?"

"As you wish, sir," Donnelly replied with a teasing obedience in his voice. He laid out his plan to the group, and by the time he finished, there was a sober silence all round.

"So, that's how I think it could work. What do you think?"

"You can put me down for 'Hell yeah,'" Kerry announced without a moment's hesitation.

"I would do all of that and more if it meant getting him out of there," Sandler said solemnly.

They turned to Brandt.

"I counted seventeen places where things could go disastrously wrong," he said flatly.

Both Kerry and Sandler looked crestfallen.

Donnelly looked him in the eye. "So, you in or are you out?"

They all looked at him, not a breath being drawn around the table.

"In, of course," Brandt answered with a chuckle and a shake of his head, as if surprised that the question needed to be asked at all. "But we have a lot of work to do."

"Fuck yeah," Kerry said, and held up her hand for high fives all around. "Break it down, chief. Where do we start?"

Brandt took a deep breath before answering. "From the beginning. We start there and work our way through. If we hit a wall, we back up and think through it again. Before we leave this table, the plan needs to be bulletproof."

"You don't think there will be guns, do you?" Sandler asked, clearly spooked.

"Not unless someone goes rogue on us," Brandt replied, deadly serious. But then he burst out laughing. "Just pulling your leg, Sandler. I don't foresee having to do anything more than a few warning shots over people's heads."

"My sociopath fiancé is trying to make a joke," Donnelly said, then turned and punched Brandt in the arm. "Stop that."

"All right, all right," Brandt replied, holding up his hands in surrender. "Let's get started. The first move is yours, Gabriel. Take us through it."

Donnelly nodded seriously, and they began to plan.

Another hotel

DONNELLY KNOCKED on the hotel room door, willing his knees to stop knocking along. He hated this moment the most—the first three seconds of being undercover, when scrutiny is the greatest, always made him the most anxious. If he could get through that, he could pull it off. Mostly he held his breath and tried to keep his heart from pounding out of his chest.

The door swung open, and instead of a suspicious glare, he was met with a welcoming smile.

"Right on time," Mr. Hendricks said as he waved Donnelly into the room. "I remember you were always a responsible young man, Randy."

As far as Donnelly knew, Mr. Hendricks had never met Randy Filkins, but the misplaced compliment was what allowed Donnelly to let out that first anxious breath. In Donnelly's experience, people liked their past to line up with their present, even if they had to make up their past wholesale. His impersonation had worked well enough that Trevor's father was remembering him fondly.

"Thank you for letting me have dinner with Trevor," he said as he stepped into the room. Mrs. Hendricks was at the vanity putting on earrings and smiling at him in the mirror.

"You really are so nice to do this for us," she said, smoothing her blouse and tucking a stray bit of hair back into place. "No one's offered to let us just have dinner together for years and years."

The warden complains about how hard it is to keep prisoners, Donnelly thought. But he kept his solicitous smile firmly in place. "That must be really hard, with all that you do for Trevor." The bitter taste of sucking up nearly clogged his throat, but he forged ahead. "You take your time tonight. I have a lot to tell Trevor, updating him on what our classmates are up to—especially my sister." He managed a sly wink at Mrs. Hendricks that instantly made him feel dirty. But it was for a good cause, he reminded himself.

"Now, Trevor should be nice and calm tonight," Mrs. Hendricks said, picking up her purse. "I gave him a higher dose of his mood medicine than usual because we need him to be focused tomorrow."

Donnelly saw in the mirror that he winced at this before he had a chance to stifle the instinct. "You really do so much for him, don't you?" he blurted, covering his disgust at the way they manipulated Trevor's emotions.

But the comment hit home. Mrs. Hendricks stepped closer to him and laid a hand on his arm. "You don't know how wonderful it is to hear that someone notices all we do," she said, a proud smile on her face. "Mostly it's a lot of thankless effort. I appreciate so much that you would say that."

Donnelly summoned up his most shit-eating smile and willed himself to be silent.

"Reservation was for five minutes ago," Mr. Hendricks called from where he was standing next to the open hotel room door.

Mrs. Hendricks fixed him with an icy glare, then turned back to Donnelly. "I've ordered dinner for you boys—I hope you don't mind." Were she actually concerned he might mind she would have paused here, but she did not. "They have a few of Trevor's favorites on the menu, and he eats the same meal every night."

"I'm sure that'll be just fine," Donnelly answered. "Now you two should get going before they give your table away." He smiled, hoping his true emotions were not visible under his vapid grin.

"Thank you again for your interest in Trevor," Mrs. Hendricks said as she joined her husband at the door. "I wish everyone he went to school with was as concerned as you are."

"Enjoy your dinner," Donnelly said, willing them to just leave already.

"We will," Mrs. Hendricks said with a smile as she stepped into the hall. She immediately stepped back in. "Just so you're prepared, when Trevor has just taken his mood medication, he tends to be pretty quiet. He may not talk much tonight. But you can be sure he hears you, even if you can't really tell he's listening."

Donnelly smiled until his face ached, and finally the door closed behind the Hendrickses. He rubbed his sore cheeks and walked quickly to the connecting door, thinking about what Mrs. Hendricks had just said. It did not bode particularly well for the plan they had in mind.

He knocked on the door, which was slightly ajar. "Trevor? It's Randy. Can I come in?"

There was no answer.

Donnelly slowly opened the door, and found Trevor sitting in the same chair, wearing the same getup as earlier in the day: a blanket and a knit cap. He sat staring at the window, though all he could see of it was the heavy curtains that covered it.

"Trevor?"

If he heard, he gave no outward sign.

Donnelly approached gradually, not wanting to startle him. He lowered himself gently into the chair opposite Trevor's, with a small coffee table between them. He studied Trevor's face, looking for some sign of awareness, any indication at all that Trevor knew he was here.

Nothing.

"Trevor?" Donnelly repeated, this time a little more loudly.

More nothing.

With a rising desperation in his chest, Donnelly leaned across the table and set his hand on Trevor's knee, much as he had done earlier in the day.

He was unprepared for Trevor's shrieking.

Recoiling from the screaming, Donnelly threw himself backward, knocking over his chair and tumbling to the floor with a great thud.

Trevor wailed until his breath failed, and then he brought both hands up to his face as if shielding himself from Donnelly.

Donnelly was surprised by how loud the pounding in his head was, but as he righted the chair, he realized the pounding was coming from the door. He ran to it and looked through the viewer. He saw a fish-eye view of a frantic Sandler, who continued to knock. Donnelly opened the door and waved him in.

"What the—" Sandler demanded, falling silent when Donnelly made wild shushing motions at him.

Donnelly pulled him into the room and shut the door behind them.

"What was that awful noise?" Sandler demanded in a harsh whisper. "I know you told me to wait down the hall until you came out to get me, but I saw the Hendrickses leave and then that horrible moaning started. What happened?"

Donnelly put his hands on Sandler's shoulders. "It was Trevor. He wasn't responsive, so I called his name a couple of times and then put my hand on his knee. I did the same thing earlier today, and he was fine, but this time he just went ballistic."

They both turned and looked at Trevor, who sat with his face buried in his hands. His agitated panting was the only sign of life.

Donnelly turned back to Sandler and saw his friend frozen, staring at Trevor from within a mask of expressionless shock. "Sandler?"

Nothing.

"Sandler, are you okay?"

Sandler jolted as if awakened suddenly but didn't take his eyes off Trevor. "That's him," he whispered. "It's really him?"

"It's really him." Donnelly looked over at the still-frozen Trevor. "Though right now it kind of looks like we've lost him."

"No," Sandler said, his voice flat and low. "No. I didn't suffer all those years and come all this way to lose him now. No." He took a step toward Trevor.

Donnelly grabbed his arm and stopped him in his tracks. "Hold on. Do you think that's a good idea? Maybe we should wait until he snaps out of it."

Sandler lifted Donnelly's hand off his arm. "I have to go to him. You understand that, don't you? I'm all he has. I'm not leaving here without him."

This was not going at all the way Donnelly had hoped, and his instincts told him to call it off and work on a plan B. But he saw in Sandler's face exactly the pain and desperation he would feel if someone were to try to keep him from Brandt, and he gave his instincts the night off. "Take it slow, okay?"

Sandler nodded. He walked over and knelt next to Trevor. "Trev?" he said softly.

Trevor fell still, as if holding his breath.

"Trev, it's me. It's Sandler."

Trevor's hands dropped from his face, but he didn't turn to Sandler. He stared down at his hands, now lying in his lap, and moved no more.

"Trevor, it's Sandler." He reached out and put his hand gingerly atop Trevor's, which made Donnelly wince and step back.

But instead of a recurrence of Trevor's banshee turn, there was silence. Then, slowly, Trevor turned to look at Sandler. Their eyes locked for a long moment.

"Yeah, it's me," Sandler said, smiling broadly.

Trevor studied his face for another few seconds, then dropped his gaze back to his lap, his face expressionless.

"Trev?" Sandler said with a catch in his voice. When there was no reaction from Trevor, he began to softly sob, though he didn't take his eyes off him.

"Maybe we should leave him alone for little while," Donnelly suggested. "See if he comes around?"

Sandler shook his head. When he replied to Donnelly, he didn't take his eyes off Trevor. "No. I'm going to sit with him for as long as it takes. I'll reach him. I have to."

Donnelly looked at the two of them, his heart breaking. They had been kept apart so cruelly, and now that they were finally together, they might as well have been on opposite sides of the globe. He wished there were something he could do to help. But the only thing that came to him was to offer them the dignity of privacy. "I'll be in the other room if you need me, okay?"

Sandler, crying softly, nodded.

Donnelly backed out of the room and shut the connecting door behind him.

"TREVOR, I'M right here next to you. I came as soon as I found out where you were."

Trevor sat motionless, expressionless.

"They didn't tell me where you were, or even that you were alive," Sandler continued, his voice steady and even. "I've spent every day since the accident trying to find anything like the happiness we had together. It doesn't work without you, Trev. Nothing works without you."

Sandler studied Trevor's blank stare and felt rage against the injustices they'd suffered rise in his chest, thick and hot, squeezing out the air in his lungs. He had to come up with some way to reach him, to make him realize that they were back together again and that things would be better.

"Trevor, can you hear me? It's Sandler, Trev." He fell silent, looking into Trevor's wide, blank eyes.

A few minutes later, Donnelly stepped back into the room. He looked inquisitively at Sandler, who got up and walked over to the connecting door.

"How's he doing?" Donnelly asked.

Sandler shook his head—the sadness that welled up in his throat kept him from saying anything.

"Keep trying," Donnelly said, putting his arm consolingly around Sandler's shoulders.

"It's not working. I don't know what to do," Sandler whispered.

Donnelly pulled Sandler into a hug. It was exactly what Sandler needed—once again, he was surprised by how effortlessly Donnelly seemed to know what to do to help the people around him.

Sandler tightened his grip on Donnelly, drawing strength from him, feeling the warmth of hope flicker back to life. "Thank you," he whispered.

Donnelly stroked Sandler's back and held him tight. "You can do this," he murmured.

Sandler stepped back from their embrace, took a deep breath, and nodded. "I can do this," he said, almost believing it.

Donnelly smiled bracingly, then stepped back out through the connecting door, while Sandler returned to kneel at Trevor's side.

He whispered soothingly to him, hoping to make some connection.

Nearly a half hour later, Sandler heard Donnelly walking up behind him. Trevor, having taken no discernible notice of Sandler, seemed likewise unaware of Donnelly's approach.

Sandler craned his head up at Donnelly, who stood behind him. "I don't know how much longer I can do this," he said.

"Dinner arrived, if you think food might help."

"I'll try anything."

They brought in the meal that Mrs. Hendricks had said was composed of Trevor's favorite foods. It was clear that his culinary tastes were frozen in high school; the tray contained pizza, french fries, and what the Swiss apparently considered hot dogs.

"Ugh," Sandler said under his breath. "No wonder he's not feeling great."

"They're probably trying to keep him fed and happy while they prep him for the doctor," Donnelly said, shivering visibly.

Sandler picked up some pizza, put it on a piece of hotel china, and held it out to Trevor. "Trev? Want some pizza?" He noticed his hand was shaking, betraying his desperation. "Please, Trevor?"

There was no response.

Sandler set the plate down on the coffee table with a clatter. Even that sudden, sharp noise brought no reaction. "I don't know what to do," he said quietly. He felt all of the promise that seemed to fill the world an hour ago was gone, gone utterly.

"Sandler?" Donnelly said softly. "We may have to consider whether what we're doing is really best for Trevor. We didn't expect him to be this way."

"What are you suggesting?" Sandler said, getting to his feet. "That we just leave him here?"

"No, I'm not suggesting that," Donnelly said calmly. He led Sandler through the connecting door, closing it behind them. "I just think we should consider whether it's responsible of us to remove him from the care of his parents before we know his condition."

"His parents don't care about him," Sandler said, anger and frustration and despair rising in his chest. "They wouldn't be doing this if the cared about him."

"You're right. Of course you're right. I'm not saying we leave him here. I'm just suggesting that we may not be able to take him to our hotel tonight. We may need to get him into another doctor's care right away, and that will take some additional planning. Otherwise, if we seek medical help for him nearby, we risk the Hendrickses showing up and just taking him back. They do have the power of attorney."

"But they want to make him worse, not better," Sandler blurted angrily. "That's not what he would want, you know that!"

Donnelly took a deep breath and looked at Sandler, encouraging him to do the same. Sandler mirrored his exaggerated breathing motions.

"Good," Donnelly said, calmly. "Now, we don't know what Trevor's medical issues are—setting aside his parents trying to drug him into being straight. We don't know what injuries he suffered in the accident, and he can't tell us what medication he's taking. We may need to take a step back and reevaluate our plan."

"I won't leave him here."

"I'm not saying we should leave him here. But unless we have a solid plan, we won't help him at all. We don't want to do more harm than good. We don't have the information we need right now to know we're doing the right thing for Trevor."

"I can't… I don't know what to…." Sandler shook his head, clearing it of all the impossible half thoughts that filled it. "I need to see him again."

He bolted through the connecting door, back to the motionless Trevor. He threw himself at the side of Trevor's chair, and summoned up the courage to try again. "Trevor—"

Then he saw it.

The piece of pizza he had set down on the coffee table had one perfect, serrated half-moon bite out of it.

That. That was hope. Sandler was not going to let this opportunity go.

"Gabriel," he called, not taking his eyes off Trevor. Donnelly ran into the room. "Kerry's downstairs, right?"

"Yes, she's holding a town car for our getaway drive."

"Get her up here, now."

"Okay…." Donnelly moved immediately to the hallway door. "What should I tell her?"

"Just tell her to get up here."

Donnelly disappeared through the doorway.

"Trev, want some more pizza?" Sandler said, a soft singsong in his voice.

He thought he saw a flicker in Trevor's eye, but no other motion was forthcoming. He repeated his question several times, waiting an agonizing minute or more between offers.

"Fine," Sandler said. "I'm gonna eat it if you don't want it." The teasing in his voice more prominent now, he danced the pizza in front of Trevor's blank face. He was sure he was about to break through.

Sandler took a bite of the pizza, purposely chomping the part that Trevor had bitten, subsuming the earlier half-moon with a huge, gaping wound in the side of the pizza slice.

"Ha. You always did have a little mouth. It's too full of all of those perfect teeth."

The hallway door swung open, and Kerry and Donnelly came barreling into the room.

"Sandler, what is it? How can I help?" Kerry demanded as she stormed over toward the window.

"I need you to do something for me," Sandler said, barely taking his eyes off Trevor.

"Anything," she replied without hesitation. She cast a look behind her at Donnelly. "Good lord he's cute—look at those cheekbones."

"I need you to look at his medications," Sandler continued. "See if you can figure out what they're treating him for. We need to be sure when we move him that we know what's going on medically."

"Got it," she said, and darted into the bathroom. Just as quickly she came jogging back through the room. "Nothing there—they probably keep his meds in the other room." She disappeared through the connecting doorway.

"Gabriel, can you find a suitcase or something for him?" Sandler said, not really a question. "They may have something packed for his visit to the clinic, but in case they don't, I want to be sure we're ready to roll."

Donnelly looked around the room and, as Sandler had expected, found nothing of use. "I'll go check next door," he said, bounding through the connecting doorway.

Sandler stared at Trevor's expressionless face, and knew he had one last chance. He got to his feet, moved the coffee table bearing the twice-bitten pizza aside, and stood directly in front of Trevor. He took a deep breath—he knew he needed to do this, but he felt anxious about it nonetheless—he unbuttoned and unzipped his pants, then pulled them down a little. Then he slipped a thumb into the waistband of his underwear and tugged them down, exposing his left hip.

And the tiny winged sandal that was tattooed there.

He stood in front of Trevor, not moving, willing him to move his blank and glassy eyes toward the tattoo that they had talked about that first idyllic weekend together, back before the accident, back before a decade of separation.

Trevor didn't move.

Sandler stood there for a full minute, then two, feeling hope flow out of him. How cruel life was, he thought, to bring Trevor back to him in body but not in mind—not in spirit.

"Trev, I need you," he managed to say before a sob caught in his throat. "Trevor, please. *Please.*" Unable to speak any further, he gave himself over to the tears that rose from the pain he felt deep inside.

Whether it was from the pleading or the crying or simply that by standing in front of him Sandler was blocking out so much of the room—what made Trevor turn to look was a mystery. But look he did.

When he caught sight of the tattoo, he froze.

Sandler, eyes blurry with tears, blinked hard and focused on Trevor's face, desperate for a sign of recognition. So intently was he studying Trevor's eyes that he was unaware of the hand that rose up before him until he felt the fingertips brush lightly across the tattoo. Startled, he jolted but willed himself not to step back.

For a long moment, Trevor stared at the tattoo while his fingers made small circles around it. Then, gradually, Trevor lifted his gaze up Sandler's body to his face.

Sandler could see the change come over him: his eyes locked into focus, his brow furrowed. He opened his mouth.

"It's… you," Trevor said, his voice just above a whisper.

"Yes, it's me." Though Sandler wanted to shout, he found he could only make a rasping murmur, so tight was his throat with emotion.

"Sandler," Trevor said, looking down at the tattoo then back up to his face. "It's really you."

"It is. I'm here, Trev. I'm here."

Like a storm that sweeps in so suddenly its first raindrops glitter in sunshine, Trevor smiled widely and began to cry at the same moment. Sandler dropped back to his knees and threw his arms around him, and to his amazement felt Trevor's arms close around him as well. Across a separation of more than a decade, the lovers embraced as if they'd never left each other's side.

Trevor was finally able to catch his breath. "You came," he said simply.

"I never would have left you," Sandler replied, his tears flowing now too. "They wouldn't let me see you, and then they took you away. I thought you were... I thought you were dead."

"I felt like I was," Trevor said, then fell to crying against Sandler's shoulder. "And then today some guy shows up pretending to be Randy from the forensics team, and then he brings you. I didn't know what to think. I thought it was a trap."

"A trap?" Sandler asked.

Trevor nodded. "She's done it before. For a while she brought in every girl I ever knew—or at least girls who said they knew me, but I could never be sure. Things were blurry for a few years after the accident. Then she got more desperate and would try to trick me into thinking you were dead, or were a criminal or something. Eventually I got into the habit of just closing down when someone new shows up. Especially someone like Randy. He was one of the only straight people who knew about us. I knew he wouldn't be talking to me about his annoying sister."

"You told Randy Filkins about us?"

"I didn't do it on purpose. I called you from the bus once on the way back from a forensics competition, and he just wouldn't let it go. He was cool about it and never told anyone. But then when someone showed up claiming to be him and telling me that you were here and that you were going to get me out of here... well, I figured she was trying one of her tricks. Like she wanted to make me do something crazy so she would feel justified in sending me to that clinic tomorrow. So I did the only thing that seems to work when she tries to trick me—I just shut down and pretend I'm somewhere else. That's the only way to make them give up. Until you showed me that tattoo. It's right where I told you to put it. You are the only person who would know about that. That's when I knew it was you."

Sandler looked at him, marveling at how strong and alive he suddenly seemed. "The part of Randy Filkins was played by Gabriel Donnelly, who's about the best guy you're ever likely to meet. He says your mom told him she'd upped your dosage of meds tonight to keep you calm for tomorrow. It looked like she'd practically drugged you into a coma."

Trevor smiled. "Here's why it didn't work," he said and reached under the blanket. He pulled out two small tablets and showed them to Sandler.

"Is that... the medication your mom gave you?"

Trevor nodded. "I wanted to be clear in case you really were able to come back."

"You wanted to be clear? What does that mean?"

Trevor sighed. "I know she's been drugging me. She thinks I don't notice that the dosage goes up every time I mention you."

"How long has she been doing this?"

"For a few years," Trevor answered, looking down at the blanket where his hands had fallen still. "At first, right after the accident, I didn't know what she was doing. But as I got stronger, I noticed that how much I recovered depended on her mood. If I said something that upset her, I suddenly had trouble sitting up—or keeping food down."

"Have you talked to anyone about this? Any of your doctors? She shouldn't be doing this to you."

"I tried. But because she has some legal paperwork making her my custodian, they won't talk with me about it. And anyone who tried to do something about it ended up getting removed from my case. The last one they ended up fighting in court. That was when I knew no one would ever help me, and I… I just kind of gave up."

"I'm here now," Sandler said, his definite tone leaving no room for doubt. "We are going to get you out of here, and you will never be under her control again. I will never leave your side."

Trevor brought his hands up to Sandler's face and cradled his jaw in his hands. "I had given up on ever being able to do this again," he whispered. He leaned forward and kissed Sandler.

Sandler felt the years fall away, and they were right back on his aunt's sofa, feeling the heady rush of first love. He ran his fingers across Trevor's face, remembering every feature—though his sharp cheekbones and angular chin had softened a little with the decade that had passed, it was terrain he knew well. They sat and smiled stupidly at each other for a long while.

"Your friends think we're insane," Trevor murmured, looking over Sandler's shoulder. Sandler turned around to see Donnelly and Kerry standing by the connecting door, arms around each other, tears running down both their faces.

"Gabriel, Kerry, I'd like you to meet Trevor. The only man I've ever loved."

The two rushed across the room to cheer the reunited couple. There were hugs all around.

Finally, it fell to Donnelly to get the group back on track. "If we're going to get you out of here, we need to move now," he said. "Trevor, I found a bag your mom packed for you. Do you think it has everything you need in it?"

Trevor nodded. "I don't have much. She keeps me in pajamas all the time so I couldn't get very far if I did try to escape."

Donnelly turned to Kerry. "What did you find in terms of meds?"

"It's like a pharmacy in there," she said, shaking her head. "Lots of stuff that shouldn't be taken together, plus some stuff that you can't get in the US anymore. All of it is psychotropic, though. There's nothing for physical issues at all, at least as far as the meds go."

Sandler's ears pricked up at this. "What does that mean, 'at least as far as the meds go'?"

Kerry paused for a moment, and Trevor answered for her.

"She means she found my wheelchair." Trevor turned to Sandler. "I can't walk, Sandler."

Sandler sat back in shock. He felt as though his stomach were going to lurch up into his throat. "I… I am so sorry." He sucked in a deep breath, but all that came back out were great coughing sobs. "I am so sorry I did that to you." He broke down completely.

Trevor put his arms around Sandler and pulled him close. "It wasn't your fault. I don't blame you—no one would. This just… happens sometimes."

Sandler continued inconsolably sobbing.

Donnelly, who knew a thing or two about paralysis from his friend Will, asked, "Trevor, are you paralyzed, or do you have some function in your legs?"

"It was a sacral injury, but an incomplete one. I was in physical therapy for a while, and I was making progress, but then Mom got paranoid that I was developing a crush on my therapist, so she wouldn't take me anymore."

"Good God, these people," Kerry fumed. "What parent would do that?"

"One who wants to be sure her sexually defective son doesn't ever escape," Trevor said bitterly. "She never had to worry that I'd run away if she kept my wheelchair under lock and key." One look at Sandler and his face softened. "She wouldn't let me walk if the only place I wanted to walk to was back to you."

Trevor's words jostled Sandler out of his guilt-ridden fugue state. He wiped his eyes, slapped his cheeks a couple of times, and shook his head to clear it. "We're done," he said, the resolve back in his voice. "We're getting you out of here."

"I'll have them bring the car around," Kerry said, bolting for the door.

"I'll grab Trevor's bag and meet you down there," Donnelly called, racing through the doorway to the Hendrickses' room. He returned seconds later, pushing a wheelchair in front of him, a duffel bag sitting on the seat. "Ready to roll." He shoved the wheelchair in Sandler's direction and shouldered the duffel. "Trevor, is there anything else you need me to grab?"

"I don't need anything from this place, now that I have him," Trevor said. Then he turned to Sandler and stuck his tongue out. "That sounded a little sappy."

"I love it. Now let's get you into this chair and get the hell out of here."

"Do you need help?" Donnelly asked, already halfway out the door.

"I think I can handle this guy myself," Sandler replied with a grin.

As Donnelly disappeared into the hallway, Trevor threw off his blanket, revealing a lightly built body clad in gray sweatpants and a thermal shirt.

"Grab on to me," Sandler said, leaning down to Trevor. He scooped one arm behind his knees and one under his buttocks. Once Trevor's arms were around his neck, he lifted, amazed at how light Trevor was. "We need to get you into the gym."

"That's obviously the worst part about being held prisoner—you can't reach your fitness goals."

Sandler pivoted slowly and set Trevor gently into the seat of the wheelchair. "Prepare to breathe the sweet air of freedom, buddy."

"Wait," Trevor said as Sandler began to wheel him toward the door. "I should leave a note."

Sandler swallowed what he wanted to say—something along the lines of his parents not deserving any explanation at all—and grabbed up a pen and notepaper from next to the telephone. These he handed to Trevor, and stood back to let him write.

It took no more than thirty seconds for Trevor to write a few lines, fold the paper over, write "Mom and Dad" on it, and set it on the bed. He settled back into the chair and nodded to Sandler. "Good to go," he said.

Sandler rushed at the chair and shoved it toward the door once again. In a blur they were out the door, down the hallway, and into the elevator.

As they descended, Trevor looked up at Sandler. "Look at me, rescued by a knight in shining armor," he said with a wink.

"I don't do this for no damsels," Sandler replied, sounding like a Knight of the Jersey Shore. "Youse gonna put out, or what?"

"Oh hell yeah. I've got *years* to make up for," Trevor said with a giddy grin.

They were sharing a kiss when the elevator doors opened onto the lobby, which even at this hour was alive with activity. There were guests, and bellhops, and—

Mr. and Mrs. Hendricks.

"MR. AND Mrs. Hendricks?"

They turned away as the elevator doors opened, clearly startled to be called by name in a hotel lobby so far from home.

Brandt smiled diplomatically. "I'm so sorry to intrude on your evening," he said, drawing them away from the elevator, "but there's a matter of some importance that I must discuss with you."

"I don't understand," Mrs. Hendricks objected. "What is this about? Who are you?"

"I'll explain in a moment," Brandt said. "I'd like to introduce you to Dr. Schwegler, the director of the clinic—the clinic at which you have an appointment with your son tomorrow? He would like to speak with you about Dr. Rauthmann."

The mention of the doctor's name got the attention of both of Trevor's parents. The exchanged a look, but followed Brandt as he led them toward a group of chairs where Schwegler awaited their arrival.

At the edge of his vision, Brandt could see Sandler rushing to the exit… pushing a wheelchair? He knew when Kerry and Donnelly had sped through that things were reaching a critical stage, but clearly their plan had dissolved into madcap improvisation.

Brandt hated improvisation.

He turned back to the task at hand. "Dr. Schwegler, this is Mr. and Mrs. Hendricks."

Schwegler stood. "Pleased to meet you, Mr. Hendricks, Mrs. Hendricks," Schwegler said, shaking the hand of each in turn.

They nodded politely, but their expressions remained bemused.

"Is it your habit, Dr. Schwegler, to seek out patients the night before they are admitted to the clinic?" Mrs. Hendricks asked. Her graceful words carried an unmistakable accusation.

"Not at all, Mrs. Hendricks," Schwegler replied soothingly. "Please, sit, so that we may have a quiet discussion on the subject of your son's upcoming treatment." He gestured to the chairs next to the one in which he'd been sitting, and the Hendrickses reluctantly followed his lead and sat.

Brandt remained standing.

"Is she on her way?" Schwegler asked him.

"Yes, she should be here any minute," Brandt replied, looking toward the street doors of the hotel.

As if on cue, the doors were hauled open by the doorman and Kerry swept into the lobby, looking pink and flushed after having gotten Sandler and Trevor securely away in a town car. She hurried over to Brandt, tucking her hair behind her ear.

"Dr. Schwegler, this is Kerry Mercer."

Schwegler stood again, and extended his hand. "Ms. Mercer, thank you for joining us."

"If I can be of help, I'm glad to be here," she said. She and Brandt took chairs opposite the Hendrickses.

"This is all very strange, Doctor," Mrs. Hendricks said. "If you think we're going to discuss the care of our son in a hotel lobby with strangers—"

"You should know, Mrs. Hendricks," Schwegler broke in gently, "that I spoke with Dr. Rauthmann this afternoon, and I have some concerns."

"Concerns?" Mr. Hendricks demanded. "What kind of concerns?"

"I question whether his protocol is of any credible therapeutic value."

Mrs. Hendricks made a noise that established her offense at this remark to all within earshot. "Are you insinuating that we don't have the best interests of our son foremost in our minds?"

"Not at all," Schwegler replied, using a voice that had doubtless dissuaded numerous psychopaths from attempting rash action. "But I would be remiss in my duties as director of the clinic—as a doctor—were I to let you proceed without all of the facts."

"I believe we have all the facts we need," Mr. Hendricks said dismissively. "We didn't fly to Geneva on a whim."

"There is no doubt in my mind that you intend the best for your son," Dr. Schwegler replied, his voice calm and even. "But when we grow desperate for a particular outcome, we may become willing to take greater risk than is reasonable." As Mrs. Hendricks drew breath to take issue with Schwegler's characterization, he cut her short by turning to Kerry. "Ms. Mercer is a chemist employed by the firm that makes the drug Dr. Rauthmann uses in his protocol. She happened to be in Geneva this week on another matter, and agreed to consult with me on this case."

This unexpected turn left the Hendrickses glancing blankly at each other.

"Ms. Mercer, would you summarize your concerns for Mr. and Mrs. Hendricks?"

"I would be happy to." She turned her smile up to full clinical strength, and trained it on the Hendrickses. "Mr. and Mrs. Hendricks, the protocol Dr. Rauthmann uses has been studied by my company, and we have found that it poses a significant risk to the patient who receives it. We have repeatedly demanded that Dr. Rauthmann cease offering the treatment, but he has so far refused. We expect to have a court order within the month to force him to stop using our drug this way."

Mrs. Hendricks fixed her with a fearsome glare. "We are aware that Dr. Rauthmann's treatment is controversial. But we have studied every possible avenue for our son, and we believe that he is our only hope."

"Mrs. Hendricks, I know you want to do the right thing for your son—"

"You don't know anything about my son," Mrs. Hendricks interrupted in high dudgeon. "And I don't have to justify the decisions we've made in his best interest, not to you, not to anyone. My son is a very ill young man, and I will do anything— *anything*—to make him healthy and strong again."

"I was unaware that you were seeking Dr. Rauthmann's care for a physical condition," Schwegler said. "From talking with Dr. Rauthmann, it seemed your son's condition was psychiatric."

"I may not have a medical degree, but I am the world's authority on the well-being of my son," Mrs. Hendricks announced. "Only when he is freed from the defective impulses that haunt him can he ever be physically strong again." She drew herself up with an adamantine certainty. "And I will not listen to anyone tell me I don't know what's best for my son."

"Mrs. Hendricks," Kerry said gently, "we are trying to help you help your son."

"You are doing nothing of the kind if you're telling me that our last hope—our last hope in the entire world—doesn't fit your politically correct view."

"Politically correct view? Who said anything about politically correct views?"

"I know how you people are. You find out that someone is using your drug to help people recover from homosexuality, and you just have to shut it down. As if you know best for the entire world. Well, some people don't think having a son with those... defects... is what's best."

"Now wait a minute," Kerry said, her voice rising. "The people treated by Dr. Rauthmann are in no way better off afterward. In fact, a number of them have committed—"

She was interrupted by Schwegler standing and clearing his throat loudly. Brandt's instincts kicked in and he turned to follow Schwegler's sight line. He saw a somewhat harried man in a suit walking toward them. Schwegler extended his hand as the man approached.

"Doctor Rauthmann, I believe you know the Hendrickses. This is Mr. Brandt, and this—"

"We have met," Rauthmann broke in to finish the introduction. He bowed courteously to Kerry, but his eyes flicked from side to side, as if his brain was working feverishly to work out what had brought together this particular configuration of people.

Brandt noticed that every bit of color seemed to have left Kerry's face in an instant.

Schwegler sat, and gestured for Rauthmann to join the group, but Rauthmann stood imperiously erect. "Dr. Schwegler," he said, his voice courtly, "I do hope you have not convened this group for the purpose of dissuading patients, both current"—he nodded toward the Hendrickses—"and prospective"—a nod to Kerry—"from seeking my care?"

"Not at all, Dr. Rauthmann," Schwegler replied, with commensurate dignity. "I simply seek more information, both for myself and for your patients. Surely you can have no objection to that."

"I do object to you asking me to meet you here, and then finding that you have assembled what appears to be a tribunal."

Without warning, Brandt erupted into a coughing fit, bolted to his feet and grabbed Kerry's hand. He gestured frantically, pleading for her assistance. She jumped up and made a show of guiding him away from the group. They walked around a corner and out of sight before Brandt stopped his fake coughing.

"Are you okay?" she asked. "There's gotta be a drinking fountain or something around here—"

"I'm fine," Brandt cut her off brusquely. "What the hell was that? Rauthmann referred to you as a 'prospective patient'?"

The fire returned to Kerry's cheeks, and she looked down as if hoping to find the answer to Brandt's question woven into the sumptuous rugs of the hotel lobby. "We kind of went off-script," she said meekly.

"Off-script? How far off?"

"As we were walking over to the clinic, we decided that we'd be able to get better intelligence from him if we pretended to need his services."

Brandt blinked in disbelief. "You were supposed to approach him as a colleague, and try to get his agreement to stop using the drug. That's it."

"We weren't sure he would even talk to me if he knew who I worked for. And we wanted to be sure he didn't lie or gloss over the true intent of the therapy. We had to be sure, Ethan."

"And so to keep him from lying to you, you lied to him?"

"To be fair, we both did."

"Wait—let me guess. Sandler pretended to be a closet case looking for a pharmaceutical escape, didn't he?"

"Exactly right. See, you understand what we were doing."

"I understand it. I just don't share your opinion that it was a good idea. Look, we know that Gabriel needed to lie to the Hendrickses—it was the only way to get close to them. But the rest of us were supposed to go in as ourselves and try to help."

"We just thought it would work better this way," Kerry said, a little lamely.

"And that's why you failed to mention this change of strategy at lunch today, when you reported the info that you got from talking to Rauthmann?"

Kerry took an exasperated breath. "We lied. We lied to that dick of a doctor so we could save Sandler's friend. So what? What difference does it make?"

"The difference it makes may be the difference between getting a conviction and not getting a conviction. Evidence gathered under false pretenses is tainted!"

"Evidence? Conviction?" She stared at him, her expression puzzled. "You're talking like this is a police investigation. That's not what we're doing. We're just trying to keep Trevor from getting his brain fried by Dr. Jekyll out there."

"No, what we're doing is trying not to fuck up the legal case your company has working against him, because if something we do gets in the way of that, then a lot more Trevors are going to get hurt. Did you think of that? Did you?"

She fell silent, and chewed on the corner of her mouth as if trying to decide whether to come back swinging or let him win the point. "I get what you're saying. I'm sorry we didn't tell you at lunch what we'd done, but we thought it would just add pointless drama to the whole thing. But, honest to God, Ethan, all we wanted to do was save Trevor. He deserves to have someone on his side for once. And we thought we'd have the best shot at helping him if we went in with a story."

Ethan sighed. "But what we have now is a situation where Schwegler thinks you're a reputable chemist and an expert on that stupid drug, while Rauthmann thinks you're someone so unhinged that she's ready to drug her gay boyfriend into being straight."

"Husband," she said.

"Husband? You two got married along the way? Nice."

"Sorry. It seemed to add the right note of pathos."

He shook his head and pinched the bridge of his nose. "I don't know how to pull out of this, Kerry. We can't go back out there. No one would ever believe you now."

"You're right, Mr. Brandt." It was Schwegler, with Rauthmann standing by his side. "I have some questions about your veracity as well that I'd very much like some answers to. And I'd appreciate the truth this time."

Brandt, backed onto a ledge and needing to decide whether to jump or fight, did what he always did. He fought. "I'm sure this looks unusual, Doctor, but I can explain. Why don't we go back to the Hendrickses and we can all talk this over honestly and—"

"The Hendrickses are gone," Rauthmann said, with a slight smile. "They went to make sure their son gets a good rest before his procedure tomorrow. They didn't seem particularly interested in what you have to say."

Brandt took a moment to consider the many and varied ways in which this little adventure had gone off the rails. He had lost the goodwill of Dr. Schwegler, Kerry's hijinks had apparently steeled the resolve of Dr. Rauthmann to neuter more gay youths, and in a matter of seconds the Hendrickses would discover that their son had disappeared, embroiling them all in what probably looked like a kidnapping. At least he had the consolation that there was nothing left to go wrong.

The appearance of four police officers rushing toward the elevator proved this an optimistic assessment.

CHAPTER SEVENTEEN

Thursday
Just after midnight, Hôtel Genève

SEVERAL HOURS later, Brandt and Kerry returned to the suite. They found Donnelly in the parlor, not watching the television. He switched it off and ran to Brandt as soon as the door opened. They embraced for a long moment.

"Where are they?" Brandt asked, still holding tight to Donnelly.

"In the smaller bedroom." He looked at Kerry apologetically. "We hoped you wouldn't mind sleeping on the couch here. I had housekeeping make it up for you."

"Surrounded by reunited lovers on both sides? If I can make it through the night without jumping from the balcony, I'm sure I'll be perfectly comfortable." She winked at Donnelly to show she was teasing. Mostly.

"How's Trevor doing?" Brandt asked, back to business.

"Much better now. Sandler really jarred him loose—all of a sudden, he's happy and talking and... well, aside from the being held prisoner by his own parents for more than a decade, he seems just fine. If I hadn't seen him myself earlier today, I would never believe that he'd been basically comatose before Sandler showed up."

"That's terrific," Brandt replied. "That's really great news."

"How'd it go with Schwegler and the Hendrickses?"

"That's the bad news."

Donnelly froze. "Oh, shit." He took a deep breath. "What's the damage?"

"It's kind of a cluster. Can you bring Sandler and Trevor out here? We need to have everyone on this."

Donnelly nodded, then walked over and knocked on the door to the bedroom.

"We're busy" came Sandler's joyful voice from inside.

"We need you guys out here. Ethan and Kerry are back, and we have to talk about where we go from here."

"Give us a sec," Sandler replied.

Donnelly walked back to where Brandt stood looking out the window into the night, and put his arms around him from behind. "How bad is it?" he whispered.

"It's bad," Brandt replied in a low murmur.

"Good thing we've got the brains and brawn on our side," Donnelly said, then kissed him on the neck.

"I don't think it's going to be enough. Not this time."

Donnelly tightened his grip, and Brandt could almost feel his confidence flowing through his embracing arms. But in that same moment he felt himself keenly unworthy of Donnelly's optimism.

"We'll find a way," Donnelly said, his voice serene.

Brandt took in those words like a breath of incense, and felt himself calmed despite the storm they were sailing into. He could only nod, and hope that Donnelly was right.

"Ethan Brandt, I'd like you to meet Trevor Hendricks," Sandler called as he wheeled Trevor out of the bedroom.

Brandt turned, wearing the smile he used whenever he had little to smile about. It generally won people over. "I am thrilled to meet you, Trevor," he said, extending his hand to take Trevor's more delicate one in his.

"I can't tell you how much I appreciate you—all of you—taking all this trouble to help me." Trevor beamed at the entire group. "I'd forgotten what it feels like to be happy."

Sandler bent down and threw his arms around Trevor, and the two kissed.

Donnelly cast a look at Brandt. It said all he needed to hear without a single word. They would have to find a way.

"All right, I need to bring everyone up to speed on where we are," Brandt announced. "Dr. Schwegler agreed to meet me in the lobby, and I was able to grab the Hendrickses as they were on their way to the elevator."

"Thanks for that, by the way," Sandler said. "When the doors opened and they were standing there, I didn't know whether to scream or pee. It was not my finest moment."

"You did a great job, both of you," Brandt said. "Once Kerry returned from getting you into the getaway car, I introduced her to the Hendrickses and to Schwegler, and she started telling them about Rauthmann's treatment. They were having none of it, as you might imagine, though I think she was starting to make some progress with them. Then Rauthmann himself showed up."

Sandler, Donnelly, and Trevor gasped in unison.

"Yeah, so that happened. I faked a coughing fit and pulled Kerry aside, but while we were trying to figure out what to do the good doctors must have compared notes about the various identities of our Ms. Mercer here, and they came and found us strategizing behind a row of potted ficuses."

There were groans from the room.

"But wait, friends, it gets worse," Brandt continued. "I told them we'd like to explain the whole thing to them and the Hendrickses, but Rauthmann told us they'd already gone upstairs."

Sandler reached over the arm of the wheelchair and laced his fingers into Trevor's.

"It was about then that the lobby filled with"—he turned to Kerry—"what was your charming term for them?"

"Members of the *gendarmerie*," Kerry replied with a wince.

"Right. A lovely way of saying that the lobby was awash in serious people in uniforms responding to reports of a kidnapping. Of which, by the way, they take a very dim view here."

"Please tell me this is where you and Kerry took advantage of the confusion and slipped out the service entrance," Donnelly said, his voice not terribly hopeful. "Please?"

Brandt scowled. "No, Officer Donnelly, this is where we sought out the head of the police contingent and let her know we had material information regarding the alleged kidnapping."

"Can we not call it that?" Sandler interjected. "How about liberation?" At Brandt's glare he fell silent.

"Any other suggestions for how we could have made an even greater mockery of a police investigation?" He looked around the room, expecting to see none, and he didn't. "Thank you. We sat down with the chief inspector, and explained to her the circumstances under which Trevor came to be somewhere other than where his parents had left him. I focused on his being an adult fully capable of making his own decisions about his care, and I think I almost had her convinced to take a big step back and calm things down."

"Almost?" Donnelly asked.

Brandt sighed. "It's not an easy story to unspool in a hotel lobby crowded with police and shocked passersby. But I was getting there, I'm sure of it, when the Hendrickses showed up. Good God, the screaming was bone-rattling."

"Dad's got some lungs on him," Trevor muttered.

"True story," Brandt replied with a rueful shake of his head. "Anyway, they were clearly distraught, and I think we might still have gotten everything calmed down if your mother hadn't started waving around the note she found in the hotel room and screaming about how you were incapable of making your own decisions and had clearly fallen into the clutches of nefarious manipulators with a homosexual agenda."

Trevor dropped his chin to his chest. "That's a direct quotation, isn't it?" he asked dismally.

"The directest. Though she delivered it two octaves higher and about thirty decibels louder. She was... unhinged."

Trevor looked up at this. "Good."

Brandt look at him, uncomprehending.

"I'm glad. She deserves to be unhinged for what she's done. To me and to Sandler."

"I agree with you," Brandt said, "in principle. The reality of it, though, is that she can cause a great deal of trouble for you. And what you wrote in the note didn't really help things much."

Sandler jostled Trevor's arm. "What did you write?"

"May I?" Brandt asked. "After all, your mother repeated it so many times I think everyone within her considerable blast radius has it memorized."

Trevor nodded, grinning slyly.

"It said, 'I didn't choose to be gay, but I chose Sandler. And he chose me.'"

"Aww," intoned Kerry, looking at them with a sappy expression.

"That's so sweet," Sandler added, kissing Trevor's hand.

"Yes, but it was pretty much the last straw in terms of your mom's tenuous grasp on sanity. When she started actually whacking people with her rolled-up power of attorney I knew we needed to get things back on a more productive footing."

"That's when he dropped the bomb," Kerry said, pride in her voice.

"What?" Donnelly asked. "What did you do?"

Brandt shrugged modestly. "I simply suggested that a power of attorney drafted in the United States is not likely to be compliant with the European Union's Declaration of Human Rights, much less Switzerland's even stronger protections."

"Nice move," Donnelly said. "But how would they be able to determine that? Wouldn't they need to have it reviewed by a judge or something?"

"Right you are." Brandt turned to Trevor and Sandler. "We have a court date the day after—" He stopped to look at his watch. "Actually, now that it's after midnight, it's tomorrow. Anyway, we'll be expected to show up in court with Trevor and explain why he should be free of his parents' conservatorship."

"And they're going to let him stay with us until then?" Sandler asked, eyes wide.

"Well, since they don't know where to find him…." Brandt said, looking casually at the artful crown molding high on the wall.

Donnelly threw himself at Brandt, and with a giddy "I fucking love you!" tackled him and knocked him backward over the arm of the sofa. They sprawled on the bed that had been pulled out for Kerry. Between kisses, he managed to say, "You didn't tell them." More kisses. "You didn't tell them where he is!"

When Brandt was finally able to extricate himself from Donnelly's effusive affection, he straightened his shirt (Donnelly had tugged on it rather vigorously) and stood again. "With that undignified display concluded…."

"Sorry, I just can't believe you were willing to lie to them to keep the Hendrickses from finding out where Trevor is," Donnelly interrupted.

"I didn't *lie*," Brandt replied. "I just kept them from asking the question of where he is by pointing out that until the hearing he should be presumed to be in control of his own life."

"And just like that they were willing to set aside his parents' power of attorney?"

"Not exactly. That's where Ms. Mercer stepped in to seal the deal." He looked to Kerry to pick up the story.

"All I did was move the conversation along toward the subject of antigay reparative therapy."

"All she did," Brandt added, "was whip Mrs. Hendricks into a frenzy of homophobic ranting. Which the Swiss take a pretty dim view of." He smiled at Kerry. "She knew just where to stick the knife."

She laughed modestly. "I may have idly mentioned that I imagined Trevor's legs were probably getting more action than they'd seen in a long while, seeing as they were probably writhing against Sandler's shoulders."

"Wooo!" Sandler hooted. "That probably put her right over the edge."

"It probably would have," Brandt said, "but just to be sure, our demure Ms. Mercer drove the point home with a pantomime of frenzied pelvic thrusting."

"Sexy," growled Trevor. Then he dissolved into laughter with the rest of the group.

"Thank you, sir," Kerry replied, with a delicate curtsey. "Your mom launched into a five-minute highlight reel of every batshit conservative Internet rant about the homosexual agenda you've ever seen. It was epic. And by the end of it, the chief inspector was wiping Mama Hendricks's spittle off her uniform and backing away slowly. Her credibility was gone, and so was any chance that the police would start chasing y'all down for the abduction of someone who was clearly better off on his own."

"I hinted I might be able to find you two," Brandt continued, "and the chief inspector agreed not to start a manhunt if you contact her office in the morning. She gave me a hell of a look—like she figured if she searched the trunk of my car she'd probably find you hiding there—but there was no way she wanted to get Mrs. Hendricks any more wound up. So she let us slide."

"The fact that you flashed her your badge didn't hurt," Kerry added.

"Well played, both of you," called Sandler, clapping joyfully.

"You guys are awesome," Donnelly chimed in, kissed Brandt again and even laid one on each of Kerry's cheeks.

"We're not out of the woods yet," Brandt warned. "We still have that hearing tomorrow. We'll need to prepare for that."

"You mean *we*"—Sandler pointed to himself and Trevor—"will have to prepare for it. You three need to get to a little castle in Devon for someone's wedding."

"There's no way we're leaving you until we're sure you're safe," Donnelly said without hesitation. "Right, Ethan?"

"As I always say, the right thing and the legal thing are almost always the same. And that's the case here, since the chief inspector asked us not to leave Geneva until the hearing is concluded. She felt the judge might have some questions for us. So I gave her my word as a fellow officer. Plus," Brandt said, pulling Donnelly close to him again, "we won't leave until you're safe, Trevor."

"But you're getting married in two days!" Sandler objected.

"Plenty of time," Donnelly said. "I'll call the travel agent in the morning, and we'll work it out. We'll do the hearing, hop on a plane or train or whatever, and get married the next day. Easy."

Brandt slapped his palm to his forehead and closed his eyes. "You *know* better than to say that, Gabriel."

"C'mon, where's your spirit? Eventually something has to go as planned, right?"

Whitford Castle, Devon, England

"BUT THERE'S no one here," Bryce repeated for the third time, his voice rising to a register normally reserved for the bleachers of a wrestling tourney when a singlet malfunction exposes something unexpected.

"Well, you're here," the general manager of the property replied. "As if you'd let any of us forget it," she added under her breath.

"But the wedding is the day after tomorrow," Bryce continued, his panic unabated.

"Which you have pointed out every hour since the sun came up."

"But where are the grooms?"

"When they called, they said they were needed in Geneva for a day or two, and then they would come right here."

"But the rehearsal is tonight. Where are the guests?"

"As I believe I've explained twice already today, there's a volcano in Iceland that—"

"We are quite aware that some pile of rocks and lava in Iceland does not want our dear troopers to be wed," Bryce growled. "But I have never been one to let reality get in the way of the way things should be." He took a deep breath and patted his already perfect coiffure. "Now, I have no doubt that the grooms are making their way here as we speak, very likely fighting crime and saving puppies from burning buildings along the way. But in case they are delayed, we must make alternative plans for the rehearsal."

She looked up from her paperwork with a sigh. "What do you suggest?" There was a distinct lack of curiosity in her voice.

"I was thinking that we might recruit a couple of the locals to stand in for the happy couple. That way everyone else will be able to know their parts."

She drooped as if exhausted. "It's a wedding, love. The grooms will stand at the front. No one else has a part."

Bryce gasped as if he'd been cut from the cast in a last-minute rewrite before opening night. "I must ask to speak with the director."

The general manager's face lit up. "That's a terrific idea. Let me call the chapel director, and you can tell him all about your concerns, and your plans, and your hopes and dreams. Tell him all of that." She grabbed up the phone and stabbed at the buttons. "Arthur, I have some people here who absolutely need to see you. Yes, right away. It's *urgent*."

"There we are," Bryce sighed, satisfied. "I told you we'd get this all taken care of. Our distress will finally be lifted."

Nestor, who did not seem to have been laboring under anything like distress, smiled and patted Bryce's hand lovingly.

"No. No, no, no!" Bryce cried. "Cut! Cut!"

Arthur sighed deeply and rubbed his brow, as he had repeatedly over the last two hours. "We don't say 'cut' during a wedding rehearsal," he said. Again.

"But it's all wrong," Bryce protested.

"What, exactly, is all wrong?" Arthur asked, gesturing at the head of the aisle, where stood the two farm laborers Bryce had recruited to stand in for Brandt and Donnelly.

"They're not standing correctly."

Arthur threw his hands up and sat with a plop into a pew at the back of the chapel.

"Excuse me, sir," the farmhand playing Brandt said softly. "What's wrong with the way we're standing?"

"You don't look…," Bryce said, struggling to find words that these simple folk would understand. "You're not standing like you're in love."

The farmhands exchanged a look.

"That's it," Bryce cried. "That's what's wrong."

"What's wrong?" the one playing Donnelly asked.

"The kilts. They're all wrong."

Both farmhands looked down at their legs. They shrugged.

"Don't move," Bryce ordered, marching down the aisle. When he reached the dais at the front, he stood between the grooms, glanced from one to the other several times, then tipped his head to one side, then the other. "Yes, that's the problem." He fell to his knees. "Now, I'm a professional, so please don't move." Without warning, he thrust his hands up under the kilt of the Brandt stand-in and grasped the young man's underwear. With a quick flick of his limber wrists, he sent them flying down to his ankles. He turned and did the same to the other groom.

They stood at the front of the chapel with their boxers pooled around their ankles, unable to speak. Bryce stepped back and appraised their new look.

"Yes, that's much better," he said, nodding. "Now, if you would kick your knickers over to Nestor for safekeeping, we can get on with the show."

The grooms obediently stepped out of their underwear and handed them to Nestor, who spirited them away. They wouldn't be getting those back.

"Excellent," Bryce said. "That's the authentic look we were lacking. Oh, and one more thing. I happened to notice, during my momentary explorations a moment ago, that you"—he pointed to the Brandt stand-in—"were already getting into the spirit of true love. Now, if I know anything about wedding-induced boners—and I know *a lot*—I think that you are practicing something more than method acting when you look at your friend here."

The poor boy flushed bright red and studied the floor.

"Ah, yes." Bryce turned to the other farmhand. "Now you, were you aware that he felt this way? About you?"

The startled young man shook his head, the blood draining from his face.

"And yet earlier this evening, when I required you to put the kilts on, I noticed that once his pants came off, you couldn't tear your eyes away."

It was his turn to blush. They were now a matched set.

"Perfect," Bryce hooted, bouncing up and down, clapping. "Now, let's begin again."

Bryce took the position of the wedding officiant and began the vows once more. This time there were two blushing grooms shifting nervously in their kilts, the outline of something more sometimes visible as they did.

"Now, you may kiss," Bryce concluded happily, and watched as the two farmhands regarded each other warily, no more than a foot of distance between them.

"I said *now*."

They drew near one another, in kilts and in front of God and Bryce himself, they shared their first kiss.

Applause, from Bryce and Nestor and even Arthur, echoed through the chapel. It lasted almost as long as the kiss.

"If you two boys would like to further explore what you've begun here," Bryce said lightly, as if suggesting a glass of lemonade, "Nestor and I would be happy to host you. In our room."

The farmhands looked shyly at each other. "I think we'd like that," the Brandt stand-in murmured.

"Perhaps we would," the Donnelly stand-in agreed.

"Arthur, do you have plans for the evening?" Bryce called up the aisle.

Arthur laughed. "My days of breaking in farm labor are well behind me, Bryce. But you enjoy yourselves."

"We shall," Bryce assured him. "We shall."

Hôtel Genève

"I LOVE you more at this moment than I ever have before," Donnelly said, gazing over the coffee table in the sitting room, the light of the dawning sun warm on his face.

"You're just high on endorphins and caffeine," Brandt replied.

"For the caffeine I thank the good people of Guatemala," Donnelly said, holding his cup high. "And for the endorphins I thank you. You really ripped me up this morning."

"Ew, guys," Kerry said, sitting up in the fold-out bed where she'd spent the night. "I'm as big a fag hag as the next girl, but even I have limits."

"While you were busy holding down that pillow and snoring, we were down in the gym lifting. Some of us care how we look," Brandt replied, then took a sip of coffee. "Girl, please."

Donnelly's mouth dropped open. "Did my butch fiancé just throw shade?"

"I have no idea what you're talking about," Brandt said coolly. He turned back to looking out the window.

Donnelly thought he saw a flash of a smile, but it disappeared so quickly he couldn't be sure. He wondered when Brandt would cease to surprise him—he hoped that day would never come.

"Just so you know, he wasn't like this when you weren't around," Kerry said to Donnelly.

"Like what?"

"You know, fun." Kerry burst out laughing.

"Shut up about my fiancé," cried Donnelly, who picked up a throw pillow and threw it at Kerry's head. Several other pillows followed in kind, and the melee only wound down when an errant pillow threatened to upend the coffee tray.

Brandt seemed ready to scold them when the phone rang. "Yes?" he said into the receiver, then fell silent for a moment.

Donnelly watched his expression cloud as he listened. Whatever he was hearing through the phone had him concerned.

"Please, send him up." Brandt replaced the receiver, then looked over at Donnelly. "We have a visitor."

"Who?" Donnelly replied. "The only people we know in Geneva are chief inspectors, doctors of questionable ethics, and homophobic psychopaths."

"And, apparently, someone from the embassy."

"The US Embassy sent someone? Holy shit, what for?"

"Not the US Embassy. The British."

"The British Embassy? I don't understand."

"I don't either, and the front desk seemed just as confused. She said a man got out of a diplomatic car with union jacks waving on the fenders and asked for our room. Actually, he asked for Sandler's room. And... yours."

Donnelly was trying to figure out how to respond when there was a knock at the door.

"Since he asked for you, it's probably most appropriate for you to answer," Brandt said.

"Can you hang on a sec, chief?" Kerry asked, leaping up from the fold-out sofa. In a ninja-like blur of motion, she tied a robe around her waist, threw the bed linens into rough order, folded the bed back into the sofa, and arranged the pillows on top. It took her no more than twelve seconds. "I call first shower," she said lightly as she walked past them and into their bedroom.

"If I'm perfectly honest, she terrifies me," Donnelly said as she closed the bedroom door behind her.

"Me too," Brandt said with a good-natured shudder.

Donnelly went to the door and laid his hand on the knob. He paused and looked back at Brandt.

"Well, open it," Brandt said. "That could be Prince Charming on the other side!"

Donnelly rolled his eyes and pulled the door open.

It was Imre.

"Gabriel," he cried, his refined diplomatic accent paired with a delighted inflection.

"Imre?" Donnelly replied, staggered. "Imre, come in, come in." He held the door open for the diplomat to enter.

"Thank you." Imre strode elegantly into the room, embraced Donnelly, and planted a kiss on each cheek. "It's only been a couple of days—how can you possibly have gotten younger and better looking?"

"Stop it, you," Donnelly said, blushing.

"Ah, unless I miss my guess, *this* is how," Imre said, walking over to Brandt. "You must be Gabriel's fiancé." He extended his hand, which Brandt took—but not before shooting Donnelly a look that asked some uncomfortable questions. "I am sorry to call so early, but although Birkin's message afforded me precious little in the way of detail, it did ask me to make all possible haste. I came right from the train station. I hope I didn't wake you."

"No, not at all," Donnelly replied, trying to regain his balance. "Imre Romanov, this is Ethan Brandt. Ethan, I met Imre on the ship when Sandler's diplomatic pouch went missing. Imre's the one who found it."

"I'm the one who stole it, he means," Imre told Brandt.

Brandt's raised eyebrows conveyed that the questions in his head had multiplied.

"Well, technically, because Imre is officially attached to the mission originating the pouch, it wasn't a violation of the Vienna Convention," Donnelly said helpfully. "Plus it was sort of meant for him anyway, so all he really did was receive it early. Technically."

"Thanks for that... clarification," Brandt said slowly, still taking the measure of the diplomat who had burst into their midst.

"Imre, can I pour you some coffee?" Donnelly offered.

"That would be lovely, thank you."

"Here you go," Donnelly said, handing Imre a cup. "Now, I'll go let Sandler know you're here. I'm sure he'll want to untangle himself and come right in to see you."

"Oh, is he still carrying on with that waiter?" Imre asked with a laugh. "That's a level of service the cruise line should include in their advertising."

"Actually, Ankur's probably on his way home to India right now, so he can marry the nice girl his parents have chosen for him. He was quite looking forward to that."

"Well, how… versatile he turned out to be," Imre replied with a smile.

"There seems to have been quite a cast of characters on this ship," Brandt observed blandly. "I wonder if I've heard about all of them now."

"I don't know… have I mentioned Fabienne?" Donnelly asked as he bustled past on his way to roust Sandler.

"I don't think so," Brandt said.

"Oh, you would remember Fabienne," Imre added, laughing.

This did not seem to reassure Brandt.

Donnelly knocked on the door to the smaller bedroom. "Sandler?" There was no response. He knocked more firmly. "Sandler? Trevor?"

There was inchoate mumbling from within. Donnelly looked back at Imre and Brandt. "I'm going in," he said bravely. He pushed open the door and slipped into the dark room. "Sandler? Imre's here."

In the light filtering through the drawn curtains Donnelly could see Sandler sit up in bed.

"He's here? Already?"

"He said he came straight from the train station."

"I only called him last night when Brandt told us about the hearing tomorrow. He must have dashed out the door as soon as we hung up."

"It seems like he really wants to help."

"It seems like we could really use the help," Sandler said, throwing back the covers.

"Hey" came a plaintive voice from the other side of the bed. "It's cold."

"Sorry, love," Sandler said, leaning over to kiss Trevor. "Do you want me to tuck you in nice and tight?"

"That I can do. Getting you to take your loud conversation outside so I can get back to sleep? Now that's something I need help with." He grabbed the covers and rolled over, cocooning himself in the downy duvet.

"Sorry, I guess he's a little crabby in the mornings," Sandler said with a chuckle. "His mom used to get him up every morning before dawn for a nice cold enema."

"And thank you for sharing that with everyone," Trevor said from under the covers.

"Awkward disclosures are part of the boyfriend experience, Trev," Sandler replied as he got up. From somewhere under the covers a pillow sailed at his head, glancing off and landing on the floor.

"I'll tell Imre you're on your way," Donnelly said, looking away from Sandler's naked silhouette.

"No, hang on a minute. How did Imre seem? He told me to get in touch if I ever needed him, but I feel like I asked him for a huge favor right away." Sandler walked past Donnelly on his way to the bathroom. He switched on the light and stood before the toilet, the door wide open.

Standing just outside the bathroom, Donnelly focused on Sandler's face in the mirror, but the memory of Sandler's sweat-glossed body thrusting powerfully into Ankur on the balcony of the ship flooded his consciousness. He was growing erect before he could even answer Sandler's question. "He seemed happy to be here, actually," Donnelly said, raising his voice to be heard over the waterfall Sandler was making. "I think he'll be glad to help out."

"That's awesome," Sandler replied, the muscles in his arm flexing into view as he vigorously shook something just out of Donnelly's range of sight. He walked over to the sink to wash his hands, and to splash some water on his face.

This, of course, gave Donnelly the reverse view, which aroused memories similar to the ones occasioned by seeing the front. He cleared his throat. "Are you going to get dressed before you go out there? I'm not sure this is what Imre came to see."

Sandler smiled as he dried his face. "You don't think he'd be even more willing to help if I met him like this?" he teased.

"Let's try to maintain at least a semblance of decorum, please?" Donnelly said, though Sandler's infectious good mood was making him smile. "I'll go tell him you'll be right out."

"Thanks," Sandler said, and then he padded across the room to sort out his clothes.

Donnelly stepped back out into the sitting room, where he found Brandt and Imre standing before the window, talking.

"And then he told me that he used to be straight, which I had honestly never heard of happening before. But now, meeting you, I'd have to guess that he's not the only one."

Brandt laughed. "We are each other's first and only," he said, smiling at Donnelly as he approached.

"I leave you alone for two minutes," Donnelly groused. "Honestly."

"I simply asked how you and Imre met," Brandt replied, holding up his hands innocently. "Turns out there was quite a tale of intrigue there."

"Don't worry," Imre leaned toward Donnelly and stage-whispered, "I didn't tell him about the kiss."

"Kiss?" Brandt asked, eyebrow up.

Donnelly sighed. "Sandler had this crackpot scheme for me to get close to Imre and find out if he knew anything about the missing pouch."

"And he acquitted himself quite well, I must say," Imre added. "But he made it clear nothing more was to follow that one kiss… that one magical kiss… under the stars, on a balcony overlooking the sea."

Donnelly could feel the heat rising in his cheeks.

"That's my boy," Brandt said with a proud grin. "Those lips could kiss secrets out of a marble statue."

Donnelly beamed at the man he loved more than anything in the world.

"Now, where is Birkin? I am intrigued beyond reason by this thicket he seems to have waded into."

"He'll be out in a minute," Donnelly replied. "It's all a bit convoluted, but the short version is that his first love was being held captive by his homophobic parents, who nursed him back to health after a car accident but now seem determined to drug him into being heterosexual. So, with his consent, we abducted him. He's here with Sandler now."

"Oh. My," Imre said, frowning over this précis. "Birkin's message hardly hinted at anything quite so dramatic—he mentioned only a court hearing. You do seem to stumble into the odd improbable muddle, don't you?"

Donnelly and Brandt raised their coffee cups to each other in silent salute to the messes they kept stepping into.

The bedroom door swung open, and Sandler hurried into the room. "Imre, you are so good to come." He held out his hand, but Imre set his coffee cup down and they embraced instead.

"After what happened on the ship, it is the very least I could do. Donnelly has given me a hair-raising hint of what you're going through. I have, as you might imagine, some questions."

"I'm sure you do," Sandler replied. "Why don't we order in some breakfast, and we can all sit down together and get this sorted?"

"Get more bacon this time!" came Kerry's voice from the other bedroom. The door flew open, and Kerry swept into the room, having accomplished her now customary roll-out-of-bed-and-look-fabulous routine. "Morning, love." She danced over to Brandt and laid a smooch on his cheek. "And good morning to you." She kissed Donnelly on the cheek and then squeezed his biceps. "Rawrrr!" she growled, winking at him.

Imre's eyebrows shot up. "So we're still a little bit straight, are we?" he asked the troopers as he and Sandler settled onto the sofa.

"Oh honey, ain't no one straight around this girl." She smiled at him as she poured herself some coffee. "And good morning to you, sweetie," she cried, making her way over to Sandler. "How's our boy? Did he sleep well?" She laid a kiss on his cheek as well.

"He's exhausted. He woke up screaming three times, which according to the Google search I did at two in the morning when he did it the first time, is actually pretty good for someone who's just been freed from captivity. The rest of the night he just held on to me like a baby koala." He grinned. "It was absolutely awesome."

"That's terrific," she said. "He deserves to be loved by someone as good as you."

Sandler blushed, then realized he had let his social obligations drop. "Imre, this is Kerry Mercer, a dear friend and coconspirator. Kerry, this is Imre Romanov, the cultural attaché to the British mission in New York. He's kindly offered to help us prepare for tomorrow."

"Pleased to meet you, Imre," Kerry said. She seemed surprised when he rose gracefully and took her hand. He brought it to his lips. "Enchantée," she said, utterly glowing at his attention.

"Moi aussi, bien sûr," he replied, kissing her hand again.

Kerry dissolved into giggles and sat down on the sofa on the other side of Sandler. Imre sat as well.

"Now, Birkin, tell me what this hearing tomorrow is about," Imre said.

"We're going to convince a judge to release Trevor from his parents' control. Because he was partially paralyzed in a car accident when we were in high school, they've been able to completely control him. They're convinced that being gay is a mental disorder, and so they've been dragging him from doctor to doctor. For a long time, they kept him drugged up on prescription psych drugs, trying to 'cure' his basic humanity. Once he caught on to what they were doing, he started cutting back on the dosage himself, and over the last few years had been only pretending to swallow the pills they gave him. He got very good at faking a near-catatonic state."

"That's horrid," Imre said, his face transforming from rapt attention to barely contained outrage as Sandler spoke. "How have they been allowed to do this?"

"He was in a coma for months after the accident, and his recovery was slow. Because he was unable to care for himself when he turned eighteen, they got a power of attorney that allowed them to make all of his medical decisions."

"But surely some authority must have reviewed his case at some point?"

"They had to justify the conservatorship every couple of years, but it was apparently pretty easy to convince a judge that he was still dependent on them. The last time, one of the specialists who examined him dissented, but they were able to get him overruled—they just hired new 'experts' who were more devoted to consulting fees than to the well-being of their patient." He shook his head, still clearly disturbed by what Trevor had been through.

"I cannot see why a magistrate would order him back into such horrible abuse," Imre said. "Do you expect to face any serious challenge to his release?"

"There may be 'expert' testimony on the other side," Brandt said from across the sitting room. "Trevor's parents brought him here to have him treated by a doctor who specializes in chemically altering the sexual identity of young gay men. We have to assume he will be there, testifying on the parents' behalf."

"Gay reparative therapy?" Imre asked, clearly astounded. "At the risk of sounding juvenile, I have to ask—that's still a thing?"

"Sadly, it seems to be," Donnelly said. "The director of the clinic seemed skeptical, and we hoped he would help us stop the treatment. But when push comes to shove, professional courtesy apparently takes precedence over the Hippocratic oath, and he may end up standing with the doctor."

"So what we need is our own experts," Imre concluded. "Backed up, of course, by an attorney who will utterly destroy whomever they have on their side."

"Now we're talking," Sandler cried joyfully. "I knew you'd be able to help us."

"I think with a few phone calls I'll be able to assemble the right team." Imre pursed his lips and pondered for a moment. "Yes, we should be able to take care of this without much difficulty."

"I could kiss you," Sandler replied, glowing.

"I rather wish you would," Imre said with a wink.

WHEN THE breakfast cart was rolled into the suite, Sandler went to wake Trevor. "He's had a steady diet of pureed vegetables and parental disapproval, so I think he'll light up when he sees this spread."

Imre watched him go. "He's a changed man," he said wonderingly.

"When I met him at the airport—wow, was that only two weeks ago?—he seemed... unsettled, I guess? He certainly didn't seem unhappy," Donnelly said.

"Birkin has a bit of a unique reputation among the diplomatic community," Imre replied. "As a man he's personable and pleasant enough, but as a courier he's superhuman. I've often thought that without a package in his hands, he's a dear man but a little lost. Once he puts on that messenger pouch, though, he's focused like a laser, and no one ever doubts that his delivery will come through." He fell silent for a moment. "Now it makes sense."

"How's that?" Brandt asked.

"He couldn't care for the one he loved, so he lavished that devotion on the parcels entrusted to his care. And Ankur, of course," he added, winking at Donnelly, who laughed at the allusion. "I am delighted to find him fulfilled in this way."

Donnelly had summarized for Imre the major events in the case by the time the door to the smaller bedroom opened. Trevor, looking strong and happy, rolled out under his own power, followed by a beaming Sandler.

"Imre, I'd like you to meet Trevor Hendricks, the love of my life."

Trevor glanced up at Sandler, a look of embarrassed adoration on his face. "I'm very happy to meet you, Imre," he said.

"I imagine after what you've been through, you're happy to meet anyone at all," Imre replied, smiling warmly as he crossed the room to shake Trevor's hand.

"I've been so lucky," Trevor replied. "All of Sandler's friends have been just amazing to help me the way they have."

"Let's get you some breakfast," Sandler said, wheeling Trevor over to the breakfast trolley.

"Go easy the first time," Donnelly advised. "Give your stomach a chance to get used to freedom."

"Gabriel's got the mom thing pretty much down," Brandt cracked.

"I think he's awesome," Trevor replied. "He was the first real person I'd seen in years, and less than twenty-four hours later, I'm free. I'd be happy to have him as my new mom."

"If that would make Brandt your daddy, I'd be totally on board," Sandler added, teasing Brandt for the first time since they'd met.

Brandt repaid the gesture with a furious scowl, which quickly dissolved into a grin. Then he blew Sandler a kiss.

"Stop it, you two," Donnelly scolded. "We have work to do and cannot be distracted by cuteness-induced boners."

A silence fell across the room.

"Or is that just me?" Donnelly deadpanned.

"Nope," Imre replied, inspiring a high five from Kerry.

"Rock-hard ladyboner," she said with a laugh.

Once the laughter in the room had died down, Imre asked if he could make some calls in the larger bedroom. He disappeared for about ten minutes, then returned to finish his breakfast.

"We have twenty-four hours until the hearing," Brandt announced. "How about we brainstorm some strategy?"

"We could do that," Imre replied. "Or we could just cut to the chase, and I'll tell you what we need to do."

Donnelly turned to see how Brandt would handle someone else wanting to take the reins.

"That would be fantastic," Brandt said, relief evident in his voice. "The floor is yours, Imre. Tell us what to do, and we'll get it done."

"Thank you, Ethan," Imre said. "Item the first, we need to get Trevor to a professional."

"Great idea," Sandler said. "We should make sure we're prepared for all of their medical objections."

"Oh, no," Imre replied. "I meant we need to get him to a tailor. He must wear an immaculate suit for the hearing tomorrow. As luck would have it, I have the name of the best bespoke tailor in Geneva, as well as a name to drop at his shop that will get him stitching forthwith. You'll hie yourselves thither as soon as we have breakfasted."

"A suit?" Sandler asked, his face a mask of stupefaction.

"Yes. What we need to show the judge tomorrow is a confident, fully capable young man ready to attend to his own affairs. That may be more important than the medical evaluation."

"Do you really think the judge is going to be swayed by something like his clothes?" Brandt, who seemed to be having second thoughts about relinquishing the reins, asked.

"Well, to some small extent the judge may be, but then again maybe not. But the attorneys and experts on the other side will surely attempt to paint him as a broken, psychotic half-wit who will wilt in the glare of everyday life. If they must make that argument while looking at this strapping lad in his sharply tailored suit, they will appear quite foolish. And, more to the point, they will feel themselves to appear foolish. Break the attorney's spirit and you break his case."

"Yes, let's do that," Trevor said. "I like the breaking part."

Imre chuckled. "Agreed. Item the second, we must indeed get you to a doctor whose reputation is beyond reproach for a complete examination. And then to a second one. And a third if we have the time."

"Sounds awesome," Trevor said, his enthusiasm quickly fading.

"It'll be okay," Sandler said, stroking Trevor's arm. "Your mom won't be there telling lies to the doctors. They'll actually be trying to help you. And I'll be with you every second."

Trevor set his jaw and nodded, clearly grateful for the support.

"Item the third," Imre continued, "we will meet with a legal team based here in Geneva that has a fearsome reputation when it comes to constitutional issues. By the time they finish filing in to the hearing tomorrow, the lawyers on the other side will have soiled themselves."

"Now you're talking," Trevor cheered, his spirits revived.

Imre turned to Kerry. "Gabriel mentioned you have some particular expertise when it comes to this 'procedure' that Trevor was brought here to undergo."

"I do," she replied, turning serious in an instant. "I work for the company that makes the drug, and we'd very much like him to stop using it."

Imre nodded, then turned to Brandt. "And am I to understand that you were somehow able to convince a chief inspector of the cantonal police to turn a blind eye to Trevor's disappearance?"

Brandt shrugged modestly. "Well, I wasn't working alone. Kerry and I did a sort of good-cop bad-cop thing. She goaded Trevor's mom into an incoherent rage, and I simply gave the chief inspector a credible way to walk back the entire thing."

"Brilliant," cheered Imre. "That's exactly what the attorneys need to hear. Would you and Kerry accompany me to their office this morning?"

Both Kerry and Brandt nodded enthusiastically.

"Excellent," Imre pronounced, then lifted his arm and looked at his watch. "It is now nine-fifteen. The tailor's opens at ten. Gabriel, will you order a car and accompany Birkin and Trevor?"

"Of course," Donnelly replied, setting aside his half-eaten breakfast to reach for the phone.

"Keep the car with you, and I will send you an itinerary of physician visits as soon as I have made those arrangements."

Donnelly acknowledged this instruction with a thumbs-up, then dialed the front desk.

"Our appointment with the attorneys is at eleven," Imre continued, looking to Kerry and Brandt, who nodded. "I expect we will be engaged there for the rest of the day." He looked around the room. "Is everyone clear on the plan?"

A resounding affirmation was heard from everyone except Trevor, who raised his hand as if he were a student in a boisterous class.

"Questions, Trevor?" Imre asked.

"Not a question, really," Trevor began, his voice hushed. "I just want to say… how much I appreciate…." He wiped his eyes and, with a great sniffle, continued, "I just want to thank you all for doing so much for me. I can't believe… I can't believe this is my life."

"It is now, buddy," Sandler said, tears in his eyes as well. He ruffled Trevor's hair, then ran his fingers down and stroked his neck.

"Let's get to it, then," Brandt announced, standing. The group dispersed, eager to prepare for battle.

AT PRECISELY ten o'clock, Donnelly stood by the open door of the town car while Sandler rolled Trevor alongside.

"Hold the chair while I pick him up?" Sandler asked.

"I can do this, Sandler," Trevor said. He rolled the chair closer to the open door, locked the wheels, then lowered the armrest. He lifted himself off the chair and into the car, then swung his legs over. "See?"

"Wow," Sandler replied. "That's awesome. Your mom actually let you do that?"

"Not once, ever," Trevor said with a laugh. "I would sometimes practice moving from my wheelchair onto my bed and back again. But I could only do it when she forgot to take my chair away, so I didn't often have the chance."

"You are fucking amazing and I love you so much," Sandler said, lowering himself into the car as Donnelly wheeled the chair around back to stow it in the trunk.

Donnelly stepped in from the street side and sat next to Trevor. Given his small stature, they fit comfortably together across the back seat. "Clothes shopping is probably not what you dreamed of doing on your first day of freedom," he said as the town car pulled away from the hotel.

"Oh, you have no idea how much I wanted to have something other than cheap sweats and slippers. I tried some of Sandler's clothes, but they basically fell off me— all except this amazing fleece thing, which is the best thing I've ever worn." He pulled the collar of the pullover up over his mouth and nose. "Probably because it smells like him."

Sandler put his arm around him and pulled him close.

"You guys are just too cute," Donnelly said.

"Cute's nice," Trevor replied. "But I think I heard something about 'sharply tailored'?"

"Right you are," Donnelly said. "I think Imre's exactly correct. We need to show the judge that you are just fine now that you're out of your parents' clutches."

"You have always been fine," Sandler added, a lover's growl in his voice. "But now you're going to be superhot." He kissed Trevor on the cheek. "And, you know, all independent and stuff."

"I'm fine with independent as long as I have you. I did dependent and alone for a lot of years, so now it's time for independent and not lonely."

They rode in quiet for a few minutes.

"Gabriel?" Trevor said as they entered an older quarter of town.

Donnelly turned and smiled.

"You don't think they really have a chance, do you?"

"Your parents? I'd like to think that they will see what you've become after one day out from under them, and they'll give up without a single word from the attorneys. But I've seen parents do really awful things when they think they're doing the right thing. It seems like your parents are pretty bought into the whole 'gay is a disease' thing, and that can be hard to pry loose once it takes root."

"So you think there's a chance they'll win, and I'll have to go back to them?"

"You're asking two questions there," Donnelly replied. "To the first, I'd have to say there's always a chance of anything. You can't go in certain you're going to win because that might lull you into taking your eye off the ball. So I would say it's a vanishingly small chance—like 'a meteor hits this car as we drive up to the tailor's shop' small—but there's always a chance. But, more importantly, to your second question: you will never have to go back to them. Never. I would never allow that to happen, and neither would Ethan or Kerry or Imre. And Sandler would pick you up and carry you out himself if they tried to take you. You are free, Trevor, and you will never have to go back to them. No matter what happens in that hearing tomorrow."

Trevor's expressions had run from relief to terror to resolve during Donnelly's answer, and now tears sprang to his eyes. "I am the luckiest man on earth," he said softly.

"You earned your luck, mister," Sandler said. "You've seen some shit, and now things are going to get better."

The car slowed and pulled to a stop in front of the tailor's shop. Donnelly got out first, checked the sky for meteors, and then retrieved the wheelchair from the trunk. They rolled into the shop, where the proprietor himself was awaiting their arrival. He stood amid a luxurious sea of cashmere, leather, and silk.

"Right on time," he called in greeting. "I am Anshel, and I welcome you to my shop. And you must be Trevor. Imre has given me very clear instructions, so let us get right to work." He swept open a curtain to reveal a fitting room surrounded by mirrors.

Sandler and Donnelly introduced themselves on their way past Anshel, and with a great flourish, he drew the curtain closed behind them.

"Imre only gave me the barest hint of your situation, my dear boy. You have my every sympathy. That such a thing can happen in our own time… well, it shakes my very faith in humanity itself. Such as my faith was, anyway. My parents were victims of the Holocaust, so when it comes to the human spirit, I am more realist than optimist."

Everyone in the fitting room took a long, sad breath.

"But today we will strike a blow for freedom," Anshel cried, dispelling the heaviness in the air. "Now, Trevor, my boy, we will start with measurements. I can do neck, arms, shoulders, and chest while you sit, of course." He rubbed his tidy gray goatee. "Yes, we start there, and we figure out the rest." He pulled out a tape measure and unfurled it with a practiced flip of his wrist.

The old man was a blur of motion as he took Trevor's measurements, not even pausing to write down any of the numbers. In under two minutes he had completed the top half, and stood back to consider. "Are you able to stand at all?" he asked. "Please don't think me rude—if you cannot stand, I will make you such trousers that people in Paris will take to sitting just to look like you."

Trevor laughed. "I don't get many opportunities to try," he said.

Sandler started to move toward him, but Donnelly put his hand on Sandler's arm, and gave a subtle shake of the head when Sandler turned to look.

Trevor locked the chair's wheels, then reached down to put his feet on the floor and swing the footplates out of the way. He gripped the arms of the chair hard enough to turn his knuckles white, but he got himself nearly to an upright posture. As soon as he had, though, he seemed unable to arrest his forward momentum, and he pitched toward the mirror. His right foot shuffled forward a half step, but it wasn't enough to catch him. Sandler did that, wrapping his arms tightly around Trevor and holding him upright.

Donnelly feared Trevor would be crushed by his failure to stand, but when he caught a glimpse in the mirror, he saw a broad smile on Trevor's face.

"Did you see that?" he said, winded a bit from the effort of standing. "I actually took a step! That's more than I've done in months."

Sandler's smile matched Trevor's, and he cast Donnelly a look that conveyed a silent thanks for allowing Trevor to try standing on his own. "Amazing, man," he said, still holding Trevor tightly.

Anshel shrugged and held out his measuring tape. "I should maybe measure both waists together, then subtract yours?" he said to Sandler with a chuckle.

"No, I got this," Trevor said, a look of utter concentration on his face. He released his hold on Sandler's shoulders, and pushed himself back. He wiggled and waved a little, but he was able to stand with just one hand on Sandler for balance.

As Trevor and Sandler kept their eyes locked to each other, the one willing himself to stay upright and the other trying to give him strength through the intensity of his gaze, Anshel flitted around them, getting the measurements he needed.

"Perfect," Anshel announced when he had completed his wizardry with the tape. "Now, we have some choices to make." He clapped his hands. "Victor! Bring the bolts!"

As Trevor sank back into his chair with a heavy exhalation, the curtain surrounding the fitting room flew open, and a young man stood as if he had been conjured up by Anshel's call. He bore an armful of fabric rolls, which he proffered to Anshel.

"This, and this, and this," Anshel said, tapping three of the bolts, which Victor then handed him. He turned to Trevor, now settled back into his chair. "Tell me, my boy, which of these will you wear?"

Trevor wore an expression of utter, Christmas-morning delight as he looked at the three bolts. He slowly raised a hand and tapped the fabric in the middle, which Anshel set aside.

"That is, of course, the perfect one. You have a very good eye." Anshel handed the other two back to Victor. "Now bring the ties," he said, and Victor dashed away, returning an impossibly short time later with a tray bearing a dozen ties in different hues. He took the tray and held it before Trevor. "And which tie will you wear?"

Trevor scanned the jewel-like strips of fabric and, without hesitation, put his finger on one in a crystalline blue.

"Just like your eyes," Anshel said with a wink. "Again, perfect." He turned to Sandler. "Hold on to this one—he knows things."

"Indeed he does," Sandler replied, smiling widely.

"One last thing." Anshel handed the tray of ties back to Victor, then whispered to him. He turned and dashed away again. "We will fit the shirt now, and that will let me fit the suit without you having to stay here all day. Come back in the evening, and we will make sure it is perfect."

"You can make an entire suit in one day, just like that?" Sandler asked.

It was clearly a question Anshel had been asked before. "My dear boy, the finest tailors in the country—in all of Europe—I have working here. I have made tuxedoes in two hours. *For royalty.*"

Victor returned once again, this time with a single white shirt on a hanger.

"Thank you, Victor," Anshel said, then closed the curtains once again. "Trevor, will you put this on?" He took the shirt off the hanger and handed it to him.

"Of course," Trevor replied, and pulled the fleece off over his head.

He was about to do the same with the T-shirt underneath when Donnelly said, "I should wait outside, give you some privacy."

"No, stay," Trevor said. "I don't mind you being here." He pulled the shirt off, and began to put on the starched and brilliant shirt Anshel had given him. "I kind of feel like if I lose sight of you, this amazing dream will be over."

Donnelly stayed, smiling at Trevor as he pulled the shirt on over his thin and somewhat frail-looking chest. He buttoned it up, and Anshel tugged and pinched and muttered, buzzing around him like a one-man swarm of bees.

"Done," Anshel announced. "Now you may get dressed and leave the shirt here. When you return this evening—say, six o'clock?—I will have it done. Give us a half hour to make final adjustments, and you'll have such a suit."

"I don't know how to thank you, sir," Trevor said.

Anshel looked at him seriously. "Imre tells me what happened to you, and I say to myself, I have to help. So I help." He smiled. "Plus, George Clooney cancelled." He shrugged. "His loss."

"All right, gents," Donnelly said, looking at his phone. "Imre's set up our next appointments, and we need to get moving." He held out his hand to the tailor. "Thank you so much, Anshel. You're a miracle worker. We'll see you at six."

"Very good, very good," the tailor replied as he threw open the curtains for the final time. "Best of luck to you—to all of you."

Late in the day the group convened in the hotel restaurant to recount the day's progress.

Trevor told the story of the tailor and then all the doctor visits—there had been three—while they ate dinner. Each of the doctors had reacted similarly to his summary of the past ten years, and all were willing to present their findings at the hearing.

Then over dessert Brandt and Kerry discussed their marathon meeting with the legal team, and though the details were intricate, the outcome was much the same as with the doctors: the experts were confident in a ruling in their favor.

At the end of the meal, Imre stood for a moment. "I would just like to say how very impressed I am with what this group has been able to accomplish in such a short time. I am proud to have a small role in helping bring this fine young man to freedom. I've only just met most of you, but I am certain that tonight I am in the presence of the most caring and dedicated people I've ever had the pleasure to know. I thank you for letting me join with you in this cause." He raised his glass to the table, and there were cheers all around.

"We'd better get you to bed," Sandler said to Trevor. "Big day tomorrow."

"You just want to get me in bed," Trevor joked, but then his face turned serious. "You do want to get me in bed, don't you?"

"Every night for the rest of our lives," Sandler replied. Their kiss was met with hooting from Kerry's side of the table.

"All right," Brandt said in his daily-briefing voice. "There will be a van to take us to the hearing tomorrow at eight sharp. Whatever you get up to tonight"—he raised an eyebrow at Sandler and Trevor—"make sure you wrap it up in enough time to be bright-eyed and ready to roll at eight. Got it?"

"We've got it, Sarge," Donnelly cracked, but he laid a kiss on Brandt's cheek.

"Once the hearing is over, resulting in our overwhelming victory," Brandt said, then paused a moment for the cheering to die down, "Gabriel and I will be heading for the wedding. You're all invited, of course. Who's coming with us?"

Kerry's hand shot into the air and waved frantically. Sandler and Trevor looked at each other, then raised their hands, clasped together.

"I'm fine with that, as long as Trevor doesn't wear his suit," Donnelly said. "I can't have him looking better than me at my own wedding."

"Imre, we'd love to have you there as well," Brandt said.

"I would be honored to attend," Imre said with a bow. "Your gracious invitation is entirely in keeping with your character, and I very much appreciate it."

"We'll kick ass and take names at the hearing, then go get hitched," Brandt said. "Good times."

Donnelly leaned over to whisper in his ear. "Fuck yeah."

SANDLER CLOSED the bedroom door softly, and padded over to Trevor, who sat on the edge of the bed. He sat down next to him. "Big day, right?"

"A big, unbelievable day," Trevor agreed. "I probably would have enjoyed it more if I weren't so scared about the hearing tomorrow."

"You have nothing to be afraid of. Gabriel said it exactly right: we can't be sure of what will happen at the hearing, but we can be sure that you're not going back to them. None of us would allow that. I wouldn't allow that."

Trevor smiled weakly. "I don't know what's going to happen when I see them tomorrow. For so many years it's just been me and them, and they were always in control."

"They aren't anymore," Sandler said soothingly, running his fingertips along the side of Trevor's face.

Trevor closed his eyes, leaning into the caress, but when he opened them, they were filled with even more concern. "It's not just that they controlled my life; they controlled me. They were able to make me think they were right about me—that I was damaged in some horrible way, and that we needed to find a treatment of some kind that would rip the disease out of me." A sob caught in his throat. "I believed them, Sandler. There were times when I was sure they were right. There were times when I just wanted to stop fighting and give them what they wanted."

"They were wrong—about you, about everything," Sandler replied. "There is no disease in you, Trev. And I will be here to remind you of that every single day until you can feel as sure about it as I am. You are your own person, and no one can tell you how to feel. What you and I had back then, and what we have now, is more real and more true and more... *you* than anything your parents ever said or did."

"I'm scared," Trevor said meekly.

"And that's okay," Sandler replied, pulling Trevor to him. "That's natural, given what you've been through." Sandler held him for a long time, until he could feel his body relax. "How about we get some sleep?"

Trevor pulled back from Sandler's embrace and looked him in the eye. "How about we do something else first?"

"What did you have in mind?"

"Something that would make my mom's head explode," Trevor replied with a sly grin.

"Is that what you want? Not for your mom's head to explode, of course," Sandler said with a shrug, "though I guess that's not a bad side effect." He looked Trevor in the eye. "I don't want you to do anything you're not ready for."

"Sandler Birkin, it's been more than ten years since we last touched each other that way. I think I'm more than ready."

"Nothing would make me happier than to end your decade-long dry spell, but are you sure you're up for it?"

Trevor laughed and tugged at the crotch of his sweat pants. "I am definitely up for it."

Sandler slid his hand down to join Trevor's, and was rewarded with a healthy handful of hard, hot cock. "It's just like I remember," he murmured.

"Let's see if it still works like you remember."

"Being under supervision all the time, how did you…?"

"Not much, is how," Trevor replied. "I think I went a year once without even touching it because of how warped they made me. They got into my head, and I really started to believe that all my problems came down to my dick wanting the wrong thing."

"What did it want?" Sandler asked, continuing his gentle stroking.

"You. Through all those years, all it wanted—all I wanted—was you."

"You've got me now." Sandler slipped his hand inside the waistband of Trevor's sweats.

"I'm going to ask you something, and I want you to give me an honest answer, okay?" Trevor asked.

"You don't have to tell me to be honest, Trev. I would never be anything but with you."

Trevor swallowed hard. "Have you been with other… guys? Since me, I mean?"

"Will you think any less of me if I say I have?"

"No, I wouldn't. I'd be happy for you. After I gave up on ever seeing you again, I just hoped you were happy. I pictured you with a great guy and a nice house and maybe some kids—all the things we talked about. I hoped you'd have those things, even if I never could."

"I've been with some guys. Not one of them meant anything like what you did to me. It took a few years before I could even think about being with anyone else, because I kept hoping I'd be able to get to you. I finally…." He fell silent.

"Finally what?" Trevor asked.

"I finally had to convince myself you were dead so that I could go on living. It just about destroyed me to know that I was driving that night, that I was the one who—"

"Shhh," Trevor interrupted. "It wasn't your fault. I never blamed you."

"I blamed myself. Every single day. I tried to forget that night and to find someone else who might take your place in my heart. But there was no one who could do that, ever. So I was alone, a lot."

"Yeah, me too," Trevor said with a grim laugh. "Well, fuck all that. Let's pick up where we left off, back when we were horny high schoolers."

"I'm going to show you some new tricks, mister," Sandler said, standing and tugging at Trevor's sweats, sliding them down his slender legs. He repeated the motion with Trevor's underwear. "There he is," he cried, elated to see that lovely penis—the first one he'd ever touched besides his own—spring into view. "Make yourself comfortable, sir, and I will treat you to the blow job of your dreams." He fluffed a few pillows into place and helped Trevor scoot back onto them until he was in recline, naked from the waist down.

"That's a pretty tall order, given how much I've dreamed of getting a blow job from you."

"I'm willing to work as long and as hard as it takes to get it right," Sandler said, saluting smartly before leaning down and taking Trevor into his mouth.

It was just like old times.

CHAPTER EIGHTEEN

Friday
Geneva

THE GROUP gathered for breakfast, as they had the morning before, and spoke in hushed tones about the upcoming hearing. The debut of Trevor in his new suit was the highlight of the morning, and it was with a spirit of great expectations that they left the suite for the hearing. Sandler tried to stay calm as he pushed Trevor's wheelchair into the courtroom and sat next to him, holding his hand tightly, bracing for the moment when the Hendrickses would enter. He knew Trevor and his team had done everything they could to prepare for this moment, but the stakes were so high. It was all he could do to keep his smile pasted in place and try not to let Trevor see how nervous he was. Trevor, for his part, seemed to Sandler to be almost preternaturally calm, as if the outcome were in no way doubtful to him. He tried to breathe in some of Trevor's confidence.

When the Hendrickses arrived, with two attorneys and Dr. Rauthmann, Trevor did exactly what he had said he would do: he looked straight ahead and ignored them completely. For their part, his parents shot dagger-filled glances at each and every person in Trevor's entourage, reserving particularly venomous squinting for that turncoat Randy Filkins.

The tone of the hearing itself, as Imre had predicted, was set by the procession of the attorneys he'd hired. There were five of them, and the arrival of each one elicited the same expression of bleak recognition among the Hendrickses' attorneys. Sandler could see them exchanging funereal glances and shaking their heads hopelessly. The attorneys were followed by the trio of physicians who had examined Trevor, at the sight of whom Rauthmann's eyebrows jumped skyward. He clearly recognized what he too was up against.

The judge, having read the briefs filed by the attorneys for both sides, asked for a private audience with Trevor before formally opening the hearing.

"I want Sandler to come with me," Trevor said in a clear, steady voice.

The Hendrickses' attorneys made instant and strenuous objections that his parents should be, as his guardians, the ones to accompany him into chambers, but they were put down quickly when Trevor's attorneys reminded the judge that Trevor had the right to choose his advocate.

Sandler escorted him to the judge's chambers, and stayed with him while he was questioned gently for less than a quarter hour. The conversation, however, contained none of the drama Sandler had feared; it was, in fact, rather anticlimactic, especially after the flurry of preparation they'd all gone through the day before. The judge seemed most interested in Trevor's ability to make decisions consistent with his own welfare. He was quickly satisfied by Trevor's answers, and in the end seemed somewhat bemused that his courtroom had become the site of senseless domestic drama.

Back in the courtroom, the judge had only one question for the doctors who had examined Trevor. They all answered in the affirmative when asked if they believed him to be of sound mind and capable of directing his own affairs. Each took pains to point out that Trevor's ability to care for himself was well established by his surreptitiously weaning himself off the psychotropic drugs and fighting to maintain his own health. The judge seemed more than satisfied, and without having asked the many attorneys present a single question, he declared that the Swiss constitution left no doubt that Trevor Hendricks should be freed from any limitation on his self-determination.

Mr. and Mrs. Hendricks sat for a long moment, Mr. Hendricks looking hatefully upon the attorneys who had raised only a single objection during the brief hearing while Mrs. Hendricks glared ferociously at her son and the man whose arms were wrapped around him. They rose slowly, and walked out of the courtroom without a word.

Dr. Rauthmann gathered his papers and followed the Hendrickses up the aisle. Sandler glanced up and noted, with no small measure of satisfaction, that Dr. Schwegler had appeared at the back of the room. The expression on his face as Rauthmann approached was… severe.

Trevor could hardly stop grinning, laughing, and repeating "Oh my God, it's finally over" all the way back to the hotel. Once there, everyone gathered up their belongings and headed for the train station.

When Brandt got to the ticket counter, the agent asked to inspect everyone's passport. Brandt made the rounds collecting them, but then he got to Trevor.

"It's not in here," he said, frantically pawing through the duffel bag that represented all his worldly possessions. "Oh fuck."

"What is it?" Sandler asked.

"My parents still have it. They kept them in the safe in the hotel room."

"Do you think we have time to go get it before the train leaves?" Sandler asked Brandt.

"The last train leaves in a half hour," Brandt answered.

"You guys go on ahead," Trevor said. "We'll get the passport and follow you tomorrow."

"No," Donnelly said flatly. "We're not leaving anyone behind."

"But it's your wedding," Sandler cried.

"Yes, but we don't know if you'll be able to convince your parents to give up Trevor's passport," Brandt replied.

"And if they don't, it would be Monday before you could get the court to force them to release it to you," Imre warned.

"I don't think your victory at the hearing today changed their minds one bit," Donnelly added. "I saw the way they looked at you—at all of us. You may have won, but if they get the chance to cause you trouble I think they will. I'm going to hail a couple of taxis to take us to their hotel." He headed out to the curb.

Trevor was distraught. "You guys have done so much already—I can't make you miss your wedding."

"It's not until tomorrow afternoon," Brandt said. "We'll get there."

"ARE YOU sure you want to go up alone?" Sandler asked as Trevor rolled toward the elevators.

"For the thousandth time, yes. I need to do this myself, or they will never believe it's what I want. If you go with me, they'll think that I'm under your control, just like I was under theirs. I need to do this myself."

Sandler nodded reluctantly.

"But if I'm not back in an hour, I want you to break down the door and rescue me, okay?"

"It's a deal." Sandler smiled widely, then grew serious again. "You're the bravest person I know."

"I think you're the brave one, taking on someone with a family like mine."

"I don't have a choice. The heart wants what it wants." He shrugged helplessly.

"Such a man, always thinking with his... heart."

The elevator doors slid open.

"One hour. Then I'm coming in, and I'm bringing Gabriel and Ethan with me. Muscles will be flexed." Sandler kept his tone light, but he was dead serious.

"I may stall a bit just to see that," said Trevor slyly as he rolled into the elevator. "I love you."

"I love you," Sandler replied as the doors slid closed.

TREVOR KNOCKED at the door of his parents' hotel room. He listened to his heart pounding, trying to slow its panicked rhythm while he waited for them to answer. It seemed an eternity to him.

Finally he heard shuffling, and then the light coming through the peephole flickered as someone looked through. As quickly as the shadow had come, it disappeared, and he imagined his father telling his mother that their wayward son had rolled unexpectedly back into their lives to gloat over his victory. He was sure they would simply decide not to open the door.

The door bolt slid back, starting his heart pounding even more frenetically than before. Then his father stepped through the small opening he had created by opening it only slightly, and the two Hendricks men were alone in the hallway.

"Dad." Trevor tried to keep his voice even and calm.

His father simply stared imperiously down. Trevor saw only hate in his eyes.

"I came to get my pass—"

"You came to make sure you've destroyed her. It's not enough that she's given her entire life to you—you want to see the wreckage your perversion has wrought." Mr. Hendricks looked ready to spit at his son. "I won't let you do that. It's over my dead body that you'll ever see her again."

Though Trevor had expected this reaction, he was still shocked by it. He swallowed hard. "That's not why I came."

His father leaned down until his enraged face was nearly touching Trevor's. "I don't care why you came. Leave. Now."

"Not without my passport." Trevor surprised himself with the force of his own voice. Having Sandler back in his life had shown him strength he didn't know he possessed. "Just give it to me and I'll leave."

Mr. Hendricks looked him straight in the eye, not even blinking. "Now you listen to me, you ungrateful punk," he snarled. "You made your choice. You decided that perversion and fleshly indulgence was more important to you than the life your mother and I have given our entire lives to provide for you. You are on your own, and that's a choice you made. You don't get to come crying to me when it turns out life isn't as easy as you thought it was."

Trevor looked at the man who had picked him up when he fell off his bike, who had helped him with his algebra homework even when he was tired from a long day at work. The man who always smiled upon his only son. What he saw now was a mask of bitter hate, of betrayal, of empty loathing. It was like watching his father die in front of him.

"Dad—"

"Don't call me that. I am not your father. Not anymore." He stood upright. "That's a choice you made. Live with it." He turned and opened the hotel room door.

A wave of frigid nausea blasted into Trevor's chest as the door slammed shut. He had expected anger, even fury. He hadn't expected to be disowned. He hadn't expected to be orphaned. What had he done to deserve this?

He heard the answer in Sandler's voice. *Nothing.*

He didn't deserve this. His sexuality, his identity—everything essential about him—was far more a part of him than who his parents were. He loved them still, but he was not going to accept their version of him. He didn't need a court order to prove his own humanity.

He knocked, hard. "Open this door." His voice was loud—not yet a shout, but on its way. "I will come back with the police if I have to."

No answer.

Trevor rolled closer to the door, and pounded on it. "You have no right to do this," he shouted.

The door swung open without warning. "Stop that," his father hissed angrily, looking up and down the corridor. "You will not cause a scene!"

"I will do whatever it takes to get what's mine," Trevor replied, his voice deadly. He looked past his father. "Mom? Mom, are you there?"

The slap came before he even registered his father's hand coming toward him. It nearly sent him sprawling out of his chair. From within the hotel room he heard a gasp.

Mr. Hendricks's lip curled in disgust. "You stay away from us, you degenerate."

"Let him in," his mother's voice said quietly.

"No," his father replied without taking his eyes off Trevor's throbbing cheek.

"Mom, I just want my passport. That's all." He struggled his way back into his chair, ashamed as he did so to feel a pang that his father, who should be proud of him for being able to do so, would only see it as further proof of his disobedience.

"Leave. Now," his father growled. He pushed the hotel door, and it would have slammed shut had it not been for Trevor's foot being in the way.

Without thinking about it, Trevor kicked out his right foot—the one that he hadn't even been able to move reliably since stopping physical therapy. His father looked down at it in surprise, as did Trevor. Their eyes met, just for an instant, and Trevor saw a flash of his father in the face of the bitter man who stood before him. It vanished as quickly as it had appeared, but it gave Trevor the confidence he needed. He pushed as hard as he could against the door, rolling his chair with every ounce of strength in his arms. It jolted back, striking Mr. Hendricks in the forehead and causing him to stagger back into the room. Trevor rolled in, and the door swung softly to a close behind him.

"Did you see that?" his father demanded. "He hit me with the door!" He raised his hand up to his forehead to feel the red welt that was already forming.

"After you slapped him," Mrs. Hendricks replied quietly.

Trevor turned toward the sound. His mother stood near the window, tissues in both hands, shaking her head slowly at the scene playing out between father and son.

"Let's not compound tragedy with melodrama," she continued.

Hope sprang into Trevor's chest at hearing his mother's calm voice. He rolled toward her.

"Stay away from me, you ungrateful obscenity."

Trevor's arms fell limply to his side as his mouth dropped open in shock. He shook his head, unable to form words.

"Mom, why…?"

Mrs. Hendricks looked at him for a long moment, dabbing at her eyes every few seconds. "My conduct is not under question here, Trevor." She daubed and continued. "I devoted every hour of every day to bringing you back to life. Even when everyone else had given up on you ever having a normal life, I stayed by your side. And this is how you repay me."

"This isn't about you, Mom. This is about me."

"It's always been about you," she replied. "Everything I've done has been for you."

"You tried to make me what you thought I should be."

"I tried to *restore* you. I built you back up from nothing. I gave birth to you twice—once when you came into this world, and once when that horrid Birkin boy tried to take you out of it."

"The accident was not his fault."

"There are no accidents," she replied, turning to look out the window. "When you took up with him, you left the right path. You lied to me and your father for that entire year, sneaking around, rolling in filth with that boy. That wasn't an accident. It was God setting you back on the right path."

Trevor's mouth dropped open. "Are you actually telling me you think the accident was a good thing? That being in a coma for a year and stuck in a wheelchair ever since was a gift from God?"

"That's exactly what I'm saying. God brought you back to us. And once we had you back, we restored you to health, body and spirit." She took a moment to daub at her eyes again. "But the demon that has you is stronger than I am."

"You drugged me into thinking I was sick. How was that supposed to help me?"

A steely glint sparked back into her eye. "You *are* sick. You have made that abundantly clear. Look what you did the first chance you got to slip away from us. You went right back into that perversion."

"I am not sick, and I am not perverted. I was born this way."

"Don't you dare come in here and parrot that crap to me. We are all born imperfect, but you are sick, and all you've accomplished this week is to refuse treatment for your illness. The judge says that's your choice to make. I won't be a part of it."

"I'm not asking you to be a part of it. All I want is for you to accept me for who I am."

"Accept what? You don't even know who you are. You've somehow convinced yourself that your happiness depends on sodomy. You're like a dog that keeps running into traffic, no matter how much its master tries to keep it safe. Eventually it's going to get hit by a car."

Trevor sat, stunned. "Did you just blame me for the car accident?"

"If you hadn't been with him, you wouldn't have been in danger."

"I was with him because I love him. That's why I'm with him now. If you can't understand that, I don't think there's anything I can say that will help. Just give me my passport and I'll get out of here."

His mother sighed deeply. "You are choosing death. I gave you life—twice—but I can't do any more. I fought so hard to make you better, and you are throwing all that away."

"What I'm throwing away is a suitcase full of drugs that you used to keep me under your control for years. I had three doctors look at what you were giving me, and they were honestly surprised I'd even survived. Don't talk to me about choosing death. You did that for me for years."

"How dare you," she replied, her voice offended, guttural.

"You managed to convince me I was sick. For years I believed it. I actually wanted those horrible treatments and all those drugs to burn it out of me so I'd be normal—I'd be the son you wanted me to be. It's what I wanted more than anything."

"That's all I ever wanted for you."

The sudden compassion that crept into her voice should have relieved him, but instead it enraged him. "Once I realized I'd never get any better, I spent my few moments of mental clarity every day plotting how to kill myself. You'd taken Sandler from me, you'd drugged me into being a vegetable—I had nothing to live for. So for three months I stockpiled all the pills I could trick you into thinking I'd taken, and took them all at once."

Her face dropped as the sudden realization seemed to sweep over her. "Two years ago. Christmas Eve," she whispered.

He nodded.

She closed her eyes, clearly badly shaken. "We thought we'd lost you. Again." A sob caught in her throat.

"Waking up on New Year's Day was the worst moment of my life," Trevor said simply. "I spent every day after that wishing I'd managed to die."

"When they said they found such high levels of those drugs in your system, I thought it was my fault."

Trevor felt a calm come over him. "It was your fault."

"How dare you say that," she replied. "You try to commit suicide—suicide!— and you say it's my fault?"

"You were trying to make me straight. That was never going to work."

"I wasn't trying to make you straight. I was trying to heal you."

Trevor could see this was going nowhere. "Can we stop doing this, please? Just give me back my passport so I can go."

"You can have it. And when we get home you can pick up all of your belongings from the trash can. We'll have nothing more to do with you."

Orphaned twice in one day, Trevor could only shrug. "I have everything I need."

Mrs. Hendricks nodded to her husband, who rose and went to the safe. He punched angrily at the buttons on the front and yanked it open. Pulling out a stack of three passports, he quickly found Trevor's and threw it at him. It bounced off his chest and fell to his lap. He looked down at it and started to laugh.

"What's so funny?" his mother asked, her voice full of disgust.

"I'm finally free," he said. "I'm finally free to be the person I was meant to be." He looked up at his parents. "I don't hate you."

His mother looked away. "Someday you will grow up and realize what you've done. If your perversion doesn't kill you first, you will understand that I was right. And I will be here when you realize that."

"I don't think that will happen anytime soon," Trevor replied. "But someday I'd like us to be able to be civil with each other."

"It will be a cold day in hell," Mr. Hendricks muttered.

"Every day with you was like that," Trevor said with a good-natured shrug, a smile rising to his lips.

"Get the hell out," his father said.

Trevor nodded, then rolled to the door, which he pulled open without assistance. He glided down the hallway into his new life.

TREVOR RODE the elevator back down to the lobby with a heart surprisingly light for someone who had just broken up with his family. He had told his mother that he had all he needed in the world, and that was exactly what was waiting for him in the lobby. Right in front of the elevator doors, in fact—Sandler didn't seem to have moved from the spot Trevor had last seen him.

"How'd it go?" Sandler asked once he had finished squeezing Trevor tightly.

"It was awful, and then it got worse," Trevor replied. Then he pulled his passport out from his shirt pocket. "But, in the end, successful."

"Awesome!" Sandler replied. "Let's go tell everyone. They've all been out of their minds waiting for you to get back."

"We're good to go," Trevor announced as they rolled toward the chairs where Donnelly, Kerry, and Imre were waiting.

"Was it horrid?" Kerry asked, studying Trevor's face for clues.

"It was," he answered. "But it's over. I learned some things about them, and I think once they have a chance to work through their bizarre prejudices, they might realize they learned something about me." He turned to Sandler. "But for now, I kind of don't have parents anymore."

"We're all we need," Sandler replied, hugging Trevor again, as he had every minute or so since he had returned to the lobby.

Trevor beamed. "Okay, enough Hendricks family drama. Let's get you guys to your wedding."

"Yeah, about that," Donnelly replied. "The last train today with a direct connection through London has already left. We can take the next one, but that one won't get us to Whitford in time. Ethan's just gone to let everyone know that we'll be late." He looked across the lobby, where Ethan was just pocketing his phone and walking back.

"You're not going to believe this," Brandt said, rejoining the group.

"After the past two days," Imre said drily, "I'm disposed to believe anything that happens to you lot, no matter how bizarre."

"It's just easier that way," Kerry agreed, nodding compassionately.

"So, let's hear the details," Donnelly prompted.

"I just talked to Wendell, our wedding planner," he told the group. "Because the volcano keeps erupting, there haven't been reliable commercial flights all week—and the ones that do get through are jam-packed. There was a surge in the ash cloud two days ago, and the diversions around it are now longer than most airlines want to take. James arranged for a private plane to bring all of our wedding guests over yesterday, but just before they were going to take off there was an incident with another private jet that got too close to the ash cloud and lost both engines. They managed to restart one of them and limp back to land. Now they're not letting any private jets try to make the trip either."

Donnelly got up and stood next to Brandt. "So not only will we not be at our own wedding, neither will any of our friends and family?"

"Looks that way. James is insisting that the place be kept ready just in case a miracle happens and everyone can get there, but there's really no chance of that at this point." Brandt kissed him softly. "Sorry, buddy. We just have the worst luck."

Donnelly looked around the group, all eyes on the unlucky couple. He shook his head. "Nope. I think we're extremely lucky. We've got each other, and we've got these amazing people around us, none of whom we would even have known if it weren't for our good bad luck."

"And we wouldn't have found each other again if it weren't for you," Sandler added.

"We were happy to help," Donnelly replied.

"You did more than help," Trevor said. "You saved my life. Not in a figure-of-speech way either. I had given up on life so completely that I was considering letting my horrible parents smash their way into my brain and break things. I figured it would either kill me or make me not care anymore, and either way it was a win. But now I have my life back, and I have a reason to live it." He ruffled Sandler's hair and smiled happily. "And we have the best friends in the world."

"So, do we just stick a fork in this wedding adventure and head back home?" Donnelly asked.

"What a picturesque image," Imre replied with a chuckle. "But I doubt you'll be flying home until the ash cloud finally clears. How about this—why don't we take the train to London as we'd planned? I have plenty of room. My grandfather has, for the last half century, owned perhaps the least-used town house in the city, and I would be delighted to host you there until the air clears over the Atlantic."

"What a generous offer," Donnelly replied. He turned to Brandt. "I guess we'll get a honeymoon even without a wedding."

"Doing things in the right order has never really been our strength," Brandt said with a laugh.

CHAPTER NINETEEN

Wedding Day
The Chapel, Whitford

UNDER THE soaring cathedral ceiling they sat. After some spirited discussion about which groom's side they should sit on, they had decided to sit across the aisle from each other.

The intricately carved walls of the vast stone edifice echoed with the shuffling footsteps of the ushers, who had no one to ush, and the officiant, who had no one to marry. The appointed time had come and gone an hour ago, and still no one, celebrant or guest, had appeared.

"You know," Bryce whispered across the aisle, "I'm starting to think they're not coming."

Nestor nodded, then shrugged and held his arms up with a good-natured smile.

"I am inclined, just this once, to adopt your attitude," Bryce replied, and mirrored the gesture of submission to forces outside his control.

A few minutes later, the sharp click of quick footsteps shattered the calm. A young man Bryce recognized from the front desk walked down the aisle to the front and then up the steps of the dais to the officiant. He whispered in the old man's ear, then retreated even more quickly back up the aisle.

The officiant, a spry if elderly man in a finely tailored suit, approached the first row of pews. "I am terribly sorry to be the bearer of bad news," he said. "I've just been informed that the grooms, and the entirety of the guests aside from yourselves, are not going to be here for the ceremony. I'm afraid the wedding's been cancelled."

"That's it," Bryce harrumphed. "I shall never sleep with another Icelandic man."

The officiant laughed, his deep voice filling the cathedral. "It is a loss to the entire nation."

"I assure you it is," Bryce agreed peevishly.

"I guess there's nothing for me to do here," the officiant said, looking about. "Unless you and Nestor here wish to take the grooms' place."

Bryce cast an appraising look across the aisle. Nestor smiled demurely and batted his big brown eyes.

The officiant raised an expectant eyebrow.

Bryce got up, stepped delicately across the aisle, and lowered himself in an elegant curtsey. He ended on one knee.

Nestor gasped, and held a fluttering hand to his throat. Bryce took his other hand.

"My darling Nestor, will you forswear all other men, and have only me for the rest of your life?"

"Oh, *Dios mío*, no," Nester replied, shaking his head.

"You always know just what to say," Bryce murmured, clutching Nestor's hand more tightly. "Will you do me the honor of becoming my bride, as I shall be yours?"

"Si, si, si!" Nestor cried happily, bouncing up and down on the pew.

They embraced, squealing and kissing with wild abandon, while the officiant looked on, beaming at the joyful explosion before him.

"We are ready to be wed," Bryce said, with Nestor visibly vibrating with happiness next to him.

"It would be my honor," the officiant said, and he invited them with a grand sweep of his hand to join him on the dais under the sparkling beams of afternoon light that shone through gothic windows. Once there, he looked up from the gilded leather book before him. "We'll need witnesses."

Two ushers—the strapping young farm lads recruited by Bryce himself to serve when none of the wedding party showed up in time for rehearsal—rushed forward from the back of the chapel. "We'll do it!" they called in unison.

"Well aren't you two just darling, pitching in for us," Bryce replied.

"It's the least we can do, to see you off into wedded bliss," said the taller of the two ushers.

The shorter chimed in, "It will help us deal with our grief, as now you won't be available for—"

"Oh, pish," Bryce said with a giggle. "Just because we're getting married doesn't mean we have to spend our evenings knitting. We can pick up right where we left off last night, you handsome boy."

"But, my darling, last night you say you never take both again," Nestor murmured.

"As I always say, never say never," Bryce said lightly, winking at both blushing farm boys.

The officiant cleared his throat. "Shall we, then?"

"Yes, yes," cried Bryce. "Let the betrothal begin!" Then he leaned in close to whisper a last-minute instruction. "My religion does require one thing."

The officiant leaned forward, a rather startled look on his face.

"Just a little adjustment. We need to leave out anything about 'forsaking all other men.' That won't cause a problem, I trust?"

"Not for me," the officiant replied. "I can't speak to how it may affect you."

"It will suit us just fine," Bryce replied with a smile, mirrored by a beaming Nestor.

A short time later, this most fabulous wedding concluded with the grooms kissing. And then the grooms kissed the ushers.

It would be a wedding night unlike any in the history of the castle.

CHAPTER TWENTY

Honeymoon
London

"WE CAN'T thank you enough for your hospitality this week," Donnelly said to Imre as they unloaded their bags from the limousine.

"It was my pleasure," Imre replied. "I don't think my grandfather's house has ever hosted that much laughter. I doubted I'd ever be able to live there after I discovered his secret life, but you have sanctified it with joy."

"Hard not to be joyful with those two around," Brandt said, jabbing a thumb at Sandler and Trevor, who were parked at the airport curb, kissing and looking into each other's eyes.

"Cutest thing ever," Kerry said, her head tipping as she regarded the canoodling couple.

"You're just happy they helped you bag a straight guy," Donnelly cracked.

"I didn't need any help, thank you very much," Kerry sniffed with an admirable play to regain some dignity. "The memory of his sister being in a wheelchair may have rendered him temporarily vulnerable, I will grant you, but it's not like I wouldn't have had a shot even if Trevor hadn't been there, being all brave and stuff."

Brandt raised a critical eyebrow.

"Okay, so maybe they gave me a head start. But meeting him in New York next week? That's all me, baby."

"He's a great guy, Kerry," Donnelly said, putting his arm around her.

"Thank you, darling. And after spending all week with this group, he's got a gold-plated hetero guarantee. If he ain't gay around this beefy bunch, he ain't gay."

"Hot enough to be, though," Trevor chimed in.

"Right?" added Sandler.

"Shut up, you two. Keep your mitts off my man."

"It would have been hard to get anything on him with you wrapped around him all week," Sandler replied. "But he did seem very happy, and we're very happy for you."

"Thank you," Kerry said with a bow.

"So where are the two of you off to?" Donnelly asked Sandler and Trevor.

"Don't know yet," Trevor replied.

"I have miles in the millions that I've never used, so we're going to pick whatever sounds good on the departures board," Sandler said. "We'll try that for a while, and if we get bored we'll find someplace else."

"But once you two finally arrange a wedding, we'd love to come," Trevor said.

"Yes, let's get the band back together!" Kerry cried.

"We've decided not to tempt fate another time," Brandt said. "We're going to go to the courthouse after we're back home."

"Small and simple," Donnelly added. "We may not even tell anyone this time. Just slip off one day and get hitched."

"Because that way nothing could possibly go wrong," Brandt groaned sarcastically.

"At least you can be comforted that when bad things happen to you, good things happen to those around you," Imre said.

"True story," Sandler said, pulling Donnelly—and then Brandt—into a hug. "You guys are awesome, and you'll be even better once you're the new married power couple."

Kerry piled on to the hug. "But you're going to tell *me*, right? I gotta catch as many bouquets as possible."

"I CAN'T believe we're finally on a plane together," Brandt said as they climbed the steps.

"I can't believe James sent a private jet to pick us up," Donnelly replied. "This thing is amazing."

"Welcome aboard, gentlemen," the flight attendant said as they reached the top stair. "Please, let me take your bags." She relieved them of their carry-ons and handed them each a glass of champagne. "Please, have a seat, and the pilot will be back to greet you in a moment."

They settled into the impossibly plush leather chairs and looked around at the polished wood and gleaming metal that accented the plane's cabin. Then the doorway to the cockpit opened, and a man in a pilot's uniform stepped into view.

"Good morning, Mr. Brandt, Mr. Donnelly," he said, extending his hand. "I'm first officer Tyson, but you can call me Jake."

"Pleased to meet you, Jake," Brandt said, shaking his hand. "Please, call me Ethan. And this is Gabriel."

Donnelly shook Jake's hand as well.

"We'll be getting underway shortly. Captain Ballard is doing the final checks. Make yourself comfortable, and we'll get you a nice smooth ride across the pond."

Jake smiled and went back to the cockpit, leaving Brandt and Donnelly to sip their champagne and enjoy their first and probably only trip in a private jet.

Two hours later, as they cruised high over the north Atlantic, they made their way back to the stateroom.

"It's a beautiful room," Brandt said, looking at the fine linens.

"It is," Donnelly said lightly, closing the doors behind them. "I imagine it's also built to withstand a lot of turbulence." He pressed down on the mattress, feeling its solid strength.

"You aren't actually proposing that we...?"

"Of course I am. Why not?" Donnelly asked, starting to unbutton Brandt's shirt. "You heard the flight attendant—she said a lot of people enjoy spending some quiet time together in here during the flight."

"I'm sure that's not what she meant."

"She said the shower is big enough for two, Ethan. What else could she have meant?"

Brandt smiled. "Okay, maybe that's what she meant." He started to unbutton Donnelly's shirt for him.

"Bet you never figured on being a member of the mile-high club," Donnelly teased.

"Safe to say you're absolutely correct about that," Brandt replied. "Then again, this isn't exactly a cramped bathroom in the back of the coach section."

"Right you are. So let's take advantage of it."

In a giddy rush, they disposed of the rest of their clothing and pulled back the covers on the bed. They had just laid themselves down when the plane dipped suddenly.

"Whoa!" Donnelly whooped, laughing.

"That's what you do to me every time," Brandt replied. He kissed Donnelly, and the plane surged upward again.

"It's like making out while bungie jumping," Donnelly cried.

"Fuck making out," Brandt growled. He grabbed the bottle of lube he kept in his jeans pocket. He lay back on the bed and squirted some gel into his hand, then spread it all over his already hard cock. He tossed the bottle to the side and beckoned to Donnelly with a jerk of his head. "Come here," he commanded.

Donnelly, delighted at the speedy turn this was taking, threw his leg over Brandt and straddled his hips, eager for the invasion that was about to come.

"No, up here," Brandt said. In case his meaning wasn't clear, he stuck out his tongue and wiggled it sinuously.

"Oh fuck yes," Donnelly breathed and shuffled his way up over Brandt's strong chest and broad shoulders, until his knees were next to Brandt's ears.

Brandt wrapped his arms around Donnelly's hips and pulled him down. Donnelly widened his stance until he was nearly resting on Brandt's chin. Then, without warning, Brandt surged upward and impaled Donnelly's ass with his tongue. Donnelly gasped and fell forward and clutched the headboard, resting his forehead against the wall in an attempt to stay upright while Brandt savaged his asshole.

The plane dipped and shuddered, then surged upward again, forcing Donnelly down onto Brandt's lips; then, just as suddenly, the bed seemed to fall away from underneath them, and he floated up until only the tip of Brandt's tongue anchored him. The plane rocked and jolted, the vibrations working through Brandt deeply into Donnelly.

A few minutes was all Donnelly could take. "I need you in me," he groaned.

Wordlessly, Brandt lifted him and slid him back down until their pelvises met. Donnelly raised himself up high enough to place the head of Brandt's hard, slick cock at his entrance. He was in no mood to take it slow, but he was rather unprepared for the plane to bring Brandt crashing into him. With one mighty bounce of the bed Brandt slammed balls deep, taking his breath away.

"You okay?" Brandt asked, alarmed by the unintended pillaging Donnelly's ass had gotten.

"Oh hell yes," Donnelly replied with a long exhale. As the plane dipped and surged, he simply tried to hang on. Brandt's prick crashed repeatedly into all of his sensitive spots, and he was soon on his way to a bouncing, heaving orgasm when the world slipped sideways, throwing both of them off the bed.

Brandt was still inside him as they hit the floor, and that one last thrust was all he needed. Donnelly's cock exploded, sending jets of white streaking all over both of them—and the bed, the floor, and the pillow that had been launched into the air with them when the plane shimmied sideways. The contraction of every muscle in Donnelly's pelvis throttled the cum right out of Brandt's cock, and it surged into him, filling him with warm, slippery delight.

The plane continued to rock and bob as they clutched tightly to each other, waves of bliss amplified by the jostle of the aircraft. Finally, as they stopped quivering from the exertion of launching all of that semen (into Donnelly, and all over the room, respectively), the plane stabilized. All was suddenly smooth and quiet.

"That was amazing," Donnelly sighed, letting himself drop onto Brandt's sweat-glossed chest.

"Did the air move for you too?" Brandt asked.

"We could have hit the ocean and I wouldn't have pulled off that amazing cock of yours."

"Let's be glad it didn't come to that," Brandt said. "Though looking around here, there are few places you didn't already come."

"You!" Donnelly cried accusingly. "You did this to me!" He laughed, then leaned down to lap a stray splash of his semen off Brandt's shoulder.

"And I'd do it again," Brandt said, before lifting his head up to kiss the cum out of Donnelly's mouth.

They lay, on the floor and wrapped in sheets, exhausted and kissing, for a long moment.

"We should probably get up and mop this place up a bit," Donnelly said finally.

"But don't you dare put any clothes back on," Brandt warned. "I'm not through with you, mister."

"We're just getting started," Donnelly promised.

They put the room back in order, then climbed under the sheets to relax with a bottle of mineral water from the minibar while they plotted their next moves. A knock on the door roused them from their quiet reflection. They exchanged a look, then pulled the covers up to their chests.

"Come in?" Brandt called, a little tentatively.

The door swung slowly open. "Hope I'm not disturbing you," the first officer said, "but I wanted to apologize for the turbulence." He poked his head around the door, then caught sight of the bare-chested men. "Oh, I'm sorry."

"No, don't worry about it," Donnelly said. "We're decent. Mostly."

"Wow. Um, you two make 'mostly decent' quite… attractive," said Jake, who was apparently unable to tear his eyes from their pectorals.

Donnelly couldn't stifle a chuckle. "Thanks, I think?"

Brandt eyed them both mischievously. "Let's not dance around it. Jake, we've been having sex in your plane. I hope that's okay."

Jake laughed. "No worries. I've, umm"—he cleared his throat insinuatingly—"made similar use of the stateroom recently." He looked around slyly, as if checking for eavesdroppers. "It was during a deadhead flight across the Pacific, and we had two guys who were supposed to be cleaning the plane, but were actually taking the long way around the world to get to England. For a wedding or something. Anyway, I'd never done anything like that before while working, but they were very persuasive. Especially the one with the accent—he was Cuban, I think? Man alive, he was the most flexible thing I've ever had wrapped around me." He sighed and looked into the middle distance. "Anyway, I'd better get back up there. Sorry again for the turbulence—we're finally around the storm, and it should be smooth sailing from here on. We're still about three hours out, so if you'd like to… carry on, you certainly have the time."

"Thank you," Donnelly said. "Though I think we both kind of enjoyed the shaking and bouncing."

"Well, now we'll know whom to blame if it starts shaking and bouncing again," Jake said with a laugh and a wink, then turned to walk back to the cockpit.

Brandt turned to Donnelly. "Two guys, one with a Cuban accent?"

"Who seduced a pilot after basically stowing away?"

"You don't think…?"

"No, couldn't be," Donnelly said with every bit of finality he could muster.

Even he didn't really believe it.

CHAPTER TWENTY-ONE

Reception
Home

"Do WE have to go?" Brandt asked. "We just finished unpacking, and there's a game on."

"He said we absolutely 'must, must, must, *must*' be there," Donnelly replied. "You know three 'musts' is life or death—I have no idea what could possibly make Bryce throw in a fourth. We have to go."

Brandt sighed, casting a woeful look at the television where he had hoped to settle in with a six-pack and his fiancé. "All right. I'm assuming there's a dress code?"

"It's at Burn, so it needs to be something you can dance in."

"Does it? Does it really?"

Donnelly pulled him close. "Yes, yes it does. *Really*." He kissed Brandt on the nose, then smiled brightly. "You remember what we did after the last time we danced at Burn."

"Barely."

"That's my point exactly. Let's do that again."

Brandt couldn't help but grin. "Okay, you win." He turned to go get dressed, since the sweatpants and jersey he was wearing weren't exactly club wear. "Maybe Oliver will be there, and he'll make that drink again."

"If it gets you out on the dance floor, I'll buy as many as it takes."

THE CLUB announced its presence with sparkling blue lights and a deep thudding dance beat that could be heard down the block.

"Well, this place hasn't changed," Brandt said, deadpan.

"Why mess with a good thing?" Donnelly replied. He pulled open the door and a wave of powerful bass crashed into them. "Wow, they are really cranked up tonight."

"Awesome." Though his tone was dark, he smiled teasingly.

They made their way into the club, and were immediately met by Xander, the waiter who had hosted their bachelor party. "Gabriel! Ethan! Great to see you," he called as he approached. "Are you all married now?"

"Not exactly," Brandt said.

"It's a long story," Donnelly added.

"I'd love to hear it sometime," Xander replied. "But Bryce will kill me if I keep you from his table, so please, follow me." He led them to the large, U-shaped booth in the back of the club, where Bryce and Nestor held court with a large group of friends.

"Troopers!" Bryce hooted as they approached. "My darling menfolk." He hopped up and ran to them, embracing both and showering them with kisses.

Brandt, overwhelmed by Bryce's effusive greeting, had almost extricated himself when he felt Nestor's sinuous arms slip around them from behind. They were now the meat in a rather fabulous sandwich, and he gave up trying to get free.

"Please, please, join us," Bryce said, leading them to the table once he had his fill of gripping them tightly. Arrayed around the table were several faces they recognized from shops on Alta Avenue—it was something of a shop-boy convention.

"Officers!" came a voice from across the bar, and Oliver, Burn's most popular bartender, raced across the floor full of bouncing men. "Great to see you," he cheered, pulling them both into a hug. "I'm so sorry about everything that happened—James was so frustrated that you weren't able to get married at his place in England. And I was really looking forward to seeing you two finally tie the knot."

Donnelly leaned close to be heard over the pounding music. "Like I told James, please don't feel bad about—"

"Can I have your attention, please?" Bryce blurted—he'd never shared a spotlight in his life, and though he loved Brandt and Donnelly dearly, he was clearly not about to start sharing this one. "Now that our most muscular guests have arrived, you are no doubt frantic to know why I've asked you here." He scanned the crowd for signs of frenzy, which his cohorts dutifully offered—they were accustomed to pretending far more strenuous things in exchange for free drinks.

Bryce paused for effect. And then paused a little longer, as if he were a reality show host dangling over a commercial break.

"My love, we tell them now?" Nestor prompted.

"Yes, yes, I was just about to." Bryce cleared his throat theatrically. "As you may know, Nestor and I traveled to merry old England last week to be of assistance at the wedding of our beloved troopers here." He bowed gracefully toward Brandt and Donnelly, who exchanged looks of purest confusion.

"You were there?" Brandt asked, once he'd caught his breath.

"Of course, darling. We said we would be."

"Everyone said they would be," Donnelly said, eyes still wide with surprise. "But we didn't think anyone actually made it."

"Apparently the rest of your guests are simply less resourceful," Bryce tutted, consulting his fingernails.

"Apparently," Brandt said, utterly confused.

"In any event," Bryce continued, "we were there. And in that groomless cathedral, we sat for a long while, contemplating the vagaries of life and the nature of love, and it occurred to me—why waste all the flowers?"

Brandt and Donnelly, having just gotten their jaws to close, dropped them open again.

"You didn't," Donnelly murmured.

"Oh, but we did," Nestor sang, and he giddily embraced Bryce.

"Yes, my dearest friends, as well as a few bitterest enemies—you know who you are, and I trust you are infuriated by how happy and well-dressed I am today— Nestor and I had our turn as blushing brides, and we stand before you now in wedded bliss." The two grooms kissed, reenacting the vigorous lip-lock that had so startled the officiant at their wedding.

Brandt and Donnelly erupted into cheers and good wishes, clapping both grooms on the back and giving each a kiss for good luck. The shop-boy chorus, however, was having nothing of it. They sat in stony silence, as if a particularly elegant rug had been yanked out from under them.

"My darlings, whatever is the matter?" Bryce asked, seeing their bereft expressions.

"I think I speak for the group," one willowy lad ventured—Brandt recognized him as the inseam specialist at the tailor shop up the street—"when I say, what the fuck, Bryce?"

"I'm sorry?" Bryce asked.

"Who's going to arrange our social events now?" the seamster demanded.

"I'm sure Bryce and Nestor will still make time to socialize with their friends," Brandt said, hesitant to get into the middle of a catfight but wanting to defend Bryce's honor.

"We're not talking about high tea," answered another of the crowd. "We're talking about shore leave and wrestling tournaments and Republican conventions. Places where sailors and athletes and closet cases gather to work out their kinks. Bryce, you invented the all-you-can-eat cock buffet, and now you're abandoning us!"

"I am doing no such thing," Bryce sniffed. "Do you think that just because we're married we'll stop having sex? With other people, I mean?" He burst out laughing, joined by Nestor. "No, no, no, darling. We take marriage far too seriously for that. We will have a traditional marriage in every sense, just as mankind has had for millennia. And as in every good traditional marriage, the male partner shall be free to indulge in whatever—or whomever—he wishes."

"We'd expect nothing less, Bryce," Donnelly replied with a laugh.

"Thank you, dear. Now, everyone, drink up and dance the night away. Or, rather, the early evening. Promptly at midnight we will all be heading to a graduation party at a charming little dive near that strict, strict military academy just outside town. There will be several dozen muscular cadets who've been locked up for a year with nothing to do but work out and stew in male hormones. They'll be free, frisky, and utterly incapable of holding their liquor. Hope you brought your appetites, darlings!"

A cheer rose from the shop-boy chorus.

"I think we'll have to beg off," Brandt said.

"Oh, sweetie, they've been living in barracks for months. *Barracks.* You wouldn't have to beg."

"I think what Ethan's trying to say," Donnelly added helpfully, "is that we hope you have a lovely time, but we won't be joining the party."

"Well, a girl can dream," Bryce said wistfully.

"THANKS FOR dancing with me tonight," Donnelly said, raising his red plastic cup to Brandt.

"I didn't want to be the only one in the club who wasn't," Brandt said with a grin.

"Come on. You enjoyed yourself out there."

"Not as much as Bryce's friend with the skintight leather pants. I thought I'd have to come out there with a crowbar to get him off you."

Donnelly looked gleefully over the top of his drink. "Whatever it takes to get you on the dance floor."

Brandt rolled his eyes, but then wiped his brow—they had danced for quite some time. "Well," he said, looking around the club, "it's not exactly a honeymoon at the Villa Hermes—"

"It's better," Donnelly said.

Brandt raised his eyebrows.

"We've had so many amazing adventures, and we've gotten to know so many amazing people along the way," Donnelly said. "And how many people can spend two weeks traversing the globe on the way to getting married and then still have a wedding to look forward to when they get home?"

Brandt laughed but had to agree. "You're right, of course. But I think at some point I'd like to actually be married to you."

"Nothing would make me happier."

"How about we head to the courthouse on Monday and make it official? Then we can head south and at least enjoy the second week of our honeymoon. Winnie said no one's booked the honeymoon suite until next month."

"Sounds like a dream come true." Donnelly leaned over and kissed his soon-to-be-groom. "Plus, everything that could possibly go wrong already has."

"Don't you ever," Brandt growled into Donnelly's ear, "*ever* lose your optimism."

"Now you're just teasing me," Donnelly replied.

"I'm not." Brandt was dead serious. "I depend on it more than the air I breathe."

"Ethan, you don't need optimism. You are a force of nature, and you always do what you set out to do."

"Without you, there's nothing worth doing." Brandt smiled. "I may give you shit about your sunny disposition, but I would be lost without it. Completely, utterly lost."

Donnelly reached out and took Brandt's hand. "Then we stick together. And heaven help anyone who tries to keep us from getting married on Monday."

"When we're together, what could go wrong?" Brandt beamed. He tossed back the last of his drink and tugged Donnelly's hand. "Now, I believe we have some unfinished business on the dance floor."

Xavier Mayne is the pen name of a writer who has been both a university professor of English and a marketing professional for software companies. He currently manages a team of writers for a large technology company based in the US Pacific Northwest. Versed in academic theories of sexual identity, he is passionate about writing stories in which men experience a love that pushes them beyond the boundaries they thought defined their sexuality. He believes that romance can be hot, funny, and sweet in equal measure.

The name Xavier Mayne is a tribute to the pioneering gay author Edward Prime-Stevenson, who also used it as a pen name. He wrote the first openly gay novel by an American, 1906's *Imre: A Memorandum*. Unique among early gay novels, it tells the story of two main characters who are straight until they meet each other.

Website: www.xaviermayne.com

FRAT HOUSE TROOPERS

XAVIER MAYNE

A Brandt and Donnelly Caper: Case File One

State trooper Brandt's new assignment to infiltrate a sex-cam operation puts him in a very uncomfortable position, especially since he'll have to perform naked on camera for his audition. Fortunately his partner and best friend, Donnelly, has his back—whether that means helping Brandt shop gay boutiques for sexy underwear or offering Jäger and encouragement while he researches porn.

Despite his mortification, Brandt gives the audition his best "shot"—and becomes an overnight sensation. But to meet the man behind the operation, he'll have to give a repeat performance, this time live on webcam opposite the highest bidder. Donnelly makes sure to win that auction for his partner's sake, but their plan has a flaw: faking it is not an option.

In the aftermath, Brandt is a humiliated mess trying desperately to come to terms with what he's had to do for the job and his own mixed feelings. But Donnelly has been on a journey of discovery of his own. Suddenly everything the two men thought they knew about themselves and each other gets turned inside out. Meanwhile, they still have a case to solve… but it may not be the case they thought it was.

www.dreamspinnerpress.com

A BRANDT &
DONNELLY CAPER
CASE FILE TWO

WRESTLING DEMONS

XAVIER MAYNE

A Brandt and Donnelly Caper: Case File Two

Jonah Fischer's high school wrestling career has been stellar, but now he's the unwilling star of a series of videos that have hit the web. The whole world may have seen the evidence that his best friend turns him on. Jonah's conservative family wants him cured, and his conventional town and school want him normal. The only person who still wants him just the way he is is Casey Melville, the same best friend who turned him on for all the world to see. Meanwhile, Casey begins to wonder if there's more to his feelings for Jonah than he thought.

Officers Brandt and Donnelly—lovers as well as partners on the job—have been assigned to find the culprit who posted the video. While investigating the case, they also help Jonah and Casey find their way through their feelings, and steer them toward refuge when Jonah's family turns against him. But the mystery remains: who wants to hurt Jonah badly enough to post those videos, and why? Thank goodness Jonah and Casey have found friends—they're going to need all the help and support they can get.

www.dreamspinnerpress.com

A BRANDT &
DONNELLY CAPER
CASE FILE THREE

A WEDDING TO DIE FOR

XAVIER MAYNE

A Brandt and Donnelly Caper: Case File Three

When a high-profile gay celebrity couple asks two of the city's most established vendors to provide cake and flowers for their wedding and they refuse, a resulting boycott threatens to shut them down. It's up to the next generation in the family-owned businesses to save them from ruin. Justin Capella, baker's son, and Roman Montgomery, floral scion, work together to plan the gay wedding of the year.

Justin and Roman haven't seen each other since that fateful day in third grade when a single kiss shocked Justin and sent Roman to boarding school. As fate would have it, Justin and Roman rediscover love while working on the wedding. But disaster might pry them apart again.

Troopers Brandt and Donnelly are working with a statewide task force for the rights of LGBT citizens—all while searching for a killer wedding planner. As guests at the "wedding of the year," they are the first responders when all hell breaks loose. In investigating, the troopers are led to a shadowy figure they believe seduced Roman into doing his bidding. But the real murderer will cover his tracks at all costs, including Roman and Justin's lives.

www.dreamspinnerpress.com

SPRING BREAK
AT THE
VILLA HERMES

XAVIER MAYNE

A BRANDT &
DONNELLY CAPER

CASE FILE FOUR

A Brandt and Donnelly Caper: Case File Four

Troopers Ethan Brandt and Gabriel Donnelly celebrate the one-year anniversary of their engagement by flying south for a week of calm relaxation at the Villa Hermes, a gay boutique hotel on the beach. But when the rest of the guests turn out to be college guys on spring break (unwittingly booked into a gay hotel by a passive-aggressive travel agent), their week turns out to be anything but calm.

Ted, one of the spring breakers, has harbored a crush on his roommate and best friend, Bark, since they met freshman year. Now, on their fourth and final spring break, Ted knows they must soon say good-bye. A lacrosse star and ladies' man, Bark has no idea Ted has fallen for him—until a storm forces the entire group underground for twenty-four hours of stress and truth-telling. Bark doesn't want to say good-bye to Ted at graduation either. He just didn't know how to put his feelings into words or if he could face the consequences of speaking them. Brandt and Donnelly help the college guys through their crisis by showing them what love between best friends can grow into.

But Ted and Bark aren't the only spring-breakers with secrets.

www.dreamspinnerpress.com

BACHELORS PARTY

XAVIER MAYNE

A BRANDT & DONNELLY CAPER

CASE FILE FIVE

A Brandt and Donnelly Caper: Case File Five

Med student Oliver Mitchell has discovered a way to make more tips as a bartender—put on ripped workout gear and serve drinks at the hip new gay club, Burn. The only catch is Oliver is straight. The staff and patrons don't mind, though, and Oliver fits in well—until he meets James Buchanan Whitford, a local politician with a secret: he's married. When James's scheming wife attempts to catch him in flagrante with Oliver, they flee the city for the refuge of James's cabin in the woods. There, Oliver faces a new challenge—he's starting to feel more for James than friendship. Their new relationship must survive political intrigue and small-town politics before they can be together.

With their wedding two months away, it's time for Troopers Ethan Brandt and Gabriel Donnelly to have a bachelor party. Ethan's older brothers are excited, but Ethan is not. As a straight guy who fell in love with another man, the whole ritual is fraught with complications, and he struggles to reconcile newly granted marriage equality with old traditions. Brandt and Donnelly work to help James and Oliver find their way to happiness while pulling off the bachelor party of the year.

www.dreamspinnerpress.com

www.ingramcontent.com/pod-product-compliance
Lightning Source LLC
Chambersburg PA
CBHW050024030726
47506CB00001B/105

* 9 7 8 1 6 3 5 3 3 1 9 7 4 *